THE

BAILEY

CHRONICLES

Catherine Cookson

SUMMIT BOOKS

New York   London   Toronto   Sydney   Tokyo

SUMMIT BOOKS
Simon & Schuster Building
Rockefeller Center
1230 Avenue of the Americas
New York, New York 10020

Designed by Nina D'Amario ≠ Levavi & Levavi
Manufactured in the United States of America

10 9 8 7 6 5 4 3 2 1

Library of Congress Cataloging in Publication Data

Cookson, Catherine.

The Bailey chronicles / Catherine Cookson.
p.   cm.
ISBN 0-671-62387-7
I. Title.
PR6053.O525B25   1989
823'.914—dc19
88-27153
CIP

*This is a story for young women
disillusioned with boyfriends and looking
out for a more stable companion;
For young widows with children,
and those without;
For widows not so young;
For a one-parent family;
For divorcees with children;
For those on the loose;
And for dream-shattered women of
all ages with hope springing eternal who
long to meet up with an ordinary
bloke like Bill Bailey.*

CONTENTS

PART

I

Bill Bailey

I

"A PAYING GUEST?"

"No, Mother; a lodger. As I said, he works on the buildings . . . he's a lodger."

"You're getting coarse. And what do you think people will say in the avenue?"

"They'll say, Mother, they wish they'd had the chance to take . . . a lodger. I know of three redundant managers in the street, and their wives are scraping for jobs."

"Well, far better to go out to work again than take in a person like that."

"Perhaps you've forgotten, Mother, we've had all this out before: I have three small children and it was costing me practically all I worked for in paying someone to look after them, and travelling expenses. Anyway, since that do in hospital, I haven't felt up to standing all day smiling and saying, 'Yes, madam; that was made for you,' and generally to old bags who still don't know how the other half lives."

"You needn't have paid anyone to look after them; I offered, didn't I?"

"Yes, Mother, you did. But look what happened when I was in hospital. There was chaos. I was hardly round from the anaesthetic

11

when you told me you were on the verge of a nervous breakdown, and you listed all the things Mark had said and done. Anyway, don't let's go on: I am taking a lodger because I cannot make ends meet otherwise."

"Well, you know who's to blame for that. And I'll say it again: if he had been any kind of a husband he would have seen that you were properly cared for by taking out an insurance."

"He did take out an insurance, Mother. I have the house."

"Yes, and nothing with which to keep it up. He was irresponsible right from the beginning. A free-lance journalist! Huh! He should have got a proper job. Your father provided for me."

"But only just, as you often tell me, Mother. Only just."

At this point the kitchen door was thrust open and a blond nine-year-old boy cried, "He's here! He's here, Mam. In a whopping big car," then turned about and disappeared.

As though caught up in the boy's excitement, Fiona Nelson and her mother went to the window and looked down the long narrow garden towards the gate, where a man was taking luggage from the boot of a car. He had placed two cases inside the gate on the pathway when the boy reached him and attempted to pick up one of the cases. They saw the man rumple the boy's hair, at the same time apparently turning him towards the car for, together, they went back to it.

"Well, he's a good age."

Fiona glanced at her mother, saying, "That at least should put your mind at rest."

"Well, it hasn't. The whole idea's obnoxious. And look." She pointed. "Golf clubs!" Mrs. Vidler's voice held a note of utter disbelief. "You said he worked on the buildings, a bricklayer."

"I said no such thing; I didn't specify what he worked at. You made up your own mind about that after I said he worked on the buildings. And that's what he does, so he told me, along with his men."

"*His men?*"

"Yes. He's a builder, Mother. He's building those detached houses above the park."

"*What! ... Really!* They're expensive."

"Yes, Mother; they're expensive."

Fiona watched her mother's countenance alter. It was as if her face was changing its skin. She had seen that look before. It meant the chase had begun, for under that refined exterior was a hunter. But that she had never chased a quarry like this one approaching the front door now Fiona would have been willing to bet.

12

There was a tight smile on Fiona's face as she left her mother arranging her hair and hurriedly nipping at her lips. She crossed the small hall towards the open door to greet her future companion by saying, "Well, you've got here, then?"

And the man, dropping the cases just inside the door, answered, "Yes, I've got here, in the flesh. And don't attempt to move those." He indicated the two big cases with his foot.

"I had no intention of doing so."

"Huh!" He was looking her straight in the face, as he added, "No; you wouldn't, would you?"

Fiona felt herself rearing slightly. She wanted to step back from him, but she didn't; she returned his stare, thinking that she had never been able to stand men with sideburns, even short ones like his; and they were grey, and yet his hair was still dark, in fact mostly black. He was only slightly taller than she, and she was five foot seven; what was more, he was thickset. She had never liked thickset men. His whole appearance, like his voice, had a roughness to it. If there had been any romance left in her, she told herself, she would have said he looked rugged; but no, he was rough, all rough; and loud, as he proclaimed now by yelling down the garden, "Hi, laddie; don't attempt to carry those."

He left her side and hurried down towards the boy and took the golf bag from him; he brought it swiftly back, dropped it near his cases, then went back to the car again. He hadn't even glanced at her this time.

When Mark came into the hall she put a hand on his shoulder; he looked up and said, "It's a Volvo, Mam, the car."

She did not remark on this, but watched her future lodger-cum-paying-guest place one more case on the drive, then lock the car door, after which she turned her son about and pressed him towards the far door, saying, "Go on into the garden; Katie and Willie are in the playhouse. Stay with them until I call."

"But Mam . . . "

"Do as I say, Mark, please."

The boy lifted his shoulders in protest but did as he was bidden.

Then there was the man again, placing another large case against the other two, and she knew she should say to him, "You'd like to get unpacked, I'm sure." But she told herself she might as well get the family introduction over, because her mother, in her present mood, would stay on until she met him.

"Would you like to meet my mother? She's in the sitting room."

"Anything you say." His tone implied I'm in your hands, so she led

13

the way into the sitting room where, looking from one to the other, she said, "This is Mr. Bailey, Mother. My mother, Mrs. Vidler."

Fiona watched her mother move slowly towards him, her hand outstretched, and in her most refined tone say, "How do you do?"

She also watched the man hesitate a moment, seeming to take her mother in in one hard blue glance; then taking the outstretched hand, he said, "I do very well, ma'am. How do *you* do?"

Fiona had to turn her head away. The chase was on, but the scent was misleading.

"I'm so pleased my daughter has decided to take a paying guest. . . . "

"Paying guest?" His head turned sharply towards the young woman who was now his landlady, and he said, "That's what I am then, a paying guest? Does that mean it will cost more than being a lodger, or are the rates the same?" His blue eyes were twinkling and for a moment she imagined that he winked. "Your advert said lodger."

He turned quickly again to Mrs. Vidler when she said on a light laugh, "Oh, that was Mrs. Green's doing in the paper shop. She's a very . . . well, ordinary person; her trade is mostly with the council house estate. . . . "

"Oh, aye, I see. I see." He was nodding. "And they are a *very ordinary lot, very* ordinary that lot." And he drew in his lips and knobbled his chin to emphasise how ordinary the council house lot were.

Fiona closed her eyes for a moment. Her mother wasn't stupid; couldn't she tell she was on the wrong scent? It seemed not.

In an effort to save the situation she said, "Would you like a cup of coffee? I've just made it."

"No; thanks all the same. I had a pint or two before I landed."

"Would you like a drink?"

Her mother's tone was one of polite enquiry, and the answer came, "Oh, yes, ma'am; I have the same intake as a whale."

"You're joking, Mr. Bailey. . . . Are you married?"

William Bailey looked at the well-preserved, once pretty woman. She was kicking sixty if he knew anything. But they never let up, did they, her sort? He allowed a pause to ensue, then, with a sad note in his voice, he said, "Four times, ma'am. And four divorces. I made the mistake in each case marryin' a woman older than meself. I did it because I wanted to steer clear of the young 'uns, you know, like your good-looking daughter here." He now thumbed towards Fiona, then ended, "I run along the middle track of the jungle now, ma'am, well away from the hunters on both sides."

14

"*Four times divorced!*"

"'Struth, ma'am. Sad but true. Four times divorced." And now pulling a wry face, he said, "If you don't mind, I'll sit down. I stand most of the day, and so when I can I always take a pew." With that he lowered himself into an easy chair whilst looking across at the open-mouthed woman. "I'd get me legs up an' all, if I was you, ma'am," he told her, "for there's nothing brings on varicose veins in advancing years like standin' about."

Fiona daren't look at her mother, whose face was almost purple now. Her mother was right; she had made a mistake in thinking that this lodger business would solve her problems, for this one was going to be a problem in himself.

She now followed her mother as she made her stiff-backed exit from the sitting room without wishing the paying guest good-bye, and she made sure that she closed the sitting room door behind her, for she knew what would happen in the hall.

"*He's impossible, dreadful.* Get rid of him. Tell him you've changed your mind."

"Mother, I . . . I have a notion he was just pulling your leg."

"Pulling my leg indeed! Varicose veins, and indicating that I was an old woman! He's dreadful, coarse, ignorant; the worst of his class I've ever come across. You simply can't let him stay."

"He has paid a month in advance, Mother, and I've already spent a third of it in stocking up the freezer, et cetera."

"I'll make it good; I'll do without my holiday."

"*Mother*"—she pressed her towards the front door—"leave it for the time being. If I find him impossible, he'll go. Believe me."

"And this business that he doesn't like young women, that's all my eye."

Fiona smiled primly now as she said, "You're using a common expression, Mother."

"Oh, girl! Don't you start. Now look, get on that phone if he starts any funny business. Do you hear me? Get on that phone."

"I hear you, Mother. And the minute he starts any funny business I'll shout for help."

Her mother had taken three steps from the front door when she turned about and came back, saying in a stage whisper, "It isn't right, you being in this house alone with him."

"Hardly alone, Mother, with three children. And I have a son who will guard me, never fear."

"*Fiona!*" The finger was wagging now. "There's nothing funny about this business. I wouldn't trust that man as far as I could toss him."

15

Her mother was indeed worried, as her speaking in the vernacular proved. And she herself wasn't seeing anything funny about this business, either; for at this moment she was wishing that she hadn't spent so much of his advance payment, for she still retained enough of her mother's character to admit she didn't really know how she was going to put up with him.

And so, a moment later, when she entered the sitting room she was startled by his first words: "I know. I know. You don't know how you're gonna put up with me. I'm brash, loud, vulgar—the lot. Well, that's me. But not as bad as I have just portrayed meself to your mother. Sit down and let's talk this out."

"I haven't time to sit down, Mr. Bailey."

"Oh, then that means me gettin' to me feet. Well now, here I am on me pins, standing trial, and I'm going to add to me brashness by telling you straightaway I could see what your mother was after as soon as I set eyes on her. And the reason why I'm here at all is that I have just escaped from a similar type. They're the very devil, you know, women like your mother."

"You put a high value on yourself, don't you, Mr. Bailey? How do you know my mother isn't married and has no need of ... er ... another man?"

"Oh, I learned that from Mrs. Green; she gave me the rough details. You have been widowed for three years, your mother for four. Would you like to know her recommendation in her own words?"

"Not necessarily, thank you."

"Well, I'll give them to you, necessarily or not. The old 'un, Mrs. Green said, is a bit of an upstart. But the young one's all right. She couldn't have been fairer than that, could she?"

They stared at each other; and then he, laughing, said, "Let's clear the air a bit further, eh? I'm not after anybody's blood, young or old. As I said, I steer a middle course; I value me freedom. And that was a lot of boloney about me being married an' divorced four times. It was once. And that was more than enough. Not that I don't enjoy meself, mind." His chin was knobbled again. "But if I have a love, it's me work." He leaned towards her now, saying, "You were surprised the other day, weren't you, to know I was the boss of the show? Thought I was a brickie, didn't you?"

"I had no thoughts about you at all, Mr. Bailey. We were discussing a business deal, and as you are a businessman you will know that it is wise to keep personalities in their place."

"Oh, come off it. Sayin' that proves you know nothing about

16

business, and once you tell them to keep their place that's when you have trouble. Like now, with the strikes. But speaking of places, the way you meant it, don't worry, I know me place, and I like it, and I mean to stick to it. So now, if you will excuse me"—his voice changed into one of pseudo-refinement—"I'll go and see if my valet has unpacked. What time is dinner?"

She had to force herself to say, "I'll make it for whatever time is convenient to you."

"Well, say, it being Saturday, make it for five; I like a long Saturday night out."

He was walking away from her when he turned his head towards her and added, "On the tiles."

He was hardly out of the room before she flopped into a chair. Resting her elbow on the arm and her head in the palm of her hand, she swayed herself slightly and muttered as she did so, "Oh, my God! What an individual!"

2

"ARE THE CHILDREN READY?"

"Yes; they're in the sitting room waiting."

"It wouldn't do any harm for you to come to church this morning.... And washing on a Sunday! You never had to do anything like this before. Are you giving him notice now this month's up?"

"No, Mother. He has already paid another month in advance."

"You're asking for trouble; you know that. I saw Minnie Hatton the other day, and she says he's got a name."

"Oh, Minnie Ha-Ha says more than her prayers, and she whistles them."

"*What!* The way you talk. I suppose you've got that from him. And where is he today? Still in bed?"

"No, Mother; he's in Liverpool, visiting his father."

"Liverpool? Is that were he comes from? Well, what can you expect, coming from a place like that?"

"Mother, let up for goodness sake! ... I'll call the children."

At this Fiona marched from the kitchen, banging the door behind her.

In the sitting room, she said, "Come on ... And I told you to sit up straight, Katie, and not lie about on that dress."

18

"I don't want to go, Mam; I don't like going to church with Grandma."

"When's Mr. Bill coming back? He said he might be earlier."

"When did he tell you that, Mark?"

"Just before he left. He's going to get us tin whistles and we're going to practise 'Bill Bailey.' "

"You're going to practise no such thing. . . . And stand up straight, Katie."

"I want to go to the toilet."

"You've had plenty of time to go to the toilet, Willie. Now all of you get yourselves out, your grandmother's waiting. And behave yourselves; I want no bad reports."

When, standing together, the three of them all looked up at her, she made a sudden dive for them and put her arms around them. And they clung to her and laughed.

"Be good," she said softly. "It isn't for long, only an hour. And I'm making you a chocolate mousse for your lunch."

"Oh, goodie!" They were all about to make a rush for the door when her voice checked them in a harsh whisper: "Walk!"

As if governed by one set of muscles, their faces dropped into a blank mould, and, forming into a line, Mark first, followed by Katie, and then Willie, they fell into step and marched from the room.

Fiona did not immediately follow them to hear the reception they would get from their grandmother when they entered the kitchen doing their turn, as they called it; but leaning her hips against the back of the couch, she drew in a long breath as she muttered, "The little devils!" Then she almost sprang into the middle of the room as her mother's voice came from the hall, crying, "Fiona! Fiona!"

"Yes? What is it?"

"I've told them they're coming back with me for lunch, but they have informed me in one voice that they are coming straight home. Will you please tell them that they are to do what they're told? I've already prepared the lunch—I'm doing this to give you a break. So will you please tell them what they've got to do?"

Fiona told her small brood what they had to do, and promised them she'd keep the chocolate mousse intact for when they came home. At the door she watched them walk dejectedly down the pathway behind her mother: Katie as if she had a hump on her back, Mark dragging his feet, and Willie aiming to kick the toes out of his best shoes.

Returning to the kitchen, she emptied the washing machine into the dryer; then made herself a cup of coffee, sat down by the table that overlooked the back garden, and told herself she should now mow the lawn, then start on the weeding of the vegetable patch at the bottom. But she also told herself she was going to do none of these things, she was going upstairs, take a bath, give her face a do—and that definitely needed it—then put on a decent dress and sit in the garden and have a read.

She looked at the clock. It was half past ten. Taken in all, she would have at least three hours to herself, which didn't often happen on a Sunday.

The hall clock was striking twelve when she came downstairs; going into the small room that had been her husband's study, she took a book from the shelf, then stood looking around her as she thought, Why can't I let him use this to do his paperwork. I never liked the room when Ray was here because he was always shut away in it, it was forbidden territory to both me and the children. So why . . . ? Oh! She jerked her chin up, then went out, took a deck chair from the outside store and placed it under the silver birch, the one big tree in the garden, and settled down to read.

But she hadn't read the first chapter of the book when she dropped it into her lap and, leaning back, let her thoughts wander over the happenings of the past few weeks, which weren't all unpleasant. A restful form of sleep was about to overcome her when the voice hit her.

"So this is what you do when you're left on your own!"

She pulled herself up so quickly that she almost toppled sideways out of the chair.

"I . . . I didn't expect you back until this evening. You said . . . "

"Yes, yes; I know what I said. But here I am. Where is everybody? Where're the kids?"

"At church."

When she made an effort to rise his hand came out, the palm vertical like that of a policeman on traffic duty, and he said, "Stay where you are. I'll get another chair."

She watched him stride across the lawn towards the shed. He looked smart. His clothes were always good, well fitting. There was something different about him, but she couldn't put a finger on it at the moment.

He placed the chair at an angle to her own, and then she saw the difference: his sideburns were gone, and his hair was cut much shorter.

During the few weeks they had been together he had developed the unfortunate knack of picking up her thoughts, as he did now, saying,

20

"Yes, you see, they're gone." He rubbed his forefingers up each side of his face. "Think you'll be able to tolerate me better now? Oh, don't get on your high horse." His hand was out again, flapping towards her now. "Anyway, you didn't like them."

"What do you mean, I didn't like them? It's of no interest to me how you wear your hair: clean-shaven, or bearded, or . . . "

"Well, why did you say you couldn't stand men with sideburns?"

"Me say that! I never . . ."

"Well, your daughter must be tellin' lies."

Oh, Katie. Katie. She turned her head to the side.

"Anyway, I feel I look better scraped and scalped."

She was looking at him again, saying now, "You're such a modest man, aren't you, Mr. Bailey?"

"Yes, Mrs. N. That's one of my virtues, no vanity about me." He grinned. Then looking around the gardens, he said, "The place is dead without the kids. And this lawn wants a cut. We'll have a bite, and then I'll do it."

"There's no need; I always see to the lawn."

"Yes, you see to everything, don't you? Bloody little wonder, you are. Oh, I'm sorry." He pursed his lips. "But you know, you would make a saint swear at times. Here I've been in the same house with you for four and a half weeks, and you're still Mrs. N. and I'm still Mr. Bailey. Look"—he leaned towards her—"I'm not after anything. I've told you not one but a dozen times since I came here, I'm a middle-of-the-road man."

"Please. Please." She looked over her shoulder. "There's people in the garden next door."

"Well, it'll give them something to talk about, pass their time. And I'm not far wrong in thinkin' that they're interested already in the goings on in number sixteen, two doors down"—he thumbed over his shoulder—"always manages to be at the gate when I draw up. And she seems very interested in the weather. She asked me yesterday if I thought it was going to rain."

Fiona lowered her head. There was a gurgle in her stomach; it was rising up to her breastbone. She mustn't laugh at him, because what would happen if he were given encouragement she didn't know. He was leaning towards her again, his voice low now as he went on, " 'How long is the heat goin' to last?' she said. And I answered, 'Oh, as long as the weather does, ma'am.' And then she asked if I was going away for the weekend. And I said, 'Aye, ma'am; yes, I am. I'm going to Greenham Common to keep the lasses company because they couldn't have seen a good-looking fella like me for a long time, and I bet some of them need more than the weather to warm them up.' "

"*You didn't!*" The words came out almost on a hiss. And he hissed back at her. "I did! and then, you know what she did?"

Fiona waited.

"She flounced. That's a Victorian word, you know; the ladies flounced about then. Well, she turned and she *flounced* up her drive. I think, in future, when she wants to know about the weather she'll turn on the television."

"You're impossible!" She was gulping in her throat now and her eyes were moist.

"I know. And now do you think I could have a bit of something, I'm starvin'?"

"Yes, of course."

He put out his hand and helped her to her feet, and they went into the kitchen together. As she took the cold chicken from the fridge, she said, "How did you find your father?"

"I didn't find the old . . . budgerigar, he had gone off to Morecambe with his girlfriend and had never let me know. I had left him this telephone number an' all."

"Your father . . . had gone off with . . . ?"

"Yes, that's what I said, his girlfriend. And don't look so surprised. He's seventy-four, but he doesn't look his age; he could pass for sixty any day, and he acts fifty. And she's just on that. Look, the way you're holding that knife, you'll cut yourself."

She said now slowly, "You must take after your father."

"Aye, I do. And I couldn't have a better pattern. He's been a good father to me. And I had a good mum an' all. She was a gentle woman, in the real sense of the word, except for her hands. She had a hand like a steel brush and she laid it across me at least once a week. But mind, I deserved it. You know, it's funny, they say men usually marry women that represent their mothers. You know? But in my case I went and married one that was exactly the replica of meself, brash and bouncy. I never knew what it was to live with meself until I woke up one morning an' discovered that that was what I was doing. It's all right for a man to be loud-mouthed. Well, it all depends upon how he uses it. If it's with panache—that's a good word, isn't it—like I do . . . well! But with a woman it's different, gets on your nerves. I can't stand a brash woman. Of course, I had to learn that. I also had to learn that you can't change people. Rub off some edges here and there, but you don't really change them. . . . Here, give me the knife, or that poor chicken'll wish it was dead."

She handed him the knife; then, dropping into a chair, she folded

22

her arms on the table, bent her head over them, and began to laugh. Her body shook. The tears ran from her eyes, and all the while he stood at the opposite side of the table, the knife in his hand, making no attempt to carve the chicken. He just stood looking down on her, and when, gasping, she raised her head, he said quietly, "That's the best sound I've heard you make since I came into this house, and it was a belly laugh, no refined giggle. An' you know what? I'm goin' to look upon it as a start. And now the next thing you must do is get yourself out."

She was sitting back in the chair, wiping her face; she blinked her wet eyelids as she looked up at him and said, "Out? What do you mean, out?"

"Just out. Out to enjoy yourself. Oh, I'm not askin' to be your escort, so don't let your face drop to your bust; what I'm sayin' is, I'll stay in some night and see to the kids if you want to go to a dinner or something. I haven't seen any men around, but that's not sayin' you haven't got a boyfriend somewhere?"

"Really!"

"All right. All right. I won't go on. But you've surely got some woman friend you could do a show with or something. . . . Anyway, if you're stuck for someplace to spend an evenin' there's always your mother's."

She got to her feet now, saying, "You're impossible, you know that? But nevertheless, thanks for the offer. I might take you up on it some night."

"Bikini or bones?"

"What!"

He pointed down to the chicken. "Do you like breast or leg?"

"Anything. Oh, the top part of the leg."

"The top part of the leg it is, madam. By the way, I've promised to take the kids in the car to the fun fair at Whitley Bay sometime, if that's all right with you."

"Oh, the fun fair? Oh . . . well, I think they're much too young. . . ."

"Young for a fun fair? Don't be daft, woman. Kids are never too young for fun. But if you feel worried about their safety you can come along an' all."

"I've never been partial to fun fairs."

"Eeh, by! You know, at times you sound just like your mother. You're not, but you sound like her." He pushed the plate towards her, saying, "Not much salad for me." Then added, "Well, if the fun fair's out, what about Whitley Bay sands?"

"Yes; yes, I'm sure they'd like that."

23

"And you?"

"We'll see."

"Negotiations pending."

She bit on her lip, and again she was laughing, but silently now. And she kept her head down as she put a small cloth on one end of the table and set it for their lunch.

They were sitting opposite each other, but she hadn't swallowed her first bite and he was on the point of saying something further when there was a commotion in the hall and the children burst into the kitchen, only to stop for a moment before exclaiming excitedly, "Oh, Mr. Bailey. You're back, Mr. Bailey."

He was standing up now, and they were gathered round him, all talking at once.

"Did you bring us the tin whistles?"

"You said you wouldn't be back till tonight."

"I can sing that song, Mr. Bill."

"Can you, Willie? Well, I'll have to hear it."

"*Fiona!*"

Fiona looked at her mother, who was now standing in the doorway, every part of her bristling with indignation.

"Yes, Mother?" Fiona went towards her and actually pressed her back into the hall.

"Well! What is this? You knew he was coming back early."

"I did nothing of the sort, Mother."

"Then why are you all dolled up?"

"Dolled up? I've had a bath and put on a clean dress. If you call that dolling up ... "

"Look at your face, all made up."

"If you recall, Mother, I used to make up every day."

"There was need for it then; you were going out to work. There's something going on here."

"*Mother!*" The word was ground out. "There is nothing going on here but what's in your mind. And I would thank you not to suggest there is. And now, listen to me." She actually pushed her astonished parent in the shoulder. "I'm a married woman with three children. I'm twenty-eight years old. I've been on my own for three years, and you haven't been much help except to criticise. Now I'm going to tell you this. If you want to keep in touch with me you'll stop treating me as if I were a fifteen-year-old."

"How ... how dare you!"

"I dare, Mother. And I should have dared a long time ago. And now I'm going to tell you something else: I'm going to give you

24

something to talk about, you and Mrs. Minnie Hatton, and the rest of your clique. I'm going to Whitley Bay with him this afternoon. It's supposed to be a treat he's giving the children, but it's really for me, because he's sorry for me and the nun's life I live in this house, dominated by you."

"*I . . . I can't believe it.*"

"No, I don't suppose you can, Mother. Now will you kindly go, because I have to get ready."

For a moment Fiona thought her mother was about to faint, but her next words proved that she was far from fainting: "It's a long time since I used my hand on you," she said, "but at this moment I have the greatest desire to slap your face."

"No doubt, Mother. But do you remember the last time you slapped my face? You did it in such a way that I fell onto the stone hearth, and Father told you that should you do it again he would do the same to you? . . . You didn't know I knew that, did you? Now, Mother, will you please go home!" She went to the door and pulled it open.

Mrs. Vidler's plump body looked as if it was about to burst. "I'll never forgive you for this, never!" she sputtered, and marched out of the house.

As Fiona slowly closed the door and stood with her back to it, the kitchen door opened. Although she had her head bent down she knew he was coming towards her.

He stood in front of her for some seconds before he said, "Well, that's a battle you've won. And not afore time I should say. Now go upstairs and get yourself ready. . . . Yes, yes; I listened in—we all did. And those kids have got her measure. And they're all right. They're digging into the chocolate mousse, so come on."

He now drew her gently from the door, turned her about and pressed her towards the stairs, saying, "She beat me to it in one way: I should have told you you look different, smashing in fact. . . . Now don't turn round; keep on going up them stairs, and tell yourself you're starting a new life."

A few seconds later she entered her bedroom. As she stood with her back to the door she exclaimed, "That man!" but she didn't explain to herself the meaning those words now conveyed.

3

HE STOOD IN THE KITCHEN DRESSED IN A DINNER JACKET: THE DRESS SHIRT, NO big frills just small pleats, was topped with a narrow black tie. His face, well shaved, showed no blue haze and his hair was meticulously brushed.

"I might be a bit late; you know how these things go on, once a year do's that seem to last a year. . . . What you lookin' like that for?"

"Like what? I . . . I was just thinking you look very . . . smart."

"Thank you. You're surprised, I suppose, to see me wearing a dinner jacket?"

"No, not at all."

"You should see me in grey tails an' topper. Oh aye, yes"—he nodded at her—"by courtesy of Moss Brothers. I was invited to a wedding last year, one of the county nobs. I'd just done a good job for him. It was Sir Charles Kingdom. I'd made good an old part of his house. It was more like gutting it and starting from scratch. But anyway, the old boy was pleased. And so was his daughter. And they asked me to the wedding. It was a great do. Talk about knees-up among the hoi polloi; that lot could show you a thing or two, apart from wearing kilts. But as the night wore on some of them were missing an' all. Oh! Oh, I'm sorry." He flapped a hand at her. "But these things happen."

He now stood looking at his fingernails and saying, "It's a devil of a job to get these clean for the occasions like this; I've scraped them till all the enamel's gone off the inside."

"You could put some nailwhite on."

"What's that?"

"Oh, it's for making the nails look white underneath. Hang on; I'll get some."

"No, no." He put out a hand and stopped her. "Sounds pansyish to me. I'll sit on me hands, eh?"

She smiled at him now, saying, "Nobody would notice your hands."

"Think not?" His voice was quiet; his blue gaze deep.

"No, of course not," she said. "As you frequently point out, you're a very presentable fellow."

"Aah! You're getting your own back now, are you?" He slanted his gaze at her before saying, "Always hitting below the belt. Anyway, I must be off; and I promise you I'll come in quietly, no matter what hour. And I'll try not to sing."

Taking up his mood, she told him, "Do that. But if you cannot overcome the urge, please make it a different tune, because I am heartily sick of 'Won't You Come Home, Bill Bailey,' both verbally and as demonstrated on tin whistles."

He laughed now, saying, "But they love it though, don't they? And let me tell you, they're learnin' to play those whistles properly. They could move from them to flutes, you know. That's how things start. Things have always got to have a start. Like me from tea-boy to tycoon. Well, not quite a tycoon yet, but I will be one day. I must tell you about me rise sometime. Yes, yes; I must. . . . Well, goodnight Mrs. N."

"Goodnight, Mr. Bailey. Have a good time."

She followed him into the hall, and as he lifted a black coat from off a chair and went to put it on, a chorus of voices from the stairhead called, "Goodnight, Mr. Bill. Goodnight, Mr. Bill." And a female voice piped, "You do look pretty."

He walked to the bottom of the stairs and, looking up, said, "Thanks, Katie, me love. Goodnight, Mark. Goodnight, Willie."

"Will you come and sing to us when you come in, Mr. Bill?"

"Yes, Katie, yes; I'll come and sing to you when I come in. Go on now, off to bed. Goodnight."

As he turned towards the door he muttered under his breath, "You won't blame me, will you, if I keep me promise?"

Her voice as low as his, she replied, "I would prefer that you broke it."

He paused now as he murmured, "Do you think I'm pretty?" and when for answer he got a bleak stare, he laughed, saying, "Do as I always tell you; mind, don't answer the door to anybody. There's some nasty types about, including your mother. By the way, have you heard from her this past week?"

"No."

"Good."

Hastily she closed the door on him, then went into the sitting room and dropped onto the couch. But she did not switch on the television, which had been her intention; instead, she sat looking at the artificial flames coming from the electric fire and she tried to recall what her life had been like before this middle-of-the-road man had come into it.

4

HE HAD BEEN WITH THEM FOR TEN WEEKS NOW AND IT WAS THE FIRST TIME HE had been so late coming in for his meal. It was half past seven when he entered by the back way, and she was ready to say, "If you are going to be as late as this you should at least let me know," but at the sight of his face, she said, "Is anything the matter?"

"I've lost a mate."

"Oh!" was all she could find to say.

He took off his coat and sat down at the corner of the table, "He was comin' back from visiting his wife's people in Wales; a lorry ran into them. His wife and four-year-old boy went with him; the three-year-old child's in hospital. I had to see to . . . to things. God, you wouldn't believe . . . " He dropped his head onto his hands. "Three miles outside the town it happened. Can you imagine it? Practically on the doorstep. And he wouldn't have gone if I hadn't said, 'Take your last week's holiday now; if not, you won't get it afore Christmas as we are up to the eyes.'"

She felt helpless as she watched him now join his hands and bang them hard on the table.

"Can I get you anything? A drink? Something to eat?"

He straightened up and leaned back in the chair; after a moment he said, "Nothing to eat, but a strong coffee, please. I'm going to slip

29

out again, call at the hospital to see how the child is. Then I want a drink. By God, yes, I want a drink.... Is there any hot water?"

"Yes, plenty."

"Then I'll have a quick sluice. Don't make the coffee yet."

As he left the kitchen she hurried after him and up the stairs and into the attic playroom, just in time to stop her small brood from engulfing him as they usually did. Then she returned downstairs and waited. Twenty minutes later he was in the kitchen again, shaved and looking spruce, as he usually did, except that his face was grim. He gulped at the coffee, gave her a brief, "So long!" and went out.

She busied herself for most of the evening, then sat in the sitting room and awaited his return.

It was half past eleven when she heard the key in the door. She didn't leave the room, thinking he would go straight upstairs, but within a minute or so the sitting room door opened and he entered, saying, "Saw the light."

She could see immediately that he had been drinking, and more than usual, but he was steady on his feet and his speech was only slightly slurred.

"Still up?" he said.

"Yes."

"Got any of that inferior coffee of yours waitin' to be golloped?"

"I think I might manage a cup." She passed him, but as she opened the door she turned and said, "Don't talk, please, until we get into the kitchen. Mark's been restless; he's just gone to sleep."

With exaggerated steps now, he tiptoed across the hall and followed her into the kitchen, and sitting down by the table, he said, "I like this. Best room in the house." Then added immediately, "You've got your stiff neck on again 'cos I'm tight."

She did not answer, and he said, "So would you be if you had gone through what I have the day. You know something? I looked on him almost as a son, 'cos I started him the same way as I'd been started, tea-boy, everybody's dog's-body. I made him do all the things I'd done. My dad was a brickie, you know, and I couldn't wait to get on the buildings with him. Played the nick most of my last year at school. Well"—he tossed his head—"nearly all my time at school I played the nick. But what d'you think? He wouldn't ask for me to be taken on with his lot, putting up skyscraper flats. Muck, he called them. But he got me set on with a small man, Carter. Funny that, you know. Dad seemed a funny man to me then, but he was right. Oh yes, he was right. Mr. Carter had six blokes working for him. The same six had been with him twelve years, and what those blokes didn't know

30

about building wasn't worth knowing. And I watched them. I copied them, and each of them let me into his own private tricks. I was fifteen when I started, and I was thirty when old Carter died. And his wife said to me, 'You've been a good lad, Bill. He thought the best of you. I've had offers for the business, but you go to the bank and get a loan, and it's yours.' And that's what I did. There's none of those six alive now. But I gradually picked me own team, kicking out the scum on the way an' them that say, what's yours is mine, and what's mine's me own. There's a lot of bloody double dealin' scroungers in this business, you know, setting your stuff on the side, under your bloody nose. Anyway—" He took a sip of the coffee, and, looking across the table at her, said, "You know, you make rotten coffee, Mrs. N. Do you know that?"

She gave a tight smile as she answered, "I'm so glad you like it, Mr. Bailey."

"You're all right. You know that?"

"Yes; yes, I'm very much aware that I'm all right."

"You're laughing at me behind that face of yours, aren't you?"

"Yes, Mr. Bailey, I'll agree with everything you say tonight."

He bowed his head now, saying softly, "I'm in a hell of a stew. You see, he was fifteen an' all when I took him on, an' just like I'd been, full of tongue and backchat. He thought he was the bloody cat's pyjamas, good as the next an' better than most, and he was an' all. And like me, he was a worker an' wanted to learn. I made him go to night school like I did. . . . Oh, that's stretched your face a bit, Mrs. N., hasn't it? Me goin' to night school. Well, you see it was all right being able to do every job on the site, but there was a business side to it; things had advanced in that way since I ran round with the tea can. And I was out to learn. Still am. But you wouldn't believe that, would you? No; no, you wouldn't By the way, how's your mother these days? You don't mention her. She comes up, I suppose, when I'm out of the way?"

"No, I haven't seen her; but she's started to phone, in order, you understand, to tell me what a dreadful daughter I am. But . . . "

"So, you haven't seen her? My! My!"

"No, but I understand she's not too well and I've promised to go across tomorrow afternoon." She smiled now, adding, "I'll have to put my armour on, though."

"Aye; aye, that'll be necessary." He now looked down on his joined hands. He remained like that for some moments, and then he said vehemently, "I'd jail every mother's son of them that pass on a hill. There's a type of driver whose one aim in life seems to be to get in front and stick there. They don't give a damn what they pass, from a kid on a tricycle to a thirty-five articulated tonner. That type wouldn't take any notice if it was the pope escorted by a bloody chorus of archangels."

She bit tightly on her lip, as she, too, now bowed her head. Even in his sorrowing he was himself.

His hand came out and caught hers, and she jerked her head up as he said, "I wasn't intending to be funny; that's just me, 'cos I'm not in a laughin' mood."

"I . . . I understand." She did not withdraw her hand; and now he said softly, "It's a long time since I felt het up like this inside. I'll never forget the sight of them lying there in the hospital. They phoned me straightaway, the police. You know why: Because he had me name in his wallet! I was the one he'd chosen to be informed if anything happened. He thought as much about me as I did of him, you know. He was almost half my age, but we were close. More than mates; like father and son."

They both turned now when a small cough came from the direction of the open door, there to see Mark standing.

"I've got a pain in my tummy, Mam."

As Mark came towards them she withdrew her hand, then rose from the table, saying, "Come along. I'll make you a hot drink."

"I'll be going up," he said, rising from the table.

She looked towards him and said, "I'm sorry I can't be of any help."

"That's all right. Nobody can help much in a situation like this. Goodnight. Goodnight, laddie." He ruffled Mark's hair as he passed, and the boy turned round and watched him leave the room. Then, sitting down on a stool by the stove, he said, "Mam."

"Yes, dear?"

"Are you going to marry Mr. Bill?"

"What! Marry Mr. Bill? Whatever put that into your head? No, of course not."

"Well, you were holding hands."

"Oh, that was because a friend of his has . . . is ill, and he's rather worried about him. Is that what's been worrying you, about me marrying?"

"Well, no; but I think about it."

"Well, don't think about it anymore because I shall never marry Mr. Bill."

"Would you be his girlfriend?"

"What! No, I certainly would not; never be his girlfriend. What makes you say such a thing?"

"Well, people have girlfriends and boyfriends."

"Well, I'll certainly never be Mr. Bill's girlfriend. A friend, yes, but not ... well, his girlfriend. Do you understand?"

The boy did not indicate whether he understood or not, but when a few minutes later she handed him the hot drink, he said, "I like Mr. Bill. It ... it would be nice if you married him."

"Mark." She pulled a chair forward and sat down near him; bending until her face was close to his, she said, "You're nine years old; you won't understand this, but Mr. Bill is not the marrying kind, he doesn't want to marry; he is what he calls a middle-of-the-road man. You won't understand that either, as yet, but it means that he neither wants to marry, on the one hand, nor be entangled with ... girlfriends on the other. Do you understand that at all?"

He screwed up his face, then took another drink and said, "Katie says you'll marry him; she bet me ten pence; but then she's reading this story about a princess and them living happy ever after."

"Oh, my dear." She put her arm round him and pressed him to her, saying softly, "Why would I want to marry anyone when I have you and Katie and Willie. Come along now, and finish that drink, then up to bed."

A short time later, when she put out the light in her room she turned her face into the pillow, saying as she had done once before, "Oh, my God!"

It was four o'clock the following afternoon when she returned home from a visit to her mother. She was feeling worn out. Her armour had been dented in several places: she had listened to a tirade against ... that man; she had heard of all the things her mother had sacrificed on her behalf to send her to a private school, to dress her in the best, for her to then marry a free-lance writer who would leave her roofless when he died but for her insistence that he take out an insurance.

She had expected a greeting from the children en masse as she entered the house. It being half term, she had left Mark in charge, instructing them that no one must go out until she returned. But there was no sound from the sitting room or the kitchen or the study, and the only light showing was in the hall.

She ran upstairs, calling, "Mark! Katie!"

She opened the playroom door in some anxiety, then heaved a sigh as she saw them all sitting on the old couch.

"What's this? What's the matter with you?"

It was Katie who answered, her voice breaking, saying, "He's gone. Mr. Bill's gone."

"What! What are you talking about?"

33

Mark got up from the couch. His eyelids were blinking rapidly, and his lips trembled before he said, "He . . . he came this afternoon and took his cases . . . and his golf clubs."

She put her hand out against the stanchion of the door, and her voice croaked as she said, "Did he say anything? Leave a message?"

"No. I asked him where he was going, and he said that he might be going into a hotel for the time being, and he left you a letter. It's on the desk in the study."

She seemed to slide down the stairs, and there was the letter lying on the pad.

Tearing it open, she read:

I've had enough, Mrs. N. I'm not one for suffering for suffering's sake; and yesterday was a bad enough day. And I knew that sometime, my lugs being what they are, ever at the ready, I was likely to hear something that would knock the stuffing out of me, and I did just that, for I happened to step back towards the kitchen to tell you that I'd be going out early this morning when I heard the lad's question. And if anything sounded final and underlined, your answer did.

Enclosed is a couple of month's pay in lieu of notice. And it's funny, isn't it? This is the first time I've written at this desk. Such is the irony of life. . . . Anyway, I'll get to sleep now nights instead of wanting to come along the landing and bash your door down. You can tell your mother she was right. That'll make her happy.

Bill

She put one hand tightly over her mouth, the other hugged her waist, and like this she walked up and down the narrow room half a dozen times. Then she stopped abruptly before rushing from the room and into the hall and to the telephone table and grabbing the yellow pages directory from its drawer. There were two hotels in the centre of the town: The Grange and The Palace. There were three others, but they'd be farther from his work.

She rang The Grange.

"Can you please tell me if a Mr. Bailey has booked in this afternoon?"

"I'll enquire, madam."

She kept tapping her teeth with her fingernails while staring at the mouthpiece.

"No, there is no such name on the register, madam."

"Thank you."

She rang The Palace. "Can you please tell me if a Mr. Bailey has booked in this afternoon?"

"Hang on. I'll enquire." The voice sounded chummy.

"A Mr. William Bailey?"

"Yes."

"Yes, he booked in just a short while ago."

"Is he still in the hotel?"

There was a pause before the voice said, "Yes, he must be; his key isn't here."

"Is there a phone in his room?"

"Yes, of course, madam."

"Would you put me through, please?"

There was a pause before the voice said, "Yes, right."

She had the feeling that everything inside her head had come loose.

"Hello. Yes?"

"Bill."

There was a long pause.

"Oh, you've done a bit of detective work? And quick at that. It's all right; you don't need to apologise."

"*Bill.*" She had yelled his name. "Listen to me. If you had let those ... lugs of yours remain just a little longer outside the kitchen door you would have heard why I gave my son the answer that I did, when I went on to explain to a nine-year-old in the best way I could that you are not the marrying kind of man, but a middle-of-the-road one. That's what you have impressed upon me, isn't it, since the day you came into this house? You know what you are.... You are a big, loud-mouthed egotist. You consider no one's feelings but your own. How do you know I haven't been waiting for you to come along the landing and bash my door in? But I had to tell myself it was something that a middle-of-the-road man wouldn't do. Now you've booked in, haven't you? Well, you can book out just as quick again and get yourself home. Do you hear me? ... Are you there?"

"Aye.... Aye, I'm here."

"Well, then, what do you want me to do? Sing, 'Won't You Come Home, Bill Bailey?'"

There came a rumbling chuckle from the earpiece; then, in his quiet voice, he said, "I'll be back there, lass, in quicker time than it took me to come. But that's if I can get past the receptionist; she's had her eye on me from the time I came in. She doesn't know I'm a middle-of-the-road man."

When she heard the click of the phone, she thrust the receiver back

35

on the stand; and once more she was holding her mouth tightly with her hand; then she was running up the stairs.

They were waiting for her, all standing facing the door. And going to them she gathered them into her arms and almost spluttered, "He's coming back."

"Oh, Mam! Mam!"

"Now listen." She pushed them away from her. "I want you to stay up here and be quiet for a time. Now you will, won't you? You may have a picnic. I'll ... I'll bring your tea up. And there's jelly and blancmange."

"Oh, goodie!" Katie was now dancing from one foot to the other.

Ten minutes later they were settled; and now she dashed into her room, dabbed at her face, combed her hair, and took in several deep breaths in an effort to compose herself; then she went downstairs.

When she reached the foot of the stairs, the phone rang. She ran to it.

"Fiona?"

"Yes, Mother."

"He's gone then?"

"Who's gone?"

"Don't be obtuse, girl. Mrs. Quinn from two doors down phoned me. She knew I'd be pleased to hear that he had gone, bags and baggage, this afternoon."

Fiona gritted her teeth before she said in the softest tone she could muster at the moment, "Mother, she must have made a mistake; Bill and I are going to be married ... or live together. We haven't decided yet."

"*What!*"

"I think you heard; marriage or sin. Whatever suits us both."

"You wouldn't! Not with that man."

"I would, Mother; and am. And I'm only too pleased to be doing so. Now phone Mrs. Quinn and tell her to keep you informed of the proceedings." She forced herself to put the phone gently down, then she went into the kitchen.

The daylight had gone. She drew the curtains, then looked at the clock. It was twenty minutes since she had phoned. It shouldn't take him five minutes by car from the town centre, but he would have had to do some repacking.

Her heart hit her ribs as she heard the sound of the car drawing up at the gate.

She made herself go to the sink and turn on the taps ready for washing up dishes that weren't there.

36

When the back door opened she had to force herself to turn round. She picked up the tea towel and dried her hands; then she looked at him standing within the doorway.

He came slowly towards her, took the tea towel from her hand; then, holding her gaze, he put his arms about her and, his voice husky, said, "You mean all that you said on the phone?"

She had to swallow deeply before she could answer: "Every word."

She was being kissed as she couldn't remember ever being kissed, and it seemed never ending. When eventually he released her, he said, "I've got a lot of time to make up, because I've wanted to do that since the minute I stepped into this house. You know that?"

"No, I don't know that, Bill Bailey. I only know that you're an idiot to have played the game you have."

"What ... well, what else could I do? What would have been your answer if, within the first week or two, I, in my polite refined way, had said, 'What about it, Mrs. N.? What about us two gettin' hitched?' You were as prickly as Margaret would be at the Labour Conference. And of course, don't forget, there was your mother.... Anyway, my question to you is"—he paused—"Do you think you could ever *really* love me, not just take me on?"

She pursed her lips and wagged her head as she said, "I could try."

"Enough to marry me?"

"Oh, Bill." Her voice was soft, her whole expression was soft. "I love you enough to do whatever you want."

"*No, no!*" He made a pretense of pushing her away. " 'Cos that's temptin'. You know what you said last night? ... Not his girlfriend." Then his tone became serious, and he said, "I don't want you for a girlfriend, Fiona; I want you for a wife."

Slowly she put her arms around his neck and laid her lips gently on his; then, her voice a whisper, she said, "You're the best thing that's ever happened to me, Bill Bailey."

His throat swelled, his eyelids blinked, and he turned his head to the side for a moment, and no words came. But when they did, they were in the form of his usual cover-up: "But mind," he said, "I'm not taking you on simply because of yourself, it's because I want charge of those three kids in order to further their education and grammar like, and their usual musical instruction."

They were clinging together now, and almost between laughter and tears she said, "Never change, Bill Bailey. Promise me you'll never change."

5

"GET ON WITH YOUR TEA. I'VE TOLD YOU, IT'S NO USE LINGERING; HE WON'T BE back for a long time yet."

Fiona looked impatiently down on the three of them sitting round the kitchen table: Mark was slowly munching his last piece of cake; Katie was doing a tattoo with a spoon on an empty jelly dish; and Willie was picking at a spot on the back of his hand.

Fiona now gently smacked at Willie's hand, saying, "You'll make it bleed again. Leave it alone."

"Mam."

"Yes, Katie?"

"After the funeral will Mr. Bill's friends go straight to a house in Heaven?"

Fiona turned helplessly towards the stove, as if to find an answer there. But she was saved by Mark saying scornfully, "There are no houses in Heaven; people just float about."

"They don't! There are houses, big houses, mansions. 'Twas in the hymn."

"Don't be silly."

"I'm not being silly, our Mark. They've got to have a house; they can't fly about all the time. Anyway, I'm going to have a bungalow when I die, a nice little one, all to myself. And . . ."

38

"When I go to Heaven, I'm going to play marbles all the time."

Fiona, Mark, and Katie now turned their full attention on Willie; and he stared back at them and emphasised, "I am."

Katie sniffed, then said disdainfully, "That's daft; there'll be no marbles in Heaven."

"*There will! There are!*" The statement was firm and defiant. "The minister said so, the black one."

When Fiona said, "Who?" Mark explained, "He was from the monastery, Mam. He comes some Sundays for the children's service."

"Oh, oh." She nodded her head. And now her young son, looking up at her, said, "And Danger House . . . and com . . . muter games."

"You mean computer games." Mark was quick to correct him; and Willie was about to retort when Fiona picked him up from his seat and hugged him for a moment before putting him on the floor again, saying, "Upstairs with you all!"

Katie, however, was slow to rise from her seat; she looked up at her mother and, her face heavy-laden with the importance of her question, said, "When is Mr. Bill going to be our father?"

Fiona's answer was interrupted this time by her son's saying, "Who art in sixteen Woodland Avenue."

Fiona brought her lips tightly together in an effort to prevent herself from laughing outright. Mark was clever at catching and turning a phrase, but she pretended to ignore him. And so, looking down on Katie, she answered her, "I'm not sure yet, but sometime soon."

"Then he won't be a lodger anymore, will he?"

That thin resemblance to her mother was about to retort, "He is not a lodger, he is a paying guest," but she thrust it aside, saying, "No, you're right; he won't be a lodger anymore."

"What'll we call him?"

"Father Bill . . . Poppa Bill . . . Daddy Bill," sang Mark now as he marched towards the door; and his sister, taking up his mood, followed after him, chanting, "Mr. Bill went up the hill to get a pail of water," and Willie, as usual coming up in their train, took up the marching routine, and Fiona's voice followed them as she cried, "Get on with your homework, Mark. And you, Katie and Willie, you have an hour in the playroom before bed. And don't dare come downstairs, any of you." And she was about to turn and clear the dirty dishes from the table when their concerted voices hit her, "Well, tell Mr. Bill to come up and see us, else we will."

"*Get!*"

As she heard their footsteps scrambling up the stairs and the

39

thumping of their running feet across the landing, she looked up towards the ceiling and sighed.

She couldn't remember feeling so happy ever before; the only thing that was marring her present state was the fact that Bill was very cut up about the young fellow and his family dying like that, and the little girl in hospital.

She stopped in her clearing and now asked herself if she had said there was only one thing that was marring her happiness; she was forgetting her mother.... Oh, her mother ...

It was almost four hours later when she heard the car draw up at the gate, and she hurried from the sitting room to open the door.

A few minutes later he was in the hall, and she was in his arms, her slim body seeming to be lost in the bulk of him.

As he took off his overcoat and dropped it onto a chair, she said, "You hungry?"

"No, no. I'll have a cup of tea, but not yet. Come in here." He put his arm about her and led her into the sitting room, and when they were seated on the couch before the electric fire, he pointed to the artificial logs, saying characteristically, "We'll have that out of that; I can't stand make-believe things. We'll have an open fire put in there, eh?"

"I like my artificial logs."

He pulled her tightly to him, saying, "You'll like what I like or else." Then his mood changed suddenly; he lay back against the couch and became silent.

"Bad day?" she asked after a while.

"Horrible. I knew I'd miss him, but God! When it came to the final act I nearly howled aloud. As I said, lass, he was like a son, the one I always wanted and never had. I love kids. Well, you know that. By the way, they're quiet." He looked upwards.

"They've been in bed for some time now, and don't you go in to them tonight."

"Oh no. You needn't stress the point; I haven't a joke in me tonight. You know something, lass?"

"No, what?"

"They say blood is thicker than water ... that's all in me eye and Betty Martin. Those two, Dan's parents and the pair they had with them ... I can't get over it. All right, his mother's crippled with arthritis, but she's not yet sixty. And his dad's had two slight heart turns. But nevertheless, that little lass in hospital is their grandchild. But they were adamant they couldn't take her on. Get a kind of housekeeper in, I said, and I'll stand half the racket; 'cos they're not

40

without money. I know that. But no, no. And then there was his nephew and his piece, both in their thirties. But no, no; again no; they couldn't have the child. They were both in business, you see. And what was more, they had made up their minds when they married they didn't want children. What they should have said was that they are a couple of upstarts, too big for their bloody boots, moving into a bigger house in the Welsh upper belt. . . . And talking about houses. The old man might have a dicky heart, but he hasn't got a dicky head. You know what he's been up to over the last three or four days? He's made arrangements for all the furniture to go to the sale, and he's put the house in the hands of an estate agent. You know, Fiona"—his voice was grim now—"if it hadn't been I'd just come back from the funeral, I would have shot me mouth off, 'cos they didn't give a damn about that child lying there. The only thing I got out of him was that he'd come back within a week or two when her arm was properly fixed and she was fit to leave hospital and decide then what was to be done with her. And I'll tell you what they'll do, I know it, they'll have her adopted. You'll see, they'll have her adopted. But whatever happens to her, I'll damn well see that what is made out of the house and furniture and insurance goes into trust for her."

She held his hand tightly, but could find nothing to say, and after a moment he went on, "It came to me today why Dan and Susie only went up once a year to see them. Sometimes they'd stay a week, but more often only two or three days; and before he got married he made just flying visits. Somehow he didn't seem to belong to them. I could recognise nothing in either of them that was in him. I suppose he missed something right from the start and that's why he cottoned on to me. And I was ready for a son." He now turned his face fully towards her and, lowering his voice, said, "And I'm ready for a wife, lass. I asked meself the day, if I hadn't you to come back to what would I have done? Oh, I know"—he tossed his head—"got blued, really stinkingly blued. And now we're on the subject of you and me, it's gettin' harder each night not to come along that landing and bash your door down, as I've said afore; and I nearly did last night; you know that?"

She made a small motion with her head.

"Well, you were lucky you have three kids; I somehow couldn't do it with them scattered about. I imagined just as we'd be gettin' down to it Katie would put her head round the door and say, 'What you doin', Mr. Bill?' "

She choked and gulped, then dropped her head onto his shoulder, saying, "Oh, Bill." And he, his voice now almost a broken whisper, said, "But there's no fear of that happening the night, lass. Put your arms around me and hold me tight 'cos all I want at the moment is a mother."

They got out of the car in the hospital car park, and once again Fiona asked in an undertone, "Are you sure it's all right to take the three of them in there?"

"Woman, I've told you, there were squads in there yesterday."

She now looked down at the three pairs of eyes staring up at her, and after drawing in a sharp breath she muttered, "I've told you now, behave yourselves."

"They always behave themselves. Come on." He held out his hand to Katie, adding, "What does she think you're going to get up to in there, coup your creels? That's what the Geordies say, don't they?"

Katie, glancing mischievously over her shoulder at her mother, said, "She thinks we might all sing, 'Won't You Come Home, Bill Bailey?'"

He, too, now glanced at Fiona; then, looking from Willie to Mark, he said, "That's a good idea, isn't it?" and they both laughed, while Willie piped up, "We didn't bring our tin whistles."

"Oh, what a pity! Why didn't you think of it beforehand?" And at this, Willie, now hanging on to Bill's other hand, grinned up at him knowingly.

A few minutes later, after walking along two corridors, they entered a wide room with beds and cots along both side walls. Every cot had a child in it and with the exception of one all were surrounded by people and toys, some of the latter almost as big as the children.

Bill led the way to the cot where the child was sitting with her head lowered as if looking at the plastered arm lying on the coverlet.

"Hello there, Mamie. Look who I've brought to see you."

The child raised her head and there was a dazed look in her eyes for a second; then her face brightened and she said, "Oh, Uncle Bill."

"Look who's here!"

Katie was now standing wide-eyed and wide-mouthed and hugging a small parcel to her breast, and Bill had to tug her towards him by the arm while saying to the child in the bed, "Look! This is Katie. And you're nearly as big as her and you just turned three and she all of seven. My, my!"

There was no response from either child, and now Bill, turning his head to the side and speaking into the back of Katie's neck, said, "Say hello to her."

Katie made an effort: she closed her mouth, then opened it, then shut it again while she stared at the bandaged head and discoloured chin; then she uncharacteristically burst into tears.

Taking the parcel from her, Fiona lifted her into her arms and, smothering her head against her shoulder, whispered, "There now; there now. She's all right; she's all right. Now look! If you don't stop you'll have to go outside."

Bill now took the box from Fiona's hand and gave it to Willie, saying, "You give it to her." And on this Willie, utterly composed, moved up by the bedside, grinned at the small occupant, and, handing her the box, said, "They're mixed, some's got chocolate on, t'others just toffee. There's half a pound."

It was some seconds before the small hand came out and took the box from Willie. But when she made no verbal response Bill leaned over her, saying gently, "What did you say to Willie for those nice sweets?"

The child looked up into Bill's face and her lips trembled, and her eyelids blinked, and she said, "Uncle Bill, I want my mammy."

Bill now turned quickly from the bed, muttering softly, "Oh, God!"

Fiona had put Katie down on the floor again and she now stared at this man who, she imagined, could never be lost for words on any occasion: he was the quick thinker of the rejoinder, the man who could take the words out of your mouth and make them funny. She looked from him to the pathetic figure of the child in the bed, and now pushing him to one side, together with Willie and Katie, she drew a chair towards the head of the bed and, sitting down, she took the hand from the box and stroked it gently whilst saying, "It's all right, my dear; your mammy . . . has gone on a little holiday."

The round red-rimmed eyes looked into hers and the quivering mouth said one word now, "Daddy."

"Well"—Fiona swallowed deeply—"he's with your mammy. She's . . . she's not very well." There was a break in her own voice now and she turned a desperate glance onto Bill. But she got no help from him for he was still standing with his back to the bed and stroking Katie's hair with quick movements of his fingers, as if endeavouring to brush something from it.

"When you are better you can come to our house."

They all looked at Mark now who was standing at the other side of the bed.

He had caught the child's attention. Her face seemed to brighten for a moment, and when she said, "And Johnny?" Mark said quietly, "Yes, and Johnny. And Katie's got a dollhouse and it's got six rooms, and I've got a rocking horse, it's called Horace."

Fiona stared at her son. There had always been something different about Mark since he was quite young. She recalled the times when his father and she would be arguing, especially if the children had been making a noise and he couldn't get on with his writing, which, as he would inform her loudly, was their livelihood. At these times Mark was apt to come between them and ask some irrelevant question but one that needed an answer. She recognised, as time went on, that he was trying to divert their attention from each other and onto himself.

She was smiling her approval across the bed at him when Willie burst in with, "Horace's not yours now, he's mine. I scratched my name on his belly."

"Willie!"

"Well, I did, Mam." He looked up at Fiona.

"She means you should say 'stomach.'" It was Katie now, tears forgotten, and at this Willie grinned.

Then all their attention again was drawn to the child in the bed, for she put her hand to her head and, her small face screwing up, she had begun to cry.

Bill immediately drew the attention of a nurse, and when she came to the bed she said quietly, "Head aching, dear? Oh, we'll soon give you something to ease that." Then turning to Fiona she made a gesture that they should all move away, and when they were in the aisle she said, "She'll have a drink, then she'll go to sleep. She sleeps a lot; her head was badly bruised."

"Seriously?" Fiona spoke the word gently, and the nurse said, "No, not as far as we know. There was no visible damage, only grazing and cuts, but mainly on the scalp. She'll be all right." She nodded reassuringly.

Fiona moved towards the door, but Bill did not immediately follow; he stood at the foot of the bed gazing at the child whose face was now awash with tears. Then he turned abruptly and joined the others, but he didn't speak. Not until he was seated in the car, with his hands on the wheel and his head bent over it, were his feelings expressed, in the word, "*Hell!*"

"Eeh, Mr. Bill. He swored."

"Be quiet, Willie."

"Well, he did, he said ... "

"Willie!"

Fiona was looking straight ahead through the windscreen as she said, "I feel like an afternoon out. Would you like to take us all to tea somewhere?"

Bill slowly straightened himself and turned his gaze on her; then slowly he said, "Yes, woman. Yes, that's what we'll do." And leaning his head back, he said, "Right kids?" And after a small pause they all answered as in one voice, "Right, Mr. Bill."

They had driven to the coast; they had walked along a cold and windy beach, and for a time the children had joined in a game with others and a dog and a ball. Then they'd had tea in a hotel where Katie had caused a stir among the occupants of the room by remarking, and none too quietly, "They've got real tablecloths on here."

At home they'd had another tea, followed by the usual routine that led up to the children's going to bed. And so it was some time before Fiona and Bill went into the sitting room, where Bill, dropping onto the couch, said, "You know what I'd like to do?"

"Yes."

"You don't, 'cos I'd like to get really bottled up."

"I know that."

"You do?"

"Yes, because every time there's a crisis your reaction is to go and get bottled up."

"But I've only been bottled up once since I came here, the night of the accident."

"Yes, that's right, but the urge has been on you at other times, too."

"You see too bloomin' much, woman."

"I don't mind if you go and get bottled up"—she sat down close to him—"the only thing I would object to, even if I hadn't to stay back and see to the children, would be if you expected me to accompany you."

He gave a short laugh, saying, "That'll be the day when I see you bottled up. I'll know then that the last vestige of your mother has been wiped out.... By the way, did you see your mother's stooge from two doors down"—he thumbed towards the street—"in the nursery when we were there?"

"You mean Mrs. Quinn? No, I didn't notice her."

"Well, she noticed you, she noticed us. And she was there when we came out an' all. I bet by now the jungle wires have been singing."

"Well, she couldn't make much out of that, could she, visiting a children's ward?"

"Well, we were together, and if we're together so much in the day, we will definitely be together much more in the night, will be the general opinion if I know anything. Anyway, I want to talk to you about that. When are we going to make our wicked thoughts respectable? Do you want it done in church or ... ?"

"Oh no!" She held up her hand. "Not in church, not in our church anyway. Mother would have a protest meeting outside. No, I wouldn't do that. And you being a divorced man, and an agnostic into the bargain ... "

"I'm a what!"

"You know what I mean, neither one thing nor the other."

"That's wrong. I have me own idea of why, seeing that He's built us as we are, we've got to do nothing about it, until we sign our names."

She laughed gently as she pushed him away from her, and said, "That's like a current; it's running through your mind all the time."

"Aye, you're right, and it's a wonder it hasn't given you an electric shock before now." And in his turn he pushed her, and they both leaned against each other laughing gently.

Releasing herself from his embrace, she said, "All this is sidetracking the main issue, isn't it?"

He thrust out his lower lip, then ran his hand through his hair before he said, "The bairn; aye, I can't get her out of me mind. You see, I saw her soon after she was born, before Dan even. And later when he saw her the tears ran down his face: he loved his boy, but he always wanted a girl. I've watched her grow. She was chatting before she could walk. She took after her mother in that way, 'cos Susan was a chatterer." His voice now rose almost to a shout as he demanded of her, "Can you understand those grandparents? Can you?"

"Shh! You'll have the lot of them downstairs in a minute."

"I'm sorry. But can you?" His voice had dropped to a mere whisper, and she said, "Yes, in a way; they are ill and they're old. But not the nephew and his wife. Tell me"—she took his hand now—"if you hadn't come here and things hadn't turned out as they have, what would you have done about her? The truth now."

He turned his head away, saying, "Well, the truth is, I would have tried to adopt her in some way."

"And that's what you would like to do now?"

He looked at her, and after a pause he said, "I wouldn't ask it of you; you've got enough on your plate in bringing up those." He raised his eyes to the ceiling.

"What if I want to do it?"

"It would just be to please me and that would make me feel under a sort of ... oh, I don't know, taking advantage. No, it's no go."

"Would you allow me to have some thoughts on the matter and to tell you that my mind was already made up when I saw that child in

46

that bed today? Of course, too, it was how you felt about her, but I knew as soon as I saw her. And then when she asked about her mother, that settled it completely. Now what's the alternative? If we don't take her, she'll be put into care somewhere. And"—she raised her eyebrows now and poked her head towards him—"what kind of a life would I have with you after that? You would become unbearable; you'd go on the razzle, and I would then have to admit my mother was right, I must have been blind. She took your measure, you know, the minute you stepped in the door, the middle-of-the-road man. . . . "

His arms were tight about her, his mouth was equally tight on hers; then, when at last they drew apart, he said, "Boloney! She thought I was right for her, the old bag. But lass"—his voice dropped to a tender note—"I've got no words to tell you what I'm feeling at this minute: I'd only make a hash of it and come out with something brash, in tune with me character. Yet I'll manage this—and don't expect me to repeat it." He tweeked her nose gently with his finger. "I've thought about you as a lady from the first minute I set eyes on you, a real lady every inch of you, inside an' all. I pass women in the street every day and I'm comparing them with you, and if we never married, if nothing ever happened after this moment, I'd know that me life had been worthwhile in just meeting you."

"Oh, Bill. Bill."

When she laid her head gently on his shoulder he held her for a moment; then reverting to his usual self, he said, "Oh, for God's sake, woman, don't start bubbling. I've had enough of it today. Come on; let's have some of your horrible coffee . . . or tea." And lifting her head up, he held her face between his hands, ending with, "And let's discuss the day I can make an honest woman out of you. And it's got to be soon, or else this town'll experience something that'll put the rape of the Sabine women into the shade."

6

SHE WAS SINGING, HER VOICE RISING ABOVE THE SOUND OF THE HOOVER, WHEN the phone rang. She was still smiling when she picked it up; then the smile slid from her face at the voice coming over the wire, "*Fiona.*"

"Yes, Mother."

"I suppose you're going to tell me you've been too busy, that's why you couldn't come round to see me."

"Yes, Mother, I have been busy. But even so, I can see no point in coming to see you when we do nothing but fight."

"I do not fight, girl: I have never fought; I merely state facts and point out things that you would see yourself if you weren't at the moment hypnotised by that awful man."

"Well, Mother, your facts are wasted. And let me tell you I'm very happy to be hypnotised by that awful man whom I intend to marry."

There was a long pause, and she was about to put the phone down when the voice came again, "The minister won't allow it, he's divorced."

Smirking now, she gave the reply that Bill himself would assuredly have given: "Oh, we don't mind the minister's being divorced."

"*Fiona.*" The word seemed to make the wires ring in her ears.

"All right, Mother. But we are not going to trouble the minister."

"Girl, you wouldn't go to a registry office?"

48

"We'll go to a voodoo man, Mother, if we want to."

"*Really!* I don't know what to make of you, Fiona. You never came out with things like that before. Voodoo man, indeed! You're getting almost as common as him, if that's possible."

"It's a nice feeling. And I'm busy, Mother; have you finished?"

"No, I haven't, and I can tell you this: you're getting your name up in another quarter."

"Really? That sounds interesting."

"You may take it lightly, but imagine how I feel when I'm told that men, workmen, are coming to your house at all hours and staying all hours. Talk about having an affair with the milkman. I'm telling you, girl, you're the talk of the street. And what's more ... "

Fiona banged down the phone and stepped back from the hall table and stared at it. That woman! What was she to do with her? And that Mrs. Quinn. She must be ever on the watch. Of course she had nothing else to do: she didn't go out to work and her husband was abroad most of the time. But what would the new people next door think if they listened to her? She had always considered herself fortunate that this house was the end of the avenue and there wasn't another Mrs. Quinn to the right of her.

She went into the kitchen and stood leaning with her hands on the sink looking through the window, down the garden. Her teeth were tight together. Women like her mother and Mrs. Quinn were the very devil.

She recalled the incident that her mother was referring to. It happened only two days ago when Mr. Ormesby, one of Bill's men, came by with a message from Bill to say that he had been trying to get through to her all afternoon from Newcastle but the line seemed dead; and so he had phoned the works and asked Bert Ormesby to stop by and tell her he was being held up and to test the telephone to see if it was all right.

It had been pouring with rain and she had invited Mr. Ormesby in; and she had made him a cup of tea and they had sat at the table talking, mostly about Bill and how, if he brought off this deal he was after, which was the building of a small estate at the top of Brampton Hill in the best part of town, it would be a good thing for them all for the next year or two.

She knew quite a bit about Mr. Bert Ormesby; in fact, she knew quite a bit about each of his eleven men, the permanent ones, because, in a way, he considered them his family. Bert, she knew, was the only bachelor among them and he was the butt of the gang because, not only was he a teetotaller, but he also didn't smoke and he attended church. Result of his father running a pub and his mother being a Presbyterian, Bill said; and guess who won.

The children had come into the kitchen and he had talked and laughed with them. He had surprised her further by telling her he was also a Sunday school teacher. His visit had lasted over an hour, during which time he had gone through three cups of tea and two tea cakes.

She wanted to cry but she wasn't going to. She wouldn't allow her mother to mar her happiness. Nevertheless, the brightness had gone out of the day.

At half past three she picked up Willie from nursery school and was thankful that his stay there was drawing to a close and that his next school would be nearer to Katie's and Mark's. Then she drove halfway across town to collect them, and as usual, having tumbled into the back of the car, they all talked at once, telling her the happenings of the day; and to each she made the appropriate sounds, until Katie remarked, "I smacked Josie Morgan's face."

"You what! Why did you do that?!"

" 'Cos she said I couldn't be a bridesmaid at a registry office; they didn't have bridesmaids at registry offices."

The car wobbled just the slightest, and Fiona's hands on the wheel tightened before she said, "Katie, haven't I told you not to talk in school about anything that happens at home?"

"I didn't, Mam."

"You must have."

"Well, I only told her last week that when you got married to Mr. Bill I'd be a bridesmaid, and she said her mother said you couldn't be bridesmaids at registry offices. But Anna said you could."

"Anna?"

"Yes, Anna Steele, she's my new friend. I've picked her instead of Josie because Josie swanks about their car and says it's a better one than Mr. Bill's Volvo."

"Your big mouth'll open so far it'll swallow you one of these days," Mark now said. And for answer, he was told vehemently, "Well, it's far better to have a big mouth than a big nose that could poke a drain."

"Stop it! Both of you."

Except for the hum of the car there was silence for some minutes; it was broken by Willie saying, "I wish I was old and six."

Her eyelids blinked. She pressed her lips tightly together. She wanted to laugh and at the same time she wanted to cry. It was one of those days.

50

Bill came in at his usual time; he took her in his arms, kissed her hand, then said, "Hello, Mrs. N."

"Hello, Mr. Bailey," she said.

Holding her away from him, he said, "What's the matter with your face, Mrs. N.? Something happened?"

"Only Mother . . . and Katie, and oh"—she shrugged her shoulders—"one of those days."

"Oh, God, not your mother again. What is it now?"

"I'm having it off with one of your men."

"No! Where is the . . . bugger? I'll break his bloody neck. How long has this been goin' on? I knew I should never have come to this house. I knew you would let me down."

"Shut up! And that language; they'll hear you upstairs." She was smiling now.

"What happened? What vitriol has she been pouring over the wires now?"

"Get your wash and have your meal and then I'll tell you."

He had his wash; he had his meal; he had romped with the children upstairs for half an hour; then got changed; and now they were in the kitchen. And when she told him, he didn't laugh or joke, as she might have expected; what he said was, "I'm sorry to say this, Fiona, but your mother is dangerous."

"I know that, Bill. I've known it for a long time. And lately things my father said to me that I didn't really understand years ago are beginning to have a real meaning. Once, I recall, she had been to his office and when he came in there were words; and later he said to me, apropos of nothing that had gone before, 'Men can be vile and cruel but they don't create as much harm as women who are sweet and poisonous.' I know now he had his reasons, because there are people who still think she is sweet, such a nice lady, so refined."

"Yes, so refined. That's the worst sort; you know where you are with slack gobs. . . . Well, Mrs. N., I can tell you, it's been one of those days for me an' all. I had a phone call from the old man about the child. Oh, of course, he said, they agreed that we should adopt her, oh yes. But there was the question of the money. What money? I said. Well, the company that was liable for the accident would have to provide for her until she came of age. Hadn't she lost all her family at one go? She had to be compensated. What were my thoughts on the subject? he said.

"Well, right away I told him what my thoughts were on the subject: I didn't want any of the money; if I was going to adopt her I would work for her and whatever money there was should be banked, together with the money from the house and furniture—I got that in—in a kind of trust in her name for whatever she needed later on.

"Yes, yes; he said he agreed with that wholeheartedly, but there should be a proviso, he thought, that if she went away on a holiday or to a private school she should be allowed to draw on it to meet expenses.

"You know, Fiona"—he wagged his finger at her—"I may be wrong, but I think I'm right when I tell you what was in the old boy's mind: they'd be willing to have her for her holidays and things as long as she was provided for. You see, they wouldn't expect, they wouldn't have the bare face to ask me to pay for her when she went to stay with them, but a trust is kind of an inanimate thing, it doesn't argue or feel, it just pays out."

"Oh, no, Bill."

"Oh yes, Mrs. N. You don't know that old boy like I've come to know him. He's been on the phone nearly every day. He would have signed her away to a workhouse in the old days rather than have the responsibility of her; he's that kind. And his wife an' all must be of the same calibre. Oh aye, there's a lot of odd bods in the world, Mrs. N., and it's been my misfortune to meet a number of them, all types and from all classes, you wouldn't believe." He now shook his head as if in perplexity, saying, "Can you understand anybody not wanting a lovable bairn like that? And ... and isn't it wonderful that she's taken to us. Which reminds me, if I want to slip along there I'd better go and get changed." He pulled her to him. "I hate this business of going out on my own at night now. Once we're made respectable we're going to have a baby-sitter and full-time daily help for you."

"No, thank you. I don't want full-time daily help. Baby-sitter, yes, and someone for a few hours in the morning. . . . "

"When you become Mrs. Bailey, Mrs. N., you're going to have someone to do the chores. I'm not going to have my wife taking in washing."

"Go on, get yourself away." She went to push him, but then said, "About the estate deal, has it come off?"

"No, not yet. I'll know tomorrow, but I think it's nearly sure, and if it is, I've got ideas for the chaps. It'll be a big thing and they've got to be in on it. They're all good lads, and they work like hell—an'—be merry for me. I know they lose nothing by it, but if this estate business comes my way, I'm going to form a kind of ... well, board, something like that, and they'll have a percentage of the profits at the end of the year. That's for the eleven permanent ones. Of course I'll have to take on a good few besides, and you never know what you're gettin' these days: joiners who think a dovetail is something that comes out of a pigeon loft; and painters who've never used a brush, just one of those rollers. Boy, I've had 'em all. Well, here I go, off to see ... our youngest daughter." He gripped her chin between his large hard hands now and, shaking it, he said, "What with the six I'm going to give you you'll be the finest mother of the ten best bairns in the world."

The thrust she gave him sent him out laughing, and she stood looking towards the door through which he had passed. What on earth had she done before he came into her life? What? She couldn't recall; she only knew that from the first sight of him her world had changed.

7

IT WAS TWO DAYS LATER WHEN, AT FOUR O'CLOCK IN THE AFTERNOON, HE
literally bounced into the kitchen, pulled her floured hands from a
bowl, and waltzed her round the room, singing, "There is a happy
land far, far away." And then he cried, "And it's not so far away the
day, Mrs. N.," and he gave her a smacking kiss before drawing in a
long breath and adding, "I've got it! And not only the estate but two
superior dwellings for the gentlemen on the finance board." His voice
had assumed a high and mighty air. " 'We are very impressed with
your work, Bailey.' But Sir Kingdom Come, as I call him, you know
from Brookley Manor. And you know what he said?"

"No, what did he say, Sir Kingdom Come from Brookley Manor?"
She was smiling widely at him.

"Well, he said, and in a very ordinary voice, 'I'm glad you've got it,
Mr. Bailey. I've seen your work and I would have been surprised if
they had given it to anyone else.' And he held out his hand to me and
shook it hard. . . . You know, there's nowt as funny a folk, is there,
dear? The old boy can trace his line back to when one of his ancestors
put a chastity belt on his wife and went off to the Crusades. By, I've
often thought those lasses must have had an awful time of it. . . . Don't
choke." He thumped her on the back. "And Mr. Ramshaw and Angus
Riddle and Arthur Pilby, well, they all spoke highly, too. But there

54

was one exception, Brown. To my mind he's the only fly in that financial company, a tsetse fly at that, poisonous individual, and compared to any of the others he's got as much breeding as a runt sow in a pigsty."

"Oh, Bill. You are the crudest, rawest individual."

"Aye, yes, I know; I know what I am, but you love me, don't you?" He was kissing her again. "And look at me! I'm all flour."

"Serves you right. Are you home for good?"

"No, I just dropped in to tell you . . . no to see, ma'am"—he pulled at his forelock—"if it would be all right to bring half a dozen or so workmen around the night, the ones that have hankies and don't spit."

"Bill!" she protested, slapping him, the while still laughing, "don't be vulgar."

"Well, it's those that have been with me longest," he said. "I want to talk this thing out, tell them where they stand. Anyway, as I said, ma'am, with your leave." He again touched his forelock, and she said, "What for, tea, a meal, or what?"

"No, nothing like that; they'll want to have a wash and brush up first. They'll come about half past seven or eight, and you, Mrs. N., can put on your best bib and tucker; I don't want to let them think I've been shootin' me mouth off for nothing."

He kissed her yet again, and was making for the door, humming, "There is a happy land," when she stopped him by hissing, "About this happy land, when I can get a word in, you've got to be more careful with your translations. They did their marching bit down the drive this morning to the car, singing it—and in no small voice."

"They didn't!" There was a large grin on his face. "The lot?"

"Yes, the lot."

"Well, if they say nothing worse than bum you won't have any need to worry."

"You've forgotten about our neighbour but one."

"Oh, I hope she heard them." Then poking his head towards her, he said, "She saw me coming in, Lady Quinn, and if she's still at the gate I'll sing it to her."

"Don't you dare."

"I dare, Mrs. N.," and on this he banged the door.

Quickly, she opened it again, and watched him walk down the drive; then she drew in a breath of relief when she saw him getting straight into the car.

They came in a bunch at a quarter to eight. Bill introduced them, seemingly in seniority of age: Barney McGuire, a sort of foreman,

Harry Newton, Tommy Turnbull, Bert Tinsley, Dan McRay, Jack Mowbray, Alec Finlay, Morris Fenwick, and Jos Wright. They all said either, "How d'you do, ma'am?" or, "Pleased to meet you."

She had placed extra chairs around the dining room table, and it looked like a boardroom. They filed in; an hour and ten minutes later they filed out again and into the sitting room where she had sandwiches and coffee and tea ready. She had, in a way, expected some quip from Bill about her not supplying any beer or hard stuff, but no, he did not make one joke about her but treated her with a dignity she found quite new to his character. He joked with the men, and they gave him as much as he sent. The chipping was mostly about the work, what he expected them to do and what they had decided not to do; but not once did he allude to her in any jocular way.

She was pleased by his attitude, yet at the same time it constricted her conversation with his men.

Five of them had come in their cars and had given the others a lift and, as it was a fine windless night, she walked with Bill down the drive and onto the pavement, and there, they once again shook hands with her and thanked her for her hospitality. And as they got into their cars Bill chipped them about what would happen if they were late for work in the morning. This he emphasised loudly to three of them who had openly arranged to go to a certain pub and have a drink before it closed.

She and Bill stood close together on the pavement and waited until the last car moved away; then arm in arm they went up the drive and into the house. And in the sitting room once more he looked at her and said, "What d'you think about them as a bunch?"

"They're very nice fellows, and they think a lot of you."

"Aye, sometimes; but you should hear what they say behind me back. They're going to tell me to go to blazes and as far beyond. I hear them and when I face them and say, 'What now?' all they come back with is, 'One of these days I'll walk out.' I'd like a pound for every time Jack Mowbray has said that. And you know something? He did walk out once, but he was back the next week. I hadn't got anybody in his place because I knew what would happen. 'What's brought you back?' I said. 'I didn't like the boss,' he said, 'he had a bigger mouth than yours.'"

She shook her head slowly, saying, "Well, in that case the man must have been quite unbearable."

"Watch it. Watch it, woman." He was about to grab her when a thin voice penetrated their preoccupation, calling from the stairway, "Mam, I want a drink; my throat's dry."

She clicked her tongue.

"Katie! I bet she's been awake all this time, in fact, all of them. I warned them they hadn't to come downstairs, so you had better go up and tell them what it was all about else there'll be no peace. Make it short and snappy."

"Yes, ma'am." And turning from her, he called, "Get back to that bed this minute else I'll give you a drink all right. . . . "

The scrambling she now heard overhead confirmed that they were all up and waiting.

Life was good.

At least that's how she felt until half past eleven the next morning when the phone rang.

"*Fiona!*"

"Yes, Mother?" She closed her eyes, drew in a long breath, and waited.

"You are determined to disgrace yourself, aren't you?"

She opened her eyes and stared at the mouthpiece, then replied, "Yes, Mother, if you say so. But what have I done now to disgrace myself?"

"Holding drunken parties. I couldn't believe it. But then I could. What that man has brought you to and what you seem to forget is that you've got three children to bring up. And what an example you are showing them: cars lined up outside, and the street raised as they piled into them late at night."

"*Shut up!*"

"What did you say?"

"You heard me, and I'll say it again: *shut up!* The drunken orgy to which you are referring was come by with tea and coffee, and the men were all gentlemen . . . yes gentlemen, having a board meeting to discuss a big new venture. Do you hear that, Mother? A big new venture, which spells money, big money . . . *great big money.* That should impress you. And the next time we have a board meeting here I'll invite Mrs. Quinn in and from then on you'll hear no more gossip from her, because, Mother, she is like you, she is jealous and would give her eyeteeth to have a man of her own. Again, like you, Mother."

"How dare . . . !"

"I haven't finished, so shut up. And I'll say this, and it's been in my mind for a long time, if you had looked after Father and treated him as you should have he might have been here today. But when he was ill and needed comfort, where were you? At your meetings, terrified, if you missed one, you wouldn't be the next chairwoman; and running after the Reverend Cottsmore, much to the annoyance of his wife. Now there you have it."

The perspiration was running from her brow into her eyes; her hand was trembling as she held the phone. She waited for the torrent of abuse, but it did not come.

She replaced the receiver, then leaned back with both hands on the small table and for a moment she felt she was going to pass out.

Her step was erratic as she walked towards the kitchen, and there, sitting down, she dropped her head onto her hands and started to cry, not because of what her mother had said to her but because of what she had said to her mother. She felt full of remorse, telling herself she should not have brought that up. She knew her father had been aware of her mother's feelings for the Reverend Cottsmore and that it had hurt him, but he himself had done nothing about it. Then she recalled something he had said to her the day before her wedding. He was sitting in the little summerhouse at the bottom of the garden. They had the place to themselves, and on that very day her mother had been out arranging the flowers in the church. He had taken her hand and said something she considered very odd at the time. "One day, my dear," he said, "you'll reach what is called the change. You've likely heard all about it. With some it lasts for years, all depending on the person's constitution. But during it never think of divorcing your man."

He had laughed, and she had laughed with him, but she knew now that he was telling her that her mother was experiencing the change and that she wasn't accountable for her instability. But if she remembered rightly, her mother's instability must have preceded the change for a long time. Yet this knowledge did not lessen her feeling of guilt, and she felt that her father, had he been alive, would certainly not have applauded her outburst.

She rose from the table, thinking she would go and have a sherry to help pull herself together, but almost aloud, she said, "No! Don't start that." Her girlhood friend, who was two years her senior, had begun with an early sherry when they moved to London six years ago, and what was she doing now? Attending Alcoholics Anonymous, and with a divorce on her hands. And so she made a strong cup of coffee.

But this didn't help and an hour later she lifted the phone again. When a small voice said, "Hello," she said, "I'm sorry, Mother." There was no reply, and so she went on, "I shouldn't have said what I did, but I was so upset because, as I said, it was just a business meeting and . . . and they only had tea and coffee." She was feeling like a child trying to explain some misdemeanour.

The voice came pitifully small now, saying, "You hurt me very deeply. You hurt me so much, Fiona."

"I'm ... I'm sorry, Mother. I really am. And ... and I'll call in sometime, sometime soon."

"Very well. Very well."

There was a pause and then the click of the receiver being put down.

She felt miserable all day, so much so that after picking up the children from school she had to make an effort to be interested in their chatter. And Mark, always sensitive to her change of moods, asked, "You got a headache, Mam?"

She replied, "Yes, rather a bad one." And later she gave the same excuse to Bill, because she didn't want him to think worse of her mother than he already did.

It was exactly seven days later, however, that all the feelings of remorse and guilt towards her mother were swept clean away.

She should have been prepared for her mother's visit, because two days previously, when picking up Katie from school, the child had informed her that her grandmother had been to the school and talked to her at dinnertime. Apparently she had questioned her about the child she had visited in hospital, and Katie had told her that it was Mr. Bill's and they were going to adopt it.

She had stopped the car and looked at Katie and said, "Is that what you said, exactly? Try to think."

So Katie thought; then she said, "I said its mother and father had died in a car accident and now it was Mr. Bill's."

She had stared at her daughter's apprehensive face, then smiled and said, "That's all right then." Yet for the remainder of the journey she had continued to ask herself why her mother should go to the school, if not to find out something to add to what she already knew.

It was known in the ward that negotiations were going on about the adoption of the child; so some talk may have filtered from there to her mother through Mrs. Quinn, whom she herself had seen on two occasions visiting another child in the ward. It would also be known that they were bringing Mamie home in a fortnight's time. But what was not widely known was that she and Bill were to be married in a fortnight's time.

It had rained almost incessantly for three days, and because of it the work on the clearing of the new sight had been held up, and this had brought Bill home at half past three this afternoon. And he was now in what was to be his study going over papers and plans.

She had picked up the children from school, settled them with their tea in the kitchen, taken Bill a cup of tea, and was crossing the hall when the front door bell rang. And there, under an umbrella, stood her mother. She felt her mouth drop open as she watched her close the umbrella, shake it, then lean it against the wall under the small porch.

"I've got to talk to you. . . . The children in?"

"Yes, they're in the kitchen having their tea." She watched her mother look round the hall, then march towards the sitting room; and she herself followed, yet not before casting a glance towards the study. Once in the room she pushed the door tight.

Her mother was standing to the side of the couch. "I'm not going to stay," she said, "but I must talk to you. You . . . you said you would call in, but you haven't seen fit to do that, so I just had to come. I felt it my duty to warn you because I know you are deaf to what anybody else but that man says. It's about this child that he's making you adopt."

"Nothing of the sort, Mother; he's not making me adopt the child. You don't know what you're talking about."

"Oh, don't I, girl. Can you tell me of any man who's hoping to marry a woman with three children who would want to adopt another one unless there was something behind it?"

"Mother! Be careful." Her jaws were tight, her teeth moving over each other now: the sound was almost audible.

"I am careful, and careful for you. He's . . . he's a disgrace. Of course he wants you to adopt this child. Of course he wants to bring it into a family, because it's *his*. He had been carrying on with that woman for years. Oh, she was married all right and had another child, but he was never away from her house. Mrs. Poller could tell you a thing or two."

She heard herself say grimly, "Mrs. Poller? Who is Mrs. Poller?"

"The woman, of course, he lived with before he came here."

"Oh, not Mrs. Quinn this time? And so you have been to this Mrs. Poller, have you, to investigate?"

"No, I did nothing of the sort. I happened to meet her in the paper shop and she was on about him. She had heard about the adoption and it was she who told me that he was never off her doorstep, supposedly because the young husband worked for him. But she had seen them both in the car together. What more proof do you want? And it was he who had to take the girl to hospital when she was having the child. The husband was down with flu, so he said. He's a disgrace. He had been carrying on with her for years, all the time he was staying at Mrs. Poller's. And God only knows how many more flyblows he's got kicking around the town. And he's duped you into . . . "

Fiona let out a high cry as the door burst open. She saw a man who didn't look at all like Bill spring across the room and grab her mother. Her own screams were joined by those of her mother and the cries of the children in the hall.

"Bill! Bill! For God's sake! No! No!" She was tearing at his hands that were gripping her mother's shoulders close to her neck, and he was shaking her like a rat as he cried, "You dirty-minded old swine! I could kill you this minute. Do you hear?"

It wasn't Fiona's efforts that loosened his hands but the realisation of what he had said that slackened his grip on her mother. And he watched her fall back full length onto the couch, where she lay straddled, gasping and moaning, her eyes staring wide in terror.

After some seconds Fiona made to go towards the couch, but Bill thrust her roughly aside, crying, "Don't you touch her, she's putrid!" Then he was bending over the couch, yelling into the frightened face, "You're putrid, filthy! Do you hear? Your mind, all of you, dirty, rotten. And listen to this: I'm master in this house now whether I'm married or not, and I'm telling you I give you fifteen minutes to get out and never put your face in that door again, because I won't be responsible for what I'll do to you."

He stepped back from her but stood panting, his jawbones moving and showing white through his skin. There was no sound for a moment except the whimpering of the children. Turning slowly about, he walked towards them; then picking up Willie, whose face was awash with tears, he went towards the kitchen, Mark walking on one side of him and Katie holding on to his trouser pocket at the other.

Fiona continued to stare at her mother; she was feeling now she couldn't go towards her, she couldn't touch her, whereas she might have a few moments ago when she thought she was gasping her last. She watched her slowly pull herself into a sitting position and push her skirt down over her knees. She watched her mouth open twice before managing to say haltingly, "I'll ... I'll have him to court for ... for attacking me."

Fiona's own voice was trembling as she replied, "That's if he doesn't have you up for defamation of character before, together with your friends. And I'll tell you this: the mother and father of that child were like a son and daughter to him; he thought of them as his son and daughter; he had looked after the man since he was a young boy. It is a serious accusation you've made against him and it will surprise me if he doesn't go to a solicitor."

It would have surprised her if he had because he was a man who fought his own battles, mostly with a laugh, as she had found out.

61

Nevertheless, this was different: she herself had been afraid of him and he could have throttled her mother. My God! Yes, he could have. But that her mother was far from being dead she now realised when she said, "You must take me home; I can't walk that distance."

"I'll not take you home, Mother; I'll order a taxi for you." And on this she went into the hall and did just that. But instead of returning to the sitting room she went to the kitchen.

The children were sitting at the table again, and so was he, but none of them was eating. She didn't look at him but at Mark to whom she said, "Finish your tea and then go upstairs," and he answered quietly, "Yes, Mam." She had turned about and reached the kitchen door when Willie's voice piped up, saying, "Are we not gonna have the baby then?"

She turned and looked at him. They all must have been in the hall listening. She was about to answer when Bill yelled, "Yes, we're going to have the baby."

The children were startled and frightened for a moment and he, bowing his head now, said, "It's all right. It's all right. I'm ... I'm in a paddy. But yes, we're going to have the baby." And he put out one hand to ruffle Willie's hair and the other towards Katie to take hold of her hand while his eyes rested on Mark. And he smiled at him and again he said, "You bet your life we're going to have that baby."

She closed the door and walked slowly across the hall, pausing to steel herself before entering the sitting room.

Her mother was sitting quite upright now. Her bag was open to the side of her and she was dabbing her face. She still used powder, and she had covered her entire face with it giving her complexion a sickly pallor. And as Fiona watched her, any grain of sympathy that she might have had for her fled. She knew that she would make straight for one of her cronies and would give her a detailed description of what had happened. And so she said, "Mother, if I hear one derogatory word that you have said against Bill, I shall tell him. And I can assure you that won't be the end of it. He's a determined man and he values his good name, and it is a good name. So you'd be wise to take this as a warning." She turned her head, saying now, "There's the car."

Fiona watched her mother rise slowly to her feet, pick up her handbag, adjust her coat, and, with a steadier step than she herself had so far maintained, walk past her without a glance. She stopped at the front door, but only to open it, picked up her umbrella, and walked down the drive to the waiting taxi.

8

SHE WAS WEARING A SLACK, OFF-WHITE COAT, A SMALL TURBAN-TYPE HAT TO match, her brown hair curling inwards onto her shoulders and picking up the tone of her tan-coloured, close-fitting woollen dress.

He was standing close by her side in a well-cut dark grey suit. He looked very well groomed and could, at this moment, have been termed handsome.

One of the two men behind the desk, pointing to the card in Bill's hand, was saying, "Repeat after me: I do solemnly declare ... "

And after Bill had made his declaration, Fiona was asked to make hers; yet both seemed deaf to what had gone before and to what precisely followed after until the man smiled, and said, "I suppose you know it's customary to kiss the bride?"

As they kissed Katie giggled. Mark made a shushing sound, and Willie looked up at his new granddad, as he had been told to address the strange man who had arrived with a strange woman at their house yesterday, and in whom he was more interested than in his new father, because, after all, *he* was still Mr. Bill, and he knew Mr. Bill, whereas he had to get to know this other tall man who made him laugh.

They were now in the outer hall of the registry office. Fiona had been kissed by her Alcoholics Anonymous friend from London, and then embraced by her friend's boyfriend, a member of the same society; there had been more hugging by her new father-in-law and by his girlfriend about whose age Bill had erred, for Madge would never see sixty-five again; then handshaking by Barney McGuire and his wife, who had acted as their two witnesses. And then it was her turn to do some embracing. First she kissed Mark who smiled at her but said nothing. With Katie it was different. "Can we stay up for the party?" said her daughter.

"Yes, for a short while."

When she came to her small son he brushed her kiss aside, saying, "I don't want to go to the party, I want to go to the hospital."

"Presently."

Bill now put his arm about her shoulders and they all went out into the bright sunshine and got into their respective cars and drove to the hotel where, in a private room, a table had been set for them: no wedding cake, just an ordinary meal. Later, the present party and all of Bill's men and their wives were to have a wedding dinner in the main hotel of the town, followed by a dance. It had been arranged like this because the family had something of import to do in the afternoon.

It was a merry meal that went on for two hours, and afterwards Fiona's London friends went back to their hotel, Barney McGuire and his wife returned home, and Bill's father and his girlfriend went back to the house. Bill and Fiona, meanwhile, having ushered the children into the Volvo, drove to the hospital. Upon arrival there they went straight to the superintendent's room, where a nurse was sitting on the couch holding the free hand of a little girl who was wearing a pinafore frock that enabled her plastered arm to be free.

As soon as she saw her new family she wriggled from the couch and came towards them. But her hand wasn't held out to her uncle Bill, as she thought of him, nor to that of her new mother, nor to Katie or to Mark; it was to Willie she gave her hand. And it was he who grinned at her as he said, "You all ready?"

She nodded at him and smiled.

Everybody was smiling, and the superintendent took Bill to one side and briefly told him that he understood the adoption papers would be ready in a few days when the legalities were gone into. Bill thanked him, and with the child in his arms they all went out together.

The children in the car and Fiona in her seat, he then placed the little girl on her lap, and, taking his place behind the wheel, he drove them home. But the excitement and pleasure was pierced when, with

64

all of them settled in the sitting room and surrounding her, the child said, "My Mammy coming soon?"

No one spoke for a moment, but all eyes were turned on Fiona, and she said, "Yes, soon, dear." Then came the question, "And Daddy?"

It was the first time since their first visit, to their knowledge, that the child had asked about her parents. And it was Willie who saved the day, albeit unconsciously—who was to know—by saying, "I've put your name on my horse's belly next to mine, an' you can ride him."

"Stomach, Willie."

"Its stom . . . ack." He pursed his lips and pulled a laughing face at his mother and the tension was broken.

With regard to leaving the children so that they could attend their own wedding party, it had been arranged that Barney McGuire's sister-in-law would come and baby-sit. Then only this morning Barney had come early to say his sister-in-law had a stinking cold, but he'd shop around and try to find someone else for them. It was then that Mr. Bailey Senior said there would be no need, that he and Madge would be only too happy to stay put with the bairns. And so it had been arranged; and also that the old couple hadn't to stay up, as the newlyweds naturally didn't know at what time they would be able to get away.

It was seven o'clock when they saw Katie and Willie and their new daughter to bed. They had put another single bed next to Katie's and had left them happily playing with their dolls and bears.

When a short time later Fiona stood in the hall in her evening dress, a cloak around her shoulders, and Madge put her arms around her and hugged her as a mother would, she felt for a moment she'd burst out crying, because not for the first time on this, her special day, she had imagined how different she would have been feeling if she'd had a mother who could have been happy for her.

When Bailey Senior jerked his head and said, "By, you're a good-lookin' piece, girl," Bill demanded of his father, "Do you think I would have picked her if she hadn't been?" Then he won her heart in yet another way by bending down to Mark and saying quietly, "You'll see to them up there, won't you? Don't stand any nonsense." And she watched her son's eyelids blink and his neck stretch as he said, "Yes, Mr. Bill. I'll . . . I'll see to them."

"That's the ticket," Bill said, touching Mark on the shoulder; then turning to Fiona, he took her arm, saying, "Come on, love," and they went out together, leaving Mark standing on the step between Bill's father and Madge. And when the old man called, "Come back sober,

65

mind," Bill did not answer him with any quip, but, as he took his place beside her in the car, he took her hand and held it firmly as he said, "Tonight, if only for once in me life, I'll aim to join Alcoholics Anonymous."

It was two o'clock in the morning when they tiptoed up the stairs, and on the landing when she whispered, "I'll just look in on them," he hissed back, "No, you won't. There's only one person you're going to look in on tonight, or this morning. Come on."

They had taken off their shoes and outer things downstairs, and now in the bedroom they stood looking at each other. He did not make any attempt to embrace her, but he took her hands and held them tightly against his chest as he said softly, "You know, I'm speaking the truth now, but I never thought I'd make it. Honest to God, I didn't. Right up till this mornin' I thought something would happen: your mother would put the 'fluence on us in some way and I'd have a crash in the car; I felt sure that some disaster was bound to happen. I've been worried for weeks, me with me big mouth acting as if I was God's secretary. Still, I never thought I'd have you. And that night when I almost throttled your mother, I thought that in some part of your mind you might believe I really had been the gay lothario. See, I know some big names."

For a moment he was silent; then softly he said, "You know, most of my life I've been full of just wind and wishes. Not that I haven't been about, but I'm certainly not the skunk she made me out to be. And when I've thought of what might have happened that night which could have separated us for life, and I might have done life at that for her, if some part of my mind hadn't warned me what I'd be losing if I hadn't you—" Again he paused; then, tracing his finger across her cheek, he said, "I love you, Fiona. I can't tell you to what extent I love you, that would be impossible, but I'll show you in the years to come. I've got ideas, whopping ideas. And one day I'll put you in a big house standing in its own grounds with two or three cars on the drive and servants and ... "

"You'll do nothing of the sort, Bill Bailey, so get your whoppers out of your head. All I want is ... oh, shut up!" And turning her back on him, she demanded, "Undo my zip!"

He let out a high laugh, then choked it as he pulled her round to him and whispered, "You know what? You're talking just like me; you sounded right common."

They were clinging to each other now, their bodies convulsed with their silent laughter.

After a moment she pressed herself from him and, looking into his streaming face, she said, "Remember that day you told me about your father and his girlfriend, and I was surprised at him having a girlfriend at his age and sarcastically I said that you must take after him, and you replied that yes, you did, and you couldn't take after a better man. And so I say to you now, Bill Bailey, if I'm talking like you and acting like you, I couldn't have a better pattern. And at this moment I know what you're wanting to say in your own inimitable way." Her voice now changed as she finished: "Stop your chitchat, it's me weddin' night. Let's get to bed."

His mouth went wide, he put his hand across it; then she was lifted off her feet and waltzed round the room. Of a sudden he stopped, put her down, turned her round, and deliberately and slowly undid the zip of her dress.

9

"WHY ON EARTH COULDN'T YOU LET HER WEAR HER GOOD COAT?"

"Because, Mr. Bailey, her good coat is not half as good or as thick as her school coat and, as you yourself pointed out in your own polite way, it's so cold outside that it would cut the lugs off a cuddy, not to mention its tail and other extremities. And—" She now turned from her husband and looked at her ten-year-old son and his six-year-old brother and added, "And you two stop that giggling, because if your sister doesn't put in an appearance within the next minute none of us will see the school concert tonight; I'm not going in there once it's started."

"Oh, woman, be quiet." Bill went to the foot of the stairs and yelled, "You! Katie. Come on, pronto!" At the same time the sitting room door opened and a young woman appeared and, looking at Fiona, she said, "Shall I go up and get her?"

"No, Nell; nobody's going up to get her; she knows her way downstairs. But if she's not here within the next minute we're going without her. She's been playing up of late."

"You wouldn't do that." To which Fiona answered, "Wouldn't I just!" But she smiled at her neighbour.

During the last four months, apart from having acquired a new husband, Fiona had also acquired a friend from among the family who had come to live next door. These were a Mr. and Mrs. Paget, a

68

couple in their fifties. It was as though the husband had arrived to join the rest of the redundant managers in the street. And with them had also come their daughter-in-law, Nell, and her husband, their son Harry, who had only last week found a job after two years unemployment. Only Nell had been employed and then part-time in a store in the town. So she was very glad to do baby-sitting or anything else that came her way. And, too, she was about Fiona's age and of similar tastes, so they got on well together. And tonight, because Mamie had a cold, Nell was once again baby-sitting.

Fiona now asked, "Is she all right?"

"Fine," Nell answered, "she's galloping with Bugs Bunny." Then their attention was drawn to the stairs, for there at the top stood the cause of the holdup. But she was making no attempt to come down; instead she stood sniffing.

"Do you hear me, Katie? Come down this minute, or you'll go straight to bed."

As Katie now descended the stairs a chorus of sniffs rose from the hall.

"What . . . on earth . . . !"

"Phew! She smells."

"What have you been up to, child?"

"I couldn't help it, Mam. I was only going to put a drop on, and . . . and it slipped and tipped, all the way down."

Fiona now pushed Katie none too gently to one side and dashed up the stairs, but within a minute she had returned, her arm outstretched and in her hand a scent bottle with just a drain left in the bottom.

Holding it up to her husband, she said, "Look! Look at that."

And Bill looked at it; then, turning his gaze down onto Katie's snivelling face, he said, "You know what I paid for that, Katie Bailey? Forty-nine quid. A bottle of Chanel she said she wanted. And where's it gone? On your school coat. And now, when she wants to smell nice, she'll have to wring it out. Aw! come on now; stop your crying. Worse things happen at sea. But, by God, forty-nine pounds down the drain."

"No, down the school coat." He turned to a grinning Mark; then looked at Willie whose nose was now distorting his face as he said, "She stinks."

"I don't! I don't! I'll slap your face."

"Come on; come on, we'll have none of that." Fiona grabbed her daughter's hand and pulled her back to the stairs and up them. And Bill, turning to where Nell had an arm tight round her waist to stop herself from laughing outright, said, "I must have been barmy, right up the pole to saddle meself with this lot. I didn't know when I was well off. A middle-of-the-road man, that's what I was, Nell, a middle-of-the-road man. And now look at me, lumbered."

"I'm sorry for you."

"Aye, I know you are." He glanced now at Mark, saying, "And you're not much help." Then looking down on Willie, he added, "As for you, you should be shut up in a home, or sent to your gran's. Aye, that's the place to send you. Aye, that's what we'll do with you, we'll send you to live with your gran. I'll have to see about it."

As he turned away to look up the stairs Mark said, quietly, "Mr. Bill." Then he nodded towards his young brother, and when Bill turned it was to see Willie's face screwed up now, not against the smell of the scent, but with tears.

Going swiftly to the boy, he swung him up in his arms, saying, "Come on, Willie-wet-eye; you know I was only jokin'. I wouldn't send a dog with rabies to your granny's, unless"—he poked his face towards the wet cheek—"it was to bite her."

As he growled and pretended to bite the child's ear, Fiona, preceded by a still-snivelling Katie, came down the stairs, only now Katie was dressed in her best coat.

"Ah! Ah!" Bill put Willie down on the floor and looking towards his wife, he said, "If you'd let her have her own way at first I wouldn't have lost forty-nine quid."

Without looking at him Fiona marshalled her small horde towards the door, saying, "You lost it when you bought the bottle. And please don't remind me again what you paid for it."

"Not remind you? By God, I will; every chance I get. So be prepared. Well, get moving, the lot of you. Bye, Nell."

"We won't be all that late." Fiona turned towards Nell, and Nell answered, "Oh, it doesn't matter. Go out to supper after; have a fish and chip do."

"That's the idea. That's what we'll do." Bill took up Nell's words. "A fish and chip do to get over the misery of the school concert."

"We'll do no such thing. It'll be ten o'clock before we get out of there."

"Pattisons in the town is open till half past eleven."

"*Bill.*"

"Yes, Mrs. Bailey?"

When the door closed on them Nell Paget went back into the sitting room where Mamie was bouncing on the couch, and, sitting down beside the child, she sighed not a little in envy of this family, of her new friend who could have three children of her own and adopt another, whereas she, who had been married thirteen years, had no hopes of ever having a baby.

IO

SHE WAS BROUGHT FROM HER FIRST SLEEP BY THE SOUND OF THE WINDOW BEING opened. And in a kind of panic her hand shot out and switched on the light. Then she almost splattered, "What . . . what on earth are you doing, Bill?"

"Letting a little air in. The room stinks," he whispered hoarsely.

"You'll freeze. Get back into bed."

"Far better freeze than be suffocated with that smell. I don't know how you can stand it."

As he snuggled down beside her again, she said, "It's supposed to go on a drop at a time and not a whole bottle. I'd only used it twice. But the carpet got more of it than her coat. I'll wash it tomorrow. What time is it?" she asked now.

"Half past one."

"Haven't you been to sleep yet?"

"No, I've got tomorrow on my mind. Four of those ten I set on are a dead weight; it would take a gaffer to watch each of them. They'll go as soon as I get in in the morning. I didn't get back into Newcastle until they had all gone, but Barney was waiting for me. There was a drizzle of rain," he said, "and there they were in the hut while our own fellas kept at it. And as Barney said, no matter how loyal our lot is they're not going to put up with shirkers like that. And there's another one I'd like to get rid of an' all and that's that Max Ringston.

He's a good enough worker but I don't trust him somehow. I can't pin anything on him, but when there's stuff being lifted as I told you about afore, such as door frames and floor boardings, he's been one of the two who've been on the lorry that day, the other being Tommy Turnbull. But I'd trust Tommy with me life. And Dan, Dan McRay. He usually takes the other lorry, but he's been in hospital for some weeks now, as you know. And so Ringston's been doing the driving."

"Can't you have him watched?"

"It's difficult. And when he brings in the loads they always check with the lists. Barney sees to that. But it's not until they start putting the window frames or the doors up that they find there's some missing. And they're all locked up at night in the shed. Barney and me are the only ones who've got keys, and added to that, there's the watchman. Oh, I'm tellin' you, Mrs. B., life ain't easy." He hugged her to him, then added, "Except when I've got you like this."

There was a pause while they both lay quiet; and then, in his voice soft, he said, "You know, I sometimes ask meself, what kind of a life did I lead before I had you? Before I came in as your lodger?"

Laughing softly now, she said, "I know what kind of a man you were, as you were forever telling me: a middle-of-the-road man; but you didn't go on to say that you drew your women in from both sides."

"Aw, that was mostly talk."

"Mostly?"

"Do you love me?"

"Yes, Bill Bailey, I love you. And I, too, can't imagine what my life was like before you came into this house as a lodger. And as for the children, if you were their father they couldn't love you more; in fact, I must admit that they love you as they never loved their father. And then there's Mamie. She's like one of our own now."

"Do you think she's forgotten about her parents and her brother?"

"Well, it's some weeks since she mentioned them. You remember that night at the table when of a sudden she said, 'Will my Mammy soon be back from her holidays?'"

"Yes; yes, I remember that. God in heaven! I didn't know what to say. Then when Willie put in, 'When I die I'm going to have wings on my heels so I can fly upside down.' Remember, we both sat there dumb."

They laughed and held each other tight, and Bill repeated, "Wings on his heels so he can fly upside down. He comes out with things, that fella."

He stroked her hair back from her face now as he said softly, "You know, I was thinking the night when I saw you walk across that schoolroom after you had been talking to the teacher, I thought you looked so young, so girlish. And you are young and you are girlish, and I wondered if you would like to go to a dance sometime, a nice dance, not a romp; you know, a dinner dance. Aye, that's it."

She giggled now and her body shook against his as she said, "Thank you, Mr. Bailey. I'll think about it, but it's on two in the morning and if I'm not mistaken you've got a stiff day before you tomorrow. That's what's kept you awake. So we'll discuss taking this young girl out to a dance some other time, but now go to sleep."

"Yes, Ma. Goodnight, Ma." He kissed her long and hard; then almost caused her to choke by saying, "The only thing I thank your mother for was getting pregnant with you."

"Mammy B."

"Yes, darling?"

"When will I get new teefths in?"

"Oh, they'll soon grow, dear."

"Big ones?"

"Yes. Just a nice size to fit your mouth."

"With a band on?"

"A band, dear? What do you mean, a band?"

"Like Katie's."

"Oh. No, you won't have to have a band like Katie's. That's just to keep Katie's teeth straight; your teeth will be nice and straight to begin with. Come on; we'll go and meet her and the rest of them, eh? Tie your scarf nice and tight because it's very cold outside."

She helped the child to knot the pom-pommed scarf, and pulled the woollen hat down around her ears; then lifting her up, she went out the front door, locking it behind her, and hurried down to the car. After strapping the child into the back seat, she drove away from the house.

Five minutes later she stopped outside the playground of the junior school. In the distance she saw Willie, but he did not rush towards her as was usual; instead, his step was slow and his head was down. She got out of the car and went to meet him.

"What is it? What's the matter?"

When he raised his head her mouth fell into a gape for he had the nearest thing to a black eye.

"What have you been doing?"

He walked past her, pulled open the car door, and sat himself beside Mamie.

73

Fiona was seated behind the wheel now, half turned in her seat, and he said, "Betty Rice hit me with a ruler."

"Oh? And what had you done to Betty Rice?"

"I . . . I punched her."

"Why did you punch her?"

"Because she took my book and wouldn't give it back." He now put his hand in his pocket, and as he handed her the envelope across the seat he said, "Teacher said to give you that."

"Oh." She did not open the envelope because she knew it would be a further explanation of what had happened; time enough to go into that when she got home.

"Is it sore?" It was Mamie asking the question of him now. And in true boyish fashion he answered, "Yes, of course it's sore. If somebody hit you with a ruler wouldn't it be sore?"

"Yes, Willie; yes, it would be sore."

Already Fiona knew that nothing Willie could do could be wrong in Mamie's eyes. She started up the car, saying, "We'll talk about this when we get home."

She knew that Mark was playing football today, and, as on other occasions when this happened, he was always a little earlier than Katie, so he was the next one she picked up.

"Cor! What's happened to you?" were his first words when he took his seat beside his mother and looked behind him to Willie.

"I was hit by a hephelant's trunk."

Fiona bit on her lip. That was Willie. There was nothing much wrong with him except that his pride was hurt.

Then she had to check her elder son when he said, "Oh, just a hephelant's trunk?" He mimicked his brother's inability to pronounce some words correctly, then added, "I thought he must have stood on your face."

"Mark!"

Mark laughed; then leaning towards his mother as she started up the car, he said, "What happened?"

And in an aside she answered, "A little girl got the better of him."

Two blocks farther on, she stopped the car again and Mark, looking out the window, said, "She's not there; she's likely waiting inside out of the cold."

"Go and fetch her."

She watched Mark run across the schoolyard. Less than a minute later he was running back towards her.

Opening the door, he said, "She's not there. They say she's gone."

"Gone? She can't have gone."

74

She got out of the car now and looked beyond the gate, towards where three girls were standing. They were well wrapped up, but they were hopping up and down. She recognised one of them; she was in Katie's class. She went up to the children now and asked, "Have . . . have you seen Katie?"

The two older girls shook their heads, but the smaller one said, "Yes; she went home, Mrs. Nelson."

"She went home? She walked?"

"Oh, no." The child smiled. "Her new father came for her. He came along there." She pointed. "He called her name and she ran to him and she got in the car."

Fiona stared at the child for a moment. She wanted to say, "Oh, that'll be all right, she'll be at home," but she couldn't, for a great fear was assailing her. Bill had never come and taken any of them home. She heard herself say, "What . . . what did the man look like?"

"Her father? Oh, he was in his working clothes. I don't know what his face was like but she told us her new daddy built big houses."

Of a sudden she was running back to the car.

"What is it?" Mark said.

She didn't answer him but started the car noisily with her foot hard down on the accelerator pedal, and then she was speeding, not towards home, but towards the works.

Five minutes later she was swinging the car into the rough road that led to the buildings; and having brought it to a stop outside some sheds that formed the office and the men's cabin and the tool house, she jumped out and gabbled at a surprised workman: "Where's Mr. Bailey?"

It was one of the new men. She didn't know him, and it was obvious that he didn't know her, for his manner was quite offhand as he said, "You'll likely find him in the office, there."

When she thrust open the door of the hut Bill was sitting at his desk, but before she could speak he was holding her by the arms, saying, "What is it? What's the matter?"

"Where . . . where is she? Katie? Why did you? You never have . . ."

"Stop it! Stop gabbling. What about Katie?"

"They . . . they said you came and took her from school."

His arms dropped from her and his words came in a thin whisper from his lips, "Who took her? Who said I took her?"

"Oh, my God! My God!" She was holding her head. "The little girl, she said Katie's daddy had come in the car and called her and . . . and she got in."

"*Almighty God!* When? When?"

75

"Just a short while ago. It must have been immediately she came out of school."

He turned now and grabbed up the phone and dialled a number. His voice was a gabble in answer to someone speaking from the other end: "My ... my daughter's been picked up. Someone ... someone impersonating me. Yes! Yes! Yes!"

She watched him close his eyes, then say, "My name is William Bailey. I'm a contractor; I'm building the new estate just beyond the top of Brampton Hill."

"What? What?" He looked towards Fiona. "The child's school? It's the junior in Mowbray Road. No; no, I can't give you other details. I've just heard. My wife's here. Look. Get crackin', will you? For God's sake do something."

He did not thrust the phone back on its stand but laid it down as if in slow motion. Then he stood, his head bent, drawing in deep breaths for a moment before he turned to her where she was still standing holding her head in her hands. Taking her into his arms, he said, "Can ... can you think of anything else the child said?"

She shook her head. Then looking at him, her eyes wide and staring, she said, "But ... but it must have been someone who knew what time she would be coming out of school. It couldn't be just a passerby, because he ... he called her name. That ... that was likely why she ran to him."

"Well, well. Now ... now try not to worry; that'll narrow things down a bit. Try not to worry, I said; my God, what prattle! Try not to worry."

"Oh, Bill, Bill. If anything should happen to ... "

"*It won't. It won't.* It can't, not to Katie. I ... I love them all, you know that, but ... but Katie was somebody special, she was. Oh"—he lifted his head—"that must be the police car. Well, I can say this, they were quick off the mark; they must have got hold of one of the patrol cars."

When they went outside two policemen were getting out of the car and before they could speak Bill was relating all he knew.

In a few minutes it seemed that from every one of the partly built houses men came pouring out, so quickly had the news gone round that the boss's bairn had been picked up by some bloke.

It was Barney McGuire who said, "What can we do, boss? Every man-jack will stay on an' help look."

But it was the policeman who answered, "We'll likely need all your help later on, but the inspector will be here any minute and he'll go into things first."

76

Taking Fiona by the arm, Bill led her towards the car, saying, "Take the bairns home."

"I can't. I can't, Bill."

"*Listen!* Take the bairns home. Get Nell to come in and see to them. Then if I don't turn up within half an hour or so you can come back here, and by that time something should be under way. Go on now, there's a good lass. It'll be all right. It'll be all right. I swear to you, it'll be all right, else by God I'll—" He shook his head, then pressed her into the car, saying, "Steady now." And looking down at Mark, he said, "See to your mother, lad."

"Katie?"

"She'll be all right. She'll be all right."

Fiona didn't know how she had driven the car home, and she sounded so incoherent as she tried to tell Nell Paget what had happened. But now the three children were aware that Katie was lost and all of them started to cry, including Mark; and this upset her still further and, taking him aside, she held his face between her hands and told him, "You're the eldest, dear; you've . . . you've got to help me. See to the others and try . . . try to keep them happy. Nell will do her best, but you know them better, and I rely on you."

"But"—his lips were trembling—"but Mam, what . . . what if they can't find her?"

"They'll find her. You know nothing gets past Mr. Bill; you know that, don't you?" When he suddenly leaned against her and put his arms around her waist she felt she would not just give way to tears but that she would howl aloud to release this dreadful feeling inside which was being probed by the poignancy of her son's love. She kissed him now; then pressing him away from her, she said, "Go and help Nell to get the tea. I'll . . . I'll be back shortly."

But she did not immediately leave the house; she ran upstairs and into her bedroom and, throwing herself on her knees by the bed, she began to pray. She prayed as she had never done in her life before. During the years her mother forced her to attend church, she had never really prayed; but now she beseeched God to keep her daughter safe and to let her be found soon. Oh yes, God, soon.

After washing her tear-streaked face she went downstairs. Bill had said if he didn't return home in half an hour . . . well, the half hour wasn't up, but she couldn't remain here. She said to Nell, "Can you stay this evening?" And Nell, gripping her arm, said, "Girl, I'll stay as long as I'm needed, today, tomorrow, a week. Don't worry about them, I'll see to them. You go on. But what you could do if you are

77

not coming straight back is phone me and let me know what's happening."

"I'll do that. Thanks, Nell."

As she ran down to the car she wondered why she should think that God provided because he had sent her someone like Nell. It was a ridiculous thought when her child had been abducted; yet she would have had to stay at home if Nell hadn't been there.

The yard was abuzz when she arrived. There were four police cars and a number of policemen and strange men standing in small groups.

In the hut she found Bill, the inspector, and a sergeant. The first thing Bill said to her was, "Do you know the name of the little girl that told you about Katie?"

"Yes, it's Rene Smith. But I don't know where she lives."

"And you don't know the name of the other two girls?" It was the inspector speaking now.

"No."

"That's all right. We can consult the headmistress. Well, now." The inspector rose from a chair and, looking at Bill, said, "We have the names of five men you dismissed. Had you any hot words or arguments with them before they left?"

"No, but they weren't very pleased."

"Anyone of them that might bear a grudge you would think?"

"Two were a bit mouthy, Ringston and a fellow called Flint. Flint had only been here a week."

The inspector now looked at the sergeant. "We'll check on the schoolgirls first, and we might get a lead. They will likely remember the colour of the car at least. I've got no hope that they would take the number, although some of them do." Looking at Fiona now, he said, "Try not to worry, Mrs. Bailey. I know that's easier said than done, but I'd go home if I were you."

"I've just come from home." Her voice was terse.

"Well, I'm afraid there's little that can be done at the moment. As far as I can judge it's no use sending out search parties, because if the man knew her name it points to a local job, and that narrows it down considerably."

Without further words he turned and went out, followed by the sergeant.

And now Bill, coming over to her, put his arms about her, saying, "As he said, it narrows it down, and that's a hopeful sign."

"Do . . . do you think it was one of your men, one you sacked?"

"I don't know. They didn't seem that type, only lazy devils. It's

78

more likely someone she's spoken to before; she's a chatterer. I've seen her chattering to different people in the street. The very look of her made people want to stop an' talk to her."

He turned from her now and, supporting himself by his doubled fists on the edge of his desk, said, "Whoever it is I swear to you I'll kill him. No matter what the consequences, I'll kill him."

"*Oh, don't say that, Bill.* Don't talk like that." She pulled him round to her, then whimpered, "As long as we get her back.... I'm frightened, Bill. That child a fortnight ago, they ... "

"*Be quiet!*" His voice was a bawl now. "Look, as the inspector says, you can do nothing; get yourself away home. Now go on, see to the kids, do something. It'll take you mind off it."

"Take my mind off it?"

"You know what I mean." He pushed her roughly from him, then turned and hurried out.

Dropping into a chair, she leaned her elbow on his desk and lowered her head to her hand. Why was it that things never ran smoothly? They had been so happy. She was in a new life. Yes, she was in a new life. Like the song, everything was coming up roses. But then roses had thorns, although the only thorn in her life up till an hour ago had been her mother. The thought brought her to her feet. What time was it? Close on six. If it was on the local radio, and it just might be, because there was always a reporter hanging around the police station and they got news like this very quickly, and if her mother was to hear it she would be over and her tongue lashing out as usual. And if she found only Nell there she'd take control, even after all that had happened.

When she went into the yard there were still a lot of men about. And it was Barney McGuire who came up to her and said, "I'm sorry, Mrs. Bailey, I am to the heart of me. But pray God they'll find her soon. She was such a bonny bit. She romped through here the other day chatting to the men. She picked the house that she would like. And the boss was barmy about her, that was plain to see. He carried her shoulder high at one time over the puddles and she laughed her head off.... "

She had to stop him. "Are ... are you staying on, Mr. McGuire?" she put in quickly.

"Yes, ma'am, as long as I'm needed."

"Well, if you hear anything, will you phone me? That is, if Bill isn't back."

"I'll do that. I'll do that, ma'am, pronto, the minute I hear anything. You go on home now."

She went home and when she entered the house it was unusually quiet, so much so she thought that Nell had taken the children next door, until she opened the sitting room door, and then from the couch they all rushed to her.

"You found her, Mam?"

"Is she coming home?"

"She can have my spaceman. Mam, Mam, she can have my spaceman. She wanted it and I wouldn't . . . "

She picked up Willie from the floor and held him tightly, saying, "It's all right. It's all right. Yes, she knows she can have your spaceman, dear, and she'll soon be back to play with it."

"Mammy B."

Mamie stretched out her arms towards her from where Nell was holding her, and she put Willie to the floor and took the child.

"Mammy B., I want Katie and Uncle Bill."

"They'll . . . they'll be back soon, dear. Have . . . have they had their tea?" She was looking at Nell, and Nell said, "Yes, but for a change nobody seemed very hungry."

Fiona now looked down on Mark, saying quietly, "Take them up to the playroom, will you, dear?"

He stared at her for a moment before turning to Willie and saying, "Come on, you. And you, too." He held his hand up to Mamie, and Fiona put her on the floor, where she started to snivel a little but nevertheless took Mark's hand, and the three of them left the room together.

Fiona and Nell looked at each other, and it was Nell who spoke, saying, "It's no use asking if they've made any headway, it's too early."

Fiona didn't answer but sat down on the couch, and what she said was, "I'm sick, all my body and brain is sick, Nell. I'm thinking all the time what he could be doing to her."

"Don't." Nell sat beside her friend and put her arms around Fiona's shoulders. "If, as you said, the man knew her name, then it's someone local. It could be someone from this very street, you never know people. I'll tell you something: I was kidnapped once."

"Never!"

"Yes. It was a man three doors down. He had a wife but no children. He had just retired from a decent job, too, highly respectable. He gave me a ride in his car, which he had done once or twice before. But then he had put me off at the bottom of the street; this time he kept on driving. He took me to a fairground; then we went to the pictures, and afterwards into a cafe for tea. Then when I wanted to go home and started to cry he drove round and round. It was in the summertime and he said we would sleep in the sands. Fortunately the police caught up with him. They stopped the car; his wife had tipped them off. He had done this before but had always brought the child back the same day. I don't think he intended to this time. Anyway"—Nell turned her head to the side and looked towards the window as she ended—"I wasn't upset about this man until I got home and found Dad was going round the bend. But Mam had taken it in her usual stride, and she greeted me as if I'd just been out to play in the street. I can see her now looking down on me, saying, 'You enjoyed yourself then? Causing trouble as usual.'"

"No!"

Nell now turned her head and nodded at Fiona. "Oh yes, yes."

"How old were you?"

"Seven, nearly eight."

"Really?"

"She couldn't stand me because Dad made a fuss of me. She led me hell until I left home. Quite candidly I ran away when I was fifteen. I went down to my aunt's in Wales, her sister, who was as different again from her, and my dad said I could stay there. It was there I met Harry." Again she looked towards the window, saying now, "I was married when I was nineteen. Thirteen years." She said the last words with a sigh. "And the only thing I've wanted is a family, and the only thing he didn't want, and will never want, is a family."

"Oh, Nell, I didn't know."

"Well—" Nell smiled at her, adding, "You can see why I'm so pleased to have a secondhand one next door."

Their hands joined for a moment and then they put their arms round each other, and both of their faces were wet when they separated. And it was Nell who now said, "I wouldn't like to be the man who's done this if Bill gets his hands on him."

"That's what I'm frightened about, too. He swore that he'd kill him."

"I don't blame him."

It was at this point the phone rang and they both sprang up. Then Fiona ran through the room and into the hall and, grabbing the mouthpiece, she was about to say, "Yes?" when the voice said, "Fiona."

She closed her eyes, "Yes, Mother."

"What is this? What is this? It can't be. The local wireless, it's just said that Katie is missing. What have you been up to?"

"*Mother! Mother!*"

81

"Never mind, 'Mother, Mother,' why didn't you pick her up from school as usual?"

Fiona held the mouthpiece well away from her and glared at it before bringing it slowly towards her again.

"I was at school, Mother, to pick her up, but she had been picked up before."

"What are you doing at home then? Why aren't you out looking?"

"Don't be silly, Mother."

"Don't take that tone with me, Fiona; I'm not going to stand it any more. Now I'm coming round."

"You're not coming round, Mother."

"You try and stop me. She is my granddaughter."

"Mother!" The line went dead. Slowly she put the mouthpiece back, then turned and, leaning her buttocks against the telephone table, bent her head.

"Your mother?"

"Yes, Nell, Mother. You've not met her, have you? Well, you're about to. My dear, dear mother, who has always done everything for my own good. You'll hear all about it and the dreadful man I have married, and Katie's disappearance has come about just through that. You'll hear it. Oh, my God! I can't stand much more, I just can't, not Mother tonight."

"Come on." Nell took her by the arm. "Come on and have a drink; that'll fortify you."

"Nothing can fortify me against my mother."

"Funny about mothers. Mine was a swine. I can say that now, a selfish swine. But there's Harry's mother and father next door, you couldn't find a more caring or nicer couple in the world. They're thoughtful, even loving. Yet Harry hasn't inherited any part of them, not any that's noticeable, at least. Although I say it, and only to you, life ain't all roses. The world owes Harry a living and Harry owes the world a grudge."

For a moment Fiona forgot her own trouble and said, "I wouldn't have thought so. He seemed so ... well, quite charming."

"Oh yes, yes; that's the outward skin. But like all of us, he has a facade. I can only wish it was hiding a nature like his father's or his mother's. Anyway, what is it to be? Sherry? Gin and lime? A whiskey?"

"Gin and lime, dear."

She didn't care for gin and lime, but she imagined it had a much more sustaining quality than sherry, and at this minute she needed sustaining.

* * *

It was only fifteen minutes later that the sitting room door burst open and Mrs. Vidler stared at her daughter sitting on the couch with another young woman ... drinking.

Fiona was on her feet, gasping slightly. She needn't ask how her mother had got in, she had come by the back way, perhaps thinking she wouldn't be allowed in the front door.

"Well!"

"Yes, Mother, well!"

Mrs. Vidler took four steps into the room and glared down on the glasses on the small table to the side of the couch; then lifted her gaze to the open wine cabinet at the end of the room before exclaiming in icy tones: "I can see how troubled you are that your child is missing. Disgraceful!"

"Be careful, Mother."

Nell now rose from the couch, saying quietly, "Your daughter was exhausted and distressed; she has only just sat down...."

"Who are you, may I ask? And I don't need any explanation from a stranger with regard to my daughter's odd conduct, and I'll thank you to leave the room, as I wish to speak privately...."

"I'll leave the room when Fiona says so and not until, and I'll thank you not to use that tone with me, or I'll consider it insulting and take the matter into my own hands. So I'll advise you to moderate not only your voice but your whole attitude."

At any other time Fiona would have almost cheered Nell's approach; it was so like Bill's would have been, only said in a more refined tone. But at the moment her emotions were very mixed, that of fear being dominant, and so, her voice low, she said quietly, "Mother, this is Mrs. Paget, my neighbour. She has been of great help to me, and so I would ask you ... "

"Oh, and I haven't of course. That's what you are inferring, isn't it? Oh, I know you of old; oh, I know you...."

What happened next startled both Nell and Mrs. Vidler, for Fiona, grabbing up the wineglass, threw it with force at the marble-framed fireplace and her scream mingled with the sound of the shattering glass: "Go! Get out! Leave me alone. Do you hear?" She took two steps towards her mother, but how she would have followed up this action she never knew because Nell gripped her arms and, looking at Mrs. Vidler, she cried, "You had better go, hadn't you?"

But Mrs. Vidler did not immediately react except to gulp before having the last word: "She's drunk. Disgraceful!" Then she marched regally out.

83

Fiona, dropping onto the couch, burst into tears, and Nell, holding her, said to no one in particular, "By, I thought mine took some beating, but that one takes the cake."

It was nine o'clock. The children were in bed but only Mamie was asleep, the other two were wide awake, sitting up waiting, as she had been waiting, seemingly for years. Bill had phoned her twice: the first time to say the little girl who saw Katie get into the car thought the car was blue. Through her they had traced the other two girls. One said the car was black and the other said she thought it was dark green.

The second time he phoned he said the police had interviewed the men who had been sacked. Two of them hadn't cars. The third, a young fellow, owned a battered old mini with stickers plastered on it. And it was considered the children would surely have picked that one out. The other one was a grey Austin 13. His last words were, "I'll be home shortly. They say there's nothing much more they can do tonight."

Following the second phone call, she had walked from the sitting room to the dining room, then into the study, back into the hall again, and, finally, as she had already done numbers of times, ended up in the kitchen because there she could find something for her hands to do.

She had been alone for sometime now as Nell, at her husband's suggestion, had gone home. She didn't care for Nell's husband, and it wasn't because of what she had learned of him through Nell. Although his manner could be quite charming he was, she considered, a cold fish. And this evening he had seemed a little irritated that his wife should be more concerned with the loss of a neighbour's child than with his achieving the enviable job of a clerk in an accountant's office, and the duties thereof.

She started to pray again with, "Oh, dear God! Oh, dear God!" only to stop abruptly as she reminded herself she had always condemned people who went to church in the last resort to beg for something. Why couldn't she just think positively, her child would be all right. But she couldn't think positively. When children were taken away, as Katie had been, they were never all right; even if they were found alive, it left a mark on them.

It was as if in panic that she rushed out of the kitchen and into the hall, there to see the front door opening. And with an audible cry she fell into Bill's arms.

"There now! There now! Stop it! Stop it! You'll make yourself ill."

84

He pressed her gently away, took off his hat and coat, then, once again holding her, led her into the sitting room.

When seated, she didn't actually ask if there was any news, she just stared at him through her streaming eyes. And in answer he said, "They can do nothing until daylight. They'll be out at first light, the inspector said. And I've just come from the site. I've had to send Barney and four of the fellows home; they've been going out in relays. Tommy Turnbull and Dan McRay have never been home. So everything that can be done has been done, at least for tonight."

He turned from her, lay back against the head of the couch, and, gripping his hair with both hands as if intending to pull it out, said, "And I made all that fuss about that damn scent. And the last thing I said to her this mornin' was, 'I'm going to keep it out of your pocket-money, miss. Forty-nine quid you've got to pay me for that bottle,' and she said, 'Well, there's still some left, it wasn't all spilt.' Oh, God Almighty!" He leaned forward now and, his hands between his knees, he rocked himself and groaned, "Forty-nine quid. I'd sell me all down to the last penny and buy a scent factory if she was only up above at this minute."

It was her turn to comfort now. Putting her arms about him, she murmured, "She loved you. I . . . I can tell you she never showed the same affection for her father. She worshipped you."

"Don't say it like that"—he almost pushed her from him—"as if she was gone, dead. Oh, I'm sorry love." He pulled her to him again. "Look"—he rose abruptly to his feet—"what I think we must do is have a bath, then get a couple of hours sleep. That's if we can. We'll put the alarm on for five. And if we've never prayed afore, we'll pray the night."

II

IT WAS ON THE EIGHT O'CLOCK NEWS; IT WAS ON THE NINE O'CLOCK NEWS; AND it was announced on the one o'clock news that the inspector had stated in an interview that he felt the search must now go beyond the town, for although it was being assumed the abductor knew the child, he must have driven her away. He also stated that every man in Mr. Bailey's firm had been interrogated and the premises searched.

Bill had stopped by the house and so heard this latest news, but he made no comment, except to say, "I'll be away; I'll keep in touch."

"Mr. Bill."

"Yes, Mark?"

"Can ... can I come with you? I ... I can help look."

"I'm sure you could laddie, but there's a lot lookin'. You stay and look after your mother, eh, and these two?" He patted Willie and Mamie on the head, and the children remained silent and watched him as he walked from the room followed by Fiona.

At the door she said, "Where are you going now?"

"To the bank. It's payday and I'll get it over early on because some of the lads are coming out with me over towards ... " He didn't finish but put his hand out and patted her shoulder as he turned away, pulled on his coat and cap, and went out. But he was only halfway down the drive when he turned and, almost at a run, came back as she was closing the door. Pulling her into his arms, he said, "Look, love, I'm not being offhand, but I'm just near the breakin' point. We both are, I know. I've ... I've never felt so womanish in me life, 'cos I just want to sit down and howl me bloody eyes out."

"I understand, dear, so don't worry about me, please. That's the last thing you need do."

He kissed her, then again made his way down the drive.

At the bank he drew out enough money to meet the wages and what was needed for his own requirements. But here he found he was again on the verge of breaking down because everyone was so sympathetic. Another time he would have laughed at the idea of the manager walking with him to the door and opening it for him.

When he arrived at the site Danny looked at him and he looked at Danny but said nothing; and after a moment Danny said, "You want to get away, don't you? Will I call them up?"

"Aye, do that."

He went into the hut and, sitting down at his desk, opened his big leather bag and lifted out an assortment of notes and silver. Then he drew towards him the ledger and a small stack of pay slips and envelopes.

Checking the slips against the ledger he put money into named envelopes. He came to the name, T. Callacter. After staring at it he went to the door from where he could see the men emerging from different parts of the building and, seeing Danny talking to one of them, he shouted, "Here a minute!"

Back in the hut he pointed to the name, saying, "He was cleared on Wednesday."

"Aye, boss, I thought so an' all at the time I made the slip out. It's my fault: twice he did an hour's overtime and I never booked it. I'm sorry."

"Why didn't he ask for it on Wednesday?"

"He said he didn't notice it until he got home, and that when he did he thought, Oh, to hell. But I think he's a bit tight now for cash. Anyway he said he'd left some tools here kicking around and wanted to pick them up. But as I said, it's my fault, he's due for that."

"He didn't seem short of a penny from the place he lives in."

"Aye, it's a biggish house, but it's dropping to bits. It used to be a farm. His dad ran it. But it's gone to pieces, I understand, since he died. From what I can gather he and his dad didn't get on. He used to live on his own but after the old fellow dropped down dead—and he wasn't all that old either—he came into the place. But there was no money to keep it up and as far as I can gather it was mortgaged to the hilt. I got all this from Morris. He lives quite near him. He tells me he's a queer fish and says he doesn't know if he's just gay or glad."

At another time Bill would have let out a laugh, but now he said, "What the hell are we bothering about him for? Let them in."

The hut was a long one and Bill's desk was at one end of it. Eight men came in, stood in a line, and received their pay, but with no back-chat today. Then some of them went out and so made room for the rest. The last one to reach the desk was Thomas Callacter. He was dressed, not as the others, but in a good-quality black overcoat and a trilby hat, and he was carrying a small leather bag with an open top, showing a number of tools. And when Bill's gaze was drawn to them, the man said, "They're mine. Would you like to examine them?"

"I'll take your word for it."

"Thank you." The words were stressed and caused Bill's jaws to stiffen. Picking up the small envelope from the table, he held it out and as the man leaned forward to take it from his hand, Bill's nostrils stretched, his eyes widened, and his mouth dropped into a gape for a moment. Then his two hands sprang out like an animal's claws, he gripped the lapels of the dark coat and pulled the man more than halfway across the desk and, like an animal, sniffed at him. Then the cry that escaped his wide, open mouth startled the remainder of the men who were in the hut. And they couldn't believe their eyes when they saw their boss grasp the man by the throat, then drag him round the side of the table, the while screaming, "Where is she? Where is she?" and then begin to rain blows on the man who retaliated with both fist and feet.

"Hells bells! What's up with you?"

"Give over!"

"God's sake! Stop it, boss."

"Come on! Come on, boss! Let up! What's he done anyway?"

The clamouring appeals came from the men trying to separate them, for by now Bill had his fingers on the fellow's throat and they were both writhing on the ground.

The commotion had brought other men from the yard and the hut was now a mass of workmen, some holding Bill and some the man who had worked with them not so long ago.

"It's him. It's him." Bill's voice was a choking scream.

"Give over, boss. Give over."

"Let me go, blast you! I tell you it's him; he's got her."

It was evident from the looks exchanged between the men that they thought the boss had flipped, and they looked with something like pity on the man who was still struggling to breathe evenly and whose lip was bleeding and one eye almost closed. But their attention was once again drawn to their boss when he shouted to Danny, "The scent! Danny. I told you about the scent and the bairn spillin' it all over her. It stank. It stank, I tell you. And his coat, smell it! Smell his coat."

There was silence in the room except for the heavy breathing of all of them. Then Danny took three steps forward and as he went to bend his head to smell the man's coat, the fellow's foot came out and only just missed Danny's groin. But now Danny had him in his grip, not by the throat but by the lapels of his coat and he sniffed at it. Then still holding him he turned his head towards his boss, saying, "You're right. You're right, Bill; it's scenty."

"Some fellas use scent." The voice came from one of the men. And another said, "Aye, it could be deodorant."

"Leave go of me. It's all right; just leave go of me." Bill looked from one side to the other, then down at the hands that held him and slowly the men released their grip on him. And looking at them, he said, "My kid spilt a big bottle of Chanel scent over her school coat. It was saturated; the house stank. It's ... it's an expensive scent. I had it in me nostrils, couldn't get rid of it, and it's on his coat. She was wearing her school coat when she disappeared."

One of them now looking at Callacter demanded of him, "Well, what have you got to say to that?"

And the man, who seemed to be foaming at the mouth now, said, "Big shot. Come up from the gutter. Scum. All he can do is bawl. . . ."

The arms were on him again, and Danny was entreating him: "Steady, Bill. Steady. Let him go on."

And he went on, the while rubbing his throat, "Marrying a lass young enough to be your daughter. Playing the big daddy to her kids."

"Shut your mouth or I'll shut it for you." It was Bert Ormesby stepping forward now, which was surprising, for he was the church-man who neither drank nor smoked. And his threat was followed by someone else saying, "And I'll help you."

Bill now shrugged off the hand and picked up the phone without ever taking his eyes off the man. And when he got through to the station he said, "Bailey here. Is the inspector there?" And the voice answered, "No, sir, he's out."

"Well, get in touch with him and tell him we've got the man. Tell him we're at the buildings. We'll wait for him here."

"You'll never find her until she's rotten." It was a scream, and when Bill's hand sprang to a heavy steel paperweight on the table,

Barney McGuire and Harry Newton, as if of one mind, got on each side of him and almost dragged him through the press of men and into the yard. And there they talked to him and at him until ten minutes later the inspector's car, followed by two others, came into the yard.

Slowly, as if he was finding difficulty in forming the words, Bill explained to them what had happened. When he had finished the inspector said, "There's barns there, but the men went right through them."

It was when one of the sergeants said, "But he may not have left her there," that Bill turned his eyes on him and the man returned his look for a moment, then looked away.

It was half an hour later and they had searched the barns and all they had discovered were some of the stolen window frames and doors and floorboards that had been missing from Bill's stock. The rest had evidently been sold. Bill had not been with the police when they first went through the place or he would have recognised his own materials then.

The house was an old one, with steps, some going up, others going down leading into the different rooms and after searching it from top to bottom, the police and Bill were now standing in the yard once more. Suddenly, the inspector turned from Bill and went to the car where Callacter was being held and, bending down to him, said, "It's no good, you know we'll find her, so you might as well tell us now."

"I know nothing about it."

"I understand you've already made the statement that the child would be rotten when we come across her."

"I just said that to get one back on him. He's a big mouth, no education, nothing. He's a lout and I've always hated his kind."

"That's as may be, and your opinion, but you'll help yourself if you tell us where the child is."

The man now sat back into the corner of the car and there was a sneer on his face as he again said, "I know nothing about it."

Returning to Bill, the inspector said, "I don't think we'll get any further here."

"*She's here.*"

"Well, we've searched, Mr. Bailey."

"I've got a feeling that she's here; I know it somehow. I want to go through the house again."

The inspector sighed, then said, "Just as you say, Mr. Bailey. Sergeant." He beckoned the sergeant towards him and he in turn beckoned a young policeman, and again they entered the house.

90

"Where do you want to begin, sir?"

"Upstairs somewhere, near the lumber room."

"That's at the end of the house."

"Yes, at the end of the house."

They went into the lumber room. And it *was* a lumber room: there were a number of broken chairs, an old sideboard, two tables that had evidently been in a fire, some large empty boxes and a pair of steps. Just as they had done before they moved everything and examined the floorboards. They next went into a back room. It had one small window, and two of its walls were obviously cavity ones, but showing no sign of having been cut into.

Then they were standing in the bathroom. This must once have been a small bedroom. The fittings were old and dirty. The inspector looked at the sergeant, raised his eyebrows and was on the point of going out when Bill glanced up towards a trapdoor in the ceiling. Then he stared at it, his head back on his shoulders, his eyes fixed tight on it, and he said slowly, "That's been moved recently."

The inspector followed his gaze, saying quietly, "It's hardly big enough to get through."

"Somebody gets through; there'll be a tank cupboard up there.... There were steps in that lumber room."

"You'll never get through there, sir."

Bill turned and looked at the young sergeant and said, "Maybe not, but he could."

The young policeman now glanced at his superior, and the inspector said, "Bring the steps."

The steps had four rungs and a flat platform, and when the young policeman stood with knees bent on the top, Bill said, "I don't know how long it could be since the wiring's been done there but once you lift the trap up you might find a switch. Grope round and see if there is one."

"I have a torch, sir." The young man patted his pocket.

They watched him push up the trapdoor; they watched his shoulder moving as his hand groped around the sides of the open space; and then there was a click and the dark hole was illuminated.

The policeman looked down towards them for a moment before hoisting himself through the hole. They waited, their heads back on their shoulders as they listened to the sound of his steps overhead; then his voice came muffled, saying, "There's nothing up here except two tanks." Then again the sound of his footsteps and his voice once more: "And there's nothing in the tanks except water." The next words that came were faint but sounded like, "Eeh, God!" And they all had hold of the steps when his face appeared above the hole. It

91

looked whiter than the light around it and he brought out on a stuttering gabble, "Sh . . . she . . . she's here, be . . . be . . . behind the tank . . . trussed."

As if he had been shot from a cannon, Bill was at the top of the steps, but when he attempted to get through the hole his shoulders stuck. And it was the sergeant who said tersely, "Take off your coats, sir."

The next instant both his overcoat and jacket were thrown to the floor, and then he was squeezing himself through the aperture.

He had to bend double to get behind the tank, and what he saw brought his mouth wide and his eyes almost lost in the contortion of his face, for there was the child. She was lying on her side: her arms were tied behind her back, her ankles were tied with a leather belt, and in her mouth was a gag held in place by a piece of cord tied round her face. Because of the sloping roof he could not lift her up from the position he was in, so he pulled her gently towards him, and then she was in his arms and he was staring down into her closed eyes.

His head went to her breast, and when he felt the soft beat of her heart it was as if his own had come back to life. There was no way he could untie her here and so, bent double, he passed her through the hatch into the arms of the sergeant. And seconds later he was kneeling beside her on the floor tearing the gag from her mouth while the inspector undid the strap on her legs. But when it came to freeing her arms it was the sergeant who said, "Don't try to bring them forward yet, sir, they'll be in cramp, just rub them gently."

And this is what they did, the inspector at one side, the sergeant at the other, while he held her slight body and longed to cry his relief while at the same time the desire to murder the man who had done this to a child gathered strength.

When they reached the yard Bill had his jacket on, but Katie was wrapped in his overcoat. And at the car in which Callacter was sitting, he stopped just long enough to bend and look into the man's face and growl, "I'll get you! By God, if it's the last thing I do, I'll get you."

"Come along, sir." The inspector touched his arm and drew him away, saying quietly, "He'll get his deserts, never fear."

"Aye. Ten years; time off for good behaviour and come out and do the same again. I tell you, I'll . . . "

"Sir"—the inspector's voice was firm—"be thankful you've got her in time." And he added, "She must go straight to hospital."

"What! She'll be better at home."

92

"The doctor will have to ascertain if everything's all right with her, and she seems to be in an unnatural sleep. The sergeant has already got through." He motioned back with his finger. "They'll be expecting us. You understand?"

Bill let out a long deep breath, then nodded. He understood.

The sergeant had taken over the wheel of Bill's car, and he was about to take his place beside him when he turned to the inspector once again and said, "Will it be possible to inform my wife?"

"Yes, we'll do that, sir. I'll get on to the station and they'll do that straightaway. Don't worry anymore. But let's get her into bed." He smiled gently, then closed the door; and they drove off.

12

AFTER LAST NIGHT, FIONA NATURALLY DID NOT EXPECT TO SEE HER MOTHER again, at least for some time, but here she was and unbelievably still in fighting form, albeit quietly so.

"You've never known any luck since you got entangled with that person," she said.

What was she going to do? She couldn't tackle her; she was so tired. Oh, Katie. Katie.

But as if it were in another's voice, she was saying, "He is not that person; he is my husband, Mother. Please don't forget that. As for luck, I hadn't much luck before."

"Well, no matter how ineffectual Ray was he was a gentleman."

"Oh, that's news to me. I always understood that you saw him as a worthless free-lance journalist, who couldn't look after his wife and family and left them penniless; even the roof over our heads was your suggestion because he was so useless he wouldn't have thought about it."

"You're exaggerating as usual."

"I can tell you this much, Mother, you never have nor ever will meet a man as good and as caring as Bill, who is my kind of gentleman."

"Good and caring, you say, when your daughter ... "

"Mother!" Her voice was a scream now. "How could Bill help that? Don't be such a fool."

"Calm yourself, girl; we want no more hysterics like last night, and I'll overlook the fact of your speaking to me as you do because you're in a state; but, in a way, it's only to be expected that you now feel remorse for you've been so besotted with that man that your children have come to mean little to you."

She was choking; she had the greatest desire to do what Bill had done recently, go for her, grab her by the throat, and shake her like a rat. But what she said now from behind her clenched teeth was, "If I've no love for my children I'm following your pattern, Mother, because you never liked children, you never wanted children, you didn't want me. The only love I ever had in my childhood was from my father. And when you were fighting your refined fights in the bedroom you told him once you had been forced to have me, but never again. So don't talk to me of loving children. You've never loved my children; in fact, you don't like them. You're incapable of loving but not incapable of jealousy: jealous that I had three, and love them; and now you are jealous that I have Bill because, let's face it, you wanted him for yourself. And why you hate him is because he showed you up as a middle-aged or old middle-aged woman."

She shouldn't be saying this. She didn't care a scrap what her mother thought of the children; all that was consuming her at the moment was the loss of her daughter. So why was she talking like this? Why was she bothering? She was so tired, so tired. She wanted to drop down and sleep but her eyes wouldn't close; they were staring as if into her brain, looking at the pictures there that presented the different ways her daughter could have died. But her mother was talking again. What was she saying? She had become deaf to her voice for the moment. She was saying: "You have become utterly vulgarised by that individual, and it's a sort of comfort to you to imagine that other people might have wanted him and are jealous of you. But let me tell you, Fiona, I would never have demeaned myself to allow a man like that even to touch me. There is such a thing as dignity and you are utterly without it. What you have said doesn't upset me, it only makes me sorry for you and pity you that you are so in need of a man that you had to take that ignorant, brash, loud-mouthed individual."

Fiona did not see her mother leave the room, for she was leaning against the mantelpiece trying to stop herself from passing out. She had never fainted in her life, but she knew she was near to it now. And as she gripped the mantelpiece, endeavouring to steady herself,

95

she asked if there was anyone in the world who had a mother like hers. Other mothers, she imagined, would be comforting their daughters, or would be upstairs in the playroom assuring the children that Katie would come back.

When the phone rang she had to pull herself from the support of the mantelpiece and her hand was trembling when she lifted the mouthpiece.

"Mrs. Bailey? I . . . I have news for you. Your daughter has been found."

Her head drooped forward onto her chest, then jerked up again as she stammered, "All . . . all . . . I mean, is she . . . ?"

"As far as I can gather she is all right. Your husband is with her. She has been taken to St. Clive's."

"Tha . . . thank you. Oh, thank you. Thank you." She rammed the phone down; then, as if imbued with new life, she sprang up the stairs, thrust open the playroom door where Mark was sitting looking out the window, Willie was curled up in the corner of the couch, and Mamie was doodling with some blocks on the low table.

"She's found! She's found! They've got her!"

They were all hanging on to her at once, all gabbling: "Oh, where? Where?"

"Is she all right, Mam?"

"Katie coming back?"

She lifted Mamie up into her arms and, hugging her, she said, "Yes, yes, she's coming back. She's coming back. Don't cry. Don't cry." She put the child down, then put her arms around the three of them now and pulled them towards the old couch. And speaking directly to Mark, she said, "You'll see to things, won't you? Nell's had to go into Newcastle, but I'll ask her mother to come in and give an eye to you."

"No need, Mam; there's no need." The boy moved his head from side to side. "I can see to things. They'll both stay up here"—he thrust his finger from one to the other—"and I'll answer the phone. And I won't open the door to anyone except I know them. So please don't worry."

Gently she touched his cheek, saying now, "No, I needn't worry when you're in charge. So I'll go now, but I'm sure I won't be long."

"And you'll bring Katie back?"

She looked down on Willie, saying, "Yes, yes, I'll bring her back."

"I'm going to give her my Ching Lang Loo book."

"Oh, she'll love that, Willie. She always liked to read your Ching Lang Loo book."

The small fair-haired boy nodded at her, then said solemnly, "And not for a lend; she can have it for keeps."

"That's very kind of you, Willie. I'll tell her." She smiled down at them, then hurried out and into her bedroom, where she grabbed up a coat; but then, about to leave her room, she stopped at the door and, looking upwards and very like a child, she said, "Thank you."

13

IT WAS THREE DAYS LATER AND KATIE WAS STILL IN HOSPITAL: THE DOCTORS' reports were that she hadn't been interfered with but that she was still in a form of shock, so much so that as yet she hadn't spoken a word.

The police had ascertained from their questioning of Callacter that he had given her strong sleeping tablets, solely because she had been kicking her heels against the tanks. And the local papers had run headlines suggesting that he had abducted the child to get his own back on her stepfather because he had bawled at him about his work, and then questioned whether the man would have let the child die up in that tank room, for he showed no remorse. One newspaper headlined the case: SCENT TRAIL, FATHER RECOGNISES ABDUCTOR THROUGH PERFUME SMELL.

Now, three days having passed, the headlines had changed; and there were no more reporters coming to the house or waiting outside the hospital for them. The only reference to the affair today was contained in a small paragraph at the bottom of the middle page; it opened with "Kidnapped child still unable to speak."

Bill and Fiona were now talking with the doctor, and it was Bill who said, "Once she's back home with her brothers and sister she'll have more chance of coming to."

"Yes, perhaps you're right; but she'll still need careful attention."

"Oh, she'll get that." Bill pursed his lips in confirmation, then asked rather tentatively, "How long does this state generally last?"

The doctor looked down at the pad on his desk. "There's no knowing," he said.

"You mean, it could be permanent?" Fiona's voice was small.

"As I said, there's no knowing. She's had an awful shock. I won't say that another kind of shock could bring her speech back, but love and contentment, which, summed up, means living in a happy atmosphere, could work wonders. Still, there's no guarantee. Subconsciously she feels that if she talks she will create the experience again. Anyway"—he rose to his feet—"you may take her home. I'll get in touch with your local man and he'll pop in on and off for the time being to see how she's doing."

They didn't thank him but they looked at him and he at them, and he smiled.

It was the evening of the same day. Katie had been home for some hours. She had been greeted joyously by the three children; she had then been put into bed in her own room, which was bright with her toys and fresh flowers. She had eaten a light meal but she had neither smiled nor spoken.

Willie, the potential actor who already had a sense of timing, had left the presentation of his rag book to a period in the evening when there seemed to be a pause. Leaving his mother and Bill and Mark and Mamie in the bedroom, he went out, and returned bearing in his hands the Ching Lang Loo book, the pages of which were made of rough-edged linen with a poem written on one side and a picture depicting it on the facing page. There were twenty-six poems in all, and the first poem carried the title.

Advancing slowly towards the bed, Willie placed the quite weighty tome on the counterpane while looking at Katie and saying, "It's for keeps, me Ching Lang Loo book."

There was silence in the room. All eyes were turned on the little girl in the bed who seemed, in a way, to have shrunk during her short absence. They watched her look down on the book, then put her hand on it and stroke its rough cover, then lift her hand and put it out towards Willie. And they watched him grab it, then take a big breath before bursting into tears and turning to fling himself against Bill's knee.

"There now. There now. She's pleased with it. Be quiet now. Be quiet."

99

"What?" Bill bent his head towards the mouth that was dribbling now, and what he heard was, "She . . . she didn't laugh."

"No, no; but she will." And Bill now looked up towards the bed where Mark was standing and he said loudly, "Come on, Mark, do us Ching Lang Loo." And when Mark muttered, "No, you do it," Bill cried, "Oh, I can't do Ching Lang Loo like you, McGinty is my piece."

"Come on, Mark." Fiona's voice brought the boy close to the bed and, looking down on Katie, he said, "Would you like me to do Ching, Katie?"

His sister looked at him. Her eyes blinked but she didn't speak. He now glanced towards his mother, and when she nodded he picked up the book, and it was evident he had to force himself to take the pose of a small sea captain. However, he did so and went into the poem. His voice taking on a pseudo deep note, he began:

I said to Ching Lang Loo today,
What shall we do, O' mate?
He said, We'll board a windjammer
And feel the fresh sea spate.

Leav'ee it to me, captain, said Ching,
And I will take you where the waves sing
And the breakers, with rolls and tosses,
Gallop upon their pure white hosses.

We'll stand firm upon the rolling decks,
With coloured hankies round our necks;
And we'll shout: Ahoy! there. Sails away!
Full tilt, my brave lads, for Biscay Bay!

And dipping down then rising again,
We plough our way through the mighty main;
Our hair standing straight with wind and spate,
We tear along at a mighty rate.

Then far, far in the distance we spy
A ship that looks like a little fly,
Until we look through BIN . . . OCK . . . U . . . LERS. . . .
Why! She's a pirate. . . . After her! sirs.

Ahoy, there! you shipmates, east by northeast;
We are right on her heels, the nasty beast.
After her, lads, and into her hold,
For she's bound to have treasures untold.
If she has *Oranges,* and *Lemons* too,

Won't the galley cook be pleased with you,
Said my brave Chinese mate, Ching Lang Loo.

With the exception of Katie they all laughed and clapped; then they looked at the white-faced, big-eyed child staring at Mark. They watched her hold her hands out for the book, and when Mark placed it on her upturned palms, she brought it to her small chest and hugged it; then sliding down in the bed she lay back as if meaning to go to sleep. And at this Fiona made a signal for them all to say goodnight, and in turn the children kissed her and hugged her. Then Bill, leading Fiona to the door, said, "See them off, then get yourself to bed; you're all in."

"Not half as much as you are."

"I'm all right. I'll arrange the bedchair by her side. We must find out how she reacts in the night, and you don't want her to wake up and find herself alone here, do you?"

"Oh, Bill."

"Now, now, stop it. We've got her back, and by hook or by crook she'll talk. Being Katie she'll talk ... you've got to believe this, woman." He gripped her shoulders. "We've all got to believe it."

He kissed her now and pushed her out of the room, and when he returned to the seat by the bed Katie looked at him and held out her hand, and he sat down and took it in his.

At two o'clock in the morning when Fiona gently opened the door she saw them both still hand in hand fast asleep.

14

IT WAS A FORTNIGHT LATER. KATIE WAS UP, AND TO OUTWARD APPEARANCES HAD
apparently returned to normal, but as yet she hadn't spoken a word
and except for the movement of her upper lip she hadn't really
smiled, nor had she played with toys; the only thing she seemed to
want was the clouty book. And although she seemed to read the
poems for herself, each evening she would push the book into either
Mark's or Bill's hands and listen to them reading and acting the
rhymes; but their antics failed to elicit any laughter from her.

During the first week, Fiona and Bill had taken turns sleeping by
her side in the chairbed, but she'd had no nightmares. So now they
were in bed together and Fiona was asking, "Who do you think gave
them the story about the scent and the school concert?"

"Oh, likely one of the lads."

"It'll certainly be a good advert for Chanel . . . 'Kidnapped Child
Saved By Chanel Scent.'"

"Well, they deserve it all, 'cos that's what saved her. He must have
held her close to him; likely she was struggling. And that school coat,
as you know, was soaked with it. She swanked, didn't she, about going
to school in a scenty coat?" Then his mind jumped ahead, "His case
comes up in three weeks' time. God!" Then, grinding his teeth, Bill
said, "They'll likely give him life, so I'll have a long time to wait to
get at him."

"Don't! Don't!" Fiona beat against his shoulder with her clenched fist. "Don't carry that hate with you over the years. We've got her back, so be thankful."

"Yes, we've got her back, a dumb child, whereas before she lived to talk, didn't she?"

"Well, she will again."

He turned from her and looked up at the ceiling, then said, "I had an idea today. I don't know whether it will work. You know the Chinese restaurant in the marketplace?"

"There are two about there."

"Chang's House, the posh one."

"I know it, but I've never been inside."

"Well, I used to eat there often before I came under your indifferent cooking." He slanted his eyes towards her and she said, "Yes, go on: before you came under my indifferent cooking."

"Well, as I said, I have an idea."

"Well, what's the idea?"

"Oh, I'd better keep it till tomorrow night as you mightn't see eye to eye with me."

"Don't be so infuriating, Bill."

"Well, I'll tell you this: I want to buy something from him but I don't know whether I'll have enough money to do it, that's speaking metaphorically." He now took his heel and kicked her leg gently as he said, "That's another big one. Surprise you, did it? All right. Well, what I mean is, I've got enough money really to buy his business, that's if I sold mine, but there are things people put value on and no money can buy them."

"Well, what is it?"

"It's a Chinaman."

"A Chinaman?"

"Yes, dear, a Chinaman. Now that's all I'm going to tell you. I'm going to sleep; I'm very tired and I don't want you to disturb me or make love to me because I've got a headache." Turning swiftly, he pulled her into his arms and all she could say was, "Oh, you! You!"

Nell had picked up Mark and Willie from school. It was a new arrangement because Fiona felt she couldn't leave Katie because Katie couldn't leave her: she followed her wherever she went, even to the toilet, which proved that the fear was still rampant in her, and she always wanted her hand to be held.

The doctor had called earlier in the day and suggested that the child be taken for psychiatric treatment. Even the word sounded ominous. What was more, she had become puzzled all day about the

Chinaman that was coming. What did Bill expect her to do with a Chinaman? Did he mean her to take him on as a kind of daily help? Likely it was a Chinese boy or young man he meant. She had nothing against Chinamen, they were always so very polite, but she didn't know how she was going to go on with one in the house even for a few hours a day. She wished he was home and knew what he was up to. Whatever it was, she knew he was thinking of Katie.

Bill was a little late in arriving home. It was close on six o'clock. Nell had just taken the children up to the playroom and she herself was on the point of leaving the kitchen when the back door opened, and there he was by himself, no Chinaman, except he was carrying a very long box. It was all of four foot.

"What's that?"

"Wait and see. Here, hold it." He put it into her arms, and she was surprised that it wasn't as heavy as it looked. He pulled off his hat and coat, then took the box from her, saying, "Come on. Where are they, in the sitting room?"

"No, in the playroom, with Nell."

"Good." He bounded up the stairs before her, burst open the door, crying, "Abaft there, shipmates!" Mamie, jumping down from Nell's knee, ran to him, crying, "Uncle Bill. A present for me?"

"No, not for you, dear, not for you." He wagged his finger at her. "And not for you." He pointed to Willie. Then to Mark, "And not for you either. This is for who?"

The three children now looked towards the sofa, and one after the other they cried, "Katie!"

"Yes, this is special for Katie. Stand aside everybody." He thrust out his arm, and it accidentally pushed Nell back against the chair and she, joining in the chorus, said, "Yes, sir. Yes, sir. As you say, sir." And the children laughed.

Before whipping the paper from the long box he glanced at Fiona who was staring at him; then he looked fully at Katie and said quietly, "Who do you think I've got for you, Katie, eh? Who do you think I've got in here?" He patted the box.

She was sitting forward on the edge of the couch now; her eyes were wide but she said not a word, nor did she smile.

Slowly now Bill lifted the lid and exposed a long colourful object. Then in standing upright he slowly drew it forth and there emerged a beautifully clothed Chinese figure, held upright by strings attached to wooden rods that Bill was now slowly manipulating. The figure was that of a Chinese boy with a long pigtail and dressed in a blue satin gown with an orange sash and black calf shoes. When the arms were lifted it looked as if the gown had wings. But what had been added to the figure's head was a pirate's scarf. They all stood spellbound as Bill awkwardly, yet definitely, moved the legs and so walked the Chinese pirate towards Katie. And as he did so he almost let go of the strings for the muscles of her face were moving upwards into a smile. And when he made the Chinaman bow to her she thrust out her arms and grabbed the puppet to her, and her mouth going into a gape and her small breast heaving, she brought out the words: "Ching . . . Lang . . . Loo."

The room was in an uproar; they were all crying now both verbally and tearfully.

"Ching Lang Loo. Yes, Katie, it's Ching Lang Loo." Bill was sitting on the couch beside her, holding both her and the puppet tightly in his arms.

"Mine?" The word was whispered as she looked up at him.

"Yes, love, yours, all yours."

Her mouth now opened and shut three times; then she swallowed before she said, "Mr. Bill."

"Aw, lass. Aw hinny."

Bill knew there was something about to happen to him and that he must do something quick to prevent it, and so, pulling her upwards, he shouted to Nell, "Put her on a chair, Nell, and get her to work him." Then thrusting the puppet into Nell's hand, he hurried from the room, and Fiona after him and into their bedroom. And there, dropping onto the dressing table stool, he covered his face with his hands and let the tears flow, and as she held him, her tears joined his; and after a while he turned his head from her, saying, "Bloody fool I am."

"And the best bloody fool in the world. And that's their sign, isn't it? It used to hang in the window sometimes, and someone worked it, and everybody used to stand and watch it. It's a beautiful thing. How on earth did you manage to persuade him to let you buy it?"

"I didn't."

"You didn't?" She moved away from him in a sort of horror, then said, "You didn't?"

"No, no, woman, I didn't." His voice sounded more like himself now. "Pinched the damn thing? No, of course not. But he wouldn't take a penny for it; he said he can get another one made quite easily. And what's more, he's invited us all to dinner. That'll save a bit." He grinned at her before again wiping his eyes and blowing his nose.

Smiling at him now through her own tears, she said, "What gave you the idea?" And to this he answered thoughtfully, "I don't know.

105

I just don't know. The same thing I suppose that made me look up to the trapdoor into that tankroom. Funny that. D'you think I could be physic, or psychic?"

Her smile was soft as she said, "No, I don't think you could be physic or psychic, Mr. Bill Bailey, only overflowing with love."

15

"I'D NEVER THOUGHT I'D MISS HIM SO MUCH."

"Well, it was your idea."

"Aye, I know it was. But you were for it, weren't you?"

"Yes; yes, of course, Bill, I was. And it's early days; we'll get used to it. And don't forget there's other three upstairs."

"Aye, well; they're missin' him an' all, the kingpin's gone."

"Oh, Katie's taken over I think. She had a row with Willie in the car, so that's healthy."

"D'you think they're settling down in the new school?"

"Yes, I do. And it's different altogether; there's more personal attention. Yet they did very well at Beecham Road."

"Aye. But Beecham Road is a good mile and a half away whereas this place is practically on the doorstep, and no matter what time you turn up there's a teacher there with them."

"Bill."

"Yes, love?"

"This is going to cost a packet, not just this year but every year, three of them to pay for. Mamie's will come out of her trust, but . . . "

"Look, woman, we've been into this. But, mind you—" he laughed now and pushed her in the shoulder as he said, "a thousand quid a

107

term! When he said that I let out so much surprised air me trousers nearly dropped down."

She was laughing as she said, "Yes, and by the look on your face I was expecting them to. But I warned you before we went. Then there are the others...."

"Well, they're two for the price of one really."

"Yes, but they are just day pupils; you've got to take that into consideration. And I told you what it would be...."

"Look, who's grumbling, woman? Not me. I want to do it. And I'll go on doin' it. I'm just saying what these blokes and blokesses charge. And what about Katie's and Willie's Miss Widdle! Did you ever hear a name like that? It asks to be called wet pants, doesn't it? And a private school at that, kids calling their headmistress, wet pants. I wonder if she knows."

"Very likely; they've got to be broad-minded."

"How long will it be before half-term?"

Fiona burst out laughing. "He's only been gone three days. It'll be sometime in November."

"And we're still in September."

Fiona's voice now changed and she said softly, "Look, if you think we've made a mistake we can always bring him nearer home; he can go into Newcastle as a day-boarder and be home at the weekends."

"No, no; we've made no mistake. What was good enough for Sir Charles Kingdom's sons is good enough for mine." They fell against each other and laughed. "That's what made me want to send Mark there, 'cos the elder one, Sir Percy, went and Norman, the one that's in America on the films now, he was there an' all. And the old boy's a nice fella, no side."

"You know something, Bill Bailey?"

"What, Mrs. Bailey?"

"You're a snob at bottom."

"Is that what I am? Oh, I'm so pleased; it's much better than being a brash ignorant slob. Of course, slob and snob don't seem very far removed, do they? Oh! Who's that now?"

The phone bell was ringing, and Fiona went out into the hall and picked it up and heard Nell's voice saying, "Fiona?"

"Yes, Nell."

"Can ... can I come round?"

"Nell, what a question to ask, of course you may come round."

"Well, you know how I feel about coming round at night when...."

"Don't be so silly. Get yourself round here. What's the matter anyway?"

"I'll tell you in a minute."

As she reentered the room she said, "That was Nell. She asked if she could come round. She sounds as if there's something wrong."

"She asked if she could come round? Why? She doesn't usually ask."

"Well, if you were given to noticing anything, Mr. Bailey, but the requirements of your stomach and how quick you can get upstairs and act the goat with that lot you would have noticed that she never comes in at night unless it is to baby-sit; she wants us to have time to ourselves."

"Oh, that's thoughtful of her. But with regard to music lessons, they ain't actin' the goat."

"Music lessons I agree aren't acting the goat, but to my mind tin whistles don't fit into that category."

"Well, it won't be tin whistles any longer, I've ordered flutes, three different sizes."

"You haven't! Oh, my God! Anyway, I wonder what's happened to bring Nell round."

"Well, the quicker you let her in the quicker you'll find out. The back door's locked I suppose?"

"Yes, of course." Fiona now hurried from the room and through the hall and into the kitchen, and she was just opening the door when Nell appeared.

It was evident that she had been crying. But she didn't immediately say anything, only sat down at the kitchen table, joined her hands together, and sat looking at them for a moment. And then she said, "Bill's in of course?"

"Yes; yes, he's in the sitting room. Come on in there, it's warmer."

"No, no."

"What's wrong?" Fiona now drew a chair up close to her. "Had a row?"

"Huh!" Nell now jerked her head back and laughed, but it was a sad, bitter laugh and, looking at Fiona, she said, "Do you know what it is to feel like dirt, of no consequence? No, you wouldn't, dear, no. You've had your mother to put up with but she's never rejected you, quite the reverse."

"What are you talking about? What's happened? Something to do with Harry?"

"Yes, something to do with Harry. He's gone."

"*Gone!* You mean he left you?"

"Just that. He's gone; he's left me. And he didn't even tell me to my face, he told his mother. She and Dad are in a state. After all, he's their son. But as Dad's just said, he's known for a long time he's bred something rotten. He hasn't been five minutes in that new job . . . he was supposed to be doing overtime, but Dad saw them out together and tackled him."

"He's gone off with someone then?"

"Yes; yes, Fiona, he's gone off with someone."

"Oh, oh, I'm sorry."

"I'm sorry, too." Nell put her hand out and gripped Fiona's. "I . . . I don't know where I am at the moment."

"But . . . but as you say, dear, he hasn't been five minutes in the job, he couldn't have known. . . . "

Nell was nodding her head now. "Oh, he was only five minutes in the job but he's known her, as far as I can gather, for some time, and she got him the job. I'm stupid and mental, besides being blind. But then I've told myself it's happening all the time, why should I be an exception to a man walking out on me? And that's another thing. When I get meself sorted out I know that I'll see it as just hurt pride because I haven't lost love; love flew out of our window many years ago. But he was there and I saw to his needs and life had become a pattern you get used to. . . . "

The kitchen door opened and Bill put his head round, saying, "Is there any room for a good-looking, interesting, and successful man in his prime in here?"

"Stop fooling, Bill." Fiona's voice was flat.

"Trouble?" He came to the table and looked down at Nell, but Nell turned her head away and looked towards the window while Fiona said quietly, "It's Harry. He's walked out."

"No!"

Fiona and he now exchanged glances, and when she made a little motion with her head he said, "Bloody fool." Then, taking Nell by the arm, he pulled her up from the chair saying, "Come on. What you need is a drink. And I repeat, he is a bloody fool, 'cos he doesn't know a good thing when he's on it. But I'll say this an' all: he wasn't worth you, not your little finger from what I can judge, and I'm no mean hand at that, at least where blokes are concerned. So come on, let's all get drunk."

Nell resisted being pulled towards the door, saying now, "Thanks, Bill, but I must go back home; they're upset, upset for me. They're nice people, Bill. I can never understand why he was so different. I . . . I love them both, and . . . and she's been a mother to me. You understand?"

"Yes, lass. Yes, we understand. And the morrow night . . . look, bring them in for a meal. How about it?" He now looked at Fiona, and she said, "Yes, that would be nice."

110

When the door closed on Nell they looked at each other, then they walked slowly side by side into the sitting room again and, going straight to the wine cabinet, he poured himself out a drink, saying, "You want one?"

"No thanks."

She watched him sip at his whiskey before coming and sitting down beside her and saying abruptly, "How's she fixed?"

"You mean financially?"

"Aye, I mean financially. Can't you understand my language yet?"

"It's difficult at times, Mr. Bailey." She pursed her lips. "But to answer your question in your own jargon, most of the time she's on the rocks. She hasn't said so much plainly, but I know she hasn't bought a new thing since she came here, and the fact that she doesn't like talking about clothes told me a lot."

"Well, we'll have to see to things, won't we? You could take her on in place of Mrs. Thingamajig. I don't like her anyway. Twice I've come up with her and she's smelt of beer. Funny, but I don't like women who smell of beer or spirits. Now what d'you think of that?"

"I think you're a very odd man, Mr. Bailey. But I don't know whether Nell would want to be a mother's help."

"She likes being here with the kids doesn't she, baby-sitting? Anyway, you can tap her, see what she says. I'll make it worth her while."

"I know you will." Her voice was soft and she leaned against him.

When the phone rang again she said, "What now?" then added, "No, stay where you are; you're an elderly man who needs his rest."

He gave her a not too gentle slap across the buttocks as she passed him and she was still holding the offending part when she picked up the phone.

"Hello, Mam."

"Oh, Mark. Mark." She turned her head to the side and actually yelled, "Bill! It's Mark. Where are you? I didn't think you'd be allowed to phone, I mean so early. Are you all right? Nothing the matter?"

There was a short silence before his voice came again, not very steady, saying, "I'm missing you all."

Her own voice dropped now. "Yes; yes, of course you are. And we are missing you, terribly, but . . . "

The phone was snatched from her, and Bill, his voice hearty, now said, "Hello there, boy."

"Hello, Mr. Bill."

"How's things?"

"Oh, all right."

"You settling in?"

There was another pause before Mark's voice came: "Yes; yes, I am."

"I didn't think you'd be allowed to phone."

"Mr. Leonard gave me leave. He's ... he's my housemaster."

"That was nice of him. Well, stick it out, boy. Have you eaten all your tuck? Would you like another box?"

"We ... we are only allowed one a month, you know."

"Oh yes; yes, I forgot. Anyway, boy, here's your mam."

"Hello, darling. Oh, you'll never guess who are pouring down the stairs? Can you have a word with them?"

"My ... my time is nearly up; I'll just say hello."

Bill had grabbed Mamie up in his arms; Willie and Katie had their hands on top of their mother's holding the phone and they both yelled together, "Hello, Mark. Hello, Mark."

His voice came back, saying, "Hello, Katie. Hello, Willie. Hello, Mamie. I've got to go now. Mam, Mr. Bill. Be seeing you."

"Yes, darling."

She heard the click; then, turning and looking at Bill, she swallowed deeply before saying, "Wasn't that nice? He must be a very understanding man, Mr. Leonard. I ... I didn't think they were allowed to phone, except under special emergencies. You don't think he's sort of pining?"

"No, no, no." He put Mamie down on the floor. Then, looking from one to the other of the children, he said, "Wasn't that fine, hearing him?"

It was Katie who answered first, saying, "It didn't sound like him." Then Willie, always to the point, muttered, "Tisn't the same as him being here. Why can't he come home every night like us?" He looked from Bill to his mother, and it was for her to answer, "It's a different school, dear; they learn different things."

"We learn different things." Willie stared up at her. Then turning his gaze on Bill, he added, "He could learn different things here and save a lot of money and we could go on a holiday."

With this statement of fact he walked towards the stairs; and as usual Mamie followed him, but she was snivelling now. And after a moment spent looking to the side as if considering the matter, Katie said, "Anyway, it was nice hearing him." And then she, too, went upstairs.

In the sitting room Bill took another sip from his glass of whiskey, then, running his hand through his hair, he said, "The verdict of the family spoken by the now male head of the upstairs apartments."

Flopping down into the corner of the couch, he looked up at her, saying, "He could be right. What d'you think? Have I persuaded you into something that you really didn't want to do?"

"Oh no, no. You're doing for him what I would never have been able to do and what his own father would never have done even if he had had the money. He was against private schools—in fact, schools of all kinds. I think he'd had a rough time himself. No, no," and she moved her head from side to side as she said this; then, sitting down beside him, she took his hand in hers, saying quietly, "Anything you do for them, Bill, I know it's for the best."

After a moment he said on a laugh, "That Willie's a character, isn't he? He had thought it all out, even to the holiday. That's a point: we've never had a holiday, what with one thing and another. And when I come to think about it, Mrs. B., you've never mentioned it."

"Well, now, if I had, what would you have said? I know exactly what your answer would have been: What! Go on a holiday with that so and so Brown breathing down my neck? He's out to get me that fellow. It's a good job I've got Old Kingdom Come on my side. That's exactly what you would have said, now isn't it?"

"No, Mrs. Bailey, not exactly. You've left out a number of adjectives such as"—he raised his hand now, palm upwards, almost blotting out her face—"I'll use the alternatives, budgerigar Brown and blue-pencil neck."

"Oh"—she thrust his hand away—"that's what I wanted to have out with you."

"Oh, my God, what now?" He turned away and put a hand to his forehead, then sighed deeply as she said, "This is serious. You know what Master Willie came out with in the car coming home?"

"No. Tell me; I can stand it." He thumped his forehead.

"He was addressing his sister and called her a budgerigar bitch, and I nearly went into the back of the bus because it was a full-mouthed, yelled retort."

"He didn't!" He was laughing at her.

"Bill, I'm serious." Her voice was a plea now. "It's a very nice school, as you know, and just imagine if he comes out with something like that."

"Well, you can't blame me for the bitch, I never use that word. I know a lot of them but I never use it on them; with one exception, and you know who that is. As regards the other, who's going to translate budgerigar into bugger? Aw, come on, don't look so worried. Just think of poor old Nell next door. Now *she* has something to worry about."

113

"Yes, yes; you're right. It must be a terrible feeling that, to be rejected, just left without a word.... If you ever walked out on me, Bill..."

Her shoulders were suddenly gripped and his face came within an inch of hers as he said, "Don't joke along those lines, Fiona; nothing could ever make me walk out on you. Nothing. Nothing. Do you hear? But I can tell you something and I mean this, as I meant what I've just said, if you ever decided to walk out on me you wouldn't last long, 'cos I'd shoot you, by God, I would, and the bugger you went with. And with him I'd aim for the place where it hurts most."

"Oh, Bill. Bill." She fell against him, her body shaking with laughter, and as she did so part of her mind was thanking God once again for bringing this man into the narrow household life she had led for years.

16

THE WEEKS SPED BY. NELL HAD GLADLY ACCEPTED THE POSITION OF MOTHER'S help. Her husband had asked for a divorce and she had willingly conceded.

She and Fiona spent long coffee breaks talking about the past, the present, and the future. They had become very close during these weeks, and Nell had expressed openly how grateful she was for the friendship and wondered what she would have done if they hadn't come to live next door. She had definitely become one of the family, and the children were fond of her, as was Bill. But, as he stated bluntly, she was a tactful piece for she knew when to make herself scarce, which was in the evenings when he was at home and most of the weekend, except on a Saturday night when he would take Fiona out to dinner and she would baby-sit.

But now it was November 9 and the night when Mark was coming home for his first leave from school.

On Monday they'd had a little bonfire in the garden when they'd eaten baked potatoes and sausages on sticks. Mr. and Mrs. Paget and, of course, Nell had come in from next door, and such was the success of the evening that before it was half over Katie and Willie, agreeing for once, said they were keeping some of their fireworks back so they could have a repeat performance on Saturday night. And now the two of them, together with Mamie, were bursting with excitement because Mark would be home and they'd have some fun.

They had left the children at home in Nell's care, as usual, and were now speeding towards the school. It was a forty-minute run from Fellburn and situated in its own extensive grounds in which were a covered swimming pool and two rugby pitches. The house itself was an imposing structure, not as large as great country houses were apt to be and apparently not large enough to provide all the classrooms necessary, for to the left of the house were three fabricated buildings that were used as classrooms. It was close on four o'clock when they arrived and the front of the mainhouse was lit up. The forecourt was busy with boys getting into cars and parents calling good-bye to other parents.

As they entered the hallway a senior boy stepped forward and, smiling at them, said, "Good evening." And to this Bill answered, "Mr. and Mrs. Bailey."

"Oh yes, yes." And the boy, nodding towards another standing some way back, said, "Take Mr. and Mrs. Bailey to Mr. Leonard."

They followed the boy across the hall, along a corridor, up a flight of stairs, and along another corridor, at the end of which he tapped on a door, and when he was told to enter he stood aside to allow Fiona and Bill to pass him.

"How do you do?" Mr. Leonard sounded very hearty. He shook hands with both of them; then addressing Fiona, he said, "I know you are dying to see your boy."

"Yes. Yes, I am . . . we all are. We've missed him so much."

"How's he been doing?"

Mr. Leonard looked at Bill. "Oh, very, very well. He took a bit of time to settle in. It's all strange, you know, coming away from a good home into a madhouse composed only of boys"—he laughed heartily—"but as I said, he's settling in. He hasn't been very well this last week. Matron kept him in bed."

"He's not . . . ?" Fiona began, and Bill put in, "He's ill? What's the matter with him? Why weren't we told?"

"Oh, it's nothing serious, just a cold. Anyway I'm sure you'd like to see him." He pressed a bell on his desk and was about to say something when Fiona asked, "How do you find his work?"

"Oh, well, varied, like most of them you know." He again laughed. "But he's very good on the maths and science side. He leans towards them, these subjects. History, art . . . well, he's improving in that quarter."

"What about sport?"

116

The housemaster now looked at Bill, saying, "Well, truthfully he doesn't take too well to rugger. I think soccer was his favourite game. He's good at running, too. He came second in the last cross-country. Oh, he'll do nicely, never fear. And as for his character and disposition, I'm sure he must take after his parents."

His smile encompassed his face, but Bill's eyes narrowed as he stared at the man and said flatly, "I'm not his father."

"Oh. Yes, of course. Ah!" The exclamation came as the door opened; and there he was, a pale-faced boy who seemed to have grown inches during the last few weeks. He hesitated somewhat before approaching them; and then he seemed to have difficulty in saying, "Oh, Mam." He kept an arm's length from her but took her hands; then looking at Bill, he said simply, "Mr. Bill."

"Hello, there." Bill put his hand on Mark's shoulder, saying with forced heartiness, "By! You have sprouted. What have you been up to?" He checked himself from adding, "Standing in manure?" but said instead, "The gang won't recognise you. We left them, yelling their heads off; they can't wait to see you."

Bill watched the boy gulp, then smile a little as he said, "I can't wait to see them. It seems years."

"Well, now, if that's the case don't let's waste time." And Bill turned to the headmaster, saying, "We'll be off then."

"Yes, yes." Mr. Leonard came and, bending his long length towards Mark, said, "Will you be all right, old chap?"

And Mark, looking into his face, said, "Yes, sir."

"That's it then, away with you."

There was more handshaking, and then they were outside on the drive, and Bill, turning to Fiona, said in an undertone, "Sit in the back with him."

This she did, and they'd hardly got out of the gate when Mark suddenly leaned his head against Fiona's breast and put his arms around her waist; and she held him tightly to her, but neither of them spoke, nor did Bill, who could see what was taking place through the mirror.

It wasn't until they were home and Mark had been swamped with hugs and kisses from Katie and Mamie and none too gentle punches of affection from Willie, and the four of them had got through a fancy tea set out by Nell and were now up in the playroom that Bill, looking from Fiona to Nell, said quietly, "What d'you two think? I know what I think, everything in the garden isn't lovely at Swandale."

"He looks peaky."

117

"Yes, Nell, he looks peaky. Well, what about you?" Bill turned to Fiona, and she put the tray down on the draining board before turning towards them and saying, "I feel the same way as you do: he's changed, he's not chirpy anymore. He used to cap everything you said; in fact, he was quite witty at times."

"Aye, yes, he was. But not anymore, seemingly; you've got to ask him a question before he speaks."

Nell walked over to the sink and, pushing Fiona gently with the back of her hand, said, "Leave those, I'll see to them. The both of you go up and have a game with them; that might loosen his tongue. Get him to read the Ching Lang Loo book again; he was really funny when he read and acted those rhymes."

"Aye, perhaps there's something in that." And Bill held out his hand to Fiona, saying, "Come on, woman." Then, as he made for the door, he looked back at Nell, saying, "Life never runs smoothly, does it?" And her answer was, "I wouldn't know, would I?"

Outside in the hall, Fiona said, "What a thing to say to Nell."

"Aye." Bill wrinkled his nose. "I suppose it was tactless. But she understands me by now."

They played games for two hours on that Friday night. On the Saturday morning they all went into Newcastle shopping. In the afternoon they saw a Disney film and when they came out they had tea in a posh restaurant where, yet again, Katie remarked aloud, "On white tablecloths."

Later that evening they played more games, and after a great deal of coaxing Mark was persuaded to read something from Katie's Ching Lang Loo book while Katie manipulated the doll. But what they all noticed was that he just read it, he didn't act it:

McGinty is the gardener
And he sometimes swears;

Pongo is the poodle
With only half his hairs;
Father is the parson
Reading from a book,

Says I'll take some saving
   By
     Hook
       Or
         By
           Crook.

And there's also my Chinese doll Ching Lang Loo
Who wants to be in
And says, "How do you do?"

They all clapped and laughed, with the exception of Willie, who stated flatly, "You didn't do it properly. You didn't act them, not any of them."

But when Mark came back with a shadow of his old self, saying, "What do you want, blood?" Willie joined in the laughter.

By arrangement Fiona managed to get Katie, Willie, and Mamie to bed, and so left Mark with Bill. And Bill, diplomacy not being his strong point, came straight out with, "What's up with you, lad? Something wrong at that school?"

"No, no."

"Aw, come on. You're not yourself; somebody been gettin' at you?"

"Well—" Mark wagged his head now, and in an off-hand manner said, "Everybody gets someone at them when they first go to school ... any school. It's a recognised thing."

"What is a recognised thing?"

"Well ... well, bullying."

"A lot of it there?"

"It ... it goes on."

"Have you been bullied?"

"I've ... I've had me share."

"And ... and you found it bad, you couldn't stand up to it? Is that it?"

"*No; no, it isn't.* I did stand up to it, I did."

"All right, all right, boy, don't shout."

"I'm sorry, Mr. Bill."

"Don't be sorry, lad. Have you made any friends?"

"Yes. Yes, two. Like me, new starters, Arthur Ryan and Hugo Fuller."

"Fuller? Hugo Fuller? Is that the Fuller who has the good tailor shop in the town?"

"Yes; that's his father."

"Oh, you're in good company. I might get a suit cheap." Bill grinned and Mark smiled, but a small, tight smile.

There was silence between them for a moment before Bill asked quietly, "Is there anything you'd like to tell me, lad, on the side like, that you don't want your mother to know?"

There was another silence before Mark replied, "No. Nothing. I'll get used to it. I ... I was homesick at first ... very. I ... I missed you all."

"And we missed you, lad. Well, if there's nothing seriously wrong, come on and get yourself to bed." He put his arm round the boy's shoulders and led him to the door and onto the landing, and there, pointing along it, he said, "Listen to them! Those two are separated by a wall and they are still going at it. Sometimes I wish Katie's tongue hadn't been loosened so much. Goodnight, lad."

"Goodnight, Mr. Bill."

It was some three hours later. They had been in bed for more than half an hour. They had talked and loved, and now, their arms about each other, they were approaching sleep when both of them became aware of the door being opened and the small voice hissing, "Mam!"

Fiona was sitting stiffly up now, having switched on the side light, and, blinking at Katie and Willie approaching the bed, she muttered, "What on earth!"

"What's the matter?" Bill's voice was thick and gruff. "Got a pain? Why are you both up at this time?"

It was Katie who answered in a whisper. "Willie came in to me. I was asleep. He woke me; he said Mark was crying."

"Crying?" Fiona swung her legs out of the bed and grabbed at her dressing gown, but Bill's hand stopped her from rising: "Wait a minute. Wait a minute," he said; then he was leaning across the bed, his face close to Willie, asking now, "Why . . . why was he crying?"

Willie not only wagged his head but his whole body as he said, "He'd punch me if I told you and Mam."

"Tell." Katie now dug her brother in the side with her thumb. "They've got to know."

"Well, come on, spill it." Bill was now out of the bed and sitting on the edge holding Willie's hand, and Willie, looking up at him, said with a quivering lip, "It's his bum . . . bottom." With the last translation he cast a glance up at his mother. And it was she who said, "What's wrong with his bottom?"

"It's all burnt . . . and his leg."

"*What!*"

The word was so loud that Fiona said, "Shh! Keep your voice down, Bill."

Bill now said, "Go on. What d'you mean, burnt?"

"Well, I was going into the bathroom and he was standing with his pyjamas down looking at his bottom in the glass, and it was all down one side . . . burnt. And he said I hadn't to tell you, or else. They put a lighted firework down it, his trousers, on Guy Fawkes night."

"*My God! God in heaven!*" Bill was now on his feet and making for

120

the door. He hadn't bothered to put on a dressing gown. And Fiona, following him, said, "What are you going to do?"

"What d'you think I'm going to do? I'm getting to the bottom of this."

"He'll hammer me."

Bill now turned towards Willie and in a more gentle voice, he said, "No, he won't, Willie. Don't you worry; you were right to go to Katie; and Katie was right to come to us. Now Katie"—he pointed at her—"you go back to bed. We'll tell you all about it in the morning. That's a good lass. And you, Willie, come on and get into bed an' all and under the clothes and pretend you're asleep."

"I can never pretend I'm asleep, Mr. Bill." This was a whispered comment, and Bill, bending down on him, hissed, "There's always a first time. Now go on in ahead. Don't let him hear you."

He now stood looking towards Fiona who was pressing Katie before her into the bedroom; and when she returned he said to her, "It's no use hanging on till the mornin' to get to the bottom of this, his defences will be up again, so come on."

One thing was immediately evident as they stood by Mark's bed, and that was that he, unlike his brother, could feign being asleep.

"Mark." Fiona's voice was soft. "Come along, you're not asleep, sit up. Now don't worry. Come along, sit up. We know all about it. I'm going to put the light on."

"No, don't, Mam. Don't."

Fiona switched the light on to reveal the tear-stained face of her son. And it was Bill who said, "Turn over."

"No, Mr. Bill."

With one movement Bill stripped the clothes down the bed; then gently he lifted the boy up and turned him onto his face. But when he went to pull down Mark's pyjamas he found them fastened, and he motioned to Fiona, saying "Untie them."

Fiona now put her arms around her son's waist, untied the cord of his pyjamas, and gently pulled them over his buttocks. Then both she and Bill stood staring down in disbelief at what they were seeing, for there, on his left buttock was evidence of a bad burn about four inches wide and three inches long, and, like drips from a candle, smaller ones linked up halfway down his thigh.

A muttered blasphemy from Bill broke the silence, but such were Fiona's feelings at the moment that she made no comment on it; instead, throwing herself on the bed, she laid her head on the pillow near that of her son. And when his arms came around her neck she held him close to her, but she was unable to speak any words of comfort: her throat was full, her whole body was full of rage and indignation. And it was Bill who voiced her exact thoughts when he said, "That flaming lot saying he had a cold! It could have turned septic. It could, even yet. By God Almighty! They'll pay for this. You'll see if they don't."

On the last words, Mark loosened his grip on his mother and swung round, only to wince as his raw buttock touched the bed. And now, looking up at Bill, he pleaded, "Don't . . . don't do anything, Mr. Bill, 'cos . . . 'cos the masters and the matron and all them, they . . . they are all right, they were good. It was only him and . . . "

When he stopped and hung his head, Bill sat down on the edge of the bed and, taking the boy's hand, he said, "Who's him? Come on, you might as well tell me because I'll go to that school and I'll get to the bottom of this. By God, I will."

"I . . . I can't, Mr. Bill, 'cos . . . 'cos when I go back . . . "

"Listen to me, boy: you're not going back."

"No? I . . . I won't have to go back?"

"No, not to that place. By God, no. So come on, spill the beans."

Both Fiona and Bill watched as the boy leaned back against the bedhead and looked up towards the ceiling and slowly let out a long breath. Then, his eyes once more on a level with Bill's, he said, "He's the dorm captain. He's the biggest and . . . and a year older than the others. There are seven of us in the dorm, but . . . but he made me fag from the beginning."

"What d'you mean, 'fag'?"

"Well, I had to clean his shoes and make his bed."

"*You what?* I thought all that was finished with."

"They all have to do it, fags. But . . . but he kept picking on me. And . . . and he took most of the tuck box. . . ." He now looked at Fiona.

"Never!"

"Yes, Mam. You see, they get the pick of the tuck boxes in each dorm, the captains. But he took the best bits, the big cake, and the shortbread. . . . "

Bill rose from the bed and walked towards the door, then back again, saying, "I can't believe this. I just can't believe this."

"It's the rule, and . . . and it doesn't matter."

Bill was now bending over Mark, saying, "Didn't you stand up to him?"

"Oh yes; yes, Mr. Bill, I did . . . I did. One time when he called you . . . I mean, me, names."

Bill lowered himself down to the edge of the bed again and he brought his chin tight into his chest as he said, "He called me names? Why did he call me names?"

"That was . . . what I mean is . . . "

Bill now held up his hand, "What you mean is, that was a slip of the tongue. But slips of the tongue nearly always speak the truth. Now, what name did he call me?"

"Well"—Mark bit on his lip—"it . . . it wasn't really what he called you, he called me Brickie Bailey."

There was a short silence before Bill said, "He said I was a brickie then?"

Mark didn't answer and Bill said, "Did you tell him I wasn't a brickie? Anyway, how did he know I had anything to do with buildings? Did you tell him?"

"No. He . . . he told me his father knows you."

"His father knows me? What's his name?"

"Brown. Roland Brown."

Bill's mouth went into a gape. He looked at Fiona, and she returned the look and nodded knowingly, and Bill said, "Now there's light upon the subject. When did all this happen?" He was addressing Mark again. And the boy said, "Last Sunday after his father brought him back. He came with some friends and they took him out for the day. I saw them when they first came. I was passing through the hall, and I'd met Mr. Brown before, you know, when we were on the site, and he looked at me but he didn't speak. And it was when Roland came back that he called me Brickie Bailey and said things about . . . " His voice trailed off, and Bill said, "I've a good idea who he said things about, laddie. And you stood up to him?"

"Yes . . . yes, I hit out at him. It wasn't hard enough to knock him down, but he tripped over something. It was really Arthur's foot, he had stuck it out, and everybody laughed, even Roland Brown's pal Roger Stewart. And then it was on the Monday night they caught me, and they pushed the lighted firework down my . . . my trousers. I . . . I couldn't get it out and I . . . I screamed. The doctor came on the Tuesday and they kept me in bed."

It was Fiona who asked now, "But why didn't you tell us this before?"

"Well, because the head said you would only be worried and Mr. Leonard said the same, and matron said that nothing like that had ever happened before, well not as bad, in the way of pranks, and it would get the school a bad name. She's very nice, the matron."

"Get the school a bad name. Don't tell your parents 'cos it'll worry them. The shifty lot of buggers."

123

"Bill!"

"Oh, to hell!" He waved his hand back at her. "That's how I feel, an' that'll be nothin' to the language I'll use on Monday mornin' when I confront that lot. But it's all right." He turned swiftly to Mark and, thrusting his arm out and pointing his finger at him, he said, "You'll never darken that door again, I'll promise you that, laddie. Nor will you go to any bloody boarding school. There are good schools in Newcastle, and you can come home at night. But that'll be after Monday. Here, get yourself up and come across into the bathroom, I want to see that in a better light."

In the better light they were even more shocked at the sight of the scars. When Bill said, "Have you any ointment that you can put on?" Fiona answered, "No, better not; just let the air get at it as much as possible. And it's drying."

"Well, we'll see tomorrow morning. I'll get onto Davey."

"It'll be Sunday tomorrow."

"I know it'll be Sunday, Mrs. B."—he nodded towards her—"but Davey will come out on a Sunday, or in the middle of the night if he's needed, you know that. He's not a nine-to-fiver. So come on, let's all get back to bed 'cos I want some sleep afore the morrow; I've got a lot of thinkin' to do." He put his arm around Mark's shoulder and walked him out of the bathroom. And at his bedroom door, he said, "Go on now, you don't need any tucking in. You'll sleep now, won't you?"

"Yes, Mr. Bill." The boy really smiled for the first time since he had come home. Then turning swiftly to his mother, he put his arms about her and kissed her before running from them and into his bedroom.

Doctor Hall said, "Fireworks! They want banning altogether, as does the one who did that." He jerked his head upwards towards the ceiling. "It's healing all right, but it's still nasty. He must have gone through it having to sit on that side and not let on. You think he would have gone back and not said anything?"

"More than likely. You know somethin'? I can't wait until the morrow mornin'."

"I understand how you feel. But if I were you I'd have a photograph taken of it."

"That's an idea. I've got a good camera and I'm not a bad hand at snaps. Yes, that is an idea."

As Fiona entered the room carrying a tray of coffee and as Bill went to take it from her, the doctor rose to his feet, saying, "How's that pain? Any more twinges?" But before she had time to reply, Bill,

124

looking from one to the other, demanded, "What pain?" And when neither of them answered he said, "Come on. Come on." And he banged the tray down on the table, spilling the coffee here and there as he said, "Come on. What's this about a pain? You've never told me."

"It's nothing. It wasn't worth mentioning. Grumbling appendix." She looked towards the doctor as did Bill as he demanded, "Is it?"

"Yes, it could be; or, on the other hand. . . . "

"Yes, on the other hand, what d'you mean?"

"Look, Bill, stop it!" Fiona's voice was sharp. "This happened long before you came on the scene. I was in hospital for a few days because I had a pain in my side and they could find nothing wrong."

"But that must be over eighteen months ago if it was afore my time. Has this been a recent visit?"

He was now looking at the doctor, who, obviously slightly embarrassed now, was about to speak when Fiona said, "Yes, yes. I popped in the other morning just to see if everything was all right."

"Because you had a pain, woman, that I knew nothin' about? Eeh! My God! This house." He turned from them. "You talk about a secret society: first the son and then the mother."

"Don't be silly, Bill. The trouble is I've got a grumbling appendix and will have to have it out sometime."

"Aye, when it gets perforated I suppose."

And now turning to the doctor, he said, "And you'll let her hang on until then, won't you?"

"Yes; yes, that's what I'll do Bill." As he took the cup of coffee from Fiona he smiled at her, adding now, "But don't you have me up in the middle of the night; I've been out three times in the past week and I'm going to report to the union that any more and I go on strike."

"You can be funny, but I don't see it that way."

"Bill!"

"Oh, shut up, woman. He knows me. And I'll tell you something you didn't know, his father was a brickie an' all."

"No, he wasn't"—the doctor's voice was indignant—"he was a carpenter."

"Not much difference when you're on the job. Anyway, the brickies earn more money."

And so the chipping went on until Bill closed the door on the doctor, but then he almost bounced back into the sitting room, saying, "That's a nice thing to do, to keep it from me, making a bloomin' fool of me. What am I supposed to be? Your husband or still the lodger?"

"Oh, Bill, please, don't go on." She slumped into the corner of the couch. And he, dropping down beside her, demanded, "Well, woman, don't you understand how I feel?"

"Yes, Bill." Her voice was quiet and patient. "It's because I understand how you feel that I didn't worry you with a trivial thing like a pain in the side. You see. Listen." She smacked his cheek with her fingertips. "Listen to me. They don't know if it's a grumbling appendix; it could be a little twist in the bowel, diverticulitis."

"*What?*"

"Diverticulitis, it's a weakness in the bowel; it's nothing. Hundreds, thousands of people have it."

"Well, you could have told me about the diver . . . tickle . . . itis, or what have you."

"Look, forget about it. And tell me, what do you intend to do tomorrow?"

And he told her what he intended to do, which caused her to plead, "Oh, Bill, please be careful."

"Well, d'you want me to pass it over?"

"No, but I know you when you get going, so please keep your temper. Promise me."

"I promise you," he said.

At seven o'clock that evening the phone rang. Bill happened to be passing through the hall and he picked up the receiver and heard a pleasant voice ask, "May I speak with Mr. Bailey?"

"Bailey here."

"Oh, good evening, Mr. Bailey. Is anything wrong? Mark hasn't returned."

"No, he hasn't returned and he's not returning." And with that he banged down the phone.

Later, he asked Mark if he was in the same form as the Brown fellow. And Mark said he was.

"And where would you likely be on a Monday morning?" Bill had gone on.

"In room two in the annex."

"About what time?" Bill asked.

"The first lesson after hall."

"And what time would that be?"

"Nine o'clock until half past; then we go to the labs."

17

BILL ARRIVED AT THE SCHOOL ALMOST ON THE POINT OF NINE.

As he entered the main doors it seemed that he was about to be engulfed in a wave of boys when an adult voice called an order to the unruly group; and so he made for the man, saying abruptly, "The headmaster, is he out yet?"

The man stared at him for a moment, then apparently realizing who he was, turned his head towards the far end of the hall and pointed, saying, "He ... he has just gone into his study. If you can wait a moment, I ... I will announce you."

"You needn't bother, I'll announce meself."

He had been in the headmaster's study before when he had been smiled on and given a cup of tea. This time he knocked hard on the door once before thrusting it open and entering the room, to see two men, one seated behind the big desk, the other standing at his side, both their faces showing a mixture of surprise and indignation.

Bill was the first to speak. Walking towards them, he said, "Have no need to introduce meself, have I? And you know why I'm here."

The headmaster, Mr. Rowlandson, said quietly, "Take a seat, Mr. Bailey."

"I've no time for sittin', thank you; I've just come to do two things: to tell you something, and to ask you something. And the first is, I think you should be damned well ashamed of yourself to allow the things to go on that go on in this school."

"This is a well-run school, sir!" It was the assistant master, Mr. Atkins, speaking now. And as Bill turned his steely gaze on the man, the headmaster made a motion with his hand for his second in command to hold his peace. But he endorsed the statement by saying, "We have never had any complaints about the way the school has been run, Mr. Bailey."

"Then there's something radically wrong with the parents of the lads, that's all I can say. Now, first of all, you must have known that my boy had been badly burned and, two, worried enough to get a doctor to him. And I'll have something to say to him an' all, for he should have informed us. But perhaps he wanted to and he left it to you. And then what do you do? You get my lad to keep his mouth shut."

"I did no such thing, sir! You should be careful what you're saying."

"I know what I'm sayin': play up and play the game, it's all in good fun, or words to that effect. You translated it into telling him that he wouldn't want to upset his parents, didn't you? And so it would be better if he kept his mouth shut."

"What happened to your son was merely the outcome of a prank. He was party to it: they were playing with fireworks." It was the assistant master again. And now Bill bawled at him, "They were not playing with fireworks, at least my son wasn't. The bully boy Brown doesn't play with anybody; he punches them into submission. Makes them clean his boots, make his bed, as my son's done since he came into this damn place. And what is more, he steals their food, not only my boy's, but from every tuck box that goes into that dorm he takes the lion's share. And don't tell me you don't know these things go on."

A quick glance was exchanged between the headmaster and his assistant. And it was the headmaster who said, "The former things you state are a form of discipline that helps the boys to be of service to others."

"Aw, come off it." Bill flung his arm wide. "It's degradin' to make one kid clean another's boots. It'll have one of two effects: make him feel damned inferior as he grows up or turn him into a bully an' all to get his own back."

"No, sir, you are wrong. We have proof from all the old boys that return here that such training makes them into men, fine men."

Bill looked at the assistant head, then glanced at his watch before saying, "I haven't much time, I have things to do. Will you be good enough to bring my son's clothes down? I've a list of them here." And he thrust the piece of paper across the table to the headmaster, and he, handing it to his assistant, said, "See to that, Mr. Atkins."

As the man made towards the door Bill again looked at his watch and said, "I'm in a hurry." And to this the assistant master cast a disdainful glance back at him before going out. And now Bill addressed the head once again: "The second thing is, what has happened to Master Brown?"

"What do you mean, sir, 'what has happened to Master Brown'?"

"Has he been expelled? That's what I mean."

"Expelled? Certainly not! As I have informed you, it was the outcome of a prank. Unfortunate, very unfortunate. No one realises that more than I did, but we did everything for your ... your son. He's had the best of care."

"Best of care." Bill's voice was grim, and now he went on, "And what punishment did you mete out to a boy who got his cronies to hold my son to the floor, then thrust a lighted firework, and not a small one, down his pants, then roll him onto his back so that he was sitting on it?"

The headmaster's eyelids were blinking rapidly and his words were slightly hesitant as he said, "Well ... well, that is not the version that I heard. I understood they were all larking on."

"They were not larking on. That Brown scum of a boy had been taunting my son by deriding me. Now I ask you again, what happened to Master Brown for his bit of fun?"

"He ... he was given lines."

"*Lines?*"

"It is a punishment that boys don't like. They would rather have anything than their spare time taken up with lines and being kept from the playing fields to work at them."

"Really!" The sarcasm in the word was not lost on the headmaster and he came back, saying now, "You are not conversant with the rules that govern a prep school like this, Mr. Bailey. We spend our lives in aiming to turn out decent, honest citizens with a cultural background...."

"And no thought of making money out of the cultural background, eh?"

The headmaster's face became diffused with colour, and his jaws tightened before he said grimly, "One has to live. And there's nothing in this business compared to that made by developers."

"I'll take your word for that. But when we've hit on money, I paid you a year in advance, I'll want two terms back."

129

"We don't do things like ... "

"Well, if you don't do things like that, sir, the Newcastle papers are going to sing, and they'll be accompanied by a photograph of my son's backside, and leg, and a report from my doctor."

"You cannot blackmail me, Mr. Bailey."

At this point the door opened and the assistant master dropped a case none too gently onto the edge of the headmaster's desk, then threw onto the floor, almost at Bill's feet, a tennis racquet and a cricket bat with a pair of boots attached to it by the laces.

Bill lifted the lid of the case, flicked through the vests and pants, pyjamas and shirts, then, looking at the assistant master, he said, "Where's the burnt pants and vest? Done away with them, I suppose. Aw well, it doesn't matter." He banged the lid closed, locked the case; then gathering up the racquet, the bat, and boots, he looked at the headmaster and said, "If I don't hear from you within a week you'll be hearin' from me." Then he inclined his head from one to the other and went hastily out.

On the drive he threw the things into the back of the car, then hurried along by the side of the school to where the annexe was situated. It was now three minutes to the half hour. The three classrooms were merely prefab buildings; number two had a half-glass door. He looked through the door and saw a young master talking to a class of about twelve boys. Then pushing the door open, he entered the room to find all eyes turned in his direction.

His voice was level and even pleasant as, looking at the young man, he said, "We've met before, haven't we?" And at this the young fellow hesitated, then said, "Oh yes; yes, Mr. Bailey."

"This was my son's class, wasn't it?"

"Yes; yes, Mr. Bailey, it is. I ... I hope he's all right."

"Yes. At least he will be; he's suffering from shock at present." He smiled as he said the words and nodded his head. Then he looked at the sea of faces staring at him. It would seem that each boy in that class knew who he was and why he was here. Bill was still smiling quietly as he said, "You have Brown here?"

The young fellow hesitated just for a fraction, then turned his head and looked in the direction of a boy sitting in the end seat of the front row. His head seemed to be on a level with the rest of the class; his face was longish and thin, but he had a breadth of shoulder. After having glanced at the visitor he was now looking down towards his desk. Bill said, "Ask Master Brown to come out."

"Mr. Bailey"—the young man's voice was just above a whisper—"please."

"What is your name? I've forgotten."

"Howard, sir."

"Well, now, Mr. Howard"—Bill put his hand out and laid it gently on the young man's shoulder—"will you oblige me by going to the back of your class?"

It seemed for a moment that the petrified class came alive, for a slight titter passed over it.

"Please, Mr. Bailey, I . . . I wouldn't do anything that . . . Let me dismiss the . . . " But Bill was leaning forward and whispering in the young man's ear, "You wouldn't like me to use force, would you? It wouldn't be seemly. Perhaps, though, you could just resist a bit so the boys can verify that you put up a stand, eh?"

The poor young fellow stood gaping at this man who wasn't any taller than himself but emanated such strength that he found it formidable. And now he muttered, "Yes; yes, it would be." At this, Bill's bark almost bounced the boys in their seats and it certainly shook the young teacher as he made play of pushing Bill, only to find himself turned around and thrust none too gently up the aisle between the desks. Then Bill, looking into the startled face of a small boy sitting in the front seat, said quite gently, "Would you like to get up, sonny, and go and join the master?" Before he had finished speaking the child had scrambled out of his desk and dashed up the aisle.

And now, looking towards the boy who was staring at him wide-eyed, Bill raised his finger and beckoned him. And when the boy made no effort to get up, he said, "Come here, Brown."

"I'll not. I'll not. If you touch me I . . . I'll tell my father."

What happened next brought a gasp from the whole class when they saw bully Brown lifted almost by the collar of his shirt and plumped in front of the desk that the boy had vacated moments earlier.

"Take your pants down."

"I . . . I'll . . . I'll . . . I'll not. You'll get wrong. My fa . . . father knows you, you'll . . . you'll get."

As if Bill had been used to stripping boys of pants every day of his life, Brown's pants came down, his underpants with them. He was twisted round and pushed over the desk, so exposing two very white buttocks.

He was yelling at the top of his voice now as Bill, thrusting a hand into the inside pocket of his overcoat, brought out a ruler and began to lay it across the screaming boy's bare pelt. When he had counted six he looked over the startled faces, shouting now, "Who's Arthur Ryan?"

131

When a wavering hand came up, he said, "Would you like a go, Arthur, for all you've had to put up with off this bully?"

Arthur's hand came down but he didn't move.

"Who's Hugo Fuller?"

A boy who had crouched away from the proximity of Brown's flailing arms, stuttered, "M . . . m . . . me, sir."

"Well, I'll give him one for you, Hugo. And here's another for Arthur."

By now there was a commotion outside the door; and when it burst open the assistant master rushed in, only to come to a dead stop at the sight before him.

Bill pulled the wailing Brown onto his feet and, thrusting him towards the master, said, "I didn't burn him as I should have done. I thought of it, mind. But there, he's all yours. Now get on the phone and tell his father what's happened. If you don't he will. And let this be a lesson to you, sir, to know what goes on in your school under your bloody nose."

The boys outside had to make a pathway to let him pass, and when he reached the end of it he turned and, raising his arm and wagging his finger from one startled face to the other, he said, "Brown is a bully. He's got his deserts and you all know why. Now, should anyone bully you in the future, stand up to him. And if you're afraid write home to your parents and tell them. It isn't cissy. D'you hear me?"

Mouths opened here and there but no one answered.

A few minutes later as he was turning his car in the drive he had another audience of boys. And when two hands, held at cheek level, made waving motions to him, he waved back at them and gave them the *V* sign.

He now drove straight to the works, and there, seeking out Barney McGuire, he gave him a brief picture of what had happened. "So there you are, Barney, he'll be out for blood. And you know what that means, he'll never be off the site."

"Aye, you're right there, boss. We can look out for squalls."

"Aye, so that being the case, tell our lot to hang on for five minutes or so the night; I'll put them in the picture so they'll keep on their toes. I'm going down home now but I won't be more than half an hour."

A short while later he thrust open the kitchen door to see Fiona and Nell sitting at the table having coffee while Mamie sat on the rug in front of the stove stuffing dolls' garments into a miniature washing machine, and at the sight of him the child jumped up, crying, "Uncle Bill!" But when she ran to him he did not lift her up,

132

or make some facetious remark about hard-working housewives; instead, he pointed to the coffee jug and said, "Any of that left?"

They had both risen from the table and Fiona, looking hard at him, said, "Yes, yes;" then added, "What happened?"

He gave a short laugh before answering, "Well, you know our marching song, 'There Is a Happy Land'?"

Before she had time to make any comment the small voice piped up, "Far, far away, where all the piggies run three times a day." And seeing that she had the attention of all the elders, Mamie went on gleefully, "Oh, you should see them run when they see Bill Bailey come, three smacks across their—" she now put her hand over her mouth and whispered "bum" and finished on a laugh, "three times a day."

Bill now playfully smacked her bottom, saying, "And that's what you're going to get, my lady, three times a day."

"You didn't! I mean?"

He looked at Fiona, nodded his head, then said, "Yes; eight of the best."

"Oh, Bill."

"Good for you."

At this Fiona turned on Nell, saying, "Tisn't good for him, Nell," and she, holding out her hand to Mamie, said, "Come and help me tidy up." And as she led the child to the door she said to no one in particular, "Cannons to the right of 'em? Cannons to the left of 'em, into the valley of death rode the six hundred." Then as she closed the door they heard, as if from far away, her voice ending, "And they were all called Bill."

A grin on his face, Bill nodded towards the door, saying, "I've noticed Nell always gives you something to look forward to."

"It's no time for joking, Bill."

"I'm not joking, lass." He went to her and put his arm around her and she said, "Couldn't you have let it go with a talk to the head?"

"Oh, I knew what that would mean afore I met him. And you know what punishment Brown had? He was given *some lines*. But there's one good thing I've done if nothing else, I've put the wind up the rest of the bullies in the school, and there's bound to be more than one. And you know something?" He grinned again. "Two little nippers gave me a wave on the quiet as I was coming out. Huh!" His head went back now and he laughed. "I must have appeared like Superman to those bairns. Oh, and that poor young teacher. Anyway, we worked out an alibi, him and me."

"What do you mean?"

"Oh, I'll tell you all about it the night but I must get back. Where's Mark?"

"He's up in the playroom; he's reading."

"We must go into Newcastle and see about a school."

"I've already been looking."

"Well, I'd better get back, as Nell says, into the valley of death. And that's what it'll be if dear papa has his own way. But what Mr. Brown doesn't know is, I'm covered with battle scars."

"But what can he do really?"

"Oh, he can make life a bit hot for us. He can find complaints about the workmanship, an' with some of the new squad I've taken on that won't be too hard for him. Anyway, I'm goin' to spread them out among our own fellows. Some of them are all right, quite good, in fact, but there's always some and some. And then there's the schedule; we're getting behind time: it takes no account of rainy spells when the brickies and tilers can't get at it, the job. But Hey! ho! I must be off."

"Do the others come around like Brown does?"

"No, Old Kingdom Come's been once on the site. Ramshaw and Pettie, they've been two or three times but couldn't be more pleased with things. And the architect, you know, is Pettie's brother-in-law. Anyway, love, I must tell you . . . you still make rotten coffee." He drained the cup.

"Bill."

"Yes, love?"

She put her hand up and stroked his cheek as she said, "Promise me you won't do anything more? I mean, when Brown comes. You won't lose your temper and . . . and . . . ?"

"Hit him?"

"Something like that."

"Don't worry. I'll try me best not to." She smiled at him as he said, "Remember what Katie says when Willie gets at her. 'Sticks an' stones will break me bones but callin' will not hurt me.' Oh, that saying, like lots of others, is daft when taken to pieces, for I'd rather have a black eye than turn me back on the fellow who said me mother didn't know who me father was or words to that effect. And that, Mrs. B., actually happened when I was on the buildings. He was an oldish bloke, oldish to me anyway, he was in his thirties then, but before he gave me a black eye I split his lip an' told him his trouble was he had never had the chance to turn a young lass into a woman. Think that one out, love."

"You're an awful man, Bill Bailey."

"I know that. Good-bye love." As he went out of the door he turned and grinned at her, saying, "If the police ring up, you'll know I'm in the clink."

He was halfway down the path when her voice halted him. "Be careful, for my sake." He made a face at her, then went on.

Mr. Brown did not put in an appearance, but his wife did. Bill happened to be at the far end of the estate when one of the men came hurrying up to him, saying in an undertone, "Mrs. Brown's in the cabin, boss."

"You mean, mister."

"No, boss, missis."

"*Mrs. Brown?*"

"Aye."

He straightened his collar, pushed his tie up into a knot, tugged his coat straight, pulled his tweed cap to a slight angle, then, as a somewhat deflated man but one ready for battle, he made his way to the cabin.

Mrs. Brown, he saw immediately, was one of the unusually tall women that seemed to be bred these days. She looked like a Miss World type: she was plainly but expensively dressed; she wasn't good-looking by his standards, he would have called her arresting, but when she spoke her voice stamped her class.

"Mr. Bailey? I'm Mrs. Brown."

"How d'you do? Won't you sit down."

"Thank you." She sat down at the other side of his desk, crossed her legs, then leaned her right forearm along the edge of the desk and, looking straight at him, she said, "You will, of course, know why I'm here."

For an answer he gave a small huh of a laugh and said, "I'm trying to guess, but candidly I was expecting your husband."

"He happens to be in London and won't be back until tomorrow evening. My son phoned me from school, as did the headmaster. I understand from both of them that you thrashed the boy."

"Yes; yes, I did, ma'am, I thrashed him. But do you know why?"

"As a result of a prank I've been informed. But I felt there was more in it than that to warrant your action."

Bill stared at her for a moment, then leaned to the side, pulled open a drawer, took out three snaps, and, laying them on the table, he twisted them around, then pushed them towards her, saying, "That's the result of your son's prank on mine. I brought them to show your husband. These were taken by an Instamatic, but there'll be some clearer ones later on that I took with a proper camera. My boy was held down by your son's crony and your son pushed a lighted firework down his trousers. Would you call that a prank, Mrs. Brown? And this happened because my son stood up to him. I think Mark objected to cleaning your son's boots, making his bed, havin' to give him the best part of his tuck box. But the final thing that broke him was to hear me slandered. So he retaliated."

He watched her pick up one snap after another and stare at it, and then, when she looked at him without speaking, he said, "I could, of course, have made a case of it, which would have hurt a good many people, so I decided on the old Jewish maxim, an eye for an eye, a backside in this case. What is your opinion, Mrs. Brown?"

She didn't speak for some seconds, and when she did, she said, "In your place I would have come to a similar decision. But I must tell you that my husband won't see it in the same way, and I hope that what I am now going to say you will do me the kindness to forget that I've said it. It is simply this: my husband should have followed your example years ago. Had he done so, this incident would never have happened."

She rose to her feet; he, too, and, moving round the table, he held out his hand to her, and she placed hers in it. And they stared at each other before he said, "Thank you, Mrs. Brown."

He now escorted her to her car, and as he held the door open for her she again looked at him and said, "Of course, you understand, my husband will make more of this, although I shall indeed put the facts to him as you have given them to me."

"I understand, Mrs. Brown . . . perfectly."

She turned her head away now and looked towards the buildings, saying, "I like your houses, Mr. Bailey; they have individuality, they're not merely boxes. It's going to be a fine estate."

He had to check his tongue from saying, "I wish you'd tell that to your husband." He smiled at her, inclined his head towards her, then closed the car door on her after she had taken her seat behind the wheel.

He remained standing where he was until she had turned the car around, and as she passed she glanced at him and smiled, and he smiled back.

When he opened the back door at his usual time there were no cries from the children, and the kitchen table was clear of food. Taking off his outer things, he went quickly into the hall, there to meet Fiona coming out of the dining room.

"What's up?" he said.

"What d'you mean, what's up?"

"Where is everybody?"

"Oh, that. They've had their meal; they're all upstairs. I ... I thought we'd have ours in the dining room tonight. I lit the fire."

"Celebrating something?"

"No, but I thought you'd be coming in, well, full of steam and you'd want a little quiet. But"—she gave a slight shrug to her shoulders—"you appear normal. What happened?"

"He never turned up ... but his wife did."

"His wife?"

"Look, Mrs. B., my stomach's yellin' out for substance. Get it on the table and then I'll tell you all. By the way, what is it?"

"Roast lamb et cetera."

"Good."

As she made to move away he checked her, saying, "Here, woman."

"Yes?"

"You haven't kissed me."

"You didn't proffer your face, Mr. Bailey, so now you can wait."

"You'll pay for it later." He laughed as he turned from her.

They had been seated at the table for some minutes when Fiona said somewhat impatiently, "Well, tell me what happened. Why did she come? And what is she like?"

"To answer the first part, she came to apologise. As regards the ... what is she like?" He now placed his knife and fork slowly down each side of his plate and, looking along the length of the table, he said dreamily, "Smashing."

"Don't be silly." She gave a laugh. "Was she as bad as that."

"No." He picked up the knife and fork again, put a piece of lamb in his mouth, chewed on it, then said, "That's what she was, smashing. No kiddin'."

"Really?" The word came out on a high note, then she added, "You were definitely impressed?"

"I'll say. Who wouldn't be? Five foot nine, I'd say, a figure like, you know ... pounds, shillings, and pence, and clothed to match."

He glanced at her. She was looking down at her plate while she chewed slowly. And when he said, "She was your type," she looked up at him, saying, "I am not placated."

"Well, you should be"—he again put down his knife and fork and, reaching out, caught her wrist—"because every inch of her put me in mind of you. And I'm going to tell you something more: I know you took a step down when you married me, but, by God, that one took a

137

big jump when she got hooked with Brown, because he's a slob at bottom and his veneer doesn't cover it. How in the name of God that woman married him will always beat me."

"She impressed you that much, did she?"

"Jealous? Go on ... say you're jealous. Oh, I'd love you to be jealous."

"Don't be silly. And that lamb is congealing. Anyway, let's get to the point: why did she come in place of him?"

Again he took up a mouthful of food and chewed on it before he said, "Well, it's like this. The old boy's in London on business. He's got his fingers into a number of pies that one, money talks. But to keep to the point. Her son had phoned her, and the head had phoned her ... all about the prank the dear child had played. Well, she didn't call her son a dear child. Believe it or not, in a way, she actually thanked me for what I'd done, and off the cuff, of course, and mustn't be repeated, words to the effect that she was glad I did it and that her husband should have done the same a long time ago."

"She didn't."

"She did though." His voice had a serious note to it now. "I couldn't believe it. Yet all the time she was talking I couldn't help thinking, how in the name of God had she got linked up with that fellow, 'cos she's county and he, you could say, came from the same backyard as me, except"—he wagged his head now—"he hasn't got my charisma. But seriously love ... By the way, you haven't seen Brown, have you?"

"No, I haven't."

"Well, you'd have to see them together and listen to them to get the full value of my meanin'."

"I'd like to meet him, I'd likely find him very interesting."

"Aw, there we go again." He was grinning now and flapping his hand out towards her. "Don't worry, my dear, I'm not goin' to walk out on you."

"*Bill!*" The movement she made thrusting her chair back from the table startled him somewhat. "Don't say things like that, even in fun. Remember Nell."

"Oh, honey"—he was out of his seat bending over her—"you should know by now it's just me and me tactlessness; I must be funny or die. I'm sorry, love."

He kissed her; then, pushing her roughly by the shoulder, he said, "Anyway, it's your own fault; you should have been working on me an' smoothing off me corners."

"I'm no magician."

He laughed now as he said, "Aw, hitting below the belt. And you know what? You sound just like your mother there." He sat down again, saying now, "Had any word from your dear mama lately?"

"Yes, I had a letter from her. She's thinking of moving."

"Good. How far? Australia?"

"No, only a quarter of a mile nearer here."

"Aw, no."

"It's a smaller house, a bungalow. I can understand her doing that, because, as she said, what does she want with nine rooms now and on her own."

"Poor sod."

"*Bill!*"

"Well, there's nobody else to hear me except you, and you should be used to it by now, and that's what she is, at least the latter word. Now tell me some nice news. What have the bairns been up to?"

Some seconds passed before she said, "There was a bit of a to-do with Mamie today. It started in the car. I couldn't understand it at first. Apparently Japan had come up in one of Willie's lessons, and you know how he goes on when he's excited about anything. And he happened to say 'I'm going on my holidays to Japan, Mam; I'm going to save up.' And that's as far as he got because Mamie turned on him and hit out at him and shouted, 'You're not going on holiday. You're not! You're not!' In fact, I had to stop the car and bring her into the front seat. And when we came in I couldn't pacify her for a time and she kept begging me not to let Willie go on holiday. Then it dawned on me."

"What dawned on you?"

"The word *holiday*."

"Oh aye; aye." He nodded at her. "You've always said Susie and Dan and the lad were on holiday. Well, we'll have to do something to change the meaning of that word for her, won't we?"

"I don't know how; it will be engrained in her mind, and the word is bound to come up among them, it's only natural."

"How is she now?"

"Oh, she's all right. I made Willie tell her that he's not going on holiday. I explained to him as simply as I could why. She adores Willie. And there's another thing. I was on the phone to the headmaster of the Royal Grammar School. He said to bring Mark down tomorrow. He'll have to go through a test of some kind, for the prep department."

"Well, that'll be nothing to him. He's got a head on his shoulders."

"He may have, Bill, but inside he's afraid of another new start. Yet

139

he's relieved that wherever he's going it's as a day pupil. But to get back to the Brown business. Do you think he'll turn up?"

"Oh yes; yes, he'll turn up all right. But I'll be ready for him, more so than ever I was now I know his home situation."

"Yes, of course, now that you know his home situation."

"Drop that tone, Mrs. B., now I'm tellin' you, else I'll skelp your lug for you. Eeh!" He closed his eyes and rocked his head on his shoulders. "Will I ever get to know women?"

She rose from the table, smiling at him now and saying, "Oh, I shouldn't worry; your practice is bound to pay off, just keep at it. . . . Do you want rice pudding or apple tart?"

It was Wednesday morning when Brown came into the yard. Although he was on Bill's mind his entry into the office touched on surprise because the door was thrust open and there he was.

Bill remained in his seat as he said, "People usually knock; this is my office."

"Yes, yes; and you'd better cling on to it, Bailey, for it mightn't be yours much longer." He was now at the other side of the desk, his hands flat on it, and leaning towards Bill, he growled out, "Who the hell do you think you are, daring to lay a hand on my son!"

As he had done two days earlier, Bill opened the drawer and took out three snaps and, again as he had done on that day, he laid them flat on the table, saying, "Look at those. That's the result of your son's venom."

Brown hardly glanced at the snaps before scattering them across the table with a sweep of his hand, saying, "It was just a prank."

"A prank that frightened the headmaster and his staff into coercing my boy to keep quiet about it. There were two options open to me: to let the newspapers deal with it, or take matters into my own hands. And which would you have preferred, *Mr. Brown*? You'd rather have your son skinned alive, wouldn't you, than let the newspapers get hold of it?"

"There was nothing for the newspapers to get hold of. They would see it as something petty. They would have seen it as another way of blowing your big mouth off. Anyway, I'm warnin' you, you'll have to keep your nose clean in future else you'll find yourself suffering the same medicine as you doled out to my son. But it'll be more lasting because you'll be plumb on your arse outside."

"Well, I can promise you this, Brown, that if I go, I swear to God I won't go alone. Keep me nose clean, you say. Well, here's some advice to you. Keep your fingers out of little men's pockets. You're on

140

the council, aren't you? As far as I understand it's not only frowned upon but illegal to extract your pound of flesh by ten percent in pushin' jobs here and there."

Of a sudden Bill had the satisfaction of seeing the man's face become suffused with colour. He watched his mouth open and shut twice before he managed to say, "You'd better be careful what you're insinuating."

"I insinuate nothing that I can't prove. You sent me a letter two years ago, and if you remember I refused your offer of help because"—now his voice became a growl—"I've worked too hard all me bloody life to get where I am today to give backhanders to swines like you. Now get out of this office. And if I see you round this plant again before it's finished, I'll put it before the next meetin' why I object to your presence here. And I'll make it plain to them some things that'll not only surprise them, but you an' all. Now get!"

"You'll regret this day. Oh, you'll regret this day."

After the door had banged on the man Bill slumped in his seat. He knew only too well that he might regret this day, because anything he brought up against the man he'd have to prove; and fellows like Brown were wily, they never put anything in writing, except in that one letter he'd sent to him. And a clever lawyer would read it as a suggestion helpfully put. For there was no talk of a rake-off in it as such.

Yes, he might regret, not only this day, but this whole week.

18

HE HAD GONE OUT AT HALF PAST SEVEN TO THE WORKS. HE RETURNED HOME AT half past nine, had a bath, got into a smart suit, came down and had his breakfast; then he was ready to go.

In the hall Fiona helped him on with his overcoat; her hands had a nervous tremor to them as she patted the lapels, saying as she did so, "I like you in this. It's very smart."

"Damn good right to be, two hundred and forty quid."

"Well, you shouldn't go beyond your station and have your things made."

"Well, don't forget Mrs. B., I had it made before I met you an' was saddled with your crew. As far as I can see there'll be no more handmade things; it'll be off the peg or nothin' at all."

"Poor soul."

Dropping her bantering tone, she now said, "How long do you think it will take?"

"God knows. It might go on till tomorrow. You can never tell with juries; there's nearly always one ... budgerigar decides to be awkward."

"You've fixed the television?"

"Yes, I've fixed the television; so don't worry. I've changed it over to the video channel and if she puts it on she'll get nothing but a loud

142

noise and a snowy screen. But anyway I hope to be back before the six o'clock news."

"It isn't the six o'clock I'm worried about; it probably won't be mentioned on there, but it'll likely be reported on the Tyne Tees news or Mike Neville's programme. It's nearly sure to be one or the other, and just imagine if she saw his face on the screen, for they are more than likely to show a picture of him."

"She won't, so stop worrying about that. The only thing that's worrying me at the moment is his sentence. If he gets off lightly ... by God, I don't think I'll be answerable for me actions."

"Please, Bill." She had her hands on his shoulders now. "Don't cause a scene, please, whatever happens. Try not to look at him."

"What! That's askin' too much. I'll look at him all right, love. In fact, I won't take me eyes off him. I have one regret, that I won't be able to put me hands on him. I had a word with Sergeant Cranbrook first thing on the phone from the office. He didn't say anything outright but there seemed to be a hint in his words that there'll be more revealed than Katie's case. Well, now, I must be off. Oh, by the way, when you're giving me orders I'll give you one. Tear up the *Journal* or put it in the dustbin, there's no picture of him but there's that report, and you know she goes through the headlines of both papers, not only the front but the back. She said she had the first clue in the *Telegraph* crossword the other day. She hadn't, but I let her think she had. Anyway, love, I'll be back as soon as possible." He kissed her and they clung together for a moment, then she watched him walk down the drive to the car.

After closing the door she stood with her back to it for a moment. She was alone in the house: Nell had gone to the dentist—she was having three teeth out—she had been suffering from toothache for some time now.

She started to walk towards the sitting room but stopped halfway across the hall, telling herself, no, she mustn't sit down; she must keep busy in order to keep this awful feeling at bay, for her mind would keep jumping back into those hours when Katie was lost.

An hour later she was wishing it was time to pick up Mamie from nursery school; she was wishing Nell was here; she was wishing one of the children were here. She wanted someone to talk to. She even wished her mother would ring; and having wished this, she knew she was in a bad way. She cleaned the odd bits of silver and brass, she turned out the china cabinet and wine cabinet.

At twelve o'clock she picked up Mamie from nursery school, made

143

her a light lunch, then found herself talking to the child as if she was Katie or Mark.

At one o'clock when the phone rang she was only a few feet from the table and, grabbing it up, she shouted, "Hello!"

"Hello, love." Bill's voice was quiet.

She drew in a long breath before saying, "How are things?"

"Oh, complicated, at least from my point of view. You know, it's the first time I've been in a court, and don't say isn't that amazing! But the procedure and the waffling is nobody's business. I've seen it on the television but it's different altogether when you're in the middle of it."

"Is . . . is he there?"

"Oh yes, he's there. My God, Fiona, that fellow looks evil. I sense it coming from him. You hear a lot of chatter about good and evil, but in the main it's only words. . . . Anyway, I'm going to have a bite. I'll give you all the gen when I get back."

"Do you think it will be finished today?"

"It could be, it seems all cut and dried. It all depends on the jury. But these blokes, the defence lawyers, the prosecution fellows, my God, how they talk. It's just as if they were on telly in a play. I'll believe all I see and hear on the telly after this. Anyway, love, be seeing you. You all right?"

"Yes; yes, Bill, I'm all right. Just waiting for you to come back."

"I won't be long, at least I hope not. Bye."

"Bye."

It was half past one when Nell put in an appearance. Her face looked a sorry sight.

"Oh, Nell, what's happened to you? What did they do?"

Through her swollen lips Nell muttered, "Used a street drill on a molar, and there was an abscess on two of them. God, never again."

"Have you just got back? You've been a long time."

"I . . . I must have passed out. Came to on a couch somewhere."

"Come and lie down and I'll get you a drink."

"Thanks. All the same, I think I'd better go to bed and sleep it off. I . . . I haven't been home yet. How are you feeling?"

"Oh, I'm all right, Nell. Don't worry about me. Do as you say, get yourself to bed. Shall I come with you?"

"No, no. But . . . but I feel I've let you down; this is the day you want company."

"Don't worry about that. Everything's going fine. Bill just phoned. It shouldn't be long before he's back."

"Good. I'll away then."

144

She was alone again. Mamie was having her afternoon nap.

When the phone rang she ran out of the kitchen, across the hall and grabbed it up.

"Fiona?"

"Yes, Mother."

"I didn't expect to find you at home."

"Well, why did you phone?"

"Well, naturally to find out. The case is on, isn't it? I would have thought you would have been there defending your daughter."

"Mother, my daughter doesn't want any defending."

"Well, you know what I mean."

"No, I don't, Mother. As usual I don't."

"Then all I can say is, girl, that you are going dim. As I see it, the presence of the mother of the child would have emphasised the wickedness of the man. And you are her only relative."

"Bill is there, Mother."

"Bill? What is he? Katie is not his child. The word *step* can never bear any relationship, in whatever way you look at it."

"What you forget, Mother, is that the man was one of Bill's workmen."

"I forget nothing, girl, nothing at all. But I can tell you what I'm thinking at this moment, and that is you have become a most unnatural mother. And what is more . . . "

The phone was banged onto its stand. What kind of a woman was she? She was asking the question of the mirror above the telephone table. And now she actually spoke to her reflection. Her hand out towards herself, she asked, "Can you understand her? There are mentally defective people who would act with more sense than she does. Has she always been like this?"

She was nodding at herself now, saying, "Yes, yes; more or less. Yes, she has."

Her hand now dropped to her side and she gritted her teeth against the pain there. Then, looking in the mirror again, she said, "Oh, don't you start. Please, please, not today."

She told herself to go and have a drink, only to tell herself once again she certainly wasn't going to start that in the middle of the day, and that it would likely do her more harm than good. "Go and have a bathe," she said to herself now, "and tidy yourself up."

As if obeying an order from a mature and elderly individual, she went towards the stairs, and as she mounted them she repeated to herself, "Hurry up, Bill. Hurry up."

Two hours later she picked Katie up from school. She hugged her

145

tight—it was as if she had just got her back again—then having settled her in the front passenger seat and herself behind the wheel, she turned her head and looked at Willie, who was ensconced with Mamie in the back of the car. And he said, "I should be sitting in the front; I'm a boy."

"Oh, what a surprise! He's a boy, Mam."

Katie was looking at her mother, her face wide with laughter, and Fiona, joining into her mood, said, "Is he? I never noticed."

This brought forth a bawl from the backseat as her son exclaimed, "Oh, you! Our Mam," and was followed by Mamie, his faithful champion, saying, "He is a boy," only to be bawled down by her hero yelling, "Shut up, you."

"Willie!" Fiona's voice was stern. "We'll have no more of that talk. Tell Mamie you're sorry."

"Not."

"I don't mind Willie not being sorry, Mammy B., 'cos I love him."

No one capped this in any way; and almost complete silence reigned until, scrambling from the car, Willie rushed towards the house, exclaiming, "I want to see Bugs Bunny."

"Get your things off first." Fiona's voice was steadying. "Then you'll have your tea and there'll be plenty of time to see Bugs Bunny."

Willie and Mamie followed Fiona into the kitchen; but Katie did not. Fiona knew she had made straight for the sitting room and the television and she waited for the cry of despair, and it wasn't long in coming.

She came rushing into the kitchen. "Mam! There's something wrong with the television. It's making a funny sound and there's no picture."

"Oh, dear me. I suppose the valve's gone now."

"Oh no, Mam; I wanted to see ... "

"I want to see Bugs Bunny."

"And Henry's Cat." This pipe came from Mamie. And now Fiona cried at all of them. "If the television is out of order, it's out of order, and Bugs Bunny and Henry's Cat and what have you are out of order, so stop it! Come and sit down and have your tea."

When Katie's mouth opened wide Fiona thrust a finger at her, saying, "Not another word. Not one more word. Sit!"

The three of them looked at her, then looked at each other, then sat down at the table. It wasn't often their mother's voice sounded like that, but when it did they knew it was time to shut up ... or else.

* * *

146

It was just on five when Bill returned. When he kissed her lightly on the cheek she didn't put her arms about him but stood looking at him. His face looked grey and drawn. She asked quietly, "Was it bad?"

"It wasn't good, neither for me nor him."

"What did he get?"

"Ten years."

She let out a long slow breath. "That's good."

"He should have had life, not less than twenty by what came out after."

"What came out after?"

"Let's have a cup of tea; I'm frozen." He had taken off his outer things and now he made towards the stove and stood with the back of his hands against his buttocks, and he went on talking while she made a fresh pot of tea. "The paraphernalia, the way they put the questions. You know, at one time I thought that his counsel was trying to get him off. In a way I suppose he was. He put him over as a sort of deprived child. His mother had done a bunk or something like that when he was twelve. He had been in Borstal for two years and after that he did two robberies and stole from his father, for which he did six months in jail; then only three years ago he was up for indecent exposure. My God! You never know who you're employing, do you? But this didn't come out until after the jury had found him guilty and it was up to the judge to pass sentence. And you know he might have got life at that only he denied flatly having said that she'd be rotten when she was found, even when Barney, Bert, and meself were up on the stand and we all said the same thing."

He stood shaking his head now. "By, that's a funny feeling being up there. You know I've always prided meself that it would take a lot to put the fear of God into me, but there I was and I was tellin' the truth, but his counsel kept comin' at me, twisting me words. I was in a rage, he said. Didn't I try to throttle the defendant all because I smelt the scent on his coat?

"I had told meself to keep calm, 'cos I knew these fellows try to bamboozle you, but there I was bawling at him. Huh!" He gave a short laugh now. "You know what I said? Don't be a bloody ass, wasn't the child found in his house, trussed up behind the tank? Oh"—he laughed again—"didn't that judge go for me. But towards the end he softened and said, 'We are well aware of your feelings on this account, Mr. Bailey, but please remember where you are.'

"By God! I was glad the child hadn't to put in an appearance. I've got to thank the doctors for that. And that came out an' all about her

147

losing her power of speech. There was only one light moment in the proceedings and you'll never guess who caused it." She handed him the cup of tea and he drained the cup before he said, "Bert."

"Bert caused light relief?"

"Aye, in his own way. The fella got at him, the defence counsel. Did he think he had heard aright? Was he not being loyal to his employer? At this there was objection from our bloke and a warning from the judge to the interrogator to mind what he was saying. And then Bert caused a rumbling belly laugh in the court by stretching himself to his full height, all of five foot eight, and in tones that outdid the counsel with their dignity, he said, 'Sir, I am a Sunday school teacher.'

"After the judge had knocked his mallet on the bench he looked at Bert and said, 'I would discount the fact that religious work of any kind would have an effect on your hearing.'

"There was another burst of laughter and another banging of the mallet and what d'you think came next? Bert looked at the judge straight in the eye and said, 'My Lord, I neither drink nor smoke nor lie.' And what he was gonna say next I'll never know 'cos some bright spark from the back of the court put in in a loud whisper, 'Or go with women.' Eeh! It was like an explosion. Another time I would have bellowed me head off with them but I wanted to shout at the lot of them to shut up, that this is no laughing matter.

"Anyway, everything went flat after that. The policemen were on the stand. The young one told how he found her and the sergeant told what had been said when seated in the car outside the house. I thought it would never end. The jury were out for an hour and a quarter. That gave me the jitters. I thought they would see that he was proved guilty beyond a doubt. But as I've said before, there's always one or two stubborn buggers who just want to be different. But it was after they came back and they said that their verdict was guilty that the judge got underway, and didn't he lay into him. He said in a way he was a lucky man he wasn't facing a murder charge and that even in his early youth he'd had a grudge against society and had taken it out on innocent people, in the last case an innocent child. After he brought out the fact that the psychiatric treatment he'd had had proved that he was normal inasmuch as he knew what he was doing and wasn't mental, he sentenced him to the ten years, and the full ten years, and no remission for good behaviour."

Bill now moved from the stove and, sitting down at the table, put his elbows on it and rested his head in his hands as he said, quietly, "I wonder if in ten years time I'll be over this feeling, 'cos every minute in that court all I wanted to do was to climb over those benches and into that dock and get me hands on him, 'cos, let's face it, love"—he looked up at her where she was standing to his side—"it was firmly in his mind to leave her there until she died and that could have been a day or two the way she was trussed. You didn't see it. He meant to do her in all right."

She was putting her arms around him when the kitchen door opened and there stood Katie. She walked slowly towards the table and stood at the other end and, after looking from one to the other, she said, "I . . . I heard my name on the radio, Mam. That man, he's been put in prison for ten years, so I won't see him again, will I? I'll be old then."

They exchanged a quick glance in which they said they hadn't thought about the radio, because none of them bothered with it.

They seemed to spring round the table together and then she was engulfed in their arms. And it was Bill, his voice shaking, who said, "That's right, love, now you can forget all about him 'cos you'll never see him again, never, not even when you're old. Now I'll go and mend your television, eh?"

"Can you?"

"Can I?" He pulled back from her. "Did you ever know anything that I couldn't do?"

"No, Mr. Bill."

"Well, come on then an' watch my magic. That fella Daniels isn't a patch on me where magic is concerned." And as Fiona followed them, she thought, And how right you are, Mr. Bill.

19

FIONA STOOD IN THE HALL DRESSED FOR OUTDOORS AND SHE LOOKED AT NELL, who was holding out a scarf towards her, and said, "I hate scarves, Nell. One never looks dressed in a scarf."

"All right, go on, feel dressed and get a cold on top of all the other things."

"What other things?"

"Well, that pain; it isn't indigestion or constipation or . . . "

"It's the appendix, Nell."

"Well, if you think it's only the appendix, it's only the appendix. But if you think it's only the appendix why are you worrying yourself sick, and keepin it from Bill? What if he should phone up?"

"Just say I've gone out shopping."

"Shopping! On a morning like this, rain, wind, hail, the lot?"

"My appointment's for quarter to ten; I'll be back by eleven or so. Anyway, there's no reason why he should phone. Stop fussing."

"Somebody's got to fuss. I can't understand how he hasn't noticed when you're doubled up with pain."

"Because it's only happened at rare times, thankfully. when he hasn't been there."

"What if he wants to keep you in?"

"Nell, I'm only going to the surgery. Where do you think he's going to keep me? In the backroom? Stop it; you're worse than Bill. Here, give me the scarf. I'll put it on. But the trouble isn't in my neck it's in my tummy."

"Your trouble's in your head, doing the brave little woman stunt; it won't work. When he finds out there'll be an explosion, if I know anything."

"Good-bye."

"And the same to you."

Fiona hadn't come back by eleven o'clock; but just after, the phone rang, and when Nell picked it up she heard Fiona's voice, "Nell."

"Yes? Yes? Where are you?"

"I'm just outside the surgery. Look. Now listen and don't go off the deep end, but the doctor wants me to slip along to hospital and have a test. If I go straightaway his colleague can fit me in, if not I'd likely have to wait another week or two. He thinks I should take the opportunity . . . Are you there?"

"Yes, I'm here, Fiona. Which hospital are you going to?"

"The General."

"I could wrap Mamie up and come along."

"Oh, for goodness sake!"

"All right but somebody should be there to drive you back. You'll likely feel wobbly after a test if it's one of the barium kind. I've had it. Half your stomach seems to drop out."

"That was in 1066, they have different ways now. Look, I haven't any more change; I've got to go."

"I knew this would happen. You should have seen to it before now. And Christmas coming on."

By now Nell was talking to herself. She put the phone down, then stood looking at it, after which she bit twice on her lip and said half aloud, "He'll go mad. Oh, I hope he doesn't phone."

It was just after one o'clock when he did phone.

"Does a Mrs. B. live there?"

"It's me, Bill, Nell."

"Oh, hello there, Nell. Where's the little woman?"

" . . . She's popped out, Bill."

"Popped out? Where?"

"She . . . she wanted something from the shops."

There was a pause now before Bill said, "It isn't the weather for a dog to be let loose today. What's she popped out for?"

"I'm . . . I'm not quite sure, Bill."

"*Nell.*"

151

"Yes, Bill?"

"What's the matter?"

"Nothing . . . nothing, Bill."

"Are you tellin' me the truth?"

When she made no reply his voice barked, "Are you there?"

"Yes, Bill, I'm here, and . . . and I'm not telling you the truth."

"What's up?" His voice had dropped to almost a whisper now.

"She'll likely kill me for telling you, as you will her for keeping it from you, but she's had that pain again and never let on. She went to the doctor's and expected to be back about eleven, but he's sent her for tests."

"Where?"

"The General."

She actually pulled her head back when she heard the receiver banged down, then turned sharply as a small voice said, "Mammy B.'s a long time."

"She'll soon be home."

"I . . . I want Mammy B."

"Now don't you start." She held out her hand to the child. "Come on and let's get the sails trimmed because there's going to be a squall if I know anything."

The squall started in the hospital reception area. It was surprising to the spectators and certainly amusing when the tough-looking individual pushed open the main door, then stopped when he saw his wife standing at the desk talking to someone at the other side. There was another man and two women waiting in the hall, and two young men in white coats going one way while a nurse went the other when Bill almost bounced up to the counter and, in what he imagined to be an undertone but was clear to everyone, hissed, "What the hell are you up to, woman?"

"Oh!" It was evident that Fiona was startled, but she smiled and said, "It's you."

"Of course it's me. We see each other at times you know. What you doin' here?"

As she took the card from the wide-eyed nurse across the counter, she facetiously replied, "Performing an operation."

"Well, here's someone that'll perform another one when I get you home."

The two young men had stopped and were now approaching the counter. They didn't look at Bill but at Fiona and one of them asked quietly, "Are you all right?"

She smiled broadly at him now, saying, "Yes, thank you. This is my husband." And she made quite an elegant motion towards Bill. "As you can gather he's a very mild person. Takes things in his stride." She looked at Bill now and asked quietly, "Shall we go and continue this in private?" and before he had time to make any response she turned to the two young doctors and, still smiling, she said, "It's very nice to be cared for."

They both grinned at her now, but Bill, glaring at them, said, "I wouldn't make any rejoinder to that if I were you; I'm in a mood for wipin' grins off people's faces." And with that he took her arm none too gently and marched her out the door.

But once outside her manner changed and, endeavouring to free herself from his grip, she said, "You are the one for making scenes, aren't you?"

"And you are the one for gettin' people stirred up. What the hell's all this about anyway? Frightening the liver out of me. Why couldn't you phone me and put me in the picture? With one thing and another I'm about right for Sedgefield."

Quietly now, she said, "And that's why I didn't want to worry you more than is absolutely necessary."

"You've gone a funny way about it."

"In my opinion it was the best way."

He was leading her towards his car now and she said, "I'm quite fit enough to drive."

"Well, if you are or you aren't, you're not goin' to. Get in."

"Bill."

"Get in."

"But what about my car?"

"I'll send a couple of chaps along."

Few words were exchanged on the journey home, but once inside the door Fiona, looking at Nell, said, "I told you." And Nell replied, "Well, you try fobbing him off next time." Then both she and Bill turned quickly to Fiona, saying, "What is it?"

"Nothing. Nothing." She stood drawing in deep breaths for a moment. "I just feel a bit muzzy, that's all."

His voice soft now, Bill said, "Come on." He put his arm around her and led her into the sitting room and, looking at Nell, said, "A strong cup of tea, lass."

When she sat on the couch he lifted her legs up, pushed a cushion behind her head, then, kneeling by the side of the couch, he took her hands and said, "Got a pain?"

"No, no; nothing like that, only a bit queezy inside."

"What did they do? Why did you go to hospital?"

"I"—she drew in a long breath—"I never intended to go to hospital. I . . . I just went to Dr. Hall because I had a twinge in the side this morning, and I explained it to him, and when I said I'd had really nothing to eat since we had our meal last night, he phoned up the hospital and spoke to a colleague of his; and it should happen that this Dr. Amble could fit me about twelve. No waiting, I was lucky I hadn't had that breakfast." She smiled at him now, saying, "It's good to have friends at court; it's amazing the strings that can be pulled. And by the way, he asked after Mark and how he was liking his new school. He's got a son there, in Mark's department. Not for much longer, he's going on to the upper school. By the way, what did you phone up about? Trouble?"

"No; I just wanted to tell you I was going into Newcastle to a meeting and that if it was over early enough I'd pick up Mark and we'd do a bit of shopping."

"Oh, I'm sorry . . . I mean, about the meeting."

"It's all right. It's all right." He stroked her hair back from her forehead. "I phoned them up. I asked for Remington. He hadn't arrived yet they said, but Old Kingdom Come came on. And when I told him that my wife—" he stressed the word, then tapped her cheek as he said, "had been taken into hospital, he was most concerned. 'Don't worry old fellow,' he said, 'everything will be all right. Don't worry.' Don't worry. He must have been joking. But he's a fine old bloke, and at the present moment I need the support of fine old blokes if never before, for although I haven't seen much of Brown I've got the feeling that there's something in the wind. One thing I'm sure, he's not goin' to let up on me; he's the kind of fellow who keeps his promises. Oh, but why worry, lass; all that is secondary. What I should be doing now, woman, instead of sympathising with you, is giving you a good going over with both hands and tongue, for Nell had me scared silly."

"Nell should never have told you. It's ridiculous."

"What is? That you're bad enough for a doctor to send you straightaway for a barium? Anyway, when will you know the result?"

"Not for a few days."

"Well now"—his voice sank low—"promise me you'll never keep anything from me again. Promise me. Good, bad, or indifferent, whatever the news, you'll tell me?"

"I promise."

He stared at her; then he asked quietly, "What does he think it is?"

"The appendix, of course."

154

"Well, if it's the appendix why don't they take you in and whip it out?"

"They don't do that these days, especially for a niggling little pain that I've got. And as I've said before, it mightn't be the appendix; it might be a twist in the bowel or . . . Oh, it doesn't matter. Anyway, here's the informer with the tea."

As Nell put the tray on the table near the couch, Fiona said, "I'll have a word with you later, Mrs. Paget."

"Very well, Mrs. Bailey, ma'am. In the meantime sit up and drink this tea and stop pretending you're poorly." She now looked at Bill, saying, "She's only after sympathy. I know her kind; my mother used to be the same. Oh, by the way." She wagged her finger down at Fiona. "Speaking of the devil, she phoned."

"Mother?"

"Yes, Mother."

"You didn't tell her?"

"That you'd gone to hospital? No, no. They've got enough trouble in the hospital without her going there, I should imagine."

"What was she after?" It was Bill asking the question.

And turning to him, she said, "She demanded that her daughter be put on the line. I said that her daughter was out, and that no, I didn't know when she'd be back; she was with Mr. Bailey." She inclined her head towards Bill, then said, "I thought she had gone, there was such a long pause, and then she said, 'Tell my daughter I'm moving next Wednesday and I need help.'"

"Well, now." He turned quickly to the couch and, stabbing his finger at Fiona, he said, "No go Wednesday, you understand? No matter how you're feelin', 'cos if you don't promise me to stay put, I'll go along there an' raise hell. And you wouldn't like that, would you, Mrs. B.?"

"I have no intention of going to help her. And please don't bawl anymore, Bill; I feel . . . well"—she shrugged her shoulders—"you know, a bit weary."

And with this she put the cup on the side table and lay back, and Nell and Bill exchanged a startled glance because this wasn't like Fiona. Each in their own way could not have been more worried at the moment if she had voiced her inner thoughts and said, "I'm frightened. I couldn't bear that. I'd rather die."

20

IT WAS FOUR DAYS LATER AND ONLY A WEEK TO GO UNTIL CHRISTMAS WHEN THE doctor's secretary phoned Fiona and asked if she would care to come to the surgery.

When at ten o'clock she faced him across his desk and, looking at him, asked, "Well?" he said quietly, "I would like you to see Mr. Morgan. I've made an appointment for the day after tomorrow. You remember him? He saw you about three years ago when you were in for tests."

"Yes, yes." She moved her head twice and swallowed the words that were sticking in her throat and would have asked, "What did the X-ray show?" She knew he would know what they had shown but that he wasn't going to tell her unless she asked. And she couldn't ask; she must put it off a little longer, for Christmas was near, and there were the children, and the tree, and Bill. Oh yes, and Bill.

Her mind started to race now: it was fortunate she had Nell. It was funny how things happened. Nell had to come on the scene when she was most needed. And Nell was so good, and the children loved her, and . . . and . . . "

"Now don't worry." Dr. Hall's hand had come across the desk and was gripping her twitching fingers. "There's nothing definite, nothing to worry about as yet."

As yet. As yet. As yet. The words were going away like an echo in her mind. She stood up, telling herself that she must get out in the air.

He walked to the door with her, where he again said, "Now don't worry. Enjoy Christmas with the children. It's their time, isn't it?"

"Then I won't have to go in?"

"No; no, I shouldn't think so. No, no." He patted her shoulder. "Anyway, I'll pop in in a day or two. Now do as I tell you and don't worry."

She was out in the air and she gasped at it. She had read somewhere, or someone had told her, that if you took ten slow, slow breaths and counted each one as they came, it settled your nerves amazingly.

She was sitting behind the wheel of the car when she finished the tenth, and yes, it seemed to work, she did feel calmer.

Nell seemed to have been waiting at the door for her, it opened so quickly, but she didn't ask any questions as she helped Fiona off with her coat; instead she said, "The coffee's brewing. And listen to them." She thumbed towards the stairs. "They are so excited; they won't last out until Christmas. They'll burn themselves up before then. I'm glad Mark breaks up soon; he'll help keep them in order."

She led the way towards the kitchen, and not until she had poured out the coffee did she ask quietly, "Well, what did he say?"

"Nothing that I can go on. I've got to see Mr. Morgan the day after tomorrow. The only thing he implied was that whatever it is there's no rush, and not to worry."

"Well, that's a relief. Now drink that and get on the phone to that fellow of yours, because if not you'll have him round here at dinnertime. And there's only so much my nerves will stand." She smiled now, then added somewhat sadly, "You're lucky, you know, Fiona; he's one in a thousand or more."

"Yes, I know. . . . Oh yes, I know, Nell."

"I had a letter from Harry this morning."

"You did? Does he want to come back?"

"Want to come back? He wants the divorce to go through as quickly as possible! If it wasn't that he never wanted children I would have imagined that she's pregnant."

"He'll have to support you."

"I hate that idea. I want nothing from him now, but his dad says he's got to pay. Funny, you know, but they're both more bitter than I am, and he's their son. Anyway, enough about me. Drink up then get on the phone."

157

It was as if Bill, too, had been waiting at the other end of the line, for before she even got his name out he said, "Well, love, what did he say?"

"Oh"—she made her voice light—"not to worry. I've got to go and see Mr. Morgan the day after tomorrow. But there's nothing to worry about, no hurry."

"Is that straight?"

"Exactly his words, to which he added that Christmas is near and it was a time for children, and I must enjoy myself. I don't know whether he was classing me with the children or not."

"Oh, lass, you've taken a load off my shoulders. Now I'll be able to carry the tree back on me own."

"You've got a tree?"

"Aye. Bert, the one who hasn't any truck with either wine, women, or baccy—by, they are pullin' his leg, but he's takin' it—he's a good fella in all ways is Bert—he tells me he's picked one up from the forestry. It's all of ten feet high and he's got it along at his place. He says it's practically the length of his garden. So you'd better get cracking and make room for it."

"Where do you think I'm going to put a ten-foot tree?"

"In the dining room, of course, in the bay window. I'll have to get a tub for it though. Anyway, I'll see about all that when I get back. And, oh, love, you've got no idea how relieved I feel.... I love you, Mrs. Bailey."

"Gert ya."

"Gert ya."

She put the phone down, turned her back to the hall table, bowed her head, and closed her eyes.

By the following night, not only was the tree installed in its butter tub, but it had coloured fairy lights entwined from the top branches.

Bill was standing on top of a pair of steps and the children were arguing among themselves which glass bauble would be suitable for which branch. Willie, holding a white glass swan, handed it up to Bill, saying, "Put this on the top, Mr. Bill," only to be shouted down by Katie, crying, "Don't be silly! The fairy goes on the top."

"Needn't."

"She does, doesn't she, Mam?"

"Well, yes, she usually does. But Willie's swan, I think, would look better on that branch sticking out there." She pointed. "See, Bill? What do you say to that one for Willie's swan?"

"Aye, yes, I think it would show better there. Hand it here, fella."

158

When the swan was resting precariously on the swaying branch, Fiona stepped back, apparently in admiration, saying, "Oh, it looks lovely with the pink light shining on it."

"Swans are not pink."

"Katie!" There was a warning in the name, and Katie, giving herself a shake, said, "Well, he's always contrary."

"Oh, oh! Look who's talking." Mark now laughed, and Katie rounded on him, saying, "Don't you start on me, our Mark."

Then a voice boomed over them all, crying, "An' don't anybody start on anybody! And if you want my opinion, everybody is a little tired, so I think we've all had enough for tonight. Look at the time, it's nine o'clock. It's past my bedtime. So come on, scram Sam, the lot of you."

Bill stepped down onto the floor and amid oohs and aahs and protestations he bundled them all into the hall, where Willie exclaimed loudly, "I want something to eat, I'm hungry." And Bill, looking at Mark, said, "Captain, would you mind taking this crew into the kitchen and feedin' them milk and two biscuits each. No more! Two's the limit because we don't want anybody being sick in the night. Do we now? Do we?"

"Will do, sir." Mark saluted smartly, and with this he marshalled the small gang of protestors kitchenwards. Then as Bill, laughing now, went to follow Fiona into the sitting room, the phone rang and they both stopped and Fiona whispered, "That'll likely be Mother."

"Let me deal with her."

"No, no."

"I say, yes."

He went and lifted up the phone while keeping his eyes on Fiona. But the voice he heard wasn't that of Mrs. Vidler, but that of his nightwatchman, Arthur Taggart, who said, "This is Taggart. That you, boss?"

"Yes; yes, Arthur. What is it?"

There was quite a long pause before the voice said, "Got bad news, boss. The . . . the show house, it's . . . it's been wrecked. It's . . . it's a mess. But I got him, at lest Dandy did as he was coming out of the window. He had taken the pane out, professionally like with brown paper."

Bill was no longer looking at Fiona but staring into the phone, saying, "Who? Who were they?"

"No they, boss, just one."

"A man?"

"No, no; it's a lad. I've got him. He's in the toolshed. Dandy's

159

standing guard. He's petrified now. There's another thing, boss. You . . . you know who he is."

"I know who he is? What d'you mean?" He was yelling now.

"Well, I know who he is an' all. You see, I told you I worked there for a time afore you set me on. I did odd jobs for him, but never liked him."

"My God, no! The Brown lad?"

"No other, boss. I . . . I was gonna call the police straightaway, but thought, what'll I do? Will I ring 'em, boss?"

Bill held the phone some distance away from him and didn't answer for a moment until the nightwatchman's voice came again, saying, "You there, boss?"

"Yes; yes, I'm here, but I'll be with you in a few minutes. And no, don't phone the police, I'll see to it meself."

He put the phone down, then turned and looked at Fiona, who was standing close by his side now, and without any preamble he said, "That Brown bastard has wrecked the showhouse."

"Oh no!"

He moved from her. Going swiftly to the wardrobe in the hall, he took down his coat and cap, saying as he did so, "Now get yourself to bed. I don't know how long I'll be."

"Oh, Bill, what next?" She put out her hands and buttoned the top button of his great coat, while he repeated her words, "Aye, what next? But I've been expectin' something—I didn't know what—yet I never thought it would come from the lad."

"If . . . if you've got to stay very long will you phone me?"

"Yes; yes, I'll do that, but don't stay up. Now promise me? Go straight to bed, and don't tell them I'm out." He thumbed towards the kitchen.

"But they'll hear the car."

"I'll run her out quietly into the road." He kissed her hurriedly, then went out.

In less than ten minutes he was on the site. The light was on in the men's cabin and also in the toolshed. Arthur Taggart met him in the yard.

"Has he said anything?"

"No, nothing. He would have defied me if I'd been on me own. He used his feet on me when I caught hold of him. But he's scared stiff of the dog. D'you want to see him first?"

"No, let's look at the damage."

The showhouse had been just that, a showhouse. He had been proud of it and proud of Fiona's choice of furnishings and colours.

160

The sitting room had been done in tones of mushroom, shell pink, and grey; the dining room had been furnished with very good reproduction furniture. Now, as he stepped onto the paint-smeared carpet and looked at the ripped upholstery of the couch and chairs and the paint-smeared walls, the blazing anger died in him, and he felt the oddest feeling, such as a woman might have felt, for he had the inclination to cry.

The sight that met him in the kitchen was even worse, for the fittings had been ripped from the wall, levered off as Arthur Taggart pointed out.

Then, leading to the upstairs rooms, the bannisters had been daubed with red and green paint, and the landing walls and carpet sprayed with what looked like tar.

When Bill picked up the silk bed cover that had been torn in two he looked at Arthur Taggart and said, "It must have taken him some time to do all this. Where were you?"

"On me rounds, boss. I do it every hour, honest to God! An' I don't only go round the blocks, I go in and out of the houses; except, of course, the six that are already occupied at yon end. And Mr. Rice in the end one, he could tell you; he said the other night he timed his watch by me."

"Aye, and somebody else has timed their watch by you, Arthur. He couldn't do this kind of damage without a torch. But he knew what time you'd be round here again. Did you change your routine the night?"

"No . . . well, not exactly. And I don't keep to it strictly. You know what I mean? I might go to the east side and end up with the west, or vice versa some nights. But it was as I came round the bottom end that Dandy's head went up and he started to sniff, and I always know what that means. And I let him off, and he caught him getting out of the pantry window. It's amazing how he got through, it can't be eighteen inches. But apparently he knew where it was. Have you seen him round, boss?"

"No, he hasn't been round to my knowledge. But then there's Sunday and I'm very rarely here then, one or the other take over. . . . Well"—he ground his teeth together—"let's go and see him."

The toolshed was lit by a single electric bulb, but it showed up vividly the boy in the paint-smeared overalls crouching among the tools, with the dog lying, paws and head forward, staring at him.

Bill did not go near him, nor did he make any comment, but the boy, spluttering, said, "T . . . t . . . take th . . . th . . . that dog . . . awa . . . away."

"Not frightened of a dog are you, a brave lad like you?" This came from Arthur Taggart. And the boy, now looking towards Bill, said, "I ... I want my father."

Still Bill did not speak, until, turning and going out of the door, he muttered, "You'll get your father. Oh, you'll get your father." And Arthur, after commanding the dog: "Stay! Dandy," followed him.

Bill now unlocked his office door and, going straight to the directory, he found the number he was looking for and dialled it.

A woman's voice said, "This is Mr. Brown's residence. Who's speaking?"

Bill said, "Tell Mr. Brown to come to the phone."

"I'm ... I'm sorry, Mr. Brown isn't in."

"Listen to me, missis, you go and tell your boss that his son is in dire trouble."

"What!"

"You heard."

"Yes; yes, I heard. But ... but I tell you, Mr. Brown isn't in. He isn't here. They've both gone out to dinner."

"Where?"

There was a pause before the answer came. "The Gosforth Park Hotel."

Bill banged down the phone, thumbed quickly through the directory, and once more lifted the receiver.

"Gosforth Park Hotel. Can I help you?"

"Yes, you can. Have you a Mr. and Mrs. Brown dining with you?"

"I ... I can enquire, sir."

"Thank you. Do that." He drummed on the desk as he waited, looking now and again at Arthur Taggart. Then the voice came to him, saying, "Yes, Mr. and Mrs. Brown have had dinner. They're in the lounge. I think they're on the point of leaving."

"Well, will you be kind enough to tell him to come to the phone? It's very, very important."

"I'll ... I'll do that, sir."

Again there was a long wait, longer this time; then the recognised voice, "Yes? Who is it?"

"This happens to be Bill Bailey here. I just want to tell you that your son has completely wrecked my showhouse. And ..."

"What are you saying? What are you talking about? Now look here!"

"If you'll shut that mouth of yours for a moment you'll hear what I'm talking about. Your son was caught leaving the showhouse through a back window, and evidence is all over him. He is under

162

guard now. I thought I'd put you in the picture before the police take him."

"My God! You've set this up."

"Yes, of course, I've set this up. I hired him to come and smash the place up. Don't be such a bloody fool, man. Well, there you have it." He was about to put the phone down when the voice yelled at him, "Wait! Wait! Are the police there?"

"Not yet."

"You haven't rung them?"

"No, but I intend to when I put this phone down."

"Bailey. Look. Give me fifteen minutes. I'll be there."

Bill stared into the mouthpiece of the phone; then slowly he replaced it, and when a minute later he hadn't picked it up again to phone the police, Arthur Taggart said, "A patrol car passes around here about this time, you could get them if you phoned the station."

He looked up at the man, then said, "I'll hold me hand, Arthur; if the police come they'll yank him straight off. I want our Mr. Brown to see his son exactly where he is now with the evidence all over him. You know what he said? He said I'd fixed it."

"No! He must be bloody mad."

Bill now picked up the phone again and rang Fiona.

"Listen, love," he said, "I'm likely to be here for sometime yet. Brown's on his way."

"Is it bad?"

"Couldn't be worse if a fire had hit it."

"And you've got him?"

"Oh yes, we've got him. And I've got Brown an' all. By God, I have. And I mean to turn the screw.... Are you in bed?"

"No; no, of course not."

"Well, do what you're told, d'you hear? Because I could likely be another couple of hours if the police come in on it."

"Haven't you called the police yet?"

"No, not yet."

"I suppose you have a reason."

"Yes, I have a reason. Now get to bed, dear. Bye."

"Are you going to bring him in here?" said Arthur Taggart now.

"No; no, he's goin' to stay where he is cringing like the young swab he is, and so his dear papa can see him." Then he added, "You've got a good dog there, Arthur."

"The best. Within seconds he had torn the pants off him."

"*He tore his pants?*"

"Yes, overalls, pants, the lot, they're stripped down the back."

163

"Huh! That's funny. Poetic justice that." He didn't go on to explain about the poetic justice, but after a moment he said, "Put the main lights on outside, Arthur, so the great man can see where he's going and not run into the mixer. Not that I'd mind that happening."

It was fifteen minutes later when Brown drove his car into the yard. Bill was standing in his office doorway and he kept his surprise hidden when, not only Brown came towards him, but Mrs. Brown also.

"What's this? Now what are you up to?"

He ignored the man for a moment and, looking at the tall woman with the pale face, he said, "Good evening, Mrs. Brown."

Her reply was hesitant, but when it came it sounded cold; "Good evening, Mr. Bailey."

"Cut the pleasantries for God's sake! Where's my boy?"

Bill now motioned the night watchman towards him, saying, "First things first. Lead the way to the showhouse, Arthur."

A minute or so later they were all standing in the vandalised house. And it was evident that even Brown was shocked. As for his wife, she turned a painful look on Bill and shook her head, but she said nothing. What he said was, "Mind where you step, Mrs. Brown ... the carpet has been freshly painted."

When, after going round the ground floor, Mrs. Brown went to mount the stairs, her husband said, "You needn't go up there."

She turned and looked at him, but did not speak; then slowly she mounted the stairs.

When they were all outside once more, Brown, blustering now, said, "I don't believe it. I just don't believe it. Anyway, who was with him? He couldn't have done this on his own. Who are the others?"

"There were no others, sir," Arthur Taggart replied.

"How do you know?"

"It's my job to know, and that of my dog."

"Dog?"

"Yes, sir, my dog got him backing out of the window." He pointed along the side of the house. "He had done the job thoroughly, prepared for it, worked it out like: brown paper pasted on the window to kill the noise of broken glass. . . . "

"Where is he?" Brown was now looking at Bill.

Bill made no reply, but walked away and the others followed.

When he opened the door of the toolshed they all filed in, but the only immediate response to the crouching boy was a gasp from his mother. Yet even now she didn't speak. It was the boy who spoke, saying, "Dad, that dog, they ... they set the dog on me, Dad."

164

When Brown, making to step forward, dislodged some shovels, the dog turned its head in his direction and bared its teeth and growled. And at this Arthur Taggart commanded, "Up boy! Here!" and the dog, slowly rising, backed two steps then turned towards its master and stood by his side.

"Dad. Dad."

"*Get up!*" The boy struggled to his feet, then leaned against the partition, his hands behind him holding up his torn clothes. Then turning his head away from his father's furious gaze, he whimpered, "Mother. Mother." Then added, "I ... I didn't do it. I was just passing, and I saw."

"Shut your mouth, you idiot!"

The boy, seeming to lose all fear for a moment, straightened up and cried, "Well, you were always on about him: what you were going to do, and you never did it. And they were laughing at me at school, and ... and giving me a nickname, and ... "

When the blow struck his head the boy reeled to the side and almost fell into the tools. And now Mrs. Brown did speak: "That has come too late," she said.

They were all looking at the tall indignant figure who had now turned to Bill, saying, "Is there any place where we may talk, Mr. Bailey?"

"Yes, come into the office."

Brown did not even wait for his wife or son to precede him into the office but marched ahead.

Inside, Bill offered Mrs. Brown a chair, but she refused it with a small shake of her head while she kept her eyes fixed on her son, who was now gripping to his side a length of his torn trousers and overall in his trembling rubber-gloved hand.

"Have you notified the police?" Brown's voice was a growl.

Bill answered calmly, "Not as yet. I thought it would be wise for you to be here when they came, for anything he says then could be taken down and used in evidence against him. That's how the procedure goes, isn't it?" He glanced at the boy as he spoke.

"Well, as far as I can see, it's a ... well it's a private matter. I'll make good the damage, so we can let it rest there."

"*Oh, no. Oh, no.* Not this time."

"What do you mean, not this time?"

"I 'let it rest there' when he burned my son. And it's poetic justice, don't you think, that the dog should have got him in the same place, only his teeth didn't go far enough, not like a flaming firework. So there's no way you're goin' to settle his latest escapade in your own

165

way. I've had enough of you and your undercover tactics from the beginning, only they've increased over the last weeks. You couldn't come yourself so you sent your stooge. And you've trained him well. So . . ."

"Mr. Bailey."

He looked at Mrs. Brown.

"I'm sure you won't be troubled any further with my husband's tactics, undercover or otherwise."

"No? What guarantee have you for saying that Mrs. Brown?" His voice was quiet but held a firm enquiry.

"Oh, I suppose you haven't heard, but he is resigning from the Finance Board."

The start that Brown gave as he turned towards his wife was almost like a shout of denial. But he didn't speak, only glared at her; and she didn't turn towards him but kept her eyes fixed on Bill as she went on, "We are moving to London shortly, where, as I think you know, my husband has a number of interests. Isn't that so, James?"

It looked for a moment as if her husband was going to choke, but still he said nothing, and she went on, "And my son is going to a school in Scotland. It's near where my uncle lives; it is rather remote but there's a lot of outdoor life and I'm sure the training will prove good for his future."

Her son was looking at her open-mouthed now. And it was he who spoke, saying one word, "Mother."

"Yes?"

"I . . . I promise you, I won't do . . . do anything ever . . . ever again."

"I know you won't, dear."

Bill felt a strange chill going through him as he looked at this tall elegant woman, for in this moment she was emanating power, a cold, even ruthless power. But how had she come by it? Evidently she had some hold over Brown, and it was great enough to have turned the man's colour to a sickly grey and caused the boy to bow his head.

She was looking at him again, saying now, "So, do you think, Mr. Bailey, under the circumstances, you could overlook this final insult? And I can give you my word and I have never yet been known to break it." Did she send a sidelong glance towards her husband? Perhaps it was a trick of the light, because she went on, "So I can assure you that you or yours will never again be subjected to abuse in any form from my family."

He did not answer her right away but stared at her as if fascinated. He had been attracted to her the last time she had stood in this office.

166

Oh yes, he had. He loved Fiona and would never love anyone else like he loved her, but that didn't stop him from admiring another woman. And he had admired this one, and he still admired her; but his admiration was now tinged with something that he couldn't put a name to. But whatever it was he didn't like it, and he was damned glad she wasn't his wife. Well, of course, he told himself, she wouldn't be for he'd never got hitched to her. But how had she come to be Brown's wife? Yes, that was the question that would always puzzle him: why had she taken a fellow like Brown, a woman like her? And ten or twelve years ago she must have been an absolute stunner, she still was. But . . .

He heard himself say, "Well—" then he made himself pause and looked from Brown to his son. The boy was staring at him, but Brown was half turned away, as if he were looking towards the door. Then he went on. "If as you say, your plans are all set to move, and your husband is leaving the firm, and your son is going to be taught how to behave, and the wilds of Scotland will likely prove more effective in the long run than Borstal . . . "

Brown's voice cut in on him like the crack of a gun as he swung round, crying, "There'd be no Borstal. He wouldn't get Borstal for that."

"Wouldn't he? Well, shall we try?" His hand went to the phone.

"James!" Almost like a fierce but whipped cur Brown swung round again towards the door, and in this moment Bill had it in his heart to be sorry for the man, for as he saw it, it wasn't right that any man, particularly a husband, should be made to look small by a woman. And he asked himself again: How on earth had this marriage come about? And to what did she owe the power that she definitely possessed?

His voice was curt when he next spoke: "As I said, I'll take your word for it, Mrs. Brown. . . . And you will make good the damage?"

"Yes, of course, Mr. Bailey. Thank you."

As she now walked to the door that Arthur Taggart was holding open for her, the boy scampered after her, whimpering "Mother. Mother." But it was as if she hadn't heard him.

Brown did not immediately follow them; he remained staring at Bill. And what he said now could have been enigmatic, but Bill got its meaning; his words were: "I intend to live a long time."

21

IT HAD BEEN QUITE A MORNING. ALL THE MEN WERE UP IN ARMS ABOUT THE vandalism, and to those he termed his board he gave as much explanation as he thought necessary. And to a man, they said he had been daft; this was a chance to get his own back on Brown. Why hadn't he taken it? And to this he replied, they had made a deal and Brown wouldn't be troubling them in future. That's as far as he had gone. He couldn't have said Mrs. Brown had taken things into her own hands, which, the more he thought about it, the more he realised were frightfully strong. And more than once during the morning when his thoughts returned to the matter he would again ask himself how she had managed to get linked up with Brown.

However, around twelve o'clock, the mystery was solved for him.

It was at this time that a chauffeur-driven Rolls came into the yard and out of it stepped Sir Charles Kingdom. The old man greeted Bill heartily, saying, "You are getting on with this lot, aren't you? What are you going to do when it's finished?"

Laughingly Bill replied, "Keep hoping that you'll get me another site, sir."

"Well! Well! You can always hope, you know. Can we talk somewhere?"

"You don't want to see round, sir?"

168

"No; no, I don't want to see round."

Bill did him the courtesy of seating him in his own chair and was surprised when the old man said, "Nasty business last night." And further when, pursing his lips, he said, "You are surprised I know all about it? I knew all about it by breakfast time; Eva phoned me."

Bill's lips repeated the words but no sound came from them and Sir Charles now said, "What you don't know is I'm her godfather."

"Really, sir?"

"Yes, really. Wasted life, utterly wasted life. God Almighty! The things women do. You've met her twice. She told me she first saw you after you lathered the boy. You did a damn fine job there I'd say. Has it ever made you ponder, having seen her, why she got linked up with Brown?"

"To be honest, sir, it's made me ponder up till this very minute."

"And you're not the only one. But up home in Scotland"—he thumbed over his shoulders as if Scotland lay just beyond the yard—"if the truth isn't known it's pretty well guessed at. Do you know, she had every fellow in the county at her feet when she was nineteen? She had been sent to a sort of modern finishing school in Paris, and she comes back into that house, that mausoleum of a house. Her father was my second cousin, you know. Damned hypocrite if ever there was one. Supported the Church, could pick his ministers; he was lousy rich, mostly inherited; but he had fingers in all kinds of pies, too, the main one a distillery. Yes, yes, a distillery, and him reading the lesson every Sunday like Michael the Archangel. And she was just as bad, his wife, Liza. Well, as I was saying, young Eva comes back to that atmosphere after seeing life abroad, and she hated it. She told me so herself. 'How am I going to get out of this, Uncle Charles?' she said. 'Marry,' I said. And I can see her now ticking off on her fingers the fellows she knew, half of them belonging to the Church and half of the other given up to horse ridin' and whorin'. But that still left two or three decent chaps. But she wasn't attracted by them.... Aren't women fools, Bailey?"

"Well—" Bill hesitated, then added, "There are exceptions, sir."

"Few and far between. Well, anyway, as I was saying, more to pass the time than anything she used to go round the works. And Brown at that time was undermanager, risen up from the bottles, he had, ambitious fellow. He was a man at this time, too, eleven years older than her, and he made it his business to speak to her every time he saw her. And she chatted to him. He was different, you see, from the usual men she met. And then came the night of the staff party. By the way she had only one brother, just one, Ian, a bit hot-headed but a

169

decent enough chap, and he was very protective of her. Anyway, the wine flowed and Eva went missing. Ian looked for her and found her, but too late. She was in the old summer house in the wood, and so was Brown. . . . And apparently the deed was done. My, my, yes.

"Lord above! When Liza knew, that was her mother, she nearly went insane. And you know how her father took it? He had a damned heart attack. There were great consultations. My mother was present, we lived just down the valley. She and Liza had been girlhood friends. It was proposed that the child be taken away. But apparently Eva wasn't for this. She dug her heels in. It was pointed out to her, I understand, that no man in the county would take her on, ever. And to this she had replied, defiantly, that Brown would. So that's how it came about. Brown was quietly upgraded; he became manager of one of the many pies old George had in England. And you won't believe it, it was sort of arranged by the family that before that happened Eva and Brown should do a kind of eloping act. It made everything more normal like, as they said. And that's what happened."

The old man now took out a small snuff box, retrieved a pinch, placed it in the hollow between his first finger and thumb, sniffed at it twice, then dabbed at his nose with a large blue silk handkerchief, before saying, "Brown thought he was clever, but he didn't know what he was taking on. Eva is a formidable woman, not only in her character, but because she holds the purse strings. I'll give her father his due, the old man never altered his will. And so when he died, she got a good slice of the takings. But the old fellow had made one stipulation, and that was the money must always remain in her name. And not only did she get a big dollop of cash, but she got a biscuit factory and a share in a big healthy removal business. Oh, she's a very, very wealthy woman is Eva. But now what I'm going to say after all that is going to surprise you, Bailey, and it's just this . . . I'm sorry for Brown. Can you believe that?"

Bill was some time in answering because he was reliving the scene that had taken place in this office last night. But when he spoke he said, "Yes, in a way, but only in a way."

"Oh, I can see it from your point of view. And the man's a vindictive stinker, I know. But my God, he must have had something to put up with, because Eva is like an icicle. And really he's still only a manager; although he seems to play about with money, everything has to be okayed by her. She has her hands tightly on the reins and sees to the business side of most things. Can you believe that?"

"Yes; yes, I can believe it."

"But on the other hand, just think, Bailey, if she had married a

170

decent bloke, somebody she loved, you would have seen a woman with a heart today."

Bill now said quietly, "She's a courageous woman. She must have had that courage when she was young; why didn't she just go and have the child?"

"Simply because, I suppose, she had been brought up in luxury, and she hadn't a penny of her own and they would certainly not have given her a farthing, at least at that time, so she could see no other option."

"Is her mother still alive?"

"Oh yes; and her brother, too, of course. That's where she's sending the boy. He's got an estate up in the hills and the school that the boy will go to is quite near. And if between them they don't make him into some sort of a man I'll be surprised, because it's Brown's fault the boy is as he is; Brown's tried to get his own back on Eva by toadying for the boy's affection, giving him all he wanted on the quiet. But truth to tell, Eva's got no love for the lad. . . . How's your life? How do you find your wife?"

"My home life is very good, sir. I have an excellent wife."

"You took her on with three children, I understand; and adopted another?"

"Yes, I did."

"You like children?"

"Yes, I'm very fond of children, sir."

"Why don't you have some of your own then?"

"Give me time, sir. I promised her to make the family up to ten."

"Ha, ha!" The old man laughed loudly. "What does she say about that?"

"She's quite willin'."

"You're a lucky man then."

"Yes, I'm a lucky man, sir."

"By the way"—the old man pulled himself up from the chair—"don't go spreading round what I've told you. And I can add this, I love that girl, but I'm not proud of her actions last night, to bring him low in front of you and a watchman. She could have done it in another way."

"Why doesn't she divorce him?"

"Why does a cat play with a mouse? She hasn't said much about the private side of her marriage, you understand, but from the little I gather he must have given her a rough time at first. But don't forget she was a nineteen-year-old and he was thirty, and brute strength can prevail for a time at any rate. Anyway, he soon had to find his

171

pleasures elsewhere. He has his women on the side, a permanent one I understand."

"And she puts up with that?" Bill's nostrils had widened.

"Apparently. Do you read history at all? The Borgias were mostly women. Well, now, I must be away. I hate Christmas, always have done. My two sons and my daughter bring their squads and my son's daughter even brings hers. Can you believe that? I'm a great-grandfather."

Bill smiled tolerantly at the old man, saying kindly now, "I don't believe you don't enjoy Christmas, sir."

"You can take it from me, I don't." He now punched Bill on the shoulder. "I went missing last Christmas Day. There was a hue and cry all over the house. I heard them. There's a closet in the attic. Well, it's a kind of little room. I used to hide in it when I was a boy and so did my sons, but they didn't remember it until they became desperate. And I heard Geoffrey saying, 'He couldn't be in there, not all this time.' But I was, with a bottle of good port and a box of cigars. But the latter was a pleasure I had to forgo because they would have smelt them. Anyway, the children enjoyed finding me. They laughed their heads off, but their parents weren't amused." He went out chuckling.

The chauffeur held the car front passenger door open for him then closed it on him, took his own seat, and started the engine. But then the old man's window began to slide down and, pushing his wrinkled face out towards Bill, he said, "I've got a good wife, too," he made a deep obeisance with his head. "Very understanding. Always has been, in all ways." And now, with a mischievous grin on his face, he ended, "Never gave me any need to go hunting, never, except the fox. Understand?"

The window was sliding up again and Bill was left standing, the laughter in him making his eyes moist as he watched the car backing into the road.

There went a character. Wait until he got home and told Fiona.

At three o'clock a maid showed Fiona into a room that could have been a study or a sitting room. She took in the overall comfort as Mr. Morgan led her to a seat. Then he discussed the weather loudly as he went around a teak desk and, after seating himself, drew a file towards him which he opened, read a little, then looked at her and, smiling, said, "Ah, well, now ... how are you feeling?"

"Not on top of the world. . . . Naturally, I'm worried."

"Of course, of course. Well, now, we had the plates back and as you may have already gathered they show trouble with the appendix. But lower down it has revealed a ... er ... rather dark mass. Now, that's what we've got to think about, isn't it."

She was unable to answer. Deep in the pit of her stomach there was a feeling that told her she could be sick at any minute. There flashed through her mind the picture of the children before she left the house and Mamie crying as she said, "You going on a holiday, Mammy B.?"

It was Mamie's kind of holiday that was in her mind now, and had been for days because of the answer to the dreaded question that could lead her to that holiday.

She hadn't meant to ask. She had told herself she wouldn't ask. But she heard a small voice say, "Could it be cancer?"

"Yes; yes, it could; but of course we won't know exactly until we get inside, will we?"

My god! Just like that, straight out. He had said, "Yes; yes, it could." Why couldn't he have lied? Or put it in a different way? But to say "Yes; yes, it could." What was she going to say to Bill who was waiting outside. She was sweating. There was a buzzing in her ears. She could hear his voice. It was as if he was standing behind her, saying, "You're going to be all right, Mrs. B."

She was hearing Mr. Morgan clearly once more. "We're right on the holidays and one or two more days won't make all that difference, because I know you would like to be with your children for Christmas, but if you would care to go in sooner I could get Mr. Rice to see to it, although I would rather do it myself. However, it's up to you."

"Oh; oh, I'll wait. Yes, please. But when will that be?"

"Well, now, I don't think we should leave it too long." He drew an appointment book towards him and, after flicking the pages, again said, "Well, now." This seemed to be a pet phrase of his. "Well, now, let's see. How about Friday. You will come in, of course, the previous day. It's the Nuffield isn't it? Shall I make arrangements for that day, Thursday the twenty-seventh?"

"Yes, please."

"Well, then, that's it."

He rose from behind the desk. She, too, rose, and as he led her to the door he held out his hand and shook hers warmly, saying, "Enjoy your Christmas."

The car was across the road from the house. Bill was walking up and down on the pavement.

On seeing her, he dodged between two cars and caught her arm, but not until they were seated in the car did he ask, "How did you get on then?"

She did not look at him but through the windscreen to where a line

173

of bare poplar trees were all bending in the wind. "I'm to go in on the twenty-seventh."

"Operation?" His voice seemed to come from high in his head, and now she looked at him and said, "Yes, dear, operation the following day."

"What is it?"

She told herself she was speaking the truth when she said, "He doesn't rightly know."

"But they took an X-ray."

"Yes"—she made herself smile—"but X-rays don't exactly talk, they just indicate."

"Well, hell's flames! What did they indicate?"

She screwed up her eyes and turned her head away as she muttered, "Oh, Bill, don't shout. Don't go on."

"Oh, love." His arms were about her. "I'm nearly out of me mind thinkin' the worst. Are you sure he said he didn't know?"

"Yes; yes, dear; I'm sure. They'll know more when they take the appendix out."

"So there is more to know?"

"Yes, I suppose so. But he says not to worry."

"Oh, that's the set phrase." He clapped his hands on the wheel now. "You would think they were talking to bairns, that lot. Not to worry. They say to all and sundry, not to worry. Why can't they think up some kind of machine they can attach to us that stops us from worrying."

"Let's get home, Bill." Her voice was quiet now. And when he started up the car, she said, "Bill." And his name was an appeal.

"Yes, love?"

"You mustn't let on to the children."

"No, you're right there. But on the other hand, I think you should tell Mark, 'cos he's got a head on his shoulders, that boy. He doesn't think of himself as a child anymore, not on a level with the others."

"Perhaps you're right, but we'll just say it's for the appendix."

"Well, let's hope to God it is . . . just the appendix. . . . "

On entering the house, they were assailed by a loud chorus from the kitchen of "Good King Wenceslas."

They looked at each other and smiled and Bill, as he helped her off with her coat, said, " 'Bill Bailey' on the tin whistle sounded better. Leave them to it; come on and rest."

"No, let's go and see them."

There was a great rush from the table, and Nell's voice, rising above the hubbub, cried, "Manners! Manners!" to which both Katie and Willie chorused, "Pianos, piecrusts, and perambulators."

"Finish your tea, all of you!"

"We've finished, Mam." It was another chorus.

"You feeling all right, Mam?" It was a quiet enquiry from Mark. And looking at him lovingly, she said, "Yes, dear, I'm feeling all right."

"We've been singing Good King Whens at last looked out."

"You keep saying it all wrong." Katie now gave Willie a none to gentle push. "It's 'Good King *Wenceslas.*' That's his name, not When's at last looked out. That's daft."

"It doesn't matter if he looked out first, last, or in between, it sounds all right to me," Bill said diplomatically now. Then looking at Nell, he asked, "Any tea going?"

"I've set yours in the sitting room."

"Oh, hotel service now. We're going up in the world, Mrs. B., aren't we?" Bill jerked his head at Fiona, and she, looking towards Nell, said, "That's nice. Thanks, dear." Then bringing her attention back to her family again, she added, "Help Nell clear, then upstairs with you. You've all got your Christmas presents to do, haven't you?"

"You coming up Mammy B. to tie my bows?"

Before Fiona could make any response to the child, Katie, bending towards Mamie, said, "I've told you it's just like tying your shoelaces, only you're doing it with ribbon."

"I'll be up as soon as I have a cup of tea." Fiona stroked the head that was pressed against her side. And as she did so she looked towards Mark, and he, getting the message, took the child's hand, saying, "Come on, you. Don't think you're going to get out of your job, you've got to carry the plates."

Bill now marshalled Fiona firmly from the kitchen, across the hall, and into the sitting room, where, drawn up near the couch, was a table set for two, and on it small plates of mince pies, bread and butter, scones, and jam.

Fiona stood for a moment looking down on it, then said quietly, "What would I do without Nell?"

Bill made no reply to this, but, pulling her down beside him on the couch, he took her face between his hands, saying softly, "What would I do without you? God, woman, what would I do without you? Remember that, will you? There's a lot to be said for willpower and right thinkin'. They're gettin' on to the track of that these days, right thinkin'. You can cure almost anything with right thinkin'."

As the door opened and Nell entered with the tea tray, he sat back on the couch and reverting to his old style, said, "You've taken your time."

"My duty is to tend the first-class customers first," she retorted.

175

"And if you're not comfortable in this hotel you know where you can go."

"I'll report you to the authorities, madam, for insolence."

"Do it, fella. Anyway, in the meantime get your tea, and you know what I hope it does to you."

Fiona's head was resting against the back of the couch; her eyes were closed. She knew what these two were aiming to do with their jocular abuse. She said quietly, "Will you pop in before you go home, Nell? Because if I understand rightly from previous arrangements, this gentleman is going out to do some late-night shopping."

"I can put that off until tomorrow."

"I don't want you to put it off until tomorrow." She sat up now and put her hand out towards the teapot as she ended, "Don't forget what you promised the squad tomorrow; the pantomime's on at the Royal."

"Nell can take them."

"Nell can't." Nell's voice was vibrant. "I live next door, you know; you'll soon have me lodging here. And I've got shopping to do, too. So stick to your plans, William Bailey, and I'll stick to mine." Her voice dropping now, she said softly, "I'll be in shortly, Fiona, when he's out of the way."

As she handed a cup of tea to Bill, Fiona said, "I repeat, I'm lucky, if only for the fact that she can give you back as much as you send."

It was sometime later, after Bill had left the house to do his shopping and the children were upstairs tying up their Christmas presents, that Nell came into the sitting room and, sitting down on the couch and without any preamble, said, "What did he say?" And for answer Fiona clasped her hands tightly in her lap and bent her body forward, muttering as she did, "Oh, Nell."

There was silence between them for a moment, then Nell said, "You asked him straight out?"

"Yes; yes, I did."

"And he confirmed it?"

Fiona now drew in a long breath and lay back against the head of the couch as she said, "Not particularly. He said it could be, but he wouldn't know exactly until they got inside." Then swinging round, she caught hold of Nell's hands and, gripping them tightly, shook them, saying, "I couldn't bear it, Nell. I'm a rank coward, I suppose, but the thought of a colostomy and having, well, that thing at the side, I just . . . "

"Stop it! Be quiet! You're jumping to conclusions. But if it did come to that, they're doing wonders with that kind of operation now. There's that young woman who works on the television in Newcastle.

She's in the makeup section. She goes around talking about it now. She had that very same thing done and within six months she had another operation and everything was put back normal again. She's marvellous, better than she's ever been."

"That may be so; she's an exception; but I don't think I could go through with it, the very thought of it, in fact, I'm sure I couldn't. And . . . and I can tell you I've given it a lot of thought of late because I've known all along what the trouble was; I didn't have to wait to hear him confirm it. Yet when he did I felt like passing out. But Nell, now listen to me." She again shook the hands that were in hers. "I want to talk to you seriously. This is about the only chance I'll have before Thursday, and . . . and please don't interrupt. Let me have my say. Well, it's like this. As I see it you're on your own; your divorce will be through at any time. You'll be free to do what you like, so I'm going to ask you to take my place here and look after the children and . . . "

"*Shut up!*" Nell pulled her hands roughly from Fiona's grasp. "Take your place here, you said. I could never hope to take your place, even with the kids. And what about him? Look. You've got to think of him more than you have. That fella adores you. He'll go barmy if anything should happen to you. Well, it's not going to happen to you. If it's what you think, you're going to go through with it. *Take your place indeed!*"

"I asked you to hear me out."

"I'm not hearing you any further on that line."

"Nell, Nell, please listen to me. It will ease my mind if I knew you would stay on here and see to them."

"You don't have to ask that. Don't be so silly. You know I'll see to them. But there's not going to be any necessity to take over from you. Now you listen to me. You make up your mind, no matter what it is, you're coming through it. My heavens! There's people had the operation twenty years ago and they're still going strong. And I'll tell you something you didn't know. There's Mam." She jerked her head backwards. "She had her breast off twelve years ago. She looks as if she's got a big bust, but one's a good falsie. So come on, lass." Her voice suddenly dropped and, moving towards Fiona again, she put her arms around the woman and, her voice thick now, said, "You mean a lot to me. I've never had a friend like you in my life. You've saved me from despair over these past months, made me feel I was a human being again, because when he walked out, as I told you, I felt less than nothing. His mam and dad were wonderful to me, they still are, but they didn't give me the boost that you did: letting me be with the kids, making me feel wanted and appreciated. Yes, that's the word, appreciated. All my married life I never felt appreciated. So you see, I'm thinking of meself, 'cos I couldn't go on without you either."

"Oh, Nell, I'm lucky to have you. And you know something? That's the third time I've said that in the last few hours."

They kissed and hung together for a moment; then Nell, getting abruptly to her feet, said, "Upstairs with you and into bed. I'll see that Bailey gang leaves you alone, until they come to say goodnight anyway."

Fiona made no protest, she just smiled at this staunch friend and went out.

Nell now went into the kitchen and busied herself at top speed: setting the table for breakfast, putting out a tray with glasses on for the late milk drinks, and a biscuit tin by its side. Stopping suddenly, she put her hand tightly across her eyes, and as the tears welled through her fingers, she flopped down onto a chair, and, resting her arms on the table, buried her head in them and gave way to the emotions pent up inside her.

It was like this that Bill saw her when he opened the kitchen door. Startled, she rose to her feet, and he, taking her by the shoulders, said, "What is it? What's happened?"

"N ... nothing, Bill. Nothing."

"It's Fiona, isn't it? You know something that I don't? Come on, come on, out with it." He shook her.

"No; no, it isn't ... not that, Bill."

"Don't lie to me, Nell. I know she's been keeping something back."

"It ... it ... it isn't that. It's ... it's about Harry, and ... and the divorce."

"Well, you knew what he wanted, and that's what you want an' all, isn't it?"

"Yes, yes." She sniffed loudly and licked at the tears raining over her lips, then said, "I ... I got a letter from him, but ... but he didn't say anything except he wanted it got through quickly. And then ... then Mam was out this afternoon and met someone who knew the girl. She's going to have a baby."

"Ah, Nell. And the dirty bugger wouldn't give you one. Ah, lass."

His right arm slipped around her shoulder, and she fell against him for a moment. And as he patted her, he said, "There, there, lass. You know what they say, there's better fish in the sea. And there'll come along someone later on. Look at me. What I ... "

His voice halted abruptly as the kitchen door was thrust open and

178

his head jerked to the side to see two figures standing stiffly, staring at him. It was the expression on their faces that made him almost push Nell from him. Yet he still held her shoulder as he turned her around, looked towards Katie and Willie, who were about to scamper away, and he yelled at them, "Stop! Stay!" as if they were dogs. And they did just that, they stopped and they stayed. He beckoned them now with his finger, saying, "Come here."

Slowly they both came towards him, their eyes wide; and now pressing Nell into a chair, he brought them to her knees, saying, "You two stay with Nell. She's very upset about something. Now comfort her. I'll be back in a minute."

And with that he almost ran from the room and into the sitting room and, seeing that Fiona wasn't there, he took the stairs two at a time and burst into the bedroom.

Fiona had just got into bed and she looked startled as he came toward her, his hand out pointing but seemingly unable to speak for a moment. And then he said, "In two seconds there'll be your daughter and younger son diving into this room to tell you that they've seen Nell and me necking in the kitchen."

"*What?*"

"Just what I said."

"Well, would you mind explaining?"

He dropped down on the edge of the bed, drew his fingers across his brow as if wiping the sweat from it, then said, "I came in the kitchen and I found Nell howling her eyes out, and I got her off the chair and I put me hand on her shoulder, just like this"—he demonstrated—"and said, 'What's it all about?' In fact, I thought she was keeping something back from me about you, you know. And I gave her a little shake like this"—he demonstrated again —"and she said it wasn't about you, but she'd had a letter this morning from that swine of hers. And he didn't say anything about fathering a baby apparently, but her mam was out this afternoon and met somebody who seemed to know that the girl is expecting. And that cut her up."

"*She didn't tell me that.* I knew about the letter but not about. . . ."

"Well, now you know. She likely thought you had enough on your plate. Anyway, the state she was in she would have moved a brick wall and so I put me arm around her shoulders and she bent her head against me for a minute." He tried to demonstrate again, but she pressed him off. Her eyes were blinking, her lips were tight, as he went on, "Then the kitchen door was thrust open and there were the two of them goggle-eyed, struck dumb, and I could see that imp of Satan dashing up here and saying just that: 'Mr. Bill and Nell were

179

necking in the kitchen, Mam.' She's well advanced your daughter. That says nothing for your son."

"Oh, Bill. Oh, Bill." She was holding her side now and her body was shaking with laughter. "Oh, Bill. Oh, Bill. If . . . if you could see your face; a . . . a jury would hang you; there's guilt written all over it."

"Guilt be damned. And look, stop laughin' like that; you'll hurt yourself."

"Hurt meself? Oh, it's the best medicine I've had for days." The bed almost shook, and when her laughter became audible she put her hand over her mouth, and he put his arms around her, saying, "Give over now. Give over."

Her eyes were wet, but when real tears began to take the place of the moisture her laughter subsided, and, dropping her head onto Bill's shoulders, she said, "Oh, Bill. Bill."

"Don't lass, don't. For God's sake, don't cry; it'll break me down."

When there came a tap on the bedroom door she quickly dried her face, and Bill, standing up, called, "Come in." And in came Katie and Willie and, after passing Bill, they went to the bed. And it was Katie who spoke first, saying, "I cried an' all, Mam, 'cos Nell's husband's not coming back."

"I'll marry her."

Bill half turned from the bed for a moment; then swinging round, he sat on the edge of it and, looking at Willie, said, "You would? You'd marry Nell?"

"Yes; yes, I told her, when I'm ten, perhaps eleven. She said she'll wait. Didn't she Katie?"

Katie nodded, saying, "Yes, you did; but I've told you, you can't get married at eleven or twelve, you've got to be fourteen."

"Never you mind, lad." Bill patted Willie's shoulder. "She'll wait and she'll appreciate what you've done, 'cos as you know she was in a very upset state, wasn't she?" They both looked at him and nodded, and, Katie staring at him fully in the face, said, "Some men can have two wives, or more. It was on the television. A man had five and a lot of children."

Bill's eyes widened, so did his mouth, but apparently he could find no comment to make on this statement. It was Fiona who said, "But that's in another country, dear, and it's because of the religion."

They looked at her in silence for a moment; then as they both turned from the bed Willie said, "God had five hundred."

"It wasn't God, silly, it was Solomon, the king."

"It wasn't, it was God."

180

The door closed on them, and Bill, shaking his head, muttered, "Those two could do a turn on their own."

Fiona now said, "By the way, you are back quickly; you couldn't have got much shopping done."

"Oh, I got all I needed tonight, and it's a beast outside, enough to cut the nose off you."

"Bill."

"Yes, love?"

"Will you have a talk with Mark, explain things to him?"

"Tonight?"

"Yes. You can take him down to help with the rest of the streamers."

"What'll I say?"

"Well, just explain I've got to go into hospital the day after Boxing Day, and you're depending on him to see to the others over the holidays; and that I'll be back home again long before he goes to school."

He stared at her, but made no further comment. Then getting up abruptly from the bed, he went out. And she lay back and closed her eyes and thought, I can't bear it.

22

TWO THINGS HAPPENED ON CHRISTMAS EVE, BOTH UNUSUAL IN THEIR OWN WAY.
The first began with a call from Mrs. Vidler. Fiona picked up the
phone to hear the voice say, "That you, Fiona?"

"Yes, Mother."

"Thank you for your help yesterday; it's left me in a nice pickle."

"I told you I was unable to come round. I haven't been well. I'm
going into hospital on Thursday."

"Not well? What's the matter with you?"

"It's the old tummy trouble.... Are you settled in?"

"Settled in, you say. I am stranded here with boxes and furniture
all around me, and the furniture men refuse to come. They started
their holidays last night, I've been informed, but the removal was
booked for this morning. I've had to sell off half my things because
they wouldn't go into the bungalow. They took them on Thursday to
the auction rooms and were to come back on Friday, but they didn't
arrive. And then their manager said they would be here this
morning. And now he says they've started their holiday on Saturday
and the firm is closed until the New Year. Did you ever know
anything like it? What am I to do?"

"I don't know, Mother."

Fiona turned her head from one side to the other in rejection as the

182

thought passed through her mind to ask her mother to come here until she was settled, when a loud, "No?" brought her to the phone again. "Well, what can I do, Mother? I can't make the company come and move you."

"No, but . . . but"—there was a pause—"that man's firm."

"Which man's firm?"

"You know who I'm talking about, girl. He's got lorries and men and they'll still be at work. They could come and do it."

Fiona now put her head back, looked up to the ceiling, and smiled broadly, before she said, "You mean you want to ask Bill to move you?"

"I . . . I am not going to ask him, but you can ask him. You can tell him to send his men."

"I can tell my husband nothing, Mother. He isn't the kind of man that you can order to do anything that he doesn't want to do, and I don't think he would be inclined to do anything for you after the way you have treated him."

"Girl!"

"I don't have to remind you again, Mother, that I'm not a girl."

There was a long pause; the voice that next came over was small: "Fiona."

"Yes, Mother?"

"I'm at my wits' end. Everything is packed up, every utensil, everything." The voice sounded tearful now. "It isn't all that far away between the houses. Fiona, please."

"Mother, I cannot ask my husband to do this service for you, but you could ask him yourself. Anyway, I don't suppose he has any men left on the site; they, too, will have started their holidays."

"Don't make me, Fiona. Please don't make me."

"I'm not making you, Mother, but he is more likely to accede to your request if *you* were to ask him, and put it politely, and tell him that you're in a hole."

"You're enjoying this, aren't you, Fiona?"

Fiona was still smiling but her voice sounded serious as she said, "No, Mother, I am not enjoying this. I only know, after all that's been said, I couldn't ask my husband to go and move you, and at this late stage, too. Anyway, I'll leave it to you. This is his number; he may still be at the works."

She gave the number, then said, briefly, "It's up to you, Mother; I can't do any more." And at this she put the phone down, but immediately picked it up again and rang Bill's office.

"Bill."

"Oh, hello, love. All right?"

"Yes; yes, I'm all right. Listen." Then almost word for word she gave him the gist of the conversation that had just taken place, and he replied with one word, "Never!"

"Yes, yes; you are her last resort. But I don't know whether she'll take it or not; she might prefer to sit on her boxes. In that case, dear, I would have to have her here for Christmas Day; I couldn't leave her there."

"Oh no! Oh no, you don't. You're not spoiling Christmas Day."

"Well, if she phones, will you do it?"

There was a pause before he answered; then, on a laugh, he said, "Aye, lass, I'll do it. Of course, they're open lorries, but by the sound of it a couple of trips should be enough. But the few lads here are finished at twelve. What time is it, now? Ten to ten. Oh, well, lass, if she phones I'll get them goin'. But I'll go with them."

"Oh, Bill, you needn't."

"I wouldn't miss it."

"Don't be rough on her."

"You leave it to me. You remember me and me dinner jacket?"

"Yes, but what has that got to do with it?"

"Well, I'd like to give her a surprise. And it's a pity there's not a film producer goin' along of me, 'cos after the act I'll put on he might pick me for stardom; in fact, no might about it, a sure thing."

"Oh, Bill. Anyway, I must advise you, Mr. Bailey, if you're going to put on an act, watch your aitches and sound your g's."

"Nark it, Mrs. B. Bye, love."

He had hardly put the phone down when it rang again, and a voice said, "I'd like to speak to Mr. Bailey."

"Mr. Bailey speaking." The tone could have been attributed to Sir Charles Kingdom.

"Mr. Bailey, the builder?"

"Yes. What can I do for you, madam?"

"This . . . this is Mrs. Vidler."

"Oh, Mrs. Vidler."

He said no more. And the voice said, "Are you there, Mr. Bailey?"

"Yes; yes, I am here, Mrs. Vidler." His accent remained high-falutin' but his tone slightly stiff. "What can I do for you?"

"I . . . I have been on to Fiona. I . . . I've explained to her about . . . about moving. They've disappointed me, let me down. My furniture and effects are all ready to be moved into the bungalow. There's not a great deal of stuff, and . . . and as it is the holidays the removal firm

184

has closed. I explained to Fiona and . . . and"—there was a pause—"and Fiona suggested that you might be able to help me."

"*She did?*" There was surprise in the tone now.

"Well . . . well, she said as it was an emergency . . . "

"What exactly are you asking me to do, Mrs. Vidler?"

"Well, I thought you might have emp . . . empty lorries and such, and your workmen and you might oblige by re . . . removing me today."

He knew that this was the space where he should have put in, "I'd take great pleasure in removing you, Mrs. Vidler, and as far away as you like," but what he said, was, "Well, well now. I just don't know about this. Most of my men finished on Friday. It's a holiday you know; I've only a few here who have come in to tidy up. . . . Where are you moving to, Mrs. Vidler?"

"Oh, it isn't very far, not a long journey, just to Primrose Crescent."

"Oh, Primrose Crescent. Yes; yes, I know those bungalows. Well, now, under the circumstances, I will see what I can do."

"Thank you. When can I expect you?"

"Oh, well, now, let me see." He paused for a full minute before adding, "Let's say within the next hour."

"Thank you."

Hearing the phone being put down, he replaced his own receiver, sat back in the chair, and let out a bellow of a laugh. But it stopped abruptly as he thought: If Fiona had only been all right we'd have made a thing of this. It would have given us a belly laugh for weeks.

Barney McGuire, and Bert Ormesby, and Jack Mowbray all knew of the situation between Bill and his mother-in-law. In fact, Jack Mowbray seemed to have her twin sister as his mother-in-law . . . and living with them. So when Bill said to them, "What about it? Will you do it?" they said as one voice, "Anything you say, boss." And then he said, "Well, now, I'll tell you something. It's like this. I intend to put on an act when I get there. You'll see what I'm at when I open me mouth, an' so I want you to fall in with it. Touch your forelocks, be sort of deferential-like. You know what I mean. But don't overdo it."

And they fell in with it. When, for the first time, Bill entered the house in which his wife had been born he realised yet again the wide difference in their upbringing. And when Mrs. Vidler, standing amid the ordered chaos in the hall, which was as large as the sitting room and dining room put together at home, and he saw that she had

185

difficulty in speaking, he opened with, "Good morning, Mrs. Vidler. Will you show me exactly what has to be removed?"

She stared at him. This wasn't the broad Liverpudlian, the big, raw, wise-cracking individual who had spurned her. She decided that he was either acting, or Fiona had been working on him. Perhaps she had sent him to one of those speech therapists.

"*Mr. Bailey.*"

Her tone imediately pointed out to Bill that his facade could be blown at any moment, and so, still keeping up the gentlemanly pose, he swung round, saying, "Oh, excuse me; I'll tell my men to get on with it; time is pressing. They are due to be finished at dinnertime you see." And now he called, "McGuire!"

Barney actually bounced in, touched his forelock and said, "Yes? Yes, boss?"

"Get the men to start moving. Look round and see what has to go on first."

"As you say, boss."

Bill turned away now. He thought Barney was slightly overdoing it; and he was no actor. But Bert Ormesby apparently was, for, crossing the hall, he lifted his cap to Mrs. Vidler and in a quiet voice he said, "Mornin', ma'am."

But Jack Mowbray coming in on Bert's heels completely ignored her, likely thinking of his own mother-in-law; but addressing Bill, he said, "How long is this likely to take, boss?"

Bill thought for a moment; then, looking at the perplexed lady, he said, "You said a lot of your big stuff had been disposed of?"

"Yes; yes, it's gone to a sale."

Turning his head now towards Jack, he said, "Oh, then, about a couple of hours I should say. You might have to make two runs each." Again he was looking at the perplexed lady, saying now, "Of course, you know, Mrs. Vidler, I have only lorries not pantechnicons."

"Yes; yes, I understand."

"But we have brought tarpaulin covers in case it should rain. Thankfully it's dry."

"Yes, yes." Her head was nodding now as if it was on strings.

"Boss." Jack Mowbray stopped as he was on the point of moving away and in a low voice that was very carrying he said, as he thumbed across the hall towards an open door, "Mr. McGuire tells me you've got a committee meeting at twelve. You forgot?"

"No; no, I haven't forgotten, but that's quite all right; I've already told them I might be a little late. They'll wait."

Now with a slight nod towards Mrs. Vidler, he followed the man into the first room where the other two were already standing grinning widely, and when there was a slight splutter, he put up a warning finger to his nose; then quite loudly he said, "Yes; yes, I'd get this room cleared first."

And so it went on until the two lorries were packed high with furniture. And Bill wondered himself how long he could keep up the farce after handing his mother-in-law into his car and leading two lorries on the journey to Primrose Crescent.

He purposely kept silent in the car, all the while thinking, Wait till I tell her. She won't believe it.

The bungalow was well built, but with now half the accommodation of the house they had just left. And here the act became more difficult, for he found that she was addressing him solely as to where the carpets and furniture should go. He then had to tell his men. Once or twice his natural tone came to the fore, but if she noticed it she showed no sign, although he knew, being Mrs. Vidler, she would likely be thinking, What's bred in the bone will come out in the flesh no matter how thick the veneer.

In order to make a temporary escape, when one lorry was emptied he left Barney and Jack to see to the unloading of the other while he himself went back with Bert Ormesby to get the remainder of the furniture. And it was evident that Bert saw himself as an actor, for no sooner had they been seated in the cab than he said, "How did I do, boss?"

"You did so well, you could take it up; it'll pay more than bricking."

"Eeh! I've never enjoyed meself so much for I couldn't tell you how long. Is she as bad as all that?"

"Worse. And I can tell you it must have cost her somethin' to ask me to do this job. By, it must. Some women are the limit, you know."

Bert's voice had a serious note in it now as he said, "No, I wouldn't know, boss; I've never been tangled up with them." He glanced at Bill now, saying, "Scared, and that's the truth. I only have to sit next to one and I become like a deaf and dumb mute."

"You've talked to my wife."

"Yes; but she's different, she's married."

"And you've talked to Nell. I saw you the other night when you helped to bring the tree in. You were chatting away when she gave you a cup of coffee."

"Yes, but she was easy. I mean ... well, she's married an' all."

"Not for long. Her divorce is coming through any time now."

187

"Funny that: a man can have a woman like her and drop her. She seemed nice."

"She is nice." Now he nudged Bert. "There's a chance for you. We'll invite you round for the New Year."

"You'll do no such thing, boss."

"But I will, that's if—" he drew in a short breath now before he said, "My wife's for hospital, Thursday."

"No!"

"Aye."

"Anything serious?"

"That's the point, we don't know."

"She seemed so bright and lively."

"Oh, that's just on the surface."

"Oh, boss, I'm sorry. But it'll be all right, you'll see. It'll be all right. God looks after his own."

"Aye"—Bill's voice was sharp now—"and God takes them young and good and beautiful."

"Aye. He does 'cos He's a jealous God."

Bill looked at this tough-looking individual by his side in something like amazement. He had worked with him for ten years but he knew so little about him except, as they all knew now, he neither drank, nor smoked, nor apparently went with women. But what was apparent, he believed in God.

It was a funny world. . . .

It was close on one o'clock when Mrs. Vidler stood at the door of her bungalow and, smiling at Barney, Jack, and Bert in turn, handed them a note, saying to each, "Thank you so much. I'll always be in your debt."

And each man touched his forelock and said, "Thank you, ma'am." And Bert, going one better, said, "Been a pleasure that doesn't come our way every day, ma'am. It's good to be of service."

Her smile was wide when, a moment later, she turned back into the small hall where Bill was buttoning up his overcoat. And looking at him steadily for a moment, she said, "I must be frank, Mr. Bailey: I never thought the day would come when I would change my opinion of you. I . . . I am always one to admit my faults and I can see that I've judged you harshly. We all live and learn and I can see that you have learned over the past months. And I am grateful to you for the service you have done me today. It all augurs more favourably for our future."

Oh, Gord! The words in his mind sounded like those issuing from a Cockney's lips. And he asked himself what would happen should

188

she visit the house and find she had been the butt of a joke, because there was one thing sure, he couldn't keep this kind of patter up; it was too wearing. Another thing he had learned this morning: actors certainly worked for their money, whether it be in acquiring an accent or getting rid of one.

"I'm having dinner with friends tomorrow. But will you tell Fiona that I will call round to see her on. . . . "

He interrupted her here by saying, "I thought she may have told you, but she's going into hospital on Thursday."

"Oh, yes, yes. Anyway, if I can't call before I shall visit her in hospital."

"I'm sure she'll be pleased to see you."

Holy Harry! Let him get out of this. He made hastily for the door now, and she followed him, saying, "I'm sorry you'll be late for your committee."

He had forgotten about the committee business. Then, making one last effort, he turned and smiled at her as he said, "Oh, they'll wait. They're used to it by now. Good-bye Mrs. Vidler."

He was halfway down the path when she called out, "Oh, you . . . you must send your bill in."

"Bill?" He turned round, his face screwed up. "There needn't be any talk of bills." His tone was pompous. He lifted his hand as if in final farewell, got into the car, started her up straightaway, and didn't seem to draw a breath until he had rounded the corner of the crescent. Then he let out a long "Whew!"

Wait till he got back home and told Fiona. She wouldn't believe it.

As he entered the yard he saw Jack Mowbray and Bert Ormesby making for their cars, and Jack shouted, "She gave us a fiver each, boss. What did she give you?"

And when he answered, "Only the promise that she's going to call," they roared laughing.

He stopped the car outside the office, and as he got out said to Barney, who was standing there, "I'll lock up, then I'm away." And Barney said, "You can't go home yet, boss."

"What d'you mean?"

"You've got a visitor; the watchman put her in your office."

"Who is it?"

"As far as I can gather, Mrs. Brown."

"*Mrs. Brown?*"

Why should that name disturb him? Whenever he heard it, it was as though his arm would go up as if warding off a blow. But her? What did she want?

He turned to Barney now, saying, "Well, get yourself away home. And thanks for this morning. Meself, if I was to speak the truth, I would say I enjoyed it, although it was a strain. My God, yes. I'll say it was a strain."

"I hope the missis comes through all right, boss. Can I give you a ring?"

"Yes, do that, Barney. And thanks."

"Well, try and have a good Christmas anyway. And my regards to the missis."

"Thanks. And you, Barney. And you. And thanks for all the good work."

"You're welcome. Oh, you're welcome."

On this they parted, and as Bill approached his office he straightened his tie and stretched his neck out of his collar. Then, pushing the door open, he said, "Mrs. Brown."

He had forgotten for the moment to revert back to his natural way of speaking.

She rose from her chair, saying, "I hope I haven't called at an inconvenient time?"

"Well, you're lucky to find me." He motioned with his hand that she should again be seated. Then he sat down behind his desk, saying, "What can I do for you?"

"Oh, nothing in particular, Mr. Bailey. I just called to ask if you have an estimate out yet for the damage done to your showhouse."

"No; it's too short a time. My accountant has already started his Christmas holiday and there won't be anything doing here until the New Year. I'll send the damage to your husband then."

"That is really the point I came to make: I would prefer that you send the bill and any future correspondence to me."

He narrowed his eyes at her as he said slowly, "You're comin' down hard on him, aren't you?"

"What do you mean?"

"Just what I say. If I'm to go by what you said the other night, you're removing him to London."

Her face became stiff as she said, "On that occasion I explained that I . . . we have many concerns in the South."

"And all of them under your name?"

Her face now slipped into a tight smile as she said, "You're a very discerning man, Mr. Bailey."

His voice was somewhat grim as he replied, "It wouldn't take a very discerning man to realise who wears the pants in your household, ma'am."

190

"That's what I like about you, Mr. Bailey, you don't mince words. You are what you are and you're not ashamed of it. You'll go places in the end; that is, if you don't remain in the North. There are no real openings for men of your calibre here."

"You don't say!" That return was cheap, but for the moment he couldn't find words with which to combat this woman. Yet he felt he already knew a number of things about her and one in particular he was refuting in his mind, while at the same time telling himself he was no fool where women were concerned.

She had her hand on the side of the desk now. It was long and slim and the only ring on it was her wedding ring. She had apparently noticed the direction of his gaze for she lifted her hand and, holding it before her face, she looked at it; and then twisting the ring around, she said quietly, "There should be a law passed to delete from the wedding ceremony this band of bondage."

He gave a short laugh now as he said, "You look on it as a bondage, Mrs. Brown? Well, I think that can work both ways. But there's no need for anybody to put up with bondage these days, either man or woman; there's always the divorce courts."

"Yes; yes, of course. You've explained it."

"How d'you know that?" The muscles of his jaws were tight now as he stared at her.

"Oh, one moves around here and there, little bits of gossip you know. Most women's entertainment in life is made up of gossip. I know quite a bit about you, Mr. Bailey. I know that you are an ambitious man. And that you'll be hard put to find work once this estate's finished. Money is very tight in the North. I don't have to point that out to you and I can't see the corporation stepping in. As for finance companies, apart from the present one, once your business is finished they'll be moving, too. So I can't see where your next, at least substantial, job is coming from."

He was on his feet now. However, she didn't move, but she looked up at him where he was standing at the side of the desk, and her voice changed and her manner seemed to melt as she said, "Believe me, Mr. Bailey, I am not trying to be nasty or rub it in. But, honestly, I think you, with your special kind of drive, are wasted here in this part of the country. And, quite candidly, the main object of my being here today is to offer you better prospects in one of my companies in the South."

He felt his jaw dropping just the slightest and he snapped it closed before asking quietly, "And does Mr. Brown agree to your suggestion?"

She didn't answer; but rising slowly, she hitched the shoulders of

191

her mink coat around her neck, turned up the collar at the back, wrapped the wide fronts of the coat over her slim body; then, looking directly at him, she said, "I am divorcing Mr. Brown on the grounds of infidelity."

This time he couldn't restrain his jaw from dropping. His mind was yelling at him, he hadn't been wrong. My God, no, he hadn't. What lengths some women would go to. There was one thing he was sure of now, he was really sorry for Brown. Yes, he was.

What he said now definitely surprised her. His voice had a note of enquiry in it; it was low and his words were slightly spaced. "Are all business concerns in your name?" He watched her pencilled eyebrows move upwards. She looked slightly to the side; then she smiled and said, "There speaks the businessman. Yes; yes, Mr. Bailey, they're all in my name, every one."

"Will he get a share?"

Her gaze was even wider now. There was a smile on her face.

"Very little. I've already told him if he takes me to court he will get less than I will allow him in redundancy pay. After all, he's only been a mouthpiece/manager; I have seen to the businesses from the back-room, so to speak."

"You know something, Mrs. Brown?" His voice was still and quiet.

Her face was bright and her lips apart in a smile when, looking at him straight in the face, she said, "No, Mr. Bailey. You tell me."

Going to the door now, he opened it; then turning to her, he said, "I'm damned sorry for your husband. I've always hated his guts, but I can understand his actions now, for, living with you, he had to take it out on somebody. And let me tell you, Mrs. Brown, I'm wide awake to what you're offering me, and if you were the last woman in the world I wouldn't touch you with a barge pole.... Have a happy Christmas."

When he had first seen her he had admired her pale alabaster-type skin, but now her whole face was scarlet, her eyes were blazing.

"How dare you!"

"I dare, Mrs. Brown, because I'm a man who's had a number of women through his hands, so to speak. Like siftin' for gold dust, you know. And at last I've found a nugget. But my experience has taught me to recognise dross when I see it. One last word, Mrs. Brown, if you go through with that divorce, you'll never get another puppet like the one you've got now."

He watched her march to the car; and it seemed she couldn't even have taken her seat before it swung round, just missed a piece of heavy machinery, and sped out of the gates.

Sitting down once more at his desk, he held his head in his hands. He couldn't believe it. But yes, he could. And Brown. My God! What he must have gone through. No wonder he was the bastard he was. Wait till he told Fiona. . . . Should he tell her? No; no, he wouldn't, not now anyway. Sometime in the future. He'd make a big laugh over it.

But Madam Brown was right about one thing: when this big job finished there wouldn't be a similar one on his doorstep. That would mean sacking men. But sufficient unto the day the evil thereof, for he had enough on his plate to worry about at the moment. Fiona was his main concern.

But that woman! If she had stripped off before him she couldn't have made the offer more clear. And to him, with his Liverpudlian voice and as brash as they came, because he knew himself. Oh, aye, he knew himself, both inside and out. And he had no desire to change. He'd had a little experience of altering his image this morning, and that had been too much like hard work.

23

CHRISTMAS DAY STARTED AT SIX O'CLOCK, AT LEAST FOR THE CHILDREN. THERE was no knocking, or "May I come in?" but a small avalanche descended on the bed. Apart from carrying things, Mark was wheeling a bicycle that he had found outside his bedroom door; Katie had a pair of ballet shoes hanging around her neck, a fur hat on her head, one hand in a fur muff, and both arms supporting numerous gifts; Willie was pushing a smaller bicycle, and over its handlebars was draped a space suit, and across its seat lay a large puppet; Mamie came in attired in an imitation fur coat and hat, nursing a doll on each arm. And bedlam came second best in the source of noise pervading the room for the next hour, until at last, shouting above the mêlée, Bill cried, "Get this clutter back to the playroom! Your mother wants a cup of tea."

"I can make it, Dad."

A silence came on the room, and they all looked at Willie's flushed face, and when he, tossing himself from side to side, muttered, "Well, 'cos you are in a way," Bill said, "Yes, I am in a way, and it sounds ... well, good coming from you."

"Better than Mr. Bill?"

"Yes, Willie, better than Mr. Bill."

"What's the matter, Mam?" Willie was addressing his mother now. "You're going to howl."

194

"No, I'm not." Fiona's voice was definite. "Howl? Why should I howl? But I'll tell you what, Willie, I think that's the best Christmas box I've had."

"You haven't had ours yet. They're downstairs around the tree. I spent a lot on yours."

"Did you Willie? Well, I'm sure I'll love it. But what I want most at the moment is that cup of tea, so away you go and make it, and take Mamie with you."

The other two didn't follow Willie, but they stood rather sheepishly looking at Bill, then with a rush Katie threw her arms about his waist muttering, "Dad. Dad." But as Bill bent to kiss her Mark grabbed her arm crying, "Come on, pick up your things," and when surprisingly she obeyed him without any comment and they were both scrambling from the room, Mark, who was now pushing his bike, turned and grinning at Bill said, "Be seeing you . . . Dad." Bill didn't laugh, but he stood by the side of the bed and he nipped on his lip as he asked her, "Did you put them up to that?"

"*No, no. Honest.* I never dreamt of it."

"Well, now I feel sort of established. And I can tell you this, I'll never have a better Christmas box, no matter how long I live. Happy Christmas, love." And he bent and kissed her gently on the lips.

And that was the beginning of a long day. There was the usual business of preparing dinner, and there were nine sitting down at the table, for Nell and Mr. and Mrs. Paget had joined them. After the meal, which went off with a great deal of laughter and jollity, especially reading out the riddles from the crackers, there was the usual chore of washing up. And this was done by Bill, Mark, and Mr. Paget, while Katie, Willie, and Mamie contented themselves in the playroom, thus leaving Fiona in the sitting room with Mrs. Paget and Nell.

It was when the conversation touched on Fiona going into hospital that Nell, nudging her mother-in-law, said, "Tell Fiona about the light."

"Oh no; no . . . really!"

"Oh, Mam, go on." Then turning to Fiona, Nell added, "She never swears, never. It's funny, I've never heard her, not once. Here, take another sip of your port, Mam, and tell her. Go on."

Mrs. Paget sipped her port, giggled, then said, "Well, Fiona, you know about this light they're using for internal examinations, well, there I was in the theatre lying face down on the operating table and Mr. Corbit, the specialist, was talking to me . . . as they do you know, not expecting any answers. 'Now I am going to insert this light, Mrs.

Paget,' he said. 'It won't hurt; it will just enable me to look around. . . . Just relax now. That's it, just relax.'

"Well, there was a sister and a nurse present and a young doctor, and as the specialist pushed this thing up"—she giggled again—"he told them what he was looking for." She took another sip of the port before going on. "You know, as I said, he said it didn't hurt, well, it didn't, not at first, it was just uncomfortable, but of a sudden he gave it a push and cried out, 'Ah! that's it. It's all lit up!' As you can imagine I let out a good imitation of a scream, but at the same time my mind, jumping back to the Review of the Royal Navy, at Plymouth, I think it was, oh, many years ago, when a BBC announcer was describing the lights going up on the ships. He got excited and he said—" She almost choked now and she looked from one to the other and spluttered as she ended, 'The whole bloody fleet's lit up!' Oh, that poor fella. He got the sack, I think because you know, language such as that was unheard of on the BBC in those days."

Nell and Fiona were both laughing with her now as she went on. "You see it was because I thought about this that I began to shake, and the specialist, he pulled the thing out quick because he must have imagined I was having a fit or something. And when the nurses turned me over, there I was, my face running with tears, and when he said, 'You all right, Mrs. Paget?' What do you think I said? And I hadn't had any"—she lifted her glass—"port that day. But I said, 'The whole bloody fleet's lit up!' Then, you wouldn't believe it, but he threw his head back, put his arm around me, and he roared. You see, he was in his sixties and knew what I was laughing about, but the others didn't. And when he said, 'That was a night, wasn't it, when the whole bloody fleet was lit up,' you should have seen their faces. Oh, dear, dear! It's many a year since I've laughed like that. I shouldn't, I really shouldn't drink port."

They had their heads together now and the tears were running freely down their faces, and Fiona thought how strange it was that you never really knew people, for who would imagine this refined and delicate-looking woman coming out with a thing like that. She was so genteel.

Oh, it was a nice Christmas Day. If only there wasn't tomorrow.

It was Willie's turn to keep them amused, and he did at teatime and later on when there were charades. And the surprise of the evening, even to Bill and Fiona, was the appearance of Laurel and Hardy. Willie, of course, was Laurel, and Mark a pillow-stuffed

Hardy. And their acting and the patter, which must have been well rehearsed, caused them all to laugh so much that when Fiona bent over double Bill bent, too, and whispered, "You all right?" And partly straightening up, she gasped, "Never better, Bill. Never better. The whole bloody fleet's lit up."

"What? The body's flattened up? What d'you mean?"

"Oh, Bill, be quiet. I'll tell you later."

"Now, give over; you'll make yourself ill."

Later, when Mr. and Mrs. Paget said their goodnights, they both confirmed they had never had such a happy Christmas Day that they could remember. Nell didn't say anything; she just kissed Fiona, looked at Bill, then punched him in the chest and went out.

And Katie expressed the thoughts of them all; when Fiona went to kiss her goodnight, she put her arms around her mother's neck and said, "It's been a lovely, lovely day, Mam. Thank you."

It was all too much.

Like a child who had had too much excitement, she sat on the edge of her bed as she tried in vain to prevent herself from crying; but by the time Bill entered the room she had not only dried her eyes but creamed her face and was in bed awaiting him.

For a time they lay quiet, resting in each other's arms; then her voice low, she said, "Bill, I want to talk."

"Look, love, you've had a long day. Won't it keep?"

"No; there won't be any time tomorrow, no privacy."

"Well, what d'you want to say, love?"

"I'm frightened, Bill."

"So am I, love. But really, there's not all that to be frightened of . . . or is there? Are you keepin' something back?"

"Yes. Yes, I've been keeping something back. I think I've got cancer."

The room was quiet, the house was quiet, the world was quiet.

"Did he tell you that?"

"Not exactly. When I asked him point-blank, he said, 'It could be.'"

"Look. Look here." He pressed himself from her, raised his face from the pillow, and, looking down into her eyes, said, "All right, let's say it's the worst, but they work miracles. Every day they're working miracles."

"Bill, I've got to say this. If . . . if it was my breasts, I . . . I would hate it, but I would likely face it; but if it's inside and what the consequences are after, I don't think I'm up to taking it."

"Now look here, you're up to takin' . . ."

"Bill, please don't raise your voice."

"I'm not raisin' me voice, but you're scarin' the bloody wits out of me, woman."

"Well, you asked me to tell you the truth, and I don't want it to come as a shock to you after. It's better to know now I think. And so, I've thought things out and I've ... I've talked to Nell. If anything happens ..."

"Shut up, will you."

"I won't shut up, Bill. Listen to me, please. If anything happens she'll see to the children, she's promised me. And she's a good woman, still young, so kind and nice. ..."

"God Almighty!" He lay back from her, put his hands above his head, and gripped the back of the bedhead. "I can't believe this. I just can't believe this. You've got it into your head if anything happens to you I'd jump at Nell."

"No, not that way."

"Not that way, be damned! Look, I haven't convinced you, all these months I haven't convinced you, you're the only one in me life. The only one I ever want in me life and nobody's ever going to take your place but I'll tell you something, that's the second offer I've had in the last two days."

"What do you mean, the second offer?"

"Well, now, Mrs. Brown called at the works. She offered me a job in London looking after her affairs or some such. And then she told me she's divorcing him. I tell you, if she had stripped off naked and done a belly dance she couldn't have been more invitin'."

The bed started to shake. "Oh, Bill, Bill, stop it, stop it. I don't believe a word of it. Mrs. Brown!"

He now pulled her round to him, his nose almost touching hers. He said, "I'm serious."

"You are?" There was amazement in her voice.

"Yes. She told me openly that he's just a kind of manager like he was in the brewery, as Sir Kingdom said. She's the power behind the scenes; she's the queen in that setup, all right. He isn't even a regent, or consort; he's been a despised individual right from the beginnin'. And you know I can understand the man now, and as I told her, I told her to her face, I feel sorry for him. And you know what else I told her, Mrs. Bailey?"

"No, Bill. What did you tell her?" Her voice was quiet.

"I told her that I had found a nugget, that's the word I used, and I was quick to detect imitations or something like that, and that if she was the last woman on God's earth I wouldn't touch her with a barge

198

pole. Now those are the very words I did use. I said straight to her face, 'I wouldn't touch you with a barge pole.'"

"Oh, Bill, you didn't."

"I did, woman, I did."

There was a puzzled note in her voice now as she said, "But that's only the third time you've seen her, isn't it?"

"Yes, only the third time."

"And you were struck with her at first, weren't you?"

"Struck? No, woman, not struck in that way. I saw that she was class. And I remember pointing out to you that you had stepped down to take me, but she had dropped a great deal farther to take him. But now I take all that back, for what I saw the other day was a cold, ruthless, vindictive bitch. And I take back an' all what I said about him, because I do pity him. She must have treated him like a serf. And no wonder the lad has turned out to be like he is. So there you have it, Mrs. B. Which one am I going to take after your demise?"

"Bill, don't look like that. I'm sorry, but I ... I love ... I love you so much, and I can't bear to think of you being lonely, because the children won't fill your life."

"I'm not goin' to be lonely; you're going to have the operation, and no matter what it is, you're going to get over it. Even if you have to go through hell and high water, you're going to get over it. D'you hear me?"

"Yes, Bill."

"Now go to sleep. Come on, snuggle up and go to sleep. Because this has got to last me for a week or ten days, for that's all you'll be there."

"Put out the light, dear," she said. And he put out the light.

24

SHE WAS IN AT ELEVEN O'CLOCK AND HE STAYED WITH HER TILL THREE, THEN returned home, promising to bring the children.

When he entered the house, it was Mamie who came running towards him, sobbing, "Mammy B.'s gone on holiday."

He picked her up, saying, "No; no, she hasn't gone on holiday. She's got a pain in her tummy and the doctor's going to put it right."

Both he and Fiona had decided that in the future the child must be told the truth, at least as near as possible. This business about her mother and father and brother going on holiday meant that they were never coming back. Although she no longer mentioned her parents or brother, the fear of loss through the word *holiday* had seemingly taken a permanent place in her mind.

"Look, I've just come from your Mammy B., and I'm going to take you and Mark and Katie and Willie to see her as soon as I have some tea. You'll let me have some tea, won't you?"

"Yes, Uncle Bill. And we're going to see Mammy B.?"

"Sure, sure as life, cross my heart." He didn't add, "Hope to die." Nell, coming from the kitchen, said, "All settled in?"

"Yes, Nell, and very calm and composed."

"Good."

"What time are we going?"

"Well, as I've just said to this one here"—he humped Mamie farther up into his arms—"I'd like some tea; I've not had a bite since this morning."

"No lunch?"

He smiled now, saying, "No. And the dinner they brought her would have satisfied a navvy. She picked over it just to please them. She wanted me to finish it, but I told her I wasn't doing any of her dirty work; if those dishes had gone out empty they'd have wondered why she was in there. Where are the others?"

"Up in the playroom. They've been at sixes and sevens all the time. Open war between Katie and Willie. I've suggested that they all write letters to their mother and give them to her when they go in."

"Good idea."

He put the child down on the floor now, and tapped her bottom, saying, "Go upstairs and tell the others they've got to be ready by five o'clock."

In the kitchen Nell said, "I've got a combination of hash-cum-shepherd's pie in the oven. Would you like that or some cold bits?"

"I think I'll have the hash. And if you don't mind, I'd like you to come with them and bring them back. I'll order a taxi; they'll enjoy the change."

"I don't think they'd enjoy the Royal Coach today."

"No, perhaps you're right." He went and stood by the stove and, leaning his elbow against the wall, he rested his head on his hand as he said, "What am I going to do, Nell?"

"Well, like they say on the old flicks, keep a stiff upper lip."

"I'm serious."

"I know you are."

"If anything happens to her I'll go mad."

"No, you won't. You'll face up to it; you have four bairns to look after."

"Damn the bairns! Damn everything! Why should this happen?"

"Don't you bawl at me, Bill; I'm not Fiona."

"Oh, Nell, I'm sorry, but you know what I mean."

"I know what you mean, and I know how you feel, and I know how I feel at this minute. I want to sit down and howl my eyes out. Since you left the house this morning I don't know how I've kept a dry face, because, let me tell you, it's only her friendship that's kept me going over the past months. If I'd been on my own I know I would have taken a shortcut out, because when you feel less than dust there's not much lower you can go. In a way I love her as much as you do. And you know something? I'm going to tell you this, likely she's put it to

201

you, too. She's got it all planned out if anything should happen to her that I'll see to the bairns. Well, I'll promise to do that at least for a time, but as regards seeing to you, that's a different kettle of fish, because Bill, I couldn't put up with you, not your type of man. And you couldn't put up with me, 'cos I'm not your type of woman. So whatever she said to you, you can make your mind at rest, there'll be no pressure from this end."

His body suddenly began to shake. He turned his face to the wall and bumped his brow twice against it. Then, turning and looking at her, his eyes moist, he said, "Aw, Nell, that's done me the world of good. Yes, she had it all planned on my side an' all. Anyway, now we know where we stand, give me that stew-cum-shepherd's pie. Oh, now look, don't start cryin' 'cos I might be tempted to comfort you again. And what would happen if the two moles appeared at the door. Fiona would never believe it the second time."

They were both laughing now, and Nell said, "When she comes out and I describe these last few minutes to her she'll die."

The last two words brought them to silence until Nell had placed a steaming plate before him, and then she said, "The English language has got all twisted up, hasn't it?"

"It has, Nell, it has."

The night staff had taken over before he left the room. They held each other closely and the last words he said to her were, "See you tomorrow about three."

"Yes, dear, see you tomorrow about three. I love you, Bill."

"I'm quite fond of you an' all, Mrs. B." He went out quietly, and she lay staring up at the shaded light above her head. And when the night nurse came in and said, "Would you like something to make you sleep?" her reply was eager: "Oh yes, please, yes."

Everyone was so kind, but then she told herself they were always kind to people going on a holiday from which they might not return.

When Bill reached home he saw there was a light still on in the kitchen and not in the sitting room, so instead of letting himself in the front door he went in the back. And on entering he was surprised to see Bert Ormesby standing at one side of the table and Nell at the other. And Bert began straightaway in a slight fluster, "I . . . I just dropped in to see how . . . how the missis was and everything like."

"Oh, thanks, Bert. Sit down then, sit down."

"No, I was just about to be off."

"How was she when you left?" This was from Nell. And he answered her, saying, "Apparently calm, you know, on top."

"What time will it happen the morrow?"

He looked at Bert again, saying, "She goes down at half-past nine and it all depends on how long she'll be there as to when she comes round. Would you like a drink?"

"No thanks, boss."

"Oh, aye, I forgot, man." He smiled weakly. "I don't know where I am."

Bill took off his outdoor things, and they all stood in awkward silence for a moment until Bert said, "Well, I'll be off then." And he nodded at Bill. "Don't worry about things back there on the site; I'll pop in now and again over the holiday. Goodnight then. Goodnight, Mrs."—he paused on the name—"Paget." And Nell said, "Goodnight, Mr. Ormesby."

At the door Bill suddenly said, "There was no car outside. Did you walk?"

"Oh, aye, it's only a couple of miles. I often have a brisk walk at night; it helps me to sleep. Goodnight then."

"Goodnight, Bert."

He closed the door and looked at Nell who was coming in from the hall shrugging her arms into her coat, and he said offhandedly, "Very nice of him, don't you think?"

"Yes. He seems a good fellow, thoughtful."

"Yes; yes, he is. He's a good bloke." Then with a quirk to his lips he added, "He wouldn't bawl at you."

"Bill!"

"Aye, Nell; there's many a true word spoke in a joke, they say."

"Well, I don't think this is the time for jokes."

"Don't put me in me place, Nell, unless you want me to bawl."

"I'm sorry, Bill; we're both on edge. I'll be off. Try to get some sleep. Goodnight."

"Goodnight, Nell."

He now went into the sitting room and to the drinks' cabinet and poured himself out a stiff glass of whiskey. But he didn't drink it there, he carried it up to the bedroom, laid it on the side table, got undressed, then he went out of the room and, gently opening Mark's and Katie's bedroom doors, he glanced in. The night-light in Katie's room showed the two girls fast asleep. But in Mark's room, although his bed was illuminated only by the light from the landing, he had the suspicion that the boy, although snuggled down under the clothes, was far from asleep. He did not investigate further, however;

203

he just gently closed the door, then went back into his own room; but before getting into bed he threw off the whiskey at one go. It was now eleven o'clock.

At half past one he was sitting wide-eyed propped up against the headboard. The whiskey had had no soporific effect on him whatsoever, apparently just the opposite, for he had never felt more wide awake nor his head more clear. Nor could he remember thinking along the lines on which his thoughts had travelled over the past two hours or so. When had he ever before felt emotion the like of which was filling him at this time? And he questioned it.

Before he had met up with Fiona his life had seemed free and easy. He couldn't recall any real worries except those connected with the job, and then they weren't in the same league as the worries that were besetting him at the present time. And all this had come about through falling in love. And what was love after all? Some people wrote songs about it; others wrote poetry extolling it; books by the millions were written about it; films were made about it. But from whatever quarter it came, as he saw it now, it was wrongly represented. Because what did it consist of? What was it made up of? Anxiety. Worry. Pain. Fear. Dread. Yes, dread. Dread of losing all that anxiety, worry, pain, and fear. For what would his life be like without it?

He wished he could go back to just before the time he first saw Fiona in the newsagent's shop. *He did. He did.* . . . No, he didn't. He'd have to stop thinking along these lines or he'd go round the bend. He'd go down and have another drink. No, he wouldn't. He put his hand out and gently switched on the radio. There was always somebody talking in the middle of the night. But what he heard now was someone singing in low deep melancholy tones. The voice appeared for the moment to be his own as it sang:

> Do not go, Do not go, my love, from me,
> For no blankets can warm my frozen heart.
> Do not go, Do not go, my love, from me,
> For the years ahead are stark.

He almost brought the radio from the bed table, so quick did his hand switch it off. Then with a heave he slid down the bed, turned on his side, pulled the clothes almost over his head, and growled, "Go to sleep, goddamn you! Go to sleep."

He had been waiting in the hospital from eleven o'clock, but it was half past twelve before she was wheeled out of the operating room. It

204

was twenty minutes later when he confronted Mr. Morgan and the surgeon told him the result of the operation.

He had sat for hours by her side, during which time the nurses had popped into the room and popped out again. At one point the sister came and said, "Would you mind waiting outside?"

When he stood outside the door he was amazed to hear the sister saying, "Come along, Mrs. Bailey, come along. That's a good girl." He heard a groan and a sound of vomiting. He closed his eyes tightly but did not move away from the door. When eventually the sister and the nurse appeared, the sister smiled at him and said, "I'm afraid you'll have a long wait. We've made her comfortable, but she'll sleep for some time yet."

"I won't be in the way if I sit with her?"

"No; no, not at all, Mr. Bailey. But it could be some hours yet before she revives completely. Then, I must warn you, she'll be in some pain. You could go home and get some rest and I'm sure in the morning she'll be . . ."

"If it's all the same to you I'd rather stay."

It was near eleven o'clock. The whole ward was quiet: there was no rattle of crockery from the kitchen, no buzzing up and down the corridor. He was sitting in an armchair near the bedhead. He had closed his eyes and when his head nodded forward he realised he had almost fallen asleep. He yawned and turned his head and looked towards the figure in the bed. Her eyes were open. She was staring at him. The jerk he gave not only pushed the armchair back and caused it to squeak on the wooden floor, but his hands on the side of the mattress bounced it gently, and the movement caused Fiona to close her eyes.

"Love." He was bending over her. "It's adhesions."

"What?"

"It's all right. It's only adhesions."

"What . . . what d'you mean, adhesions?"

"That's what the mass was, the dark mass, nothing else, just a bundle of adhesions sticking your guts together."

"Oh, Bill. Bill." She screwed her eyes up tight, opened her mouth wide, then again muttered, "Oh, Bill. Bill . . . Adhesions?"

"Aye. That's what it's all about. Never heard the word before, but it sounds wonderful. How're you feelin', love?"

She looked at him tenderly. A smile spread across her face, then she answered simply, "All cut up."

He put his hand across his mouth to still the sound and stood away

205

from the bed so his shaking body wouldn't again disturb the mattress.

When the spasm passed he sat looking down at her. His face was almost solemn now. This is what love was about, too: besides the anxiety, the worry, the pain, and the fear, there was relief, and joy, and hope. But, by God, he wouldn't like to go through these past few days again. And what he said now was characteristic of the Bill she knew.

"You've got no idea what I've been through these last few days, lass, so never do this to me again. I couldn't stand it. My God, no!" Then he was a little surprised to see her hands hovering over the counterpane above where her stomach was. And her face was almost contorted when she said, "Bill. Oh, please Bill, don't make me laugh, it's, it's painful."

For the first time he really couldn't see that he had said anything funny. In fact, he had been very serious, very serious indeed: there was nothing funny about what he had gone through, but he had to concede that Fiona's sense of humour was at times a little off key, especially as now when she was getting over the effects of the anaesthetic, and this was proved when next she said, "Oh, Bill Bailey, you are funny. One day you'll be the death of me. . . . Oh, oh!"

"Don't, love. Don't; you'll snap your stitches."

PART

II

Bill Bailey's Lot

25

"GET UP THOSE STAIRS."

"Mam! Mam!"

"Don't 'Ma'am,' me. Get up with you."

"It . . . it was only a little swear, Mam, it wasn't a big one."

"Yes, it was a little one, but one of the worst little ones."

"*Oh, Mam.* Don't smack me. *You're hurting my legs.*"

"That's nothing to what you're going to get. Get in that room there!"

Fiona pushed Willie into his room, and when he jumped onto the side of the bed and sat on his hands, she said, "Get your things off."

"I . . . I haven't had my . . . tea, Mam."

"And you're not going to get any tea; you're going to bed."

"Oh, Mam. Mam, I'll not say it again."

"No, I can assure you you won't say it again." She now grabbed her son by the shoulder and, twisting him round, pulled off his coat and dragged his pullover over his head, then she said, "So do you want me to take your trousers off or are you going to?"

"Oh, Mam." The tears now were washing Willie's face. "I'll . . . I'll never say it again. I . . . I promise. It was only once."

"It wasn't once. Don't lie. I heard you at least three times using the same word."

"Well, it was because he used it at me. He . . . he said he wanted to come and see our house and . . . and he wanted to see inside. And I . . . I knew you wouldn't like him to come in."

"Why wouldn't I like him to come in?"

Willie's head now swung from side to side as he tried to explain.

"Well, 'cos . . . 'cos he's from Bog's End and . . . he's the one I made you laugh about when . . . our school won and . . . and the nun ran him off the field 'cos he was tearing into everybody."

"Get your trousers off."

"Oh, Mam. Are you going to tan me?"

"No, I'm not going to tan you."

Fiona now stood stiffly, watching her son divest himself quickly of his trousers and his pants and then struggle into his pyjamas. This done, she said, "Get into bed."

"Mam . . . I'm hungry. I . . . I didn't eat much of the school dinner. I didn't like it."

"That's your fault. Get into bed."

Fiona now saw the look she knew only too well come over her son's face; his nostrils twitched, his lips came tightly together. And when he said in a small voice, "I'll tell Mr. Bi—Dad when he comes in. He'll give me my tea," her own face stretched and her hand began to rise, but he saw the warning sign too late, for as he was about to scramble into bed, her hand caught him none too gently across the buttocks, which brought a yell from him: "Now I will! I'll tell him. And . . . he won't hit me for saying a four-letter word."

"Won't he just! He'll wipe the floor with you if he hears just one whisper of a four-letter word."

The tears were sniffed loudly. He rubbed the back of his hand across the bottom of his nose as he cried, "There's lots of four-letter words, like like and love, and I don't like you and I don't love you, and I'm going to make myself die now and you'll be sorry."

As she straightened the cover on the bed Fiona said, in a much cooler voice now, "I don't think I will because I just do not want anything to do with boys who use filthy words." She walked towards the door where she turned and, pointing a stiff finger toward him, said, "And don't you dare get out of that bed until I tell you."

On the landing she stood and drew in a long, slow breath. It was odd, she thought, how her four children, including Mamie, would all revert to the name of Mr. Bill when they wanted him to champion them. It was only a few months since they had started calling him Dad, and she could still picture his delight and the emotion their acceptance of him as their father had evoked.

210

She was passing the landing window when she caught sight of her husband. He was standing on the drive and there, right in the middle of the daffodil border, stood the awful boy who had caused all the trouble.

Unaware of "the trouble caused by the awful boy," Bill looked at him and demanded, "What were you going to do with that brick?"

"Nowt."

"Standing opposite a window, swinging a brick in your hand, and you were goin' to do nowt with it? You were goin' to throw it through the window, weren't you?"

"Aye, I was. And I will an' all."

"Well, you try it on, laddie, and I can tell you this for nowt, you'll beat the brick to that window."

"Oh aye? Well, you'd better not lay a finger on me, mister, else me da'll wallop you. He's a big fella, six foot three he is."

"Oh aye? So he's a big fella, six foot three; but you're not a very big fella are you, and you're ruining the daffodils. Come out of that!" And as his voice rose his hand went out and grabbed the diminutive figure and before the boy knew what was happening to him he left the ground and landed on the drive at Bill's feet. And still with his hold on the boy's shoulder, Bill said, "What's your name? Come on'; you've had enough jaw up till now. What's your name? If you don't tell me I'll yank you along to the police station."

"I've done nowt."

"Haven't you? You're trespassing and you were about to throw a brick through my window. That's enough to put you along the line for some time."

"Sammy Love."

"*Sammy Love?* That's a gentle name for the likes of you. Well, Sammy Love, what you doin' here in my garden?"

"Settin' Willie home. Are you his da?"

"Whose da?"

"Willie's?"

"Yes; yes, you can say I'm his dad."

"Well—" The boy attempted to shrug himself free from Bill's hold, saying, "Leave loose of me shoulder, mister; you'll crumple me jacket, then I'll get me brains knocked out when I get home if it's messed up. An' yer hands are mucky."

Bill slowly released his hold on the boy's jacket, then looked him up and down, remarking to himself that he was decently put on. But his rig-out certainly didn't match his attitude or his tongue, both would have been more fitted to those of a ragamuffin.

211

"Well, go on, tell me, what are you doing here? All right. You set Willie home, but why the brick business?"

"Well—" The small figure kicked at a broken daffodil lying on the path, one of the victims of his boots, before turning and looking at Bill and saying, "He wouldn't take me into his house. I just wanted to see like what it was, I mean, inside. He said his mam wouldn't like me to go in. So I told him what I thought about his mam."

"You did?"

"Aye, I did. And we had an up an' downer and she came out and she went on and she lost her hair yellin' at me and him, an' she yanked him inside. She's a starchy bitch."

"Careful! Careful!"

"Well, she is. As me da says, our old girl's not much good but there's worse, and she's worse."

Bill curbed the urge to take his hand and swipe the little beggar back into the middle of the daffodil border. But then he saw something that stopped him: the boy's chin started to knobble; his lips were drawn in between his teeth, his eyelids were blinking rapidly. And then he turned, not only his head, but his whole body away and kicked at the offending daffodil once more. "Have you any brothers or sisters?" Bill asked quietly.

"No, none."

"What . . . what does your father do?"

"Nowt. He's on the dole."

"Does your mother go out to work?"

The face came round to him, the look in the eyes almost fierce now as the boy said, "Not anymore. She did off. She's always doin' off." Another kick at the daffodil and a mutter now as he ended, "But she comes back. She always comes back. Me da says, wait long enough an' she'll come back. An' she always does, she always comes back."

He was nodding his head now as if reassuring himself. But when Bill's hand came swiftly out to catch at his, he tugged away from him, saying, "I've done nowt. I didn't throw it. I'm not goin' to any police station."

"Shut up! Whose talkin' about police stations. You wanted to come inside, didn't you, and see what it was like? Well, come on."

The boy swayed back on his heel and looked up at Bill and said, "Eeh, no. She'll pepper me if I go in there. She told me I hadn't come back here anymore, else what she would do."

"What did you do to make her say that? Did you hit Willie?"

"No; no, I didn't. It was the language I suppose. That's what she said, using bad language."

"Did you use bad language?"

"No, I only said, f...."

Bill turned his head sharply away; his eyes closed for a moment. But when he again looked at the boy and spoke his voice was low and it conveyed horror to his small companion as he said slowly, "No wonder she nearly lost her hair. That's a very, very bad word. And her son, I mean our son, never uses words like that."

"Well, he did. He shouted it back at me, he yelled it. That's what brought her out."

Bill's shoulder heaved with the breath he drew in. Aye, it would bring her out if Willie came out with that particular four-letter word. Oh, my! But anyway, he had asked the youngster in and in he must come, and for more reasons than one.

"Well, let's go and face the music," he said.

The boy said nothing more but kept pace with Bill at a run as he strode up the drive, round the side of the house, and into the kitchen.

Fiona turned from the stove, her mouth in a slight gape, but the mouths of Mark, Katie, and Mamie were wide open. Mr. Bill, or Dad, as he was, had brought in that boy who was the cause of Willie being walloped. He was the one that used language; they had all heard the language, and both Mark and Katie had been warned about what would happen to them if they ever said such a word. As for Mamie, she wasn't sure of what she had heard, and she wasn't very interested in words in any case. But she was interested in Willie, and she had just stopped crying because he had been sent to bed. And Mammy B. had warned her that she'd be sent to bed, too, if she didn't stop her howling. So they all gaped at the boy their dad was holding by the hand.

"Hello, hello, Mrs. B." Bill looked towards Fiona, and what she said, and with emphasis and meaning, was, *"Bill!"*

"Yes, Mrs. B?"

"Bill!"

"Yes? I heard you." He looked down at the culprit, saying, "That's my name ... Bill."

The boy made no reply. He did not even look at him; his eyes were fixed on the tall young woman who was staring at him.

"You're lucky, you know"—Bill now nodded towards Fiona—"he intended to put a brick through your window. Didn't you?" Again he looked down at the boy. And now the boy, glancing sideways at him, gave him what could be called a deprecating look and kept his silence.

"Anyway, all he wanted was to see inside your house, Mrs. B, 'cos it's such a nice house. He asked Willie if he would bring him in but apparently Willie said he didn't think you would like him to. That isn't true, is it? You'd like him to see your house, wouldn't you, Mrs. B?"

Fiona turned towards the stove. Her shoulders were slightly hunched and Bill, allowing his gaze to drop to Mark, conveyed by his look a need for cooperation. And in answer Mark gave him a little grin.

Bill was now divesting himself of his coat, but as he did so he looked towards the boy again, saying, "Sit down," and indicated the chair by a motion of his head.

"Don't wanna."

For the second time in their short acquaintance Samuel Love was picked up by the collar, and when his bottom hit the hard kitchen chair with a resounding smack he lay back against the rails and gasped. Then Bill's attention sprang on Katie, saying, "And don't you dare move away along that table."

Her face now puckering itself into primness, Katie said, "I wasn't moving along. Anyway, I've finished my tea; I was just going to get up."

"Well, you can leave your departure for a little longer. Sit where you are; he hasn't got fleas. Well, he doesn't look as if he has. . . . Have you got fleas?"

"No, I 'aven't got fleas." The voice was indignant, and to it was now added, "I get a bath every Friday. Me da sees to it, he stays in. . . . Fleas!" The word held indignation. "And I 'aven't no dickies in me head neither, or nits."

Bill turned away; his Adam's apple was jerking quickly in his neck. He made his way towards the sink where Fiona was standing and, pressing his shoulder to hers, he looked down into the soapy water as he muttered, "Go easy on him, love, he puts me in mind of somebody you know, but I'll tell you more about him later."

But when she showed no sign of complying with his mood he played on the mother instinct. Taking his finger and whirling it around the suds, he muttered, "He's from Bog's End. Apparently his mother goes off and leaves him. The fact that Willie has a mother and lives in a nice house has drawn him like a magnet. Besides, from what Willie has told us about him . . . well, you know he made us laugh, but he cottoned on to him an' all. Come on, lass, give him some tea."

"*What!*" The word was hissed. "If you had heard him, *the language.*"

"Oh aye, I know all about it. But down that quarter it's just like God bless you."

"Oh, be quiet!"

"Dad." Mark's head was pushed between them and they both looked at him as he whispered, "I . . . I think he's crying."

They turned and looked at the small figure sitting on the kitchen chair, head bowed, and as Bill took a step towards him the head came up and the voice bawled at him, "I ain't cryin'. I never cry. It's just me nose runs."

"By! Lad, you've got hearin' as good as mine and I've got a pair of cuddy's lugs on me. No, of course you're not cryin', but if your nose runs use your hanky."

It was evident within the next few minutes that the boy didn't possess a handkerchief. Katie slipped from her chair and went to the wall at the side of the fireplace, pulled a paper square from a roll, then, turning to the visitor, but keeping a good arm's length away, she offered it to him.

There was a moment's hesitation before it was taken; then there followed the sound of sniffles and a long blow.

"Do you drink tea?"

"Aye."

"What have you in the name of eats, Mrs. B.?"

Bill looked towards Fiona, and she, going to the fridge, took out a small plate on which there were a number of sandwiches covered with cling film, and on the sight of them Mamie piped up, "That's Willie's tea, Mammy B.!"

"There'll be plenty more for Willie."

Taking the cover off the plate, Fiona now placed it in front of the boy and forced herself to say, "Do . . . do you like egg sandwiches?"

He stared up into her face. This was the woman who had yelled at him, told him to get away and never to come back near her house nor her son. "Go back where you belong," she had yelled, "you dirty-mouthed little urchin!" He remembered all her words, and here she was asking him if he liked egg sandwiches. His mind presented him with two answers. One was to say, "No!" and throw the plate of sandwiches into her face; the other was to say, "Ta, yes." He decided to choose the latter, but just because he liked the fella that had brought him in. He had a big mouth but he seemed all right.

"Ta, yes."

"Well, eat them up."

He took up one of the sandwiches and bit at it almost delicately because he was under surveillance from three pairs of eyes, not counting the bloke and his missis. Then of a sudden everything changed; the big bloke was yelling again; "Come on you three, scram!

215

Upstairs with you and get on with your homework. And I don't want to hear anything from you until I've had my tea."

"I don't see why we can't have our tea in the dining room an' all."

His hand outstretched, he made a dive for Katie's bottom, but she was out of the door, giggling now, and with Mark following, pushing Mamie before him.

Bill hadn't asked where Willie was, but he knew where he'd be after that fracas. And so, slipping out of the door, he pulled Mark to a halt, saying under his breath, "Tell Willie I'll be up shortly."

"Okay. Then, under his breath, Mark said, "He looks a rip," and jerked his head back towards the kitchen. "There's a lot of them about, Mark, more's the pity," Bill answered.

Back in the kitchen, he noticed immediately that the sandwiches had gone from the plate on which there was now a piece of fruit loaf, and although he purposely took no notice of the boy, he nevertheless noted the swiftness with which this, too, vanished.

When presently Fiona placed a bowl of red jelly in front of him, the boy looked up at her for a moment but didn't speak, nor did he touch the spoon that was stuck in the jelly until she went into the pantry and the fella followed her. Only then, the kitchen to himself, did he pick up the spoon. But he didn't use it straightaway to ladle up the jelly but looked at the handle. It was like one of those his granny had in a box: she always brought back a spoon from a day trip. On one it said, "A present from South Shields," on another "A present from Scarborough," and she had one "A present from The Isle of Man." She'd had to go to Liverpool and get a boat to go there, and all that week his ma kept saying she was praying for storms and shipwrecks. He hadn't understood what she meant at first 'cos the sun was shining all the time, until his da called his ma a vindictive bugger and reminded her that his mother was a good swimmer although she was sixty, which was dead old.

This spoon hadn't any writing on it—well, not writing that he could read—but it had things like two crossed swords and some letters in between them.

And he gobbled up the jelly. It was nice. This was a nice house. A nice kitchen, warm and bright; theirs was pokey. His ma used to be always on about the pokey kitchen, but then she was always on about every part of the house. When she kept on about it his da used to sing, "I Never Promised You a Rose Garden." His da could be funny.

"Have you finished?"

It was the fella again. He jerked in the chair as if coming out of a dream. His hand came out of his pocket and was laid flat on the table, the fingers spread.

Bill said, "Well, your one aim was to see inside the house, wasn't it? Don't you want to look round now?" and held out his hand, and the boy slid from the chair. He didn't take the proffered hand though. He looked at Fiona standing next to Bill, but his question was put to Bill, "She let me?"

"Well, if you're not sure you'd better ask her."

He didn't but stared at Fiona until she forced herself to say, "Well, if you want to see the rest of the house you'd better come along, hadn't you?" and she moved towards the door, leaving Bill to indicate with a jerk of his head the boy should follow her.

In the hall, Bill, spreading an arm wide, said, "The Baronial Hall, sir. It isn't as big as some I've seen but it's nicer than most."

Sammy did not look around the hall as one might have expected, but down at his feet at the carpet over which he was walking. When they entered the sitting room his head came up, and after gazing from one thing to another, his disappointment evident in his voice, he said, "You ain't got no telly?"

"Oh yes, we have, sir; it's behind those closed doors there." Bill pointed to a cabinet in the corner near the fireplace.

"Coloured?"

"Yes of course it's coloured."

He did not ask for proof of this but turned his gaze on the window and the long pink velvet curtains topped by a French pelmet.

Fiona was walking towards the door again, and once more Bill piloted the boy after her and into the dining room.

Here it was evident the boy was immediately impressed, for his gaze travelled swiftly from the silver on the sideboard to the china cabinet, then to the long table running down the middle of the room with its accompanying eight chairs, his gaze coming to rest on the far end of it, which was set for a meal.

Turning to Fiona and his head bobbing, he said, "We're gonna have a big house someday, we are."

For the first time Fiona looked fully at the boy and her voice was soft as she said, "Yes, I'm sure you shall."

"And a gardin."

"Yes, and a garden, too. Yes, a garden."

She turned abruptly from him now and hurried from the room, and as she made for the stairs she pointed along the passageway, saying in an offhand manner, "There's a room along there; it's my husband's study. It isn't very interesting."

"What do you mean, it isn't very interesting? It's the best room in the house. . . . Go on. Up you go!" Bill pushed the boy towards the stairs. And when they reached the landing Fiona, still leading the

217

way, did not turn round as she stated, "We won't do an inspection of the bedrooms; I think you might just like to see the playroom."

When she pushed the playroom door open, Mamie wriggled her plump body down from the old couch and ran towards her, while Katie and Mark, sitting one at each end of the worktable, both looked at their mother in not a little amazement. But she stared hard back at them, defying them to make any comment on her apparently altered attitude.

"There now, what do you think of this? It's the busiest room in the house." Bill looked down on Sammy, but Sammy didn't look at him or speak, he was once again gazing from one object to the other in the room, taking it all in yet not believing what he saw: the big dollhouse in the corner, the battered rocking horse, the train set taking up part of the floor under the sloping roof in the far corner of the room, the long bookshelves holding two rows of books, the bottom row seeming in order, the top row all topsy-turvy; and then, hanging from a peg in the wall near the window, what he took to be a great long puppet of a Chinaman.

"You going to stay with us?"

Sammy turned and looked into the round bright face of Mamie and he repeated, "Stay with you? No; no, I'm goin' home. I'm late as it is." He now turned quickly about and, looking up at Bill, he said, "He skelps the hunger off me, me da, if I'm not in." Then, walking past Bill and Fiona, he turned a half circle and made for the door, only to find he was looking into a cupboard.

When there was a burst of laughter from Katie, Mark, and Mamie, he turned on them, crying, "Think you're clever don't ya, think you're clever buggers. Me da's right, yer all a lot of nowts up here, a lot of nowts."

Before Bill could bawl a reprimand Mark rose swiftly from the table and, moving towards the boy, said, "We didn't mean anything. I mean, we do that, daft things like that, and we live here. We are always doing daft things, aren't we . . . Dad?" He turned to Bill, and Bill said, "You're tellin' me. I had no notion at all what a daft lot you were when I took you over. If I'd had an inkling of it I'd have run a mile." He now nodded towards Sammy. "I haven't been here all that long, you know. I'm their stepfather, but you've got a real dad, so you say."

Sammy was definitely nonplussed at this change of front: the big-mouthed fella said he wasn't their father but their stepfather. Stepfathers were terrible; his ma always said that. You don't know you're born, she would say; you should have had a stepfather like me.

218

He thinks too much of you, she used to say; and that was after his da had belted him. He couldn't understand his ma, he couldn't, but he wished she'd come home. He wanted to get out, away from this swanky house and these people. He turned from Mark and made for the right door this time, and Bill, signalling to Fiona to stay where she was but beckoning Mark to follow him, escorted his visitor downstairs.

Sammy made straight for the front door, which he found difficult to open, and as Bill unlocked the door he said to the boy, "By the way, where do you live?"

"Rosedale House in River Estate, flat fourteen."

Rosedale House, River Estate. Bill pursed his lips as he looked down on Sammy. That estate was deep in Bog's End, a good distance from here. "That's some way," he said. "Have you got your money for your bus?"

"I can walk; I've got legs."

"You're so sharp you'll be cuttin' yourself one of these days, lad." Bill was yelling again. "I can see you've got legs, and any more answers like that, and in that tone, you won't be standing on them but sitting on your backside. You understand me?"

From the look on Sammy's face he understood but said nothing. And when Bill put his hand in his pocket and brought out a ten-pence piece and offered it to the boy, Sammy just stared at it; but then he jerked backwards when Mark grabbed the coin from Bill's hand and, thrusting it at him, said, "Look, take it. Come on."

Sammy took it, thrust it into his pocket, then turned away without further words and walked towards the gate, Mark at his side now.

Outside the gate Mark was somewhat surprised when Sammy, looking up at him, said, "Will she keep him in bed all night?"

"Who? Willie?"

"Aye, who else?"

"No; no, he won't be kept in bed, not all the evening anyway."

"Will she give him his tea?"

Mark stopped himself from smiling. This kid was really funny: bossy, cheeky, as coarse and common as they come, yet he was enquiring if Willie was going to get something to eat. And so he said quietly, "Yes, he'll get his tea. Mam never remains angry long, she'll have forgotten about it by tomorrow. Willie an' all. He'll likely greet you like a—" He had been about to say "brother," but that would be stretching things too far, and so he substituted, "Buddy."

"You a Yankee?"

"*Yankee? American?* No. What makes you think that?"

"Then why do you say 'buddy'? Only Yankees say 'buddy' on the films."

"Oh, I think it's a very common word . . . name."

"No, it isn't."

"All right. All right." Mark's voice was loud now. "We won't go into it. Go on, get yourself away."

"I don't need tellin' twice."

Sammy got away, but in a slow defiant manner: his hands thrust in his pockets, he strode down the street. But he had not passed Mrs. Quinn's gate when he turned and yelled, "I don't like your house anyroad," before breaking into a gallop.

Bill was still standing at the front door when Mark came running up the drive; laughing, he called out, "I heard that. He had to have the last word."

As Bill closed the door Mark said, "He's a type right enough," and Bill answered, "Yes. Yes, Mark, he's a type, but he's got guts if nothing else. And I would say he's got little else."

They both turned now as the kitchen door opened and Fiona came into the hall carrying a tray, and as she passed them and made for the stairs she remarked to no one in particular, "If you're wise you'll make no comment. You may begin your tea, Mr. Bailey, it's all ready. And you, Mark, finish your homework."

They both stood and watched while she mounted the stairs. Another time Bill would have taken the tray from her or told Mark to do so. What he did, however, as she disappeared from view was to push Mark in the shoulder, and Mark pushed him back. Then they both hurried from the hall, along the corridor, and into Bill's study in order that their laughter shouldn't penetrate up the stairs.

When Fiona entered her son's bedroom and saw the round tear-stained face just visible above the bedclothes, she had the desire to run to him and gather him into her arms. But she put the feeling aside, walked slowly to the bed, laid the tray on the foot of it, then said calmly, "Sit up and have your tea."

Willie did not obey her. His face crumpling, he whimpered, "Oh, Mam. Mam, I'm sorry. I . . . didn't mean it, what I said, I didn't, I didn't."

The urge overcoming her outward demeanour, she pulled the clothes back from him and drew him upwards, and when his arms went about her neck she hugged him to her, saying, "There, there; it's all over."

"I'm sorry, Mam. I do love you. I didn't mean it, I didn't."

"I know you didn't, dear. I know you didn't. Come on now." She pressed him from her and as she dried his face, she said, "Do you know that your sparring partner has been here?"

He nodded and gulped, then said, "Mark ... Mark told me Dad brought him in. Did you ... wallop him?"

She pressed herself back from him, saying, "Wallop Sammy Love? I'm not big enough; nobody's big enough to wallop Sammy Love."

"Oh, Mam." He tossed his head from side to side, sniffed again, then said, "He ... he was all right until tonight. He ... he used to wait for me at the school gate, I ... I told you, because he gets out sooner than us. But he's only ever walked with me a little way. It was the first time he came right home, and ... and then I knew you wouldn't want him to ... to come in."

She lifted up his chin by placing her finger beneath it and looked into his eyes. "Did you want him to come in?" she said.

And shamefacedly now, he muttered, "Yes ... well, yes, I did because he seems—" He shook his head at this stage as Fiona urged, "Seems what?"

"I ... I don't know, Mam, sort of"—his head was still shaking—"I don't know, Mam."

"Do you know that he nearly threw a brick through the window? Mister ... your dad just caught him in time." It was odd, she thought, how she, like the children, would at times revert to Mr. Bill, but then he had been Mr. Bill the lodger longer than he had been her husband.

She rose abruptly from the bed now and, lifting the tray, said, "Come on, eat this up and then you may go into the playroom for half an hour. By the way"—she pointed down to the tray—"that's part of tomorrow's tea; he ate your egg sandwiches."

"He didn't!"

"Oh, yes, he did. And your cake and your jelly."

Then putting her hands out quickly, she held her son's face tightly between them for a moment before hurrying from the room.

Bill was already in the dining room and had started on his meal, but on the sight of her he rose from the table while still chewing on a mouthful of food. Pulling another chair from under the table, he said, "I just had to start; I could eat a horse between two mats."

"Didn't you have any lunch?"

"No; I hadn't time. I've had a rough day."

Taking his seat again, he put his elbow on the table and rested his head on it for a moment, saying, "I was like a bear with a sore skull when I came in that gate tonight. I was fuming inwardly against the big boys who can scale down their options until it's impossible to try and compete. And then I met Mr. Samuel Love and he took me back

221

to a part of my childhood and I saw myself in him, gob, brick, an' all, because although I had decent folks I was a hell-raiser. And that little chap's a hell-raiser because he hasn't got decent folk, I should imagine by what he came out with."

"Never mind about Mr. Samuel Love." She put her hand out towards him. "You don't think you stand a chance to get the estate?"

"Not a pigmy's stand."

"But Sir Charles Kingdom?"

"Yes, there is Sir Charles Kingdom, or there would be, but he's out of the picture for a time, he's in hospital having an operation, old man's water trouble."

"Well, he's the big noise in all this, it's his land they're going to build on, or it was before he sold it, he should have the main say. Are the same members on the finance board as before?"

"Yes, there's Ramshaw, Riddle, and Petty. Of the old lot there's only Brown missing. But they are all naturally hard-headed businessmen, and it seems even if Sir Charles were there the score would be three to one. But there must be more; in fact, someone said there were ten; and I'm not surprised for there's a great deal of money at stake. By yes, I'd say there is."

"But it was Sir Charles himself who told you to put your estimate in, wasn't it?"

"Yes, he did. But even so I couldn't see him letting sentiment stand in his way when it means a thousand or so off each house. And there's a hundred and ten of those, besides the two rows of town houses, one at each end, and the six shops, and the children's play centre. It takes a lot to cover sixty acres. There's been nothing like it around here for a long, long time; each house having its own quarter acre of garden and the designs all different. God!" He thumped his head with the palm of his hand for a moment. "Me and McGilroy have worked on those plans for months. It means as much to him as it does to me."

"Who are the firms that are in for it?"

"Oh"—he tossed his head back—"I understand there's even a London one trying. I do know there's one from Carlisle and another from Doncaster. Anyway, what kept me busy part of the day was I had to talk to our fellas. You know, when these two houses are finished that'll be the finish of us around here because there's not another thing going. And when Barney McGuire put it to me that I should lower my estimate and this would give me a better chance I had to hold my temper and say, aye it would, and yes, I'd do it if they would all agree to me cuttin' their wages, say by a third. Oh, the moans and groans. But you know what? After they shambled out they put their heads together and came back to me and said they'd all be willing to take a cut, twenty percent they said. I was touched. I . . . I was"—he nodded towards her now—"because most of the time they're wantin' a twenty percent raise. They're no better or no worse than the rest of 'em. But they were willin' to stand by me to a man. Anyway—" He smiled weakly at her, took another bite of food, then said, "It's a nice bacon pie. Any more taties?"

"Yes, plenty."

She helped him to some potatoes and peas, then she said quietly, "You're not to worry about us, Bill. Do you hear? Those three went to the local junior before you came on the scene; they can go back there and then to the Comprehensive; it's not going to hurt them in the long run."

"Like hell they will."

"Bill, listen to me." She gripped his hand. "Before you came on the scene as the lodger"—she pulled a face at him now—"I was really up against it. We were living then from hand to mouth but we were surviving. That's why—" she now pursed her lips as she ended, "I had to suffer my mother's indignation and wrath at my letting the side down."

He laughed and squeezed her hand. "Have you heard from her today?"

"No, but the phone could ring any time now."

"It's a form of torture, isn't it, she's putting us through? Ever since Katie blew my gaff."

"Well, you shouldn't have pretended that you are what you're not. You took the mickey out of her and she'll never forget it."

Bill sat back in the chair and laughed. "Eeh, but I did enjoy meself that day," he said. "And not just from the knowledge that I could do it . . . pretend to be what I wasn't. I can see her face now when I went in, talking like the county lot with marbles in their mouths. And the lads playin' up around me, touching their forelocks, jumping to my word. Eeh! I did enjoy that. And do you remember when she came in unexpectedly at New Year, I was forced to go into me act again? And Katie had to come out with 'Who you imitating, Mr. Bill? You do sound funny. Doesn't he, Mam? Anyway, Gran knows how you really talk.' Trust Katie."

"Well, as I said, you shouldn't haven taken on the part. And you know, I've had to suffer for it every day since. Before, I wouldn't perhaps hear from her for a week or more."

"She says she saw through my game. She didn't you know, I had her really gulled. She wasn't sure whether I had been taking

223

elocution lessons or you had been instructing me. Anyway, enough of her. And, by God, I've had enough of her. You'll never realize what I suffer because of you; you know when she looks down her nose at me I want to spit in her eye. Last time she came in I wondered perhaps if I threw her on the couch and half raped her it would satisfy her, because, you know, that's what she wants, a man."

"Oh, Bill!" There was a shocked note in Fiona's voice now. "How can you say such a thing. She doesn't. She's not . . ."

"She does, and she is. I know her type; I ran the gauntlet of them while in digs. They might be in their fifties, but they're not past it. Oh no, you believe me."

Fiona sighed; then, reaching over, she took his empty plate and asked, "Apple crumble or fruit salad?"

"Why can't I have both?" He grinned at her, then said, "Apple crumble."

Left alone, Bill let out a long, slow breath and looked about the room as if seeing it for the first time. He should feel he was in heaven: this good solid home, a wife like Fiona, and four good kids ready made. But here he was, amid all this, worried to death and really scared. Aye, at bottom he was really scared, because when these two houses were finished there was just nothing in this town, unless he could pull off this gigantic deal. And if he was honest he knew there was little hope. He hadn't told Fiona the whole of it. There were fifteen firms at least in for the job. Besides the London, Doncaster, and Carlisle ones, there were the two leading ones that had been building in the North for years, and sixty-acre plots were just their cup of tea. Ah, well, he could always go on the dole.

"Dole be damned!" He had spoken aloud. And now he pushed his chair back and marched towards the door, only to run into Fiona, but before she could say anything he said, "Love, I'll have it in the study."

"But Bill, you'll be there all evening in any case."

"I know, but I've been thinkin' about something, something I could alter on the plans. It's been in the back of me mind all day. Look, give it here." He took the tray from her. "I'll do a couple of hours; and after I've had a bath we'll have a natter. Then you'll go to bed."

And now, holding the tray in one hand, he stuck the index finger of the other hand into her chest, saying, "And tonight you go to bed, and you sleep."

"How can I sleep when you're not in bed at one o'clock in the morning?"

"Well, you'll have to get used to that. But of course, there'll be nights when I come to bed earlier when I want me rights. You've got to be of some use to me."

"Oh, Bill! Stop joking."

"I'm not joking, it's a fact and you know it. Go on. By the way, get Katie downstairs to give you a hand with those dishes."

"You go about your business, Mr. Bailey, and I'll go about mine."

When Fiona reached the kitchen she didn't immediately start with the washing up, she stood at the kitchen window looking down the back garden and into the long, slow twilight. It would break him if he didn't get that job. Not only was he worried about the family but also about the men who had worked with him for years; they were part of his family, too. They had been his only family until she had come onto the horizon. And oh, every day she was thankful she had. Yet she often had to smile when she thought back to her first impression of him, the thick-set, middle-aged, brash, loud-mouthed egotist. That's how she had seen him. But now she knew; in fact, he hadn't lived in the house long before she knew that behind that off-putting facade was a deep sensitivity that, in a way, he was ashamed of and did his best to hide.

She wanted him to succeed, to get to the very top in this building business. Yet if he didn't she knew it wouldn't matter to her, not really; as long as she had him and the children, they would scrape along. But it *would matter* to him. His pride would be dashed because he wanted to be more than just a breadwinner, a meals' provider. As he himself often said, men or women like him who had pulled themselves up by their bootlaces never wanted to tie the laces at the top.

There was a tap on the kitchen door and she turned and greeted Nell: "Hello, Nell. Oh, that face of yours. How many this time?"

"Four."

"Why didn't you have them all out at one go and get a set in?"

"I want to keep my front ones."

"Sit down. Have a cup of tea."

"No thanks; I've just had one."

"Anything wrong?"

Nell shook her head and held her swollen jaw for a moment before she answered, "That's what's brought me across. Mother's just said there were some ructions in the garden earlier on. She would have come across, but as you know she's full of cold. And you never get Dad interfering. Mind your own business is his motto."

She tried to smile.

Fiona now laughed, saying, "Oh yes, there were ructions. Our dear

225

Willie was escorted home by a little tyke from Bog's End who apparently wanted to see inside the house. And when Willie told him that I might object"—she pulled a face now—"there was a battle of words, four-letter ones."

"Oh! Four-letter ones?"

"Yes. It's a wonder you didn't hear them, they were yelling them. And, of course, I did my own share of yelling, but my words were a bit longer. I dragged Willie in and smacked him all the way to bed."

"Poor Willie."

"Poor Willie, indeed! And the the other one was aiming to throw a brick through the window when Bill caught him. Anyway, you know Bill and his reactions. Well, he brought him in and it was entertainment from then on; but not my kind, at least not at first, for I certainly didn't take to Mr. Samuel Love.

"Yes, that's his name, Sammy for short. But as Bill, in his usual way, pointed out, there are two sides to every question, especially so to little boys whose mothers . . . go off at times."

"Oh, another one of them?"

"Yes, that's what Bill said, there's many of them. Anyway, forget about us; you want to get yourself inside and into bed."

"Yes, that's where I'm going." She rose to her feet, then turned to Fiona and said, "Heard any more about the big deal?"

"Yes, but the news isn't very good. Too many in for it, I understand. But you know Mr. William Bailey, if he goes down it will be fighting."

"Oh yes, in all ways. You know, Fiona, I've never come across anyone in me life with such a loud voice. He's just got to say hell and it's like a blast."

"Go on!"

She followed Nell to the door, saying now, "You stay in bed in the morning. I'll pop across once I get them off to school."

"Oh, I'll be all right by then. See you."

Fiona returned to the sink and the dishes. Life was strange. One time you were on your own with three children to see to, no one to back you up but a mother to point out that everything you did was wrong, the next minute you had a fellow like Bill and a friend like Nell, not forgetting an adopted daughter called Mamie, one of the results of Bill's hidden sensitivity. Life was good. If only Bill could manage to pull off that deal it would be more than good, it would be marvellous.

26

IT WAS HALF PAST EIGHT BY THE TIME BILL FINISHED HIS BATH, BUT BEFORE going downstairs again he went into the bedroom that Katie shared with Mamie. The latter was already in bed and was sitting up talking to Edward Muggins, her teddy bear. There was no doubt about the bear's name, it was written across the chest of his sweater. And after Bill had kissed Mamie goodnight he then had to shake hands with Mr. Muggins and tell him that he must go to sleep and stop talking and keeping Mamie awake. Next he put his head round the door of the playroom, and when three eager faces were turned towards him, he said quickly, "Not tonight. Not tonight, comrades."

Katie, getting to her feet and coming towards the door, said, "You can spare five minutes."

"No, not even five minutes because I know what your five minutes is: I'd be roped into something. Keep your distance, woman. Goodnight, Mark. Goodnight, Willie. And by the way, you've got a do you two, haven't you, and I'll see about that tomorrow night. I won't forget. And you know what it's about don't you?"

Willie made no reply except to pull a face. And when Bill now said, "Goodnight all," they all answered. "Goodnight, Dad."

Fiona was in the sitting room. He went to the back of the couch and, bending over it, rubbed his face in her hair, then said, "I'll give you another hour then get yourself upstairs."

"Do you want a drink before you start?"

"Not one of yours, thank you, Mrs. B."

He now walked to the drinks cabinet in the corner of the room and, opening it, poured himself out a measure of whiskey; he drank it raw. He then came round to the front of the couch and, looking down on her, said, "Why don't you put the telly on?"

"I prefer to read."

"Have it your own way." Dropping down on his haunches, he caught hold of her hand, and said, "I'm sorry I've been stuck next door so often of late, but it's got to be done if. . . ."

"Oh, Bill, you don't have to apologise to me. You should know that by now. And who do you think's keeping you next door with your nose to the grindstone until all hours? We are, I and my lot."

"*Our lot*, Mrs. Bailey."

"Sorry, our lot. But it's true: if it wasn't for us you wouldn't give two hoots about getting that contract."

"Oh yes, I would. Let me tell you, I was an ambitious man before I set eyes on you. You forget, from tea boy to little tycoon. Little, I admit, but nevertheless a tycoon. Because I'm very proud of that last job of mine, every house has been sold and could have been twice over. The finance company made a nice little pile out of that; and *I'm* not grumbling, I didn't do too bad either. So don't ever suggest, Mrs. B., I lacked ambition before I entered your portals and met your mother."

He threw his head back now. "I often think of that day. She was after my blood, wasn't she?"

"Oh no, she wasn't."

"Oh yes, she was; until I told her I had been divorced four times and that my intake of whiskey was that of a whale. But the last bit that did it was when I suggested she get off her legs because she was such a poor old soul."

"You were a terrible man then."

"You never thought I was a terrible man, did you, not from the first."

"Oh yes, I did. Don't kid yourself. I not only regretted your entry into these portals, as you say, on that first day but for a number of days afterwards."

"But when I left, you came running after me, didn't you?"

When he found himself overbalancing and thrust onto the hearth-rug, he lay there laughing for a moment; then jumping up with the

228

agility of a twenty-year-old instead of a man on the road to fifty, he punched her gently on the jaw, saying, "A sandwich and a cup of your rotten coffee in about an hour's time," to which her answer was, "If you're lucky."

He was on his way toward the door when he turned and said, "I'd better be." Then, just as he opened the door, the sound of the front doorbell ringing brought him to a stop. Turning his head swiftly, he said, "I bet that's your mother."

"No, no." Fiona had risen quickly to her feet. "She wouldn't come out in the dark, at least not on her own."

He pulled the cord of his dressing gown tight, saying, "I can't go and open it like this, but I'll be behind the door just in case; you never know these days."

A moment later when Fiona opened the front door she was amazed to see that the unwelcome visitor of earlier in the evening had returned, only now he was accompanied by an extremely tall and bulky man. And it was the man who spoke, saying in a deep Irish voice, "You Mrs. Bailey, ma'am?"

"Yes, I'm Mrs. Bailey."

"Well, you know all about this 'un. You've had him here the night, I understand?"

"Yes, he was here."

"Well, he has somethin' to tell you and somethin' to give you."

It was at this point that Bill stepped from behind the door and looked at the visitor, and the visitor looked at him and said immediately, "Hello there, Mr. Bailey."

Bill screwed up his eyes and peered at the man. "I . . . I know your face. You're . . . m'm . . ."

"Davey Love. I worked for you a bit about two years gone."

"Oh aye, yes. Well, come in, don't stand there." He pressed Fiona aside, pulled the door wide, and allowed the very big fellow and the very small boy to enter the hall. Then after closing the door, he said, "You had better come into the sitting room."

"Thanks, I will. . . . After you, missis." Mr. Love's arm went out in a courtly gesture that caused Fiona's features to twist into what could have been taken as a smile or an expression of surprise.

In the sitting room they all stood looking at each other for a moment until Bill, pointing to a chair, said, "Well, sit yourself down." And when the big fellow had seated himself he and Fiona sat on the couch. That left Samuel Love standing to the side of his father, but with his eyes directed towards the carpet, until a very ungentle nudge from his father's elbow that nearly knocked him sideways

229

brought his head up. And now he was glaring up at his parent who was saying to him, "Well, tell them why you're here. That's what we've come for, isn't it? Well ... in part. But you get yer say over first. Go on, don't stand there like a stook, go over and tell her what you did, how you repaid her kindness after her stuffin' yer kite with the other lad's sandwiches and his cake an' jelly. You did enough braggin' about that, an' if it hadn't been for yer granny I wouldn't have known how you repaid these good people. Go on, tell 'em."

The boy now took two steps towards Fiona, then, putting his hand in his pocket, he drew out a spoon and thrust it towards her, saying, "I pinched it off ya."

Fiona took the spoon and looked at it. It was one of a set that someone had given her for a wedding present at her first marriage. They were silver plated, but she had never liked them and the children had used them from when they were babies.

"His granny had a few but not as good as that 'un. Presents from here, there, and every bloody where, day tripper things you know. And this 'un here thought he would add to her collection. I'm ashamed of him, bloody well ashamed of him. He's standing now 'cos he won't be able to sit down for a week; he'll be lying on his face the night. I'll bet you a shillin' he won't repay anybody's good tea pinchin' their cutlery after this.... Well! What have you got to say to the lady?"

Sammy cast his father a glance that should have shrivelled him; but the man was too big, and so he looked backwards towards Fiona and said, "Sorry."

"You're sorry who? Begod! I'll knock some manners into you afore I'm much older."

Again there was the glance, then, "I'm sorry missis."

The boy's gaze was now jerked towards the fella who bawled even worse than his da because he was making a funny noise in his throat as if he was choking. He had his head bent and a very white handkerchief held to his nose. And when his wife said to him, "Mr. Bailey!" he lifted his head and replied, "Yes, Mrs. Bailey?"

Bill wiped his eyes; then, in a voice he had to control, he said to Davey Love, "If I remember rightly you were with us only a short time."

"Aye, that's right."

"And if I also remember rightly you're the only man who's ever been on my books that left with two days pay owing him and never came back for it."

Mr. Love laughed now as he said, "Aye, that's right an' all. But when I had time to come back you had finished that job and started another 'un. So, I said, to hell! Pardon me, missis; it just slips out, you know. But as I said, what odds."

"Did you get another job?"

The head went back again, and now there was something in the laugh that was not quite bitter but which you couldn't say was jolly, and the man said, "Sort of. Ah, well, you might as well know, I went along the line."

"You did?" Bill nodded. "Along the line?"

"Aye, along the line. Well, you might as well know. You might have seen it in the papers at the time but didn't link me with it. Of course, me name's not that unusual, but you see, his mother had walked out on me again." He thumbed towards the boy. "She'd gone off with her latest fancy man. Oh, missis"—he flapped a hand towards Fiona—"don't look so troubled, he knows all about it." He again thumbed towards his son. "He's been brought up on it. She's like the swallows, she does a flit every year but she usually comes back, mostly on her own. This time, though, she landed in the town with him. Well, if she comes back on her own we have it out an' that's that. But I ask ya, for a fella of my size an' appeal to be passed over for a little runt! Five foot five he was an' she's all five foot nine or ten if she's an inch. That's why I took her at first, 'cos she was near me size. Anyway, the sight of her latest choice was too much for me; I wiped the floor with him, an' a couple of walls an' all." He grinned widely now. "He had his quarters in hospital for two months after that an' mine was in Durham for nine."

Bill could hold it no longer. His body was already shaking before the sound erupted; and then almost to his joy he saw that Fiona was in a similar state. When the man joined in, their laughter mingled, and it didn't die away until Fiona, noticing that the boy was not laughing, held her hand out to him; and he took it, and when she brought him to her knee and she said in a voice that she aimed to control, "It's all right, I understand: you wanted it for your grandmother. Well, there you are, you give it back to her." She picked up the spoon from where it had been lying on the side of the couch and added, "And I think I have another one somewhere; I'll look it out for you."

"What d'you say?"

The boy turned his head sharply and looked at his father and, addressing him now as one adult to another, he said, "I know what to say, but let me have me breath." Then, directing his gaze on Fiona once more, he said, "Thanks, missis. Ta."

"Well, that's over. But not quite." The big man had both Fiona's and Bill's attention again. "But mind"—he wagged his finger towards Bill—"I would have brought him along in any case. Oh aye. That's one thing I won't stand for in him, is light fingers. As far as I know that's the first time; and it'll be the last, 'cos the next time it'll not be the belt across his backside, I'll string him up. Begod, I will."

When Fiona closed her eyes for a moment Mr. Love put in more moderately, "Well, that's what you call stretchin' it a bit, missis, but you get me meanin'."

She was unable to answer him but she inclined her head towards him. And he, looking at Bill now, said, "When you've done a stretch, whatever for, your name's mud. But believe me that was the first time I'd been up, an' that'll be the last. It was an object lesson with a big O for me. Begod, it was. I hope I'm never tempted to bash anybody again. But if I am I'll do it in the dark with a stockin' over me head 'cos they won't get me into Durham again, not in that van anyway. So, what I'm inferrin' like is, jobs have been few an' far atween, sort of. And I'm a man who likes to work, to use me hands, and I give worth for worth, no shirkin' when I'm on the job. So, what I'm askin' you for is, can you take me on 'cos I hear you're startin' on two new houses shortly?"

Bill looked at the big fella. It was his intention to set on two extra men on Monday because of the time limit set on this last piece of work he had in hand, which, if not met, would mean the loss of money on the contract. Considering what he had just heard, and such was this man's need and the appeal of his raw child, he made his decision.

In the brusque businesslike manner he usually adopted when dealing with new starters, he said, "You're lucky. I was thinking about setting two on on Monday. If you show up then we'll see what we can do." He could have added jokingly, "If you don't reach Durham again in the meantime." But he resisted the temptation, because Durham must have been an experience in this man's life that would be best forgotten. But perhaps not best forgotten, perhaps the thought of it would keep him out of trouble in the future.

Davey Love stood up now and his whole attitude seemed to change: the tone of his thick Irish voice had dropped several levels when he said, "That's real kind of you, sir. I won't forget it, and you won't regret it. No, begod, I'll see you don't."

Bill, too, got to his feet, saying, "Would you like a drink?"

"Aye, thank you very much, I would that."

"Whiskey? Gin? Beer?"

"A beer would be welcome, sir; you get more in a beer." He turned a laughing face on Fiona now, and she smiled back at him. Then looking at the boy again, she said, "And would you like a drink of milk or orange juice?" And he glanced towards his father as if for permission, and when it was given with a nod he said, "Got any Coke?"

The bawl was as loud as Bill's: "Milk or orange juice, the lady said. Take your choice an' be thankful, you ignorant scut."

Again that look was levelled at the big man; then Sammy said, "Orange juice."

"What else? God an' His Holy Mother! Won't you ever learn?"

There was an actual sound of a sigh before the boy said, "Please."

Fiona had to hurry from the room, and when she reached the kitchen she stood with her back to the door for a moment, her hand tight across her mouth. She had never thought that this evening would end in laughter, not after the fracas she had had with that small piece of humanity back there, and then knowing of the worry that Bill was experiencing.

Quickly now she poured out a glass of orange juice and put a large piece of cake onto a plate, then both onto a tray. And she was crossing the hall when there was a hiss from the top of the stairs; and there they were, the three of them, and it was Mark who whispered, "There's company?" And she whispered back, "Yes. Tell you about it later."

"What's that for?" Katie was pointing downstairs; and Fiona, stretching her head forward, whispered back to her daughter, "It's great for the guest. He only takes orange juice."

"Mam!" It was a loud whisper.

"Yes, Willie?"

"Hurry up and come up and tell us."

"I will. Go on now and get ready for bed, you two."

"Mam."

"Yes, Katie, what is it?" Her voice showed her impatience now. "Can we . . .?"

"No, you . . . can . . . not! Now you, and you Mark, do as I say, get ready for bed. If you don't I won't tell you a thing that's happened." She moved away amid the muttered grunts.

In the sitting room she put the tray on a small table and, beckoning Sammy to a seat near it, she said, "There you are."

"Ta!" said young Master Love with deliberate emphasis now, and his father, shaking his head, said, "My! My! You won't forget this night, will you, laddie? There'll be no livin' with you after this. You'll not only want to move from the flats you'll want yer meals brought to you on a tray." He now turned and made a face towards Bill, and Bill smiled, and Fiona smiled.

Five minutes later, when Mr. Love had finished his beer and Sammy Love had got through his juice and his piece of cake, the big man said to his son, "Go and stand in the hallway; I'll be there in a minute."

The boy rose from the chair, looked from one to the other of the three adults, then slowly walked out, closing the door behind him.

Davey Love now turned to Bill, explaining: "I yammer on about things and his ma and the situation atween us in front of him 'cos he knows all about it; he's heard it since he was on the bottle. But there's some things it's better him not to know, 'cos kids talk. It's like this: I've a piece of news that might be of some use to you. You see I get around. Well, you do down at Bog's End. It's a particular bar I go to and you hear things. I sometimes give a hand behind the counter. I'm not s'posed to serve you see, being on the dole." He stretched his upper lip over his lower one and his face took on a comic, grotesque look. But he continued straightaway, saying, "One or two things have happened to your lads lately, haven't they?"

"You mean, Mark and Willie?"

He turned to Fiona, laughing and saying, "No, I wasn't meanin' the kids, missis, I was after meanin' the boss's men on the job."

And at this Bill said, "Aye, yes; one or two things have been happenin' to them. It started when they were clearing the site for the new houses."

"One had his car pinched?"

"Yes, he had."

"Well, I can tell you where it is."

"You can? That's interestin'. But how do you come to know that? Did you have a hand in it?"

"Now, Mr. Bailey. No, I've told you, haven't I, nothin's gonna get me to Durham again." There was indignation in the tone.

"Sorry. But ... well, go on."

After a moment's hesitation, Mr. Love went on: "There's two fellas have come to live round our way. I don't know where, but I recognised one right away. He was one of the residents like when I was on holiday in Durham. Well, Kit Bradley, he's the man who runs the pub, and atween you an' me I think he runs with the hare and hunts with the hounds, as the sayin' goes, 'cos to see him chattin' to a smilin' bobby you'd think they were brothers at times. Anyway, these fellas were in the pub and they put it to him on the side if he would be interested in a car that was goin' cheap. They had bought

234

it, they said, from a fella who was a brickle and who said he needed spare cash; they said his boss was soon goin' out of business.

"Now them words was the link up for me: his boss was goin' out of business. It didn't hit me at the time, but it did after, if you get what I mean. Anyway, one said it had always narked him that brickies could go to work in their cars. The world had turned upside down, he said. I got all this from Kit, you understand?"

Bill made a small motion with his head signifying that yes, he was following Mr. Love. "Anyway, Kit went round to the spare plot aside Gallagher's junkyard where the car was parked. He said it wasn't what he was wantin' but he'd pass the word round. I asked him if he was gonna tell the cops, and he said, no, let 'em find out for themselves. That's what I mean, you know, about running with the hare and huntin' with the hounds. He's a deep 'un is Kit. But anyway, news gets round, an' I heard about this fella who was hoppin' mad an' had been to Gallagher's junkyard lookin' for his car, 'cos apparently it was an eight-year-old banger but he had looked after it like a baby. I never saw the bloke meself, but somebody happened to say he was one of Bailey the builder's fellas. Well, as you know, this all happened a couple of weeks ago an' I suppose I could have let on then, but I said to meself, Love, mind your own business. And anyway, anythin' to do with the cops brings me out in spots. An' I'm not kiddin' about that! I have a rash that comes out in me sometimes and I'm covered from head to foot with it. Saint Vitus' dance has nothin' on me when that hits me, I can tell you. Well, there it is." He spread his fingers wide.

"Do you think the car will still be there?"

"Well, they were in it up till yesterday. It's a bit changed: they've painted it a different colour and the number plates are sure to be changed. It was a kind of grey but now it's a blue. They're barefaced buggers those two, an' I don't think they'd be clean fighters. It would be the knife, or chains. So I'd tell your bloke if he goes after his car not to go alone."

"Well, if I've got anything to do with it"—Bill's tone was grim—"he'll be accompanied by the police."

"Well, that's up to you. But as I said, one good turn deserves another. Or did I?" He grinned now at Fiona, and she was forced to smile at him.

Bill, too, smiled now as he said, "Well, thank you very much anyway. It's been an eventful evening. Our *antique silver* has been returned, then ... given away again"—he glanced towards Fiona—"Tommy Turnbull has the chance of getting his car back, an' you've

235

got the chance of a few weeks' work. I hope it may be longer, but at the moment I can't promise anything."

"You're in for the job of makin' that big estate some way out, I hear, on Sir Charles Kingdom's estate? Is that right?"

"You get about."

"Oh aye." Davey Love grinned widely now. "The Job Centre has more information than Pickford's tourist's office.... Ah, well, I'll have to be goin'." He buttoned up his coat; then, with an elaborate bow towards Fiona, he said, "It's been a pleasure, ma'am, a pleasure. An' you can always look back on this night as the night that you had a visit from an honest burglar." And he thumbed towards the hall, then added, "But it took a very red backside to make him come clean. As I said to him, there's honour among thieves an' as I've always said to him, don't do as I do, do as I say. At least I used to afore I took that holiday, you know. Anyway, I mustn't keep you good folks any longer."

In the hall they stopped and looked at the small figure sitting on the second step of the stairs, and it was apparent he had been in some sort of whispered conversation with the three heads at the top of the stairs.

Mr. Love looked upwards, a wide grin on his face, and he called loudly, "Goodnight, kids," and he was answered almost simultaneously by the three voices, saying "Goodnight, Mr. Love."

Fiona's eyes were wide, her face straight. That was how they used to address Bill, calling Goodnight, Mr. Bill. She was about to issue a stern order to her offspring when Mr. Love, looking at her, said, "You've got somethin' to be proud of there, missis." Then, turning to Bill, he added, "And already made, I understand. He told me." The jerk of his head was towards his son who was now standing near him. "He gave me the whole rundown on the family. Never misses a trick, that 'un. Well, come on you." He placed his hand between the small boy's shoulders and pushed him none too gently towards the front door, which Bill had opened.

"Be seein' you, Mr. Bailey."

"Yes, Davey, be seein' you. Goodnight."

"Goodnight to you. And it's been a good night all round, it's been a good night. Indeed it has that."

Bill and Fiona stood watching the tall and the small figure walking side by side towards the gate, and not until they had disappeared into the darkness did Bill close the door. Then, striding towards the stairs, he bawled up to the three faces still there. "Goodnight, Mr. Love," mimicking them. "You've changed your allegiance have you? Goodnight, Mr. Love. It used to be, Goodnight, Mr. Bill, didn't it?"

"Well, you're not Mr. Bill anymore, are you?" This was from Katie. "You're Dad now."

"She's right." Mark was nodding.

But Willie, and in a small voice, said, "He asked if he could come back again, Mam, Sammy, and I said yes. Is that all right?"

Fiona did not take her eyes from her small son, although she knew that Bill was looking at her intently, and her answer was noncommittal. "We'll see," she said. "We'll see. Now get yourselves to bed this minute."

"Goodnight, Mam." "Goodnight, Mam." "Goodnight, Mam." The voices followed one after the other; then steps could be heard crossing the landing and now, like the descending notes on a scale, there followed "Goodnight, *Mr.* Dad," from Mark; "Goodnight, *Mr.* Dad," from Katie; and "Goodnight, *Mr.* Dad," from Willie—and a quick scampering of feet. Laughing, Bill put his arm around Fiona's shoulders; leading her back into the sitting room, he pulled her down to the couch and, holding her tightly, kissed her, then said, "Well, it's certainly been an evening. What d'you say?"

"Yes, it's certainly been an evening, Mr. B. And wouldn't it be a shame," she added, her head now to one side, "to waste it by spending the rest of it in the study."

He stared at her, his eyes twinkling as he said, "You know what, Fiona Bailey? You're a brazen woman, and before you were a brazen woman you must have been a brazen girl called Fiona Vidler. All this refined veneer of yours is just mush; you're sex mad. I could say I've got a headache but I won't." With a jump he got to his feet and pulled her upwards. "Come on; I'll give you half an hour, then I'll return to the job."

"Not if I know you," she said.

"Aw, lass." He pulled her to him and kissed her again hard on the lips before almost running her from the room.

27

MARK HAD TAKEN THE BUS TO SCHOOL IN NEWCASTLE, AND FIONA HAD DROPPED Katie and Willie and Mamie off at their respective schools. Then, having done quite a bit of shopping, she was now lifting two laden bags from the boot of the car in the garage when she heard the phone ring; and it had rung six times more before she managed to open the front door, drop the two bags, and pick up the receiver.

"Fiona?"

Fiona drew in a deep breath. "Yes, Mother," she said.

"You've taken your time to answer. Where on earth have you been?"

"I've been out shopping, Mother; and before that I took the children to school."

"I thought that person next door took the children to school?"

"Only sometimes, Mother."

Fiona pulled a chair forward and sat down; this was going to be a long session.

"I'm not feeling very well. The lights flickered last night, then went out just as I happened to be coming downstairs and I got a shock and I slipped off the two bottom stairs and twisted my ankle."

"I'm sorry. Can you walk?"

"Only just. But ... it isn't only that. I phoned for the electrician. I got his private number; he lives above the shop in the High Street.

238

And when I asked if Mr. Green could come round at once and find out what was wrong his wife laughed at me. She's the one that serves in the shop, a common place if ever there was one. And you know what she said?"

Fiona didn't say, "No, Mother," she just waited, and Mrs. Vidler went on, "Her husband was at the club and when I asked if she could get in touch with him she said, 'You're asking something, aren't you?' Those were her very words. And she said that if the whole High Street was plunged into darkness he wouldn't leave the club at that time. And it was only nine o'clock, you know."

"Well, he'll likely come today, Mother."

"He won't. I was on to him immediately the shop opened and he said he would be round as soon as he could. How soon was that, I asked. Sometime tomorrow, he said; he was full up with work ... so ..."

Fiona stared at the mouthpiece waiting for her mother to go on; when she didn't she repeated, "Well, so? What d'you mean by that? You don't think I can come round and fiddle with electricity, do you, Mother?"

"No, I don't. But ... but that ... your ... well, your Mr. Bailey, he has men who do all kinds of things on his job, he could send one of them, couldn't he?"

"He could, Mother"—Fiona's voice was sharp now—"but he wouldn't, or he won't. He did you a big service at Christmas and what was the result? You insulted him just because he had altered his voice. ..."

"Altered his voice indeed! He pretended to be what he wasn't, he ridiculed me."

"You always said he was a big-mouthed individual. Well, he just wanted to show that there was another side to him."

"Yes, and one that he couldn't possibly keep up."

"Oh, yes, he could, Mother, if he wanted to. Anyway, I don't know how you have the nerve to expect him to send one of his men round there. There are other electricians in the town you could contact; surely one of them would come straight out?"

"Yes, I suppose they would, but do you know what they want for coming out? I've already contacted two and the first one said there'd be an eight pound road charge; and the other one was apparently a self-employed man, asked if I could pay on the spot, sort of cash on delivery. I put the phone down. So you can't say I haven't tried."

"Well, Mother, you'll have to try again because I'm not asking Bill to send one of his men round."

There was silence on the line for a moment; then Mrs. Vidler's voice, changing from a plaintive whine almost to an undignified yell, said, "Of all the most ungrateful women in this world, you are one. You would let me sit alone here in the dark, a woman entirely alone while you are sitting comfortably in the light, surrounded by your children, my grandchildren whom I never see, and your servant friend next door, not forgetting your loud-mouthed husband. But there'll come a day when you'll regret your treatment of me. Oh yes, there will."

When the phone had banged down Fiona sat back in the chair and, puffing out her cheeks, she let a long lingering breath slowly deflate them before placing her own phone down.

Her children, her servant friend ... poor Nell ... and her loud-mouthed husband. Her mind did not say poor Bill. Why did she always feel so terrible after her mother had been on the phone?

Slowly she rose from the chair, took off her coat, picked up the bags of groceries, and went towards the kitchen, saying to herself again, "Four children, a servant friend, and a loud-mouthed husband."

Her mother was right there. She was very lucky. Oh, she was very lucky.

The groceries put away, she made herself a cup of coffee, and as she sat sipping it she told herself that she would go next door to see how Nell was. She had phoned her early on and told her to stay put for the morning, that she could manage and that there wasn't anything to do really. Now that Mamie was at school she had more time to do things, because Mamie was a child that demanded a lot of attention. There was a great need in her for love that had been brought on by the loss of her parents and her brother.

So she worked it out, as she sipped at her coffee: after she had been in to see Nell she would tidy the children's rooms and get down to some cooking. The freezer needed packing up again.

But having arranged all this in her mind, she still sat on. Then of a sudden she sprang up, saying, "Damn!" It was a loud damn. And now she walked to the kitchen window and looked down the back garden, and the sight of the daffodils there reminded her that she must straighten that patch in the front garden where the young visitor had trampled the flowers down. What she actually did next though was to walk smartly from the kitchen, across the hall, and pick up the phone again.

She had to wait some minutes before a voice answered and when it said, "Bailey Building Company. What can I do for you?" she said, "Oh, is that you Bert? I recognised your voice."

"Oh, hello, Mrs. Bailey. D'you want the boss?"

240

"Yes, please."

"I'll get him in a minute; he's on the job. I just happened to be passing the hut."

It seemed a long wait, but it was only two minutes; then Bill's voice hit her, saying, "What's the matter? What's wrong?"

"Nothing's wrong, at least not here, not with me or any of ours. But something's wrong with ... Mrs. Vidler."

"Oh, my God! What's happened there? Is she dead?"

"No, she's not dead, Bill Bailey."

"That's a pity; I could do with a break the day."

"Listen."

"I'm listening."

She then went on to tell him what had transpired on the phone a short while ago, and before she had finished his voice came loud and clear, "No way, Mrs. B. No way."

"All right. All right. Anyway I told her that it was an imposition. I said she had a nerve, but she said you had ridiculed her. And you know you had. Now you can't get over that; you know you had."

"Well, you should be able to stand a bit of ridicule when you get a job done for nowt. Well not quite nowt: she gave the fellas five pounds each. But instead of fifteen pounds she would have had to pay fifty, if not more for that double journey. Oh aye, she would at that, especially with the firm she picked. So no, no way."

"All right. All right."

"Then why did you get on the phone and tell me?"

She paused, before she said, "Well, to tell the truth I'm lonely: Nell's off colour, her face is in an awful state; our four offspring are at school; my husband doesn't come home to lunch; I have a long day ahead of me and no one to talk to. So I thought it would be nice just to have a word."

"You're a liar, you know that, and you're not going to soften me up."

"Bill"—her voice had changed—"I have no intention of softening you up; I'm just putting it to you straight because she said something to me and it keeps going round in my head. And I'll tell you exactly her words. She said, there she was on her own, but what had I got? My children ... her grandchildren, a servant friend, that's what she called Nell, and a loud-mouthed husband. Yes, a loud-mouthed husband. Well, taking them singly or lumped together, I thought to myself, I'm very lucky. She is alone, and no matter how bitchy she is, she happens to be my mother and at times I feel responsible for her."

"Then all I can say to that is, you're a bloody fool."

241

"All right, I'm a bloody fool, but that's how I'm made. And ..."

"Don't say it."

"Don't say what?"

"That if you weren't a bloody fool you wouldn't have taken me on."

She hesitated for some seconds before she said, "Bill, I wouldn't ever say that even in joke."

His voice sounded flat now as he said, "All right, all right. Leave it, will you? Leave it."

"Bill."

"Aye?"

Again there was a slight pause before she said softly, "I love you very, very much."

There was a longer pause before he said, "Doing seventy, I can get home within five minutes."

She pushed her head back and laughed, saying, "You've got the mind of a frustrated monk."

"Well, because I'm not the only one, because I can see you climbing the convent walls any day."

"*Bill!*"

"Good-bye, love."

"Bye, my dear."

Having replaced the receiver she stood looking down at it. Would he do anything? She didn't know.

A short while later, she went next door and was surprised to see Mrs. Paget in the kitchen in her dressing gown.

"Why are you up?" she said. "You still look full of cold."

"Oh, it's only the sniffles now, I'm much better. But Nell's in bed. I came down to make a drink."

"Well, you go back and I'll see to the drink."

"No, my dear, no. I'll tell you what you can do though, you can go up and have a talk with her. She's ... she's in a bad way this morning."

"Do you think she should have the doctor?"

"No; no, no doctor can cure what's wrong with her at the moment. She'll likely tell you herself."

When she entered Nell's room she saw that Nell was lying in the middle of the bed, her head almost buried under the bedclothes, and it wasn't until she touched her shoulder and said, "You feeling awful?" that Nell bounced round in the bed, saying, "Oh! Oh, it's you, Fiona; I thought it was Mother. Yes; yes, I'm feeling like nothing on earth this morning."

"Your face aching?"

"Not . . . not so much as I'm aching here." She pointed to her chest. Then, pulling herself up onto the pillow, she said, "Sit down." And at this Fiona sat down on the end of the bed, saying now, "What is it, what's happened?"

"Well, really nothing that I didn't know was going to happen, but when I heard it had, it just hit me. I suppose because I was feeling low at the time. But I got a letter from a so-called friend this morning. It would have to come this morning, wouldn't it?" She made an effort to smile. "The baby was born last Saturday. It was a girl. You know, Fiona"—she leaned forward now—"although I knew it was going to happen and that's why he left me—perhaps he might have left me in any case, but that made him put a spurt on—when I read those words I was overcome by the most frightful feeling. You know, if he had been near me I . . . I—" She moved her head slowly and closed her eyes and swallowed deeply before she ended, "I could have really killed him. For a second I longed for a knife. Just to have a knife in my hand to stab at the air and pretend he was there. All those years humbling myself, making myself a doormat just so he would soften up and give me a child. That's all I wanted. I could have forgiven him anything, his selfishness, his laziness—he was lazy—he had such an imagination he should have been writing books—but I could have forgotten all that and looked upon him as the best man in the world if he had only given me the chance to have a child. I mightn't have been able to carry one, or have one, but . . . but no, he always saw to it that there were no slip-ups. When I accepted the idea that he couldn't stand children, as he said, and there was no possible hope for me ever being satisfied in that way, I still had to put up with being . . . a wife to him. God!" She turned her head on the pillow now and looked away from Fiona. "The indignities that one has to suffer, the degradation."

When Fiona pulled her gently into her arms, Nell laid her head on her shoulder, and with tears in her voice she said, "What I would have done all these months if it hadn't been for you and that horde next door and the big fella, but mostly you, God alone knows. Mother and Dad are good people and they haven't a good word for him, but he was their son, so I couldn't let go in front of them, they were suffering enough. But to know that you were there. . . ."

"Nell, listen to me." Fiona pressed Nell from her, and now she was wagging her finger into her face: "Bert Ormesby is a good man, he's an attractive man and a sober fellow, as you know. He's got a nice house, everything all ready, and the main thing is, he's more than sweet on you. But he's shy; as Bill says, he's had no dealings with women; but it's evident that he wants dealings with you. But from what I can gather you've kept him at arm's length. And I can understand it. But you've got your divorce, you're free, and there's still time enough for you to have a baby."

"What! Nearing forty?"

"Yes, nearing forty. It's happening every day."

"Not with the first one."

"Yes, with the first one. They do wonders now, caesareans, and all kinds of things. Anyway, first things first; let him know that he's free to speak. You know something? I'm sick of him coming next door to make excuses to see Bill about this and that which could be done at work, and the look on his face when he finds you've just gone."

Nell lay back now on the pillows and, wiping her face gently with her handkerchief, said, "I'll think about it."

"Don't think too long. And what's more, don't lie there crying your eyes about him. Because I'll tell you something; that young mother will get her eyes opened before long."

"Oh, I hope so. I'm being vindictive, I know, but I do; I hope she sees what she's taken on when she has practically two babies on her hands. You know, he would never do a thing in this house, wouldn't lift his hand to dry a cup. That was his mother's fault, I suppose. No; no, it wasn't; he was born lazy. And there's his father just the opposite, always frantically doing something."

"Well, anyway"—Fiona rose from the bed—"get yourself up, that is if your face is not paining too much. Come the weekend, go to the hairdresser and get your hair styled; it's like a dog's tail at the back. It's lovely hair but it will look better if it's trimmed. And put a bit of makeup on. You never wear makeup."

"Yes, Mrs. B. You know, in a way, you're as bossy as Bill. The only thing is, your voice is not quite so loud, but that'll come I suppose."

Fiona flapped her hand towards Nell, then said, "I'm off to do some baking. That freezer was packed this time last week with pies, cakes, and what-not, and now it's almost bare. Oh, I've got something to tell you, but not now because you can't laugh properly with a face like that. You know, I told you last night about our first visitor; he was Mr. Samuel Love. Well, we had him return with his father later. The little devil had pinched a spoon you know, the one with the coat of arms on the top."

"Never!"

"Yes. But I'll tell you about it later. Now come on, get up out of that."

"Yes, ma'am; and I'll be in shortly."

"You needn't bother being in shortly; except for a drink; there's nothing to do and, as your mother-in-law says, dust eats no bread."

"I've just made the coffee," said Mrs. Paget as Fiona went into the kitchen, and Fiona answered, "I won't stay, dear. Anyway, Nell's getting up."

"She is?"

"Yes; she feels better."

"Oh, thanks Fiona. You always do her good." Then her head drooping, she said, "Have you ever thought, Fiona, that you might one day dislike one of your sons?"

"No; no, I couldn't think that way."

"Well, it's possible. Oh yes, it's possible. And at this moment my feeling for my son goes deeper than dislike. He had one of the best girls in the world. She had one fault, only one, she didn't stand up to him; and she could have because she's not without spunk, but she kept hoping that if she gave him his own way he'd give her what she wanted, the only thing she wished for in the world."

"There's still time, Mrs. Paget; she could get her wish yet."

"You mean ... Mr. Ormesby?"

"Yes, I mean Mr. Ormesby. It all depends on her; I'm sure he's willing."

"Oh, then, please God, something will come of it. She deserves a little happiness. And I understand from what she says he's a churchman?"

"Yes, he is."

"There's not many about these days. More's the pity. You're sure you won't stay and have a cup?"

"No thanks, dear. I'm going to get down to some baking. I'll be seeing you."

"Yes, yes."

As she walked up her own garden Fiona wondered yet again how a nice couple like those two could have such a stinker of a son.

After tidying up she eventually got round to her baking, and by three o'clock she had cleared away and was about to get ready to go and fetch Mamie when there was a knock on the back door. And when she opened it she was surprised to see the man who had been the topic of conversation between Nell and her earlier on.

"Oh, hello, Bert."

"Hello, Mrs. Bailey."

The tall, rather gangling fellow moved from one foot to the other, then quickly explained his presence by saying, "I just called round to see if Nell was ... well, all right, after her teeth, you know. I ... I was just quite near at Mrs. Vidler's seeing to her electric . . . her electric light, you know."

"Oh, you've been to my mother's?"

"Yes; yes; the boss said the old lady was without light and . . . and, as I said to myself, it's not so far away"—he made a motion with his hand indicating the short distance—"and knowing what Nell had been going . . . through with her toothache. . . ."

"Come in a minute, Bert."

"Oh, well, Mrs. Bailey, the boss'll be expecting me. But all right, just a minute."

Two long strides brought him just within the door, and Fiona said, "I was just about to get ready to go and pick Mamie up from school."

"Oh aye, she's at school now. They do grow, don't they?"

Fiona made no comment on this, but said, "Nell hasn't been across today; she hasn't been feeling at all well. . . ."

"It's those teeth of hers, they do play her up."

"Bert, it isn't her teeth at the moment that's making her feel . . . well, off colour."

"No?" He stared at her and waited, but Fiona did not go on straightaway to explain what was making Nell unwell, for she was questioning herself if she would be doing the right thing in playing cupid. But she felt that if one or other wasn't given a push the situation could meander on, then fizzle out. As it was now, the situation lay between a shy man and a woman who was afraid to be hurt again.

"Of course, you know, Bert, that Nell is divorced?"

"Oh yes. Aye, I know she's divorced. And I think the fella must have been blind or daft."

"He was neither blind nor daft, Bert, but he was cruel. Perhaps what you don't know is that he left Nell because he had got . . . well, the girl into trouble as the term is."

"Aye; well, it's generally the way."

"But not in this case, Bert. You see, Nell had always wanted children and her husband was adamant that there would be no children of the marriage. He couldn't stand children; he didn't like children, et cetera. So for thirteen years Nell lived in frustration. But imagine how she felt when she learned why he had left her. And then this morning she got a letter from, as she says, some kind of friend who told her that the child was born on Saturday and that it was a girl. She had always wanted a girl. I'm . . . I'm telling you this, Bert, because . . . well, Nell never would. And I think you are fond of her, aren't you?"

She watched him wet his lips, then gulp before he said, "Yes; yes,

246

I'm fond of her. I've never been fond of anybody before. I mean, I've never felt about anybody like I have her. For one thing . . . well, I can talk to her; I don't feel all at sixes and sevens. And thank you, thank you, Mrs. Bailey for puttin' me in the picture. I'm a stupid individual, you know, thick." He dabbed his forehead with his finger, and at this Fiona smiled and said, "You're neither stupid nor thick, Bert; you're a very caring man, and Nell needs someone to care for her in a special way. We all love her, but that isn't enough."

"D'you think she'd have me?"

"Why don't you ask her? Why not call in tonight and see how she is?"

He turned from her now and pulled open the door; then he paused on the step for a moment before turning and looking at her again. He said quietly, "Thanks, ma'am."

"Bert. Call me Mrs. B., will you?"

She watched his face go into a wide grin and he said, "Willingly, Mrs. B., willingly. And again, thanks."

She watched him bring his bicycle from the wall and hitch himself down to the back garden gate, which made him look like an overgrown schoolboy from behind.

She had picked the two girls up from their separate schools. She'd had to wait fifteen minutes for Katie. There had been a rehearsal for the chorus of the concert the school was putting on, and now Katie was sitting in the passenger seat describing with some elation that she had also been chosen to do a walking on part. She had four lines to say, then toss her head and walk off; and she was about to deliver the lines yet once again, and with actions, when she turned her head and exclaimed, "There's Willie! and Sammy's with him."

Fiona pulled up sharply, and, her head out of the window, she called to the two meandering backs, "Willie!"

At this Willie came running back towards the car. Sammy's approach was a little slower, but nevertheless he was at the window when Fiona, addressing her son, said, "Well, get in."

"Okay," said Willie, now, and, turning to Sammy, he pushed him towards the back door of the car, saying, "Well, get in."

Fiona was forced to exchange the glance that her daughter was casting on her now while Mamie was greeting Willie in her usual enthusiastic way: "Willie, I've made a box to put my beads in," to which Willie's retort was, "Move along."

"Hello, boy." Mamie was now addressing the newcomer; but Master Sammy Love gave her no reply.

"Sammy's dad says he can stay to tea, Mam."

Fiona said nothing. She started up the car, but she did so with a jerk. And when her son's voice came at her on a high laugh, saying, "You'll be all right, Mam, once you've passed your test," she exclaimed loudly, "Willie!" and the tone seemed to be sufficiently meaningful to silence the backseat passengers, at least for the moment. "Don't forget, mam, that Mark's going to tea straight from school with Roland Featherstone."

"I haven't forgotten, Katie."

"Well, I just thought you might have."

"Mam"—Willie's head was on Fiona's shoulder—"Sammy says his dad says he can come to tea whenever he likes."

Fiona allowed a number of seconds to pass before she said, "Oh, did he?"

Then before Willie could confirm his statement Sammy's voice came loud and strident, "But that's only if you asked me, missis; and I hadn't to ask, I had to wait."

Katie's giggle was audible, and Fiona muttered at her, "That's enough!" Then, in a clear voice she said, "Well, Sammy, you may come to tea now and again, let's say . . . er, once a week."

"Fair enough. Ta. I know where I am now."

"Which night, Mam?" There was a disappointed note in Willie's voice.

"We'll make it a Friday, the day after tomorrow. Will that suit you, Sammy?" There was a note of sarcasm in her tone, and Sammy answered, "Aye, I suppose so . . . ta."

Because she was endeavouring to negotiate a corner, Fiona could not put her hand out and slap Katie who had swung round on her seat and, addressing Sammy, had said, "When can Willie go to your house for tea?"

And she was slightly taken aback when the answer came, "Any day, except a Thursday like. Tisn't posh like your place, but he can come."

Katie could find nothing to say to this, but when her mother pointedly said quietly to her, "I'll have a talk with you when we get home," she gave a grunt and slid further down into the seat.

Fiona had just got them settled round the table and all munching away, Willie doing the most talking, when the phone rang.

It was her mother's voice that greeted her, saying, as usual, "Fiona?"

"Yes, Mother."

There was a pause before Mrs. Vidler's voice came again, prim-sounding and definitely reluctant, with thanks. "Well, he sent a man

248

round and I must say that his men could teach others quite a lot in civility. He was a very nice well-spoken man. I'll remember to send for him if I ever have any need in that way again."

"He works for my husband, Mother. You seem to forget that."

"Oh, no, I don't forget that. I asked him what they were working on now and he said they were building two houses. And when I asked him what they were doing after he said that it was all up in the air. And I could have told him that for I get around, and from what I hear there are twenty firms in for Sir Charles Kingdom's estate. Whoever gets that will be made; it's bound to go to an experienced builder, I mean a well-established firm. So, have you thought, Fiona, what you would do then?"

Fiona stared hard into the mouthpiece before she said, "Go on the dole, Mother; and we'll live as we did before Bill came on the scene, three years from hand to mouth when you didn't offer a crumb to help me. But there'll be one difference now, Mother, I'll be happy, we'll be happy. We'll all be happy. And lastly, Mother, I want to tell you, you are the most un . . ."—her voice rose now—"the most ungrateful creature I've ever come across in my life."

The phone was quite used to being banged down; nevertheless, she kept her hand on it, once it was on the stand, as if she had hurt it and regretted her action. But her mother . . . that woman simply got her goat. Was there another mother on earth like her, so ungrateful and so determined to infiltrate any unhappiness she could into her life? It was jealousy, pure and simple jealousy. But how could a mother be so jealous of a daughter? There must be other mothers like her. If she only knew them, it would be a help because at times she felt there couldn't be anyone quite as vicious as the woman who had borne her. Yet there were times when she had heard people actually say to her, "Oh, your mother is such a nice person. She has such a gentle manner." Gentle manner indeed! She now marched up the stairs and into her bedroom where she flopped down into a chair and pressed her hands between her knees, as she had often done as a child when things had got the better of her; and she was amazed to hear herself praying aloud: "Oh, dear God, let Bill get that contract. If it's only to show her. Please! Please! And it's so important to Bill. It's the most important thing in his life."

She got up abruptly and, as if she were replying to the Deity, said, but with no plea in her voice now, "No, it isn't; we are the most important. But he wants it for us."

With that she marched out of the room. As she reached the stair-head Willie's face appeared at the bottom, saying, "We're all finished, Mam. We've put the dishes in the sink. Can we go up to the playroom? I mean, can I take Sammy up?"

"Yes, yes." She nodded at him, and he scrambled away. Just as she reached the bottom of the stairs the phone rang again. She delayed for some seconds her lifting of it; and then she held it as if it were hot: if it was her mother again she would scream at her, she would.

"Fiona?"

"Oh yes, Bill." The words came out on a sigh.

"What's the matter?"

"Oh, I've just had Mother on the phone."

"Well, what's the matter with her? She should be very pleased; her electricity's all right."

"Yes, I know that, dear; but you know Mother."

"Yes, I know Mother. But listen dear, I won't be home straight-away; I've got to go to the hospital."

"Hospital? Have you . . . what's the matter?"

"Nothing with me. But you know Barney?"

"Yes, I know Barney."

"Well, apparently he was mugged last night. I've just heard of it. I've been out with the architect all afternoon, going round that land again, seeing where we could cut corners. And I've just got in and Barney's wife phoned this afternoon. She apparently got worried last night when he didn't come back from the club. And they found him in a back alley badly knocked up. So I'm going along now. But you know, Fiona . . ."

"Yes? Yes, Bill?"

"There's something fishy going on here. First Tommy's car, then Jack Mowbray's shed was broken into, his bike stolen and most of his tools."

"When was this?"

"Oh, one day last week. These things are always happening, and I thought it was an isolated case. But now Barney. I don't like it. Anyway, I'll tell you more when I get back. You all right?"

"Yes; yes, I'm all right, dear; but I hope Barney's going to be all right."

"So do I. Anyway I'll know more when I see him. Ta-ra, love."

"Ta . . . bye-bye."

She was turning from the phone when Willie's guest, who had started to mount the stairs, turned round and looked at her and said, "Ta, missis. It was a nice tea."

She was forced to smile, saying, "I'm glad you enjoyed it, Sammy. By the way, are you sure your father knows you're staying?"

250

"Well, I said I might be able to, but I'll tell him it's just Friday nights after this, eh?"

"Yes, yes." She moved her head twice.

"It's a good job you didn't say the morrow night 'cos I go to confession on a Thursday night straight after school."

"Oh, you . . . you do . . . go to confession?"

"Aye."

Willie, now two stairs ahead of him, turned round, leaned on the bannister, and said, "He tells all his sins to a priest. If he doesn't the nuns whack him."

She walked towards the foot of the stairs now, and looking at Sammy, she said, "But how do the nuns know whether you've told all your sins to the priest?"

"Oh, they can tell, missis, they can see through you. If they know you've missed anything out they wallop you on the ear."

"The nuns wallop you?"

"Oh aye. Me Da went for one of them. He said what he'd do to her if she walloped me again. Well, I mean, on the ear! She could . . . well, do it on the backside, but not on the ear. Me da's dead against bein' walloped on the ear. You see, 'cos his da was deaf. He's dead now, his da. But his da was deaf 'cos of bein' walloped on the ear. So me da told the nun what he would do if she walloped me on the ear again. And so she hasn't done it, but instead she nearly shakes the bloody life out of you."

Fiona glanced quickly to the side to see if Katie or Mamie were in sight. They weren't. Then, wetting her lips a number of times, she stepped up a stair and, putting her hand out, she gently touched Sammy on the shoulder, saying, "Now, Sammy; you know what I think about swear words."

He stared up into her face, and his small bottom jaw moved from side to side before he said, "But I thought it was only the little ones, the four-letter 'uns."

"Yes, it was the four-letter 'uns, I mean, ones. They are vile words. But there are other words, too, like the one you've just said, and that's swearing. There's a difference, I know; but . . . it's not nice to swear."

He studied her for a moment, then with his head tilted slightly to the side, he said, "Everybody does it."

"No, my dear, everybody doesn't do it; except perhaps when they are very annoyed."

"Your man bawls, his da"—he thumbed towards Willie now—"or step-da, or what, he swears. Willie says he does."

251

She looked at her son, and he, nodding at her, said, "He does, Mam, at times, Mr. Bill. I mean Dad, he swears."

"Only when he is very, very annoyed. Oh"—she shooed them now as if they were two chickens—"get upstairs. Go on with you." And they both turned and ran from her. But at the top her son turned and called, "Mam!" And impatiently she asked, "What now?" And the reply made her turn quickly away, for Willie, nudging Sammy with his elbow, had said, "Sammy says you wouldn't be half bad if you let your face fall a bit more."

She was in the sitting room before she seemed to draw breath. She wouldn't be half bad if she let her face fall a bit more. Really! What were things coming to. She'd have to do something about this, and with that thought she moved towards the door. But then stopped. No, she wouldn't. She was thinking now like her mother. Better to let her children know that there was another life being lived by other children, then they would appreciate their home more. And on the other hand, Sammy might learn from them. "Huh!" and it was an audible reaction; she couldn't imagine either Sammy or his father learning from anyone but each other.

Accompanied by Mamie, Katie now entered the room, Katie saying, "Mam, I've washed the tea things and dried them, and Mamie helped." And Mamie chimed in, "And I didn't break nothin', Mammy B."

"That was a clever girl. Now away with you both upstairs."

"Mam, I'm sorry about that bit in the car when I acted snobby; because at teatime he was all right: he didn't take anything unless Willie pushed it towards him or I offered it; and then he said thanks, well not thanks, just ta, but it all means the same. He's awful, Mam, but you can't help sort of liking him after a time. Did he really say four-letter words?"

"I know a lot of four-letter words. At school today I wrote them on the board for the teacher: Cats, dogs, bears."

"Bears have five letters silly. Come on with you."

As Katie pushed Mamie before her out of the room, Fiona looked after them and mused on how that child had fallen into place in this household. It was as if she had been born of herself. And in a way she was a very lucky child, discounting the fact that she had lost her parents and family, because she would grow up to be a comfortably rich young lady. The compensation for the loss of her parents had been a considerable sum and it was growing with the interest. Whereas, Katie, what would Katie grow up to be? An independent spirit. Yes, for richer or poorer Katie would make her own choice, and she would see that she was allowed to do so.

28

BILL SAT LOOKING ACROSS HIS DESK AT TWO OF HIS WORKMEN, DAN MCRAY AND Alec Finlay. Dan was a tiler and Alec a bricklayer, but both could turn their hands to anything on the job. Bill was fond of them and appreciated their work. And now, looking at Dan, he said with some concern, "You feeling all right though?"

"Oh, aye, boss, I'm feeling all right, except inside where I'm bloody mad. As the others are sayin', there's something fishy goin' on. First, there was Tommy's car swiped. I know he's got it back, but they didn't get the blokes. Then Jack's shed broken into and his bike and tools taken. Now me being set on; but by God they got as much as they sent if not more: my boot caught the smaller one where he'll feel it for days, I'm tellin' you. But what would have happened to me? Likely landed up where Barney did, in hospital, if it hadn't been for those two blokes happening to come along at the time, which made the bastards scarper. Anyway, Alec, he's got something to tell you. He didn't think much of it, did you, Alec, at the time? But it might give us a lead. Fire away, Alec."

Because of a slight stammer Alec Finlay always had to be prompted into speech, but now he said quite naturally, "Brown, boss ... you know, I saw him at the gate one day last week. I was just on le ... le ... leavin'. You and Harry were away on t ... t'other site and I was havin' wo ... wo ... words with the w ... w ... watchman

253

and I noticed a car had pulled up at t'other side of the road. It was no po ... posh do but the driver saw me, he started up. But I cr ... cr ... crossed the road before he g ... g ... got go ... go ... goin'. And when I thought I rec ... rec ... recognised him I looked back and yes, 'twas him ... Brown. He had snooped around the estate often enough so I co ... co ... couldn't mistake him. He must have been si ... si ... sittin' lookin in on the gr ... gr ... ground, 'co ... 'co ... 'cos we were just g ... g ... gettin' the foundations goin' then."

Bill rose to his feet. "Brown." He nodded from one to the other. "Yes; yes, Brown; that could be the answer. But I understood he was in London."

"He was divorced a short time ago, I heard," Dan nodded at him now. "Aye and somethin' else has come to mind. It was rumoured he was back with his piece again, the one he had afore he left."

"Any idea where they live?"

Dan shook his head. "Not a clue, boss. All I knew about him was the gossip."

Bill put his hand on a heavy paperweight on the desk and pushed it around in a circle, watching the movement for some minutes before he said, "I'd like to bet we've got the answer to what's been going on here, because these attacks and the pinching are certainly no coincidence. It's never happened before to any of you, has it?" Without waiting for an answer he went on, as he pointed to Dan, "Go round the fellas and ask if anybody knows where Brown's hanging out now."

"That's an idea." Dan nodded. "Somebody's sure to know something, a bit anyway. And by God, if it's proved that he's put these fellas up to dirty work, he'll land up with more than one black eye and a split lip, and I can tell you, even if I go along the line for it."

The two men were making for the hut door when Bill stopped them, saying "You said you had an idea that one was much taller than the other?"

"Aye, that's what I got and from the feel of it an' all. I didn't get a look at their faces, 'cos they were between the lights. I saw them comin' towards me, and they walked past me. Next minute I knew they were on me."

"That sounds exactly what happened to Barney, same technique, yet Davey Love said those two fellas had scarpered after the car business. When the police got round there they had left their lodgings. He said he had heard they had crossed the river. Look, send Love in will you?"

"Will do."

When the two men went out Bill sat down again and once more he fingered the paperweight, pushing it round in circles that gradually merged into one.

Brown. Of course. Who else? For in a way, he had ruined Brown's career the night his son had smashed up the showroom on the estate, the night Brown's wife had treated him like a dog.

Yes; yes, this was Brown's doing; for without any doubt he had been the cause of the man's ruin; his visible ruin at least. Both Brown and his wife had been mean, vindictive types. But now Brown must be out to get his own back. It couldn't be his own men: he had eleven good men on this job, and they had been with him for years now. And he had made them feel that they were part of the company because at the end of the year they got their rake off of the profits. He had made it known to them when he was given the last big job, for he saw it then as good policy to let the men know they had a finger in the pie. But it looked as if Brown was out to disable his committee in one way or another. Well, he would see about that. By God, he would.

When a tap came on the door he called, "Come in." And when Davey Love entered, saying, "You want me, boss?" Bill said, "Yes, for a minute, Davey. You get about. You said you thought that those two fellas had scarpered after the car business?"

"Well, I did hear they went across the water down to North Shields."

"Are you sure of that?"

"No, not sure, boss, it was just hearsay. It was in the pub."

"You've heard about what's happening here to the fellas?"

"Aye, I've heard."

"Well, you're on the payroll now, it could be you next."

"No, begod, boss. I've got eyes in the back of me head."

"Oh, you can be too clever."

"Oh, 'tisn't a case of bein' clever; it's a case of whose walkin' behind you. I very rarely walk on the flags, I keep to the gutter or the road; cars are not half as dangerous as some people I know of, especially around our way. No, begod, I'll say."

"Do you know anything about a man called Brown? He used to be a big pot in the town, lived in one of those houses facing the Moor in Newcastle. Went to London some time ago, divorced and come back and took up with a woman he knew."

"That Brown, boss?"

"Yes, that Brown."

"Well, I know nowt about him, not really, but I know quite a bit about his one-time chauffeur-cum-odd-job man. He used to hire him when he was goin' out on a spree. He often had these bouts at one time, you know, goin' gettin' bottled up, mortalious, paralytic, the lot, oh aye, the lot. So Charlie Davison had the job of ferryin' him home. That was until Charlie saw my Betty, and once again it was love at first sight for her, and off they go together. Well, she had done it afore but not so brazenly. An' then she has the bloody cheek to come back, an' he follows her. God and His Holy Mother! Was I rattled. Well, I followed him. The result was that holiday I told you about up in Durham, boss, y'know?"

Bill wanted to laugh. He wanted to bellow. He had just to hear this fellow talk and it was as if every other word he spoke was a joke. He had that way with him. But this business on his mind now was no laughing matter, so he said, "Well, where is he now, this Charlie Davison?"

"As far away from me, boss, as he can get I should think, the way I left him."

"Aye, yes, of course he would be. So you know nothing of Brown?"

"Not at the moment, boss; but I could find out. One thing's certain though: his type won't be livin' in Bog's End, even if he got his piece from there."

"You never know; it might be her house."

"Aye, there's that in it. But private house owners are few an' far atween around our quarter you know, boss. But as Alec said, his car was just an old 'un, no BMW, Volvo, or such, so he wouldn't be livin' up in Brampton Hill area, now would he? No, not with a car like that he wouldn't. Middle town I'd say. Any road. I'll ask around. I'll have a talk with Kit Bradley. Aye, that's what I'll do. What he doesn't know isn't worth learnin'. Any road, as soon as I hear anythin' you'll know of it, boss."

"Thanks, Davey."

"You're welcome, boss."

"By the way"—Bill stopped him as he was about to turn about—"both Dan and Alec seemed to remember that the fellas who attacked them were different sizes, a tall 'un and a short 'un. Now you seemed to think that there was a pair like that who pinched Tommy Turnbull's car, didn't you?"

"Aye, begod! I'm sure it was that pair. An' givin' it another thought, they could easily have slipped up from Shields to do their dirty work an' get back. Half an hour or so each way would see to it. Aye, it could be the same couple. And if it is it's a setup job an' they're in somebody's pay, this fella Brown's. Is that how you see it, boss?"

"Yes, that's how I see it at present."

256

"Well, we'll take it from there, boss, eh?" Nodding now, he turned and went out.

Yes, Bill said to himself, we'll take it from there. But once I find out where you are, Mr. Brown, you can look out for sparks.

He was again pushing the paperweight around in circles. He had been in a few tight corners, businesswise, in his time but none so tight as this one. There was a time limit in getting those two houses finished and somebody ... Brown in fact knew what time limits meant and was aiming to diminish his work force. And each of his men in his own way was an expert and worth three of any casual labour he might have to take on.

Then there was the thought that when this job was finished he'd be out on his beam ends if he didn't get that contract. And the more he knew about those who were in for it the more he saw it receding from him. He had heard that although Sir Charles Kingdom was out of hospital now he was still not a well man, so there was little hope of coming across him.

He rose from the chair and took his coat from the peg on the wall of the cabin, thinking as he did so there were businesses dropping like flies around him. Well, he wasn't going to go down without a fight, and the first blow to be struck would be at Mr. Brown.

Nell said, "You look tired. What you want is a night out."

"Well, I should think that would make me more tired. What I think I really want is an early night in bed."

"We are of different opinions there." And Nell cast a naughty glance at Fiona, then said, "Get the big boy to take you out to dinner. And why you wanted to tack a new addition onto the squad I'll never know."

"I've told you, Nell; I had no option."

"But he stood at the door there and argued with you and reminded you that you said Friday night was visiting night for him."

Fiona sighed. "Oh, I know; but there he was, wanting to be contradicted. I don't know what it is about him, he's an uncouth, dirty ... no, he's not dirty, I will say that for him; however, he's been brought up, his father keeps him very tidily dressed, but there's something about him."

"Yes, I know there is, but I'm not going to let it get at me."

"Oh, Nell Paget; there you were giving him the biggest piece of cake from the plate, filling his mug before it was empty. Oh, you're a hypocrite. Anyway, you tell me to get out, how can I when you're off tonight jitterbugging?"

At this Nell put her head back and laughed, saying, "Oh, that's funny. Can you see Bert jitterbugging?"

"Yes; yes, I can; Bert to my mind is a deep well."

"Oh, don't say that, Fiona." Nell's face was serious now. "I don't want to find out anything more about him than I do now, because if I put my bucket down the well it might bring up something nasty."

"Not in Bert's case. He's a good nice man and . . . he's attractive."

"I'm glad you think so."

"Oh, come off it, Nell. You more than think so, you're positive of it. Has . . . well, has he spoken yet in any way?"

"No . . . Mrs. Bailey, he hasn't spoken yet, but the minute he does you'll be the first to know." She laughed now, saying quietly, "It's odd, you know, Fiona, but I feel like a daft girl, waiting you know, knowing what's going to come and a bit frightened of it. Well, well"—her tone altered—"I suppose I would be after what I've gone through, because, don't forget, the late Mr. Paget was also thought to be very charming. That sounded as if he was dead." She gave a little giggle now, then added, "I don't wish him dead; no, I wish him a long, long, long life and a houseful of bairns. Oh yes I do, because then there won't be any time for his wife to baby him, and he has been babied from birth. When we married, I simply took over from his mother. Ah, well, it's all over, and I'll get away before the lord of the manor comes in, and also leave you to get rid of your guest." She laughed now as she added, "It's amazing how Willie's taken to him, isn't it? And he apparently to Willie. They go to different schools; you didn't say how they met up."

"Apparently on the football field. Master Samuel was warned off, or carried off, or sent off, or some such and roused Willie's admiration. They got on talking, as far as I can gather, and the next thing Mr. Love junior was waiting for Willie coming out of school. He's at the convent along Mitchell Road. He's got to come some way from Bog's End to there."

"He's at the convent!"

"Yes, he's at the convent. And by all accounts, if you believe him, all nuns are not angels."

"Oh, I can believe that. Well, as I said, I'll be off. If there's one thing can be said about this house, it's never lost for entertainment."

She was going out of the door when Fiona said, "Let me know if it happens, won't you?"

"What happens?"

"Oh, go on with you! Get out!" As she pushed Nell out and closed the door, she heard the pounding of feet crossing the landing. She

258

hadn't reached the kitchen door before it burst open and Willie came in, followed by Sammy.

"Mam, can Sammy come to my birthday party?"

"Your birthday party? That's weeks ahead."

"Only three. It's the day after Easter Monday, you know."

"Yes, I know, I know."

As Fiona spoke she wasn't looking at her son but was returning the gaze of Samuel Love whose face had lost its wide expectancy and was now set, lips tight, the eyes unblinking. She heard herself say, "Why, yes, of course, if Sammy would like to come."

"Oh, he'd like to come, wouldn't you, Sammy?"

It seemed that Sammy had difficulty in taking his gaze from his pal's mother. And when he did, his answer was abrupt and to the point: "Aye," he said.

"Oh, well, that's settled." Even as Fiona spoke she thought of Roland Featherstone, who had been to tea with Mark just two nights ago and who spoke so beautifully; in fact, she was hoping that Mark would take a pattern from him. Not that her son did not speak well, but there was a difference between Roland's accent and that of the members of her own family. And the difference had been emphasized when Katie "did him," immediately he left the room to depart, and then infuriated Mark on his return from setting his friend off to the bus by greeting him with: "How d'you do? How d'you do, Mr. Bailey?" and turning to Fiona, had added, "I'm so pleased to meet you, Mrs. Bailey." And when Mark had struck out at her, she had come back at him with her toe in his shins after she herself had remonstrated; and Katie's last words were, "Well, he gets up my nose. He's a cissy." And she had further had to restrain Mark from dashing after the figure that was disappearing up the stairs.

It was about nine o'clock that evening when Fiona, taking yet another cup of coffee into the study, said, "Give over a minute. Sit back and leave that. Get your coffee and listen. You know Willie's birthday is looming up? Well, the latest is he's asked Sammy to come, and Mark has already asked Roland. Now imagine the party with those two, poles apart, present."

"It should be fun."

"What! With Willie ready to strike a blow for Sammy and Mark getting on his high horse if everybody doesn't admire Roland."

"Well, if you want my opinion, Mrs. B., if Master Roland doesn't like the setup, he can lump it."

"Oh, of course your sympathies lie with the poor downtrodden Sammy."

"Huh! There you've got it wrong. My sympathies might lie with him, but he's no poor downtrodden Sammy. I'd like to bet he's got more spunk and intelligence in his little finger than Master Roland's got in his whole body. Although mind, I like that lad. He's a civil enough kid, except of course that he speaks a different language." He grinned at her now.

"Yes; yes, it's evident he speaks a different language."

And laying across the desk now, he poked his face at her, saying, "And you would like your sons to speak the same as him, wouldn't you? Not common . . . like me and Sammy Love."

"Yes, you're exactly right, exactly, Mr. Bailey."

"If I come round there I'll slip your lugs for you. You're nothin' but a snob, you know that? I thought when I married you I'd knock it out of you, but I see I've still got a long way to go. You're your mother's daughter all right."

The satisfied smile slid from Fiona's face and she muttered now, "Don't say that, Bill. I mean, don't see me as you see my mother."

He was round the desk and had his arms about her, saying, "My God, woman, don't you know when I'm joking?"

She swallowed, then said, "Yes; yes, I do; but oh, sometimes I get het up inside when I say something or do something and I tell myself that's just like Mother. And I can't help it but I don't want to be like Mother in any way. She's vicious and vindictive."

"Now, now, forget about her. Give us a kiss."

A moment later he pressed his head back from her, saying, "That wasn't worth tuppence. Going cold on me, are you? Somebody else in your eye? Oh, I know; you're jealous because Bert's going to pop the question." He laughed; then went on, "I wonder if he's done it?" And Fiona had just answered, "She'll phone me if he has," when there was a ring, but at the front door and she expostulated, "Oh lord, who's that at this time?"

"Likely she's bringing him the front way all correct an' proper."

"No, not her," she said as she turned to go and answer the door; but straightaway he said, "Stay! It's after nine; who do we get at this time of night?"

When Bill opened the front door he saw whom they had got at this time of night. "Hello, boss," said Davey Love. "'Tis late, I know, but I've got a bit of news. I've just come across it, so it entered me mind that you might like to hear of it."

"Come in. Come in, Davey. Come through here."

"Evenin', Mrs. Bailey. It's nice out; there's a full moon the night. 'Tis a beautiful sight, a full moon. But it does disturb some folks, so

I'm told, at least they used to say in Ireland. But then there's some barmy ones over here an' all. Oh aye; begod, yes."

"Is ... is that so?" Her reply was stilted; Mr. Love's conversation and even his greetings were different from the usual. "Would you like a cup of coffee?" she said.

"I would that. Yes, I would that, Mrs. Bailey, ma'am, if it's no trouble. But that's a daft thing to say; everything at night's a trouble. But I accept your invitation, kindly given an' kindly received."

Fiona made her way towards the kitchen, her head making small perplexing movements.

In the study Bill said, "Sit down, Davey. What's this news you've got for me?"

"Well, it's like this, boss. I was in the Mucky Duck."

"The what?" Bill screwed up his face.

"Oh, that's me name for it. It's Kit Bradley's pub. It's called the Duck an' Drake, because, apparently, they tell me, years gone, donkeys' years, there was a farm there where the pub stood, I mean stands the day."

Bill made a small sound in his throat, then said, "Aye ... aye, I understand."

And Davey went on, "Well, I was doin' me little bit behind the bar, just washin' glasses you know—as I said, I'm not allowed to serve 'cos I would be thereby committin' a felony against the dole, but washin' glasses I'm only helpin' out a friend. Y'see? Well, there I was helpin' out a friend when this fella comes in. Now I know every customer in that place as well as does Kit himself, an' when strangers appear they stick out like sore thumbs, as did them two fellas I told you about who pinched the car.... You've never heard any more about those, have you, boss?"

"Davey, come to the point, will you?"

"Oh aye, that's me: I start meanderin' up a lane an' find meself in the middle of the A-One, an' drivin' on the wrong side. Well, I'll come to the point, aye I will. This fella asks for a large whiskey, and he gets it. An' then he asks for another and he gets it. And I happen to go round the counter and pick some glasses up from an end table an' Joe Honeysett, that's the fella I know, he stops me and wags his head to the side an' he says to me, 'He's out of the way, isn't he?' And I said, 'Who?' And he nods toward the newcomer an' said he, 'Brown, who used to be the bigshot.' So, of course, boss, as soon as he mentioned the name I said, 'Brown? Brown who used to be the builder?' an', said he, 'Aye. But he was never any builder, financier or somethin', but never any builder. He provided the money like. But his wife got rid of him an' he's back in town.' 'D'you know where he lives now?' said I. 'I only know one thing,' said Joe, 'he doesn't live round this quarter.'

"So there I was, boss, behind the counter again sayin' to Kit, 'Can I have the loan of your jalopy for half an hour or so?' 'What for?' said he. 'I'll tell you when I come back,' said I. And to that he said, 'Well, take the jalopy, but drive it back in one piece. D'you understand?' Anyway, there I was sittin' in Kit's old banger that he takes more care of than he would a Volvo when this fella comes out and gets into his car. And it was no great shakes either. An' so, as I trailed him, I felt like The Minder. And it was as Joe said, he didn't live anywhere in Bog's End, but in quite a nice part really, middle town. Seventy-two Drayburn Avenue, boss."

"Drayburn Avenue, eh? Well, not a bad part as you say. Thanks, Davey. Look—" He put his hand into his back pocket and pulled out some loose change, four sovereigns amongst it, and when he handed them across the table to Davey, saying, "Get yourself a drink from this side of the counter," Davey Love rose to his feet and with a dignity that could have appeared comic at any other time, said, "Thanks, boss, but I'm not after expecting to be paid for a service like that. Anythin' I do for you outside workin' hours is to repay *you* an' your good missis for what you're doin' for me lad. Keepin' him off the streets an' showin' him a different way of life."

For a moment Bill felt a twinge of guilt, knowing that the boy was only allowed into the house on sufferance. But in a way he could understand Fiona's reaction to the child, because Willie was talking and acting more like his new mate every day; and while this, perhaps, had amused him at first, deep down he wanted his lad, as he thought of him, to be different, better than himself, at least where speech was concerned, and so he was now less amused. But he wouldn't for the world let Fiona know this. At the other end of the scale there was Master Roland Featherstone. Now Fiona was more than willing to let her son copy Master Roland, oh yes. And wasn't he himself pleased in a way that Mark would pass himself and be able to converse like young Featherstone? Oh, to hell! What was he thinking? He had Brown's number now and, by God, he'd have more than his number tomorrow when he saw him. Pocketing the coins again, he said, "No offence meant, Davey."

"None taken, boss, none taken. Well, I'll have to be off. An' now I've got the banger outside I'll go an' pick up that scallywag of mine from me ma's."

He was making for the door when he turned and faced Bill again as if answering in protest some remark Bill had made; "I don't let him run the streets when I'm at the pub, don't think that. I push him along to me ma's; that's when she's in, 'cos she's an old gadabout. But when I can I make it worth her while to stay put. This is a very mercenary world we're in, boss. God! I'll say it is. Although it's Himself made it. Yet there's times I have me doubts; and then I have to ask myself, if He didn't who did?"

"You're right there, Davey, you're right there. It is a very mercenary world."

"Oh aye, I'm right there; you can get nowhere without money. Money doesn't only talk, it shouts, it bawls. By God, aye."

He had turned away, but now he turned yet again, and with a hand clasping the knob of the study door, and his voice lower, he said, "You'll never know how grateful I am for me job. And I can promise you this, you'll get more work out of me than you will out of a willin' donkey."

"Aw! Go on with you." Bill gave him a push, and they both entered the hall laughing.

Bill opened the front door and was feeling almost thankful to be about to say a final goodnight to his visitor when Davey, standing on the step and leaning towards him, said, "You know something, boss? I can tell you where I wouldn't tell another soul, but I've made up me mind that I'm goin' to Mass on Sunday. Tis years since I stepped foot in a church, but that's where you'll find me on Sunday, first Mass, an' givin' thanks to God for straightenin' me life out for me, an' bringin' good friends into me son's existence. For only God an' His Holy Mother know that that kid wouldn't have had a rougher time if he had been brought up in Siberia. 'Night, boss."

Bill did not reply. He watched the figure disappear down the garden path and through the gate; then he closed the door and stood with one hand pressed against it for a moment, his head bowed. And as he stood he stilled the desire to let out a bellow of a laugh, because he knew if he had, another emotion might have welled up in him and contradicted his laughter.

Fiona, coming out of the sitting room, said, "I thought you would be coming in for the coffee, but he's gone. What's the matter?"

"Nothing, Nothing, love."

"What did he want?"

"He's found out where Brown lives."

"Oh, Bill, you won't go and do anything silly?"

"Nothing silly, love. The only weapon I'll use is me mouth."

"What's wrong?"

"Nothing. Nothing's wrong, love."

"There is. Something's happened. Has he said something, something to upset you?"

"No, no; nothing to upset me. I'll tell you about it later, perhaps when we're in bed and the light out and our heads under the clothes."

He bent forward, kissed her lightly on the lips, then made his way to the study.

Life was strange.

29

BILL DID NOT VISIT 72 DRAYBURN AVENUE UNTIL LATE THE FOLLOWING afternoon, for as he saw it now, Brown would surely be working and wouldn't be at home until tea time. Yet this morning, when he arrived at the site and Arthur Taggart, the watchman, told him that Dandy had been uneasy around one o'clock, and that when he let the dog go Dandy had raced around barking his head off; he was sure the dog had disturbed someone on the site, because when he reached the road he heard a car starting up, and there wasn't another house for a couple of hundred yards along the lane. It was then that Bill had wanted to dash round to Brown's straightaway and confront him.

He phoned Fiona to say he might be a little late. When she had enquired where he was going he had replied, flippantly, to get blind drunk, so she had better look out and get the tribe to bed, because he would be in the mood to play merry hell when he got in.

"I'll do as you say, Mr. Bailey," she had answered coolly, "but should you find the door locked, there's always a hotel in the town, the one you went to before, you remember?" He had been able to smile as he put the phone down, but he wasn't smiling when, a short while later, he rang the bell at 72 Drayburn Avenue.

Waiting for the door to open he stretched his neck out of his pullover while telling himself he should have gone home and changed

265

and smartened himself up before coming here. But what the hell! He just couldn't wait to get at this fellow.

The door had opened and he was looking at a woman well into her fifties: he was a good judge of age, and her tinted hair and well madeup face didn't deceive him; she wasn't a kick in the backside off sixty. Maybe she was the mother of Brown's piece.

"Yes?"

"I'd like to speak to Mr. Brown, please."

"He's not in." The woman took half a step forward and pulled the door behind her and, her voice changing now, said, "And he won't be in to you, ever. I know who you are. You're Bailey, so get about your business. You've done enough harm, you."

She almost fell back as the door was wrenched open and there stood Brown. But he wasn't the same Brown as Bill had last seen him; he had lost a lot of weight; yet his manner was the same. "I've been expecting you," he said.

"Well, you're not disappointed, are you? And you know why I've come?"

"Oh yes, I know why you've come. Your little tin-pot business is being nibbled at."

Bill clenched his teeth, then said slowly, "You call being nibbled at leaving a man half dead, stealing a car, breaking into sheds, and last night aiming to sabotage me building?"

"Is that all that's been done?"

"Look, Brown; you're asking for it and you'll get it, not from me, for I wouldn't soil me hands on you, but from the courts because I'm puttin' up with this no longer. You must be a fool to think you can get away with it."

"The only fool I've been is that I didn't bust you years ago when I could have done."

"It was never in your power, Brown, to bust me, and you know it. In your wife's, aye. Yes, in hers, but never in yours. You're a little man. You'll always be a little man."

The woman, in some agitation, pulled at Brown's arm, saying, "Come in. Come in. Leave him; he's not worth it. He's not."

Brown brushed off the restraining arm and said slowly, "I'm going to tell you something, Bailey. You're barking up the wrong tree. I've got no hand in what's been happening to your tin-pot business. D'you hear me? And this is the truth. No matter how much I'd like to see you and your little empire go up in smoke, I've never lifted a hand towards you, for the simple reason I've been too busy arranging my own business. No, you can take my word for it, whatever's happening to you, and will go on happening to you—oh yes, I can promise you.

266

that, it will go on happening to you—it's none of my doing. But you know something else? I wish it was. And yet it's good to stand on the sideline and see your dirty work done for you. So get the hell from my door. And if the things I wish for you come about, there'll come a time when you'll wish you were dead."

The door was banged, and Bill was left standing looking at it and not knowing what to think: he only knew what he felt and that was that Brown was telling the truth.

He'd have to look for another source, somebody else, some other firm that had it in for him. And there were a number to choose from, and more probably one of those that were in for the contract for the building of the estate. He got into his car, but did not immediately drive home; he stopped in a lay-by and sat thinking.

Three of the builders in for the business were known to him, and he felt sure they would never stoop to doing another down in the way that was happening to him. Would the big boys go to that trouble? Oh yes, yes; he could understand some of the big boys going to a great deal of trouble to wipe out an opponent. But why him? Oh yes; that was the point: they must think him worth wiping out; perhaps they had heard he had been favoured by Sir Charles Kingdom.

Fiona greeted him with, "Well, what happened?"

"It isn't him."

"What do you mean, it isn't him? He's not behind this business, all the things that are happening to the men?"

"No."

"How do you know?"

"Because he said so."

"And you believe him?"

"Yes, on this occasion I believe him."

"Well, who could it be?"

"It can only be one of those in for the estate job. I must have opened me mouth too often about the good gang I have and that once they get goin' each one's as good as three of the ordinary floaters that's goin' about today. I should keep me mouth shut."

"Yes, you should."

"Oh, don't you start."

"I'm only repeating what you said. Look, there's piles of hot water; go and have a bath and change. It will make you feel better. I'll see if I can rake up some scraps for a meal, such as a meat pudding."

"Meat pudding!" He pulled a face at her.

"Well, I don't know what it will be like by now or by the time you'll be ready for it. But go on, I'll have a talk to it."

"Where's the tribe? There's no bustle, no yelling."

"Oh, they're upstairs. Katie's in a mood. The bottom's fallen out of her world: she didn't come top in the mock exam; in fact, she didn't come second or third. She really can't believe it, so she's up there now digging into her homework, screaming at anybody who dares look at her. And Willie nearly got another twanking."

"Why?"

"He came out with a polite 'bloody.' Something will have to be done about him and that boy."

"Oh, the boy's all right. He'll learn."

"And so will Willie, all the wrong things."

"It's a phase; it'll pass."

Detecting a weary note in his voice, she said, "Go on up those apples and pears."

He grinned at her, saying now, "I don't mind you turning common, that'll suit me, but it's got to be Liverpudlian common, or Geordie common, I draw the line at Cockney."

He had reached the landing when he turned and called, "Fiona!" And when she reached the foot of the stairs, he asked her, "Any news about the love birds?"

"No. She said he never said a word. They had a lovely meal and went to a show, and that was that."

"Silly bugger!"

And Fiona endorsed this as she walked towards the kitchen. Yes, he was a silly bugger.

It was about eight o'clock that night when the silly bugger came knocking at the back door. And when Fiona said, "Come in, come in," he hesitated, saying, "She's not in, is she, I mean Nell?"

"No; no, she's next door."

"Good. I . . . I'd like a word with you and the boss."

"All right. Sit down. I was just going to take him in a drink; he's in the study."

"No, I won't sit if you don't mind, Mrs. B. it's . . . it's . . ."

"Sit down, Bert. And stop fidgeting." She laughed at him. "Look, have that cup of coffee." She took a cup off the tray.

"No, no."

"Shut up and drink that; I can always make another."

She now left the kitchen and hurried to the study and, pushing open the door, said, "Come into the kitchen for a moment, there's an employee of yours waiting to see you. And if you want any work out of him in the future you'd better straighten out his love life."

"Bert?"

"Yes, Bert."

She gave an exaggerated whisper. "And by the look of him he doesn't know which end of him is up. It's dreadful to reach that age before love hits you. He's had no practice at it."

When Bill entered the kitchen Bert got to feet, saying, "I'm sorry to trouble you, boss, but . . . well, it's like this."

"Sit yourself down, man, and finish your coffee. Where's mine, woman?"

Fiona handed him the cup, and he sat down opposite Bert, saying, "What's happened? Got home and found out you've been burgled?"

"No, nothing like that, boss. That would be simpler. Oh aye, that would be simpler. No; it's something I want to ask you. How long will this job take, boss? I mean . . ."

"Well, you know as well as me, Bert, there's a time limit on it. We've got another eight weeks and then, if nothing comes up, we're all in the soup."

"Aye . . . aye, I know that, boss, I know I'm asking the road I know, but have you nothin' in mind besides the big estate job?"

"Not a thing, Bert. Not a thing, at least so far. Of course, there might be some odd bits and pieces pop up in the next few weeks, but they'll only be patching jobs, or gutting, because there's no spare land around here now, or very little, and what there is they want a gold mine for it. Anyway, Bert, you know the lay of the land, you've been with me long enough, you know I discuss everything with you all."

"Aye, I know that, boss, but it's . . . er—" He drooped his head now and watched his fingers drumming on the table before he said, "It's Nell. I want to ask her. Oh aye, I want to ask her. But what are me prospects if I'm finished after this lot? I own me own house, as you know, but there's rates and upkeep and you've got to eat, and in spite of all she's been through, she's lived a very . . . well . . . sort of middle-class life, so I can't ask her, the way things stand. It's come too late in life anyway." He turned his head to the side, only to be almost startled by Fiona, and in a voice that could have been attributed to Bill, crying, "Don't be so damn soft and blind! Nell hasn't lived an easy middle-class life; she's had to work all her days to help to keep that no-good husband of hers in comfort. So don't make that an excuse."

"Oh no! No! No!" He was on his feet now. "I . . . I don't want to make an excuse, I just . . . don't want to offer her something less than she's been used to and . . ."

"You know what you are, Bert"—it was Bill speaking in a voice that was unusually quiet for him—"you're a bloody fool. And I've known some good bloody fools being left on the shelf through the

269

same ideas as you've got. And I can tell you this: if you wait any longer, when you do pop the question you'll be refused, 'cos she'll get the idea that you don't really want her. Women are like that, you know; they're bloody awkward." He cast a glance at Fiona. "They go as far as to tell their sons that they'll never marry, at least not fellas like brickies."

"Bill!"

"Yes, Fiona? Well, you did. You did tell Mark that you'd never marry me."

"Only because you kept pumping into me and everybody else within earshot that you were a middle-of-the-road man and that you would never marry anybody. Anyway, it's just like you to turn everything into a personal fight." She looked at Bert now. "Bert, you go next door this very minute and tell Nell what's in your mind and why you didn't pop the question to her last night when she was all dressed up and waiting."

"You think she was?"

"I don't think, I'm sure. But, as Bill here said, women are queer cattle and you don't know what will happen just out of sheer pride."

"But what if I'm out of work?" He was looking at Bill now and Bill's answer was a bark. "There's always the bloody dole and social security and the odd scraps from our table here."

Bert was smiling quietly now as he looked from one to the other, and his head wagged for a moment before he said, "Well, if I never have a wife I'll always feel I've got two good friends."

As he turned from the table, Bill said, "What are you going to do?"

"Do what your Mrs. B. told me, go next door. But mind, me heart's in me mouth."

"Well, spit it out and give it to her. Go on."

Bill pushed him out of the door; and then, looking at Fiona, he said, "I didn't know there were any of them left."

"Any what left? What do you mean?"

"Just him, the likes of him, fellas who are afraid to ask a woman. He's an oddity."

"Oh, I don't think so." She went towards the kitchen door now, saying, "I think there are many men like him. It's people like you who are the oddities, the brash individuals." And she let out a squeal when he brought his hand across her buttocks; then hearing a door open upstairs she turned on him, saying in a whisper, "There you are! Prepare yourself to meet the horde."

There was only one solitary figure at the top of the stairs. "Mam."

"Yes, what is it?"

"Sammy's got a present for you. He's going to bring it on Saturday."

"A present for me? That's very nice of him. What might it be?"

"He wouldn't tell me, but he says it's lovely."

"Oh, I'll look forward to that. But he'd better not bring it in the morning because, as you know, we all go out shopping."

"I told him that. I said early afternoon."

"Oh, you did?"

"Yes, Mam. That okay?"

"I . . . suppose so."

"Do you like Sammy, Dad?"

"Yes. Yes"—Bill nodded up at him—"yes, I quite like Sammy."

"I thought you did. I . . . I told him you would, I mean like him, because he's your type. I'm off to bed now. Goodnight, Mam. Goodnight, Dad."

Fiona had hurried away, her hand across her mouth.

And they had just entered the sitting room and Bill was saying, "I see nothing funny in that, Mrs. B.," when the phone rang, and Fiona, swinging around, said, "That'll be Nell to give us the news."

But a moment later when she lifted up the receiver and the voice said, "Fiona," she turned her head quickly and looked towards where Bill was standing in the doorway. And when she raised her eyes ceilingwards she heard him say, "Oh no!" as she herself said, "Yes, Mother?"

"Now don't you get on your high horse, Fiona, at what I'm going to say. It's all for your own good. Well, I mean, the children's good."

"What is for the children's good, Mother?"

"Well, to put it in a nutshell, the company they keep."

"Oh. Well, as far as I know they all keep very good company." She closed her mind to Sammy. "Mark is very friendly with the son of a doctor whom I understand is a leading specialist in his own way, he's a gastroenterologist; and Katie has a number of friends, and their parents, I know, would pass your scrutiny. One is an air pilot who I understand makes frequent trips to America." She did not continue along this line to state that two of the fathers were unemployed, one having been made redundant recently after twenty-five years managing quite a large business concern; she paused and presently her mother's voice came over the line, saying, "And Willie's friend?"

"Oh, Willie's friend is the son of a builder."

"Son of a builder indeed! If I'm going on what Mrs. Quinn heard, the B could stand for blaggard and bad language. She happened to be following them as they came along the street and she said, the . . .

271

the *b's* punctuated every other word the boy said, and they were many and varied."

"What a pity some of them didn't sting Mrs. Quinn if there were so many flying about."

"Don't be facetious, Fiona. And don't tell me that you've sunk so low that you condone your son's keeping company with dirty scum like that boy."

Fiona held the phone away from her face for a moment; then, bringing the mouthpiece close, she almost yelled, "He's neither dirty nor scum! He is an unfortunate child who didn't have your opportunities or mine, as badly brought up as I was."

"Fiona!"

"Yes, Mother; I say again, as badly brought up as I was. In fact, there's a great similarity between young Sammy Love, and that's his name, and myself, for Sammy has never tasted mother-love as far as I can understand. And will you please tell Mrs. Quinn that if she doesn't stop minding my business I might start looking into hers and why she's on her own so much."

"Her husband works away. You know that."

"Yes, but why does he work away? And where does he work away?"

"On an oil rig. He's quite a big man."

"Oh, I admit, he's quite a big man, at least in appearance; but men don't work on oil rigs for nearly eleven months in the year. It's a long time since I've seen Mr. Quinn. Now you tell her or I'll tell her myself. Yes, I will; so don't bother, Mother, I'll do it myself. Goodnight!" She banged down the phone, then turned to where Bill was standing close to her and he said quietly, "Good for you, lass. Good for you." Then, bending and kissing her, he said, "Pick up the phone again."

"I . . . I didn't mean, Bill."

"Pick up the phone again and hand it here."

Slowly she handed him her phone; and he dialled a number and when a polite voice said, "Yes, Patricia Quinn here," he said, "Good evening, Mrs. Quinn. This is your neighbour but one, Mr. William Bailey. We have just had a call from Mrs. Vidler relating to us all the information you gave her concerning my son's companion. Now, Mrs. Quinn, I want to tell you something. You interfere with our family life, my children's companions, or anything that happens in Number Two, then I will start probing into the affairs of Number Six, and I'm sure that'll be very enlightening. Have you got my meaning, Mrs. Quinn?"

"You . . . you're a dreadful man. Don't you dare threaten me."

"Oh, Mrs. Quinn, I wouldn't dream of threatening you; I'm just saying, should you interfere in our affairs, then, on a friendly basis, too, we shall go about interfering in yours and bring to light, I'm sure, certain things that may be embarrassing. You understand me, Mrs. Quinn? You see, I have ways and means of garnering information."

A gasp came over the phone before it was banged down, and Bill, turning to Fiona, said, "Have you noticed, Mrs. B., my use of words when I'm on the phone, big words, unusual words? Garnering . . . that was a good one, eh . . . ?"

"Oh, shut up! I don't feel like laughing, Bill." She turned from him and hurried into the sitting room; and when he followed her she said, "I'm worried, really I am. I . . . I know you like Sammy, and in a way I do, too, but he's no companion for Willie. I told you how Willie's letting words slip out as naturally as God bless you."

"I know, I know, love." He put his arm around her. "But in a way I think Sammy's going to learn more from Willie than Willie will learn from him. And ask yourself, now ask yourself"—he brought her round to face him—"have you it in your heart to tell that little chap not to come back here again and to stop seeing Willie? Now have you?"

Fiona moved her head impatiently; then she said, "Well, something's got to be done. You've got to have a talk with him."

"With which one?"

When the phone interrupted their discourse, again Fiona gasped, "Oh, no! I bet she's phoned my mother."

"Leave it to me."

"No, Bill."

"Look"—he pushed her none too gently—"you leave this to me."

In the hall he grabbed up the phone. "Yes? What is it now?"

When the voice came at him, "Is that Bailey?" Bill held the mouthpiece away from him. He thought he recognised the voice, but he didn't give himself time to think before he was answering, "Yes; yes, this is Bailey, William Bailey."

"Well, this is Charles Kingdom here."

Oh, good God! He did not actually voice this but said it in protest against himself.

"You still there?"

"Yes, sir. Yes, I'm still here; and forgive me for my abruptness when I picked up the phone, I was . . . well, rather angry with someone." He allowed his voice to drop to a confidential whisper and said, "Mother-in-law."

A slight giggle came over the line; then it rose to a laugh, and the voice came on a long chuckle, "Mine's dead, but I know what you mean. How are you?"

"Oh, I'm very well, sir. And you? I heard you weren't too good."

"No, I wasn't; but I'm back home now, under protest. Nobody wants me: here, they all say I should have stayed in hospital; and there, they were glad to get rid of me." The voice dropped now as he went on, "Wife's just walked out of the room." Then resuming his ordinary tone, he went on, "Like to see you, Bailey. Now, now, don't get big ideas. It's not about the option, or the big business, but I would just like to see you and have a chat about . . . well, how you're going on. That all right with you?"

"Yes, sir; yes. I would like to very much."

"How about Saturday afternoon?"

"That would do splendidly, sir."

"What do you do usually on Saturdays?"

"Oh, well, it's usually a family day, shopping you know."

"Well, if it's fine: bring them with you."

"There's four of them, sir."

"Yes; yes, I think I remember there's four of them. Well, I think the garden's big enough to take four. If I remember rightly there were five hundred at the last garden party here for some damn charity or other. But that was some time ago now, when my wife was young and agile." The voice dropped again: "She's back in the room," which made Bill smile when he recognised that the voice wasn't low enough to miss his wife's ears; and it made him think they must be on very good terms, those two.

"Three o'clock suit you?"

"Yes, sir. Thank you very much. We'll be there at three o'clock and be very pleased to see you."

"Daffodils are still out. Great sight in the woods. . . . Saturday then?"

"Yes, sir." He heard the phone click before he put down his own receiver; then he turned and looked at Fiona, who was standing a short distance from him, and said, "Sir Charles Kingdom. Invited on Saturday for three o'clock . . . and the gang."

"No!" She came up to him, her arms about his neck now: "You've got it?"

"No. Apparently it's not about that. I don't know why he wants to see me, but he made it quite plain it wasn't about the contract."

"Oh."

"Well, I told you, didn't I, he's not alone in this. There's quite a board. He might have a big say but, after all, he's only one."

"But a very important one I should think."

"Yes, yes." He now walked her towards the sitting room, saying nothing more until they were seated opposite the fire, when, leaning forward, his elbows on his knees and his hands dropped between them, he said, "I wonder what he wants to see me about if not about that? It must be something important to ask me over there. He's a queer old card, with a mind like a rapier, for all his age. But you know what he said? He said, 'The daffodils are out. Great sight in the woods.'"

"Did he really! The daffodils are out. Great sight in the wood. Sounds so nice. What is the hall like?"

"Beautiful, not all that big. I told you, I did a job over there, gutting one wing, and making it like another self-contained house. I really think he had it done for his tribe when they descend on him. By what he said he's not very fond of family gatherings, but perhaps that's only a front he puts on."

Fiona caught hold of his hands now, saying, "I feel excited already. And oh, won't the children enjoy it. Do you think I should go and tell them? They won't be asleep."

"Can't see any harm in it. You can use it as a bribe to make them behave."

"That's an idea." She pushed herself up quickly and almost ran from the room; and Bill lay back on the couch, his mind again questioning: I wonder what he wants? He hasn't asked me over there just to say hello or to see the bairns. There's something in the wind. Ah, well, I'll have to wait till Saturday afternoon, won't I?

It was as if the two words had brought him to the edge of the couch again and he repeated, Saturday afternoon. That's when little Sammy's going to bring Fiona her present. So what are we going to do about that?

Well, he told himself, the only thing to do would be to get Willie on the quiet and tell him to tell Sammy to get here before two o'clock, for if he were to arrive at the hall at three o'clock, they would have to leave here by a quarter past two, and if not forewarned about time, Mr. Samuel Love might arrive just as they were leaving. And what would happen then? Oh, he knew what would happen: Master William would see no reason why his pal could not join the afternoon outing. And that would be just too much for Fiona. So he must see that that emergency did not arise.

It should happen that Bill could do nothing about that particular emergency, for Willie was sick in the night, whether it was from excitement about the proposed visit or something that he had eaten, Fiona didn't know, but she kept him off school on the Friday.

275

Saturday came and Fiona took the children shopping in the morning while Bill continued to work with figures in the study. But he certainly knew that they had all returned home when Katie dashed into the study, crying, "I've got a new dress, Dad. It's blue with a flared skirt and a white lace collar."

"My! My!"

"And Willie's got new pants. He doesn't like them. They're long pants and he wanted short ones like Sammy. And he started to play up in the shop and Mam said she would leave him behind and he said that was all right with him."

"Don't tell tales!"

Katie turned to Fiona who was now coming into the room and answered her: "Well, you did. I mean, he did. He's always causing a fuss."

"And, of course, you don't?"

The voice came from Mark who was behind his mother: "Blessed Saint Katie of the enlarged mouth."

"I'll hit you, our Mark." But as she made a dive for him, Bill, who had come round the desk, caught her by the collar of her coat and, swinging her about, bent over her and said, "D'you want to come with us this afternoon?"

She wagged her head, turned it slightly to the side, pursed her lips but said nothing.

"That means you do. So behave yourself, miss. Where's Mamie?"

"She's followed Willie upstairs," said Mark. "She's bought a dummy for her dolls. But how she's going to get it into their mouths I don't know because her dolls are china ones."

"Did you get anything new?" Bill looked at Mark.

"No, not a thing; I'm the last to be thought of in this house."

"Poor soul." Bill pulled a face as Mark grinned at him. Then Fiona, dropping down into the leather chair at the side of the desk, said, "It would be very nice if somebody made me a cup of tea."

"I'll do it, Mam."

As Katie made to dash from the room Mark said pompously, "There's good in the child yet," which stopped her in her tracks, whereupon once again Bill had to say, "Ah-ah. Now, now."

And to Fiona, "Tea you said?" And to Katie, "Tea you would make; so, away woman!"

Then turning to Mark, he added, "Stop teasing her so much. And I mean that, mind."

"Okay. But she can't always have her own way, you know."

"I know that, so does your mother."

"Am I being told off?"

"Consider yourself so."

As Mark went out shaking his head, Fiona muttered, "Did somebody say the other night that this trip might blackmail them into being little angels or something similar? It's the worst Saturday morning I can remember having with them. You should have heard Willie in that shop. I could have boxed his ears. I nearly did. And Mamie didn't want a small dummy; no, she wanted one of those great big monsters that clowns or drunks delight in sticking in their mouths."

As Bill laughed, Fiona said, "This has been a very funny week; in fact, a very funny two or three weeks. Do you know, I was just thinking that nothing seems to have gone right since Mr. Samuel Love showed himself in the garden; everything's gone topsy-turvy. People don't act somehow as you expect them to. For instance, Nell not phoning us; then coming in yesterday morning as cool as a cucumber and saying, 'Oh, what? Yes; yes, he popped the question.' And, 'Oh yes, I accepted him.' And, 'Oh yes; yes, that's the ring he gave me.' It was like a damp squib. You say that Bert looked as if he had lost a ten-pence piece and found a new sovereign, and he was even singing. And you tell me the fellows were chipping him all day. Well, there was no such merriment here. You know, Bill, I feel that there's something not quite right there."

"You mean between Nell and Bert?"

"No, next door. I just can't put my finger on it. Nell seems odd. She tried to be her usual self but somehow it seemed difficult for her. . . . Oh, thanks, Katie. That's lovely. And a biscuit, too. And two cups!"

"I brought you tea, Dad, because I can never make the coffee properly. I know you don't like tea, but there it is."

"You're not the only one who can't make coffee properly. You take after your mother. But thanks all the same, pet."

Ignoring the remark, Fiona looked at Katie and said quietly, "Go on up and get ready. But see to Mamie, first, will you? Wash her face and hands and put on her pink dress. Then you get ready. And in between times"—she leaned forward now and touched her daughter on the cheek—"say a kind word to Mark. I'm not asking you to apologise, just speak nicely."

"Well, if I do that, Mam, he'll say, 'What you after?' "

"Well, if he says that just you tell him, all you're after is civility."

"Oh, Mam!" Katie turned away as if in disgust; and Bill said to Fiona, "You do ask the impossible, don't you: a sister to say to her brother, all I ask is a little civility. Come on, woman, drink that tea

277

up. And then you get upstairs an' all, an' plaster your face an' put your best bib an' tucker on."

"What about you?"

"Well, from the moment I take the razor in me hand until I knot me tie the whole process takes me ten minutes, not an hour and ten minutes. So get yourself away."

They were all ready and waiting, although it was only five minutes to two; Katie and Mamie were sitting on the couch; Mark was lounging in an armchair; Willie stood at the window looking down the garden; and Nell, coming into the room, put her hand over her eyes as if cutting out the glare as she said, "My! My! I must have come into the wrong house or wandered into a BBC studio, the next programme will be fashions for children from five to fifteen," and turned to Fiona, who was behind her, saying, "Who's this lot?"

"I don't know. I've never seen them before, at least not like this; and not so quiet."

Changing her tone now, Nell smiled and said, "By, but you do all look lovely, smart. What time are you leaving?" Nell had turned to Fiona again.

"Quarter past two on the dot we are informed; that's when we're all seated and strapped in. The journey takes forty-five minutes, five minutes of which I am told covers the drive, and it's pretty rough in parts, it'll be like a military exercise."

"And what are we going for? We haven't been invited to tea." Willie had turned from the window for a moment.

"You haven't?" Nell showed her surprise.

"No; so Dad says, it's just a visit."

"That's stingy, I'd say, after a journey like that."

Nell had her back to the door when she asked, "Where's your lord and master?" and when the voice came from behind her, saying "Her lord and master is here," she turned and said, "Oh, another one got up like a dog's dinner."

Whatever response Bill might have made was checked by a cry from Willie, saying, "Here's Sammy with your present. Mam, here's Sammy with your present."

"Oh no. Oh no." Not a startling response but a kind of whimper from Fiona. "I'd . . . I'd forgotten," and she put her hand to her brow, disarranging the veil that was attached to her small hat.

"Well, we've still got fifteen minutes. Don't get in a stew. Let him in, Mark."

"No! I will."

278

"You'll stay where you are, Willie." Bill's finger was pointing down into the eager face; and Willie stayed where he was. They all stayed where they were and awaited Mark's entry into the room, accompanied by the visitor.

Sammy was carrying an unwieldy brown paper parcel. He was holding it in both hands and tightly pressed against his narrow chest, and it remained there as he looked around the company.

It was Bill who spoke to him first, saying, "Hello there, Sammy. You've just caught us in time; we are all about to go out visiting."

"Aye, I can see that, I'm not blind."

Bill brought his lips tight together for a moment, whether with vexation or amusement couldn't be told. And now Sammy, looking at Willie, said somewhat accusingly, "I told you I was comin' on Saturday with the present. I told you to tell her."

Fiona now forced herself to say, "Willie hasn't been well, Sammy. I had to keep him in bed yesterday. He was sick in the night."

Sammy made no comment; instead, moving the parcel from his chest, he held it out towards her, saying, "This's for you."

"For me?" Fiona made a good pretence of being utterly surprised, and she repeated, "A present for me? That's . . . that's very kind of you."

She took the parcel from the outstretched hands, then stood hestitating a moment until the presenter of it said, "Well, aren't you gonna open it?"

Walking to a small table, she pushed a glass dish aside and slowly unfolded the brown paper. Then there, exposed to her surprised gaze and not hers alone, was what had once been a silver-plated teapot. What little silver was left on it was bright; the rest of it was still bright but shining with a dull lustre. It had a beautifully curved spout and an ornamental lid; the handle, too, was ornamental. The whole could, at one time, have graced a Victorian tea table; it still retained its beautiful shape except that the spout seemed to be leaning at a slight angle.

"Oh, it's . . . it's very nice, really lovely." She glanced from the boy to Bill and the rest of the company who were now gathered round the table. Then remembering how Sammy had come into possesion of her spoon, she asked him tentatively, "Did . . . did your father give it to you, or . . . or your gran?"

That was as far as she got before Sammy told her in no polite tones that neither his father nor his granny had given him the teapot. "No, me da didn't give it me, 'cos we've got nowt like this in our house; nor 'as me granny. I got it from the tip."

279

Fiona glanced at Bill as if for help. And he came to her aid, saying, "You go totting on the tip?"

"Aye. Aye, I do."

"Which tip is that, Sammy?"

"The quarry where they're fillin' it in. Belmont Road. All the town's muck goes there."

"Oh yes; yes, that's a big tip."

"Aye, it is. An' you can get some good things off it an' all. They bring barrows an' carts, some with ponies, the ragmen do. Beds ya get, an' chests of drawers, just with a leg off." He was talking to Bill now as to someone who understood these things. "Not long ago somebody found a tin box an' it was full of money. But somebody claimed it. It had been thrown out by mistake, they said. There was a fight over it. Ya get all things. An' I found that last week." He pointed to the teapot. "I had to fight for it. Another lad wanted it an' he was bigger'n me, but I got it. An' I've cleaned it up proper. I washed it inside an' out. There's no dirt on it. Ya can look."

"Oh, I'm sure there's no dirt on it, Sammy. And it's a lovely piece of work." Bill picked it up, making sure that he held the spout in place; and turning to Nell, he said, "I bet that's poured some swanky cups of tea out. What d'you say, Nell?"

"Yes, I bet it has at that." Nell looked down on Sammy. "It must have come from one of those big houses, the toffs," she said.

"Aye, must 'ave. Don't see many like that about; china ones with broken spouts, an' brown ones, heaps of brown ones without lids or 'andles off, but nothin' like that." He turned now to confront Fiona again. "D'ya like it, missis?"

"Yes. Yes, I do, Sammy. I ... I think it's splendid. I'll give it pride of place in the china cabinet. Put it on the top shelf in the china cabinet, Bill, please, will you?"

They all watched Bill gently move some Coalport cups and saucers to one side to make a place for the teapot. And after closing the door he stood back and said, "You're very proud of your Coalport china, Mrs. B.; well, I'm sure at one time it had that very teapot to match it."

It was noticeable that not one of the children as yet had spoken, and Bill, looking at Willie, whose face was bright as if with pride, said, "It's good to have a thoughtful friend. What d'you say, Willie?"

Willie looked at Bill but didn't answer. Then Bill, addressing Katie, said, "What d'you think of it, Katie?"

Katie looked at him, glanced at her mother, then, looking at Sammy, said, "I think it's very nice. And I think it was very kind of

280

you, Sammy, to give it to my mother. It must have taken a long time to clean it up."

"Aye, it did"—Sammy nodded back at her—" 'cos it was black in parts."

"I've got a nice teapot. I've got a whole tea set; it's in my dollhouse."

"Yes, but those are toys." Willie was almost spitting the words at Mamie now. "This's is a grown-up teapot. Well, what I mean is . . . well . . ." But he couldn't express what he meant, and so Bill said, "It's all right, laddie; we know what you mean." Then looking at his watch, he said, "Well, we must be off." And now turning to Sammy, he explained: "We've all been invited to visit somebody, so we've got to go now."

"Well, there's nobody stoppin' ya." The aggressiveness was back in tone, the defence was up again, and as the small figure turned for the door Bill grabbed at his arm, saying, "Hold your hand a minute and let me finish. You know, you've got as big a mouth as I have."

This brought a titter from the children.

"You know what?" Bill was bending down looking into the stiff face. "You'll grow up to be the same as me. Now you wouldn't like that, would you?"

"Don't know, might. You're all right in parts."

Bill straightened his back, closed his eyes, and turned his head away for a moment; then looking down at the boy again, he said, "Well, the part that's all right is asking you if you'd like to come to tea the morrow?"

The boy didn't answer, but turned and looked at Fiona, his piercing eyes asking a question. And she nodded quickly at him saying, "Yes, that would be nice if you came to tea tomorrow."

"Thanks, missis."

"And thank you, Sammy, thank you very much for your present. I'll never forget that you gave me it, and I'll always take care of it."

Sammy's face worked: it seemed that all the small muscles were vying with each other. His eyes blinked, his nose twitched, his lips moved from side to side, and his clearly marked eyebrows were pushed up as if trying to escape his hair; then he turned from the company and marched through the hall. But just as he reached the door Nell's voice checked him, saying, "Hold your hand a minute! Look, I'm on me own, at least I am till four o'clock when I have an appointment." She sniffed now and tried not to glance in Fiona's direction. "And there's one thing this lot who are going out don't

281

know yet, and that is if they're going to be invited to tea, but I can tell you, you are."

"Who with?" He glanced sidelong up at her.

"Me of course, next door. That's if you want to come. I've just made a cream sponge and it'll go begging, as this lot don't want it."

There was a murmur from Katie, which was hushed by Bill's saying, "Well, that's settled that. See you the morrow, young Sammy, eh?"

"Aye, all right. What time?

Bill pursed his lips; then addressing Willie, he said, "What time?"

Willie did not return Bill's look but, glancing at his friend, he said, "Anytime you like." And on this he marched past Sammy and out of the front door, and the rest followed him, with the exception of Fiona who, turning to Nell, said quietly, "Thanks, Nell."

"You're welcome, Mrs. B."

"Will you lock up for me?"

"Yes. Go on, I'll see to everything. And in case you're not invited to tea, I'll bring what's left of the cream sponge round, that's if we leave any." She was now looking down on Sammy. "On second thoughts we won't leave any, will we? Will we, Sammy? We'll stuff our guts, eh?"

The small boy smiled up at the woman: she was speaking his language and he said, "Aye. Aye, we'll stuff our guts."

After Fiona clicked her tongue and said, "I'll have a word with you, Mrs. Paget, when I return," the boy stood watching her walk towards the car before, looking up at Nell, he said. "That means you'll get it in the neck for sayin' guts."

Nell put her arm around the small shoulders and pressed him to her side, and it was standing thus that the occupants of the car saw them as they drove out of the gate. And when Katie remarked, "Look! Nell's hugging him," Fiona wondered why the sight should create in her a guilty feeling; it was as if she had missed an opportunity of some sort.

They had been on the journey only two minutes or so when Katie, bending forward, tapped her mother on the shoulder, saying, "Are you going to keep that teapot in the china cabinet, Mam?"

"Well . . . for a time, yes."

"The spout's broken, did you notice?"

"Yes, she noticed, Katie." Bill's voice was not his usual bawl, but there was a definite note in it that pressed Katie back into the seat as he went on, "But spouts can be mended, and the whole can be replated and I'm going to see to it that it's done." He did not add, "And it'll probably cost twice as much as a new one would."

"I know that tip, Dad, where he got it from," said Mark.

"How *d'you* know it?" Bill half turned in his seat; then brought his gaze quickly back onto the road again. "It's yon side of Bog's End; you've never been that way."

"Oh yes, I have. Roland's father drove us round that way in the car."

"Why?"

"Well, he said that Roland should know how . . . well, everybody should know how the other half lives. He has patients up that end."

"I thought he worked in hospital?"

"He does at times. He operates there. But he also sees people outside."

"Private?"

"Roland says, some and some."

"He sounds a man after me own heart."

"It's an awful part, Dad: dreadful houses and the gangs rampage at night, Roland said."

"Then you should thank your lucky stars you don't live there, Mark."

"I wouldn't mind living where Sammy lives."

This insertion into the conversation came naturally from Willie. And it was Fiona who turned round and said, "Oh, you wouldn't? But then your wish is easily satisfied: you can pack your bag anytime you like and go round there and live with him. Can't he, Mr. B.?"

"Well, I supose so, if he wants to so badly. He could go an' try it for a time anyway. It's not a bad idea." He glanced at her; but Fiona, looking straight ahead, muttered, "You know I was only joking."

"What did you say, Mrs. B.?"

"I was merely talking to myself."

"You know," said Bill now, "I don't think this is going to be a happy visit at all. The lady of the house takes them out and buys them things and nobody is satisfied; then some kind little fellow scrapes on a tip till he finds a present for the lady of the house, spends hours cleaning it, presents to her, only for it to be criticised from all quarters."

"I'm not critcising it. I never criticised it. I think it was a very, very, kind gesture."

"I'm glad to hear it, Mrs. B. But I haven't heard much approval from the rest of the family. The only one to my mind who seemed to have a real grip of the situation was Nell. She's another one who wants sorting out; but you'll certainly have your work cut out there. Whatever's happened to make Nell behave as she's doing she'll sort

283

out herself; and mind, you'll not get to know what it is until she's ready. She's kept mum before, remember. Anyway"—his voice rose—"let's forget about everything else but that we're going out for an afternoon's jaunt and have been invited to meet Sir Charles Kingdom. And let me tell you lot back there, it is an honour you are about to partake in, for, as I sum up that gentleman, he doesn't scatter his invitations about. What d'you say to that, Mrs. B. Am I right or am I wrong?"

"What I say, Mr. B., is please keep your mind on the road else you'll still be bawling your head off when you drive us all under that bus in front."

At the sound of explosive laughter from the back seat the atmosphere changed.

From the moment the car left the long winding drive and swept round the large lawn towards the front of the house the children seemed to be struck dumb, even Mamie stopped her chattering. Not a word was spoken as they mounted the eight shallow steps to the stone balcony that fronted the house.

When Bill pulled the iron bell pull to the side of the black oak double door, Fiona had hardly time to cast a warning glance around them before the door opened and a smiling middle-aged woman dressed in a black dress and a small white apron said, "Good afternoon," as she pulled wide one half of the door. And no one of them had hardly time to take in the huge hall with the stags' heads sticking out of the wall at each side of the broad staircase before a large woman came hurrying towards them and, holding out her hand, said, "Good afternoon, Mrs. Bailey." Then, "Good afternoon, Mr. Bailey."

These greetings exchanged, she then looked at the children and said, "What a healthy-looking quartet. Will you come this way?" He's waiting for you, fuming as usual. You won't have to mind the smoke."

Fiona, holding Mamie by the hand, followed their hostess, the three children in single file followed their mother, and Bill brought up the rear. Then they were in a long room that seemed packed with furniture of all kinds, but mostly of easy chairs and couches with little tables dotted here and there.

For a moment Fiona could imagine she was back in her own home as Lady Kingdom called out, and in no small voice, "For goodness sake! Charlie, put out that cigar. Can't you leave them alone for five minutes? Here are your friends." And before her husband could make any response, she turned towards the company, saying, "Sit down; make yourself at home. But you, Mr. Bailey, better sit near his nibs

284

because he'll want to chatter. Have you had a nice journey?" She was looking at Fiona.

"Yes, very pleasant, thank you."

"You are much younger than I expected. From my husband's description I thought you must be in your forties, whereas you look as if you've just hit your twenties."

The end of the compliment laid some salve on Sir Charles's idea of her age, and, looking up at the big, hearty, red-cheeked woman, she was tactful enough to say, "I think Sir Charles was nearer the mark."

"Nonsense. Nonsense. And now tell me your names."

She addressed Mark first, and he, rising straight to his feet, said, "I am Mark, madam."

"Mark. That's a very nice name." She inclined her head towards him. And now he took it upon himself to introduce the others by saying, "This is Katie, my sister, and my brother William, and my adopted sister Mamie."

"Katie, William, and Mamie, all nice names. I have a daughter called Katie." She was bending over Katie now, but for once Katie had nothing to say. Yet, if she had spoken her thoughts she would have answered this lady, "One day I'll have a house like yours, but I won't have so much furniture in the room. This is comfortable but cluttered."

"What about tea?"

The intrusion caused Lady Kingdom to turn to her husband: "All in good time," she said. "I thought you'd like a chatter first. And for goodness sake put that cigar out, will you! Everyone isn't impregnated with smoke like I am. Some people can't stand it. You know what happened when Irene came, she was sick." She turned now to Fiona, saying, "Do you like houses? I know your husband builds them, but do you like looking over houses?"

"Yes, I do indeed, especially houses like this."

"Well, come along then and leave them to have their chatter before we have a cup of tea. I won't say I'll give you a guided tour but I'll show you the main rooms, and then Jessie can take the children around the rest."

Bill watched his squad, as he thought of them, rise quickly from their chairs, all their faces looking bright with expectancy, and he knew it wouldn't be long before their tongues were loosened.

The door closed, he now turned and looked at the old man propped up in a long basket chair, with, to his side, a table on which stood a box of cigars and an outside ashtray.

"You don't smoke, Bailey?"

"No, sir."

"Drink?"

"Oh, yes, sir; I like a drink."

"Well, what's your poison?"

"Whiskey as a rule, and neat."

"Like one now? He pointed across the room. "There's a bottle in that cabinet there."

"If you don't mind, sir, I won't at the moment. I try not to when I'm drivin' and especially when I've got five passengers."

"Well, yes, you're right. I see your point. There'll be tea shortly. Ah, now. Well"—he sighed—"I'd better get down to the reason I asked you here today. First of all, mind, I wish it was to say that you've got the contract, I do really, yes I do, but that remains to be seen. I never thought there'd be so many firms interested in it; but, of course, it's a concern that will take some long time. It'll put somebody on their feet. But it's about the trouble you've been having."

"Trouble?"

"Yes, trouble with your men, things happening."

Bill's lower jaw fell slightly. "You ... you've heard about that?"

"Oh yes, yes." The old man grinned wickedly. "I have my ear to the ground. I can hear a horse galloping five miles away, or words to that effect. You know what I mean?"

"Not really, sir. Why should you have come to know what's been happenin' in the yard to my men?"

"Because things like that get about, Bailey. You know as well as I do, one firm can't blink but the other one hears about it. And I was very sorry to hear when one of your men was hurt, attacked, mugged they call it now, don't they? And then a car was stolen; and another one had his place broken into. And it could go on if it's allowed to go on."

"You know who's behind this, sir?"

The old man reached forward, took a fresh cigar from the box, tore off the band, took up something that looked like a pair of pliers, used it to nip at the end of the cigar, then lit it, before he replied, "Yes; and it wasn't Brown as you imagined, although it's the kind of thing that I wouldn't put past him if he had enough money to pay the culprits."

Bill had moved to the end of his chair and, leaning forward, said, "It's someone that's in for the contract, then?"

"No, no. They wouldn't do things like that. But on the other hand I don't know.... No; not in this case, no. You're a sharp fellow, you know, Bailey, the kind of fellow who would say to himself, there's no flies on me; yet, you don't seem to have an inkling who's at you?"

"No, I don't sir. Except for Brown, I don't know of anyone else who would have it in for me."

"Don't you? Have you ever heard these words 'Hell hath no fury like a woman scorned'?"

Bill's jaw actually did drop now. His mouth went into a gape, his cheeks pushed up, his eyes narrowed, his mouth even went into a wider gape before he said, *"Never!* Not her?"

"Yes, her. You should never say to a woman that you wouldn't touch her with a barge pole no matter what you might think of her. That's what you said to her, didn't you? Whatever happened in your workmen's hut that day, you insulted her, you made her feel small, and that was something she had never been made to feel in her life. She admitted as much to me. She had offered you a position in London and you took it that she was offering herself."

"She was. Believe me, sir, she was."

"Oh yes, yes, I believe you. But on the other hand, it takes a lot to make a woman like Eva cry. I had never seen her cry, not even after she had let herself down with Brown and had to allow herself to marry him. She didn't cry unless it was in the privacy of the night. But I happened to come across her not less than half an hour after she had left you that morning. And she was still white-hot with rage. You know, you're not a very tactful man, Bailey. All right, you didn't want her, you preferred your wife, but you could have let her down gently."

Bill gulped heavily before he managed to say, "Sir, you weren't there, you don't know what happened. She laid herself open to me. I've had experience of a great many women in my time, I must admit, but not one so brazen as she was. And then I asked her what about Brown, and she said she was divorcing him. And next I asked her if all the businesses she wanted me to manage were in her name and she said, yes everyone of them; Brown had just been a form of manager. She inferred she had let him play the big man but she held the strings and wore the trousers. And then the final note was when she said that if he were to sue her he would get less than she was going to give him in redundancy pay. That was the word, redundancy pay. No matter what the man was, and I can say now, I hate his guts, always have done, but at that moment I was sorry for him and for the life he'd had to lead with a woman like her, a calculating cold fish: she hadn't taken into consideration my wife or the children; she had been used to getting her own way, stepping on people. It was then I told her that if she was the last woman on earth I wouldn't touch her with a barge pole. It's a well-worn saying that, common if you like, but I meant every word of it. And I still do; I don't take back anything I said that morning, tact or no tact."

The old man blew out three large puffs of smoke before he said, "Well, putting it like that shows a different complexion, at least from your side. But I know what kind of life she's had to lead and it hasn't been easy. Power's been her only pleasure. But power's an empty love and a cold bed. Come to think of it, though, I'm not without blame, at least where your men are concerned, because I can recall telling her that you had a gang of the best men throughout the area, which showed itself in the work they had turned out, especially those houses above Brampton Hill. And she then likely saw one way of getting at you was to disrupt your gang. She's a ruthless woman, I admit. Oh yes, she's ruthless. But I know one thing, she disliked Brown, in fact she might have hated him, but not with the fervour that she hates you, to go to the length of engaging scoundrels to do dirty work, as she has. Anyway, I sent her a wire and told her that it had to stop; and then wrote to her and told her I was aware of her little game. But apparently the letter didn't reach her. I understand she's gone abroad on holiday."

"But what makes you so sure she's behind this, sir?"

"Oh, a hunch, and the way she told me that if it was the last thing she would do she would ruin you one way or another, for she meant it. She also said that if I voted for you to get this contract she'd never speak to me again. And she also meant that."

"But, sir"—Bill had now risen to his feet—"I'm not going to let this go on; I'm going to the police."

"What can you prove? Nothing until they catch the fellows."

"I can say who's behind them."

"You've only my word for it, Bailey. And sit down, sit down, you look ferocious standing there. Do something for me; put on another nightwatchman just for the time being. If you do I'll pay his wages, so don't worry about that. You see, there's two or more of these other blokes and your single man and a dog won't be a match for them because they're dirty players. And another thing, if they should cause any more damage, I'll make it right."

When Bill resumed his seat he sat quiet for a moment; but he certainly wasn't quiet inside, he was raging. He wanted to strike out at something or someone. That bitch of a woman. Never would he have imagined that she would go to such lengths. It was criminal. She was worse than any gangster. And this he voiced now, saying, "It's criminal. She's worse than any gangster. Look, sir, as much as I admire you, I can't promise to keep my tongue quiet if I can nab those fellows. Anyway, like all thugs of that type, they'll squawk once they're caught."

"Well, until they are, Bailey, let's say that any damage they do to your works or your men's property will be covered. . . . I'll see to it."

"Money won't buy a life, sir, and they nearly did for Barney McGuire. He's a man of fifty, and tough. And they almost got Dan McRay. What if they kill somebody, sir?"

"Oh, they won't go that far; they'd be afraid of the consequences."

"Do you know who they are, sir?"

"No, I don't, Bailey; and if I did, I'm afraid the frame of mind you're in I wouldn't tell you, because that would involve Eva straightaway. And once I get in touch with her she'll stop this. I'll see to it."

Bill got abruptly to his feet again, and he walked the length of the long run towards the big open fireplace; and there he stood for a moment in silence.

When he turned, he looked at the old man and said, "I can't believe it, sir; I can't take it in. That some firm had it in for me through competiton, yes; yes, that would be quite feasible; but that she would take it on herself to get back at me like this . . . well, as I said, I just can't believe it."

"You said a moment ago you'd had quite a few dealings with women in your life, and I can believe that. Well, then, you should have learned that they are the more dangerous of the species. Sit down. Sit down. You get on my nerves popping up and down. And I'll tell you something about women, something that happened in this very house. My great-grandmother was the daughter of a farmer, what you'd call in those days a gentleman farmer. She had her eye on this house and all that was in it, I was told, and she set her cap at my great-grandfather. Now he was a lad of many tastes and his tastes ranged from the kitchen, through various farm barns, to the wife of his best friend. Now my great-grandmother must have known all about this before she took him, but when she found him in one of the attics with the housemaid she almost went berserk. And later, when the girl was known to be pregnant, she made her marry, at least she paid this man, a horse dealer, to marry her. And this particular fellow was known to be cruel, even to the dog he was supposed to care for. He was never seen without a whip in his hand and he whipped his bride from the day he married her. It was said he was ordered to by my great-grandmother. And when my great-grandfather discovered

289

what had happened ... he really wasn't a man who bothered with anybody's business but his own, but he had the decency to take the girl away before she was flailed to death. He installed her in a cottage with a woman to look after her. It was only half a mile from the house—the foundations can still be seen; overgrown with weeds, but they can still be seen—but the day after the child was born the cottage was burned down and the mother and the child and the woman who was looking after her were burned with it. It was rumoured that the window had been nailed up and so had the door. The horse dealer disappeared. It was also rumoured that my great-grandmother had paid him to do the deed. Anyway, from that time my great-grandfather never slept with his wife, but he made hay all round the countryside and she could do nothing about it. It was said, too, that he was heard to say, while laughing at her, 'You can't go round burning all the barns down, Cicely,' It became a catch phrase I understand: 'You can't go round burning all the barns, Cicely.' Women, Bailey, are the very devil. I've been lucky. Oh yes, I've been lucky: Bertha is a good woman; she's been a great helpmate and companion. But, you know, we've bred one hellfire of a daughter. She could be great-grandmother Cicely all over again." He laughed now and his lower set of false teeth wobbled in his mouth. Then he said, "You know people think nothing happens in the country. Let me tell you, the country makes the patterns for the towns. And you know, it isn't the day or yesterday that I've thought Eva Brown could be the reincarnation of great-grandmother Cicely. Ah, here they come."

The door opened and the children actually ran up the room, only to come to a stop at a respectful distance from the man in the basket chair. But he cried to them, "Come here! Come here! Well, what do you think of this little cottage?"

They all laughed, and it was Katie who said, "It's beautiful, lovely."

"Would you like to live in a place like this?"

Katie glanced first at her mother then at Bill, and her answer was diplomatic: "When I grow up," she said.

"Clever girl, clever girl. You like your own home?"

"It's a beautiful house, sir." The old man looked at Mark and asked now, "What are you going to be careerwise?"

"Well, sir, I would like to do physics; and I'm rather good at maths, you see; yet on the other hand I have a fancy for being a doctor, so I might have to take biology, I'm told. I haven't fully made up my mind yet. It all depends on how I do in the exam."

"Well, its' good to hear that somebody knows what road their life's going to take. Either one of those sounds good. And you, young lady, what are you going to be?"

"An actress."

There was a quick exchange of glances between Bill and Fiona because it was the first they had heard of it.

"An actress? My! My! Stage or television?"

Katie hesitated just a moment before she said, "I'll be able to do both."

The old man put his head back and let out a wheezy laugh, which caused his wife to wag her finger at him and say, "There you are! You're laughing now; you didn't laugh when Annabella made that statement some years ago, did you?"

"A lot of water's gone under the social bridge since then, woman. Ah, here's Jessie with the tea."

At this they all turned and looked towards the door where a maid was pushing in a large double-shelf tea trolley, the top laden with tea things, the bottom shelf holding plates of scones, sandwiches, and a fruit loaf.

"By, you've taken your time, Jessie; my mouth's as dry as the desert."

"That's caused by cigar smoke, sir."

"Now don't you start."

Fiona watched a mingling of glances between the mistress and the maid; then Lady Kingdom, now addressing Mark, said, "Take the things off that small table there, will you, dear, and bring it here? This room's full of tables, and for what? Just to hold stupid cups and trophies. And who notices them?"

"I do. It's all I've got left in life."

"Poor soul. Poor soul."

Again there was an exchange of glances, this time among the children. They were amused; this sounded just like home.

When Mark had duly brought the table to her, Lady Kingdom set it in front of Fiona, saying now, "Do help yourself, please; I've long since given up being polite and handing plates around. You see, when the family descends upon us it's a free for all. And so I generally let them get on with it. I can assure you of one thing, the sandwiches will be very nice: they are fresh cucumber, preseason, brought forward in the greenhouses. I said to a certain person"—she now closed her eyes and nodded her large head—"that we should start a market garden, but no. Has everyone got a cup of tea? Well, then, it's a free for all. Move along, dear; I'm going to sit in between you."

Willie hitched himself along to the end of the couch, and when the big woman sat down on the big cushions beside him he bounced

291

slightly. Then, with some surprise he watched the big woman, as he thought of her, bite into a scone, taking half of it in one mouthful.

He looked at the tea trolley. On it, there was a large silver tray and on the tray was a silver teapot and a matching sugar basin and milk jug, besides a small tea strainer on a stand.

"How old are you?"

When Willie didn't answer, Lady Kingdom followed his gaze and said, "Would you like another cup of tea?"

"No, thank you. It's the teapot." He pointed.

"The teapot, you like it?"

"Ah ha; I mean yes. It's just like the one my friend Sammy brought my mother today."

"It isn't! The strong denial came from the other end of the couch and brought all eyes on Katie. "That's a beautiful teapot, the other one's broken. He . . . he got it off the tip."

It was evident that both Katie and Willie had forgotten just where they were for the moment because Willie, bending across Lady Kingdom's knees, hissed, "I know where we got it, but it's still a lovely . . . "

"Willie! Katie!" Bill's voice brought them both back to where they were. "Apologise to Lady Kingdom."

"Oh no! No! No!" Lady Kingdom was laughing now, as was Sir Charles, and they, looking at each other, said, "It could be Rachel's lot, couldn't it?"

"Yes, to a tee, to a tee."

"Well, what about this teapot?" Sir Charles was looking at Willie now. "You say, at least your sister says, he got it from a tip. What do you mean he got it from a tip? Somebody tip him off to buy it?"

Willie hung his head for a moment; then, jerking his chin upward, he stared straight at the old fellow in the funny basket chair and said, "No, sir; he hasn't got any money to buy silver teapots, he's very poor. He's from Bog's End. But they're filling in the quarry in Belmont Road."

"Oh, that tip! Where they're filling in Murphy's Quarry. And so your friend found a silver teapot there?"

"Yes, sir. And he cleaned it up inside and out and brought it to my mother for a present." He glanced at his mother's very red face.

"Well, to my mind, that seems very kind of him. Is he a schoolmate of yours?"

"Well"—Willie hesitated—"he doesn't go to the same school. I go to St. Oswald's, it's a private school, but Sammy goes to the convent school, he's taught by nuns but he doesn't like them."

"He doesn't like the nuns? Why now, why? I thought nuns were all holy ladies."

It was evident in the glint in Sir Charles's eyes that he was enjoying this conversation. He had even brought himself more upright in the chair and had stopped puffing at his cigar. "Why doesn't he like the nuns?"

"Well, sir, Sammy says they've all got hosepipe hands."

"What hands?"

"Hosepipe hands, sir." Willie had made his voice loud and clear as if he was talking to somebody hard of hearing.

"Hosepipe hands? Nuns with hosepipe hands? What does he mean by that?"

"I suppose it's because when they whack him across the ear it's as if he was being hit by a piece of hosepipe. His dad went for one of the nuns . . . put the wind up her . . ."

Of a sudden Sir Charles had a fit of coughing and at the same time his wife seemed to be wriggling in her seat. Willie did not look towards either his mother or Bill, he kept his gaze directed to the funny old fellow. He liked him. He thought, somehow, Sammy would like him, and he would like Sammy an' all.

The bout of coughing over, Sir Charles wiped the spittle from his lips with a napkin; then, looking at Willie again, he said, "He sounds a very interesting chap, this friend of yours. How did you meet him if you go to different schools?"

"Our school played them at football, sir."

"Do you like football? Are you a good footballer?"

"Not very."

"What about him, your friend?"

"He's not very good either, sir. He was pushed off the field that day."

"What for?"

"I don't quite know, misbehaviour I suppose."

"You mean fouling?"

"Could be, sir."

"So you and he are pals?"

"Yes, sir."

Sir Charles now looked at Bill and Fiona and noting the consternation on Fiona's countenance, he said, "With your parents' approval?"

Lady Kingdom had also noticed the look on Fiona's face and, now pulling herself with some effort from the deep cushion on the couch, she addressed her husband, saying, "Mind your own business, Charlie

Kingdom. You should know by now that children pick their own friends, and they're often better at it than parents. Now do you want anything more to eat?"

"No, ma'am, I don't." And he turned to one side so he could once again see Willie, and in a loud whisper he said, "Do you get bullied like this?" And Willie, smiling back at him, said, "Yes, sir."

Sir Charles's voice changing, he looked up at his wife and said quietly, "Bring me the children's box will you, dear?" And she turned from him and went to a cabinet at the far end of the room and returned under the watchful eyes of the company and placed a box on her husband's knees.

"Have you had enough to eat?" He looked from one to the other of the children. And when they all spoke at once, saying, "Yes, thank you," he said, "Come here, then." And when they stood in a line at the side of his chair, he opened the box and said, "This was my father's children's box and each week he doled us out a certain amount according to our age. I was the second in line and got nine pence. My brother, the eldest who is now dead, he got a shilling. The baby got a penny. There were seven of us altogether. So I propose to do the same with you as I do with my grandchildren. You, Mark, are the eldest. Well, here you are." He picked out a pound coin from the box and handed it to Mark, who said with evident gratitude, "Oh, thank you, sir. Thank you very much indeed."

"Now you, Katie. Well, I think it will have to be fifty pence for you."

"Thank you, sir. Oh, thank you."

"And Willie. Well, what's half of fifty, Willie?"

"Twenty-five pence, sir."

"Well, let me see." He now counted out twenty-five pence and handed it to him.

"Thank you, sir."

"And now the little one. Maisie you say her name is?"

"No; Mamie, sir."

"Oh ... Mamie. Well, Mamie, ten pence is your allotment."

"I have a money box, a piggy bank."

"Have you? And are you going to put that in?"

"Well, some of it."

"Say thank you, Mamie." Fiona was standing behind the child now, and she said, "I have, Mammy B."

"No, you haven't."

"Oh, well. Thank you, Mr. .... sir."

"You're welcome, Mamie."

294

"I suppose you'll all be making for home now?"

It wasn't a note of dismissal but a note of enquiry and Fiona answered, "Yes, sir, straight home. We wouldn't want to spoil the memory of this visit with anything else."

"Nicely put. Nicely put. Well, it's been my pleasure, too." He now shook hands with the children one after the other. And they all said again, "Thank you, sir." And then they turned to Lady Kingdom, and as they thanked her she patted their heads; at least she patted three, with Mark she did him the courtesy of shaking his hand.

It was as they were all trooping out that Sir Charles's voice called, "Willie!"

Willie turned quickly and looked back up the room to see the funny old man leaning forward in his chair, saying, "The next time you come to visit us, bring your friend from the tip. Will you?"

"Willie's smile spread from ear to ear. *Yes, sir! Yes, sir!* I'll tell him."

Lady Kingdom had bid them a warm farewell and said they must come again.

The car had hardly started to move before Willie exclaimed loudly, "Did you hear what he said?"

Before he could continue, however, Fiona said, "Yes, I heard what Sir Charles said, but he was joking."

"He wasn't, Mam. He meant it."

"Yes, he might have meant it, but merely to be able to laugh at Sammy."

"Oh no, Fiona." Bill cast her a hard look now. "He'd laugh with the lad but not at him. He's not that kind of a man."

"Dad's right."

"Be quiet! Willie."

"Oh, Mam"—there were tears in the boy's voice now—"don't spoil the afternoon."

Fiona turned round now and angrily retorted, "If this afternoon was to be spoilt, Willie, it was you who contributed mainly towards it. You had no right to bring up the matter of the teapot."

"Enough! Enough! It was a natural thing for him to do."

"Oh, Bill." She turned and stared out the window, thinking, as she had done once before, that there had been no peace in the house since that boy had entered it. She would have to do something. But what? she couldn't think at the moment. And then the perpetrator of her irritation himself swept it away from her when his hand came on her shoulder and his voice in her ear muttered, "I'm sorry, Mam. I really am. I didn't mean to spoil anything. It's been a lovely time."

It was some seconds before she could turn her face round to him and say, "I know you didn't, dear. It's all right. And it was a lovely time, wasn't it?" Then she forced herself to go a step further and make them all laugh by saying, "And isn't it wonderful we're going to have an actress in the family."

When the laughter subsided, Bill said, "Many a true word spoken in a joke, eh, Katie?"

"Yes, Dad. I'll surprise them all one day. And when I'm picked for the Royal Variety Show . . ."

"Oh, lord! She's going to be a comedian."

"No, I'm not our Mark. And anyway, you've got it wrong, a woman can't be a comedian, it's comedienne."

"There you are. And she's right, too; what's wrong with being a comedienne? Look at Penelope Keith in 'To the Manor Born,' she's marvellous."

"I like Olive and Popeye," put in Mamie.

Again there was general laughter; then out of the blue Willie enquired, "Why did we go there this afternoon, Dad? What did Sir Kingdom want?"

"Oh, only to talk about a bit of business."

"You're going to get the big estate job?"

This was from Mark, and Bill answered, "No; no, that isn't settled yet. It was just a bit of other business."

From Bill's tone and the look on his face, Fiona couldn't wait until they got home to know what this other business was. But it wasn't until the children had changed their clothes and got through another more substantial meal and were now settled round the television that she managed to be alone with him in the study. And she opened by saying, "Well, what was it all about?"

He didn't answer immediately, but when he did, what he said surprised her: "I'm sick in my stomach," he said.

"Why? What's made you like that?"

"What Sir Charles told me with regard to who's got it in for me."

"He knows?"

"Yes. Oh yes, he knows."

"Well, tell me. Who is it? One of those in for the contract?"

"I wish it was; I wouldn't feel so bad. No." He paused, then looking into her face, he said quietly, "Mrs. Brown that was."

"What d'you mean, 'Mrs. Brown that was'?"

"Brown's wife."

"She? But . . . but why would she want to cause havoc in your business?"

"Well, isn't it evident? She's out to break me in one way or another."

"And Sir Charles knows?"

"Yes; yes, he knows."

"But how does he know the reason why? Or do you know the reason why?"

"Yes, of course I do, my dear. Don't you remember? Just before you went into hospital at Christmas she came to the office and held out high prospects if I'd go to London and work for her, but in more ways than one."

Fiona screwed up her face. Yes, she remembered something about it now; but she had been in such a state, thinking she had cancer, and, too, Bill had made fun of the incident. Her voice was a mutter now and held some incredulity; "You mean, because of that she would go to the length of ... well, engaging men ... thugs? She must have."

"Yes; yes, she must have."

"But ... but aren't you upset? Surely, if she's gone so far she'll stop at nothing."

"She'll stop all right, or, as I've told him, I go to the police. And yet, as he pointed out, I've no proof, and I won't have until I catch those buggers. All I hope is I'm not alone when I do come up with them because I'll want to do them for meself."

"What is he going to do about it? Has he any influence with her?"

"Well, quite a lot I would have said at one time, but apparently not enough. She's out of the country at the moment, but she's due back soon. He sent her a wire and a letter, so he tells me, and he's also offered to pay for any damage she does. But as I said, he can't pay for a life. And if it had been Harry that was set upon instead of Barney she would have had a corpse at her door because Harry's had one slight heart attack already. Barney's the oldest of the lot, but he's got a constitution like a horse, and so it's just as well."

Fiona turned away from him, her hands gripping each other as she said, "She's a dreadful woman, to go to those lengths all because you rebuked her. Oh, Bill."

"Now don't worry. Don't worry."

"That's a stupid thing to say, don't worry. And you're worrying. I knew something had happened as soon a I got back into that room; you looked as if you'd had a shock."

"Well, you're right there, I did have a shock. And you've just got a shock, haven't you? But there's one thing I'll say to you: I know you talk to Mark as one adult to another, but don't give him any hint of this. He'll probe to know what business it was, not out of mere

297

curiosity, I grant you, but just to know what's going on. I've always tried to make him feel important and in charge of the others, but he's as sensitive as a woman in some ways. So, I'm telling you, don't let on. Think up anything but the truth."

She went to him now and put her arms around his neck and, looking into his eyes, she said, "If you had still been the middle-of-the-road man when she put her proposal to you would you have accepted?"

"No; knowing then the setup between her and Brown, no."

"But if you hadn't known about the setup?"

One corner of Bill's mouth took on a quirk and he put his head back as if considering; then, looking at her again, he said, "I might have, being a middle-of-the-road man and havin' an offer like that made to me by an attractive woman, because, say what you like, she was attractive."

Her hands snapped from around his neck and she pushed him with both of them on the chest, saying, "I ask myself at times why I bother with you! You can lie like a trooper about other things, why can't you lie to me?"

"Because, love, you wouldn't want me to. Aw, lass"—he pulled her towards him—"don't take the pet. Tisn't you."

"Then why can't you be tactful?"

"It wouldn't be me. I've always been honest with you. Anyway, how many times have I told you it was from the minute I saw you in that paper shop that I knew I'd have you, and not just a landlady, either. But I had to work me way in, hadn't I? By, that was hard. Come on, lass, smile. I've got enough on me plate without worrying about our love life."

"Oh, Bill, you're incorrigible."

"I like that word, I must remember it. I'm collecting words, you know. I hope you've noticed.... Oh, there's the phone. You know, that phone never seems to stop ringing. What time is it? Ten minutes to seven."

Bill was making for the door when he turned, saying, "Oh, someone's answering it. That's likely Mark."

A moment later Mark pushed his head round the study door, saying, "It's Nell, Mam."

"Nell?"

Fiona went quickly past them now. She picked up the phone, and Nell must have realised this, for her voice came to her saying, "I knew you had all come back. Are you going out again?"

"No; no, Nell. Why?"

298

"May I come round for a moment?"

"I wish you wouldn't be so silly, woman, may you come round for a moment! Whatever it is, get yourself round; and don't ever ask again."

She put down the phone and turned to Bill who had come into the passageway and said, "It's Nell. She wants to come round for a moment."

"She's daft, that woman. Why on earth does she have to phone?"

"It's all because of you. I told you; she hates to disturb your slumber. Anyway, apparently she wants to have a talk, and I'm glad because she's been acting very odd, at least she has for someone newly engaged, so will you keep them out of the kitchen?"

"Leave it to me."

Fiona was only in the kitchen a minute or so when the back door opened and Nell came in. She was dressed for out and looked very smart, and Fiona, making the obvious remark, said, "You're going out?" and so she got the obvious answer: "Yes; yes, I'm meeting Bert at half past seven. I was round his place this afternoon, but now we're going out to dinner."

"Nice. I'm glad. Sit down."

They both sat down, but when Nell didn't speak and bit on her thumbnail, Fiona said, "Come on, come on. Unload." Then reaching across, she gripped Nell's hand, saying, "What is it, dear? Oh, don't cry; it'll make a mess of your makeup. What is it?"

"You never know people, do you?"

"No, I suppose that's true."

"I've lived with Mam and Dad since . . . well, since we moved next door, and before that I was always dropping in, seeing to things for them. Well, I thought they knew how Bert felt about me and how I felt about him. . . . Well, I knew Mam did. But whenever Dad spoke of it, I realise now, he did it as a sort of joke. Well, to cut a long story short, when things were coming to a head, I mean between Bert and me, and I knew he was going to ask me, once or twice I heard Mam and Dad arguing, and I couldn't believe it really because they seemed such a happy couple. And then the very night we got engaged I found out why. He . . . he ordered me out."

"He what! You mean, Mr. Paget?"

"Yes, yes. I . . . I couldn't believe it. He said if I was going to marry that man, in fact he suggested that we were already married except in name, I had either to go to his place or to my friends next door." Nell's head was bobbing now and her eyes were bright with tears. "Fiona, I just couldn't believe it. It was a bigger shock than when

299

Harry walked out on me. It was, really. He said that after all they had done for me he expected me to stay with them for life and look after them, especially Mam, being she's not well. He gave me no option: pointing to my ring, he said, 'Either give that back to him this very night or don't come back here.' Mam had to intervene."

"I can't believe it. He seemed such a nice man, and thought the world of you."

"So thought I. But I know now that his kindly manner was hiding a sort of religious or moral mania. When Harry left me I thought his father was taking a very strong note when he said that he would never speak to him again as long as he lived. But last night, he told me that he considered me still married to his son: his son may have sinned but I was still his lawful wife. He tolerated you, Fiona, I gathered, because your husband had really died. That made the difference, you see; yet not altogether, because you had been married in a registry office. It all came out. I really couldn't take it in."

"And I can't either, not what you're telling me. Anyway, why didn't you speak about this before? Why didn't you come straight round here?"

"Oh, I just couldn't. I felt it would be taking advantage of good nature; and anyway, I was sort of . . . of stunned. Do you know, it had a really worse effect on me than when Harry walked out."

"Have you told Bert about this?"

"No. How could I?"

"Well, you must, woman. Now, this very night you tell him. And you're not going to be swayed, are you?"

"Oh no, Fiona, I'm not going to be swayed because I realise that I've never known what . . . well"—she looked down towards her hands again—"what real love is; and I have it for Bert, and I'm sure Bert has it for me."

"Well, there you are then. There's a house all ready waiting for you; forget about engagements and go and get married straightaway. I know he's a churchman, but the minister might be one of those who won't marry divorced people. If the church won't do it, there's the registry office, and so get yourself to it and don't wait, dear, because if Mr. Paget's turned out to be the Jekyll and Hyde that he is he could play on your feelings until you do give in. Oh, I've heard of such, and I've had a bit of it, you know, through Mother. But again, I cannot understand why you didn't tell me straightaway."

Nell smiled now and said, "Well, there was another obstacle. You've just mentioned Jekyll and Hyde. Well, my father-in-law has certainly turned into that all right, because, you know, after telling me to get myself across here he informed me that if I said a word about his attitude he would know and would come across and tell . . ." She paused here and repeated, "He said he'd come across here and tell Bill what he thought about him as a man, and so on, and so on. And by the sound of it his opinion wasn't high, and never has been. And just look back to the times that he's been here for a meal. Remember Christmas? Could you remember a nicer or more jolly man?" Her voice and face changed now as she said, "I . . . I think he must be mental, schizophrenic or something, one of those. And I think Mam has been aware of this for a long time, because since this has happened I can recall her coming downstairs at times, saying, 'Dad's lying down. He's got that headache again.' And when I've offered to take him a drink, she's said, 'No, I'll do it,' although she could hardly get upstairs with her bad leg."

Nell rose to her feet now and looked at her watch, saying, "I'll have to be off," and Fiona went to her and, putting her hands on her friend's shoulders, she said, "Now listen to me. You'll tell Bert all this, won't you?"

"Yes; yes, I will."

"And if it gets too hot for you next door you come back here, because I can easily shuffle those beds around upstairs. If the worst comes to the worst you can take up your abode in the playroom. That old couch is as comfortable as any in the house."

"Oh, Fiona."

"Now, now, don't cry; you'll mess up that makeup. I've told you. And you look fine, like a young girl. I'm not kidding. Go on now, and no matter what time you get back, pop in and tell me that it's all settled, that you're going to be married next week."

"Oh, Fiona, that's jumping the sticks."

"Well, it's about time you did. Go on." She now pushed Nell out of the door, but within a minute she was in the sitting room and beckoning to Bill as she said, "Here!"

"Shhhh! Mam." The command for silence came from Mark and Katie; and Bill whispered, "It's a Western. They're going to get him."

"I'll get you if you don't come now."

Bill made a great pretence of dragging himself away from the television. And when he reached the study close on her heels he said, "Well, what's the news?"

"Sit down. You won't believe this."

It took her all of five minutes to relate what Nell had said, for she interspersed this with her own comments. And when there was no response from Bill she said, "What d'you think of that? Eh?"

"What do I think of it? I think we've got a psycho next door all right. And when I come to think of it now, there have been times when he's utterly ignored me and I thought he was slightly deaf. I spoke to him over the fence one morning. He was doing something in the garden. His back was half turned towards me, but my voice, as you say, carries to the end of the street, and he didn't move a muscle. I thought it was funny at the time, and I remember thinking he must be deaf in one ear, but recalling that he hadn't seemed to be deaf when he had been in here at various times before that. And that wasn't the only time he seemed to ignore me. I still put it down to this being deaf in one ear business though. Poor old Nell. She does get it, doesn't she? Likely his son took after him and she had that to put up with, too. By the way"—he wagged a finger at her—"didn't Mrs. Paget say he was from Ireland, and I remarked it wasn't an Irish name. Remember?"

"Yes, but what has that got to do with it?"

"Only these things seem to link up. You know, Liverpool floats on the Irish population and in our street we felt like foreigners with so many of them. And I remember a sort of discussion, well it would often come up, about two families where the daughters of the house never married and that in both cases they had looked after their parents. And I can hear me dad saying, jocular like, that Ireland was full of bachelors 'cos Irish parents demanded that one daughter stay at home to see them in their old age. And you know, he was right. These two were very nice and presentable middle-aged women who only seemed to get out of the house when they went to mass or confession or what have you. Aye"—he nodded—"me dad said it was an Irish strain, and if the only girl in the family should walk out an' let them fend for themselves, it was as if she had committed a crime. Now, there you have it, the strain is next door."

"Oh, that might be part of it, Bill, but it's more than that. From what she said, it's religious mania, and in a twisted way, too."

"Well, I can tell you one thing, love: if she doesn't tell Bert the night I will in the morning, and tell him to get cracking. There's nothing to stop them going to the registry office the morrow if it comes to the push. You know, there's one thing you can say for this lower-middle-class avenue, and that is there's always something going on."

"Why stick on the lower?"

"Because that's what it is. There's a lot of pretence along this street, you know. Look at our dear Mrs. Quinn. And there's the two redundant managers farther up. You said yourself you were invited to one of their coffee mornings."

302

"Well, I suppose they could still afford a cup of coffee."

"Aye, I suppose so in that case; but what about that bloke at the top inviting us to a meal and suggesting at the same time we take a bottle."

"Well, if I remember rightly, we didn't get a second invitation after your refusal of the first. You know, you are an uncouth individual at times."

"Look, Fiona"—he again pointed at her—"don't use that word on me. I'm a big mouth and I'm brash but I'm not uncouth. I know you were smiling when you said it but I still don't like it."

"Oh, I'm sorry, Mr. Bailey." She went to turn away and he got hold of her none too gently and pulled her tight against him, saying, "An' don't take the pet. And that means ever, because if I can't speak me mind to you, then I'm all at sea." And his smile widening now, he went on, "And me rudder's gone and me outboard engine's bust; I didn't bring any oars and there's a leak in the bottom of the boat. Dear Agony Aunt, what must I do?"

"Oh, Bill Bailey."

"Don't spit at me when you say my name like that." He made a great play of rubbing his hand across his mouth. "Anyway, you say that Nell's going to let you know how things go when she gets back. Well, that could be all-hours. But we'll wait up. And there's a certain way we can fill in the time, isn't there, Mrs. B.?"

She pressed herself from him, saying, "You know, with all these other things on your mind, I'm amazed at the space you reserve for that one thing."

"Well, what's life for, love, if not for that?"

"Oh, you!" She thrust him away none too gently, and as she went out she said, "I'm going to have a bath, and I don't want to be disturbed for the next hour. Will you inform the crew?"

"I'll give you half an hour, woman. That's long enough for any bath and titivating."

When she had gone he sat down at the desk and for a few moments his mind dwelt on Nell's situation; but then he was back to the main happening of the day, and once again he was experiencing the feeling that had arisen in him when Sir Charles Kingdom informed him who was behind his present troubles. But added to it now was an emotion he hadn't experienced before, and it was fear, fear of that woman; and this in itself was frightening, for never in his life could he recall being afraid of a man.

30

IT WAS WILLIE'S BIRTHDAY, TUESDAY, APRIL THE FIRST. TWO MORE THINGS HAD happened to Bill's men in the intervening time. One: Jos Wright's allotment had been stripped and trampeled flat. And Jos being a leek fanatic this had really depressed him. As he said, they could have mugged him and he wouldn't have minded so much. The second incident had to do with Morris Fenwick's pigeons. It was known among the pigeon fanciers in the district that Morris had great hopes for one of his birds winning the continental race. But in the middle of the night before the special day the birds had been let out from their lofts at the bottom of the garden, and Morris and his wife had been woken up with the flutter they made as they circled the house.

What Morris and no one else could understand was how the birds had been let out, because the coops had been locked, for it wasn't unknown that attempts could be made to steal prize pigeons or, as some vandals had done of late, to kill them. It would seem in this case that the interlopers had had keys to fit the locks.

In both cases the police had been informed; Sir Charles Kingdom, too, had been informed and by a very angry Bill who had promised Sir Charles that just one more thing, just one more, and he would go to the police and spill the whole story. What Sir Charles had said, was, "Don't do that, Bailey. As I said, I'll make everything good; but

304

don't do that, not at this late stage because you'll spoil your own chance if you do."

When Bill had asked him what he meant by that he got no answer, for the line went dead.

But now it was Willie's birthday. All the April Fool tricks that could be played had been played on him and by him. Excitement in the house was at a high pitch waiting for the party to begin at half past five, when Bill would join them, and also Bert.

It was a special day for Bert. He hadn't been to work, for he was getting ready for his wedding to Nell on the morrow. But now here they all were, ten people sitting around the table: Fiona at one end, Bill at the other; Sammy Love sat to Bill's right hand and Willie to his left; next to Willie was Roland Featherstone, and opposite him Katie; Bert's seat was next to Katie, and opposite him was Nell; next to Nell sat Mark, and opposite Mark, to Fiona's left, was Mamie.

The children had got through sandwiches, sausages on sticks, a variety of small cakes, ice cream, and jelly. Now they were waiting for the coming cake; and when Fiona paused in the doorway holding her son's birthday cake topped with nine fluttering candles, there was a concerted cheer from those at the table. And when she placed it before Willie, he looked up at her and said, "Oh, Mam; it's a big one. Where've you kept it?"

"Never you mind. Aren't you going to blow the candles out?"

His face glowing, Willie puffed twice and the candles were snuffed out; and Katie's calling across to him, "Look what it says; it's got writing on all sides," caused a stretching towards the cake and pointing now as different ones read out the words: "Happy Birthday"; and then again "To Dear Willie," which was written on the top.

"Well, go on and cut it, man," said Bill. "We're all waiting just to see if your mother's a better hand at making a cake than she is at brewing coffee." And he now nodded towards Roland, saying, "She burns the water when she makes coffee, she does."

"She doesn't, Dad! It's you, you want it so thick," countered Mark.

"You would take her a part, wouldn't you?" Bill was nodding down the table at Mark when Fiona, looking at Willie, said, "Give your dad a piece of cake, will you, Willie, to keep him quiet."

As Willie placed a piece of cake on Bill's plate he said, "It'll take more than that, Dad, won't it, to keep you quiet?"

"Never a truer word spoken, laddie."

His eyes still on Bill, Willie asked, "What's it taste like, Dad?"

Bill chewed on the cake for a moment, then nodded, first at Willie

305

and then down the table at Fiona. "Lovely!" he said. "The best she's ever made."

Fiona smiled back at the man sitting at the head of the table. She knew that her husband had no sweet tooth and that one thing he disliked was fruit cake; but there he was, munching away and grinning widely.

Everyone had been served, and Willie, looking across at his friend, said, "You like it, Sammy?"

"Aye." Sammy nodded. "It's good; not scrimped on the fruit," which brought a laugh from the company.

The ceremony of the cake over, Fiona now pointed to the two pyramids of crackers in the centre of the table. They were the leftovers from Christmas and she said so, then told Willie to pass them round.

With each motto being read out there was accompanying laughter. First, Nell. When she hesitated to read hers, Mark said, "Well, go on," and Bill added, "What's keeping you?" And Nell, pink in the face, looked at Bert and read, "You will shortly meet and marry a handsome man and live happy ever after."

"And that's true. That's true, Nell."

"Aw! Bill, man." Bert's head was wagging.

But when Mark read his: "I'm a little fairy flown from the wood, may I join your party if I promise to be good?" and added in baby talk: "Twinkle, twinkle, little star, how I wonder where you are? Up above the earth so high like a diamond in the sky," Willie and Katie fell about.

Then one and another cried at Bill, "Read yours! What's the matter? Read yours!" But he pulled a face, saying, "They're daft things," and crumpling the tiny piece of paper, he thrust it into his pocket, which for a moment caused a silence to fall on the table until Bill said to Sammy, "What's yours say, Sammy?"

"It's daft an' all."

"I know. They're all daft, but what does it say?"

"Look." He handed it to Bill, who read out, "You're a man after my own heart; don't break it."

This brought the laughter back again, and when Willie read, "You will soon be offered a high post, jump at it," Katie put in, "You could never jump a flagstone, Willie." And he, flapping his hands toward her, replied, "Oh, you! Just you wait."

There followed a desultory flatness that had to be lifted, so Willie, looking across at Sammy, said, "You tell them the Pat and Mick story."

306

"Aw! I couldn't."

"Well, you told it to me."

"Aye, that's different."

"What's this Pat and Mick story?" Bill was nodding down to Willie now, and Willie said, "Well, Pat brought his mother over from Ireland and she was very tired; and he was a big fella, so he carried her through the town. And she said, 'Why don't you go into one of them places, Pat.' And he said, 'How can I, Mother? They all say rest ... yer ... aunt, but there's no place says rest ... yer ... mother.'"

The laughter was forced but it was loud. Then Roland's cultured tones brought all attention to him when he said, "I have an uncle, in Scotland. He's a minister in the Church of Scotland and he tells the funniest jokes. He has the congregation rolling in the aisles, so to speak, when he's in the pulpit."

"You're kiddin'?" Bert looked across at Roland. "The Church of Scotland minister telling jokes from the pulpit?"

"Yes, it is perfectly true, Mr. Ormesby. People have to go very early to get a seat. His church is always full."

"I must go and hear him one day." Bert smiled across at Roland.

"Oh, you wouldn't need to go to church to hear him, you could hear him at a wedding or a little party. The only thing he draws a line at are funerals. But for weddings and christenings, people always invite him. He told a very funny one at my cousin's wedding a short while ago."

"Well, let's have it." Bill was nodding at him.

"Oh, well, it was very funny, but it takes him to tell the jokes. Like a comedian, it's how he tells them."

"Don't be so bashful; and you're not bashful, so don't tell me you can't tell a joke. Go on, let's have that joke."

Roland looked round the table; then his eyes rested on Fiona and she, too, said, "Go on, Roland."

"It's ... it's a very odd joke."

"We like odd jokes."

"Well, you see, my cousin was being married and you know the husband always has to stand up and reply. Well, the weddings I've been to, the new husbands always seem very bashful and the best men who speak for the bridesmaids they're always very dull, I mean, in their replies. And it should happen that this day the groom was very nervous and the best man, to my mind at least, very dull because he was always reminiscing about his sporting childhood with the groom. Anyway, my uncle stood up and everyone became quiet because, you see, a lot of people there were strangers to him. He had come from far away in Scotland and this was London and moreover he had a dog collar on. Well, he began by congratulating the bride and groom in a very funny way that made people titter. Then he got on to his jokes and—" Roland bit on his lower lip and said, "Well, this is the one I like but it's . . . well, it's—" He turned now and looked at Bill and said, "It's not really naughty."

"Oh, that's a pity," said Bill; and having glanced at Fiona, he went on, "Well, we're nearly all grown up here, except one." And he nodded towards Mamie who was still munching at her second piece of birthday cake. Then he said, "Go on, lad. Go on."

So Roland got on with it: "Well, I'll use the Pat and Mick names," he said; "they're easier than the Scottish ones. Well, there were these two Irish farm workers. They were on a half-day holiday and they had to take a message for the farmer to the village a mile or two away. It was very hot and they had got halfway along the road when Pat said to Mick, 'Aw, I'm not going no farther, Mick.'" Roland had dropped his southern accent and was into broad Irish. "'You go on,' said Pat, 'and I'll have a kip here until you come back.' 'I'll do that,' said Mick; 'I don't mind walkin'. You have your kip.' And so off went Mick to the village, and Pat lay dozing in the ditch by the roadside. Well, it was just half an hour later when he was brought with a start from the ditch because there was Mick, sitting in, of all things, a great big Volvo car. So he rushes up to him and says, 'Mick, where on earth did you get that? You haven't nicked it?' 'No, no,' said Mick. 'You see, it was like this. I was on me way back from the village and this young woman stopped and asked if I would like a lift, and I said, 'Thank you very much, ma'am. I'll be very obliged for it's hot it is.' So into the car I got. But she didn't keep to the road, she turned off into a thicket and out she got and, Pat, believe me, before God, she stripped off to her bare pelt, took every stitch off her, she did, and there she was, naked as the day she was born. And she comes up to the car and she says, 'Irish farm boy I'll give you anything you want.' . . . And so . . . well, I took the car."

There was a great splutter, a clatter in Bill bringing his hand quickly to his mouth to help soften the explosion, and in doing so he upset his teacup, which was half full; and this seemed to accentuate the laughter. Nell was choking. Bert had his hand tight across his brow shading his eyes. Mark and Katie were both doubled up; Willie and even Mamie were smiling. Of course, they were just following the pattern. The only one who hadn't a smile on his face was Sammy. But Roland was waving his hands, flapping them and saying between gusts of laughter, "It . . . it isn't finished, it isn't finished."

"Oh, my lord!" said Nell. "There can't be any more after that, boy."

"Yes, there is. There is. Listen. Listen." Roland was choking with laughter himself as soon as there was comparative quiet he said, "When Mick said, 'Well, I took the car,' Pat said to him, 'You did right there, boy you did right, 'cos her clothes wouldn't have been any use to you.' "

Both Nell and Fiona rose from the table, but as Nell did so she brought Roland a clip across the head with her hand, gasping as she said, "You'll go far, but where to I don't know."

"I must get something to wipe up that mess," Fiona said as she passed down the side of the table.

Bill had a hand across his forehead, his elbow resting on the arm of the chair. His body was shaking, and it sounded as if he was in pain.

"Move your carcass out of that." Fiona had returned and was sopping up the tea from the tablecloth. And as she did so she looked at Roland, saying, "You know I don't believe a word of that parson-uncle of yours."

"Oh"—the boy's face was serious now—"it's true, Mrs. Bailey. Oh yes. If I may I'll bring him to see you the next time he comes down."

"Well, I'll believe it when I see him."

"And you'll believe it when you hear him, too."

A few minutes later, seated at the table again, Bill said to Sammy, "I noticed you didn't laugh at that joke, Sammy. Mamie didn't know what it was all about but she laughed."

"I knew what it was all about; it was about a whore."

The whole table seemed to freeze. Every eye was on him. Bill had no immediate answer, and the boy went on, "Women who take all their clothes off are whores. Me da says they're bad women, and me da says a wife can be a whore, but not a mother."

Even the gulp Bill made was audible; then he nodded at Sammy and said, "Yes; yes, your dad's right in a way: mothers are precious things; wives can make mistakes but never mothers, at least from the man's point of view. Yes, I understand your father."

While he was speaking one part of his face seemed to be sending signals up the table to Fiona who had half risen from her seat, and also to Mark. He now glanced at Willie. Willie's face looked blank; he knew that Sammy had blotted his copybook again. He wasn't quite sure whether it was a four-letter word or not, but it was one that hadn't to be used. Then all eyes, as if in relief, were turned on Bert, for he was saying, "I know this game; the lads in the club love it. You can all sit where you are, but we'll have to be divided into two teams. Mrs. Bailey will take that side of the table and Mr. Bailey will take this side of the table that includes Sammy, Katie, Mamie, and myself. It's to do with words. Now you have three choices, you lot over there." He was pointing to them. "You can either choose actors and actresses, or towns, or countries. The words start with *A*. Say you pick actors and actresses, well, you must name as many surnames of actors starting with *A* during the time we at this side count twenty seconds. And we do it loudly. You know how to count a second: one-and, two-and, three-and ... like that. We'll get a pencil and we'll put down how many you get. You start first, Willie, with *A*. And then Roland will have to take *B*. And Nell will have to take *C*. And Mark *D*."

"That isn't fair."

Bert looked at Katie. "Why?"

"Well, they're all older and they'll know more. Mamie won't know any and I doubt if Sammy will."

"I ain't daft. I know towns and countries as well as you. And I go to the pictures on a Saturda' mornin', so I know actors and actresses an' all."

"There you are," said Bert loudly now. "We'll not only match them but we'll beat them."

Fiona looked down the table towards Bill, then they both looked at Nell, who was smiling widely as if with pride. Her husband-to-be was not only a good man, he was a diplomatic man; he had saved the birthday party. Oh yes, indeed, because Fiona had been ready to blow her top. Mr. Samuel Love's oration on morality and on the filial piety of mothers from a son's point of view had obliterated Pat and Mick and the Volvo car. Oh, she must remember that one.

When the phone rang Fiona put her hand up, checking Bill from rising, saying, "I'll see to it." And as she passed the bottom end of the table, Bill pulled her towards him and, above the noise of the counting, he said, "Tell her where to go to."

Fiona picked up the phone. He had been right, it was her mother. "Fiona?"

"Yes, Mother."

"It's Willie's birthday and as he hasn't called for his present and I have not been invited to his birthday party, it remains until he comes."

"Mother, the birthday party is for the children, and if I remember rightly you expressed the opinion that you can't stand children in a horde." She almost added, "You couldn't stand one, singular."

"If I'd been invited I could have looked in for a moment. I ... I feel very isolated, Fiona. And it's your doing, and . . . and . . . and that person's."

"I've warned you, Mother, that if you do not address Bill either by his name or as my husband I shall refuse to talk to you, even on the phone."

"You're hard, Fiona. You don't take after me."

No, thank God. Again she'd had to restrain herself from voicing her thoughts, but she said, "You're not very isolated, Mother, when you can play bridge three times a week, go to the theatre on a Saturday night with your cronies, have your coffee mornings, and your weekends away for relaxation. Your life hasn't altered a bit over the years, Mother. You don't need me. You never have; all you want to do is disrupt my way of living, my life. Now, look, I've got to see to the children. I'll send Willie tomorrow after he comes from school. Goodnight, Mother."

"Fiona."

As she thrust the phone down the term *serpent in heaven* came into her mind. The party had been going beautifully, and she had to ring. What was she talking about, going beautifully? That child had nearly ruined it. Something would have to be done. But what? And his father talking to him about whores. Really! If only Willie wasn't so set on the boy. Well, she'd have to put her foot down; that association couldn't be allowed to go on.

Bert's game was a great success; and it went on for a half hour or more, until Bill gave the signal for an end to festivities, at least in the dining room, by rising from the table, saying, "The slave women want to get this table cleared, so the rest of you up aloft and see what you can do with Willie's computer. Only don't break it." And pointing his finger down at Willie, he warned, "That cost me a packet."

"Yes, I know, Dad. And thank you very much," Willie said as he put his arms around Bill's waist; and Bill ruffled the boy's hair as he muttered, "Later on tonight you come back and tell me it's bad manners to say what you paid for a present, because if you don't your mother will; and I'd rather it came from you."

Bert and Nell helped to clear the table and wash up; when everything in the dining room was shipshape again they returned there to discuss the big event of the morrow. And it was as Bert was saying, "I can't help feeling guilty, boss, in taking leave at this time, when everybody's working all out to get the places finished," that the phone rang again. And Bill, stopping Fiona from rising, said, "It can't be her again so it'll likely be for me, although I don't know, who'll be ringing unless it's more trouble."

His expression was blank as he picked up the phone: "Fellburn seven-eight-four-three," he said.

"Hello, Bailey. This is Sir Charles here."

"Oh. Oh, Sir Charles? How nice to hear you. How are you feeling?"

"Very well at the moment, at least in my mind. If my body was as good as my mind I'd be running races."

"I'm sure you would, sir. Are you calling about the latest attack, about the pigeons?"

"No, but don't worry, I'll make it all good. I told you. But that isn't what I've rung you about."

"No, sir?" Bill's voice was still flat.

"Are you standing up or sitting down?"

"I'm standing up, sir."

"Well, put your hand out and hang on to something."

"I'm sorry, sir." Bill gave a slight laugh. "There's nothing within reach that I can hang on to, except a chair here, but that's rather fragile. I rarely sit on it in case I snap the legs."

There was no response to this, jocular or otherwise, only silence on the line, and he was about to enquire, "Are you there, sir?" When Sir Charles's voice said, "You've as good as got the contract, Bailey."

Bill's hand did shoot out now and grip the back of the chair.

"Did you hear what I said?"

Still Bill could not answer for a moment; then he muttered, "Yes, sir. Yes, I heard what you said."

"Well, there's been a meeting here today, the whole crew of them, and I can tell you I had to resort to a little wangling, a bit of persuasion, and in one or two cases perhaps a bit of threatening. One big boy wanted to know why such an important project should be given to a small builder, to which I replied that that small builder's work was better than any other's I'd seen."

Again there was a pause before Bill could say, with a break in his voice, "Oh, thank you, sir. From the bottom of my heart, thank you. If I can ever do . . . well, it's to say this from where I'm standing, but if ever I could do you or your family any service you've only got to say."

"Oh, well; that you might be able to, if that mad woman of whom I'm rather fond doesn't let up, and if those rascals are found she might be in need of help. Then whether the case comes up or is dropped will be up to you."

Bill didn't answer for a moment, but his tone was thoughtful as he said, "Well, I never break a promise."

"Good man. Now, what you must do is to be in Newcastle tomorrow at the Civic Centre at three o'clock. I'll be there, if I've got to be pushed in a wheelchair. But I can manage the car now, so never fear, I'll be there. Put on your best bib and tucker. And there's no need for me to ask you to answer straight because you always do that; but on this occasion, not too straight. Try a little diplomacy here and there, for there's a couple on this finance board who would still have their own favourites. You understand?"

"Yes, sir. Yes, I do. And oh, thank you very much, and not only on my behalf but on behalf of my men, the eleven that have stuck by me all these years."

"Well, you'll need many more than eleven when you start this project. It's a big deal, Bailey. You'll need to take on supervisory help, you know that. And also you'll need to have a long talk with your bank manager ... oh yes, indeed."

"Oh aye. Yes, sir, I've worked it out, just in case"; and he smiled at the phone as he said, "Night after night for weeks now, I've gone over and over it: who I would need, and what I would need? You can't work a project like this on your own. But I have the men in mind; two of my own men will be works managers; and two others will take on gangs. These are the ones who don't mind responsibility. Others are good workers; but after work they consider they've earned their clubs, and darts, and snooker. Oh yes; I've got it all worked out, sir. And again and again, I thank you."

"Well, see you tomorrow. Don't let me down."

"I'll never do that, sir."

"Goodnight, Bailey."

"Goodnight to you, sir."

He stood for a moment with his hand pressed tight down on the receiver, and actual tears welled up in his eyes, which he slowly rubbed away with his handkerchief.

He did not run into the sitting room, he walked in quietly, and straight to Fiona, who was looking at him enquiringly.

He pulled her from the couch, then drew up Nell, and, when Bert, too, got to his feet he put his arms as far around them all as he could, clutching at Bert; then his head drooped between them and there was a break in his voice as he said, "I've got it, the contract." Then, his manner changing, he threw his head back and let out a "Whoop!" and amid cries of, "Wonderful! Marvellous!" he took Fiona into his arms; and when she buried her face in his shoulder he patted her, saying, "There now. There now; I feel like that meself, but I'll wait till I get into bed."

Looking at Bert, who was holding Nell and whose face, too, was showing emotion, he said, "We're set, Bert. We're set. Work for the lads for some years ahead; and for others an' all. Oh yes, dozens of them. Oh, let's drink to it."

Gently now, he pressed Fiona onto the couch; then on his way to the cabinet in the corner he turned towards Bert and said, "I'm not going to tempt you, but would you?"

"No thanks, Bill. No thanks. I can get high as a kite on orange juice."

Amid the laughter Bill said, "How about you, Nell, sherry?"

"Yes, please."

He brought the tray to the couch, on it the two glasses of sherry, the orange juice, and a whiskey. And as their glasses clinked, he said, "Let's drink to an outsize in miracles because, believe me, when I knew how many were in for this, although I kept struggling and hoping, I felt I really hadn't a chance."

"God's good."

Looking at Bert, Bill said, "I'll believe it after this. You take it from me, I'll believe it after this."

It was eight o'clock when Bill drove Roland and Sammy back to their homes, homes set well apart in the town's layout. Roland had been effusive in his thanks for the wonderful party, and Bill had said that he had gone a long way towards making it a success, and assured him that he would never forget that story; he also hoped that one day he would bring his uncle to see them.

When he dropped the boy before the iron gates at the entrance to the short drive leading to the white stuccoed house that faced the moor, Roland turned and said to Sammy, "Be seeing you again, Sammy." And Sammy's mouth opened and shut twice before he answered, "Aye, okay."

Having watched Roland walk towards the gate, then turn and wave, Bill started the car, and Sammy leaned over the backseat and said, "He said he'll be seein' me. Think he meant it?"

"Of course he did; he's a very nice boy that."

"Not snotty?"

"No; no, he's not snotty."

"Like some."

"Well, in life you'll always find there's some and some, Sammy; young and old, there'll always be some and some. But the real ones, the real gents and ladies, they're never snotty."

Bill drove through Bog's End and when he stopped at the block of flats he said, "Will your dad be in?"

"Don't 'spect so. But I've got a key." He dug his hand into the bottom of his pocket, pulled out the door key, and Bill looked at it for a moment before he said, "Would you like me to come up with you and see you in?"

"No; no, I can go by meself; I always do."

"Yes, aye, of course. Did ... did you enjoy the party?"

"Aye. Aye, it was good. Nice food. An' ... an' did ya think that Willie liked me present?"

"He loved it."

"I didn't get it off the tip. Me da give me the money for it, and he helped me pick it. He said it was the best model car on the market."

"It is; it is that. And I know one thing, it'll start Willie on collecting them." Bill now leaned over and opened the back door, saying as he did so, "Goodnight, Sammy."

"Goodnight, mister."

The boy was standing on the pavement now, and he said, "What have I got to call ya besides mister?"

"What about Mr. Bill?"

"You won't lose your hair if I call ya that?"

"Well, I've just said so, haven't I?"

"Aye. 'Night then."

" 'Night, Sammy."

Bill watched the small figure open the paint-scratched and scarred door that led into the hall of the flats before starting the car, saying to himself, "God above!"

He, too, had had a rough childhood but nothing like that kid's. His own mother had always been at home waiting a meal, even if her hand might be outstretched toward his head if he wasn't on time to sit down with his dad and her; and when he was younger she would always kiss him goodnight after he'd had a playful slap on the backside from his father. He didn't know why he felt so concerned about this little fella, but he was. Yet it was obvious Davey did the best he could for him: he was well shod and clothed and likely got plenty to eat; and it would seem that he tried to instill a certain morality into him, even if it was about the whores. Eeh my! He grinned to himself. He had thought he would collapse when he heard him, and he had wanted to bawl even louder than he had done at Roland's Pat and Mick story. And by, that was a corker an' all. My goodness, what kids came out with these days. But that lad; he would like to do something for him, and he would. Yes, he'd do it through giving his dad plenty of work that would enable them to get out of that hole and into a decent little house.

Work. He was set. Set for years ahead; for once he had done a job like that the world would be his oyster, 'cos he'd build those houses like houses had never been built before. There'd be hardly two of the same design. He'd fight to get his ideas through. But then, they must have liked them in the first place to give him the contract.

Dear Lord—he was swinging the car round into the drive—he had never felt like praying but at this minute he wished he was going into a church where he could kneel and say thanks to whatever was there. He did that.

A bubbly feeling rose in him and his step was so light that he almost danced into the house, only to realise straightaway that the party atmosphere was changed.

Nell was coming down the stairs and Fiona behind her.

"What's up?"

"I've . . . I've been thrown out, finally."

"Come and sit down." Fiona put her arm around Nell's shoulders and guided her into the sitting room, Bill followed, saying, "The old devil threw you out?"

"Literally." Nell sniffed, then blew her nose. "Mam tried to stop him, but he nearly knocked her on her back. He had my cases and everything lined up in the kitchen, with the ultimatum that either I gave up this mad idea and stayed where I belonged or else I could go to my fancy man now and he never wanted to set eyes on me again.

"I went to pick up the cases, and he actually punched me in the chest; then, one after the other, he threw my things outside. I called over the fence for Bert, and when he saw what had happened he wanted to go in to him, to reason with him. But I told him you couldn't reason with that man, or at least the man he had become."

"Where's Bert now?"

"He got a taxi and took my things along home. Funny . . . I already think of it as home."

"He should have waited; what's my car for?"

"He . . . he didn't know what time you'd be back. Anyway, you've got a lodger for the night."

"My God! I've a good mind to go over there and give him the length of me tongue, if nothing else."

"It's no use, Bill. It's as if the devil or something has got into him. I can't understand it. He's . . . he's become a frightening creature."

"Well, this time tomorrow you'll be away from it all. Look, now that things are settled for the future, why not make Bert take a week off. What's two days for a honeymoon?"

"All I want, Bill, is to come back into that house and know that I've got a real home and a real man at last." She now turned to Fiona,

316

saying, "And yet I won't feel safe until after the ceremony tomorrow morning; I've got the feeling that something will happen, that he'll do something."

"He'll do nothing of the kind, because we won't let you out of our sight until the deed is done and you're on that train. So don't worry. And look, Mrs. B."—he turned to Fiona—"go and make some of your rotten coffee, and lace it with a little brandy before Bert gets back, because if he sees her having the hard stuff he'll think we've already got her off the straight and narrow."

As Fiona passed the bottom of the stairs two voices hissed at her, "Mam! Mam!"

She looked up to see Katie and Willie, and in stage whispers they said, "We heard Nell." And it was Katie who took up the conversation now. "I saw Mr. Paget going up and down his garden. He seemed to be talking to himself. All the lights were on in the house. Willie saw him an' all, and he came for me."

"It's all right. Go back to bed and get to sleep or else, mind, it'll be school for you tomorrow and no wedding. Go on now."

"What's the matter with Mr. Paget, Mam?" This was from Willie.

"He's . . . he's not very well."

"Then he should go to bed, shouldn't he?"

"Yes, he should. Now both of you get back to your beds; I'll be up in a minute." And hearing them dutifully scampering across the landing, she turned and went towards the kitchen to make the coffee.

This was made and she was about to lift the tray with the three cups on it when there came a knock on the back door. It was a hard knock, and she wondered why Bert hadn't come the front way, as he had been doing of late.

She unbolted the door, pulled it open, then stood gasping at the man confronting her, for she did not recognise John Paget: the man who was always meticulously dressed was wearing his under vest and trousers and slippers. He did not attempt to come into the house; in fact, he stepped back from her as if, it would seem, to give his arm and finger more length to point at her as he said, "You tell her she's got to come back. Do you hear? She owes us that much. My wife needs her. I'm sorry we ever saw this house, and you and your big-mouthed man, because it's him that's the cause of this. Yes, it is. Yes, it is. He pushed his low-type workman at her. He did it to spite me because he never liked me. But he'll pay for it. Oh yes, I'll get him. Oh yes, I'll do for him, or I'll burn him out and the lot of you."

Gasping for breath, she banged the door in his face; then stood holding on to it as if to get her wind after a long run. Even after she'd

317

heard the back gate bang it was still a full minute before she could move to the table and onto a chair.

That's how Bill found her when he entered the kitchen, saying, "Have you gone to Brazil for that coffee? . . . What's up? You've got a pain? What's up?" He had his arms about her. "You look as white as a sheet. What's happened? Tell me. Tell me."

Twice she made the effort to speak before she could bring out, "He . . . he came, Mr. Paget. He . . . he threatened."

"What d'you mean, threatened? What did he say?"

She stared into Bill's face but couldn't say, "He threatened to do you in and burn us out," because Bill would have gone round there and God only knew what would happen. So what she said was, "Oh, he was on about Nell and that she had to go back and . . . and that one of your low-type workmen had got her. And so on, and so on."

"Come on." Bill pulled her to her feet. "Look, come on, pull yourself together. And we mustn't tell her that he's been for she'll not close her eyes tonight. And I won't sleep very heavily either, I can tell you. By the sound of it that old fella's gone off his rocker and should see a doctor, a special one at that. Here, look, before you go in there, take a gulp at that coffee and let's get some colour in your cheeks." He patted each side of her face. "Then we're all for bed. Now, as arranged, Nell will sleep with you, and I'll sleep down here on the sofa."

"It isn't long enough."

"You leave that to me. My God!"—he picked up the tray now—"talk about situation. Who would believe that old fella could turn out like that." He paused as he was going towards the door and, looking at Fiona, said, "If he can change as much as he has done in the past few weeks I don't think it's something new. I'd like to get to the bottom of it."

They got to the bottom of it at eleven that same night. After Bert returned they had sat talking in the sitting room until nearly eleven o'clock, when both Fiona and Bill left the room to let the couple say goodnight and to part for the last time before their marriage.

As they went into the kitchen Bill said, "Now I won't be ten minutes running him home, and you don't open the door to anyone, not even God himself. D'you hear?"

"Don't worry. Don't worry about that."

"But while I'm away, if you're frightened or he comes back to that door, dial nine-nine-nine. This, I think, has become a police matter."

A few minutes later, after Fiona had locked the front door after

318

the two men, she went upstairs with Nell. In the bedroom she said, "Now get yourself to bed and go to sleep; I'll be up as soon as Bill comes back. That brandy should do the trick."

"Yes, I think it's starting already." Nell gave a weak smile. "It was more than a drop; he said it was."

Of a sudden Nell put her arms around Fiona, saying brokenly, "What would I have done without you? I'll never know."

"Well, you're not going to do without me. Things will go on just the same, at least for half days only. It's all arranged now, isn't it? So there's nothing more to worry about. And no more talk; get into that bed and go to sleep," and saying this, she went to push Nell towards the bed, but Nell, her old manner returning for a moment, pushed back at her, saying, "Well, let's get me clothes off first," which caused them both to laugh and left Fiona feeling easier in her mind when she went from the room to do her nightly round of looking in on her children before going downstairs again.

But she had no sooner entered the kitchen and reached the stove and was about to put the kettle on when she heard a tap on the kitchen door.

She swung round and stared towards it; then slowly, as if sliding past someone, she was making for the hall again when a small voice said, "Fiona, it's me, Mrs. Paget."

Fiona put her hand to her neck as if to assist herself to breathe. Then she hurried to the back door and was about to unlock it when she stopped at the thought that he might be behind her. And so she called, "Are you alone, Mrs. Paget?"

"Yes; yes, I'm alone."

When she opened the door, Mrs. Paget, a coat pulled over her dressing gown, stumbled into the kitchen, and Fiona rebolted the door before saying to the elderly woman, "Sit down. Sit down."

"Oh, Fiona, what can I say? What can I say? Where's Nell?"

"She's in bed, Mrs. Paget."

"I would like to have seen her, but . . . but perhaps it's better not. Will . . . will you give her this?" She brought from her dressing gown pocket a narrow black case, saying, "I . . . I couldn't get out; he . . . he wouldn't take me out to buy her anything, a wedding present. Tell her that it was my mother's. It's the thing I value most and I want her to have it because I value her, too."

"Why has your husband turned so much against her, Mrs. Paget? He was never like that."

"Oh, my dear—" The pale pink face seemed to crumple and the older woman had to fight for control before she said, "He's been like that many times, my dear, but he's never had such a long spell since Nell came to live with us. He seemed to change altogether after Nell came, and it's been the longest spell he's had from hospital in years. It's been like a small miracle, no, a large miracle. He . . . he's a good man really, the other side of him. If he hadn't been I would have left him years ago. When he comes to himself he's like a child, so sorry. But I've never seen him as bad as this before."

"Have you told the doctor?"

"Oh, the doctor knows about his spells, but he's threatened what he would do if I ever call the doctor in. I need the doctor for myself as I haven't been well. I'm never well when he's like this. It's nerves you know, nothing physical, just nerves."

"Oh, my dear." Fiona took a seat by the side of the troubled woman and asked, "Nell mustn't have known anything about this?"

"No; no, she didn't."

"Didn't her husband tell her? He must have known."

"Oh, he wouldn't have. Harry wouldn't have told Nell; he was ashamed of his father having these turns."

Remembering the threat the man had levelled at her a short while ago, Fiona put the question tentatively now as she said, "Has he ever become . . . well, dangerous in his manner?"

Mrs. Paget sighed before she answered, "Yes, twice, and . . . and he was in hospital for almost a year after that."

"How long do these turns last?"

"It's strange, but I've known them to go as quickly as they come. Other times he's got to have medication for a lengthy period. Once he . . . he went for a man, quite a big man, and the man felled him with one blow. And when he came round he had his senses back, too. The doctors found this very interesting."

The thought went through Fiona's mind that it might perhaps have been a good job if she had let Bill go round there, for his medicine might have brought the man to his senses again. But then it would take a lot for Bill to hit an old man.

"You must get the doctor to him as soon as possible," she said.

"I will tomorrow, no matter what happens. But he watches me, my every movement, and whenever I go near the phone it seems to agitate him. When he's like this he does not realise he's ill. Yet he does realise he can be put away; and oh, dear, that's pitiful."

"I'm so sorry, Mrs. Paget. I never guessed that you were in this trouble; you were always so bright, seemingly happy."

"Yes, I was because . . . well, Nell was there. To him she was like a cure. But please; oh, please, don't think I don't want her to be married, and he's a good man. Will you tell her I wish her all the best in the world? I love that girl. I must go now, but . . . but I wanted you to understand."

After unlocking the back door, Fiona turned before opening it and said to Mrs. Paget, "If your husband has to go into hospital and you're on your own . . . remember you won't be on your own: Nell will be coming here half days and we will all be at hand to help you in any way we can."

"Thank you my dear. That is something to know anyway. You will give my love to Nell? And will you tell her what I've told you?"

"Yes, right away. She'll understand then. Goodnight, Mrs. Paget."

"Goodnight, my dear."

The older woman now touched Fiona's hand, saying, "You've got a good man. Take care of him."

When the door was closed once more Fiona again stood with her back to it. You have a good man. Take care of him. It was Bill who took care of her and of all of them. But yes, she would take care of him.

31

IT WAS DONE. NELL WAS NOW MRS. ORMESBY. THEY CAME OUT OF THE TOWN HALL, Bert and Nell, Bill and Fiona, Mark, Katie, Willie, and Mamie, dressed in their best. And that wasn't all. Barney McGuire had taken the morning off, so had Harry Newton and Jos Wright. Amid laughter and chaffing they piled into their respective cars, Bill and Fiona taking the bride and groom, the children divided between Harry Newton and Barney McGuire.

It was only a short run to the hotel where the wedding breakfast was awaiting them, but before Bill drew up in the car in front of the hotel he said over his shoulder, "The first thing you'll get, Bert, is a car."

"I can't drive a car, boss; you know that."

"No, but your wife can."

"Can you drive a car?" Bert looked at Nell.

Their faces were shining and Nell laughed as she said, "Of course I can drive a car."

"You never told me."

Bill was quick out of the car, and first went round and opened the door for Fiona; then addressing Bert again, he said, "Lad, you're in for some surprises. You never told me, you said. You'll be kept awake at nights with the things she'll tell you and that you didn't know. I never got any sleep for the first month."

"Oh, Bill, shut up!"

So, laughing, they entered the hotel.

They laughed a lot during the breakfast and when, an hour and a half later they all stood on the station platform saying good-bye to the happy couple, there was still much laughter.

Nell, hugging Fiona, now said, "Tell Mam I'll be seeing her soon. . . . Give her my love. Tell her I'm happy. And things will work out all right now that I know about Dad. Oh, you don't know what that's done for me, to know I haven't been the cause of his illness."

The train was moving off as Bill yelled to Bert, "Make it a week. I've told you."

"Not on your life, boss. Be back on Friday."

"Come back on Sunday night."

Nell's head was thrust out of the window and she yelled at the top of her voice, "You mind your own business, Bill Bailey."

This caused more laughter and comments from the men, saying, "Well, now you know, boss; somebody's tellin' you straight."

"Don't they always!"

And so, amid chaffing, the wedding party divided, Bill addressing his men, saying, "I'll be changed and back on the site within an hour. If any of you are a minute late it's the sack. So you know. So long."

"The same to you, boss, the same to you. But I thought you had the big meeting this afternoon, boss. Have you forgotten?"

"Don't be such a . . . don't be such a fool, Harry. As if anybody could forget that."

"Then you won't be changin' your clothes, will you?"

"You're too clever by half. Anyway, get back on that job. I'll be looking in afore I go on to Newcastle."

"We'll see about it," said Jos Wright. "Might stop and have a pint or two, then, on top of that champagne, you never know the effect it'll have on us. Do you lads?"

In the car again, Willie said, "They're funny men, aren't they, Dad?"

"You said it, Willie, they're funny men. And I don't know whether it's funny ha-ha or funny peculiar."

"Have we got to change our clothes, Mam?" said Katie.

"Of course you've got to change your clothes. You're not going to lounge around in that dress for the rest of the day."

"Why not? She'll shortly be able to have a new one for every day of the week."

"Will I, Dad?"

"No, you won't, miss," Fiona answered for Bill quickly and

323

definitely. "So sit back there and behave yourself, and take Mamie on to your knee because Mark's leg's in the cramp. It is, isn't it?"

"Yes, Mam." Mark was pushing his foot against the back of the seat.

"I don't want to go on to Katie's knee; I'll sit on Willie's knee."

"You'll do no such thing. I don't want you on my knee. If you don't sit on Katie's you can sit on the stool."

"I'm too big to sit on the stool, and I'll stop loving you shortly Willie Bailey, 'cos you're always at me."

There was a quick glance between Fiona and Bill. That was the first time since that little girl had come under their care that she had spoken out against Willie and his manner towards her.

"Well, well. Good for you, Mamie. It's about time you told him where he stood." Mark was patting Mamie on the head now and she smiled up at him from the cracket where she was crushed between their feet, and she said, "You're nicer than Willie."

"What's the matter with you? Gone daft?" Willie was definitely perturbed: his sole female admirer preferring his elder brother and telling him off in front of the family.

"Revelation."

"What do you say, Mam?" Willie was bending forward.

"Nothing."

"Well, I'm going to say something, Mam. I'm going to wait for Sammy coming out of school, then I'm going to his house."

"You're doing nothing of the kind; you're staying at home. If you don't want to play in the garden or in the playroom then you can sulk in your bedroom."

"Dad, can I go and see . . .?"

"No, you can't!" Bill bawled at him. "Don't you dare start that prank, Willie Bailey. If your mother says you can't do a thing, you can't do it. You could talk to her and try to make her see it your way, but don't you come to me expecting me to countermand her orders. Never do that. Do you hear? And that goes for all of you."

It was some moments later when a lone voice said, "Happy wedding." But no one laughed or made any comment on Mark's statement.

At half past one Bill left the house. He had arranged to give himself time to visit the site and be in Newcastle well before three. In the privacy of the bedroom he had held Fiona in his arms and said, "Lass, I'm shaking like a leaf inside. Facing and talking to Sir Charles is one kettle of fish, this board will be another."

"But you've got it; he said you've got it."

324

"Yes, but I've still got to put myself over to the board, to gain their confidence in me, because there's only two from the old board on this one and by the sound of it there's a dozen or more altogether."

"You'll win them over, all of them. You know your job and you won't lie or prevaricate."

"What's that? Prevaricate? Oh, I must add that to the list, prevaricate."

They had kissed and clung together; then she had set him to the gate and watched him drive away in the car.

It was half past five when he phoned her from Newcastle, saying, "How does it feel, Mrs. B., to be the wife of a building tycoon?"

"Just the same as it was when I was the landlady to the fellow who had risen from a brickie; it hasn't altered. I don't think it will. I'm not the impressionable kind. . . . Oh, Bill. Everything went well?"

"Yes, yes. A bit tricky here and there. Questions flung at me that made me want to, well you know me, spit back. But I kept me cool an' convinced them that I was the man for the job. Sir Charles was delighted. He shook my hand after. But what was more impressive than words, he didn't speak at all, he just kept shaking my hand. And now, Mrs. Bailey, I have been asked to join five of the men at dinner in their hotel, so don't expect me home yet awhile. If you go to the paper shop and ask Mrs. Green for a late edition of the evening rag you'll likely find a report of the outcome of the meeting, because there were a number of newspapermen around. And I saw a TV crew, too, so it might be on 'Look North' with Mike Neville. Look love, I don't know what time I'll be home, but I'll get away as soon as possible."

"Don't hurry, dear. Don't hurry. Enjoy your meal. Enjoy your success."

"I never enjoy anything without you. Now if you were here we'd make a night of it."

"Will Sir Charles be there?"

"No, no. He went off early. He's still pretty groggy, I think, but his secretary will be standing in for him, so he said. I think the secretary is a relation. He lives in the house. I never knew he had a secretary. But, of course, with all his business he's bound to have. He's a nice fellow, not unlike Sir Charles when he was young I would think. Oh, Fiona, I don't know whether I'm on my head or my heels. But one thing I do know, there's a lot of hard work before me, and worry. Oh aye, and worry. But if I can get a crew together even half as good as my lot, then we'll manage. You know, I'm that excited I want to do a handstand, or jump up and click me heels, do something daft like

325

that; and I will do once I get home. You wait and see: I'll get all the kids up and I'll slide down the bannister."

"You'll do no such thing, because they'll be after you, and they'll break their necks."

"Don't be daft. Nobody's broken his neck sliding down a bannister. But that's what I'll do as soon as I reach home, I promise you. I won't even look at you; I'll go straight to the top of those stairs and slide down that bannister, and the noise I'll make will bring them all flyin' out of their beds."

"Oh, Bill, I'd let you do that now if you were here this minute."

"Well, it's going to be an early dinner, and I can promise you that, as I'm driving home, I'll be steady on the liquor. I must go now. I love you, Mrs. B."

"And I have a strong affection for you, Mr. B. Hurry home."

She put down the phone, then went straightaway upstairs and told the children the news.

"Will we be rich now?" asked Katie.

"No, we won't be rich, but we'll have a little more to get by on."

She knew Katie's tongue and she could imagine her going to school and saying, "My father's going to be rich and he's a friend of Sir Charles Kingdom," and so on, and so on.

And their excitement seemed to revolve around that little bit more, and so she left them jabbering about what they wanted; except Mark. He followed her to her room, saying, "I'm glad for him, Mam. And I'm glad you married him."

"Oh, Mark." She put her arms about him, and he clung to her as he used to do when he was smaller and not the twelve-year-old budding man.

"You know something, Mam?"

"What?"

"I . . . I like Bill. You know, inside I always think of him as Mr. Bill. I like him better than I liked my father. I remember my father well."

"Oh, don't say that, Mark." There was a sad note in her voice now, but he went on, "He never played with us, and I can remember him going for you. But from the minute Bill came into the house, he noticed us, he did things with us and for us."

"Look, Mark, get yourself away else you'll have me in tears. And if Bill, or Mr. Bill, or your Dad, whatever, hears you, his head will be more swollen than it is at present. But"—she gently touched his cheek—"thank you for what you've said, I mean about Bill, because he's a very special person."

"Yes; yes, I think he is, too." And then laughing, he added, "Anybody who can bring in a kid who is about to throw a brick through a window and give him tea must be a very special person." They were both laughing loudly now as they went downstairs. But in the hall Fiona stopped and in a quiet voice she said, "But something must be done about Sammy and Willie, because, you know, that child is impossible. I can't imagine him ever changing; all he can do is get worse, and he's not a fit companion for Willie."

"I shouldn't worry about Sammy, Mam. You know, I can't help it, but I . . . I like him, too."

"Well, I'm glad you haven't got a counterpart and you've picked a boy like Roland."

"I'll tell you something, Roland likes him."

"Oh, go on with you." She pushed him away and hurried towards the kitchen, saying now, "Take some ice cream up to them to celebrate."

She, too, celebrated, singing and humming to herself for the next hour. And when she heard a scream from above that caused her to jump from Bill's chair in the study where she had been sitting musing about the bright future, she rushed out to meet the horde tumbling down the stairs, Mark holding out his transistor, calling to her, "Listen! Listen, Mam. They're talking about Dad."

They seemed to be hanging above her, clinging onto the bannister, while Mark, on the bottom stair, held up the transistor and, grinning from ear to ear, looked into his mother's face and listened to a voice saying, "This is a triumph for a small company. It is understood there were fifteen firms applying for this contract, and so it must say much for Mr. Bailey and his particular small firm that they have succeeded against bigger firms more experienced in this form of contract. It is understood that he'll be able to set on at least a hundred men, and this comes at a time when only this week Brignall and Patten have closed down with the loss of seventy-five jobs.

"Tune in again this time tomorrow for more up-to-date news of what is happening in your street, your town, and your area. This is YS, YT, YA, signing off."

"Isn't it wonderful, Mam!"

Her smile was as wide as Mark's. "Marvellous!"

"It'll likely be on the news, nationwide."

"No; no, it won't be on there, dear. Perhaps on BBC North."

And it was on BBC North. They all sat around the television

staring at Mike Neville, the jovial practised announcer. He opened the programme with a repeat of the closing down of Brignall and Patten and the loss of seventy-five jobs. He spoke of the busmen refusing to drive after a certain time of night because of the hooliganism and the threatening attitude of young gangs. He next told of the attack on a crippled seventy-five-year-old woman as she was returning from drawing her pension. And this apparently took place in a quiet suburb where up till then residents thought they were quite safe and that such incidents happened only in the lower end of towns. Then his face stretching into a wide smile, he said, "Now for the good news of the evening. David and Goliath are not dead, for today David, in the form of Mr. William Bailey, a building contractor of Fellburn, brought off a scoop. He put a stone in his sling, and fifteen other firms, among them half a dozen big boys, fell. There are still Jack the Giant killers kicking around. . . . Pardon my puns." He made a face at himself. "Mr. Bailey will be celebrating with his eleven good men and true, as he told our David. These eleven men have worked for him for the past twelve years. They are, he said, the foundation, and there could be no better workmen in the country. Mr. Bailey is a Liverpudlian by birth but a Geordie by inclination. And he couldn't have been more forthright if he had been born a Geordie, because he said, 'Yes, I'll be taking on quite a number of men, but they'll have to be those who'll pull their weight and know that when we start at eight, it doesn't mean quarter past; and when we finish at half past four they don't start to get ready for that at half past three.' Mr. Bailey knows what he wants and he's the kind of man who will get it. That's how he's pulled off this very choice deal. . . . I wonder if he'll set me on; I could run round with the tea."

This must have brought forth a quip from the cameraman, which couldn't be heard but which Mike Neville made use of in his own inimitable way: "Well, Mr. Bailey admits he started as a tea boy. And what one can do another can. . . . What do you mean, there are exceptions?"

"Isn't he funny, Mam?" Katie was looking up at Fiona, who was standing behind the couch.

"Yes, he is."

"He's had a bad leg, that's why he was off and couldn't come and talk."

"He doesn't talk with his leg, stupid." Mark pushed Willie now. "And it was his foot not his leg."

"Now, now, Willie." Fiona leaned over and grabbed her son's flailing arms.

328

"I wish Daddy B. was in. He would have liked to hear that, wouldn't he?"

They all looked at Mamie now and laughed. Then ruffling the child's hair, Fiona said, "Yes, he would have liked to hear that, but—" She turned and looked at the clock, saying, "Just about now he'll be going into a slap-up meal in a posh hotel in Newcastle."

"Mam." Katie was kneeling up on the couch, looking into her mother's face. "Will you be going out in the evening all dressed up in new things? To dinner and parties and such?"

"Well, I might be going out to a dinner now and again, but I'll not always be wearing new things."

"Well, you couldn't go to a dinner two weeks running in the same dress. And you'll have to have a fur coat that you can take off and hand to a waiter, and he'll put it on the back of the chair or hang it up."

"My dear girl"—Fiona was bending over her now—"I won't have any fur coat that a waiter can put on the back of a chair or hang up. Now get that into your head. And listen to me, and not only you, but all of you: life will go on much the same for a long while, except that very likely we won't see so much of your dad, because he'll be working all hours. There'll be treats but they certainly won't be every week; nor will you be any better dressed than you are now. Your dad's brought you two rig-outs in the last few months, you know. So things will go on pretty much the same for a time."

"How long?"

Fiona looked down on Willie. "I don't know, Willie, but when your dad comes back you mustn't greet him with 'What am I going to get out of this?' "

"Oh, Mam!" Mark got up, saying, "They didn't mean that."

"I know. I know. I don't know whether I'm on my head or my heels either. Look what I did, sending all that ice cream up to you. I never meant to do that."

The giggles now turned to high laughter when Mamie, addressing no one in particular, said, "I want a big pram and a talking baby."

"She wants a big pram and a talking baby" built into a chorus that followed Fiona out of the room.

A talking baby. She wanted a talking baby, too; and she hardly dared to think about it these last few days because she had gone past her time. She had gone past her time before and nothing happened, but this time she prayed it would, for she wanted to give Bill something of his very own. She was only thirty, and so there was plenty of time; but she longed to give him two, three, or four. No, she would stop at two. But oh, how she longed to see that man's face when he held his own child, because he gave so much to others.

She stopped by the telephone table. Her mother hadn't phoned today; nor was it likely that she would now, because she was bound to have heard something of this, if not on the radio or the television then certainly from Mrs. Green's paper shop, for Mrs. Green didn't only sell papers, she gave away, free, the local gossip.

Looking at the phone, her face spread into a smile; her mother hadn't phoned her but she could phone her mother. Oh yes; yes, she could phone her mother.

As if the thought had lifted her to the phone, she already had the receiver in one hand and was quickly dialling a number with the other. And when the sweet voice came on the other end, "This is Mrs. Vidler's residence," she pressed her lips tight to quell the sound of laughter from being in her voice when she would say, "Mother, it's me, Fiona."

There was a slight pause before the voice said, "Fiona? This is an unusual occurrence, you phoning me."

"It's an unusual day, and I have unusual news, Mother. But I'm sure you've heard about it already."

Another and considerably longer pause now before the voice said, "I don't know what you're talking about."

"Oh, Mother! If you hadn't the radio, you have the television on every night, as well as, if I'm not mistaken, your routine taking you to Mrs. Green's gossip shop at least once a day."

"Fiona! I needn't listen to you, you know that. I can put the phone down."

"Yes, you can, Mother, but you won't, will you? Because you must have heard about my husband getting this wonderful contract and the praise that's been doled out to him on both the television and the radio. He's been referred to as David, and as Jack the Giant killer."

"Well, his mouth is big enough to hold either of those characters, I should imagine."

Fiona did not retort to this; instead she said, "You can't bear it, can you, Mother? To know that this brickie, as you call him, or that man, or that person, has pulled off one of the biggest deals in building in this area for a long time. And what is more, he is a friend of Sir Charles Kingdom."

"Oh, well, there you have it. As I said, it's who you know, and if you can suck up to a title."

"So you've already expressed your opinion on my husband's success. But let me tell you, Bill did not get this contract through the

330

people he knew, but because of his good work and because it is known that he has a trained group of sound workmen."

"Well, what you've got to remember, Fiona, is the old adage, 'You can't make a silk purse out of a sow's ear.' "

Fiona's teeth pressed together: her mother was winning as usual, boiling her up. But she couldn't let her get off with it this time. "It's a pity distance doesn't cut off the phone because I don't suppose we'll be staying here much longer; Bill's had his eye on one of those big houses in Gosforth, one standing in its own grounds. He had said if he got the contract that's where he would move to. He's also considering buying a chalet-type house in Barbados, where we can slip over two or three times a year for a break. And when we make these moves, Mother, I could also change our phone number; in fact, I've been thinking about being put on ex-directory, the particular type, you know, where no one can get through, no matter how much they press or ask. Goodnight, Mother."

She walked into the kitchen and stood at the sink looking down the garden. The sun was casting long shadows over the lawn from the one big tree growing there. She loved this house; she never wanted to leave it. As for Newcastle, she couldn't bear the thought of living in the city, not even on the outskirts, all that traffic buzzing about. And Barbados, well, you could keep Barbados for her. If she was going anywhere she would like to go to America or Australia, but certainly not Barbados. Lying on a beach all day would bore her to death. Oh!

She turned from the window. She wasn't going to let her mother spoil this. The children were settled, so she would go up and have a bath, give her face one of those ten-minute mud packs; put on another dress, the blue one that Bill liked; it showed off her figure, he said. What time was it now? Just turned seven. He'd likely be in the thick of that dinner now, but he shouldn't be later than half past nine or ten.

She almost skipped from the room, ran across the hall, and put her head round the door of the sitting room, saying, "I'm going to have a bath. Behave yourselves."

"You going to do your face up with that lemon pack, Mam?"

"Yes; yes, I might even do that."

"Well, I'll come up and watch you."

"You'll do nothing of the kind." Her arm was thrust out, the finger pointing. "Give me half an hour to myself."

As she turned away, she glimpsed Mark's hand pulling Katie back onto the couch, the while saying, "Sit down, hussy!"

And Katie's strident tones, likely telling her brother what she thought of him, followed Fiona up the stairs.

Oh, she was happy, happy in all ways. Just that one fly in the ointment. But her mother had always been a fly in the ointment, so why worry.

It was just nine o'clock when she thought she heard the car turning into the drive, and she went into the kitchen, because she knew he would come in the back way.

When she didn't hear the garage door bang she went into the hall again and looked through the small side window, but it was too dark to see as far as the gate. Yet she had heard his car stop there.

The night having turned chilly, she went to the hall wardrobe and put on a coat; then she walked down the drive in the shadow of the cypress hedge. But she stopped where the hedge finished, for there was a car drawn up to the curb and so parked that no car would be able to enter the drive. The car wasn't theirs; Bill's was a silver grey Volvo, whereas this car, as far as she could make out in the light from the far street lamp, was either a dull reddish colour or brown. She detected a movement inside; so she stepped back a few paces before turning and making her way back to the house again. Bill would have something to say to them when he found he couldn't get into his own drive. He had often remarked on the snoggers finding their way to the avenue when it was dark; it wasn't all that brightly lit and was certainly quiet.

About half an hour later she thought she heard a commotion in the street, and she told herself that would be Bill telling the occupants of that car where to go to. She didn't go out, but waited in the hall. However, when there was no sound of the car coming up the drive, she once again went down and stood in the shadow of the cypress hedge. The car was gone. Somebody else had likely complained and there had been a bit of an altercation. That's what she had heard. She did not go out of the gate into the street but returned to the house.

At eleven o'clock she began to worry. The children, having become tired of waiting for Bill's return, were in bed and asleep. The house was quiet.

There was the sound of a car, but it was from next door and made her wonder why Mr. Paget should be returning so late. He very rarely went out in the car at night, and in his present state of mind she imagined his driving would be anything but safe.

At half past eleven she was standing in the hall rubbing one hand

332

against the back of the other, telling herself that he wouldn't have stayed so late without having phoned her. Whom could she get in touch with? Sir Charles's secretary? He lived at the Hall, apparently. But Bill had said he was at the dinner as well.

She whipped through the pages of the directory, and then she was phoning the number. She listened to the bell ringing and ringing, but she wouldn't put the phone down. Then a woman's weary voice said, "Yes? Yes, what is it? Who is it?"

"May I speak to Sir Charles Kingdom's secretary, please?"

"Who . . . who's speaking?"

"This is Mrs. Bailey."

"Oh, Mrs. Bailey. Well, this is Lady Kingdom here. What is wrong?"

"My husband hasn't returned from Newcastle. I . . . I understood he was having dinner with Sir Charles's secretary and others and he said he wouldn't be late, but it is now nearing twelve o'clock and . . . and . . ."

"Oh, my goodness me! Yes, yes. Wait a moment, I'll get up."

"Oh, I'm very sorry."

"Don't worry. Don't worry. I can contact Rupert on the intercom."

She waited, one hand holding the receiver, the other tapping her lips in agitation. When a man's voice came on the phone, saying, "Mrs. Bailey?" she said, "Yes; yes, it's Mrs. Bailey."

"Lady Kingdom has just told me that . . . but . . . but your husband should have been home ages ago. He had a very early dinner. It was over by . . . oh, well, I'm not quite sure, about half past eight, perhaps quarter to nine. I left him in the foyer talking to Mr. Ramshaw and Mr. Pithey."

"Are . . . are they Newcastle men?"

"I . . . I think so. Yes, I think they both live in Newcastle. Look . . . what time is it now?" He paused. "Twenty minutes to twelve. What I should do first of all is ring the police and see if there's been an accident."

"But they would have let me know surely; he always carries papers on him."

"Yes; yes, that's right. But nevertheless I would do that. And then ring Mr. Pithey and the other man. Then ring me back."

"Yes; yes, I'll do that."

Her hand was shaking visibly as she phoned the police station.

"Has there been any . . . accidents on the road from Newcastle this evening?"

"No, madam; not that I know of. Who's speaking?"

"Mrs. Bailey. My . . . my husband hasn't come home, and it's just on twelve o'clock. He's the builder, and he went to a dinner, but he said he'd be back about ten."

"Ah, Mrs. Bailey. Yes, I know Mr. Bailey. I shouldn't worry; he'll turn up. Would he have gone on to another function?"

"My husband would have phoned me, sir, if he had been going on to a further function."

"He would?"

The question seemed to say, Well you're a lucky woman, and she answered it as if she had heard it: "Yes, he would. He's that kind of man."

"Yes, all right. All right. What is your address, Mrs. Bailey?"

She gave him the address. Then he said, "Well, there's bound to be a patrol car somewhere near. I'll get in touch with them right away and they'll give you a call."

"Thank you." She put down the phone. Celebrating indeed. Bill would never celebrate without her if he could help it.

It seemed to her that she had been walking the floor for at least half an hour before the bell rang; but the clock told her it was only five minutes past twelve. When she opened the door there were two policemen standing on the step.

"Mrs. Bailey?"

"Yes."

"About your husband."

"Yes. He . . . he hasn't returned home. It's very unusual and. . . ."

"May we come in, Mrs. Bailey?"

"Of course, yes, yes."

They passed her and stood in the hall, and then the taller one said, "I am Constable Anderson and this is Constable Burrows. What make of car does your husband drive?"

"It's a Volvo."

"And can you remember the number?"

"Oh." She looked from one to the other, then round the hall, before she said, "I'm dreadful on numbers. It starts with a JR."

"That's all right. That's all right." The police constables looked at each other, and then one said, "Sit down, Mrs. Bailey."

"Why should I sit down? Look, please tell me what's happened or what you know."

"Mrs. Bailey, your husband's car is outside on the road."

"It's on the . . . !"

"Yes, it's on the road. But your husband isn't in it, and I'm afraid, from the cursory glance we've been able to give it, there has been a bit

334

of a struggle. Parcels that were evidently on the passenger seat are trampled on the floor. There are bits of broken glass there and some sort of child's toy and various other articles that we haven't as yet examined. And what is more ... Please do sit down, Mrs. Bailey." The taller of the two men took her arm and led her to the hall chair, and when she was seated her voice was just a whimper as she said, "You said, what is more."

"Yes. There's evidently been a struggle because there's ... well, there's a splash of blood on the dashboard, and more on the pavement. But the blood on the pavement is near the boot of the car. Do you want a drink of water, ma'am? Get her a drink of water."

"Where's the kitchen?"

She brought up her drooping head and put out her hand, saying, "I'm all right. I'm all right."

"Have you any relatives living near who could come and stay with you?"

Her mother was the last person on earth she wanted at this moment, and Nell wasn't here, so she shook her head.

Police Constable Anderson said to his partner, "Ring the office and see if Joan Wallace is free. Ask them to send her round straightaway; and while you're on you'd better tell Sergeant Nichols to inform the inspector."

"He'll have gone home."

"Yes, I know that." The words were a hiss. "Well, he can just come back from home or from wherever he is. You tell them."

There was a great silence in Fiona's head, yet she could hear the policemen talking. They were at the far end of space; they were disembodied voices. And one of the voices floated over her head and spoke to her, saying, "Have you any children?"

The silence seemed to explode as she pulled herself to her feet, and she said, "I have four children."

"Young?"

"The eldest is twelve. He's very sensible. I'll go and wake him."

"No; no, I wouldn't ma'am, not yet. A policewoman will be coming to keep you company, and the inspector an' all because ..." But she didn't wait to hear why; she walked to the phone and dialled the Hall number again.

It was Sir Charles's secretary who spoke, saying, "Yes, Mrs. Bailey?"

She went to open her mouth but found she couldn't speak for a moment and she turned and looked at the policeman and, her voice again like a whimper, she said, "It is Sir Charles Kingdom's

335

secretary. He . . . he was at the dinner with my husband tonight. Will
. . . will you tell him, please?"

Constable Anderson took the phone from her hand, and he said,
"This is Police Constable Anderson here from Fellburn. We have
found Mr. Bailey's car outside his own gate. There are signs of a
struggle. That's all I can tell you at the moment, sir."

"Well . . . well, where is he? I mean, Mr. Bailey?"

"We'd like to know that, sir. He wasn't in the car. We are just going
on what we saw there."

"*My God!* I'll come across."

"I don't think there's anything you can do at the moment, sir, but
we'll keep you informed. Mrs. Bailey would like that."

The policeman put down the phone and, turning to Fiona, he said,
"The less there are moving around the car at the moment, the better,
ma'am. You understand?"

"Yes, yes. But . . . but what do you think? Oh"—she put her hand
to her head—"I . . . I can't believe it. Who would want to do that? But
there . . . yes; yes, there was a car outside from just after eight
blocking our drive. There was someone inside, men I think, but I
didn't like to go onto the pavement to enquire further."

"Are you sure of the time, ma'am?"

"I think it was nine. I'm not sure. I'm not sure of anything at the
moment. Then I heard Mr. Paget come in at eleven. No; no, it wasn't
quite eleven."

"He is your neighbour, this Mr. Paget?"

"Yes; yes, he is our neighbour."

"We could speak to him. We'll do that when the inspector arrives."

"No, no." She shook her head. "He's not well. He . . . well, his mind's
gone a bit funny lately and . . ." She stopped and started across the
hall, and it was as if her eyes were seeing through the kitchen into the
back garden and into the house next door. My God! He had said he
would do for Bill. And he was more than slightly mad. Had he?

"What is it, ma'am?"

"Mr. Paget, he . . . he was angry with my husband."

"What was he angry about?"

"Because his daughter-in-law was to be married to one of my
husband's men. She was divorced from his son. He didn't want to lose
her, and he blamed Bill. Yes; yes, he blamed Bill for being the means
of them losing Nell. He's been going funny lately. He's . . . oh, my
God!" She put her hand over her mouth and rushed towards the
kitchen and just managed to reach the sink before she vomited.

Constable Anderson was about to follow her, but he turned to

336

Constable Burrows, saying, "Get on that phone again and see if they've got the inspector yet. There's more here than meets the eye. I want to know if I should go next door or not."

It was half past one when the inspector and Police Constable Anderson rang the bell next door. When there was no response to the second ring the inspector kept his finger on the bell, and this time it was answered by the opening of a window.

"What is it? What is it?"

"Mrs. Paget?"

"Yes; yes, I'm Mrs. Paget."

"Would you mind coming down a moment, please?"

"What do you want?"

"We are the police. We just want to speak to your husband for a moment."

"He's in bed, sound asleep."

"Would you please come down, Mrs. Paget?"

The window closed with hardly a sound, and a moment later Mrs. Paget opened the front door, then stood pulling hard at the dressing-gown belt.

"May we come in, Mrs. Paget?"

She stood hesitant for a moment, then said, "What . . . what can you want with my husband?"

"We just wanted to ask him a few questions."

"What about, and at this time of night?"

"Would you ask him to come down, please?"

"No . . . no, I can't. He's not well."

"Mrs. Paget"—they were standing in the hall now—"Mr. Bailey has gone missing. His car is outside his gate. There is evidence that he has been attacked: there are bloodstains on the pavement and the signs of a struggle inside the car."

"But . . . but what has my husband to do with that?"

The inspector did not answer this question; instead he asked one of his own. "What time did your husband return home tonight?"

"I . . . I don't know; I was asleep. I haven't been very well."

"Do you know what time he went out?"

"About seven o'clock, I think."

"Do you know where he was going?"

"No, no. He often goes for a drive. It helps to soothe his . . . well, it helps to soothe his nerves."

"I'm afraid, Mrs. Paget, I must ask you to go and wake your husband and bring him downstairs."

"But why? Why? My husband wouldn't have anything to do—" She put her hand to her mouth, then said, "What has Fiona been saying? I mean, Mrs. Bailey."

"Mrs. Bailey is very distressed. Her husband has disappeared after apparently being attacked. She recalls that your husband was very abusive to her and threatened what he was going to do to her husband. Now I would like to see your husband and have this accusation confirmed or denied. If you don't bring him downstairs, Mrs. Paget, I'm afraid I'll have to go up and question him there."

The poor woman almost stumbled from the room, and it was a full ten minutes later when she reappeared in the hall followed by her husband who, on the sight of the police, began to tremble.

"He's not well. He's under the doctor. But he would never do such a thing. Come and sit down, dear." She led the shivering form into the sitting room, and the two officers followed. Looking at what appeared to be a tall frail man, the inspector had difficulty in believing that this man could overpower a fellow like Bill Bailey, because he knew Bill Bailey and he was a tough guy altogether. One blow from him should have knocked this fellow flying. But from what he had heard from Mrs. Bailey, this man was a sort of Jekyll and Hyde. He bent towards him now, saying, "Where did you go when you drove your car tonight, Mr. Paget?"

"I don't know. Well, I just drive. It . . . it soothes me, doesn't it? Doesn't it, Bella?"

"Yes dear, it does, it does. He . . . he hasn't been very well."

"I know. I know, Mrs. Paget." The inspector silenced her with a small movement of his hand. Then looking at the man again, he said, "Did you stop and speak to Mr. Bailey when you were out?"

"No; no, I didn't. I never saw him. His car was at the gate though when I came in, and I felt bad against him. I remember that, yes I do, but not anymore."

The policemen exchanged glances.

"Did you not get out of your car and speak to Mr. Bailey?"

Both men watched the older man blink his eyes, nip on his lip, then look up at his wife before saying, "No; no, I never did. I never did."

"No, of course, you didn't dear. Of course, you didn't."

The inspector now spoke to Mrs. Paget, saying, "Who is your doctor, Mrs. Paget?"

"Dr. Nelson. He . . . he knows my husband's case."

"What do you mean, your husband's case?"

"Well, he's been under him for five years. I have, too. That's what I mean." There was an icy touch in her tone now. "What are you trying to insinuate? My husband's not well, but, as I said, he wouldn't hurt a fly."

338

"What are you getting at? What are they getting at, Bella?"

"Nothing, my dear, nothing."

"I'm afraid we are, Mr. Paget." The inspector once more leaned forward. "As I've already said, Mr. Bailey is missing. There are signs of a struggle and blood was spilt. And we just want to know when you last saw him and if you spoke to him with regard to what you were angry about."

"No; no, I didn't. I haven't done anything. I didn't. I wouldn't. I'd never go as far as that, never. Would I, Bella? Would I?"

"No; no, you wouldn't, dear."

"Take your husband back to bed, Mrs. Paget. We'll have another talk later. I'm sorry we disturbed you. I'd get in touch with his doctor, and perhaps he will come and see him in the morning. I may be round again, too."

Both men left the room, and when Bella followed them it would seem she hadn't the strength to open the door; and the policeman, putting his hand on her shoulder, said, "Don't worry, missis, don't worry; it's just an investigation. We have to ask these questions. You understand that?"

She nodded but was unable to speak. And when the door closed on the two men they walked slowly down the drive and into the street again and stood looking at the Volvo and the stain on the pavement near the boot.

"What d'you think, sir?"

"I can't see him getting the better of Bailey in any way. Yet if he's schizophrenic ... they can get the strength of ten men when the mood's on them. Remember that young lad last year from Boswell Terrace, a respectable family, a father a solicitor? Look what he did. He's out again now, but I understand the mother's in a breakdown, because she's hardly let him see daylight since. To my mind he should never have been let home. And that's what the girl's parents are saying, too. Still, by the look of that old fellow, he won't do much more harm the night. But if he has gone for Bailey, it's to find out where he's dumped him. We'll have another go at him first thing in the morning. By that time we should have his doctor's report. But we had better go in now and see if Burrows and Wallace have been able to calm down Mrs. Bailey. She's in a state. I think we'll have to have a doctor there an' all. In the meantime I want this car ringed round; somebody on duty all the time. And it looks as if our visitor will be Sir Charles Kingdom's secretary, if not Sir Charles himself."

"I thought he was ill, sir, I mean, the old man?"

"No, I understand from the papers and the report of the meeting

339

that put Mr. William Bailey in the big money, that the old fellow was there today, and very much in voice."

They were going up the drive now when he stopped and said, "We might be jumping to conclusions about that old fellow next door. Disappointed rivals, you know, can become nasty. And they say there were twelve or more of them in for that big slice of cake. Yes—." He stood now under the outside light of the front door and, nodding to the constable, he said, "It looks as if we'll have a number of interviews tomorrow besides the old schizo boy next door. But there's one thing I'm going to have and that's a couple of hours of shut-eye before we have them. So I'll send Parkins and Steel round; they can see that nobody fingers anything. We'll leave Burrows here with Wallace. If it's a kidnapping job, and you never know, there should be somebody near that phone. In the meantime, I want you to go back to the office and tell Pringle to get names, addresses, and phone numbers of every man that was at that meeting yesterday, that's those on the board and also every firm that applied for the job. Names, addresses, the lot. Anyway, nothing much can be done till daylight, and since I've been up since six o'clock this morning preparing for the minor Royalty that was flitting through, it's more than twenty hours since I had my head down, and I need at least four hours a night or I get nasty."

When they entered the house they heard the sound of crying coming from the sitting room; and when they entered the room it was to see Mrs. Bailey holding a young boy tightly to her and saying, "It's all right. It's all right. He'll come back. You know Mr. Bill, don't you, no one gets the better of Mr. Bill. They never have and they never will. You know that. You know that, Mark, no one gets the better of Mr. Bill."

32

IT WAS NINE O'CLOCK THE NEXT MORNING. THE CAR HAD BEEN TAKEN AWAY; A policeman was standing just inside the gate and a number of reporters on the pavement outside. The news had spread early up the terrace, and there had been a crowd of sightseers to see the car being driven away. But it had thinned somewhat by the time Barney McGuire forced himself through to speak to the policeman. "I'm Mr. Bailey's foreman," he said. "We've just heard. I must see Mrs. Bailey."

"What's your name?"

"Barney McGuire."

"Stay where you are a minute."

The policeman went up the path; and when he returned he opened the gate, but as he did so a reporter tried to slip in, only to be grabbed by the collar and pushed back onto the pavement again. And the policeman, an extremely tall young man, said, "We don't want any rough stuff, do we? Now I've told you, if there's any news from inside you'll get it, but you'll get it standing on your own side of the gate."

The door was opened for Barney by a red-eyed Katie who said, "Mam's in the sitting room, Mr. McGuire. Have ... have you heard anything?"

"No, hinny. No." He took off his cap and walked on tiptoe across the hall and into the sitting room.

341

Fiona was standing in front of the fireplace. It was already quite warm outside but she had the electric fire on. She said, "Hello, Barney."

"Hello, Mrs. B. I can't believe it. I just can't believe it. We're all stunned. The fellas all wanted to come and see what they could do, but as I said, the job had to go on. That's what he would want. We had to keep at it until he came back. Oh. . . ." He stopped, lost for words.

"Why should it happen to him, Barney?"

Her voice was breaking. "Who would want to do this? And he must have put up a fight, there must have been more than one. I . . . I thought last night in my distress that it might have been Mr. Paget next door because he's been funny lately and going on about Nell marrying Bert, because he didn't want her to leave them. And he had said quite threatening things to me, what he would do to Bill. But when I thought about it, Bill would have knocked him down with one hand. The only thing is, if he had an implement. But then he would have had to lift or pull Bill into the car. Oh, I can't help it." She turned now and faced the fire. "I can't help it, Barney. I keep thinking aloud all the time, talking, talking. I think I'm going to go mad."

He was standing at her side now, his hand on her shoulder. "Look, as the lads said back there, he's a tough guy, the toughest, they don't come tougher than him. He's not going to be knocked out with one blow. It's likely somebody's done this for money; kidnapping, you know, because they've heard he's got the big job. And you'll see, you'll get a phone call shortly. But as we all said, if that was the case we'd skin our hides to help you meet it, we would that, because there'll never be another boss like him. And they all know it. Who, I ask you, would put his men onto the sort of board as he did last year on that other job and give us a percentage of the profits at Christmas? Not many, not many I can tell you." His voice was rising as if he were addressing a meeting. Then he turned as the door opened and Mark came in.

"Hello there, son."

"Hello, Mr. Barney. Have . . . have you heard anything?"

"No, lad; we've only just got to hear of it back on the houses. We couldn't believe it."

"Sit down, Mam." The boy came and took Fiona's arm and, as if she were an old lady, led her to the couch. Then looking at Barney, he said, "Sit down, Mr. Barney."

"No, lad, I won't stay. He'd want the job to go on, as I said to your ma. And I'll see it goes on. Aye, by God, I will, because he'll be back.

You'll see, he'll be back. And you know I just said a minute ago, Mrs. B. about blackmail, you know, of being kidnapped, well, as the lads were sayin', if that's the case it's been done by those blokes who mugged me and took Jack Mowbray's bike and levelled Jos Wright's allotment, not to mention Morris Fenwick's pigeons. Then there was Alec Finlay's outhouse and all his tools, and the whole thing started with Tommy Turnbull's car being pinched. D'you remember? Now they've been through us all, and it seems to be the same two fellas, they've turned to the boss, and it'll be money they're after this time, blackmail, as the lads said. By God! If we could only get our hands on them they wouldn't live, I can tell you, not to go to court. But . . . as Davey Love, the new Irish fella said, 'Blokes don't do things like that off their own bat except their gettin' paid, 'cos there'd be no money in it, would there, for levelling an allotment and letting out pigeons?' No, there's some big bloke behind it. But that fella Love's got his head screwed on the right way, and he seems to think everything stems from the fellas who took the car. He remembers what those blokes looked like, Mutt and Jeff, he said, one big and one small, well not over small, but contrast like, you know."

She wished he would stop talking. She wished he would go away.

There was a bit of commotion in the hall, and she rose from the couch and put her hand out towards Mark's and gripped it tightly. But she didn't move from where she was standing: she kept her eyes on the door expecting it to open and Bill to walk or stumble in. But it was Katie, who said, "It's Sir Kingdom, Mam."

She drew in a long breath then said, "Oh, show him in. Bring him in." Then turning to Barney, she said, "Thank you, Barney. If . . . if you hear anything at all you'll let me know, won't you? And if we have any news we'll phone you."

"Thank you, ma'am. Yes, thank you." He edged his way to the door but had to step back when Sir Charles, followed by his secretary, came into the room, the old man saying, "They didn't tell me a word of this, Mrs. Bailey, not a word did I hear until after breakfast. A lot of nincompoops. My dear. My dear. What can I say?"

He turned and looked at Barney, who was aiming to get out of the door, and said, "You . . . you one of the workmen?"

"Yes, sir. I'm the boss's gaffer."

"Oh, well, he'd want you to keep on working, wouldn't he?"

"Yes, sir. Yes, he would that. Good day to you, sir."

"Oh, my dear." He was moving towards Fiona now, his hands outstretched. "What can I say? I feel responsible. Oh, I do, I feel responsible."

"Please sit down, Sir Charles."

"Thank you. Thank you."

The old man dropped into a chair; then looking up at his secretary, he said, "I'll never forgive you for keeping this from me; nor my wife either, because . . . because I feel responsible for it all. I should have done something before now. Yes, I should. I should."

"What could you have done, Sir Charles, that could have prevented this?"

"Oh, my dear"—the old man put his hand to his head—"I should have gone to the police and told them what she was up to. What did I do? I said to Bailey I would make good all the damages to his men. But as he pointed out to me, oh yes, and truthfully, you couldn't pay for a life."

"What are you saying, sir?" Fiona's eyes were wide, her mouth slightly agape, then she went on, "You know . . . you know who has done this? You know where my husband is?"

"No, my dear; the latter I don't know, I don't know where your husband is. I'd give all I own at this moment to be able to say to you, yes, I know where he is. But her thugs must have got at him."

"Her?" She could not believe what her mind was thinking. Her, he had said. Her voice was small when she said, "Your niece, you mean?"

"No, she's not my niece, dear, she's my godchild. Strangely, I've thought of her as a daughter and put up with her whims and antics for years; in fact, I've condoned them, but not this, not this. I warned her, but she went abroad and I couldn't locate her. I tried again this morning only to be told that she's gone off again. Rupert here"—he wagged his finger towards his secretary—"got in touch with her accountant, and what he was told, well, I could hardly believe. Over the past months she has sold most of her businesses and has gone to live abroad. Where, nobody seems to be able to tell me. But you can't escape in this world for very long, and if anything happens to Bailey . . ."

Fiona turned from him, her hand shading her eyes, saying as she did so, "Please! Please, sir, don't even suggest such a thing. I . . . I can't bear it. Anyway, you should know her and I'm sure you don't think she would be capable of . . . anything like—" she couldn't say murder, but instead said, "anything awful just because my husband refused her advances and told her plainly he wouldn't leave me for her. That's what it's all about isn't it? Hurt pride, someone dared refuse her something. But . . . but even so, she surely would stop at ordering someone to really hurt him, murder him, wouldn't she? Wouldn't she?" Her voice had risen almost to a scream, and both

344

Katie and Mark rushed to her side and put their arms about her.

The next moment, however, she became full of contrition as she saw the old man bow his head and the secretary put his arm on his shoulder, saying, "Can I get you something, sir?" And he turned to Fiona, saying, "May I ask if you have any spirit, a little brandy?"

"Oh yes, yes."

"I'll get it, Mam."

Mark hurried to the drinks' cabinet in the corner of the room, and when he returned with the glass half filled with brandy the secretary smiled wanly at him, saying, "That looks like a treble, but thank you." Then taking the glass from the boy, he turned to Sir Charles, saying, "Drink this, sir," and the old man, with a shaking head, took the glass, looked at it for a moment before drinking half of its contents, then sat back in the chair, his head resting on the rail. Presently, looking at Fiona, he said, "Nothing you could say to me, my dear, could come within miles of the condemnation I'm pouring on my own head at this moment."

"I'm sorry, sir, but I'm so upset. He was, I mean he is," and she stressed the last word, "such a good man. He loves my children as if they were his own. He may be rough of tongue, but he would not do an underhand or dishonourable thing."

"I'm sure of that, my dear. Yes, I know that. I have great respect for him."

"Sir, may I speak?"

"Can you tell me who has ever been able to stop you if you wanted to, man?"

"Well, you seem to have come to the conclusion that this happening is solely at Mrs. Brown's door. But last night Mrs. Bailey seemed to think it could have been done by the neighbour next door. Isn't that so, Mrs. Bailey?" After a moment's hesitation, Fiona said, "Yes; yes, that's right. I understand Mr. Paget is schizophrenic."

"And you know, sir, such people have dual personalities, they can do the most outrageous things when their character changes. They have uncommon strength and are wily with it. So I don't think, sir, you should take it for granted that Mrs. Brown is solely behind this. Then again, as has been hinted, it could have been the work of a disappointed contender for the estate project."

A little of the strain seemed to go from the old man's face, and he looked from his secretary to Fiona, saying, "Yes, he could be right. He could be right. I only hope that he is. But whatever, the main thing now is to find out what has happened to your husband."

"But we can't find out that, sir, can we, until we know who did it?"

Their attention was all on Mark now, and the secretary said, "Yes, you're right, you're right. But the police are hard at work looking into every avenue; they are not just following one lead. The inspector said to me on the phone this morning that this case is turning out like a piece of tapestry, there are so many threads to it."

Sir Charles now drank the remainder of the brandy; then, looking at his secretary, he rose to his feet, saying, "You've eased my mind a little, Rupert. You have the habit of doing that. I suppose you get that from your mathematical mind." Then looking at Fiona again, he held out his hand to her, and when she took it he patted it and in a low voice he muttered, "We will keep in close touch. I . . . I will phone every hour."

"Thank you, Sir Charles."

"Oh, don't thank me for anything, my dear, don't thank me." His head still shaking, he went out, and his secretary, after exchanging a glance with Fiona, turned and followed the old man.

The next visitor was Mr. Paget's doctor. He stood in the hall, saying, "I've had a long talk with him. Quite candidly he doesn't really remember what he did last night when he went out in the car. This often happens in cases like this. I've attended him for years and he hasn't had a bad turn; well, not for some long time. But they were pretty frequent at one time. He seems to have been better since his daughter-in-law came to stay with him. Really, he's been a changed individual. It's been only since she talked of leaving them to get married that he's reverted. Even so, the once or twice I've looked in on him recently he hasn't seemed too bad. Of course, in cases like these they can become very sly and appear quite normal when talking to a professional man. But I can say he is greatly distressed this morning. He says he saw your husband's car there as he drove into his drive, which surely points to the fact that, whatever happened, happened before he arrived home, because your husband, naturally, would drive straight into his garage, wouldn't he?"

"Yes; yes, he would."

"But then, of course, he could have said he saw the car there. I don't know. I really don't know, except that if the police get at him and wear him down he might own up to things that he's never done out of sheer fear, and so confuse the issue. This also happens. Anyway, I'm glad they're leaving him where he is for the time being. And his poor little wife is so upset. Now she is, physically, not well at all. I know how worried you must be about your husband, Mrs. Bailey, but I do hope that whatever happens to him isn't laid at Mr. Paget's door, because all his life he's been a frightened man. He knows what's wrong with him and he's afraid of it. But when he has these turns he takes on an aggressive attitude as if to make up for the fear and timidity that has filled the best part of his life. We never know what the other fellow is thinking, do we, Mrs. Bailey? Anyway, I'll be looking in on him later in the day. I'll tell you what transpires then."

"Thank you, doctor."

It was around twelve o'clock when the next visitor appeared after having had an altercation with the policeman at the gate. Mark opened the door to him and the visitor said, "Could I be seein' yer ma, son? I'm Davey Love; you know, Sammy's father."

"Yes, yes. Come in, please. Will you come into the sitting room? My mother's upstairs; I'll call her."

A minute later Mark knocked on Fiona's bedroom door, calling, "Mam."

"Yes? Come in, Mark."

"Sammy's father's downstairs."

"Mr. Love?"

"Yes."

"Oh, tell him I'll be down in a minute."

She had turned her face towards him, and he knew that she was crying and he went out and walked slowly down the stairs. He, too, wanted to cry, like he had wanted to do in the night, but, as his mother had said, she had only him to rely on until Mr. Bill came back. He felt more in touch with him when he thought of him as Mr. Bill rather than as Dad. He was wonderful as a dad, but he had been more wonderful still as Mr. Bill. He had come into their lives like an explosion, a burst of fireworks. In those early days he had longed to get home just to hear his voice. It was different now he was their father. But it was a good difference. He supposed it was a difference without the fear that he might get up, pack up and leave as he had done once before, when he was a lodger. He entered the room to see Mr. Love sitting on the sofa holding Willie's hand and saying, "You take me word for it, yer dad's comin' back. We'll scour the town and as far afield as it takes, but we'll find him, and whole. An' the next thing you know he'll be bawlin' his big head off at you like he does us at work. Oh, God in heaven! I'd love to hear that bawl this minute, indeed to God I would that. You know, boy"—he now looked up at Mark—"I've just joined the troop, so to speak, but I've never worked with a more decent lot of men, and I've never before worked with men who had a good word for their boss. Not that they're angels, they're always on the grouse. Well, I mean, if we didn't grumble what would we have to talk about? Now I ask you.

347

But when the chips are down that lot would stand on their heads for him.... Oh, there you are, ma'am." And he rose to his feet as Fiona entered the room. "It's me dinner hour. I thought I'd come round and have a word with you."

"Thank you, Mr. Love. It's very kind of you."

"Kind? Not at all. If it wasn't that that big-mouth gaffer Barney says we've all got to stick at it, 'cos that's what the boss would expect, I would've had the half day off or the whole day since I heard the news. I have me own ideas where I could put me fingers on two blokes, the two that've been playin' havoc with the gang. But o'course there's no proof that this would be tacked on to them. They were up to their eyes in piddlin' things like stealin' bikes, lettin' pigeons out, an' things like that, annoyin' things. But I don't know if they'd be up to kidnappin'. They're sayin' now there's so many suspects fallin' over themselves, the police don't know which end of them's up. There's an old bloke next door gone off his head, they say. An' then there's that were after the big job. An' you know some blokes can't take defeat. Up to every trick in the book. Oh aye, begod! I know some of them. Don't I know. But anyway, I just want to tell you you've got all me attention and as soon as I finish on the job the night I'll be lookin' for those two blokes, and if it's only one of 'em I find, I'll kick his backside from here to hell before handin' him over to the police. Ma'am, can I ask you somethin', personal like?"

"Yes, Mr. Love, anything."

"It's about me young 'un. He missed seein' Willie yesterday, an' this bein' Thursday he's bound for confession. But what in the name of God he has to confess I won't be knowin', except his four-letter words, an' they've dropped off of late. It's surprisin'. I know what state you're in but d'you think that the morrow he could come round and have a word with yer Willie there? It's amazing, tis, how the lad's taken to Willie. An' you like him an' all, Willie, don't you?"

Willie's face was unsmiling as he said, "Yes; yes, I do like Sammy."

"There you are then. How will it be, missis? He won't be in the way, he knows better. I've threatened to knock his brains out an' slap his face with' em if he doesn't behave himself when he's in yer house. But that boy's as miserable as sin when he can't see the young chap here." He jerked his head in Willie's direction. "I've never known him to be like this, not in all his life. Such a change in him. He was always askin' when his ma was comin' back, an' when I said, never I hope, I'd find him cryin' in bed. So I had to tell him she'd come in the door one day: she'd pop in just like the bad penny she was. But lately, not a word about his ma an' no cryin' in bed. So, if you wouldn't mind. I feel that I'm imposin' upon you in yer trouble, but ..."

"Of course, Mr. Love, he may come round." Anything, she was thinking, only go.

"Thank you, ma'am. Thank you, very much. Well, I'll be off now. I'll have a bite and a pint afore I start again, but I tell you I'll be hot on somebody's trail the night if it takes me to dawn. I have me own ideas about this. Oh aye, I have. Good-bye to you."

"Good-bye, Mr. Love. Will you see Mr. Love out, Mark?"

"It's a fine family you have. I don't begrudge you them, but I can't help wishin'. No harm in wishin' is there?"

"No, Mr. Love, there isn't. No, there isn't."

"No, there isn't. And I know what you're wishin at this minute, and it'll come true. Believe me, it'll come true." He had reached the sitting room door when he turned and added, "I'm a very bad Catholic, and a bad Catholic is worse than a heathen, there's no hope for them. God forgives them who doesn't know any better, like heathens, Chinese, Indians, and Baptists"—he grinned as he said the last word—"but for a bad Catholic there's no hope, 'cos you know, we should know better, we've been given the faith. But I'll tell you what I'll do the night afore I start on me rounds after those two bug . . . blokes, I'll go into church, before God I will, and I'll make a bargain with Him and I'll give you three guesses as to what that bargain will be. Now I'll be off, rightly this time I'll be off. Good day to you."

Fiona didn't answer, "Good day." She only wished that she could laugh, but she would never laugh again. No, she would never laugh again.

The inspector called in the afternoon to tell her how things were going. His men made a house to house call in the district. They had police scouring the fields on the outskirts of the town and Brooker's woodland. He didn't mention that there were divers in the river, nor did he say that they'd had a call from someone who had likely put in for the contract, to say that he had overheard a certain man, whom he named, saying that he would like to put a bomb under Bailey's car. That was another thread in the tapestry of this case, but they were following it up.

At seven o'clock in the evening Nell phoned. They had just heard the news; they had been out all day. They were coming back straightaway.

"Oh, Nell, Nell," Fiona had almost wailed over the phone. "I think I'm going mad. I can't eat. I can't close my eyes. Oh, Nell, Nell, I'll be glad to see you."

"I'll be with you soon," said Nell. There's a train from here at six o'clock tomorrow morning, and we'll be on it."

At eight o'clock her mother rang. "Fiona. Oh, my dear, my dear, I've just heard. I'd been on a trip, I'd been to Harrogate with the bridge four, you know we go on a little trip now and again. Oh, my dear, I am, I must say it, I am extremely sorry. Believe me, dear, I am. We had our differences I know, but for this to happen. Have you heard any more news?"

"No, Mother."

"What do you think could have happened to him?"

"I don't know, Mother. It's all in the papers or on the radio. It will be on the nine o'clock news again I suppose."

"I'll come round, dear."

"No, Mother, please wait until tomorrow morning; I'm ... I'm going to take a sleeping tablet."

"But the children?"

"The children are wonderful, Mother. Mark is managing them and Nell will be back in the morning."

"Oh, Nell! I suppose you prefer others to your own kith and kin."

"Please, Mother, please."

"All right, dear, all right, I won't. But ... but I'm distressed for you."

"Thank you, Mother. Thank you."

"Fiona, I think it only right that I should come round now."

"Mother, do this for me, please: let me sleep tonight."

"But ... but, my dear, I wouldn't disturb you. I can sleep downstairs on the couch."

"Mother, you'd never rest on the couch, you know you like your own bed, but I appreciate what you're offering, what you're saying. I do really."

"I'm so glad you do, dear, and I mean it. I'm really deeply sorry. And after he had got that wonderful contract. Someone's done this out of spite. I'm sure of it. They hate to see people get on."

Fiona closed her eyes. How could people change like that? Her mother talking like a normal caring person, a normal caring mother, when only two days ago Bill's name was like a firebrand to her. She was talking as if Bill was dead and she herself already a widow.

"Goodnight, Mother," she said. "Thank you for calling. I'll see you in the morning."

"Goodnight, my dear. Goodnight."

She had said she was going to take a sleeping tablet, but she hadn't any idea of taking one. She doubted she even had any in the house. Yes, come to think of it, she had. When she had come out of the hospital at the beginning of the year she hadn't been able to sleep and the doctor had prescribed some for her, telling her not to make a habit of them: "You're a healthy human being and sleep should come naturally," he had said. So there must be some somewhere upstairs. They wouldn't be in the medicine cupboard. She didn't keep pills or anything like that in there in case the children got their hands on them. They would be in her toilet drawer in the dressing table. Suddenly, she decided that that's what she would do, she would take a sleeping tablet. She'd blot it out and when she woke in the morning he'd be there. Yes, he'd be there.

33

"DA, YA DIDN'T COME IN TILL LATE."

"I know I didn't, but I thought you were asleep."

"I couldn't get to sleep. They were rowin' next door."

"They're always rowin' next door, but you sleep through it, usually you do."

"Aye, I know. But I wasn't really thinkin' about them, but about Mr. Bailey."

"We're all thinkin' about him, lad. Eat yer flakes."

"I don't feel hungry, Da."

"Eat yer flakes."

"Why . . . why were you out so late, Da?"

"I went to see a man about a dog."

"Da, don't be funny. I feel awful inside 'bout Willie's da."

"You're not the only one that feels awful inside 'bout Willie's da. An' that's why I was out late. You know those two fellas I asked you about? It was some time ago. You remember the car that was stolen?"

"Aye, I do."

"Well, I asked you if you had seen a tall fella and a one not so tall, thick-set, fattylike. They had been in Kit's bar. And you said, you had. Would you know their mugs again if you saw 'em?"

"Aye, Da. An' I've seen them a number of times."

352

"You have! Then why in hell's blazes didn't you tell me?"

"I didn't know ya wanted them; the man got the car back, didn't he?"

"Where did you see them?"

"Oh, in the street, an' where they lived."

"Where they lived?" Davey was now on his haunches pulling his son round towards him. And the boy said, "Look out, Da, you've spilt me flakes."

"Never mind yer bloody flakes! You say you know where they live?"

"Well, I did, sometime back. It was behind Gallagher's yard."

"The scrap iron place?"

"Aye, Da."

"There's nothin' behind there, only broken-down sheds."

"There's Gallagher's Mill, the old stone house that's droppin' to bits. They took the machinery away years ago."

"Gallagher's Mill? How d'you know they're livin' in there?"

"Well, I found a bit o' scrap on the tip. It looked like lead, and I took it to Gallagher's yard and old Mr. Gallagher was in the office. But there was a man, clearin' up like, two of 'em, a tall 'un and a short 'un, and I thought they were the men who I'd seen afore. One of 'em took me scrap an' said it wasn't lead. He gave me fifty p. And when I was goin' away the other one laughed an' said, 'That's worth a quid or two,' so I knew it was lead. I went out the gate pretendin' I was goin', but I went along by the railin's and I saw them both come behind the office an' go into the mill. They had me bit of lead with 'em. Then I stayed put and I watched 'em. It was on a Saturday so I had plenty of time. An' when they came out they had different jackets on, so I guessed they were livin' there."

"How long ago was that?"

"Oh, a fortnight ago, Da, or three weeks. P'raps longer. But one thing, they didn't leave by the yard gate; they went out the back way an' cut across the fields and onto the road there."

Davey Love stood up and, looking down on his son, said, "It's God's judgment on me for not talkin' to you more. If I had, I'd likely have had those two bastards weeks ago."

"What have the bastards done, Da?"

"Now enough of that. I've told you ya keep a clean tongue in yer head else it won't be soap I'll wash yer mouth out with but a pan scrub."

"But ya said it, Da."

"Never mind what I said. Take no notice of what I say, just do what

353

I tell you. Goin' along to a fancy house like the Baileys an' pallin' up with a lad like that Willie, then comin' out with words like bastard."

Sammy looked up at this tall man. He was funny, not laughable funny, well just at times he was laughable funny, but at other times he was funny. He said he hadn't to swear and use bad language, especially four-letter words, yet his own mouth was drippin' them all the time. He was a funny man. "What're ya goin' to do, Da?" he said.

"What I'm goin' to do now, lad, is go to work. But what I'd like to do is go round there an' take those two fellas by the scruff of the neck an' bang their heads together till they were just about insensible. Then I'd half string 'em up until I put the fear of God in 'em with just their toes touchin' the ground. Then I'd punch 'em silly. After that, I'd call the police an' let 'em deal with what was left. That's what I'd do. But I've got to go to work. But you say nothin' 'bout those two blokes, mind, not a word to anybody. I'll deal with 'em after five o'clock the night. By God, I will. And may He an' His Holy Mother help me. . . . I went to church last night, you know."

"Did ya, Da?" Sammy's voice came out on a high squeak.

"Aye, I did. And I asked Him to help me find them fellas who had done whatever they had done to the boss. I made a deal with Him. Well, if He carries out His deal I'll carry out mine."

Sammy's face was one wide smile now and his father, getting into his coat, turned and looked at him, saying, "That pleased you, me goin' to church, did it?"

"Aye; yes, it did, Da. But Sister Monica told me ya would."

"Sister Monica told you that I would go to church?"

"Aye, she did an' all."

"How did that come about?"

"She asked if ya went to mass, an' when I said no, she said did ya go to confession and I said, no. Then she said, did ya go to yer Easter duties, and I said I didn't think so. Well, she said if I lit two candles every week and I said one Our Father and ten Hail Marys every night for a month, ya would go."

"She did? An did you?"

"Aye, I have. But the month isn't quite up yet."

"Well, I'll be buggered. Was that the one I was goin' to skelp if she hit you again across the ears just once more?"

"Oh no, that was sister Catherine. But as I said, Da, she doesn't hit me 'cross the ears anymore, she just shakes the bloody life outta me."

"Now, now, what did I tell you. Wash your mouth out. Ya want to go to church every night yerself and ask God to stop you swearin'."

"Aye, I could. And I could ask Him for both of us, Da, couldn't I?"

There was a grin on Davey's face as he lifted his hand, but it stayed in midair and he said, "Ya know yer gettin' too big for yer boots; they'll be givin ya corns, but that'll be nothin' to the corns that'll sprout on yer backside if I have any more of that lip of yers. Now I must be off. Do the usual, mind: wash up, make yer bed, and mine; rub the kitchen floor, then lock up. All right?"

"All right, Da. Be seein' ya."

"Be seein' you."

When the door had closed on his father and he heard him running down the iron stairs, Sammy sat where he was at the table, not eating now, but thinking. His da was a funny bloke. But he was all right. Oh aye, his da was all right. He was glad he had his da. And he didn't miss his ma now, not like he used to. He knew what he was going to do today, and if his da was to find out he'd skin him alive. Oh aye, he would, because he was one for him stayin' at school, but he was goin' to play the nick. After he'd had his school dinner he was goin' to slip out. There was something he had to do. His da had said he could go and see Willie the night. But he didn't only want to go and see Willie, he wanted to go and see Willie's mother; there was something about her that he liked. And he wanted to take her another present. He had the idea that that teapot could have been part of a set. His ma had a china one on the dresser, an' she'd gone mad when it got broke in a bloody row. People just didn't throw away a teapot like that. If they had a teapot, they wouldn't just have the teapot they would have the sugar basin and the milk jug, wouldn't they? He knew exactly where he had found the teapot, and so if they hadn't tipped any more stuff there and he did some rakin', he'd likely come across either the milk jug or the sugar basin. And then, of course, he'd have to clean them up, so he needed time. And he couldn't do all that if he stayed at school all afternoon and get to Willie's for teatime. So his day was planned.

He did his chores as he did every morning, locked the door, put the key in his pocket, and went to school.

But Sammy didn't manage to play the nick after school dinner. Sister Catherine, coming into the dining hall just as they were finishing, called out, "You, you, and you, come with me."

Sammy was one of the you's, and was about to protest, but he had recent memories of his head wagging at such a rate that he thought it would fly off his body. So he gulped the last of his pudding, joined the other boys who were all bigger than him, and followed Sister Catherine's modern skirt along the corridor. He had always thought

355

it unfair that nuns didn't look like nuns anymore, but like ordinary human beings, woman human beings.

This one, far from being a human being, now pointed to the three walls in the room, saying, "All these books have to be got down and packed before you leave tonight, before anybody leaves tonight."

When one of the bigger boys dared to ask, "Why, Sister? Aren't we goin' to have a library anymore?"

"Yes, we're going to have a library some more, Reilly, not that it would interest you as it's a surprise to me that you even know this is a library because you never use it, do you, except under force, brute force. The fact is, there's all kinds of rot here, wet rot, dry rot, and all the rest in the walls, and these shelves have to be cleared and the walls behind the racks inspected. Now are you satisfied?"

"Where have the books got to go to, Sister?"

"E block. Sister Monica is over there with her gang. But where they go from there and what's finally going to happen to them will be no concern of yours, Reilly. Now you see those cardboard boxes there?" The nun pointed to a large stack of flat cardboard in the corner of the room. "Now you, Baxter, open those boxes and set them round the shelves. And you, Reilly, get up that ladder and hand books down carefully to Watson, and dear little Sammy Love will take them from you, Watson, and pack them care . . . fully. And I'll see they're done carefully. I'll be back in a minute." And she stressed this to Sammy by pulling a face at him and with a nod of the head, and when the door closed on her he did her the courtesy to stick his tongue out as far as it would go. And when Reilly, from the top of the library steps, said, "I'd like to put a bomb up her bum," and Watson, who was standing on the bottom step, added, "Make it a rocket, Reilly, an' she'll fly straight into heaven," they all laughed until Reilly cried, "Stop it! You're rockin' the boat. I'll be landin' either on me face or me arse in a minute." Then looking down on Sammy, he said, "She's got it in for you, Love, hasn't she? Ever since your da threatened to knock her block off. When I told me ma about that and asked her would my da do the same, she said, no, because he was neither soft in the head nor a bloody fool, 'cos only a bloody fool would tackle a nun."

"Me da's no bloody fool, Reilly."

"All right, all right . . . *dear Love*. I was only kiddin'. Don't get your rag out unless you want to blow your nose."

Sammy glared up at Reilly. He'd often wanted to hit him, especially when he said 'dear Love' like that, because sometimes the others would take it up and sing songs about his name, like the one the chorus sang last year in the concert; "My Love Is Like a Red Red Rose."

Oh, but why worry about Reilly? He was stuck here for sure this afternoon, and he'd never find what he was lookin' for.

It was at this point that Watson brought up the subject that made it so necessary that he should find something to take to Willie's ma the night. He said to him, "You're thick with that Protestant, aren't you, who's da's been kidnapped?"

Sammy didn't answer, but glared at the boy who wasn't much bigger than himself and who, he promised himself, he would nobble if he didn't shut his mouth. Then Reilly put his oar in again, saying, "You know where you go to if you have any truck with Protestants, more than to be civil."

"Aw, that's all hogwash. Father Cotten said it was. He said that was all in the bad old days; we're all alike now and heading for the same roundup. That's what he said."

As though backing Sammy up, Watson, with a broad smile on his face, nodded at Sammy, saying, "Father Cotten's a caution. Me da laughed himself sick when he saw him on the telly standin' next to a Hallelujah. He said old Father Whitehead would be kicking the lid off his coffin to get out and at him."

"Me ma said he only went so he could be seen on the telly." This was from Reilly. "She says he's an abish ... abishionist, and God isn't goin' to do away with hell just because he's mixin' with the Protestants."

"If you ask me, I think your ma and da's up the pole."

"Watch it, Watson, watch it, 'cos I'll come down there an' stick that pole in one end of ya an' pull it out the other."

Watson, who wasn't much bigger than Sammy, merely shrugged his shoulders at this dire threat! Reilly, he knew, was all wind and water. As his ma said, the bigger they were the more empty space there was inside them, especially in the head. So he dared to grin up at Reilly, then turn his laughing face towards Sammy while shrugging his shoulders. And when Sammy returned his grin, Reilly purposely missed handing the books to Baxter and they landed almost between the heads of the two smaller boys.

They had been unaware that the door had opened, but when Sister Catherine's voice boomed over them, "You do that again, Reilly, and I'll whip the ears off you," Sammy thought, She's got a thing about ears, that 'un.

It had been a boring, tedious afternoon and when, all together in the main hall, they sang the last hymn to close the week's work, which was "Soul of My Saviour," Sammy, as usual, half spoke it, for he was no singer and very half-heartedly he said,

357

Soul of My Saviour,
Sanctify my breast;
Body of Christ, be
Thou my saving Guest;
Blood of my Saviour,
Bathe me in Thy tide,
Wash me in water
Gushing from His side.

He had never understood a word of that hymn except the bit about
the water gushing from His side. And then he always imagined a
spring like the one he saw up in the hills that Sunday his da took him
for a bus trip. It was shortly after his ma had left. He couldn't
remember which time it was, the first, or the second, or the third, but
he knew he had cried a lot. It was then that his da had stayed with
him all day on the Sunday and they'd gone for this ride in the bus,
and his da had gone into a weird little pub and he had sat outside and
had had ginger beer and a meat pudding. It had been a lovely day,
and they had walked and had seen this spring that was tumbling out
of a rock and rushing down the hillside to the river. He'd always
remember that day. . . .

He didn't go home and change his clothes; he hadn't time, he told
himself. Anyway, he'd just have to get into them again if he was
going along to Willie's house.

There was great activity on the top of the tip. There seemed to be
more lorries than ever the day, and the great big pusher was at it an'
all levelling the muck.

As he made his way around the side to where he could slip down
the bank and so reach the old part of the tip, he almost jumped in the
air when a voice yelled at him, "D'you want to land up in the muck?"
And there followed a string of words whose meaning he understood
but whose use was forbidden to him now. And the man, leaning out
of the cab, added to them, saying, "You should have a revolving light
on the top of your head; you could have been under the wheels, you
silly little bugger. And keep away from that side; we're emptying
slush."

He ran some way from the lorry before he turned and saw it really
was emptying slush, and he recalled hearing yesterday someone say
the park lake was being drained as it was gettin' silted up near where
the stream ran into it.

He ran on again, and didn't stop for breath until he reached the
bottom of the tip where it was now sprawling into what had been

358

pastureland. Now the quarry had been filled, they were goin' to fill this little valley up, so it was said. His da said it was a shame, 'cos this was where they used to do rabbit coarsin'.

Standing looking back along the sloping bank of the tip, it all looked the same, but he knew where he had found the teapot. And so he scrambled back among the debris until he came to the part, not realising he had rounded the curve and was almost in the same place where the lorry was tipping the slush.

He never brought a rake with him, there was always something at hand that he could rake with, and today he was more lucky than usual because he found a piece of iron with a bent end that must have been a proper rake anyway. And so with this he began to pull at the smelling rubbish.

When his rake hit something hard, he grabbed at it, but what he pulled out was just a brown stone jar that was used for pickles. Another time he would have considered it a find because there were no cracks or chips to be seen in it. It was half full of muck but that would have been easily tipped out, and after the jar had been given a good scrub, it would have been handy in the kitchen. But today he threw it aside; he was after bigger bait.

He had been raking for sometime when suddenly he cried, "Aw!" and put his hand into the muck and pulled out the remnants of what had been once a filigree butter dish holder. He didn't know this; he saw only something that was attractive but which seemed to be broken in so many places he could never get it put right to take to her in place of a milk jug or sugar basin; but he placed it to one side 'cos it might be silver and he'd get a copper for it at the scrap yard.

He had been raking for almost an hour, and he was tired and thirsty, and his clothes and hands and face were dirty, and he was feeling very sad inside when his head was brought up and back by a shout from high up on the bank. A man was standing up there near the back of a wagon. He was yelling something and waving his arms. He saw another wagon come farther along the bank and tip its load. It looked like thick treacle running down among all the rubbish. The man was still yelling at him to get out of the way.

He wasn't in anybody's way, he was at the bottom of the bank, but he thought he'd better go 'cos the man would likely scud him if he got hold of him. He had been working some way up the bank, but now he slithered down and as he did so he saw a nice boot, no it was a shoe, and although it looked mucky the sole was good. It was sticking out of something like a cardboard box. The top part of the box looked just the same as those that had been used for packing the books in this afternoon. He tried to pull the shoe from out of the box, but it wouldn't come. And so he stopped his slithering and put two hands on it to give it a tug, thinking that where there was one there might be the other, and they were men's shoes and might fit his da, at least for work. Then he let out a cry, but it was soundless because it was only in his head. Pulling at the shoe he had seen the trouser leg. And when, gingerly, he now moved the muck from the sides of the cardboard box he could see the other leg.

Quickly now he said a prayer;

> Hail Mary full of grace,
> The Lord is with thee;
> Blessed art thou among women. . . ."

But that was as far as he got because the man was shouting at him again. And now he stood and waved and shouted back. But the man simply flung up his arms and turned away. Cautiously now, he slithered farther, along what his mind wouldn't tell him was there, to more cardboard, here ridged like tent, but almost covered with all descriptions of muck. And when, with the rake, he gingerly pulled this away he exposed the knob of a bedstead.

His hand waved over the cardboard box before he could bring himself to pull it aside. And then he saw the face. It was filthy dirty and covered with dark streaks of blood, and instinctively he stood up and backed away, and in doing so he slid almost two yards of the bank to where the grass began. And with his instinctive reaction he had cried out, "Oh, Lord Jesus!" for that thing there, that man was Willie's da. He recognized the hair because he had often thought it was nearly like a punk's. Willie had said his da was always brushing it, it only stood up because he was always running his hands through it.

He now put his head back and yelled, "Mister! Mister!"

But there was no sign of the man at the top of the bank. The two lorries, however, were still there, one was empty and the other full. And then he let out an oath, one that he shouldn't have used, because the lorry was tipping up and the black slime was coming down the bank straight at him. It wouldn't hurt him because he could run, but it would likely cover the man.

He scrambled up the six feet of bank again; then he was tearing the muck and the cardboard away from the prone figure. And now he was yelling at the face, "Mr. Bailey! Mr. Bailey! It's me, Sammy. Come on! Come on! They're tippin' the slush." He looked up. It wasn't a broad stream to begin with, just as wide as the lorry, but now it was

360

spreading out. It didn't seem to be sinkin' into the debris but splashin' over it. His mind told him it wouldn't be very thick by the time it reached them, perhaps it would have disappeared, sunk into the muck by then, but he just couldn't be sure; those were big lorries, they held a lot. And it wasn't only slush that was comin', it seemed to be stones an' all, 'cos they were bouncing.

He screamed into the face now, "Mr. Bailey! Mr. Bailey! Wake up, man! Come on! Come on! God Almighty! Wake up! Wake up, man, else we'll be covered. It's slimy, all wet."

When the face made no response he caught at the arm and tugged it; then he let out a high scream for now he and the figure seemed to be embracing and were rolling down the bank. He knew he was screaming in his head as he pushed the body from him, and when he looked up there were two men again and one was shaking his fist at him and yelling, but he couldn't hear what they were saying.

What they were saying one to the other was, "That little bugger'll be done for one of these days. If I go down there I'll kick his arse for him."

"Hold your hand a minute," said the other one. "He's waving."

"Aye, he's waving. He's a cheeky little bugger if ever there was one. He's never off this tip. When he goes missin' they'll blame the likes of us for not chasin' him. There should be a watchman on here. I've said it afore. An' did you notice; it's not this side that needs the slush, it's yon side. That's burnin' underneath, hot as a volcano in parts.

"Look, man, the lad's waving us down."

"Well, he's not gettin' me down there. What does he think he's found? A gold mine?"

"He's found something. Look, he's waving and pointing. Aw, I'd better go."

"Please yourself. If you took any notice of these kids you'd be doin' overtime till midnight."

It appeared that the men weren't going to take any notice of him. So what must he do? What he did was to lift up Bill's head and pat his cheek, saying, "Aw, Mr. Bailey. Come on, man, come on." Then he asked himself how you know when people were dead. On the telly they lifted the hand and felt the wrist, the doctors did, or they opened the coat and put their head on the chest. Then they phoned for an ambulance. But he was at the bottom of the tip and everybody had gone. And oh, God! What was he going to do?

He raised his eyes upwards and said, "Please send help. God, please send help."

And God did send help. A man came round the foot of the tip and yelled at him, "Come on out of that, you young bugger, come on!"

"Mister! Come here a minute. There's a man here."

"God Almighty!"

The man was looking down onto the dirty blood-stained form, and then he muttered, "Aw, lad. You've found him."

"Aye, I did. And I know who it is. It's Willie's da, an' Willie's me pal. He was kidnapped last night. It said on the radio."

The man now knelt down like they did on the pictures and took hold of Bill's wrist. And he had no need to open his coat because it was open, as was his waistcoat.

He put his ear down to the dirty shirt; then, turning to Sammy, he said, "I'm not good at this. I can't tell if he's here or not. Look, laddie, just stay with him. I'll be back in a jiffy."

The jiffy took five minutes but it seemed like five hours to Sammy. All the time he had sat with his legs outstretched, the head on his small lap. Once he thought that the body moved and it made him shout down at the face: "It's me, Mr. Bailey. Wake up! Wake up, man! They've gone for help." But then they were still on the slope, and he might have slipped slightly.

When the man returned he said, "They're bringing the ambulance. And I phoned the police an' all. My God, lad, you've done a good rakin' the night. The 'morrow would have been too late, 'cos we've had orders to fill this part in right down to the field. Whether you've saved his life or not, I don't know, 'cos he looks a gonner to me; but, in any case, you've found him. Better for his wife to know what's happened to him one way or t'other than to go on in the dark."

A half hour ago he had been the only one on this side of the tip. He had previously reasoned this out: very few people were on the tip on a Friday, 'cos they seemed to have money then. But now the tip seemed to be swarming.

When the man said, "I'll have to go and guide them down," he was once again left with the inert body. And he talked to it, saying, "When I go to see Willie, I won't have anythin' to take. But me da says you don't have to take presents every day to friends. But still though, I wanted somethin' to take to her, your missis, 'cos she's not for me like you are, not really, and I want her to be. 'Cos as me granny says, men might wear the trousers but women wear the pants and, in most cases, what they say goes. So I want to get on the right side of her, like."

It seemed he had talked himself out. They were a long time in comin'. He thought that if he was good he should be prayin'. But, like his da, he knew he was what they called a wooden Catholic: he went

362

to mass and confession and communion 'cos he had to. He wished he was a Methodist, 'cos Methodists always seemed to have money. His da said you never found a Methodist that had to scrape the butter off the bread after he had put it on. He once said that Christ had died to put the Catholics into business and they were still at it an' doing fine. Oh aye, he had said, 'cos they didn't ask you to put a penny on the plate anymore but gave you a packet to hold a slab of your wages. His da came out with funny things. He couldn't understand him half the time except when he swore. His voice was different then: you could tell then if he was mad or just bein' funny.

It seemed that suddenly there was a crowd of people round him. He felt he had been dozin' and had just woken up. His legs were cramped. The policeman lifted Sammy up in his arms and took him down to the grass, all the time smiling at him and saying, "Stout fella. Stout fella." And after a while, as if he couldn't scramble up the bank himself, the policeman again lifted him in his arms and carried him.

In the police car one of the policemen asked, "Where d'you live, laddie?" And then his mind began to work; it was really as if he had come out of a dream. If he went home his da would likely knock blazes out of him for messin' up his good school clothes even if he had found Mr. Bailey. So he told them where he lived but he said, "I don't want to go back there, I want to go to Willie's house, I mean Mr. Bailey's. I want to tell her, Mrs. Bailey."

The policemen looked at each other; then one of them said, "It's only your due, lad, it's only your due. You want to go to Mr. Bailey's house, then go there you shall."

When the policeman actually lifted him out of the car he endeavoured to shrug him off, saying, "I can get out meself; I've often been in a car afore"; then again the policeman had to stay him with a hand on his shoulder while talking to the one guarding the gate; and when this policeman said, "I've had word through from the office. They say, let him go in and break the news," the other opened the gate, saying, "Well, it's all yours, big boy."

He knew they were being funny, so he didn't come out with anything. He walked up the path and knocked on the door; and it was the woman Nell who opened it. She looked at him, from head to foot, then exclaimed, "My! My goodness! Where've you been? What ... what d'you want?"

"I want to see Mrs. ...."

"Oh, Sammy, it's the wrong time; it's ..."

"Tisn't. I've got something to tell her."

Nell lifted her eyes from the boy to the two policemen who had stopped a little way beyond him. They nodded at her; and although their nodding didn't give her any explanation, she let them all into the house. And when Sammy said, "Where is she?" Nell, with a slight shake of her head, said, "She's in the sitting room."

She went to stop him, but the policeman's hand stayed her; and by himself, and quietly now, Sammy went to the door.

Fiona was sitting in front of the fire. Katie was on one side of her, Mamie the other; Mark was in a chair, and Willie was sitting on the mat, his head resting on the edge of the sofa. But they all turned round simultaneously and looked at the dirty apparition standing in the doorway.

The sight of him brought Fiona to her feet. She opened her mouth to speak but closed it as he came towards her. And, his face bright, he looked up at her and said, "I've found him, your man. He was buried in the tip. I've found him. I was lookin' for a sugar basin or milk jug to go with your teapot, an' I found him."

"Wh . . . what!" Her lips were trembling so much she stuttered the word out. The children were gathered round her, and Mark stuttered as he said, "Y . . . y . . . you mean that, Sammy?"

"Aye, Aye. He's been taken by the ambulance to hospital. But it was me what found him. They were emptyin' the slush down; an' they said the morrow would've been too late, 'cos they're clearin' the lake and it's muck an' slush an' he would really've been buried. He was buried enough; I only found his boot at first."

"*Oh, dear God!*" The smell of him was affecting her nostrils. But what she did was to suddenly thrust her arms out and pull him into her embrace; and his head pressed tight against her neck, she said over and over again, "*Oh Sammy. Sammy. Sammy. Sammy. Thank you.* I must go. I must go to him."

Katie was crying, Mamie was crying. Mark's face was wet. But Willie stood apart, and he alone seemed to show no emotion.

Fiona now pressed Sammy from her and, looking into his dirty twitching face, she said, "Sammy, I will love you all my life. But tell me, is . . . is he all right? I must go to hospital, but is he all right?"

Sammy looked towards Mark and hesitantly said, "I don't know. I couldn't get him to answer. I kept talkin' to him when I was waitin'. They were a long time comin', I mean with the ambulance an' that. But the police might know." He thumbed towards the door.

Fiona hurried towards it, and to the two policemen standing in the hall she cried, "Is . . . is he all right?"

"He's alive, ma'am. But as far as we can gather, he's in . . . well, in

364

a pretty bad mess. He's been badly knocked about, but he's alive."

Fiona now turned to Nell, saying, "Oh, Nell, Nell. Can you believe it?"

"Yes. Yes, I can Fiona. Where Bill is concerned I can believe it. I told you . . ." But what she was about to say was checked by a high cry, almost a scream from the sitting room, and when Fiona turned and rushed back into the room, followed by Nell and the policeman, it was to see Willie beating Mark with his fists, the while crying at him, "I told you! I told you Sammy was all right. He's my friend. I want him as a friend. He's better than your Roland. I want . . ."

Fiona picked up her son in an effort to placate him, but, his face awash with tears, he now fought her, too, as he screamed, "You didn't like him! You didn't! You didn't, Mam. You didn't want him to come to tea. Only Dad, only Dad wanted him. And he saved Dad. And I'm going to be his friend. . . . I am! I am!"

"Yes, of course you are, dear. You were right all the time. You were the only one that was right. Yes, you are. Yes, you are. No more now. No more. Stop crying. And look, I'll tell you what. Take Sammy upstairs and let him have a bath and give him some of your clothes to get into until his own are clean again." She turned now. "Would you like that, Sammy? Would you like that?"

"I have a bath on a Friday night, the night, later on. I do it meself. I fill the bowl from the . . ."

"It would please me, Sammy, if you would use our bath tonight and stay with us until your father comes."

"Huh!" He jerked his head. "He'll likely wallop me. He'll be lookin' for me now an' he won't know where I am."

She turned to the police, saying, "You'll find Mr. Love, won't you, and tell him where Sammy is and tell him to call for him?"

"We'll do that, ma'am, don't worry. And—" he now patted Sammy's dirty hair, saying, "he won't recognise you when you're cleaned up and got rid of your smell. But he'll be proud of you, I can tell you that. We're all proud of you. Aren't we constable?" He turned to his companion who said, "By, yes. You'll be in the papers tomorrow and likely on the telly."

"Nell, take Willie upstairs." She went to hand her son over to Nell, but Willie, wriggling in her arms, said, "I can walk." And when he was on the floor Sammy looked at him and grinned and said, "That's what I said to the police earlier on when he carried me up the tip. And I said I was more used to the tip than he was. He got all mucked up with slush, didn't he?" He turned to one of the policemen, and he,

365

grinning, said, "He did an' all, and he didn't like it. He's gone home an' all to change."

Turning to Mark now, Fiona said, "See to them, will you?" But before Mark could reply her second son almost barked, "We can see to ourselves!" and a relieved Nell, smiling broadly, said, "Back to normal. Oh, back to normal. And thank God. Now get yourself ready and get off," and saying this, she pushed Fiona towards the hall.

A few minutes later, when she was ready for the road, she turned to Nell and said, "I meant what I said, Nell. I'll love that boy until the day I die. And I mean to do something for him. Oh yes, yes. No matter what happens. Yes, Nell, no matter what happens. And to think I couldn't stand the sight of him."

Nell again pushed her, saying, "Love at first sight very rarely lasts. Go on now. And if he's conscious at all give him my love, too."

The relief and even the vestige of gaiety that had come back to her being when she knew he had been found slipped away, in fact was shocked away, at her first sight of him.

He was already in the theatre when she had reached hospital. "They have just taken him down," the nurse had said. "He needed some cleaning up." Then she had added, "Come and sit in the side ward; there's two newspaper hounds already in the waiting room and you'll have enough of them before you're finished."

"How . . . how long do you think he'll be?" Even as she had asked it she knew it to be a stupid question, which the nurse had answered seriously, but just as she should have expected, "Well, it all depends on the extent of his injuries."

Twice they had brought her tea and biscuits. She had drunk the tea but left the biscuits. And she had made an effort to smile at the nurse who had come to take the tray away when she said to her, "If any of my children had been here that would have been an empty plate."

"Oh, sure," the nurse had said; "I have three young brothers so I know."

It was almost two hours later when there was a commotion outside the ward door and the trolley was brought in; and on it she saw Bill. When she had last looked on him he had been a spruce, good-looking, middle-aged man, who, because of his energy, could have lied within ten years about his age. But here they were easing into bed a figure that seemed bandaged from head to foot. His head was bandaged and all down one side of his face. Both arms were bandaged from the wrist to the shoulder. He was dressed in a sort of sleeveless nightshirt. When it fell open as they put him on the bed she saw that his stomach, too, was bandaged, and one leg was in a sort of splint.

The sister did not ask her to leave the room; she and her nurse and two male nurses were obviously too preoccupied with their patient; so much so that she was thrust back against the wall, and there she stood with one hand pressed tight against her cheek. When the three nurses left the room the sister drew up a chair to the side of the bed and beckoned her forward. And quietly she said, "You may sit with him for a time; but mind, he won't wake for some hours, so if you'd like to rest there is a visitor's room with a bed in it just along the corridor. You might be able to sleep for a while."

"How . . . how bad is he?"

"I think the doctor will be able to answer that better than I could. He'll be along in a moment or so. Have you had a cup of tea?"

"Yes; yes, thank you."

The sister now put her hand on Fiona's shoulder, and what she said was, "He's alive," but her tone could have indicated, just.

She was alone with him now and, bending towards him, she muttered, "Oh, Bill; Bill, my love." Then she gently touched the fingers of one hand that was sticking out from the bandages; and the tears running down her face, she cried brokenly, "How could they do this to you? Whoever it was I hope I never have to come face-to-face with them."

She did not hear the doctor enter the room and so she started when he spoke her name. Hastily, she got to her feet and dried her face, and he, pointing to the chair, said, "Sit down. Sit down."

"Tell me"—she paused and gulped—"how . . . how bad is he? He looks"—she spread her hand wide towards him—"dreadful."

"Well, first of all I will say to you that he is a very lucky man. I understand a little boy found him on a tip. Another night, in fact a few more hours, and there would have been no hope whatever. How long he's lain smothered in that muck in his condition I don't know. But you've got one thing to be thankful for, he's got a very strong constitution. If he hadn't, well, I'm afraid all this"—he moved his hand from the top to the bottom of the bed—"would have been in vain."

"Is . . . are his injuries serious?"

"Well, yes, I can say some of them are. He's had fifteen stitches in the back of his head. There was a big gash there, but fortunately it didn't go deep, nor did the knife that went into his stomach."

She put her hand tight over her gaping mouth and repeated, "A knife?"

"Yes; they were out to do a thorough job on him, whoever they were. And I think it must have been more than one because a man of

367

his build would have been able to fight off one. I think it's what they call a gang job, because his arms and legs are lacerated."

"What damage did the knife do?"

"Oh, it penetrated the gut but fortunately it missed his kidneys and the bladder. But I would say he's gone through enough to kill ordinary men. And I think you owe a lot to that little boy. I understand he's only a nipper about eight or so?"

"Yes; yes, I know. He . . . he came to the house to tell me."

"He did?"

"Yes, yes. I didn't know what state my husband was in but the child was filthy and . . . well, it was as if he, too, had been buried among the refuse."

"He deserves a medal whoever he is. They say he's from Bog's End. They don't come tougher than they do from that quarter, children upwards. But there are good and bad as in all classes. I would say, though, there's a few more bad ones down there than good."

He smiled at her. She didn't smile back but she said, "Thank you. Thank you very much, doctor. You've . . . you've likely saved his life."

"No, Mrs. Bailey, I haven't saved his life, nor Dr. Pinkerton, who helped to sew him up; as I said, all your thanks should be to that little nipper. You don't often hear the police speaking highly of anyone from that quarter. I also understand one of the lorry drivers did his bit, too. Slush from the lake, they said they were pouring down on them." Shaking his head, he turned towards the door as he said, "The days of miracles are not yet past. I'll be seeing you again shortly, Mrs. Bailey."

She inclined her head towards him, but found it impossible to say anything; he seemed to have said it all: "The days of miracles are not yet past."

She resumed her seat by the bedside. She was feeling odd, not faint but just odd, sort of tired. She hadn't taken a sleeping pill last night but had sat on the sitting room couch and dozed while waiting for the phone to ring. And then today had been the longest day in her life, and the loneliest day in her life, and yet the most surprising, when she came to think of it: her mother had been round twice, and she'd put her arms around her and she'd cried and she'd even said she was sorry about the things she had said about Bill. But, of course, she had thought he was dead. What would she say when she knew he was alive and that he wasn't going to die? *No, no! He wasn't going to die. He wasn't. He wasn't. . . .*

She must stop her mind from galloping on like this. That's what it

368

was doing all last night and all today. She was talking to people, answering people, yet her mind was away by itself, galloping, galloping.

A nurse came and gently squeezed the bag of blood that was hanging from a hook above the bedhead; then, after she had felt Bill's wrist, she smiled before going out. And Fiona sat on, telling herself she should phone home and tell Nell to tell the children. But she was tired and she didn't want to move. She didn't want to leave him. She never wanted to leave him.

Another nurse came in and, bending over, she said quietly, "There is a Sir Charles Kingdom and another gentleman. Sister has put them in the visitors' rest room. Do you think you could go and speak to them? The old gentleman seems very anxious."

"Oh yes, yes." She rose from the chair, looked down on Bill, then went out.

On her entry, Sir Charles and his secretary rose quickly, and the old man approached her with hands outstretched, saying, "I've never been so relieved in all my life. How is he?"

"They think he'll survive."

"They think?" Sir Charles glanced up at his secretary; then, looking at Fiona again, he said, "As bad as that?"

"Oh yes, yes." Then briefly she gave them a description of what the doctor had told her. And when she finished the old man groped at the chair and sat down again, muttering to himself, "She wouldn't have meant that. She wouldn't have meant them to go as far as that. Never! Never! I can't believe there's that in her. No. No."

"Sir." Rupert bent down towards his employer, saying quietly, "I think you must face up to the fact that Mrs. Brown probably did organise this whole business. She herself mightn't have meant to go as far as murder, but she was out to destroy someone. It's right what Lady Kingdom said before we left: you have always seen her through rose-tinted spectacles."

"Don't you chastise me, too, Rupert. I've had enough of it, and in condemnation from myself, too, which is something more bitter and harder than either you or my wife can dole out to me. And I'll show you both that I mean business because I'll bring her to justice over this. Oh yes, I will."

"She's left the country, sir, and you have no idea where she is. No one seems to have. We've been into all this, sir."

"If you weren't a decent relative, Rupert, playing at secretary, I would sack you this moment, I would that."

"It wouldn't be the first time in the last ten years, would it?"

369

The man now smiled gently at Fiona and he said, "The last thing you want to witness, Mrs. Bailey, is a family quarrel."

"Oh, I don't mind." There was even a small smile on her lips as she replied, "It takes my mind off things. But, I will say this, if Mrs. Brown is behind attempted murder, and that's what it is, then she must be brought to justice."

"And she shall be. She shall be." The old man was nodding his head. "Once she can be located I will set to work, I promise you. Yes, I do, I promise you."

She put out her hand now and touched the shaking shoulder, saying "Please don't distress yourself any further, Sir Charles. You were very fond of this woman, you trusted her. We're often led away by our feelings." Her mind lifted her back for a moment to her first marriage and how, within a short time, she knew she had made a mistake. Yet it had given her three beautiful children and so she should be thankful to the man who inveigled her into marriage with soft words, only to tell her within a year that his work would always come first and that one day he would be a famous writer. He never became a famous writer. He never wrote anything good enough to really keep the wolf from the door. But why was she thinking like this? Sir Charles was now standing up and shaking her hand. "I'll be in tomorrow again. You look very tired, my dear, and that is natural. Can we run you home?"

"No, sir, thank you very much; I'm staying the night."

"Yes, well, that's what I would expect. Can I do anything for you? Anything at all?

"You could call at my house, if you wouldn't mind, and explain that my husband is as well as can"—she shook her head—"I think the term is, as well as can be expected. You can say that to my friend, Mrs. Ormesby; but tell her to tell the children that he is all right and ... and will soon be home, and that I, too, will be home tomorrow sometime."

"We'll do that. We'll do that." He was nodding at Rupert now. "Good-bye then, my dear. Good-bye. I'm a very sad man, yet at the same time a relieved one. You understand?"

Yes, she understood.

It was half past nine and her head was drooping with sleep when the night sister said, "I would go and lie down an hour or so, dear. If there's any change at all, believe me, I'll call you. But I can assure you he won't be conscious for some hours yet."

But she hadn't the opportunity of going to bed straightaway, for a policeman who was apparently on duty stopped them outside the ward door and said to her, "There's a man here. He insists on seeing you. He's the father of the boy who found your husband."

"Oh yes, yes. Oh yes, I'll see him, certainly."

"Well, if you'll go to the visitors' room, Mrs. Bailey, I'll tell him."

When Davey Love entered the room and stood before her neither of them spoke for a moment. And then he said, "How is he, ma'am?"

How is he? Could she say all right? She said, "He's alive."

"Aye. Tis happy I am to hear that. Happy indeed."

Although there was no smile on Davey's face, in fact, now that she looked more closely at him, there was a cut across the bottom right-hand side of his chin, and one eye, although not black, was dark and puffed. And when he said, "An' my lad saved him. What d'you think of that, eh? Twas my own boy that saved him."

"I think it's wonderful, Mr. Love," she said, "and I'll never forget him as long as I live."

"I'm glad to hear yerself say that, ma'am, I am. I am. An' you know, I've thought all this out, ma'am, and I've thought how strange it is." He did not go on to say what was strange, but seated himself on the edge of the bed and said, "If it's all the same to you, ma'am, I'll take the weight off me legs, 'cos to tell you the truth you could knock me down with a flannel hammer this minute. And how that's come about I'll tell you shortly. But as I said, there was I thinkin' how strange life is. I haven't got a dirty mouth meself. I swear, oh aye, I know every one in the book an' more; but I'm not gone on the four-letter ones, never have been, see no sense in 'em. Yet there was me youngster comin' out with 'em an' levellin' 'em at yer son. Now that was the beginnin' wasn't it? Then yer good man hauls him into the house. An' you don't like that a bit, do you? Now, now, now, it's all right; you needn't bow yer head. In yer place I would 'ave kicked his ar ... backside out of the door meself. But strangely he takes a shine to you. Oh aye, he does; he takes a shine to you. An' I'll say this for him, if there was nothin' else about him he would be persistent. Oh aye, like me old father, he would be persistent, 'cos himself spent four years in an Irish prison through bein' persistent. Well, now, ma'am, what's happened to yer man would have happened in any case, seems to me, 'cos it was a different thing altogether, long different lines, seemingly not connected with me lad or me. Yet if he hadn't used that language an' he hadn't been allowed to enter your house an' wanted to give you a present, he would never have gone to the tip now, would he? Well, on the other hand, he would, 'cos he was used to goin' to the tip. But what I mean to say is, after findin' the teapot he would never have gone back there lookin' for the milk jug an' sugar basin or what have you that goes to a set of such. So, as I said to the chief constable himself not an hour or so ago, God works in a strange way to clear things up. But mind you, ma'am, I didn't think I'd end up in the clink again just 'cos I went out of me way to help clear this business up."

"What do you mean, Mr. Love? You've been taken to"—she couldn't say clink so she said, "you've been to jail, I mean put in jail, tonight?"

"Yes, this very night, ma'am. But I didn't go there alone, I can tell you. And it's a good job those bobbies came in time, 'cos I lost me head an' there wouldn't have been much left of that fat swine by the time I'd finished with him. But there we were, both in the clink. And it took me some time to convince the police that this was one of the two that tried to do your man in."

"You've found the man . . . the man who was . . . behind all this?"

"The very one, ma'am. It's a good job there weren't the two together else I doubt if I would have managed 'em. As far as I can gather from what I got out of that bloke an' then the police after, it was his mate, the big 'un who liked to use the knife and lead piping. You see, it was like this, and I could kick myself black an' blue when I think those two could've been picked up ages gone if I'd listened to the young 'un. But no, I was away washin' the glasses for Kit. That's the barman in the Duck and Drake. I feed him an' clothe him, threaten him about school, swear at him about cussin', and all told consider I've done me duty. That's how I've felt, but now I could kick myself, for just this very mornin' he told me where he had seen these two fellas. 'Cos I always said these were the ones that took one of the lad's cars. You remember? I'd seen 'em in the pub that night. They weren't the usual customers an' they looked odd bods, one big an' one small but both hefty. Well, the young 'un had seen 'em at the taggerine yard when he had taken some bit he'd got from the tip. He said they were livin' in the old mill behind the sheds that Gallagher uses for an office an' where he keeps his prize pickin's for the huckster shop dealers or the market stall wallahs to look over. Anyway, there's a field and some scrub behind the old mill an' the ditch that used to carry water long ago. An' so I got in this scrub an' I waited. Then across the field came the smaller one. The lad said they went out the back way, so I thought that's the way they'd come in. The plan in me mind was to see them both in there, then scarper an' ring the police; it wasn't me intention to tackle 'em together. But when I saw there was just the one, and I made sure there was just one an' nobody else inside before I let go. I can tell you this, ma'am, I didn't come off scot free. He could use his feet that 'un, as he admitted later to the police. It wasn't him that stuck the knife in or battered the boss's head. He said he used his feet an' that was all. But when he used 'em on me he did something to me, ma'am. I almost battered his brains out. It was Gallagher, hearin' the ructions, who rang the police. An' that's how we were both hauled in. They wouldn't believe a word I was sayin' until I demanded ... aye, I did; I threatened the sergeant what would happen to him when the truth came out and to get the chief constable down there 'cos there was another murderer at large and he'd be goin' back to that hideout, and that if Gallagher told him what had happened to his mate the fella would scarper. Well, missis, you never did see such a cafuffle when they finally believed me. There was a young reporter hangin' about as usual, an' the chief constable warned him to keep his mouth shut till they got the other one."

For the moment Fiona felt herself wide awake, and she asked, "Did the man say who had engaged them to do this ... I mean, who was paying them?"

"Oh, he started to gabble, ma'am, but it was all double Dutch, too airy-fairy, I think. It seems it was the other one that did the business. He went up to London every now an' again an' picked up money from a post office in a letter like with a note tellin' 'em to continue, but it was never signed. He said it was all a funny business."

"And he didn't know who it was?"

"Well, if he did he wasn't sayin', ma'am. But whoever it was they had their knife in for the boss. By God, they had. And at first they got at him through the lads, the firm like. But him bringin' off that big deal must have been too much for whoever the swine is. I'd like to bet the son of a bitch was one of those big boys that was also after the contract, 'cos who else would be up in London, have their headquarters there like? I've worked it all out in me head, ma'am. It must have been a big boy. Oh aye. An' they've paid those two to try everythin' in the book, from simple car pinchin' to near murder. If there'd been a woman involved they'd have tried rape."

Davey Love now chastised himself: that was a damn silly thing to say because she was involved. It could have been her next, or before. Oh aye. It's a wonder they didn't think that one up. But the spite seemed all levelled at the boss. He paused now, then said, "You look very tired, ma'am. And you know, as me mother used to say, she took me to be inoculated against whooping cough but they made a mistake and used a gramophone needle on me. But don't you worry, ma'am, I'll leave you now and you can get some kip ... sleep. I'll be round first thing in the mornin'. And you know where my lad is the night?"

373

Fiona didn't answer. She was so tired, so very tired. His voice had almost lulled her to sleep. Yes she just wanted to kip. Yes, she just wanted to kip.

"He's round at yer place. Aye, he is, stayin' the night. Bert's wife fixed him up. Eeh! You know, when I got in from work an' couldn't find him an' there wasn't a sight nor hint nor hair of him, I threatened to murder him, I did honest to God, 'cos he always has the kettle on an' the fryin' pan on the stove an' the table set. An' there it was, the place, as cold as charity. Aw, ma'am, there I go again. Look, I . . . I must be off." He bent towards her and patted her hand. "It's 'cos I'm excited inside. I'm so relieved. You know, I made a bargain with the Almighty"—he pointed his finger to the ceiling—"an' now I've got to keep it. Aye, I did, I made a bargain with Him. Let's find the boss alive, I said, and I'll go to mass every Sunday for a year. I didn't promise longer 'cos I didn't know whether I would last further than that."

"Oh, Mr. Love, Mr. Love." There was something rising in her, a great burst of laughter. "Go on," she said. "Go on. I don't want to laugh. Go on."

"Aye, I will, ma'am. Aye, I will. You can laugh the morrow when he comes round. Goodnight to you. Goodnight." He backed away from her and didn't turn until he reached the door. Then, about to say something more, he gave his mouth a whacking clap and went out.

And Fiona, like a mother who had just seen her amusing child leave the room, began to rock herself. The gurgle was mounting, but when it reached her throat it stuck there. And when her mouth opened wide she gasped for air. A current of water seemed to spray from her eyes, nose, throat, and she threw herself on the bed and buried her face in the pillow.

374

34

FIONA OPENED HER EYES BUT CLOSED THEM AGAIN QUICKLY AGAINST THE glare of the sunshine. She was dimly aware of a face hanging over her and a strange voice saying, "I've brought you a cup of tea, Mrs. Bailey."

She had been dreaming she was at home. She muttered, "What . . . what time is it?"

"Just on eight."

"What!" She pulled herself up sharply in the bed. "On eight! I . . . I haven't slept all night?"

"Yes, you have; and you needed it. You'll feel better for it."

"How . . . how is he? Is he round?"

"Yes; yes, he's round to some extent, and he's all right. Don't scold yourself; there's plenty of time. Have a wash and make yourself pretty"—she smiled—"because at the moment you look all eyes and teeth."

Fiona smiled in return; then, pushing the white quilt from her, she said, "I've been sleeping in my clothes, I must look a sight."

"I don't suppose he'll really notice, just your face."

Just five minutes later she entered the side ward. He was lying in the same position, and looked exactly the same as he had done last night. She stood by the side of the bed and said softly, "Bill." And

375

when he slowly lifted his lids and she saw the deep blue of his eyes seeming to sparkle for a moment, she said again, "Bill. Oh, Bill."

"Hello . . . love."

"How . . . how are you feeling? Oh, that's a silly question."

"Fiona." He made as if to move his hand towards her, then grimaced, his eyes shut tight and his lips squared from his teeth.

"Oh, my love, don't. Don't. Lie quiet, please."

A nurse came in and took his temperature and his blood pressure, wrote on a sheet, then went out again.

Another nurse came in and replaced the almost empty blood bag. The surgeon came in accompanied by two young doctors, the sister, and a nurse. After he had indicated she remained seated, he stood looking down on Bill. Then he said, "There's a lucky man if ever there was one." And turning to the sister now, he asked, "What has he had already?" And when she told him, he said, "Oh, well, he should go off again presently." Then looking across the bed at Fiona, he said, "You could go home, Mrs. Bailey, and give your family the news, because it will be better for him to sleep. Come back this afternoon. And he's likely to be in a similar condition for a few days, you know."

She rose from the chair now, saying, "He'll be all right though?"

He raised his eyebrows, pursed his lips, and said, "Unless there are complications he should do well, but it's going to take time. As I said, he's a very lucky man. . . . Now will you follow my advice and take a short time off, eh?"

"Yes, doctor, if you think he won't be round."

"I can assure you he won't. And that is the best thing for him you know, sleep. It's the cure now, sleep; all we have to do is just stand by and watch."

All those present in the room stood aside to let the great man pass. And they did treat him as if he were a great man. She had noticed this before when she was in hospital: surgeons were as gods. Nevertheless, she thanked the God she had been praying to for days that there were such men.

She bent over Bill now and gently laid her lips against his blue ones, and she felt sure they moved; but perhaps it was just her imagination. She lingered a moment longer before leaving the ward. Then she picked up her coat from the visitors' room, spoke her thanks to the sister and the nurses, and said she would be back later, then made her way out and into the bright sunshine. She threaded her way through ambulances and milling cars and she was about to walk out of the hospital gates to try to locate a taxi when a voice hailed her from a passing car. And she turned to see Rupert waving to her and Sir Charles's head poking out of the rear window.

Making her way towards them, Sir Charles immediately said, "How is he?"

"I've left him sleeping peacefully, Sir Charles. The surgeon said . . . he'll be all right, but it'll take time."

"Where are you going?" Rupert said.

"I was going to find a taxi."

At this he seemed to jump from his seat, then hurriedly go to the far rear door, which he opened, saying, "Get in." And she got in and sat beside the old man who said, "You want to go home?"

"If you please, Sir Charles."

"How bad is he really?"

"Well, very bad I should imagine. Apparently he's had a knife into his stomach and a blow to his head, it's split open at the back. Do you know they have caught one of the men?"

She watched his blue-veined hand go to his mouth, and it was some minutes before he spoke, when he did he said, "They'll know then about . . . about Eva?"

"No."

"They haven't spilt . . . told?"

"I don't know. I don't think so. Mr. Love came to see me last night." And she told them the gist of what Davey had related to her. And when she finished the old man lay back against the upholstery of the Rolls. But that was only for a moment, for now, sitting upright again, he turned to her and said, "But Bailey won't let this pass. He can't, can he? Nor you. Because it's been a near thing, it's touched on murder. And . . . and I'll understand, because in Bailey's place I would feel the same."

Her voice quiet, she now said, "It will be up to Bill, Sir Charles."

"Yes; yes, I understand, my dear." His voice had been quiet, but now he was leaning forward thumping Rupert on the back as he said, "And don't say I will try to talk anybody round, because in this case I won't, I'll let justice take its course. I've told you, I'm finished with her."

"I've never said a word."

"No, but you've been thinking plenty. I can read you like an open book."

"Clever . . . fellow."

"Now watch your tongue."

"I'm watching the road, Sir Charles, and if you don't stop thumping me in the back there could be an accident at any minute."

377

When the old man sat back he turned and nodded to Fiona, saying, "Some people get too big for their boots."

And then the voice of the driver said, "You must finish it, sir: when their toes pinch they find they are walking in their bare feet."

Fiona wanted to laugh, as she had wanted to laugh last night at Mr. Love. But her laughter was still too near to tears to be given a free rein.

"Would you like to come in for a moment?"

"What about it, Rupert, have we time?" The question was quiet and polite.

"Yes, Sir Charles. You've got a good half hour to spare before you meet her ladyship in Newcastle."

"Then we'll come in."

A large car was parked immediately outside the house, and three men were talking to the policeman at the gate. And so Rupert stopped beyond. The men turned to look enquiringly, and when Fiona emerged on the pavement side, one of them moved forward, saying, "Good morning, Mrs. Bailey. May I have a word with you?"

"No, you can't! And get yourself to the devil out of it." And Sir Charles guided Fiona through the gate, still muttering, "I know this lot, television snoops. And I know him"—pointing back to the man who had spoken to Fiona—"that's the one with the funny name, one of that Mike Neville crowd."

Rupert and Fiona exchanged glances and smiled. And when Rupert said, "That one with the funny name did a nice piece on you last year, sir. And, if I recall, you pressed drinks on him and practically carried him out of the house."

"You're asking for trouble, Rupert, aren't you? It's one of those mornings."

"Most mornings are the same, sir. And look, the time's going on. You have now only twenty-five minutes to spare before you meet her ladyship."

The old man, walking now towards the door with Fiona, nodded at her as he muttered, "I'll get rid of him. Yes, I will." But there was a twinkle in his eyes as he said it. And Fiona knew that both of these men, the old man and the young one, enjoyed this daily exchange. There was a similarity between the two of them and Bill and one of his men. The only difference was in the tone of voice.

"Mam! Mam! We gonna be on television."

"I sat in the front." Mamie was jumping up and down now.

"And I stood at the back," Mark mimicked her, as he pretended to bounce. "And dear Katie there"—Mark now pointed—"mightn't be

378

on at all. She wasn't on the first lot because she would go upstairs and change her dress. She must look pretty, pretty, pretty."

"I'll throw something at you, our Mark. Yes, I will."

Only Willie said, "How did you find Dad, Mam?" And this quiet question brought them all round her, saying, "Yes, yes, Mam. How is he? How is he?"

She looked over their heads at Nell; then before answering she said, "Don't you see we've got visitors."

"Morning, sir. Morning, sir."

"Hello." This from Mamie.

"Morning, Sir Charles," from Mark.

The only one who hadn't spoken was Sammy. He was standing among them yet apart. And he looked at her and she looked at him. And as she addressed her family she continued to look at him as she said, "You wanted to know how your father is. Well, he's alive, but it's only thanks to Sammy here."

"You're a brave fellow." Sir Charles was now patting Sammy's head. "And I'd like to shake you by the hand."

It was noticed that Sammy had to push the sleeve of Willie's coat back before he could take the proferred hand. And when it was grasped by Sir Charles's long thin fingers, Sammy said, "The sleeves are too long, it's Willie's. Me clothes were all mucky last night."

"Yes, of course, they would be. That's a very large and dirty refuse heap. Do you often go there?"

"Aye. Ya get some good pickin's. I got Mrs. Bailey a nice teapot from it, didn't I?" He turned and looked up at Fiona. And she said, "Yes, you did, Sammy; and I'll always treasure it. That is one thing I'll never part with."

Withdrawing his fingers from the tight grip of the old fellow, Sammy said, "I'll be on television the night an' all. They took me by meself. I wanted to be with them"—he pointed to the children—"but they said, no, I had to stand by meself. An' they wanted me to smile or laugh and I told 'em I didn't smile or laugh unless I had somethin' to laugh about."

"You told them that?"

"Aye, I did."

"You're a man after my own heart, an independent spirit."

Sir Charles turned now and glanced at Rupert who was standing to the side of him, smiling, and he said, "Something must be done in that quarter. Make a note of it."

"Yes, sir."

"Would you like to come in and have a cup of coffee, sir?" Nell

379

motioned towards the sitting room. And now Sir Charles, looking at Rupert again, said, "How's the time going?"

"I don't think there's enough left for coffee, sir."

"Well, in that case we'd better get along." He turned to Fiona: "You'll be going back to the hospital today?" he asked.

"Oh, of course."

"Well, will you phone me of his progress?"

"Yes; yes, I will."

"And I'll look in tomorrow and see him myself. Well, good-bye everybody." Then giving all his attention to Sammy, he said, "Good-bye, young man. We'll be meeting again, rest assured on that."

Fiona walked with Sir Charles down the drive, Mark and Nell with Rupert and the children dancing along. From the gate, they watched Rupert help the old man into the car, and Nell said, "I wouldn't mind having the price of one wheel of that."

"Oh, it isn't the wheels that cost the money, Nell," Mark put in, "it's the engine. I'll go for the engine."

"One day I'll have a car like that."

All eyes had been on the disappearing car but now they rested on Sammy, and no one, not even Katie, said, "Some hope," because if someone like him could save their father, and had been the means of telling his own father, as it said on the wireless this morning, where the would-be murderers were, at least one of them, then having a Rolls-Royce would be a simple matter.

It was fifteen minutes later, when Nell and Fiona had the sitting room to themselves, that Fiona said, "How are they next door?"

"Oh, as they used to be. I can't believe it. And the relief they've experienced since Mr. Love caught that man. Well, it's taken years off both of them. As Mam said, there was still a strong suspicion in the inspector's mind that Dad had done it. But enough of them. How did you really find Bill?"

"Oh, Nell." Fiona sat down on the couch. "They told me last night there looked as if there was nothing left of him that hadn't been battered almost to a pulp, his arms, his legs, his head, a knife in his stomach."

"Oh, those fellows should get life and whoever's put them up to this. As Bert said, it's been a planned job from the beginning. Have you any idea at all? I mean, did Bill say anything?"

Fiona could look at Nell now and say, "You mean, who's behind it? No; no, we've no idea. Likely somebody who's jealous of him and his success."

She said this because she knew that Bill would do nothing to bring further hurt to Sir Charles. And it wasn't because of his strong backing of him to get this great contract, the contract that was going to alter all their lives, a contract that might never have come off but for little Sammy Love.

Her mind kept going back to the child. They had adopted one child because Bill had wanted to do so; they could adopt another because she wanted it. But in this case there was an obstacle, a huge obstacle, the father. He loved the boy and the boy loved him. Still, there were things that could be done for him, and she already had it half planned in her mind; and for the father, too. Yes, for the father, too. By the time Bill came home she would have it all cut and dried, and he would be so pleased, because right from the first meeting with Sammy Love he had associated himself with the boy. In some way they were akin.

35

IT WAS A FULL SIX WEEKS LATER WHEN BILL CAME HOME. HE'D HAD TWO further operations, but for the past fortnight he had regained fresh strength daily to such an extent that he had been sitting up and walking about his room now for the past five days.

He had naturally become a favourite with the staff. The first words he spoke to the sister when he had become fully conscious and seen the flower-decked room and the dozens of get-well cards arrayed around it were, "I never knew they decorated the morgue like this." And the day following his second trip to the theatre he said to Fiona, "I want a divorce because I'm going to marry Nurse Campbell here." He indicated the plump, cherry face of a twenty-four-year-old girl before adding, "You see, she knows about places inside me that you've never dreamed of." And Fiona had answered, "Oh, that's all right. I'm sure she'll love to take on your whole adopted family." She had nodded across the bed to Nurse Campbell, adding, "There's only four of them." Then looking down on Bill again, she had ended, "I didn't know how to tell you, but this lets me out. I'd been planning to start a new life with Rupert. You know, Sir Charles's chauffeur."

The nurse had gone out of the room shaking with laughter, but Bill had looked up at her and said, "Look, woman, I'm allowed to make jokes like that, but not you. There's no truth in my line, but with you

382

it's different. There's no smoke without fire, you know. And he's a good-looking fella, an' related to the old bloke, too."

"Well, I thought it was about time we both had a change."

"Fiona." The look on his face, the sound of his voice brought her face down to his, saying, "Oh, Bill, Bill. It isn't fair. You can joke like that and I can't."

"I'm always afraid."

"Oh, that hurts me," she had said. "There's nobody and never will be anybody in my life but you. All I want is for you to get well, really well, and come home. They're all longing for you. The house isn't the same. My bed is cold. I hug your pillow at night." He had slowly lifted his hand and touched her face, saying, "I'm a lucky fella"; then had added, "Talking of Rupert, which leads me to the old fella. He's worried in his mind, isn't he, about what I'm goin' to do? And that inspector keeps poppin' in. Whether the big fella gave him any hint when he was picked up of who was behind this, I don't know. But as Davey said, the little bruiser seemed to think that his partner was in the dark as well as himself. Anyway, if that big lout knows it was her, she's promised to pay him enough to keep his mouth shut."

"What are you going to do about it then?"

He surprised her when he said, "I don't really know," because she had imagined that he wouldn't do anything that would disturb Sir Charles further. And then he had added, "It narks me to the very core to think that bastard of a woman, because that's what she is, a bastard, will get off with this. And all because I turned down her offer. You can't believe it, can you, dear?"

"Oh yes; yes, I can believe it. It's a dreadful thing to be spurned."

"How would you know anything about that? Nell would but not you."

"Oh, well, perhaps not quite, but I have experienced a cousin to it, say. *Because*: there were long stretches when I was ignored; I was there only to be used in various ways as a cook, a cleaner, a shopper, a bearer of children, a satisfier of needs ... without love. I was scarcely eighteen when I married. I knew nothing about men or marriage. Well, if I thought of men I thought they were like my father. I really married to escape from home and my mother. You can understand that. But there were times even during the first year when I longed to be back."

"Oh, Fiona; I ... I didn't know. I didn't realise. And the kids have always seemed so ... so happy and...."

"It's a dreadful thing to say, but they became happy after he died, and so did I. And I swore I'd never marry again." Her smile widened.

383

"And just look what I did. Just ... look ... what ... I ... did. And oh!" Her mouth fell onto his and it was some seconds before she finished, "How I thank God every day that I did it."

"I had thought I knew everything about you. But you now somehow appear like a stranger. No, no; not a stranger, someone new, someone who hasn't been touched by anybody but me, and never will. ... Have you told me all this because you don't want me to take the matter further?"

"Yes and no. I ... I want her brought to justice, I really do; at the same time the exposure would hurt the old man, because I really think he loved her more than he did his own children ... his own daughters. And likely his affection was heightened because she'd had a dirty deal in having to marry Brown."

"Aye, there's that in it. You'd rather that I let it rest then?"

"Well, if you don't there'll be a court case, and she'd go to prison. And I think the old man would rather go himself than see her suffer that. But you've got one satisfaction: those two individuals will, as Mr. Love would say, take a long holiday in Durham."

"Funny, isn't it, how he and his lad have come into our lives? But it seems they had to, else I wouldn't be here now. I'm going to do something for him, you know."

"Are you?" She widened her eyes and raised her brows.

"Oh, yes, definitely. I don't know what yet, but I'll think up something."

"Well, I'd leave it till you come home, eh?"

He was due to go home on the Saturday, and he guessed there'd be a reception awaiting him. What was worrying him was whether he would feel fit to stand up to it. But on the Friday night, and without preliminary thought, he was forced to face a reception: his room was invaded by twelve men, some awkwardly carrying flowers, some with square boxes that suggested cakes, some with tall boxes that suggested the kind of spirit forbidden in hospitals. And they all stood around his chair. It wasn't the first time they'd been there, but it was the first time they had arrived en masse. And it was Barney McGuire, the oldest of them, who, being spokesman, said, "We would like to have come the morrow, boss, but we knew it would be your family's do. So we decided to come the night and to say we're all looking forward to you gettin' back on the job. Although that's finished, all but tidyin' up."

"Works better than if you'd been there, boss." Jos Wright nodded towards him with a solemn face yet with a twinkle in his eye, and Bill

384

answered, "The same to you Jos. And may I hope your next lot of leeks are pulled up again."

There was a burst of laughter, and Tommy Turnbull said, "Their case comes up next week, boss. We'll likely know who's behind them then, if anybody."

"I doubt it," Jack Mowbray said. "Me cousin Lisa's goin' with a young bobby. He's only just come this way—he was transferred from across the river—but he says it's his opinion that it's been organised from the beginning to sort of break us, you know. Well, break you, boss; first through us, sort of, with the car and the bikes and the lot of them. He thinks they'll likely keep quiet because it's his opinion there's big money behind it. Somebody, you know, with dough, boss, who wanted the contract an' wanted to put you out of business. In any case"—he grinned now—"we've got a bet on: thirty quid who's nearest the stretch they'll get."

"And what d'you think they'll get, Jack?"

"Well"—Jack wagged his head—"I'd say five years. I hope it's more, for I reckon it could have been murder you see. If the kid hadn't found you it could have been murder."

"If the kid hadn't found me, Jack, there'd be no case next week, 'cos I'd be well down among the dung by this time; that park lake held a lot of silt and slush."

"Aye. Aye, boss, there's that in it." And the dire would-have-been results of this caused a few shuffles all round and Bert Ormesby to say, "I would keep off the subject if you don't mind, boss, because our *mute* and *shy* friend here, Mr. Davey Love, has talked of nothin' else since. He's thinkin' of sendin' the lad to Eton."

Now there was a general movement, a spluttering; then quite quietly Davey said, "Well, now, friend Bert, I've kept me tongue quiet for this length of time so's you could all get yer nebs in. But, as they say, there's many a true word spoke in joke an' you'll be surprised if you knew where that lad is headed for."

"Surprise us then," said Morris Fenwick.

"Well, now, I'll do just that," said Davey. "He's headed for a private school, the same as ever the boss's son goes to. Oh aye, tis all been arranged. The boss's wife herself saw to it, and I meself went to the headmaster only last week. 'Would you like yer son to attend my school, Mr. Love?' said he; an' said I, 'I would, sir, I would indeed.' 'We'll be proud to have him, Mr. Love,' said he."

A small titter to his side caused Davey to turn and look at Tommy Turnbull. And he said, "I had afore mentioned the boss's wife, Tommy. If I was after imaginin' things or makin' things up I wouldn't have brought her name into it, now would I? But for two pins I feel like bustin' somebody's mouth, and it's me own, 'cos didn't I promise her that I wouldn't say a word of it till himself"—he pointed to the figure in the chair—"put in an appearance the morrow. I'm sorry, boss. It's me weakness to open me mouth when I should keep it shut."

"Well, good for you, Irish," said Harry Newton. "I've got three youngsters, and I'd be pleased to send them along there an' all. See what you can do, Love, will you?"

"Such honours have to be worked for, Harry, and I think my Sammy has worked for his. What d'you say, boss?"

"I say, you're right, Davey. Yes, you're right: Sammy's worked for the honour. And I could tell you all something else that would raise your eyebrows"—he now looked from one to the other—"but it can wait."

"You'll have to go to court next week, Love. Are you expectin' a medal for bustin' that bloke up?"

"No, no," one of the others put in now, "he knows what'll happen: the judge will pat him on the shoulder and say, six months for assault and battery. Stand down."

"You could be right at that, Tommy, you could be right at that. There's queer things happen in this world," said Davey, laughing now.

As often happens after laughing, there was silence for a moment in the room, then Bill said, "You're all ready for the big show?"

"Ready and willin', boss," came from different quarters, and all their heads nodded.

"You know I'll have to take on a pretty large crew, don't you?"

"Aye, aye." Barney McGuire was nodding at him again.

"Well, now, this is what I've got in mind. Not one of you will be doin' your own job, at least you'll be doin' it but through others. You'll each be in charge of a gang for your own particular work. And you know what I've always wanted from you, so you know what to get out of them. And as I've said afore, you don't find gold nuggets among the workers the day, but pick out the silver and let the dross go down the drain, in other words, get rid of them. There's plenty now needing jobs and there're some good fellas about. There'll always be shirkers, but you know how to deal with them. When I get home we'll have a meetin' an' we'll discuss your wages. But apart from that you'll have to meet the architects and the overall works manager. I'll have to have him until I'm fully on me feet. You understand? And there'll be an office staff and a sort of quantity surveyor type of accountant, perhaps two, one to keep the other straight."

386

There was laughter at this; then Barney, stepping forward now and shaking Bill's hand, said, "From me, I say thanks, boss. And I think that goes for all the rest."

"Aye, aye, I'll say," was the general chorus.

"And we'll be goin' now because, after havin' seen this lot perhaps they'll keep you in another week, you'll need so much more rest."

Then came the sound of a gasp from the doorway and a nurse, indignation in her voice, said, "What on earth do you mean crowding in like this! You know there's only two visitors allowed in at a time. You'd better not let sister see you."

"We're going, nurse, we're on our way."

"Goodnight, boss."

"Goodnight, boss."

"Goodnight, boss."

One after the other they shook his hand and filed out laughing; and the last one to leave, by accident or design, was Davey Love, and what he said was, "I'm never lost for words, but I'll have to find some new ones to express what I'm feelin' inside this minute, boss. Any road, see you the morrow."

"Aye, see you the morrow, Davey."

36

WHEN FIONA BROUGHT BILL HOME ONLY THE FAMILY AND NELL WERE THERE TO
greet him. And when he was at last ensconced in the armchair in the
sitting room with his family, Mamie on his knee, Katie in the circle
of one arm, Willie in the other, Mark kneeling at one side of the chair,
there was Sammy Love at the other.

Sammy was dressed in a pair of well-fitting, long grey trousers. He
had on a pale grey shirt and a bright blue tie. And over the shirt he
wore a blue pullover. His hair was brushed flat, his nails were clean,
and on his feet were the same patterned shoes as Willie was wearing.

Willie now looked down on his friend's head before he turned to
Bill and said, "Sammy's got something to tell you, Dad."

"Aw, it can wait till me da comes with the present. He should be
here now." Sammy looked towards the door; but Willie persisted. "It
won't come as such a surprise then 'cos there'll be other things. Go
on!" He dug his fist into Sammy's back. "Tell him, man."

After a moment's hesitation, Sammy twisted round on the carpet,
cast his eyes to where Fiona was sitting smiling at him, then looked
at Nell, where she, too, was sitting smiling at him. Then he looked at
Bill and said, "Guess where we live."

"I know where you live."

"No, that's where we used to live. Guess where we live now."

388

"Aw, Buckingham Palace."

"Don't be daft."

There was a giggle from the children, and Bill, looking at Fiona, said, "That's something to come home to in your own house and be told that you haven't got to be daft. Well, how am I to guess? All the streets and places in this town, and you ask me to guess where you're livin'. Not here?" He pulled a face, and Sammy said, "No, not here. But not very far away."

"Oh, Lord! Don't say we're going to be neighbours."

Sammy cast a glance in Fiona's direction and she, looking at Bill, said, "Not quite neighbours, at least to us."

"I'm intrigued." Bill nudged Katie. "That's a good word, isn't it, intrigued?" And she grinned up at him and nestled closer into his shoulder.

"Primrose Crescent."

Bill didn't make a sound, he just gaped. His mouth opened, then closed; he looked at Fiona, then at Nell, then around the children, then back to Sammy again. And his voice was a mere whisper for him when he said, "Primrose Crescent?"

"Aye. Yon end. A bungalow, three bedrooms. And it's got a dinin' room all to itself. And a bathroom, a big bathroom with two basins." His face was alight now as Bill had never seen it. Then Bill's body began to shake and he said, "Oh, don't Sammy, don't make me laugh, 'cos there's parts of me that might split open. You shouldn't make me laugh. Primrose Crescent! Do you know who lived in Primrose Crescent?"

"Aye, I do."

"You do?"

"Aye."

Bill now looked at Fiona and asked, "Does she know?"

"Yes; yes, she knows."

Again he was looking at Sammy. "Did you know that my mother-in-law lives in Primrose Crescent?"

"Aye, she spoke to me."

"And you're still alive?"

The children all began to laugh and splutter.

"She seemed all right, okay. She said she'd seen me on the telly an' read about me in the papers."

"Has she met your father?"

Sammy looked at Fiona, and she, looking at Bill, said, "I don't think so, not yet."

"Hallelujah! Hallelujah!"

"Oh, Dad, Dad, don't. But they will meet soon because Gran is coming to tea and she'll meet Mr. Love th ... then." Mark was giggling.

"And it's all set out in the dining room and it looks lovely." This was chirped in by Mamie; and Katie took it up, saying, "We had to put the two tables together because there'll be fourteen of us."

"Fourteen!" said Bill. "Who's the fourteen? I thought I was going to have a quiet homecoming among my family."

"Well," said Fiona, "it will be your family, sort of, with Nell and Bert. There are nine of us, mother is ten. Then there is Mrs. Paget—" She did not add that Mr. Paget as yet couldn't come and face Bill. But she went on, "There's Rupert and Sir Charles and Lady Kingdom, and Mr. Love. Fourteen, the way I count them."

"Sir Charles and Lady ... ? And your ... mother? An' ... Mr. Love?" His face was screwed up.

"Yes. Sir Charles and Lady ... and my mother ... and Mr. Love. Be reasonable, Bill. You've got to put a little salve on the sore, as you yourself would say."

He looked down on Sammy and he thought, Aye: aye, she's right. A little salve on the sore, and the sore would be Davey Love. It was going to be an interesting tea party.

When there was a ring at the bell, Nell sprang up and went out of the room, and they all turned towards the door. And when a voice came to them from the hall Sammy got to his feet, saying, "That's me da." And he ran to the door, and there met Davey coming in carrying a large square box done up with fancy paper and a bow.

"Hello everybody. Hello everybody. Hello there, boss. See you're all settled in."

"Yes, Davey, all settled in. Come and sit down."

"Aye, I will in a minute. Here you! Here's what it's all about." He thrust the parcel into his son's arms and Sammy staggered with it towards the coffee table and just managed to ease it onto the end. Then looking at Fiona, he said, "Could ya clear it, I mean them things off the end, books and such?"

Both Fiona and Nell grabbed up the books and magazines, the ornamental shell, and the small ebony wood figure of a seated mandarin. And when the table was clear, they looked at Sammy and he, looking at Fiona, tapped the top of the box, saying, "It's me present for ya. I got some money from the sir an' some for talkin' to a fella in a magazine, an' me da lent me the rest. So I didn't get it from the tip." He grinned at her now.

"A present for me in ... in this big box?"

390

"Aye. Well, open it."

She unpinned the bow, then undid the gold cord, and as she had to tear the paper at the top she thought it was a pity because it was such lovely paper and she always kept the Christmas wrappings that weren't stuck up with tape. And when the paper was spread out there was revealed a cardboard box, and that was sealed, too.

She looked about her. They were all gathered round the table, and they were all surprised, even amazed, as was Fiona, when at last she pulled the four pieces of cardboard to one side to reveal a number of articles wrapped in tissue paper. Gently picking the first one up, she unwrapped it. It was a silver sugar basin. And looking at Sammy, all she could say was, "Oh, Sammy."

His response was: "Go on! Look at the rest. There's a lot more."

The next article was a matching milk jug, all of eight inches high with a beautiful handle. She again looked at the boy. Her eyelids were blinking now.

When she next drew out the teapot, she just gasped because it was a beautifully shaped teapot with a small black ebony knob on its lid.

And the reason for this was pointed out to her very quickly by Sammy, who said, "That's so ya won't burn yer fingers when ya lift up the lid to put more hot water in. That's what the man said. Go on! See the rest."

The next piece she drew out was a matching hot water jug. She had never seen one like it. It was about twelve inches high and had fluted sides and was shaped in what she could only describe as an exquisite design. Like something one would see, she imagined, in an Egyptian house. Then there was this large thing in the bottom of the box. It had black ebony handles on each side, and when, with some effort, she lifted it out and put it on the table, there was a gasp from everyone in the room except Davey Love and his son, for they were all looking down on a tray over twenty-four inches long, supported on four short, curved, sturdy legs, and the handles at each end, emerging, it seemed, from a deep, two-inch rim surrounding the tray.

"Oh, *Sammy. Sammy.* Mr. Love." She looked from one to the other. "This is ... really, what can I say? It's all so beautiful. But ... but there was no need for it. And dear me, dear me." There was a break in her voice.

"P ... p ... put them on the tray and see what they look like."

Slowly she did as Sammy ordered. Then he said, "There! The man said there were very few like that about, didn't he, Da?"

"He did that, son. He did that. And it's the best quality, ma'am. Tis, tis the best quality. It's what he called Elkington silver. An' look, will you? Just look. Tis on the bottom of every piece and on the bottom of the tray an' all. We got it from a real jeweller's. Of course, you know . . . you know, it isn't new. But it's not the modern stuff, 'cos that's femmer. You've only got to spit on the silver of the modern stuff and it's gone. Oh aye. But this'll last a number of lifetimes. It'll go down to yer children, it will that. An' that's what the man said to me, it'll go down to yer children. And I said, 'Sir, it won't go down to *my* children but to that of me son's best friend's mother.' "

"Will you excuse me a moment?"

After Fiona hurried from the room Sammy, looking from his father to Bill, said, "She doesn't like it?"

"Oh, Sammy, she loves it." Bill put his hand out and drew the boy into his embrace. "She loves it. An' so do I. By, yes. It's the most beautiful set I've ever seen in me life. I might be a rich man some day but I would never be able to buy a better. Go on, she'll be in the kitchen. Go and have a word with her."

When the boy remained still, his father said, "Did you hear what the boss said? Go on. An' remember, it's not everybody who laughs when they're happy. Go on."

Sammy went. He crossed the hall slowly and pushed open the kitchen door, and there he saw Fiona sitting at the table, her elbow on it, her head resting on her hand. But she turned and looked at him coming towards her. And when he was near her knee, he said, "Ya did like it, didn't ya."

She had difficulty in speaking at first, then she said, "Like it? It's a beautiful set, really beautiful. I love it, but not half as much as I love you."

Who put their arms around the other first they didn't know, but she bent over him and held him close and he reached up and, his arms around her neck, he pressed his face against hers. And after a moment they were standing apart, both sniffling. And then she touched his face gently as she said, "No matter where you live I want you always to consider this your second home. And you'll always be loved, not only by Willie, but by all of us."

"Ya mean you an' all?"

"Oh yes, me an' all, me first."

"Me da had a letter this mornin'. Me ma wants a divorce, an' me da says that suits him 'cos she would never fit into Primrose Crescent."

Here was a place for laughter: the child's mother couldn't fit into Primrose Crescent but his father considered he could. And who knew, who knew but that he would. But, oh, what her mother's reaction would be when she saw who her neighbour was. She didn't

392

know how far along the Crescent Davey Love's house was, but that it was in the actual vicinity was a sign for foreboding.

He half turned from her now, saying, "There's the bell. I wonder which one it is?"

She rose to her feet and he, looking up at her now, said, "Your hair's all fluffed an' ya want to dab yer eyes with cold water else ya'll look a sight."

"Oh, Sammy, Sammy."

He laughed now. "I'll have to stop sayin' what I think, won't I?"

Again she put her arms around him, and again he clung to her. And what did she hear him say? It seemed like a whisper, like a repeat of his own name, but it had sounded like, "I love ya." Then he was running from her; and she hurried to the kitchen mirror, straightened her hair, wet the side of her forefinger and rubbed it in turn under her eyelashes, giving them a sweep.

Her eyes looked bright, sparkling. Her face looked good in spite of the tears, and she wanted to keep it good always, for Bill. She swung round from the mirror as she heard her mother's voice, and muttering to herself now, "Oh, dear. Oh, dear," for she couldn't imagine her mother stomaching Davey Love. The boy, yes; for as long as he didn't come out with warm language he could appear funny, amusing. But Mr. Love's form of amusement could be uproarious, and her mother had never cared for uproarious people or occasions.

Mrs. Vidler was already in the sitting room and Bill was saying, "You know everybody except Mr. Love. This is Sammy's father."

"How do you do, Mr. Love? I've ... I've heard quite a bit about you."

"How do you yerself, ma'am? I've yet to hear anythin' about you, but I'm sure it could be nothin' but good. No, nothin' but good."

"You are very gallant, Mr. Love."

"Who could not be gallant to a beautiful lady, ma'am?"

Never. Never. Never. She couldn't believe it. Fiona, thinking she had better break it up before the illusion was shattered, said, "Mother, look what Sammy has bought me."

Mrs. Vidler moved towards the table at the other end of the room and she looked down on what she recognized immediately as a beautiful Victorian tea service. And she turned to Fiona and said, "You mean, Mr. Love?"

"No, no. Sammy. The boy, the child."

"He bought you that?"

"Yes, Mother, he bought me that."

"Oh, Fiona!" She turned her head away in disbelief. But when a

393

voice said, "I did; and it was me own money from the newspaper an' the old fella, Sir Charles. I hadn't it all but me da subbed me some and I bought it. Me da went with me."

She turned and looked at Davey, and Davey, looking at Mrs. Vidler, said, "Aye, he's right, ma'am. The boy bought it for your daughter, a beautiful woman who undoubtedly takes after her mother." And without pause he went on, "And he picked it himself, ma'am. He'd seen it in a jeweller's shop. We travelled the city, we did, foot sore I was, but a tea set he wanted for the boss's missis. But nothin' would suit him till he saw that one. And it is as I said already in this room, it is Elkington silver. And you will know, ma'am, that you cannot get much better than that unless you have the real Mackay."

There came a diversion with the bell ringing, and when a moment later Nell ushered Sir Charles and Lady Kingdom, accompanied by Rupert, into the room, Mrs. Vidler became her most charming. And as Fiona watched and heard her, she thought: her morning-coffee manner and her ladies' bridge evening rolled into one.

Lady Kingdom caught sight of the tea service and the cardboard box near it and, realising it was a present, she exclaimed, "Oh, what a beautiful service! Where did this come from? You've been given this as a present, Mrs. Bailey?"

"Yes, ma'am."

And again the pattern was repeated. But it was under Willie's oration now. He described to the admiring old couple how his friend had bought this for his mother and how he had come by the money. And he finished up by looking at Sir Charles and saying, "You gave him most, else he wouldn't have done it."

"*Willie!*"

"Yes, Mam?"

Sir Charles, laughing now, said, "Glad I've been of help."

"An' not only to the boy, sir, not only to the boy. Meself, I've never had the chance of thankin' you for the house." Once again Davey had the attention of all those present. "Now who would have thought in this wide world that you'd go an' give me one of your houses?"

"Oh, now, now, now, Love ... Mr. ... er. Get things absolutely straight: I have not given you a house, I have allowed you to rent it."

"Aw, you know what I'm after meanin', sir. And I know a hundred or two in Bog's End who'd give their eyeteeth, or their false sets, to get the chance of rentin' a house like the one you offered to me. For offer it you did, sir, didn't you? Never in me wildest dreams would I have had the nerve to come and ask you for such a place, even if I'd

394

known you owned the whole Crescent. Now what's the difference atween a street and a crescent?" He looked around everyone now. And it was Mark who said, "It's the shape."

"Oh aye; yes, lad, yer right, it's the shape. I'm as dull as an Irish bog an' as ignorant as the runt of a sow's litter."

Fiona turned away from Bill's straining face, then closed her eyes for the moment; but only to open them wide as a deep bass laugh came from Rupert and an accompanying chuckle from Sir Charles, with Lady Kingdom exchanging an amused glance with Fiona, before moving towards her, saying, "How are you now, my dear? I haven't had the chance to say a word."

"Very well, Lady Kingdom, since I know everything is going to be all right health-wise with my husband."

"Naturally. Naturally."

There was another diversion when Nell brought her former mother-in-law in, with Bert following them. There were more introductions, and almost before these were finished, Nell gave the signal to Fiona that all was ready in the dining room. And so the children, following instructions, allowed the elders to go before them.

It wasn't until all were seated that Fiona realised with dismay that her mother was placed next to Davey Love, and she almost groaned to herself, "Oh, dear me! Something will happen." And eventually it did.

As usual, Bill was at the head of the table and she herself at the foot; Lady Kingdom was on Bill's right, and Mrs. Vidler on his left. Next to her was Davey Love. Sir Charles was seated on Fiona's right with Rupert next to him. The children were arranged between Davey and Rupert at the one side, and Nell and Bert at the other. Fiona had seated Sammy to her left, thinking she would be more able from this position to control any ribald remark he might make. Unfortunately, though, there would be no one to so control his father. Still, what did it matter? She was feeling happy, even elated. Yet as she looked round the table she thought, What a mixture of characters.

Sir Charles was saying, "I haven't been at a party for years."

"Don't be silly, dear," his wife nodded down the table towards him. "We have two parties at Christmas and one in the New Year."

"Yes, but that's family, people you see every day in the week. And anyway, you know I escape if I can up to my snug." He bent forward in front of Fiona and, addressing Sammy, he said, "I've got a hidey-hole in the roof; I'll show it to you when you come to my place. And some day when you're grown up and married you'll remember it and make one for yourself because you'll want to escape."

Sammy did not quite understand this old fella, except the married bit, and he said, "I'm not gonna get married, never."

He had the attention of the table now, and Sir Charles, bending forward again, said, "Why are you so dead against marriage already?"

" 'Cos ya've only got to get divorced . . . me da's gettin' divorced."

As at a tennis match all heads now were turned towards Davey as he cried down the table, "Nobody wants to know about me business, and when I get you home I'll put me foot in . . . what I'll do is to give you a lesson in tea . . . tea-table conversation."

"That a fact? You getting divorced?"

Davey looked down the table at Sir Charles and, simply as one adult to another now, said, "Aye, well, you might as well know, them that he hasn't already opened his mouth to, this morning I got a letter from me wife sayin' she wants a divorce."

"I'm very sorry," said Sir Charles. Before Davey had a chance to reply, his son leaned forward in front of Fiona and answered for him, "Oh, ya needn't worry, ya needn't be sorry."

"No?"

"No, 'cos as me da says, me ma would never have fitted into the Crescent. She wasn't the type. He says he'll look out for a body a bit more refined like."

The laughter around the table was like a smothered rustle as Davey now cried at his son, "You remember Sister Catherine an' what she did to yer ears?" It was as if the two of them were quite alone now. "Well, begod, I'm tellin' you there won't be a part of you that I'll miss the night when I get you home."

"Why? He's only speaking the truth. And what's more, I think it's very commendable of you that you should look for someone refined. I do indeed. What do you say, Mrs. Vidler?"

"Oh . . . oh, Sir Charles, I . . . I agree with you. I think every man should marry, especially if there's a child in the case, and he's aiming, as he says, for more refinement in his life." And when she turned and bestowed on Davey a beautiful smile, Fiona looked up the table at Bill and he looked down at her, and they yelled from the one to the other: No! No! *No*. She's surely having him on. But no; Fiona could read her mother only too well: Davey Love's reformation would be a crusade. And under the patronage of Sir Charles! Well, what was good enough for the gentry would indeed be good enough for her.

She could see he was beginning to laugh: his body was shaking; she knew the symptoms, soon it would explode into a bellow. And in this, he was helped when Sir Charles, once again leaning forward and his

396

mouth full of cake and grinning mischievously, said to Sammy, "What will your father really do to you when you get home tonight?" And Sammy replied with an equally mischievous grin and in no small voice, "Threaten to knock bloody hell out of me. But I don't give a tinker's cuss 'cos it's just his mouth workin'."

A tablecloth had been stained with tea at Willie's birthday party, but now Fiona looked at the chaos that was taking place up and down the table, then at Rupert who, leaning forward and thumping his employer on the back, called to her, "How long has he been at that private school?" And Sammy, as though just becoming aware that he was an actor and could make people spill their tea, laughed himself as he shouted, "Three weeks!"

37

THE PARTY WAS OVER. THE VISITORS HAD TAKEN THEIR LEAVE. THE CHILDREN were in bed. Nell and Bert were doing their last tidying up in the kitchen, and Bill and Fiona were really alone for the first time since his return home.

They were sitting on the couch, his arm about her, and neither had spoken for some minutes when she said, "Tired?"

"Yes, I suppose I am; it's been a day and a half. As long as I live I'll never forget that tea. I've never seen so much havoc at a table."

Fiona did not enlarge on this but said, "You've had presents from everyone but me. Do you know that?"

"No, Mrs. B. Anyway, I've never given it a thought. You're my present. By, aye."

When he kissed her, she gently pressed him away and, looking into his face, she said, "I've got a present for you."

"You have? Well, then, let's have it."

She took his hand and brought it to her stomach, saying, "It's in there."

His ruddy colour had somewhat dimmed during the weeks in hospital; even so, his complexion was still somewhat high; but now, to her consternation, she saw the colour disappear from around his mouth when twice he opened it without emitting a sound.

"Bill, aren't you pleased? *Bill!*"

"When? ... How long?"

"Oh." She wagged her head. "Two and a half months, a bit over. I didn't tell you in hospital because I thought it best not to excite you. But I needn't have troubled myself."

"*Oh, Fiona!*" He closed his eyes.

"What is it, Bill? What is it? Tell me."

She was asking him to tell her. Tell her what was happening inside of him? How could he when he couldn't explain this feeling to himself. He only knew that all his life, yes, all his life . . . the part that mattered, he had longed for a child of his own. He was Dad to four children, but they weren't his, he merely played at being a father. But now she was telling him he had put a child into her, his child, his own.

He heard the door open and Nell say, "Well, we are now all shipshape and Bristol fashion," then her voice quite near, saying, "What's the matter? Has it been too much for him?" And Fiona answering, "Yes, something like that. I've just told him I'm pregnant and he's going to have a baby, and he mustn't like the idea of carrying it."

The room was filled with gusts of laughter from Bert, Nell, and Fiona.

He opened his eyes and looked up at the three laughing faces, then slowly held out his hand towards Fiona. But all he said was her name and that was softly.

It wasn't a bit Bill-like, but it expressed something that went beyond his usual bawl.

PART

III

Bill Bailey's Daughter

38

"IT'S MY TURN TO LISTEN." MAMIE PUSHED WILLIE TO ONE SIDE AND HE RETURNED the gesture with more force as he said, "It's always your turn; you've always got to be first."

"Stop it! Both of you." Fiona hitched herself up on the couch and, looking from one to the other said, "I'm tired of you two squabbling. What's the matter with you these days?"

"He's always nasty to me." Then turning on Willie, she cried, "When I next go to see my grandma and grandpa I won't come back."

"Good job, too. Anyway, you cried to come back last time. Dad had to go and fetch you. You were howling your eyes out."

"Willie! Oh, dear me." Fiona lay back on the cushions and put her hand to her head, saying, "I used to have a nice family at one time. And I don't know what this baby will think when it comes." She put a hand on the high mound of her stomach; then she turned her head quickly as her ten-year-old son remarked nonchalantly, "It won't be able to think for a long time, years and years."

The mother and son exchanged a long glance, and she answered the twinkle in his eye by saying, "Who knows? It might be a genius: start composing at three like Mozart, or it might be a great sculptor or an artist."

"Some hope."

"Willie!"

"Well"—Willie tossed his head from side to side—"neither Mark, Katie, nor me, and certainly not her"—he thumbed towards Mamie—"show any signs of genius."

"Well, I never! We'll have to wait till Mark and Katie come from school and inform them that they're wasting their time studying, because their brother thinks I have a family of numskulls."

When the sitting room door opened Fiona called across the room to Nell. "You know what you're looking after, Nell?" she cried.

"Well, sometimes I wonder, but you tell me."

"A bunch of near-idiots."

"Oh, I'm not surprised at that. I've thought that meself for a long time. Of course, some are worse than others. But how has this been revealed to you?"

"Oh, by my son here."

"Well, Willie should know." And she turned to him, saying, "Your second lieutenant, Mr. Samuel Love, is in the kitchen awaiting your presence."

Almost before she had finished speaking Mamie had turned and made to run from the room, only to be stopped by Nell's arm.

"Leave go, Nell. I . . . I want to see Sammy."

"Well, I don't think he wants to see you, my dear. As usual he's come to see Willie."

"He does want to see me, he's my boyfriend."

"Oh, in that case." Nell removed her arm, and when Mamie darted from the room Willie turned and looked at his mother with a most pained look on his face, and Fiona said softly, "Don't worry, dear. You know Sammy, he doesn't like girls."

"She'll make him like her."

"No, she won't. I mean, she won't be able to."

"Why?"

"Well, if ever there was a he-boy, he's a he-boy, isn't he. Go on. Tell her to come back here, I want to see her; then take Sammy upstairs to the playroom."

"Can he stay to tea?"

"Does he ever not stay to tea?"

Her son made a face at her; then hurried from the room. And Nell, walking towards the couch, said, "The eternal triangle. How goes it?"

"The same as yesterday, dear, and the day before that. The only thing is I feel I'm going to explode. Did you ever see anything like it?" She again put her hand on her stomach. "Can you remember?

404

Was I ever slim? As flat as a pancake? You know, Nell, not one of the others was this size. If I hadn't been assured there's only one there, I would swear it's triplets, or more. When I was carrying the others they were hardly noticeable."

"Well, you must remember they had a different father; this one owes its existence to Wild Bill Hickok."

Fiona laughed. It was a quiet, contented laugh. She laid her head back on the cushion and, looking up at Nell, said, "I don't think I've ever been so happy in my life. It's odd. I've felt well all the time I've been carrying. But not only that, I've had this feeling of contentment. Well"—she now nodded her head—"I shouldn't say all the time because you know what happened when I was two and a half months. My goodness, will we ever forget that? You can't imagine, looking back, that anyone could kidnap Bill, could you?"

Nell sat down by the side of the couch and looked about the room musingly before she said, "Life's odd, isn't it? The more you think about it the odder it becomes. Who would have thought that I'd ever marry Bert and be so happy that I'm afraid?"

"Why are you afraid? What do you mean?"

"Well, that it can't last. After those thirteen years with Harry, I keep saying to myself every morning, when will he change? I mean, Bert. When will he grow indifferent? When will he walk out on me for somebody else and give her a baby that I longed for for years? And when will he say 'I want a divorce'?"

"Now stop thinking like that! What's the matter with you? Bert would never do any one of those things, you know he wouldn't."

"Yes, I know." Nell nodded her head now. "Yes, I do know, yet I can't help being afraid. When you've been made to feel worthless, it's really hard to take in the fact that someone thinks ... well, you're wonderful." She pushed her hand towards Fiona as she grinned widely, adding, "He does, he thinks I'm wonderful."

"So do I, Nell, in a different way, so do I, and I'm so grateful that I have you. I can't imagine what I would have done without you, especially during this time."

"Oh, the big fellow would have gone out and hauled somebody in. You would have managed. By the way, how's his pains?" She laughed, and Fiona replied with a chuckle, "He had a cramp in the night. Had to get up and stamp his feet on the floor."

"He's having a bad time carrying."

They both laughed out loud now. Then Fiona, becoming more serious, said, "If I've had worries at all during this period they've been about him. I've picked the wrong time to become pregnant. It

405

would have to be, wouldn't it, just as he's starting work on the estate."

"But that's going well, isn't it? Bert says it was a brain wave of Bill's to put the eleven disciples"—she pulled a face—"in charge of gangs. They're already vying with each other as to who can get the most work or the best work out of their lot. Bert says it's funny to hear them in the cabin. He calls the cabin the hen cree. One of them threw some water over him yesterday because he said they were like hens with their first brood. And yet, you know, he's just as bad with his lot. Anyway, what would you like to eat besides apples? You're getting no more apples today; there'll be pips sprouting in your ears."

"I don't feel very hungry, Nell."

"You must eat; you've got to feed it. By the way, have you decided on names?"

"Yes. If it's a boy it's going to be Samuel."

"Samuel?"

"Yes, Sam ... u ... el. Because, as Bill says, if it wasn't for the Samuel that I heard pounding up the stairs a moment ago he wouldn't be here today."

"And if it's a girl?"

"Angela.'

"Angela. That's nice. Did he choose that?"

"Yes, it was his idea. Because, as he says, it'll be his first real child and it will be like an angel to him."

"Well, well. The big fella being sentimental."

"You don't know the half."

"Oh." They both turned towards the door as the footsteps came running across the hall. "Here comes the lady of the house."

Katie had put on inches during the year. Every time Fiona looked at her she saw herself as a girl of eleven, straight, slim, luxuriant brown hair, deep brown eyes with arched brows, and a well-shaped mouth, wide but matching the face. She could not imagine, though, that her tongue could ever have been as caustic as her daughter's could be at times.

"Hello. Hasn't it come yet, Mam?" Katie grinned down on Fiona; then, with a swift movement, she put her ear down onto her mother's stomach, saying, "How's the alarm clock?"

"Get out of the way." Fiona laughingly pushed her upwards. "I've had enough of that for one day."

"The juniors have been at it?"

"Yes, the juniors have been at it."

"Their lugs want scudding."

"*Katie!*"

"Well, Dad says that."

"He might, but it doesn't sound the same on your tongue."

"Not ladylike, eh?"

"Certainly not ladylike, not even girllike."

"Where are they?"

"They're upstairs with Sammy."

"Oh, is he here again? I thought that when Sir Charles let them have the posh bungalow we'd seen the last of him. Why doesn't he bring his bed?"

"Katie!" Fiona was wagging her finger at her daughter now. "I've told you. We owe a great deal to Sammy. Never forget that. I won't and your father won't. So remember, we are all together and doing well and only through Sammy."

"I'm not allowed to forget it."

"Why do you dislike him?"

"I don't dislike him, Nell. It's only that . . . well, there seems to be only Sammy in this house."

She now turned a pained glance on her mother and Fiona said, "Oh, Katie, you know that isn't true."

"It is, Mam. And you know when Dad comes in, what does he say? 'Has Sammy been round?' At one time he used to yell out, 'Where's my gang?'"

"He still does."

"Yes, but then he says, 'Has Sammy been round?' His gang isn't sufficient for him now."

"Come here, Katie."

Slowly Katie went to her mother, and Fiona, hitching her heavy body to the side, pulled her daughter down onto the edge of the couch and, putting her arm around her shoulders, she said, "Your dad cannot forget that if it wasn't for Sammy he would now be lying very deep in that frightful tip. And, you know, Sammy hasn't a real home."

"Well, it's a nice bungalow. It's bound to be when it's in the same Crescent as Grandma's."

"But he hasn't a mother."

Katie's mouth now went up at the corner and she turned her head half to the side before she said, "Grandma's trying to sit that exam, isn't she, Mam?"

"*Katie!* What put that idea into your head?"

Fiona had lifted her gaze towards Nell as she turned away, aiming to suppress her laughter, and now, looking back at her daughter, she said, "Your grandmother is only trying to be kind."

"That's a change isn't it?"

"Katie, what's come over you?"

"Nothing, Mam, only you know she's set her cap on that big rough fella."

"She hasn't."

"Mam, please." Katie pulled herself away from her mother's hold now, saying, "I'm older than Mamie; I'm nearly twelve."

"You're not nearly twelve, you're eleven."

"All right, all right, but on my next birthday I'll be twelve. I'm not a child."

"You are a child, Katie. You are still a child."

"Mam, don't say that. I'll tell you something. Sue's mother talks to her about everything. *Everything.*"

"What do you mean by *everything?*"

"Well, you know, men and things."

Fiona felt the colour rising from her neck to her forehead, and, her voice stiff now, she said, "I've told you all that is necessary along those lines. You know you haven't got to speak to strange men."

"Oh, that!"

When her daughter flounced round and made down the room Fiona shouted, "Katie! Come here."

But her daughter took no heed and marched out of the room.

Fiona brought her hands tightly together and held them on top of the mound of her stomach. Had she really said she had never felt so peaceful in her life before or so happy? Yes, she had said that because that's how she felt. But had happiness blinded her to what was going on under her nose with her daughter? With Willie? Even with Mamie? The only one of her family who remained the same was Mark. Sometimes she forgot that her son was not yet thirteen years old, for both his conversation and concern seemed at times to be that of a young man. She wished he was home, or better still Bill, but it would be half past six before he arrived. And she should be thankful it was that early in the evening when he came home now, for during the summer months it had been nine o'clock and sometimes later. He'd had a fortnight's holiday after coming out of hospital; then he seemed to have spent the next three months on the site, for he was determined that, as far as it lay in his power, everything would go right. And up till now, except for small hitches mostly concerned with the weather, everything had gone according to plan.

But no matter what time he came home now, almost immediately after his meal he would go into the study and work until midnight. Sometimes she would sit quietly in a chair watching him; and only recently she had said to him, "If the plans are all worked out in the beginning why must you keep going over them?"

And he had answered, "Because you can always better somebody's idea of best. And I've discovered, what can look all right on paper can appear a mess when set up in a room, particularly bathroom fittings. Oh, and a thousand and one other things." And when she had asked, "Doesn't McGilroy object if you're altering his plans?" he had replied, "Oh yes. But he can object as much as he likes; if a thing doesn't look right to me then it comes out. The second time that happened we began to see eye to eye. But I still feel I cannot and must not relax."

"He seems a nice man," she had said.

He had grinned at her as he replied, "He's always nice to women. Which reminds me, have you had your caller today?" And to this she had answered, "Oh, Bill."

After the near tragedy that happened to Bill she took it as an act of kindness that Rupert Meredith dropped in when he happened to come into town. And Bill did, too, at first, until on two occasions he himself happened to pop in out of hours when on his way to a board meeting in Newcastle. On the first he found her dispensing tea to Mr. Meredith. Nor were his feelings softened when on the second occasion Rupert was accompanied by Sir Charles himself.

When later on that particular evening he had said, "What's his game?" she had stood up full of indignation, then pushed out her stomach, saying, "I'm alluring, aren't I?" And to this he had answered, "Yes, and so is your condition to some blokes. . . . "

She now lay back and stared at the fire. She had two weeks to go before the child was due. If all went well she'd be in hospital a fortnight today, that would be Monday, November third. And she was longing for the fortnight to pass. But, of course, it might happen beforehand or even after. But whatever time it came she could see herself—as she had pictured hundreds of times since first knowing she was pregnant—watching Bill holding his own child. Only she knew how much this child was going to mean to him.

Her thoughts were disturbed by the pounding steps running down the stairs, and then the sitting room door being unceremoniously thrust open, and Willie coming in, accompanied by his friend Sammy Love.

"Mam, Sammy can't stay to tea tonight."

"Oh, why? Why not, Sammy?"

"Aw, 'cos." The round brown eyes and the pugnacious face were riveted on the mound of her stomach.

"Because what?"

"Well, me da says I've got to get in and get the tea ready like I used to do in the flat so's your ma won't come in and start messin' about."

Fiona nipped on her lip to stop herself from smiling, and she kept her voice level as she said, "Does ... does my mother make it her business to go in often?"

"Aye, she does. Well, she did when me da left the key in the gutter. She asked him to at first like, 'cos she said she wanted to tidy up for us. But now me da says we mustn't put her out, take advantage like. Is it still kicking?" He now pointed to the mound. And Fiona, after a slight gulp, said, "Yes; yes, Sammy; it's still kicking."

"Let him hear it, Mam, the bumpety-bump."

"Oh no, of course not." She looked from her son to Sammy, and, seeing the defensive look she had come to know so well during the time when she could barely stand the sight of him, she said, "You ... you wouldn't want to hear its heart beating, would you, Sammy?"

There was a pause before he answered, "'Aye, if it's all right with you."

"Go on, put your head on it." Willie pushed Sammy now, and Sammy, turning and looking at his friend and in his inimitable way, said, "All right. All right, hold yer hand, don't rush me."

He now took the two steps that separated him from the couch and Fiona; and when she held out her hand to him and he placed his in it he did not immediately bend his head forward towards her stomach but looked at her, his face unsmiling. Then, his head to one side, he slowly lowered it down onto the mound.

"Do you hear it?"

He did not answer Willie's excited enquiry but remained still for a moment before straightening up and, looking at Fiona, he said, "Ta."

"You heard it, Sammy? You heard its heart beating?" Willie's voice was full of excitement.

"Aye. Well, I heard a kind of knock, knock, knock. That would be it like?" He looked at Fiona, and she said, "Yes, that would be it, Sammy."

"I'll tell me da. He'd be pleased you let me listen to it."

"Perhaps he'd want to come and hear it an' all."

"*Willie!*"

"I was only kidding, Mam."

"Well, don't kid about such things."

"Me da's got a new suit."

"Has he, Sammy? That's nice. What colour is it?"

"It's dark blue. He wore it when he went to mass yesterday mornin'."

"You went to mass together?"

"Aye."

"That's nice."

"It won't be for long, much more I mean, the year'll soon be up he says."

"What do you mean, Sammy? Your father's only going to mass for a year?"

"Aye, that's what he says. He made a promise or somethin'. He said that's what he owed Him."

"Owed who?"

"God."

Fiona swallowed deeply. She could never see either Sammy or his father altering. In the months Sammy had attended Willie's school it had made little impression on him except for the fact that he no longer said 'ya,' and, of course, she must admit that his use of strong language had become a little less frequent, only when very excited or angry did he resort to colourful adjectives.

"Me da's goin' to get a car an' all."

"Is he? Oh, that'll be nice for you both."

"I don't know so much. I won't be able to drive until I'm seventeen, and then I'll be old."

"No, you won't be old at seventeen, you'll just be a young man."

"Aye; I know, but I don't want to be a young man."

"Why?" Fiona's question was in earnest. And the answer came back in earnest. " 'Cos then you think about lasses an' you get married an' they leave you. Then your troubles start."

"Oh, Sammy." She put her hand out again and caught his, and as she did so she thought, It's true: your early environment never leaves you. Her own never had. She put out her other hand and brought her son to her side, too, and, looking from one to the other, she said, "When you are both seventeen you will be a pair of rips and you'll both have cars, racing ones. And the only trouble that'll happen to either of you won't come from girls or lasses"—she nodded her head, laughing now into Sammy's face—"but from the police for speeding."

Willie's laugh rang out at this, but Sammy only grinned and said, "Mine'll be white like the Pink Panther's."

"Mine'll be red." Willie did a zoom over his mother's head with a

411

twisting hand. But he stopped suddenly when Sammy cried, "Don't do that! You'll frighten it."

Both Fiona and Willie now looked at Sammy, who said, "Well, you can. I mean, it was on the telly t'other night. Some sheep were chased by a dog and they dropped their lambs afore time and the farmer said they were just like humans: give them a shock an' things went wrong."

"Oh, Sammy." Fiona now swung her legs slowly from the couch and, pulling herself upwards, she said, "It would have to be a big fright before a baby dropped out. But thank you for being so protective."

As she made her way slowly down the room towards the door, one hand on a shoulder of each boy, she said, "Have you ever thought about getting a dog, Sammy?"

"Aye. Me da and me had a row about it just last week. He said I wouldn't look after it and it would be thrown out and I said it wouldn't. But he said it was cruel to leave a dog in the house all day, an' that's what would happen to it. Anyway, he said, it would mess the place up."

"Well, you could come home at dinnertime and let it out. I'll get Mr. B. to have a talk with your dad. How's that?"

He looked up into her face in that odd way he had of holding her gaze, then he said, "Ta." And again, "Ta."

"Miss Slater said you had to say 'thank you,' remember?"

"Aw." Sammy pushed Willie none too gently, saying, "Don't you start. I'll say 'ta' when I like and 'thank you' when I like, so that's that. I'm goin' now 'cos me da won't say ta when his tea's not ready." There was a quirk to his lips now as he glanced at Fiona before pulling open the front door and running down the path, crying as he did so, "Ta-ra! Ta-ra!"

After Willie shouted a similar good-bye, Fiona said as she closed the door, "As Sammy has just said, don't start that. No more ta-ra's." And as he ran from her, making for the stairs, she called after him, "Do you hear?"

He was already halfway up them when he turned and grinned down at her, shouting, "So long, Mam. So long." And she went into the kitchen saying, "So long, Mam. So long!"

"What's that?"

"That, Nell, is the result of checking my son from shouting 'ta-ra!' after Sammy."

"I like the sound of 'ta-ra!' "

"You might, but I don't think it's in the curriculum at school. Sammy apparently was pulled up for ta instead of thanks."

412

"Oh, my, my! How dreadful!" Nell gave a short laugh as she nodded towards Fiona. "You set that school a task when you got them to take Samuel Love."

"He was the town's hero, don't forget that. He could have got into Newcastle University at that time, and they would have pinned a degree on him."

They both laughed now; then Nell said, "Get off your feet and sit down."

"I've got to move, Nell; it's part of the exercise."

"There'll be plenty time for your moving when you get rid of that. I've never seen anybody so big. It looks as if you're carrying a young elephant or a whale."

"More likely a whale. It'll be three parts water."

"Oh, here's the last of the tribe coming." Nell looked down towards the back gate. Then she added, "He seems to be the only one of them that doesn't run."

Fiona joined Nell at the window, and she said, "He's always walked like that, straight, steady. It's like his character."

"Well, I'm glad there's one of them that's straight and steady. But here's one that'll have to run"—she turned from the window—"if I don't want Mr. Bertram Ormesby to arrive home to a plain table. Everything's set in the dining room; and mind, see that the squad clears away." She nodded towards Fiona. "Anyway, I've been up there and I've told madam what she's got to do. And so, leave it to them, and no more interfering from you and standing at the sink till all hours. Hello there, Mark."

"Hello, Nell. Boy, it's cold. Hello, Mam."

When he leaned forward to plant a kiss on the side of his mother's face he made no remark, such as Willie might have done, saying, "I'll soon have to get a ladder," or some such, but quietly asked, "How are you feeling?"

"Fine, fine; the same as I did when you went out this morning. How are you feeling?"

"Fine, fine; the same as I did when I went out this morning."

They laughed together; then, looking to where Nell was getting into her coat, he said, "Anything filling before tea, Nell? I'm starving."

"Yes, there's plenty of dry bread and pullet."

"Oh, that'll be nice."

"Well, you know the new arrangement: help yourself to a snack until your dad comes in; then in the bottom of the oven there's a shepherd's pie big enough to feed five thousand, and there's an apple pie to go with the custard I hope Katie is going to make."

"She'll not." Fiona flapped her hand towards Nell. "I've had some of Katie's custard. Look, get yourself away and let me have my kitchen to myself for five minutes."

"That's gratitude if you like."

"Drive carefully; it's the peak hour."

"And you be careful. . . . Ta-ra!"

As she went out laughing, Mark said, "What was that last about; she generally says, bye-bye."

"Oh, I was telling her about Willie and having to chastise him about ta-ra."

"Oh." Mark pursed his lips now. "I shouldn't trouble. I bet before he's finished he'll end up talking like Sammy does now, and Sammy will be talking plain, unvarnished English."

"I'm sorry, I can't agree with you, Mark, at least about Sammy. My fear is we'll have two Sammys. Anyway, everything all right with you?"

"Yes . . . Mam."

"Yes, what is it?"

"Roland's going skiing in February. There's a party from the school going to Switzerland. There's . . . there's still a vacant place and he wonders if . . . well, if I could go. But . . . but it costs a lot of money."

"Skiing? Would you like to go?"

"Oh yes, Mam. Oh yes, I'd love it. But as I said . . . it costs. . . . "

"How much?"

"Over two hundred pounds."

"Over two hundred. It is a lot of money." She stretched her upper lip as she nodded at him. "Well, we'll have to ask your dad, won't we?"

"Yes; yes, we'll have to ask him. But it's not only that; there'll be clothes, you know. You can hire the skis and the boots, Roland says, but . . . well, there's other things."

She put her arm around his shoulder, saying, "Don't worry about that. When your dad comes in let him have his bath and his meal, then we'll get at him."

"You're for it then, Mam?"

"Wholeheartedly. And I shouldn't be a bit surprised but I'll come with you."

He leaned his head against her shoulder, and when she asked, "What did you say there?" he looked at her through blinking eyelids and said, "Nothing, nothing. I'll . . . I'll take my snack upstairs." He went to the fridge, and after opening the door he asked, "Is this mine on the plate?"

414

"Yes. And if you get all that down you, you won't have any room for dinner."

She watched him close the fridge door, then go out of the kitchen without looking towards her again. And she stood where she was for a time, her hands joined on top of her bulging stomach.

Her son had said to her, "You're wonderful."

She was so lucky.

She was crossing the hall when the front door bell rang.

She was surprised to see her mother. She phoned practically every day, but her visits were few and far between.

"Oh, this cold." Mrs. Vidler bustled into the hall. "The wind goes right through you. No, no, dear, I'm not staying; I've just come ... well, I want a word with you. Are we alone? I mean ... "

"Yes, yes; they're all upstairs."

Mrs. Vidler hurried into the sitting room. Fiona followed, more slowly, and when they were seated, she said, "Is ... is anything wrong?"

There was nearly always something wrong when her mother phoned; there was always something wrong when she visited her. She had been very sympathetic when she thought Bill was dead, but on his recovery she had reverted to her natural self; and yet not quite, because of her new interest in Davey Love and the boy. Of course, this interest could have been put down to motherly concern, but she, knowing her mother, was well aware that Mrs. Vidler held no motherly feelings towards the big raw good-looking Irishman. In a way this filled her with pity. She was well aware of her mother's need of a man, but why she should pick on this raw, uneducated yet good-hearted and amusing individual, she would never know, because refinement was her second name.

"I'm going away for a while, dear."

"Going away?"

"Yes, that's what I said, going away, and for perhaps a month."

"A month?"

"My dear, stop repeating my words. I said, I'm going away for perhaps a month. Is it unusual that one should take a holiday?"

"Where are you going for perhaps a month?"

Not immediately, but after a pause, her mother said, "America."

"America?"

"Yes; you've heard of it, haven't you?"

"Mother, please don't be facetious. Why has this come about all of a sudden? Who's going with you?"

"There's no one going with me, dear. And it hasn't come about all

415

of a sudden. I've been thinking about it and preparing for it for some weeks."

"But there must be a reason. America, of all places. And . . . and on your own, and . . . "

She watched her mother rear up now: the old defensive look came back on her face and her voice was stiff as she said, "Don't say that, Fiona . . . at your age. I am merely turned fifty. I'm not dead yet."

Turned fifty? Her mother was fifty-eight, if she remembered rightly. Of course, she must admit she didn't look it, except there were those bags under her eyes and lines running from the corner of her mouth and marking her upper lip. Yet her bone structure was good; her high cheekbones stopped the cheeks from sagging. Yes, she could pass for fifty, or a little less, when she was made up, as she was at present. But why this trip to America? She said, "Do you know anyone there?"

"Yes; I have been corresponding with someone there for some time now. And don't look surprised, Fiona. You see I have my own life to lead. You definitely have yours and haven't paid much attention to me or my doings. Oh, oh"—she held up her hand now—"I'm not blaming you. In your present condition I know how you must be feeling, but there were times when you weren't in your present condition and you must admit that then you didn't feel for me, or ask if I was lonely. . . . "

"Mother! You have been surrounded by your women"—she'd almost said cronies—"friends for years: bridge friends, coffee friends, church friends; there's hardly a week goes by that you don't take a trip with them." She could have added, "And during the years that I was lonely and struggling to bring up three small children you only came here when it suited you, and then it was nearly always to interfere and cause an upheaval about one thing or another." She sighed now as she said, "Well, all I can say, Mother, is I hope you have a wonderful time."

"There's no doubt about that, I'm sure I shall." She was about to turn towards the door when she hesitated, then looked back at Fiona and said, "By the way, did you tell Mr. . . . Love that you thought it was too much for me to pop in and see to their meals?"

"No, I certainly did not; in fact, I have never discussed you with *Mr*. Love." And she emphasised the mister.

"Well, that is something in your favour. Now I must be going."

"When are you leaving for America?"

"The day after tomorrow."

"*So soon?*"

416

"No, it isn't so soon. I told you the arrangements have been going on for some time. Anyway, I may not see you again before I go, but I do hope everything goes well with you at your confinement."

They stood facing each other at the front door now, and as Fiona looked at her mother she thought: mother and daughter, and there was the mother saying, 'I'm going off to America for a month. I hope everything goes well with your confinement.' But she had never been an ordinary mother. She recalled the day after Mark was born when her mother stood by the bedside and said, 'Make a firm stand. Don't let this happen again.' And when she had said, 'Have you seen the baby?' Her mother had answered, 'All babies look alike at this age.'

That empty place somewhere below her ribs opened its door again and for a moment she felt she was about to cry. But why should she? She had everything: a loving family and an adoring man. So why should the lack of mother love be an empty space inside her?

"Good-bye, dear."

"Good-bye, Mother."

"Aren't you going to wish me a safe journey and a happy holiday?"

"Yes, I wish you both, Mother."

Mrs. Vidler stared at her daughter, then said, "You were always so enthusiastic over my doings, weren't you, dear?" And then leaned forward for the maternal kiss, and without further words pulled open the door and went out.

Fiona had switched on the outside light, but as she watched the prim figure walking away she called, "How are you going to get home, Mother?" One heard of old ladies and young ones, too, being attacked in the streets in the dark, and the Crescent was situated almost half a mile away. But she needn't have worried because Mrs. Vidler turned and said, "I have a taxi waiting, dear."

Of course, she would have a taxi waiting; her mother always looked after number one. But taxis were expensive, as were trips to America, and she was always putting it over that she could just manage to exist in the middle class way she had been accustomed to all her life.

"Mam."

She looked up to where Katie was making her way down the stairs, two at a time as usual.

"That was Gran, wasn't it?"

"Yes; yes, that was Gran."

"Has she upset you?"

"No, no, dear. Would Gran ever upset anyone?" She pulled a face at her daughter and Katie said, "Would there ever be a time when she didn't? Come on and sit down." She took her mother's arm as if to give

417

her support and escorted her back to the sitting room and to the couch. And when, having sat down by her mother's side, she did not begin to chatter by asking a question or expressing her adverse opinion of something or someone, Fiona said, "Anything wrong?"

"Mam."

"Yes?"

"Can I ask you something, personal like?"

"Yes, of course, dear."

There was a long pause before Katie, looking into her mother's face, said, "Do you love me?"

Fiona drew her head back as if to get her daughter into focus, and then she said, "What a question to ask, Katie! Of course I love you. You know I love you. I . . . I love all of you."

"That's it."

"What do you mean, that's it?"

"That's what Sue said her mother said: she loved them all, the six of them, en masse. That's what Sue said, they were loved en masse because there wasn't time to love them singly. Sue said you got advice doled out to you singly, but the other . . . well, it was in a lump."

"Katie"—Fiona took her daughter's hands and held them tightly between her own—"you're an individual. You are my daughter and I love you for yourself."

"Do you love Mark and Willie like that, too?"

Fiona paused before she answered this, and then she said, "Yes. Yes, in a way. I love you each for yourself, not en masse."

"What about Mamie?"

"Well"—Fiona again paused—"Mamie comes into a different category. It was compassion I felt for Mamie first. But now I love her, too. You understand? You understand me?"

"Yes; yes, I do, Mam. But as Sue says, it'll be different when that comes." She now poked her finger gently into the mound of Fiona's stomach. "She says it was like that in their house because there was nine years between the last and the new one, and the new one is now three years old and Sue says life has never been the same since it came."

Fiona didn't speak for almost a full minute, but continued to look at her daughter. But she wanted to, she had wanted to say immediately, "That Sue says too much; and I don't like your being friends with her. She's a year older than you in age, but apparently much older in her ideas, which she doesn't hesitate to voice." But what she forced herself to say was, "No two families are alike, Katie. Ours is a very special family. And I can assure you when the baby is born you'll all love it, and I shall continue to love you all ... individually. Remember that. Individually."

"Where is everybody?"

At the sound of the voice Katie jumped up from the couch, crying, "That's Dad! He's early."

As she went to pull the sitting room door open Bill pushed it from the other side, saying, "Now Lady Bailey, are you pushing me out or welcoming me in?"

"You're early."

"Is that a fault?"

"No, no; but it's only about half-past five."

"I'll go back." He took two steps backwards, and Katie, grabbing his hands, said, "Do you want a cup of tea?"

"No, he doesn't," said Fiona from the couch. "We can have dinner anytime now."

"I want a cup of tea, madam." He made one flapping movement with his hand towards her; then turning to Katie, said, "Yes, hinny, a cup of tea, sweet and strong."

"Aye, boss."

"She seems in a happy mood." He came quickly up the room now and, pushing Fiona's legs to the side, sat on the edge of the couch. Then turning his head sideways, he put his ear to her stomach, saying, "Hurry up you! You've got me worried; you're comin' in between me and my work." Lifting his head, he asked gently, "How are you feelin', love?"

"Fine."

"You know something? I'll have to stop calling you love. Every time I say that word I think of Big Davey. How about pet?"

"No, I don't like pet, I'd still rather have love, even with the image of Big Davey."

"The house seemed quiet when I came in, no ructions from above."

"Oh, you just missed those earlier on before Sammy went home. ... I've got news for you."

"Good or bad?"

"Well, it all depends upon how one sees another person. I think from your point of view it'll be good. Mother's going away for a month."

"Oh, that is good. Where's she going?"

"America."

"*What!*"

"That's what I said when she told me."

"What's she goin' to do there?"

419

"Don't ask me. She says she's going for a holiday. She's been arranging it for a long time, she said."

"She's up to something."

"What can she be up to in America?"

"Your mother, my dear, never does anything without a purpose. You know that. Anyway, I know somebody who'll be glad she's out of his hair for a time, and that's Davey. I know all his little movements now, his reactions, and he's been tryin' to corner me for days. But I've had somebody with me or I've been on the site. You know, between you and me, I think it's indecent the way she's chased that fella. She's old enough to be his mother, she is really."

"You needn't emphasise the fact, I know it too well. It's most embarrassing, especially since he stopped leaving the key handy for her. Why he did it in the first place was likely because he looked upon her as a motherly old soul."

"What I can't understand"—and now Bill shook his head as he laughed—"is that she's so stinkin' uppish, so refined, she's looked down her nose on me so much that she's cross-eyed, and yet, what does she do but set her cap at a fella like Davey Love who, let's face it, even from my point of view, is a pretty rough diamond. My! My! Well, I've never been able to fathom it."

"Well, you should have, with your insight into the sexual activities of all mammals, especially the two-legged ones."

"Aye, well, that might be so, but goin' by her age there's nineteen years between them and that's indecent."

Fiona half-cocked her head and said, "Taking the argument a little further: it wouldn't be indecent if it was the other way around, the man nineteen years older than the woman, would it?"

"No; no, it wouldn't. That's nature. Anyway, it still wouldn't have been so bad if she had picked on somebody of her own standard, at least what she considers her standard. Say now she had taken a shine to Rupert. Now there, he would, I should imagine, have been up her street, socially and in every other way. By the way, has he called in today?"

"No, he hasn't dear; and I'm so disappointed."

"Watch your lug. You know, I could dislike that fella. He's everything I am not, and, too, he's had a marvellous upbringing and a first-class education. But what is he doin' with it? Secretary to Sir Charles. And what does that mean? He is just a glorified chauffeur."

"Oh, Bill, what's the matter with you? You used to like him. When you first got to know him you thought he was a splendid fellow."

"Yes, perhaps; but I've changed me mind since he started visiting you and knowin' that you more than like him."

"I don't more than like him. You know something? I . . . I feel he's lonely."

"Oh, my God!" As if he had been prodded with a fork, Bill rose from the couch. "Don't take that tack. My! He has got to you."

"*Bill*." She brought her legs from the couch and, pushing herself upwards, she said, "You've got to stop this. It . . . it upsets me that you should go on like this." When her voice broke she was immediately in his arms and he was saying, "Aw, love. I'm sorry. I am really. But I'm worried sick. I want to be with you all the time an' I've got to be on the job. And there I come in and he's sittin' an' you're natterin' away as happy as Larry. And it's at that time I should be happy for you. But let's face it, I suppose it's the old inferiority complex escaping."

Fiona stared into his rugged face. Inferiority complex. That's the last thing anyone would imagine could be tacked on to this boisterous, loud-mouthed individual. But what did one really know about the makeup of another, even as someone as close as he was to her? Inferiority complex. That was the first time she had heard him use that term; but being Bill, he knew himself better than anyone else did.

She now took his face between her hands and in a voice that was soft and full of caring, she said, "Bill, there'll never be anyone in my life but you. Never. Even if you walked out tomorrow, no one could or would replace you. I love you as I never thought to love anyone in my life. In fact, I didn't know what love was until I met you. All I want in life is to make you happy."

He said nothing; he just stared at her for a moment, then dropped his head onto her shoulder, and she held him close, as close as her stomach would allow.

"Here's your tea, sweet and strong . . . and stop necking."

They drew apart, and he turned to Katie, saying, "Thanks love. And . . . there'll never be another you. I heard that on the radio comin' over. It's a nice song. Suits you."

"Flatterer. What do you want me to do? Get out and leave you two alone?" She looked at her mother and said, "Mam, I think we had better have dinner because that shepherd's pie will soon need a crook to dig it out of the dish; from what I gathered when I opened the oven door it's going dry."

"Well, call the rest, dear, we'll have it now. And you"—she pointed to Bill—"don't blame me if you have indigestion after eating meat on

421

top of tea. Come on," she said, taking his hand now, "give me a hand to carry in the dishes."

"Carry in the dishes, she said," said Katie, looking at Bill. "She needs somebody to carry her in, doesn't she? What do you bet she doesn't go the full time."

"Katie, please!"

"Your bet's on. I bet you . . . what?" Bill pursed his lips. "Five quid that she goes to the very day."

"*Five quid.*"

"Pounds, Katie."

"All right, five quid, or five pounds, that's a lot of money. I'll have to take it out of the bank."

"Well, are you on or off?"

"I'm on. And that means if it's before or after you pay me."

"Aw, now you're stretching it. Before you were willing to bet it would be before. Well, what about it?"

"Meanie. All right, you're on. Mam." She turned to Fiona. "You put a spurt on; I can't afford to lose five pounds."

"No dear, you can't; not with Christmas coming," said Fiona as they went across the hall. And, looking at Bill, she added under her breath, "Pity I didn't arrange things better. I could have given you a Christmas box then."

Dinner was over; the children had washed up and were now upstairs in the playroom: and Bill was again settled behind his desk in the study and Fiona seated in the big leather chair to the side of the fire. She stopped her knitting when Bill stopped writing and looked at her, saying, "I set four new ones on this mornin', and it amazes me that with all the unemployed in this town there aren't men queueing up for jobs. And of the four there was only one who really showed any interest. Apparently he had been a clerk and was in his late forties, but he said he had been on the dole for two and a half years and would be willing to try to turn his hand to anything. The other three seem to have been in and out of jobs like yo-yos. 'Why did you leave your last job?' I asked one. 'Well, it was the travelling. You see, mister, I never got in until half past six at night and by the time you have a meal and a wash it was practically the next mornin', and I had to leave at seven again. That was no life.' God in heaven!"

"Yes, but how are things otherwise? I mean the schedule and so on."

"Oh, the schedule. We seem to be a bit ahead. And the board seems well satisfied. We had a contingent round yesterday, but some of them ask bloody silly questions. What would be the saving if you could cut down on this, that, or the other? I answered one particular gentleman bluntly by saying, inferior buildings. Another asked why we put lime with the cement. So you could pick the pointing out between the bricks with your fingers, I said to that one, and he believed me; I had to put him straight. Some blokes feel they must say something no matter how stupid. The fact is we've been through all this in the boardroom, minutely and minutely. . . . There's the bell. Who can this be at half past eight? Your mother likely to say she's not going to America, or will I accompany her. Now sit where you are; I'll go and see who it is, that's if one of the squad doesn't get there first."

None of the squad appeared in the hall, and when he opened the door it was to see Davey Love standing there.

"Hello, boss. I'm sorry to trouble you."

Bill suppressed a sigh and said, "Come in. Come in, Davey."

"It's a cold night; cut the ears off you."

"Yes, it is," said Bill. "We're in the study; there's a proper fire in there, not artificial logs. Come along."

As they entered the study Bill said, "Here's Davey, Fiona. He wants a word."

"Oh, hello, Davey. Do sit down."

"Ma'am, I feel I'm intrudin', but it's of necessity. You know what I mean?"

"Well, she will when you tell us why you're intruding. Sit down, man."

Davey sat on a straight-backed chair, a hand on each knee, his cap dangling from one. He leaned forward more towards Fiona than to Bill and said, "Tis a delicate subject that I'm about to bring up, but I'm troubled. And knowin' me, it isn't often, you know, that I'd be lost for words, but at this minute, as God's me judge, they're all stickin' in me gullet afraid to jump out an' into me mouth in case they upset you, ma'am . . . 'cos, you see, tis about your own ma I would speak."

Fiona, resisting casting a glance in Bill's direction, said, "Don't be afraid to speak about my mother, Mr. Love."

"Well, even with your permission, ma'am, I'm still chary of utterin' me thoughts. But afore I begin I'd like to stress this point. Aye, I would, an' it's this: me thoughts aren't made up of 'magination in this case; there's no Irish blarney coatin' the facts. The fact is, ma'am, that your ma . . . your mother has got the wrong end of the stick. Aw, begod, begod, how can I put it?"

"I'll put it for you, Davey. You mean she's been chasing you?"

Davey looked at Bill for a moment; then, with his gaze dropping away and his head swinging from side to side, he said, "Tis a rough way to put it, boss, but that's the top an' bottom of it. And"—he raised his eyes now and looked at Fiona—"I'm scared. I am. An' that's a strange thing to come from me lips, at least with regard to women, 'cos I've never been scared of a woman in me life. I get on with women, and I suppose that's the trouble in this case. But you see . . . well, how can I put it, ma'am, but I thought she was only bein' motherly. An' what man, I ask you, would say he didn't want a woman of her calibre to be motherly? Twas a nice feelin' at first: there was the table set all ready for the lad's tea, and mine an' all, when I come in. And there was me washin' sent out to the laundry. Begod!" He now slanted his gaze towards Bill adding, "Don't those bug . . . I mean those laundry blokes, charge. You could get a new shirt for what you have to pay for their washin' an' ironin'. It must be the pins they stick in that put the price up." He gave a small grin now. "But, give the devil his due, I've never been so clean in me life afore. As for the youngster, he's become sick of the sight of soap, for she's had him washin' his hands when he went to the lav. Well, tis only right, I suppose"—he was nodding his head now—"in that case. But afore his tea and after his tea! She was even there at times in the mornin', afore he went out to school, examinin' his nails. It got so that I hoped he'd give her a mouthful, you know the way he used to, an' that would've put her off. But now I don't think it would have. She's a tenacious woman, your ma."

Fiona felt the child inside her wobble, and she had to stop herself from bursting forth in high, almost hysterical laughter. She blinked her eyelids a number of times as she looked at the big raw Irishman now appealing to her, saying, "What am I goin' to do, ma'am?"

"Get yourself a woman. Bring one in."

"Oh, Bill!" Fiona shook her head.

"Never mind, 'Oh, Bill!'" Bill was nodding at Davey now. "That's what to do. Be cheerful about it. Introduce her to Mrs. Vidler. That'll knock the nail right on the head."

"You know, boss, them were me very thoughts at times, but, you see, the Crescent isn't the kind of place that you do that kind of thing, is it? They're nearly all old dears an' highly respectable people an' they've been very kind, I mean . . . well, they've been very civil to me an' the lad. Of course, it was all 'cos of the papers, you know, an' makin' Sammy out to be a hero an' all that twaddle. They fell over themselves at first; not so much now, you know, but still they've been very civil. An' the type of woman that might suit me mightn't suit them."

"To hell with them! Just say that to yourself. It's your life. And anyway, you're divorced, you could marry again."

"Aw begod, no. The fryin' pan put the fear of the fire into me; I'm takin' nobody in on a permanent basis like. No, sirree, 'cos you see I've got this bit of a temper. Well, I did the nine months in Durham 'cos of it, didn't I now? For plasterin' me wife's fancy man's face all over the wall. No; no more marriages. An' that's why, you see, that life appeared rosy when your ma took such an interest in us: I had a mother at last, I thought, not like the real one, an' the lad had a granny not like his real one."

"Tell me"—Fiona leaned forward now—"what's made you think otherwise then, that she doesn't still think of you as a mother?"

"Aw, ma'am. Ma'am. There's some things in this life you can't explain, not even God himself could put it into words. Tis the way some women have: the things they drop you know, little hints; an' the way they titivate themselves up. An' she could, couldn't she, your ma? Not that she looks her age. I've told her time an' again that nobody would take her for a day over forty."

Bill's laugh was a deep guffaw, and he ran his hands through his hair. "Aw, Davey Love, I thought you'd have more sense than that. Not a day over forty. You've asked for it. All you've got you've asked for. Anyway, she won't trouble you for the next few weeks, she's goin' to America."

"She's goin' to . . . ?"

"Yes." Fiona now nodded towards him. "She came in not so long ago to tell me that she's going on a holiday to America. And who knows? She might meet her soul mate on the journey."

"Praise be to God and His Holy Mother that she does. Praise be to God. Aw, you've lightened me day. You know what I was goin' to say next? That we must up an' leave, an' that would be a shame. I put it to the lad last night: I said, 'We might have to leave here.' 'Why for?' he said. 'Well, you don't want another ma,' I said. 'It depends,' he said. 'How about Mrs. Vidler?' I said. 'Bloody hell!' he said. Oh, dear, tis sorry, I am, ma'am, tis sorry. But he only uses language when he's troubled like. And he was troubled. Aye, begod, he was, 'cos you know what he said? 'You might have to do it, Da,' he said; ' 'cos if you didn't you might upset Mrs. B.' You gave him leave to call you that, didn't you, ma'am, 'cos that's what he said, that I might have to take on your ma, 'cos I might upset you. 'Cos he has a great feelin' for you. Oh aye, past understandin' the feelin' he has for you. But it's good news, oh aye, tis good news, America."

Bill had to make himself go down on his knees and poke the fire, then add more coal to it. And when, after dusting his hands, he sat back in his chair his face was red, not only from the flames. "Now look here, Davey," he said, "take no notice whatever of the other occupants of the Crescent—they've all got their own dark secrets; there's not a house anywhere that hasn't—you find yourself a lass, a nice one for preference, not a beer slugger from The Dirty Duck. By the way, are you still goin' there and washin' up the glasses?"

"No, boss, no. Since I've been on this job I've hardly been in the place but twice. No, I left that when I left Bog's End, and me patronage now is given to The Crown."

"Oh, The Crown. That's a nice pub, The Crown."

"Aye, it is that. An' they get some nice folk in there an' all, all types, but all respectable."

"Aye yes, indeed they do, at The Crown. If I remember rightly there's a nice barmaid in there, auburn-haired, good figure, name of Jinny." He looked at Fiona now, and when he winked at her she said, "We'll discuss her later, Mr. Bailey." And this brought a laugh from Davey, and he said, "Don't think you need to worry, ma'am, not in that direction. But, aye, she's a nice piece, that. I've had many a crack with her. And I know this about her: she's been divorced these two years back, an' no children. She lives with her brother up Melbourne Road."

"Well, now, what are you waitin' for? You'll lengthen those cracks if you've got any sense, boyo, and you'll have her installed by the time Mrs. Vidler returns."

"Aw, boss, that'd take a fast worker indeed, and I'm not all that fast in that direction. Women never take me, what you call, seriously. They have a laugh at me; I'm good for a joke. Anyway, if I was for pickin' up with a woman an' Father Hankin got wind of it, begod, he'd expose me from the altar. He's hard on me heels now 'cos I told him quite plainly, that was in confession of course, that I was only goin' to mass for a year to pay me debt to Him"—he now thumbed towards the ceiling—"and once that's done, well, we're back where we started. You'd think those fellas, 'cos after all what are priests but men, well, you'd think now that they wouldn't remember what was said to them in confession, wouldn't you? They're not supposed to blow the gaff; but, begod, they must have pockets all over their brains, and in one of 'em he's stored what I told him, 'cos before that he didn't take any notice to me, I was just one of those thick Irish blokes that go to mass 'cos they're frightened not to. They're all scared that they'll get knocked down an' die in mortal sin, 'cos they still believe in hell's flames. But there was this one"—he pointed to his chest—"tellin' him the truth. And I tell you, since then me Guardian Angel couldn't be stickin' to me closer than he is."

"Shut up, will you? Shut up! Come and have a drink." Bill's cheeks were wet. "And you stay there"—he now touched Fiona on her bowed head—"and I'll bring you one in, nonintoxicant, of course."

Davey was on his feet now and bending towards Fiona, saying, "Goodnight to you, ma'am. I'm glad we've had this crack; I feel better now. And who knows: Things'll work out; they generally do. Oh aye, they generally do. And if I'm not to see you afore your delivery, ma'am, may the Holy Mother of God be with you on that day and help you through your trauma."

"Come on away with you, will you.... Dear God in heaven! I'm talkin' as Irish as you." Bill put out his arm and almost hauled Davey from the room, leaving Fiona to sit back in her chair with the tears running down her face.... And may the Holy Mother of God be with you on that day and help you through your trauma. Oh, Davey Love, Davey Love, and Sammy Love. How they had affected this family since they had come onto the horizon, and not least with laughter.

39

SHE HAD ONLY ANOTHER WEEK TO GO, AT LEAST ACCORDING TO HER. BUT THE betting in the house was varied. You could say a book had been set up in the family Bailey. It had gone on from Katie's betting Bill, to Katie's betting Willie; then Willie's betting Mark, and Mark's betting Nell, and Nell's betting Bill, the bets being kept in the book by Mark with the amounts and dates of arrival against each case. Willie stood the lowest, aiming to gain or lose only twenty pence. Katie's bet still remained at the top of the list.

A lot of laughter had been caused by the book, but a certain amount of dissent, too: on the one hand, Bill had laughingly said, Fiona had kept her family off drugs, drink, and smoking, only for them to take to gambling, and that, in his mind, was much worse than drink; whilst on the other, it had heightened the war between Katie and Willie and caused it to be inflamed still further by Mamie's preference for Sammy. Where at one time she had adored Willie and been given the brush off every time she showed her affection for him, now she infuriated him by not only ignoring him, but also, in her childish yet knowing way, extolling the virtues of Sammy Love. And if Samuel hadn't been wise enough to abhor little girls, as he once did nuns, there would certainly have been a rift between him and Willie.

With regard to Sammy, Fiona had put her foot down: he was not

428

to be brought into the book—it was bad enough her family was betting on her. Yet Sammy's being excluded from joining the book was brought into the open at the tea table.

The old routine of the children sitting down to tea when they returned from school had been resumed, for Bill was now home much later, and the children couldn't be kept waiting for a meal. So here they were, all sitting round the kitchen table, including Sammy.

Nell, who was about to leave, said to Fiona, who was pouring tea out, "Now look, Fiona; leave that! Mark or Katie or any of them can surely pour tea out if they want more. Go and sit yourself down."

"No, Mam, you stand up, walk about." Katie was laughing up at Fiona. "And you know why?"

"Katie, stop it!" But Fiona shouldn't have glanced from her daughter to Sammy, for he, like all children, could interpret signals. Gulping down a mouthful of cake, he looked across the table at her, saying, "I know why she wants you to walk about, Mrs. B., it's so's she can get her bet. Willie told me."

As Fiona turned to look at her son she remembered: although she had told him that in no way was she having Sammy betting on her condition, she hadn't said that he mustn't tell Sammy about the silly business. And she had forgotten that those two were almost soul mates.

"It's a silly business," she said. "It'll come when it's ready, not before and not after."

"And it'll surprise everybody."

They all looked at Sammy now, and it was Mark who said, "What do you mean, it'll surprise everybody?"

"Well—" Still looking at Fiona, Sammy answered, "Babies are surprises, aren't they? And people brag about 'em bein' big. So yours will be a surprise."

Fiona smiled down at Sammy. He came out with such odd things, did this small rough child. But she was to remember his words. Oh, yes, very vividly she was to remember his words.

Sammy was now looking at Willie and saying, "Mrs. Fuller, upstairs, was gonna have a bairn. It was the time me ma was with us an' she said she was pig-sick of listening about it. But Mrs. Fuller had three all at one go! Me ma said she should have hired a sty 'cos she'd had a litter."

"Stop it! All of you, stop it! You'll have your teas over. Sammy!" Fiona had to swallow deeply in order to keep a straight face and insert admonition into his name. And the boy, recognising this, said, "I never swored, Mrs. B."

429

Both Katie and Mark took this up: looking at their mother and spluttering, they said, "I never swored, Mrs. B.," which caused Sammy to round on them. His face red, he started, "Aw, you lot are silly bug . . ." But like a crack of the whip his name came back at him: "Sammy!"

"Aw, well!" He tossed his head. "They're takin' the mickey."

"Only because you're funny, Sammy."

Mark stretched out his arm behind Willie's back to pat Sammy on the shoulder, saying, "If we didn't like you we wouldn't rib you."

"He's right. He's right." Willie was nodding at his friend now. "It's because we like you that we can rib you."

"Well, I wish you didn't like me so much, then I'd know where I stood."

It was Fiona's turn to smile, but quietly, down on the boy. He might only be ten, the same age as Willie, but he was keen witted. And the thought made her wonder what he would turn out to be, because she couldn't see the polish of the private school sinking deep. And perhaps, after all, that was a good thing.

Of a sudden Katie said, "There's a car come on the drive. It'll be Dad."

"A car? I never heard a car. It must be the wind."

"If cuddy's lugs says it's a car, it's a car," Mark said as he got up from the table.

Before he reached the hall the bell rang and, looking over his shoulder at his mother, he said, "She was right."

When he opened the door Fiona was behind him, and on seeing Rupert Meredith standing there she paused before greeting him: "Oh . . . hello! Do come in. It's a wild night. Take Mr. Meredith's coat, Mark."

"I hope I'm not intruding. Is it meal time?" He looked at Mark, and the boy answered, "Oh, we're finished, sir. Would you like a cup of tea?"

"Well . . ." He looked at Fiona, and she said, "Yes, he would. Would you see to it, Mark?"

"Yes, Mam."

"Come into the dining room; there's a proper fire in there. Bill hates artificial logs. He's going to have the sitting room fireplace out, he says. But I like my artificial logs; I can switch them on any time I'm feeling cold."

Rupert stopped just within the doorway of the dining room and, looking towards the table, he said, "Oh, *I am* intruding; you're all set for dinner."

"It's only for Bill and me. You see, he's rarely in nowadays before

430

half past six, and of late it's been sometimes nearly eight. So we've had to go back to our old system of feeding the tribe at teatime. We tried for a while to have our meal as a family, but they got so hungry they kept stuffing themselves while they waited."

"I like this room," he said, looking about him. "It always appears to me very cosy. The dining room at Brookley Manor is a fine room, but it's much too big for the three of us. It's different when the family come."

"Do sit down." She pointed to a winged upholstered armchair to the side of the fire, but he declined, saying, "No; no, you take that seat. It looks so comfortable."

"I prefer a straight-backed one." She smiled at him and turned one of the dining room chairs round towards the fire. "It's easier for me to get up ... and down."

"How are you feeling?"

"Well, very well, extremely so."

"That's good. I told Lady Kingdom I might look in after I left Newcastle, and she wishes me to convey her best wishes to you and hopes that you are not feeling too uncomfortable. Those were her words. Apparently, from what she says, she had a very bad time with all her children. And as Sir Charles pointed out, he's had a very bad time with them all since then."

"How is Sir Charles?"

"Oh, he seems to have got a new lease on life. I think it's the interest engendered by the site. He trots down every possible opportunity. I think the men must sometimes imagine he's snooping to see if they are working or not, but he seems to have caught your husband's enthusiasm and excitement. He really is much better than he's been for years, I should say. In fact, this time last year he wouldn't have thought of travelling to Scotland, but that's where they're off to at the end of the week. His younger brother is in rather a low state and apparently they're worried about him at yon end. So he feels he must go. And he might stay over Christmas—that is, if he can get round Lady Kingdom. He just does not enjoy the Christmas gatherings at home. As you know, he has a horde of grandchildren and, like all children, when space offers they run wild. For my part, I look forward to their coming."

"Why have you never thought of marrying?"

Almost as she was saying this she was chiding herself for probing. Yet the question had been on her mind for some time: here was this man, on thirty years old, handsome, because that was the word for him, and charming, and he had the kindest manner, the kindness was expressed in his eyes, deep brown like the colour of his hair. He wasn't all that tall, about the same height as Bill, five foot ten. And so, when she received no answer to her question and saw that his gaze was now levelled towards his crossed knees, she said, "I'm sorry. If that wasn't impertinent it must at least have appeared nosey. I'm sorry."

"*Oh no, no.* Please don't be sorry, and you would never be impertinent. But to answer your question: I have thought of marriage, very, very often, but there's . . . well, an impediment. I'll tell you about it sometime. Now I'm going to be sort of impertinent when I say, may I call you Fiona? It's a lovely name, Fiona. And my name is Rupert, as you know."

Oh, dear, dear, dear. There was a little hammer hitting her on the head, saying, "Bill. Bill. Bill. You must understand it means nothing; we've known him for months; it's natural that we should be on more familiar terms."

"I'm sorry. I should not have asked."

"Oh yes. Don't be silly. Well, what I mean is, we've known each other for some time now and quite candidly, I don't like the sound of Mrs. B. . . . Ah!" She paused and looked towards the door. "Mark with your tea, and all set out on a tray I hope you'll notice."

"I do indeed. And some cake, too. Thank you very much, Mark."

"I wouldn't be too thankful for the cake, sir; it's a bit dry."

As Rupert laughed Fiona said, "I suppose you have noticed by now that I have a very frank and outspoken family."

"Yes, and I find it very refreshing."

"By the way, Mam"—Mark was looking at his mother now—"Sammy is about to take his leave and he wants to say good-bye, or so long, or ta-ra. You may take your choice. He has to get home and set the tea for his father." This last was addressed to Rupert, and he, looking at Fiona, said, "Does he come every day?"

"Most days. But he'll always be welcome."

"Yes; yes, of course."

"Let him come in before he goes," she said to Mark.

"Will do."

When they had the room to themselves again, she looked at her visitor and asked, "Does Sir Charles ever hear of Mrs. Brown?"

"Yes, he hears of her but not from her; nor does he want to. But I do know he wrote her a very severe letter—I typed it—and it was to the effect that she should be serving a sentence of eight years alongside her two stooges. And it went on to say, he never wanted to set eyes on her again and that if she attempted to come back into this country he would put the police on her. It took a great deal for him to dictate that letter. But I put it down word for word as he said it.

432

It was sent to her London agent, for he would likely know where to send it. But it was strange, when I was up in town a few months ago, I called on him with the intention of trying to find out if she had really tried to come back into this country, because there was really nothing to stop her, no warrant was out for her arrest and those two villains had kept quiet as to who was paying them. But the fellow had moved. Still, Sir Charles will be ever grateful to your husband for not pressing the case against her. If she had to go to prison, I'm sure it would have had a dire effect on him."

When there was the sound of a commotion in the hall she thought with something akin to panic, Oh, dear, no! Not Bill, and *him* here.

But it was Bill. The door opened slowly and he walked in slowly, and on his appearance Rupert stood up, saying, "Here I am again, scrounging tea."

"Aye, I see that." Bill now walked towards Fiona, but, as would have been usual, he didn't bend and kiss her; instead, sitting on a chair near her, he said, "Windy outside."

"Yes, it's been blowing a gale all day. I'll go and get you a cup of tea."

He put out his hand and stayed her movement, saying, "It's all been put in order; they're seein' to it. Well—" he looked at Rupert, who was now seated again, and asked, "And what are you doin' with your life these days?"

"Oh, much the same as usual: ferrying my boss, doing his mail, running errands, the same routine."

"Good life if you can get it."

Rupert reached out now, picked up his cup, and drained it; then, putting it back on the tray, he said, and in a voice from which all pleasantness had disappeared, "It isn't the work I would have chosen, but circumstances in some cases take no account of desires. Well—" his tone changed slightly as he got to his feet and, looking at Fiona, said, "I must be off; but I'll be able to tell Lady Kingdom that you're still feeling well. Goodnight, Fiona."

She did not rise as she said, "Goodnight . . . Rupert."

"I'll see you out," said Bill.

"There's no need; I can find my way. You must be tired after your day's work. Goodnight."

When the door closed on him, there was silence between them, until Fiona burst out, "How could you, Bill!"

"How could I what? I come in here and find you tête-à-tête, that's the term isn't it, tête-à-tête? all cosy an' nice; and now on top of that it's Fiona and Rupert. It was Mrs. B. last time, if I remember, and Mr. Meredith."

"Well, now it's Fiona and Rupert as you say; so what do you make of it?"

"What I've made of it afore, just that he doesn't come here to convey messages from Lady Kingdom to you, or from you to her; he comes to see you and you're pleased to see him."

"Yes, Bill; yes, let's face facts, I'm pleased to see him."

"*Fiona!*" He was standing in front of her. "I told you afore we married, didn't I, what would happen if anybody came between us, ever, didn't I? And I wasn't shoutin' me head off when I told you. When I'm really serious about anything I never shout, and I'm not shoutin' now."

As she stared up into his face she knew a moment of fear. No, he wasn't shouting and she knew he meant what he said. Her voice was trembling now as she answered, "That being the case, you must tell him not to visit here any more."

"No, not me, but you. You must tell him."

Her throat was tight; the muscles in her stomach seemed to be throwing the child from side to side. She cleared the restriction in her throat before she said, "I never thought I would say this to you, Bill, but at this moment I don't like you. I still love you but I don't like you." And at this she pulled herself up from the chair and, almost thrusting him aside, went from the room. And he didn't stop her.

It was only a matter of minutes later when Katie came into the room and stood by the chair in which he was sitting, his elbows on his knees, staring into the fire.

"Mam's crying.... Did you hear what I said, Dad? Mam's crying."

He pulled himself upright. "Yes, I heard what you said, Katie."

"Why have you made her cry?"

"It was something you wouldn't understand."

"Oh yes, I would, and I do."

He turned his head sharply and looked at her, and she went on, "It's because you found Mr. Meredith here, isn't it? You're jealous because he's different from you."

"*Katie.* Now mind. You can go so far."

"But it's the truth, isn't it? I'm not a little girl, Dad. Well, I mean I am, but you know I was here when you first came and we all loved you and we still love you ... more. And Mam loves you. But even if her stomach is sticking out a mile, she's still attractive, and you don't like that, do you?"

He let his head drop onto his chest and moved it slowly.

"Don't be mad at me."

He was looking at her again as he said, "I'm not mad at you, lass,

I'm only amazed that you seem so grown up and so different from the little girl I knew when I first came into this house. Well, this being so, and being observant as you are, you know me, so you'll know that I can't change. I am what I am, brash, loud-mouthed, ambitious, but protective of me own. Aye, those are the words. I read them somewhere, but they apply to me. I'm protective of me own. And Katie"—he put his hand out now and laid it gently on her shoulder— "I know something that you don't know, as yet. I know men and the workings of their minds. Sometimes I'm wrong, but not very often. Ninety-five to five, I'd say."

Katie's eyelids were blinking rapidly, and in this moment she looked very much like her mother as she said, "Go on up and tell her you're sorry."

"No, pet. I'll go up, aye, and tell her I love her, but not that I'm sorry for what I said, for if he comes here again I'll give him the same cool reception, colder, being *me*, you know." He smiled grimly now.

Reaching up, Katie placed her lips on his stubbly cheek, saying, "You're a funny man, Bill Bailey, but I love you."

He put his arms about her and held her close for a moment, then said, "Go and see to the dinner. I'll bring her down."

"Perhaps she'll like it on a tray. She may have gone to bed."

"Aye, she might. A tray would be fine."

She had hardly left the room when Mark came in and, purposefully but in a low voice, said, "Dad, Mam's gone into her room. She's crying."

Bill's voice was louder now. "Yes, Mark," he said, "I know your mother's gone into her room cryin'. And I'm cryin' an' all inside. So what does a man do when he's cryin' inside, can you tell me? Now your sister Katie who's grown up . . . *Oh yes, she is.* Don't shake your head like that. She's very much grown up. Her remedy for cryin' is to say you're sorry. What's your remedy?"

It seemed a long moment before Mark said, "Well, you sort of have to arrange things and your life and that so you never have to say you're sorry."

"Oh, my God, boy." Bill gave him one hard slap on the back. "You're goin' to break under the lessons you've got to learn, whereas Katie, she'll ride the waves. But don't worry, for as the sayin' goes, it'll all come out in the wash. Now go and help Katie put out the dinner for us. Tell her I want two trays upstairs, and you give her a hand."

Mark stood where he was and watched Bill stalk from the room, and what he thought was, He's a funny man, really. I don't think he understands Mam.

40

SATURDAY AFTERNOON WAS GREY AND ICY COLD. THE SKY WAS LOW AND HEAVY and the forecast, everyone said, was snow; and yet it was only the end of November.

Bill was driving back home from the outskirts of Durham; he was feeling very pleased with himself: he had, as he thought, killed two birds with one stone. The first was reposing in the glove box. It was Fiona's Christmas box and in it lay, on a velvet pad, a heavy filigree gold necklace with matching earrings. They had been hand wrought by a young artist and, as he put it to himself, had cost him a bomb. But what did it matter as long as they pleased her. The notion had entered his mind when watching her face as she was looking at the picture of some actress attending a gala: Katie, who was sitting beside her, had said, "Look at that necklace she's wearing, Mam. Isn't it beautiful?" and Fiona had murmured, "Yes, indeed; and I bet it was a beautiful price, too." Well, it had been a beautiful price. That young goldsmith was maybe just starting out but he knew his own worth. Still, what odds; he was making money now and he'd make more.

Then there was the house. Twice in the last week he had been over to see it. The first time he had just walked round the garden, all five acres of it. But on Wednesday he had made an appointment with the

436

agent to view the house itself; the people were still in it. And by, as soon as he had stepped into the hall he knew that this was where he wanted to bring Fiona and the family. It wasn't a baronial hall in any sense, quite modern in fact; well, the whole house had been modernised thirty years ago and the man had done a good job on it: the mouldings on the ceilings had been retained, as had the eighteen-inch skirting boards; and all the doors were solid hardwood. But the furnishings, especially the carpets and drapes, were modern and beautiful. The whole house was beautiful. Three of the six bedrooms were en suite. And, too, there was an indoor swimming pool with dressing rooms. My! My! He could see them all there, the whole family, with Sammy Love, too. Aye, Sammy Love, too. It wasn't strange, he was continually telling himself, that that boy's name should pop into his mind: if ever there was a saviour it was Sammy Love.

Roll on Monday. He smiled to himself. Katie was going to lose her bet. He could picture her handing over the five pounds and him taking it and pocketing it, at least for a time. That would teach her a lesson. He loved Katie. He loved them all. But love alone didn't express his feelings for Fiona, adoration was nearer the mark. And he had sworn to himself never to upset her again as he had done the other night. By, she was in a state. And so was he. Oh aye, he was an' all. Funny about cryin': it was more painful when you cried inside; you got relief when you could let the water flow.

Blast it! He had taken the country road off the roundabout. It was that bloody lorry driver. *Maniacs!* Likely the same bloody hit-and-run driver that had finished Mamie's mam and dad and her brother.

Being a country road, he could have turned back, but he kept on although it would put another couple of miles on the journey. Had it been a pleasant day he would have enjoyed this run. The road must have gradually been rising, for it opened onto a stretch of moor. Here it was bordered on one side by a ditch and on the other by a wire fence.

He had travelled about a mile and a half along this stretch before seeing another vehicle, but there, in the far distance was one seeming to be travelling in the same direction. Presently, however, he realised that the car was stationary and was parked half on the road and half towards the fence.

He slowed down, wondering if there were anything wrong, and in such an out-of-the-way place.

There was something very familiar about the car, an elderly Rolls, at least as much of it as he could see, for the bonnet was up and the driver was bending over the engine.

He stopped and, putting his head out of the window, shouted, "Got trouble?"

When the figure straightened up and turned towards him and said, "Yes, you could say that," they both stared at each other for a moment. Then Bill, getting out of the car, walked forward, saying, "You're out of your way this end, aren't you?"

"No; no, I often take this road."

"But Brookley Manor is over there in that direction." He pointed.

"Yes, I know where Brookley Manor is, but I wasn't going to the Manor." Rupert's tone was stiff, and when he looked at his wristwatch Bill said, "Been here long?"

"Oh, about five minutes."

It was obvious that the fella, as Bill termed him, seemed to be on tenterhooks, looking first up the road, then down. "You expectin' help?" he asked.

"No. Where would I get help on this road except from passing motorists."

"Aye." Bill gave a small laugh. "There's that in it. Well, can I be of any help to you? Where do you want to go?"

The younger man now stared at Bill for some moments before he said simply, "Hetherington."

"Hetherington? You ... you mean the hospital?"

"Yes, I mean the hospital, or as some would still call it, the lunatic asylum."

"Aye, well." For a moment Bill seemed taken aback; then he said, "Well now, I should ask why, but I'm not goin' to. Anyway, I would lock her up." He pointed to the car. "And on our way there we should find a garage and ask them to pick her up. But I'd like to bet Sir Charles won't welcome the news that his baby has broken down."

"It won't be the first time; she's getting worse for wear."

"How is he, by the way?"

"He was very well when I put him and Lady Kingdom on the train for Scotland this morning."

"Oh, they've gone to Scotland then?" They were both sitting in Bill's car now and as he started her up he added, "What's takin' them up there at this time of the year? I thought he didn't like the cold."

Rupert didn't enlighten him on this subject, and they drove in silence for some way until they came to a country crossroads, when he said, "If you turn sharp right here it will bring you to the gates. And there's a garage just beyond."

438

"I've never been on this road before. I thought I knew this part very well. You live and learn."

"That is quite true. And when one is living and learning I should like to tell you now that I have no designs on your wife."

The car jerked as if it were going over a grid as his mind said, "That's straight from the shoulder anyway." But the actual words that came out, and in a casual tone, were, "Well, you surprise me. Still, accept that's so, why then your frequent visits?"

"Because I found it pleasant to talk to someone of my own age, and a woman. Sir Charles and Lady Kingdom are the dearest people in the world, but they are of another generation and once again removed. And there isn't what you would call a home life in the Manor, except when the family bring their children; whereas in your home there is a liveliness, and with the added attraction of amusing youngsters like Master Sammy Love."

"If you feel like that then, why haven't you a wife of your own? Why aren't you married?"

"Fiona asked me the same question."

The very fact that the fella was calling his wife by her Christian name and in that voice of his stirred something in his bowels, but he forced himself to say, "What answer did you give her?"

"I told her I would tell her sometime."

"Are you normal, I mean . . . ?"

Even Bill himself had to admit he couldn't have bawled any louder than the fella when he cried, "Yes, I am normal. And yes, I know what you mean."

"You can shout almost as well as me."

"You're an insulting bug-ger, aren't you?"

Bill suddenly wanted to laugh. It was the way he said, bug-ger; it sounded so fancy, it wasn't like bugger at all. "I don't know about being an insultin' bugger; I'm a plain one, I say what I think."

"Well, I think it might pay you in future to think before you speak."

"Now look here!"

"No, you look here, *Mr. Bailey*. I have no need to explain anything to you, but here we are at the hospital and I thank you for the ride. You need not wait for me. There is a garage quite near, I can walk there."

"Just as you like."

He drew up the car outside the high iron gates, and when Rupert got out, Bill watched him walk towards the small wicket gate and speak to a uniformed man standing there, then go towards the window of an office, where he stood for a few moments before striding away up the drive towards the hospital that was out of sight beyond the trees.

He turned the car around, but then drew it along by the side of the high wall and in such a position that he could keep his eye on the gate. Why should this fella be going to Hetherington? Some people called the place a nerve hospital, while others gave it its old name of asylum. But then, why should he be goin' there? Well, in the ordinary way you would have thought he would have gone to Scotland with Sir Charles and Lady Kingdom, 'cos it seemed at times that the old fella couldn't get on without him. Had he a parent in there, a mother or a father, or some relative that he felt responsible for?

He recalled that in the car he kept looking at his wristwatch, and he seemed agitated, so much so that his suave gentlemanly manner had slipped and he had reacted to the pointed questions just as he himself might have done.

He, too, looked at his watch. It was twenty minutes to three. How long would he likely be in there? Well, he would give him an hour. Aye, he would; he would give him an hour. Fiona wouldn't be worrying because he had told her he was going out shopping for Christmas boxes for the bairns before all the shops were sold out.

He switched on the radio, but after a minute or so switched it off.

That fella wasn't so soft and pliable as he looked. But then, soft wasn't the right word, perhaps courteous would be better. Still, courteous or pliable, he could swear. And he smiled to himself as he said aloud, "Bug-ger." Then for him to come out with, "I have no designs on your wife." No beating about the bush there.

But who had he gone in there to see? Someone connected with him or perhaps with the old boy? Aye. Yes, that was a possibility. That's why he had stayed behind, to carry out the visits.

Oh, hell! If he had an hour to spare, surely he could find something better to do than sitting here. By, he could that. It was weeks now since he had given himself a day off; even on Sundays he kept at it.

It would be today, when he hadn't a newspaper or book in the car. Had the kids left anything in the back? He leaned over the back of the seat and groped in the paper rack and pulled out a square hard-backed book and smiled as he looked down on it. It was one of Mamie's, entitled, *Nancy Nutall and the Mongrel*. Where on earth did these writers get their titles? The pictures were nice. Mamie loved this book.

He started to read the little story. It didn't take long, and he found himself amused that the last words of most of the little chapters were: "And Nancy's father sighed again."

Apparently Mr. Nutall was sighing over his daughter because she was in her way demanding a dog and his wife didn't like dogs. . . . He'd have a daughter soon, or a son. Somehow he fancied a daughter. Of course, a son could follow in his footsteps. He could see himself taking him to football matches;—that's if the crowd weren't wearin' steel helmets by then. Well, a cricket match then—but that was getting as bad. He could see himself reflected in the windscreen nodding at himself, and he smiled. This is what happened when you were left on your own, sitting in a car waiting, and you didn't know really why you were waiting, because the fella could have got a taxi quite easily at the garage.

But what if he did have a daughter? Well, as he said, he would call her Angela; and he would watch her growing up into another Katie, but with a difference: she'd be his, his own daughter. Looking back down his family line, he had to admit that they weren't good breeders. His father had been an only child, his mother one of twins and the twin had died. And what he remembered of his grandmother, she'd been a loner, too. Anyway he'd be quite satisfied with one, whatever sex. But being satisfied with one wasn't going to stop him trying again. Oh no. And Fiona, bless her, was more than willing. By, he'd got a prize there; and he meant to hang onto it. And the thought brought him back to the man who had gone up to the hospital.

How long had he been sitting here now? Over half an hour. Well, as he'd said to himself, he would give him an hour.

He switched on the radio again: a sports commentator was yelling his head off over a motorcycle race. He lay back in the seat, pulled his tweed cap over his brow, and prepared to doze, only immediately to pull himself upright again and look out the rear window. That was a daft thing to do, he told himself; the temper that fella was in he could have walked past him and left him sitting high and dry till the cocks crowed.

His watch said he had been sitting fifty minutes when he saw Rupert come out of the gate. And he noted that he neither looked to the right nor to the left but walked with his head down away from him as though making for the garage.

He tooted sharply on the horn, but had to repeat the process three times and start up the car before he saw the fella pause and look towards him.

He now turned the car about and stopped again alongside Rupert, and, leaning over and pushing open the passenger door, he called, and none too gently, "Get in."

441

Rupert did not immediately get into the car, but bending slightly, he said, "You needn't have done this; I could easily get a taxi."

"Get in. I'm bloody well froze. I suppose you know when these are stationary they don't give off heat."

Rupert got into the car. But Bill didn't start up straightaway; he turned and looked at Rupert as he said, "Well, put your seat belt on. If we go out lookin' for an accident you'll go straight through the windscreen."

They had gone about half a mile along the road, and Bill, glancing at his passenger, asked, "You all right?"

"Yes; yes, I'm all right."

The words were said in the usual polite cultured tone; and Bill, ever forthright, said, "Well, you don't look it. Where you makin' for?"

"The Manor. But . . . but drop me in the town; I can get a bus out."

"Who's lookin' after you there?"

"I'm looking after myself. I'm used to it. Anyway, Jessie comes in every day."

"Look, I'm sorry I opened me big mouth." Even as he said it he was wondering why he should be apologising to this fella, because he had to admit he was still furiously jealous of him; what he was and what he stood for he imagined must appeal to Fiona as they were pretty much of the same class.

"Do you mind stopping the car for a moment?"

"What d'you want me to stop the car for? Now look, just sit tight."

"Please. I'm going to vomit."

"Good God!" Bill didn't know whether he spoke the words or just thought them, but he pulled the car up to a jerking halt. And the next minute he watched the fella hanging onto a railing and vomiting onto the grass verge.

He went round the car to him, and as he was wont to do with the lads or Katie or Mamie under such circumstances, he put out his hand and held Rupert's head. And his face twisted into a grimace as the fella heaved as if he would bring his heart up.

When the bout was over he remained by Rupert's side as he leaned against the railings and drew in long slow deep breaths. But when he seemed to be making no move Bill shivered and said, "Come on; get yourself back into the car; it'll freeze you out here." He did not, however, now attempt to assist him, but hurried round the car and took up his seat again, and remained seated quiet for a while; then said, "You often car sick?"

There was a moment's hesitation before Rupert said, "No, I'm never car sick."

442

Again there was silence. And Bill noted that the fella lay back against the head rest and continued to take in the long deep breaths, after which he said, "Take your time; there's no hurry."

The silence hung heavy on him. There was no movement on the road, except for a passing car, and he sat looking straight ahead and down the long length of the road, waiting for the fella to say he was all right. But when he did speak it was to say, "You asked why I never married. Well, the reason is back there. We were going to be married on her twenty-fourth birthday. We had been engaged for two years. We had actually known each other since our schooldays when she had come to stay with the Kingdoms because her people were abroad. There was a distant connection there. Then her parents split up. Her mother remarried and her father was killed in an accident. Her mother was then in America and wanted her to go, but she wouldn't leave me. We seemed to know from the start there was only each other. I had been through University and was interested in industrial design. Sue's stepfather was in big business in the U.S., and he had an opening for me once we were married. It was all set. Then one night we were at a party." He paused and wiped his lips with his handkerchief. "We were leaving early. I went round to get the car. They were chock-a-block and so it was a while before I could bring the car to the front of the house. She wasn't there. The police found her the next morning, in the shrubbery not far away. She had been raped, and hit on the head. Just one blow, apparently just one blow to stop her screaming. She was in a coma for days; and when she came out she screamed, and when she wasn't screaming she just sat perfectly still looking ahead. And she's never spoken since, until today. They generally phone me when the fits are bad because she calms down somewhat when I'm near her. They are chary about giving her too many drugs in case she goes into that long sleep. But today she called my name."

He stopped talking, and for once in his life Bill could find nothing to say, until the silence screamed at him, and then he said, "Well, that's a good sign if she called your name."

"I thought so, too, but the doctor didn't seem very impressed. He said he didn't want me to get my hopes up; it sometimes happened, but it signified little."

"Tactful blokes, doctors. By the way, did they ever find the fella that did it?"

"Oh yes; and he's only got three years to go now."

The way those last words were spoken sent a small shiver through Bill; but he understood the fella's feelings all right; he had felt the

443

same towards those bastards who had tried to do him in, and even more towards the man who had kidnapped Katie.

Rupert turned and said to him, "Now you know why I'm not married and why I continue to carry on in this cissy job, as so-called secretary to Sir Charles."

Again Bill could find nothing to say. He sat back in the seat and looked through the windscreen as he thought: this should be an object lesson to you, lad. Your mother was always saying you never knew what was going on behind the curtains next door. People, himself included, envied those like Sir Charles and Lady Kingdom and this fella here for their position, their money, their houses, probably imagining that those things protected them from the tragedies of life. In fact, now he came to think about it, the tragedies hit them harder than most because they had to put a face on it; people like himself yelled out against injustice, the injustice of tragedy, especially when it was doled out to the innocent like this fella's lass. God, that must have been awful.

Tentatively now, he asked, "Were they long in finding the bloke?"

"No; no, the next day."

"As *quick* as that?"

"Well, it was easy. You see, he was a friend, in fact, our very good friend. He had always fancied Sue. How he had got her to the shrubbery will never be known. It was suggested that he might have said, Come on, let's hide from old Rupert. And she was high-spirited and mischievous. From what came out at the trial he hadn't meant to hit her, that was the last thing on his mind; but when she screamed he was afraid she'd be heard, and when she wouldn't stop screaming he put his hand across her mouth and his other hand, groping, must have come across the piece of wood. They showed it in court. It was only about a foot long but it had dark patches on it. He got ten years and he left the dock crying."

He let out a long sigh as if he was tired, but his voice was still level as he went on, "He wouldn't have got that for rape alone. But the verdict of the specialist was that there was extensive brain damage, and although she had come out of the coma it was doubtful whether she would ever return to normal."

He turned and looked at Bill now. "Love's a funny thing. He had told his solicitor that he loved her and he couldn't bear the thought of me having her. And there we had been for three years, almost like brothers: playing squash together, cricket, tennis; him staying at the Manor, me staying with his family. Oh yes; yes"—he nodded—"he had a warm family. It finished them, too: his father had a heart

444

attack and died three days after the case was closed; his sister and her husband went off to Australia, and the mother's now at a cottage somewhere in Dorset, likely waiting for his return . . . as I am."

Bill put a hand out and gripped Rupert's knee, saying, "Forget that part, lad; but I know how you feel. Retribution is me second name and I know how I've longed to lay me hands on Sir Charles's pet god-daughter, but it's not worth it. Anyway, have you looked ahead? You can't go on like this: you're a young fella an' you need a family. "You've already shown that to me. You must get yourself married."

"I can't do that." Rupert's voice was quite calm now. "I somehow still think she'll come round sufficiently to recognise me, and what would happen then if I had a wife? I know I would leave her, no matter who she was, and go to Sue. You see, our relationship was something rare. We often discussed it. We felt we had been here before because we recognised each other right away when we were very young. And so I have memories, wonderful memories."

"You can't live on memories, lad. Sometime or other they go sour on you. Anyway, let me say now, thanks for tellin' me. And I'm sorry about the big mouth of mine. But you see I'm as jealous as hell of Fiona; but not anymore, where you're concerned." He patted Rupert's knee. "So let's get home."

"No, no. Please drop me."

"Shut up! The matter's closed, except to say this: you're welcome there any time of the day or night; so fasten that seat belt and let's get away. I know a good firm I can ring to pick up the Rolls."

Rupert did not demur: he fastened his seat belt, laid his head back on the rest once again, and did not speak for the rest of the journey.

On entering the house, Bill was saying to him, "Get your coat off," when there was a howl from upstairs that brought their attention to the landing; at the same time the kitchen door opened and Fiona came into the hall, and the commotion on the landing gave her a shield to cover the surprise of seeing whom Bill had brought with him after the fiasco of the other day.

"I'll bash your face in!"

"*Willie!*" Fiona and Bill cried almost simultaneously while looking up the stairs.

"Well, she's torn up my picture, Mam."

"It was a picture of me"—Katie was now slowly descending the stairs, her chin thrust out, battle blazing in her eyes—"and he gave me a big nose."

"No, I didn't! No bigger than it is. And a big mouth an' all."

445

"Come down here, both of you." Bill's voice was not loud now.

"Shan't." This was from Willie, and he was about to turn away when a sound emanating from Bill's mouth shook them all and brought his stepson to a halt, his hand now gripping the top of the bannister.

"*Down!*" Bill thumped the floor three times, crying, "Get down here this minute!"

Katie, now at the foot of the stairs, said, "He's always taking the mickey out of me with his drawings and . . ."

"And you, madam, get into the kitchen and find something to do with your hands instead of using your tongue so much. *Get!*"

After a very surprised look at her hero, Katie departed for the kitchen, but not in a hurry.

Then there was Willie, chin thrust out, too; and when Bill said, "Get into that study. And the next time you say shan't to me, you won't be able to walk there."

Willie hesitated, about to appeal to his mother, but by her look he thought better of it and stamped away. And Bill was himself about to turn to Fiona when another voice piped from the landing, "They've been fighting all afternoon."

"And you, madam, stop tellin' tales and get back to the playroom if you don't want your backside smacked."

"Bill!" Fiona's voice was scarcely above a whisper and he turned to her and said, "And you, madam, shut up!"

Before Fiona could either walk away or retort there was a sound from Rupert that made them both look up the stairs again and to the figure descending.

"Well, well, well." Bill looked at Sammy and Sammy looked at him as, unblinking, he marched down the stairs.

"I didn't know you were here. Where've you been hidin'?"

"I ain't been hidin'." Sammy passed Bill and made his way towards a chair to the right of the door on which his coat and cap were lying.

"Where do you think you're goin'?"

"I'm goin' home."

"Where's your dad?"

"He's at the football match. Where else?"

Bill bit on his lip. "Will he be home for tea?"

"How do I know? Tis Saturday, isn't it?"

"Well, to tell the truth, Sammy Love, I don't know which day it is, it could be whistle-cock-Monday, nor do I know which end of me's up in this house. So don't you add to my confusion, but put that coat

446

down again and get yourself into the kitchen and see if you can be useful and rattle up some tea.... Go on, get!"

Sammy stared at him for a moment, then slowly threw his coat and cap onto the chair, mumbling something as he did so.

"What did you say?"

The small boy turned and looked at the three adults; then his eyes focusing on Fiona, he said, "He does nowt but shout."

"Bill!" She caught at his arm; then, on a half laugh, she said, "He's right. I'm sorry Rupert." She had turned towards him, but before he could answer, Bill said, "Oh, don't be sorry for him; he wants a noisy family. Look, get yourself in there and sit down, and take him along with you."

In amazement, Fiona looked from the one to the other and was surprised to see a quiet smile on Rupert's face, especially when he said, "You'd better do what you're told."

But before making a move to do what she was told she said to Bill, "And what are you going to do?"

"I'm going into the kitchen to sort that lot out and get us some tea. We're both froze; it's cold outside you know."

Bill now stamped towards the kitchen, and Fiona walked into the sitting room followed by Rupert. But she had hardly entered the room before she turned to him and said, "I'm all at sea. What's happening? He was civil to you."

"Oh, it's a long story, one for a winter's afternoon. And it's already been told. I'll leave it to Bill to relate to you, perhaps when you're tucked up in bed tonight."

She sat on the couch; and when he sat down beside her and took her hand she glanced over the back towards the door; and when he said, "It's all right. It's all right; he won't mind," she stretched her face, her eyes wide, and said, "No? Well, life is full of surprises."

"Yes, isn't it," he said, "and some are nice."

Bill did tell her the story when they were in bed tucked up together. And when he finished she was near to tears and she said, "Poor soul. Oh, poor soul."

"Now don't get too sorry for him," he said, "he's not goin' to fall for you, and you'd better not start fallin' for him because you know what I once promised you if you ever turned your eyes away from my direction—and I meant it, I wasn't jokin'—I'd murder you both."

"Oh, Bill! You do say such frightful things. But I'm glad you won't mind him coming here, for I sensed he was lost in some way. We'll have him for Christmas, eh?"

447

"Aye. Well, yes, that's an idea. . . . What is it? Got a pain?" He took his arms from around her and pulled himself up on an elbow, and she flapped her hand at him, saying, "No, not really, no; just he, she, it, is jumping about a bit. Been doing it all day."

"Oh, woman." He drew in a long breath. "I wish it was over; me nerves are in a frazzle; in fact, you've got all our nerves in a frazzle. That's what's the matter with the kids: they're all waitin'; they're tired of waitin'; their tempers are all on edge. And it's true, you know. You know what Willie said to me tonight when I was goin' for him? He started to bubble and he said, 'I'm frightened.' And when I said, 'What are you frightened about?' he said, ' 'Cos Mam's going into the hospital and she mightn't come out.' 'Don't be daft,' I said. 'She's just goin' to have a baby. They all come out after havin' babies.' And he said, 'Do they?' and when I said, 'Aye, yes of course,' he said, 'I hope it isn't a girl. I couldn't stand another Katie and another Mamie. Girls are awful.' Then he ended up by sayin', 'Sorry I cheeked you, Dad.' " He sniffed; then laughed. "That got me. That got me. He's a nice kid is Willie. They're all nice kids. I love 'em, but I've got to say it"—he laid his hand gently on her stomach—"this 'un'll be really mine. Can you understand that and how I feel about it?"

"Yes, dear, I can understand that perfectly," she said.

41

BILL WAS IN THE OFFICE CABIN GOING OVER A PILE OF INVOICES WITH HIS accountant, Arthur Milburn, when a rap came on the door.

"Right!" he called, without lifting his head; and when a man entered and approached the desk, Bill sat back in his chair and looked at his works manager in enquiry, saying, "Yes, what is it now? I can tell by your face it isn't pleasant."

Peter Honnington said, "No, it isn't very pleasant. There's been a bit of fracas on the Community Hall site with that big Irishman and one of the new fellas."

"You mean Love?"

"Yes, that's who I mean."

"What's he done?"

"He's knocked a fella about. Had to get an ambulance."

"God! How did that happen? Why did you have to get an ambulance?"

"Because the fella needed an ambulance; he couldn't get up and he was bleedin' heavily from the nose."

"How did it happen? I mean, what started it?"

"As far as I can gather the man, Potter, referred to Love's nationality in a derogatory way."

Bill stared at Honnington. Honnington's attitude stuck in his neck

449

at times, particularly his pedantic way of speaking. He was good at his job, but when that was said, all was said.

"Was it really necessary to get an ambulance?" he asked. "Simms does first aid and there's everything that's needed in the hut."

"The man was almost unconscious, and I may as well tell you the police came on the heels of the ambulance."

Bill rose from his chair. "Have they taken Love?"

"No, they questioned him. It will all depend if Potter presses the charge. Anyway, I've wanted to speak about this fellow Love for some time. In my opinion he's not the right man to be in charge of others. There's too much—" he paused here before he added, "merriment goes on."

"What have you got against merriment? As long as it doesn't interfere with the work. . . . Has it in this case?"

Honnington pursed his lips. "Not noticeably," he admitted, "but his gang don't seem to have any respect for him. What I mean is . . ."

"Oh, my God!" Bill turned his head away. "Which century do you think we're in, man? The whole lot of them have hardly got any respect for me that's noticeable. In my opinion a happy gang works better, and if they're happy they'll joke."

"Well, that's your opinion, sir."

"Aye, it is."

"What are you goin' to do about him then . . . Love?"

"Nowt. Why should I? Except have a word with him. If the police have come on the job, they'll have plenty to say to him."

"In my opinion I don't think he's the man for the job."

"Don't you? Well, we differ on that point an' all. Anyway, send him along an' we'll hear his side of it. And he'll have a side, I know that."

"Oh, yes; yes, he'll have a side." Honnington turned and went out; and Arthur Milburn, looking at Bill, said, "I don't like that fella, never have. And I think that's the opinion on the site. But there's one thing about him, and it's in his favour, he's straight. So far there's been no backhanders to the contractors that I know of, and so, of course, he's not liked in that quarter either." He smiled. "A man can't have it all ways, can he? Now back to the pounds, shillings, and pence."

But Bill couldn't put his mind wholly to the pounds, shillings, and pence, because he was thinking that if that fella was sent along the line again to Durham it would do something to him. The bloody fool. It was to be hoped the other fella wasn't badly hurt.

It was not ten minutes later when a rap came on the door and

Davey entered and, going straight to the desk, he got the first one in by saying, "I know, boss, I know. I know every word that's gonna come out of yer mouth, an' the first one is, you're a bloody fool, Love, you're a bloody fool. But I don't feel so in this case, boss. No, begod, I don't. When I give you the rights of it you'll likely see me side."

When he paused Bill said, "All right, go ahead and give me the rights of it."

Davey cast a glance at Arthur Milburn, then nodded at him and, looking back at Bill, he said, "That bloke's been a trouble since you set him on, boss. The artful dodger he's known by. Boss, me crew had been a happy lot till Jack Potter was put among 'em. I'm tellin' you, boss, he's the kind of bloke that starts riots. Ireland is dotted with 'em: they're against everybody else's God but their own. And against Parliament, works managers, an' people who go abroad for their holidays. That's the kind of bloke he is. So you can guess, boss, what he thought of me. And he showed it. Oh aye, begod, he showed it. But I put up with it. Every day for the past week I've put up with it, since Jim Ridley went sick an' you put this one in his place. But to come to the point. Just an hour gone I asked him, and I did it, boss, as you told the lot of us who's in charge of gangs, ask first, and if that doesn't work, then tell 'em. Well, I asked first. 'Take those four-be-two's down to Roger,' I said. Roger was workin' in a little room at the end, puttin' the floor in. If I'd asked the fella to climb up to the roof I could have understood it when he lifted one plank an' put it on his shoulder an' went to walk off. 'What you playin' at?' I said next. 'There's two more there on the floor beggin' to be lifted at one an' the same time.' He stopped now and lifted another, then said, 'It's me back.'

" 'Aye,' said I, 'we've all got backs, an' they ache. But you tell yours yer goin' to give it another plank an' see what it says.' Well, boss, he lifted up the other plank and he muttered somethin'. And I guessed it wasn't in me favour, boss. So I said to him, 'What was that you were after mutterin'?' And at that, you know what happened?"

Bill made a slight movement with his head, as did Arthur Milburn; and Davey, nodding from one to the other, said, "He threw the three bloody planks at me. They scraped me shins. Look!"

He stepped back from the desk, pulled up his trouser leg, pushed down his sock, and there, indeed, Bill could see that the planks had scraped his legs and drawn blood for quite a long way down from below his knee.

Davey now said, "I nearly fell on me arse; an' you can guess, boss, I let out an oath or two. Then there he was, standin' yellin' at me. And you know, boss, I'm quite used to people pointin' out me nationality—

451

well me tongue gives me away—and I can laugh with 'em that chip me, but not this time, boss. You know what he said to me? He said, 'You thick pig ignorant Irish Paddy.' That's what he called me. Then he went on to mention how the muck of the sty was runnin' out of me ears. God in heaven! I could stand no more. An' I heard no more, 'cos I went in at him hell for leather. I only had the chance to hit him three times for the lads got me off him. Then Mr. Honnington came on the scene. An' there's a man who has no love for me either—we don't speak the same language. No, begod, we don't, 'cos that man's so unbendin' you would think he has a poker up his . . ."

"All right. All right." As Bill raised his hand to check further description of where the poker might be, because he had heard it all before, he said, "Have you thought what'll happen if that fella makes a case of it?"

"Aye, boss. Aye." Davey turned sideways and looked towards the floor; then jerking his head up again, he said, "But I couldn't do anythin' else, boss; 'twas more than flesh an' blood could stand. It didn't take very long, though, after I saw him lyin' there for me to know that they'll throw the book at me. Aye, begod! Second time for actual bodily harm, they'll throw the book at me all right. An' I'd like to bet they'll not take into account that the two blokes that are inside now doin' their time are only there 'cos I collared the first one, will they?"

"I don't know about that, but they might remember, Davey, that you knocked him about an' all."

"Aye, well, he didn't miss me either, did he now? I was in a bit of a mess meself, wasn't I now?"

"But you're not this time, Davey, are you?"

"No." Again Davey looked towards the floor. "No," he said, shaking his head, "but, boss, nobody's goin' to get me to say I'm sorry for what I did. The only thing I'm sorry for—" and he now looked up at Bill again as he repeated, "the only one thing I'm sorry for is the effect this is gonna have on the lad: if I go along the line for however long or short a time, what'll happen to him?"

"I don't think you need worry about that part of it, at least what'll happen to him physically; it's what'll happen to him in his mind concernin' you. You should think about that, you big galoot." Bill's voice had risen; and now leaning across the table and his hands splayed out flat on it, he stared up into Davey's distressed countenance as he repeated, "You never stop to think."

For a moment Davey didn't say anything; then he said, "Can I ask you a straight question, boss?"

"Yes, go ahead."

"If some bloke called you a big-mouthed Scouse, would you stand an' say, thank you very much?"

Bill sat back in his chair. He had something there. If anybody had used that term on him he knew that his reaction would have been just the same as the Irishman's. "What I would do is not in question," he said. "Perhaps I would have the sense to remember I had a wife and family to see to. You know, although you care for the lad you seem to forget your responsibility at times. Now, go on. I'll send somebody to hospital to see how the fella's gettin' on. On your way, call in at E block and tell Bert Ormesby I'd like to see him for a minute."

Davey didn't move, but he said, "One last thing, boss. What'll happen if they come an' pick me up? I mean, about the lad. He won't go to his granny's on his own. He hasn't any feelin' for her nor her for him. But somebody'll have to take him an' tell her she'll have to put up with him."

"You needn't worry on that score; he can pig in with Willie if it should be necessary. He'll be all right."

"Aye, boss. Thanks. Aye, thanks."

When the door closed on Davey, Arthur Milburn looked at Bill and, smiling, said, "It's funny; even when that fella's in trouble you still want to laugh at him. He's got that way about him."

But Bill was in no mood to concur. "He's a bloody fool," he said. "And I've got enough on me mind at this moment without worryin' about him and his troubles."

He now picked up the phone, and when the voice on the other end answered he said, "You all right, dear?"

"Oh yes. Yes, Bill."

"Sure?"

"Sure."

"No sign of it?"

"Not a murmur."

He heard Fiona laugh before saying further, "If it doesn't start today Katie's lost her five pounds."

"Oh aye. And mind, I'll take it. I'll tell her I'm not goin' to wait until she gets it out of the Bank, so you loan it to her and we'll just watch her face when she hands it over, eh?"

"Oh yes; and she'll shed blood because she's been saving for as long as I remember."

"Love."

"Yes, Bill?"

"If . . . if there's any sign at all you'll give me a ring?"

453

"Please, please don't worry. Of course I will. You know I will. But the way I'm feeling I could go days." Then, her voice changing, she said, "But I hope I don't; it's getting so heavy my legs are giving way. What would you say if they were all wrong and it's triplets?"

"Three hurrah's."

"I had a card from Mother. It came just after you left. She had a wonderful journey; America is wonderful: the people are wonderful; she feels wonderful. I'm still very puzzled in that direction."

"You're not the only one. I'll be home early."

"You will?"

"Definitely. Just after five."

"Good. Good-bye, dear."

"Good-bye, love."

"No sign of it yet?"

Bill shook his head in answer to Arthur Milburn, saying, "She can't go on much longer; and she's tired. And so am I. I want this bairn badly, Arthur, but I don't think I could go through it again. I'm sure I couldn't." And when Arthur Milburn burst out laughing, he said, "You can laugh; it'll be your turn someday."

"Not if I know it . . . not if I know it."

"I said that once. Funny how circumstances make you change your mind. Aye." He picked up his pen again. How circumstances make one change one's mind. He knew all about that.

The family were together in the sitting room, Katie holding centre stage. She had just handed Bill five pounds and, as he sat looking at it on the palm of his hand, his face expressing surprise, Fiona put in quickly, "Where did you get that, Katie?"

"From my bank."

"But when?"

"When I was out on Saturday."

"But . . . but I could have had the baby on Saturday, or yesterday, or even today."

"I knew you wouldn't."

"The oracle has spoken."

"You shut up, our Mark."

"Well, well!" Bill's voice brought Katie's attention from Mark. "What made you so sure, hinny?"

"I don't know. I just felt . . . well, if the baby came, well and good, but if it didn't I wanted to have it ready, because I knew if I didn't . . . well, I mean have the money ready, Mam would offer to lend it to me supposedly and I would hand it to you; then at a convenient time you would hand it back. I didn't want that."

454

"You didn't want me to hand it back?"

"No, I didn't; I'd . . . I'd made a bet and I wanted to stand by it. It was a matter of . . . well—" She jerked her head to the side, and when Mark put in, "Ethics?" she glanced quickly at him and said, "Yes, I suppose that's as good a word as any, but not what I meant."

Fiona and Bill exchanged glances and Fiona thought, She's too young to think this way, too young to act like this; she'll be old before her time; while Bill thought, If the one that's coming is a girl and is a patch on her, she'll do. Suddenly he put his arms out and jerked Katie into them, and when he kissed her she put her arms around his neck and leaned against him for a moment, until Willie's voice brought her on the attack again as he said, "Scene one-oh-one, retake, retake."

"I will! I promise you I'll slap your face right and left."

"Katie! And you, Willie." Fiona drew in a long breath, then went on, "I might as well tell you I'm getting very tired of your wrangling. At this moment I'm tired in all ways, but more so by the fact that you two are forever at each other's throats. What's the matter with you?" She was looking at Willie, and his answer was, "Well, she must always be front of the picture. She's a know-all."

"And you're a numskull and you'll never be at the front of the picture."

"Right!" Bill's voice was not loud. "I've heard enough and I'm ashamed of you both. Yes, I am at this minute, I'm ashamed of you both. There's your Mam not knowin' where to put herself 'cos the waitin's gettin' her down, but what do you two do? Instead of being a comfort to her or tryin' to help you're goin' on like two gutter snipes. That's what you are, two gutter snipes." He now pointed at Willie. "Give Sammy Love the chance to be in your place and he wouldn't be actin' like you, I can tell you that. As for you, miss"—he was now pointing at the girl he had held closely to him but a moment ago—"there's two sides to you, and there's one of them I don't like. Now get yourselves away out of my sight and out of your mother's sight."

"Bill"—there was an appeal in Fiona's voice—"let them be. They're on edge like me, like us all. Come here." She held out her hands widely, and after a moment's hesitation they both walked towards her and she put her arms around them and looked from one to the other as she said, "How can I go into hospital and feel at peace knowing that you two are likely to keep this up. Now I want you both to promise you'll call a truce, at least until I come back. Now, now, don't you dare say it's her." And then turning towards Katie, she said, "And don't you dare say it's him. It's both of you; and you've got

455

Mamie at it, too, because she takes her pattern from all you older ones."

Then endeavouring to lighten the situation, Mark went up to Bill and said, "I want to be loved an' all," and pulled a face, but the answer he got was, "You'll be loved, me boy, with a kick up the backside, and it'll be so hard that me boot'll knock your teeth out."

At this, surprisingly, Willie started to laugh and he turned his face into his mother's shoulder; Fiona, too, laughed, and Katie gave a wriggle.

"There's somebody in the hall." Mark was hurrying towards the door when it opened and Nell entered.

"What's the matter? I thought you had gone home ages ago."

"Of course I went home ages ago, but now I'm back; and so is Bert. He's in the kitchen with Sammy."

With outstretched arm, Nell staved off Willie's dart for the door, saying, "Stay! Stop! Remain where you are; all those three at once, Master William. This is your dad's business now. Anyway, what are you all down here for?" She looked about. "You should be upstairs. As for you"—she pointed to Fiona—"why aren't you in bed?"

"I'm just about to go, Mrs. Bossy Boots. But first of all I'm going into the kitchen." She hung on to Bill's arm and he helped her up from the couch. Then, looking at the four children, she said softly, "Stay where you are now. We'll come back and tell you what's happening."

"You'll do nothing of the sort; you'll go straight upstairs following your kitchen visit, and I'll stay here and put this inquisitive lot in the picture."

Bill had scarcely pushed open the kitchen door to let Fiona enter when Sammy's voice hit them both, saying, "I'm not going to me granny's; I can stay by meself in our house. I'm used to stayin' by meself. If you send me to me granny's I'll only come back. Tis a waste of time."

"Sit down. Sit down. Well, what's the latest, Bert?"

"Well, boss, the fella must have pressed the charge. I told you I thought he was puttin' it on a bit. All right, his nose was broken and his lip's split but it would take more than a couple of punches to put a fella like him into shock. That's what the nurse said. I told you. I sort of put it to him when I saw him that Davey was sorry and that if he let the matter drop he wouldn't lose by it. But no. He's always appeared a spiteful individual since he first came on the job. Had a lot to say in the mess cabin, and by what I hear he's been in and out of more jobs than all the fellas put together. Anyway, Davey got

456

word to me after tea. It was through one of the policemen. He brought Sammy along to ask if I would take him to his granny's. And the police heard what Master Samuel"—he wagged his finger at the small boy—"thinks about his granny. And when he emphasised the fact that he could stay alone, the police wasn't having that. And so I said Nell and I would see to him. But he wasn't for staying with us either. So . . . well, boss, I thought I'd better come along and see if you had any ideas."

"I'm not askin' to stay here, I'm not; I can stay by meself. I did it all the time." The boy suddenly swung round and went towards the sink, yelling now, "Bloody people! If they put me dad in prison I'll kick all the buggers to hell. . . . I will! I will!"

"Here, here! Enough of that!" Bill had swung him up now and through the air and planted him with a none too gentle plop on the chair. "I thought you had left that language behind you. Goin' to a private school and comin' out with . . ." He stopped at a signal from Fiona and, following her pointing finger, he noted now that tears were running down the face of the drooping head. And she addressed Bert in an overloud voice, saying, "There'll be no need for Sammy to stay alone in his own house, Bert; he has stayed here with Willie before and he may stay again as long as he likes. Come on, Sammy." She held out a hand towards him, but apparently he didn't see it. So she slowly stooped and picked up one of his from where it was hanging between his knees, and she led him, still with his head bowed, from the room.

"We'll have to go and bail him out," Bill said to Bert.

"Well, it's no use tonight, boss. I said those very words to the police and he said nothing could be done until tomorrow morning when he'll be coming up before the magistrate. And he said a funny thing. He said that you'll be able to get him out if he pleads guilty, but if he pleads not guilty he'll go back inside and have to wait on his case coming up."

"No!"

"Aye. That's apparently what the system is. Guilty and you're let out on bail, not guilty and you're kept in. Seems daft. But those are the very words the police said."

"Did he say what time or give you any idea when he'll come up?"

"Well, I understand they start at ten."

Bill sighed. "I'll be there then if it's possible. But what if something happens in the night"—he thumbed towards the ceiling—"in that case, you'll have to go and stand bail for him. Whatever the amount is, put your name to it and I'll see to it. Anyway, Davey wouldn't scarper, at least I don't think so. But what I do know is, he's dead scared of Durham, and that being so, I don't understand why he doesn't control his bloody temper. Come on, let's go in and see how things are goin'. Talkin' of tempers, they've been flyin' here the night, too. Master Willie's been on his high horse, so Mr. Samuel Love's presence may do something to fetch him off it. Funny that. Talk about opposites clickin'; if ever there were two opposites they are it."

What was he talking about, opposites clicking; if there were ever two opposites like Willie's mother and himself, they were it, too. There was a lot to be said for opposites getting together.

Davey's case came up at eleven o'clock on the Tuesday morning. He pleaded guilty and was bailed on the assurance of five hundred pounds. The surety was one William Bailey.

A weak sun was shining when they came out of the court; and they walked along the street, neither of them speaking. And then Davey said, "I never thought meself to be worth five hundred quid, boss. But I can assure you of one thing: you won't lose your money; I won't scarper. Even if I hadn't a youngster to see to I wouldn't scarper. But, by God, I was sick to the bottom of me bowels in that cell last night. And I might as well tell you I've got a dread on me that's weighin' me down: just the thought of Durham turns me into a jelly, boss. It does. It does."

"You're a bloody fool. You know that?"

"Aye, boss, I know that. But it's a way a man's built. I said afore, put yourself in my place on that day. I'm unlucky, that's me. I'm an unlucky sod. Here I am, fair set, a good steady job, a house that I never dreamt of, me kid at a private school. Eeh, my, that alone should make me think twice. But no, out goes me bloody fist. But why the eighth of January before the case comes up? Why couldn't they do it next week and I'd be out of me misery? I'd know one way or t'other."

"Thank your stars you've got a little time to clear your head and get yourself a lawyer."

"A lawyer?"

"That's what I said, a lawyer; for what d'you think you're goin' to do? Talk to a judge and jury yourself?"

"Aye, I could, and do it better than some of those fellas."

"So you think. But it's a lawyer you want, and we'll have to look around."

"Is he still in hospital, the bloke?"

"No; as far as I can gather he came out this morning."

"Well, I suppose I could say, thanks be to God for small mercies. But there's part of me says now that since I have to suffer for it I wish I'd made it a three-week job. There's another thing, this'll likely have queered me pitch with Jinny. You know you told me to try me hand, well I did, and she had promised to do a show with me next week in Newcastle, a pantomime thing."

"Well, this'll test her. Look at it that way: if she can't stand by you in this then to my mind she's not for you."

"Ah, well, time'll tell, boss. But I want to say thanks for taking the boy in last night. I told him if anything should happen to go to his granny's an' not to bother you; and when I did he told me flatly he wasn't goin' there. Bairns should love their grannies, shouldn't they? And grannies should love their bairns. But still, I never loved me ma nor she me, so what can I expect. God Almighty! It's a funny life."

"Well, it's got to be lived; and so you get home and change and get back on the job."

"I'll do that, boss, an' thanks for all you've done an' that comes from the bottom of me heart. It does that, the bottom of me heart."

"You and your bloody barmy Irish tongue. Go on, get yourself off."

Bill had hardly drawn the car to a stop outside his office when Peter Honnington hurried towards him, saying, "Don't get out. Someone rang from your house about ten minutes ago. Your wife's in need of you."

His stomach turned over; and yet, even as he turned the car around, he thought, of course Honnington wouldn't say she's started, or the bairn's comin'. Oh, what odds. This was it. This was it. Damn the red lights! It was always the way, when you hit one you hit half a dozen. *Come on. Come on. Come on.* How long would she be in labour? A few hours? Some of them took a few days. Oh, my God! That would drive him mad. Not a few days; he'd had enough waitin'. But the time had come. The excitement lifted him off the seat for a moment and he cried at himself, "Well, get goin'! It's amber."

He hadn't known what to expect when he arrived at the house. Perhaps Fiona would have been sitting in the hall, her cases ready. Instead, there was Nell, asking, "How did it go with Davey?"

"Never mind, how did it go with Davey? Where is she? Why isn't she here? I mean, she should be on her way."

"Well, if she has wings she would fly, but even so she wouldn't fly until she thought it was time. She's in the sitting room. And don't barge in, Bill Bailey, walk. It'll come in its own time."

"Have you phoned the hospital, woman?"

"Yes, the hospital has been informed, sir. Your wife is all ready and waiting and she is quite calm. And don't you disturb it." The last was a hoarse whisper, and now he whispered back at her, "One of these days I'll tell you what I think about you."

"That'll be nice."

"Oh, hello, dear," said Fiona. "You haven't been long."

"Has it started? The pains?"

"Oh yes, yes. Now for goodness sake, Bill, take that look off your face. Thousands of babies are born every day. I bet you there's a hundred women in this town this very minute waiting for the next spasm."

"For God's sake! Fiona, don't take that attitude. You know how I feel."

"Yes; yes, I do, dear. Come and sit down."

"But shouldn't you be on your way?"

"Yes, and I'll go in a minute; I just want to time its next effort."

She hadn't long to wait. The next moment she was gripping his hand, her nails digging into his flesh.

Nell came into the room dressed for the road and carrying Fiona's coat, a fur hat, and a scarf.

"Get her into these," she said, handing the coat to Bill; then together they helped her up from the couch.

When she was dressed and about to leave the room, Fiona turned at the door and looked around her, and she said, "I like this room. I've always liked it."

Bill made an impatient sound in his throat but kept his tongue quiet.

In the car, Fiona turned to say to Nell, who was sitting in the backseat, "You did lock the front door?"

"Yes; yes, I did."

"And bolted the back?"

Nell sighed and said, "Yes, and I bolted the back, and I put the bars up at the windows!"

"Oh, that reminds me." Fiona looked at Bill now and asked, "How did Davey come on?" But she didn't quite hear his answer for she was once again seized by a grinding pain.

When it had passed she sat back gasping, and Bill said, "You should have got to hospital before all this started."

"You don't go to hospital before this starts. If you do they send you back."

"Well, there's one thing sure," said Nell now, "it's taken its time in coming but now its made up its mind it'll be here before you know where you are."

* * *

It appeared that Fiona's baby was indeed galloping, but obviously not in the right direction, for it was still galloping at four o'clock in the afternoon. And it was then the decision was taken that the child must be brought out. Bill was alone in the waiting room. He had a white coat over his suit. They had made him put it on hours ago, or was it years? Was this still Tuesday? Was it only twelve o'clock when he had held her hand and talked to her? How many times since had they pressed him aside, then let him go back to her? But now she was in the theatre.

He had wanted to see his child born, but an hour ago he didn't know whether he would be able to stand it or not: as he had watched her tortured body heaving, heave after heave, he swore that never again would he put her through this. Never. Never.

And now she was down there and they would have to cut her open to take the child away. It wasn't worth it. It wasn't worth it. He had longed for a child, craved for a child; every day that she had been carrying it he had thought about it. When she was asleep at night he had put his hands on her stomach and counted its heartbeats, the heartbeats that were part of him, all of him.

When the door opened he jumped round as if he was startled. The nurse came in: her face looked quiet, and so was her voice as she said, "Your wife's back, Mr. Bailey. And . . . and you have a daughter."

He gulped twice but still he couldn't speak. The nurse now said, "Dr. . . . Dr. Wells would like a word with you."

"How . . . how is she? My wife?"

"She's all right; she's asleep."

"And . . . and the baby?"

The nurse seemed to hesitate a moment before she said, "Yes, it is all right." Then she repeated quickly, "Dr. Wells would like to have a word with you. He's in his office. Would you come this way?"

There was a spring in his step as he followed her into the corridor, down it, along another one; then she was tapping on the door, and when they were bidden to enter she stepped aside and allowed Bill to pass her. Then she closed the door again.

Dr. Wells was a young man . . . well, youngish, not yet forty, Bill would have said.

"Sit down, Mr. Bailey," he said.

Bill sat down and looked across the desk into the fresh-coloured face and waited for he knew not what, only that he should now be standing at Fiona's side holding his child. He forced himself to say, "You . . . you seem to have something to tell me?"

461

"Yes; yes, I have, Mr. Bailey, unfortunately."

My God! My God! What is it? What's he going to tell me? He burst out, "Fiona! She's not?"

"No, no, no. Your wife is quite all right. Very tired, naturally, but quite all right."

"The child, it's not quite all right. Is that it?"

"Healthwise—yes, I should say it is perfectly all right; but . . . well, have you heard of Down's syndrome, Mr. Bailey?"

"Down's what?"

"Down's syndrome?"

"No; no, I can't say I have."

"Well, I'd better put it another way. I suppose you have seen what is commonly known as a Mongol child?"

His chair scraped back on the parquet floor, but he sat perfectly still for what seemed a long, long time. Then he saw his hands go out and grip the edge of the desk; he saw the knuckles whiten as if he were standing outside himself; he saw his head slowly move forward as if it were going to drop off his body while his real self was standing apart yelling, "God Almighty! No! No!" But the man sitting in the chair said, in an oddly quiet voice, "And my daughter is a . . ." Even his outside self had to help him to press the word through his lips, "Mongol?"

The doctor answered, "It is hard to take at first, but I want you to believe it's no fault of yours or your wife's. This child happens in numerous families. But I can tell you this, in nine cases out of ten, they bring happiness because they exude happiness and love and laughter. Of course, it is natural that the first reaction of the parent should be one of shock, even anger, perhaps shame, particularly on the father's side, but from my experience in such cases this turns into a feeling of protectiveness and love. I go as far as to say that these children are born with special love, some kind of gift bestowed on them by the gods."

The anger against this placid individual, this doctor, was rising in him, threatening to choke him. A special gift from the gods. He glowered at the man, but the doctor was looking down onto the blotting pad and seemed to be tracing his finger in a sort of circle. What the hell did he know? A gift from the gods!

He was on his feet glaring down on the doctor and grinding out through his teeth, "Stop that bloody prattle, for God's sake! You've just told me that my wife has given birth to a Mongol, mentally deficient child into the bargain, and you sit there prattling about gifts of love. What d'you know?"

462

The doctor, too, was now on his feet and facing him, and his tone matched Bill's own as he said, "I know, Mr. Bailey, because I am the father of a five-year-old Mongol child."

As Bill stared into the man's face he had a queer feeling that his body was shrinking, as if the fat was suddenly being stripped off it. His head was drooping on his shoulders. He knew he was going to cry and he screamed at himself, "Hell's flames! Hell's flames! Not that," when a voice penetrated through his whirling thoughts, saying quietly, "Come along and see her."

He walked out into the corridor and returned along it, and as he did so he knew he'd never again be the same man who had come down this corridor a few minutes ago.

There were only three babies in the nursery. Two had tubes attached to them; the third one was lying on its side, and a nurse was standing looking down into the cot. She moved away when the doctor approached, and he now turned to Bill and said, "Lift her up."

Bill looked down at the child. The side of its face looked rounded like any ordinary child's face. But he couldn't put his hands out towards it. He muttered thickly, "I'm . . . I'm not used to babies. I haven't held one."

The doctor now stooped over the cot and lifted the child up; then held it out to Bill, saying, "It's a simple process. It just lies across your hands."

He lifted his arms—it seemed there were weights on them—then he was looking down into his daughter's face, seeing it for the first time. Its eyes were open, its lids were blinking, it looked like a Chinese baby might, or Japanese. The small fist opened and shut; then its arm lifted upwards as if it was trying to reach his chin. This was his daughter. This was what he had longed for, lived for over the past months. Never a day, never a night had passed but his mind had conjured up the picture of when the time would come and he would hold his child. And now the time had come and he was holding his child; and it was an idiot.

No! No! No! Not that! It wouldn't be. No! He recalled his school-days. There had been a boy in his class who looked like a Mongol, but he had been bright; and he had grown up to be a man. But this child would grow up to be a woman, who should have been as beautiful as her mother. Oh, God! Poor Fiona! How would she take it? What if she didn't take it? What if she couldn't bear it?

"She is perfectly made." The doctor was taking the child from his arms. "She is very like my Nanette was, very much the same."

The nurse stepped towards the cot, and now he was following the

463

doctor out into the corridor again and he was talking quietly, "Your wife is in a side ward. We'll keep her there until she goes home. She needn't be more than two or three days here; she'll face up to it better at home. You have a family?"

"What? Oh yes; yes, four."

"Oh, that's good. We have two others. One older and one younger than Nanette."

Bill paused in his step. "Younger? Your wife had a child after?"

"Oh yes, yes. The other two are very ordinary."

"They . . . they accepted the other one?"

"Oh yes; they love her. And she's quite bright. She didn't walk until she was about three, nor really talk until then, but she's never stopped since." He smiled widely now, adding, "You'll be surprised at the difference she'll make in your home."

By God, yes. He'd be surprised all right.

He stopped abruptly and, facing the doctor again, he said, "About . . . about the mind, I mean the mentality?"

"That differs. Here and there you might find one that is exceptionally bright in some special way; but in the main we find the mental age stays around six or seven or so. Yet ask yourself what that really means; or better still, talk to a seven-year-old today: they're thinking clearer than many so-called normal adults."

The doctor kept talking until he pushed open the side ward door where a nurse was writing on a chart, and after she had clipped it onto the bottom of the bed she moved back as they both approached.

As Bill stood gazing down at Fiona, whose face looked very red and sweating, he cried at her voicelessly, I'm sorry, lass. I'm sorry, for at this moment he was feeling that he was to blame for giving her the child. She could have done without it. She had three of her own and an adopted one, but she knew how he felt and so she had given him a daughter, and her name was to be Angela. It was a farce. Oh, God! It was a farce. Yet that man standing at the other side of the bed had experienced the same thing. Still, that fact didn't help him, not one jot; such pain was a private thing, it couldn't be shared. No one else's antidote could act as a salve on it.

The doctor was saying, "She'll sleep for some hours yet. I would go home if I were you."

"I would rather stay till she wakes if it's all the same. I . . . I won't be in the way?"

"Oh, you won't be in the way. I was just thinking, you might, well, want to tell the family. You could come back later."

"Aye, perhaps. But . . . but could I stay the night with her?"

464

"Yes; yes, of course. I don't see why not. Nurse here"—he turned and smiled at the nurse—"will provide you with an easy chair, or the night staff will see to you."

"How . . . how long will it be before she wakes? I'd like to be here when she comes to. . . . You understand?"

"Yes, I understand. Well now"—he looked at his watch—"give her another two hours and a half; she should be round by then. You live in the town, don't you?"

"Yes."

"Well, that's what I should do: take a run home."

He wanted to put his hand out and touch Fiona's brow, but he resisted and, turning abruptly from the bed, he nodded at the doctor, saying, "Thank you. I'll . . . I'll likely see you later." And with that he went out, and drove home.

As soon as he got in the door they rushed at him like a small avalanche; and behind them stood Nell and Bert.

"Has it come?"

"How's Mam?"

"What is it?"

"Has it really come?"

"When will we be able to go to hospital?"

"Dad! Dad! Tell us."

He waved his hand around them, then said, "Be quiet a minute. Let me get in." Then he forced himself to say, "The baby's come; it's a girl. Your mother's all right. She had to have an operation, and now she's asleep. Now get yourselves away for a minute; I want a bath."

And Nell said, "And a meal."

"No, just a cup of tea, Nell; but I do need a bath. I'm going back."

Nell stared at him, as did Bert. They watched him throw his overcoat, scarf, and hat onto a chair. Then she cried at the children, "Go on! Do as your dad says. He'll tell you all about it when he has a minute to himself. Go on now, up in the playroom. That's good kids."

Slowly they obeyed her; that is, with the exception of Mark, and he, following quickly after Bill who was moving towards the sitting room, touched his arm, saying, "Mam all right, Dad?"

"Yes; yes, she's all right, Mark. I'll come up in a minute and tell you all about it."

The boy walked away, a puzzled look on his face, leaving Bill to walk slowly into the sitting room followed by Nell and Bert. And it was Nell who asked immediately, "Something gone wrong?"

"You could say that, Nell. Aye, you could say that."

465

"Fiona. She's all right?"

"Oh yes, yes. She had to have a caesarean, but she's all right. I left her sleeping. But I'm going back in a couple of hours time, staying the night."

"Well, what is it? The baby?"

Bill dropped onto the couch; he lay back and put his hand over his eyes before he said, "Yes, Nell, the baby."

"Oh, my God! Deformed?"

"No, not in that way, Nell, not in that way. Have you heard of Down's syndrome?" He was sitting up now looking from her to Bert. And he watched them glance at each other before Nell said, "Yes." Then, "Oh no! No, Bill. And Fiona . . . how did she take it?"

She doesn't know yet. She hasn't come round."

"No, no; of course not." Nell dropped into a chair. "Is . . . is it bad?"

"What d'you mean, is it bad?"

"Well, they look like . . ."

"Yes, it looks a bit like a Chinese, but otherwise it's all right. As the doctor said, perfectly formed."

"I'm sorry."

Bill now looked at Bert, saying, "So am I, Bert. So am I. But there you are. As the doctor said, it happens to all kinds of couples." And he added on a derisive laugh, "And he put it over very well, as if he was selling something, that these kind of bairns often bring happiness into a home. Anyway, he should know, he's got one."

"The doctor's got one?"

Bill nodded at Nell, saying, "Yes, a five-year-old; and he says she's lovely, or words to that effect. But I would have voted for one as ugly as sin itself as long as it was normal. Oh, God! How Fiona's goin' to take it, I don't know—that's if she takes it at all. . . . Give me a large whiskey there, Bert, will you?"

Bert, the staunch teetotaller, went to the drinks cabinet in the corner of the room and poured out what he imagined would be a double whiskey. And as he handed it to Bill he said, "God works in strange ways His miracles to perform."

"*Aw, Bert!* God in Heaven or whatever, don't come religion on me at this time. If you're so much in contact with Him then you ask Him why. Aye, that's it." His voice was raising now. "Ask Him why." He put his glass to his lips and threw off half of the whiskey, then coughed and choked on it. And leaning back against the couch again, he muttered, "I'm sorry. I'm sorry."

"It's all right, boss; but I've seen these bairns. I've got one in my Sunday school class. And a nicer lad you couldn't meet. And he's not mental. He's nine years old and for his type is bright."

466

"There you've said it, Bert, there you've said it, 'for his type.' "

"Well, I'll tell you this much, boss. I've got twenty-eight children, when they all come, and they're all supposed to be normal except Roger. But let me tell you, Roger is more intelligent than at least half of them. The only thing noticeable about him, apart from his eyes, is that he's got a sort of slight lisp. But I can tell you he's all there. And he's got three brothers and two sisters and I wouldn't swap him for the top two brothers I can tell you that. Now I don't know how your little girl will turn out, but all I can say is, give her a chance. And I will say this, whether it vexes you or pleases you, boss, there's nothing happens in this world that can't be laid at the door of the man, right from the beginning of time, through Christ's Crucifixion, wars, and massacres; and the only hope of relief is through belief in God. But that, of course, is only my opinion, and I don't often voice it, as Nell knows, 'cos I'm afraid it isn't hers, not totally. Anyway, boss, what about the bairns? Are you goin' to tell them?"

Bill now looked from Bert to Nell, and he shook his head as he said, "I don't think I can. Not tonight anyway."

"Would ... would you like me to do it, Bill?"

"Would you, Nell?"

"Bert and I ... well ... we'll do it together."

Bill now finished the last of the whiskey and, handing the glass to Bert, he rose from the couch and went out.

He was in the bathroom when Nell and Bert went upstairs and into the playroom. And on their entry Mamie jumped from the couch, crying, "Have we got a new baby?"

"Yes, dear; yes, we've got a new baby. It's a girl." She looked at the other three. There was no excitement on their faces. It was Katie now who spoke: "Something's not right, is it Nell?" she said. "Is it Mam?"

"No; no, dear; your mother's all right. Come and sit down."

Not until they were all seated did she glance at Bert, and it was he who started. Looking from one to the other, he said, "You all love your mam and dad, don't you?" None of the children spoke, but Mark and Katie exchanged a puzzled look, then waited. And Bert went on: "Well, I know it goes without saying that you do. Now in the future they're goin' to need all your love and cooperation because of the baby."

"Something wrong with it?"

Bert looked at Willie, and he said, "In a way."

In the stunned silence that fell on the children Nell now said, "There's a thing called Down's syndrome. You won't have heard of it, but it's when a baby's face is slightly distorted. I know you've seen children like it in the street."

467

There was a thin whisper now from Mark as he said, "You mean Mongol children?"

"Yes, Mongol children."

"And that's what Mam's got?"

There was a trace of horror in Katie's voice, and Nell said, "Yes, that's what your mam's got. Now what you've all got to remember is that the baby is your sister. And I was going to say that you will have to love her; but you will find, from my experience and those who know more about it than me, and Bert is one of them, that these children give out love and affection. That's all they seem to live for, to give out love and affection. They are not aware that they are different from other children. There is a simplicity about them."

"Do ... do they go mad?"

"No, Willie." Both Nell and Bert answered together; then Nell went on, "Of course not."

"He didn't mean mad, Nell ... well, he meant just mental, like those in the school at Burrows Road."

Nell paused a moment because she was about to say, "Not necessarily," but instead she was emphatic and said, "Not at all. The only thing is I understand they don't grow into adults. Well, yes, of course they grow up, but what I mean is their minds won't expand any further than, say, Willie's is now. And he's bright enough, isn't he?" She smiled from one to the other. "Too bright at times. Anyway, there it is. Now, naturally, your dad is upset and is going back to the hospital to be there when your mam wakes up, and it's only natural that she, too, will be upset. So when she brings the baby home, you'll all have to pull together to help her accept the situation."

"People will talk."

"What d'you mean?" said Nell, now looking at Katie.

"Well, they talk about that boy round the corner in Saville Street."

"You mean John Bent?"

"I ... I don't know what his name is, but his legs and arms and head are all over the place."

"Yes, they might be. But his brain inside his head is not all over the place, Katie. He's very bright. In fact, he's as bright as any man. And if you're going to be afraid of what people will say, then it's a bad look out for this family. And I'll be ashamed of the lot of you."

"It's come as a surprise, Nell."

It was Bert who answered Mark, saying, "Yes, naturally, Mark, it's come as a surprise, and to all of us. But the ones who are goin' to feel it most are your mam and dad, and they'll want support. That's what Nell's saying, they'll need your support every inch of the way, at least

468

at first. Now we are going downstairs to get your dad a drink and to try to get him to eat a bite. And try to understand if he doesn't come in and see you the night because . . . well, he's in a bit of a state and worried about your mam. You understand?"

He got to his feet, and Nell, too, rose, and she said, "Get ready for bed. I'll be up shortly. And another thing, your dad will be staying at the hospital all night with your mam. But don't worry, Bert and I will be here."

As they made their way downstairs Nell said under her breath, "Thank God that's over."

Fiona was still asleep when Bill reached the hospital. And he noted there was already a big easy chair placed by the side of the bed. The day staff were leaving and the night staff coming on. Two nurses came in, nodded at him and smiled, then set up an apparatus on top of the locker, from which they attached something to Fiona's arm. Then one of them explained, "This will take her blood pressure during the night, save disturbing her. Make yourself comfortable. Would you like a cup of tea?"

"I wouldn't mind. Thank you."

"Do you take sugar?"

"No; no thanks, no sugar."

The tea was weak but hot. He sipped at it, while all the time looking at Fiona.

Half an hour later she made restless moaning sounds; when she opened her eyes and saw him she said, "Oh, Bill. Bill."

"It's all right, love. It's all right."

"The baby?"

"She's all right an' all."

"A girl?"

"Aye, a girl."

"Oh, Bill. . . . It was tough going to . . . towards the end."

"Yes, dear, very tough going. It's over."

She drew in a long breath, then said, "I'm so tired, I feel I could sleep for a week."

"You go to sleep then, dear. You go to sleep."

"But . . . but I'd like to see her."

"You will in the morning. She's asleep, too, now. D'you know what time it is?"

"No."

"Going on for ten o'clock."

"Ten o'clock. Have . . . have you been here all the time?"

"Yes, except when I slipped home."

"To tell them?"

"Yes, to tell them."

"I . . . I bet they were excited."

"Yes, they were. They were."

"Oh, Bill. I'm . . . I'm glad for you."

She closed her eyes, turned her head to the side, and he realised with some surprise that she had gone to sleep.

What time he himself fell asleep he naturally didn't know, but he had strange dreams. And when he finally awoke it was to the sound of cups rattling and the feeling of bustle around him. He didn't open his eyes because he still felt very tired. It came into his consciousness that he had a slight cramp in his right leg. He pushed out his heel and brought his toes up until the pain went. Then he heaved a sigh and opened his eyes and looked on the smiling face of Fiona. She was sitting propped up in bed drinking a cup of tea. She smiled at him and in quite a casual voice, said, "Feel better, Mr. Bailey?" then added, "There's a cup of tea to your hand. Drink that, and then you'll be able to see me clearly."

He put out a groping hand, picked up the cup, and almost drained it with one go; then, pulling himself forward to the end of the chair, he leaned an elbow on the bedside and put his other hand up to her face and stroked her cheek, saying, "How d'you feel?"

"Fine. Excited. Raring to go. The nurse tells me I'll be here for a day or two; but still, what odds." She brought her head down to his, saying softly now, "I'm dying to see her. Apparently they have rules and regulations, and she's sound asleep."

When he bowed his head she said softly, "Bill. What's the matter? Look at me, Bill."

When he looked up she said again, "What's the matter? Something's wrong. She's not . . . ? No, no, no. She's not deformed or anything like . . . ?"

He gripped both her hands as he brought his words out hesitantly: "No, not what you call deformed."

"What d'you mean?"—she pulled herself back from him—"Not what I'd call deformed. What d'you mean? Tell me."

"Quiet. Quiet." He looked towards the door, then said, "Now, dear . . . my very, very, dear, there's something you've got to know. It's goin' to come as a shock as it did to me, but . . . but we've got to live with it."

She pressed her head back tight against the pillows. "She . . . she's deformed! She's . . . she's not right! She's . . ."

470

"She isn't deformed, and as far as it goes she's all right, but—I'm sure you will have heard the term, I hadn't—but she's what you call a Down's syndrome baby."

Her eyes slowly closed while her mouth opened wide as if to emit a scream, and he said sharply, "Fiona! Fiona! Please!"

"*No! No!*" She was now shaking her head on the pillow in deep denial, and again, "*No! No!* All these months I never, never, never felt so contented in my life. She . . . she can't be. She can't. They would have told me."

"Remember, love, remember you wouldn't go to the clinics? You said you felt so well you wanted none of it. When you did go it was too late, much too late."

Her head came up from the pillow and her face was hanging over his as she said through clenched teeth, "I won't have it, I won't. It can't happen to us. I wanted her for you, just for you. I couldn't give you a . . . a Mongol, because that's what you're telling me, isn't it? It's a Mongol. I won't have it! I won't have her. I won't! I won't!"

He pushed himself back and stood up, causing her to drop onto the pillow again and her mouth to open when he said, harshly: "Fiona! You've got to have it. We've both got to have it."

Through a whimper now she said, "I don't have to. I've got three healthy children. I don't have to."

Bending over her, with his hands on her shoulders, he said grimly, "You haven't only got three children, you've got four children of your own."

"*No!*" It was a shout, and the door opened and a passing nurse came in, saying "Is . . . is everything all right?"

Bill straightened up from the bed. "No!" he answered the nurse, "everything isn't all right. Would you mind bringing the baby?"

"Now?"

"Yes, now."

"I'll see sister."

"Do that, and quickly. Please."

Fiona's eyes were still closed but she was talking quietly now: "It's no good, Bill; I just couldn't. I've seen such children and I just couldn't."

He said nothing, just stood looking grimly down on her, listening to her protestations, unintelligible mutterings now.

It was a full ten minutes before the door opened and the sister came in, saying brightly, "Good morning!"

"Good morning." Bill nodded at her.

Fiona still lay with her eyes closed.

The sister now stood by the side of the bed, saying, "Mrs. Bailey, here is your baby." There was no compromise in the voice; it was a definite statement.

In answer, Fiona turned her head to the side, but in a moment Bill was round the bed, and he almost grabbed the child from the sister's arms, his action thrusting her aside.

"Take the child!"

"I . . . I've told you, Bill."

"No matter what you've told me, you've got a baby to see to. Take her!"

When there was no response and her body moved, as if painfully, away from him, he was round to the other side of the bed again in a flash. And now he thrust the child down into her stiff arms; and it was only reflex action that made her bring her hands up to stop it from rolling onto the bed.

It was as if her head and neck had been out of use for years, so slowly and so painfully did it turn. And then her eyes were forced to look down on her daughter, and what she saw were two bright eyes looking up at her, a little face that had a suspicion of a smile on it, and fingers that were clasping in and out. And when, as with Bill, the arm came up and the hand seemed to be aiming to touch the face above it, Fiona pressed her head away. But she continued to stare at the child. It had a tuft of light brown hair on the top of its head.

She couldn't bear it. Why? Why? She was normal. Bill was normal. Her mother and father had been normal. Bill's father was normal. Why? Why? As she went to thrust the child away Bill's hands grabbed it from her, and now he was holding it tight against his chest. And he startled the sister, but not Fiona because she was used to his voice, by bawling, "All right! All right! You won't have her, but she is mine. *My daughter.* My responsibility. And her needs will come first. D'you hear? So, if that's how you want it, that's how it's going to be."

42

FIVE DAYS LATER BILL BROUGHT THE CHILD HOME. AND IT WAS BILL WHO brought her home, because he carried her from the hospital to the car, placed her carefully on the backseat, then drove her and her mother to the house. And it was he who picked up the child, carried it in and straight upstairs to the small nursery that had been made by taking down a partition between the box room and the airing cupboard. And there the children had crushed in and around it.

Sammy Love happened to be present at the time, and when no comments came from any of the children it was he who looked up at Bill and, smiling, he said, "She's canny." And Bill, with a large lump in his throat, looked down on the boy, put his hand on his head and said, "Yes, Sammy, she's canny."

A short while later, when Bill stood in the kitchen with Nell, he thumped his fist against the framework of the sink as he said, "This is going to be hell! She'll never accept it. What are we going to do Nell?"

"Give her time. I can understand how she feels. She wanted to give you something. Most of what she's feeling is guilt, not so much against the child but somehow feeling she's let you down. I'm sure that's at the bottom of it. Who knows, the child may end up being a blessing in disguise."

473

He rounded on her now, crying, "For God's sake! Nell, don't come that tack. I've heard it so often these last few days. But I know, too, of such bairns who aren't a blessing in disguise."

"Well," Nell came back at him harshly, "can you show me any normal family and the parents pointing to a child and saying, they're a blessing in disguise? No; I know of people who wish their normal offspring had never been born. Anyway, she'll have to accept her in the end. Other mothers have, and they've probably been saddled with just the one. She's got plenty of support all round her; she'll just have to pull herself together. But then"—her voice dropped—"it'll take time. And I'll say to you, Bill, go canny with her; she's had a shock. And oh, I know, you've had one an' all. I'll never forget the night you came back from the hospital after seeing her for the first time. I wouldn't have been surprised if you had thrown her off then. Anyway, pray God that something will happen to make Fiona change her mind." She laughed. "I'm getting as bad as Bert, aren't I, calling on the Deity every possible occasion."

Nell was to say later, the Deity must have heard because something did happen to change Fiona's mind.

Mrs. Vidler had stayed seven weeks in America. She had written a short note to Fiona to say her friends were pressing her to extend her holiday—these were her words—and she would let her know when she was coming home.

But she didn't let her know until after she had actually arrived. It was the week before Christmas on the Friday afternoon, the nineteenth to be exact. Nell had just gone to pick up Katie and Mamie from school. Fiona had the house to herself except for the child, and it was in the nursery where it remained most of the time except when either Bill or Nell brought it downstairs. Fiona wouldn't let the thought penetrate her mind that it was strange how her children had taken to the child, even vying with each other to hold it.

She was about to enter the kitchen when the phone rang, and so she returned to the hall, picked it up, and in a flat voice said the number, but before she had finished she heard her mother say, "Fiona."

"Oh ... yes, Mother. Where are you?"

"I'm home, of course."

"You ... you said you were going to let me know."

"Well, I didn't, and I'm home."

"What's the matter? You sound ... "

"Yes, I know how I sound. I want to talk to you. Can you come round?"

474

"I'm sorry, I can't, Mother."

"Why?"

"I'm alone in the house but for the"—she paused—"the baby."

"Oh yes, the baby. You say you are alone?"

"Yes."

"I'll come straight round then." The phone clicked down.

Fiona turned, stood still for a moment, then went into the sitting room. She had always said she loved this room, but not anymore, because there was no happiness in it now. There was no happiness in the house. It was a divided house: Bill and the children on one side, Nell and Bert somewhere in the middle, and Sammy Love . . . where was Sammy Love? When he was with her he was for her, when he was with the child he was very much for the child.

It almost seemed that her mother had been standing outside the door, and when the bell rang twice she wanted to cry out, "All right! All right! I'm coming," but when she opened the door and saw the person standing on the step who spoke like her mother but wasn't her mother, yet was, she stood aside and allowed her to enter.

"Don't stare at me like that."

"What do you expect me to do?" The woman before her was dressed, not as she usually was in good class but plain clothes, but in a flamboyant imitation fur coat with an enormous collar and cuffs and a woollen hat on top of her russet-coloured hair, which when Fiona had last seen it had been a light brown streaked with grey. But then there was her face: there was a tightness at the corner of the eyes, very like—Fiona could not make herself even think, the child's—and the droop and lines from each side of the mouth had gone. Her face had the appearance of one that had just been taken out of a mud pack, smooth and unlined but ready to slip back into its natural slackness once the astringent wore off. But in her mother's case the astringent wouldn't wear off. *She'd had a face-lift.*

"Yes; yes, you can look, and you can say it: why did you have to go all the way to America to have it done?" They were going towards the sitting room now. "Because I understood they did a better job there, and they have."

"Then why are you in a temper? You should be pleased with yourself."

"It's . . . it's him, Davey. I couldn't believe it."

"What's he done? Sit down. Sit down."

In the presence of her mother's agitation Fiona felt calm for the first time in weeks. Mrs. Vidler, seated now on the couch, her open coat showing that she was wearing a tight-fitting red woollen dress which, in its turn, showed that she had certainly lost pounds in weight, was clasping and unclasping her hands as she said, "I ... I did it just for him because ... well, he gave me the impression that he was interested. But I went straight round there and what do I find? He's got a *woman* installed."

"Well, he's a young man. He looked upon you as a mother."

"*He did not, Fiona.* He encouraged me."

"I don't know about encouraging you, Mother. I do know that you threw yourself at him. But even then he saw you as a motherly figure."

"I am no motherly figure." And she wagged her head as she said this. "All that way, the dreadful journey and all the expense ... yes, the expense. I'll tell him. I will."

"I wouldn't if I were you, mother; I would save what little dignity you have left; and I'd also get out of those awful clothes and be yourself."

"I'll ... I'll never be myself again. And ... and I hate America."

"I thought it was lovely and the people were marvellous."

"Yes, as long as you're spending money. Oh"—she got to her feet and began to walk up and down—"why had this to happen to me, at my age?"

"There you said it, Mother, at your age."

Now her mother rounded on her. "And may I ask what's the matter with you? Not a kind word out of you, not a word of welcome. Are you ill? You look it. Is it this postnatal depression that all mothers seem to indulge in these days?"

"No, I'm not suffering from postnatal depression, Mother. And I'm being as thoughtful of you as you are of me."

"Here we go again. Anyway, may I ask what the latest effort is? Am I a grandmother to a boy or a girl?"

"It's a girl."

"Well, where is she?"

"In the nursery."

"You've got a nursery now?"

"We've made a makeshift one. Would you like to come up and see her?"

"Well, it's the least I can do, isn't it?"

"Yes, Mother; it's the least you can do."

The room held a cot, a small table, a cupboard, and two straight-backed chairs. The child was awake and gurgling; they both heard it as they opened the door. There was a permanent night-light glowing as the only other light in the room was from a fanlight in the roof.

476

Fiona switched on the main light; then one at each side of the cot, they stood looking down on the gurgling child.

"*Dear God!*" It was a thin whisper from Mrs. Vidler. "It's a . . . "

"Yes, Mother, a Mongol."

"*Oh, my goodness!* Oh, really! How on earth could this happen to you? Are . . . are you going to keep it?"

"Yes, Mother, we are going to keep it. And it isn't an 'it,' it's a 'she.'"

"They . . . they grow up mental."

"They do nothing of the sort, Mother!" It was a bawl that would have done credit to Bill; and Mrs. Vidler reared up and said, "Don't you dare shout at me like that! Anyway, what do you expect from that man? There's nothing like this on our side of the family; it's through him."

"It isn't through him, Mother. These things happen to all types of people."

"It's genes; it's passed down."

"It isn't genes, and it is not passed down."

"All right, all right, it is not passed down; but this has come about through him, and what will people say?"

"I don't give a damn about what people say, Mother."

"Well, you should. And don't expect me to be grandmother to it. There are homes for such children."

"Yes, there are, Mother; and this is the home for this child, my child, Bill's child." Of a sudden her arms went out and grabbed the baby from the cot, and she pulled it to her breast and, holding it tightly there, she said, "And what is more, I'll put her in the pram and take her outside, and everybody I meet I'll tell them that Mrs. Vidler is my mother."

"Stop it, Fiona. Stop it!"

"No, you stop it, Mother. And get out! Do you hear? Get out!"

She was yelling at the top of her voice now; and her mother had already backed towards the door and onto the landing. And the noise must have been heard in the kitchen, for from there emerged Nell, Katie, and Mamie; and Nell could only briefly notice the change in Mrs. Vidler because she was staring up at Fiona coming down the stairs, screaming at the top of her voice as she held the child to her, "And don't come back into this house until you're asked. Do you hear? And I hope you find a man who will appreciate your face-lift and all the money you've spent on it. As for Davey Love, he looked on you as a grannie, not even a mother."

"*Fiona! Fiona!*"

"Mam! Mam!"

Nell was holding Fiona by the shoulders now and Katie was gripping her mother's arm while Mamie, her face twisting into tears, was tugging at her dress.

"She's gone. She's gone. Come on. Come on into the sitting room. Sit down."

"Nell . . . Nell . . . she said . . ."

"It doesn't matter what she said, dear. Give me the child here."

"No; no, I want it. It's Bill's. It's mine. It's Bill's."

"Don't cry. Don't cry, dear."

"I must cry, Nell, I must cry. I've been wicked, wicked. Poor Bill. It's Bill's. It's mine."

As her crying mounted she pressed the child tighter to her and began to rock it, and Nell, turning to Katie, whispered, "Go and ring the yard. Ask your dad to come home. Quick!"

When Katie got through and heard Bill's voice, she said, "Dad."

"Yes, who's that?"

"It's Katie."

"Oh yes. What's the matter?"

"Dad, can you come home; it's Mam."

"What's happened? What's she done?"

"She's . . . she's done nothing, Dad. Gran's been here. She's upset, but I think it's a good upset."

"A good upset? What d'you mean?"

"I can't explain. Just come, Dad."

Katie could hear her mother's cries and they were mingled with Mamie's; and then Nell's voice, saying, "It's all right, dear, it's all right. Don't hold the baby so tight. Just rock it. Just nurse it. That's right, that's right."

"Nell, I hate her. I hate her."

"Yes, I know, dear. Very few people like her."

"It's wrong to hate, Nell. It's wrong to hate."

"Here, let me dry your eyes. Try to stop crying, dear."

"I want to go on crying, Nell; I want to cry forever. I've been wicked. Poor Bill. I'll not put her in a home, ever! I'll not put her in a home."

"No, of course you won't; we wouldn't let you even if you wanted to; we all love her."

"Yes, you all love her. I didn't love her, but you all loved her, Bill most of all. But it wasn't love really, not really. It was compassion. Yes, that's it, compassion, compassion."

"It's all right, dear. It's all over."

478

"No; no, Nell; it's not all over, it's only starting. Don't take her from me. No, don't take her from me. I won't hurt her. I'll hold her like this and rock her. My mind's been going round in circles, Nell; I don't know where I've been. My mother has been in me. I'm part of her you know. Yes, I am, I am. And I've been seeing Angela through her eyes. I'm glad she came. And she doesn't look younger, she looks awful. Her face matches her character, tight, stretched, selfish. Can a face be selfish? It's all right, Nell; it's all right; I'm not hurting her, I'm just rocking her."

"Lie back, dear. Lie back. Try to relax."

"Sammy said I would get a surprise. Sammy comes out with odd things and they always mean something. He's an odd boy is Sammy. Oh, Nell, Nell; I think I'm going to die."

"No, you're not going to die, dear. You're going to live and make us all happy again."

"Bill will never be happy again."

"Oh yes, he will. Once he sees you holding her, he'll be happy."

"Will he, Nell? I'm so tired, Nell, so very tired. I've been fighting inside me all the time, wanting to touch her, because she isn't bad to look at, is she?"

"No; no, she's not. We all think she's sweet."

"Well, I wouldn't say she's sweet, but she's not bad."

She had a bout of coughing and choking, but still she would not relinquish the child.

And five minutes later she was still holding it, still rocking it, and still crying when Bill entered the room. He paused for a moment, then hurried to the couch and sat down beside her, saying, "Aw, love, that's it: cry. That's it: cry."

"I'm sorry, Bill: I'm sorry."

"You've nothing to be sorry for, hinny. Nothing. Nothing. From now on everything will be all right. There now. There now."

When the front doorbell rang, Katie ran to open it, and she greeted the man on the step: "Oh, hello, Mr. Meredith. Come in. Come in."

"What's the matter, Katie? Why are you crying?"

"It's Mam. She's . . . she's come round."

"Come round from what?"

"The baby."

"Oh, has it come? I've been in Scotland you know; Sir Charles's brother died. I . . . I went to the funeral."

"Oh, I'm sorry. I mean about Sir Charles's brother. Give me your coat."

"Mr. Meredith."

"Yes, Katie?"

"Don't ... don't look surprised when you see the baby, will you not?"

"Should I?"

"You might."

"All right, Katie; I won't look surprised."

When he entered the sitting room and saw the situation he continued walking slowly forward, and Bill turned to him, saying, "Oh, hello there. You've got back then."

"Yes, I got back this morning. I thought I'd look in. So it's arrived."

"Yes, Rupert, it's arrived." Bill nodded towards him. "Show Rupert our daughter, Fiona."

"Hello, Rupert." Fiona could hardly see him through the still running tears. And he said, "Hello, Fiona." Then he looked down on the child and he smiled. "What's her name?" he asked.

"Angela."

He glanced at Bill and repeated, "Angela? Well, she'll likely turn out to be an angel in disguise."

Nell rose from the other side of the couch, saying, "Well, I think we could all do with a cup of tea. And then you Katie, and you Mamie, and the rest of the gang can get down to those Christmas decorations and rake out the things from the garret for the tree. Are you going to Scotland for the Christmas, Mr. Meredith?"

"No, Nell. I've just come back from there. Sir Charles and Lady Kingdom are staying over the holidays. But coming down in the train, I was thinking that as I am a very lonely man there might be a nice family who would invite me to stay over the Christmas holidays."

Katie made a sound between a giggle and a sniff, and Bill said, "You're welcome. More than welcome. But this'll be your bed." He thumbed toward the couch."

"It will suit me."

"This house will soon be bursting at the seams." Nell went out smiling now. And Bill, looking at Fiona, who was lying back taking in deep gasping breaths, the child still held, but gently now, in her arms, said, "That reminds me. I've got a Christmas box for you."

She looked up at him but said nothing.

"Tomorrow I'm goin' to take you to see it: in fact, I'll take the whole squad of you because I want more than one opinion." He turned to Rupert, saying, "D'you know Burnstead Mere House?"

480

"Oh yes, yes. It's a lovely place. Beautiful gardens, too. And the mere is quite a large one. I've been there. You after that?"

"Yes. It's got twelve main rooms and a small indoor pool. What d'you think about that?" He was now putting his face close to Fiona's.

"If you think it's for us, then it's for us. Wipe my face, will you?"

As Bill gently wiped Fiona's face, Rupert caught hold of Mamie's hand and took her from the room. But in the kitchen, before he had time to say anything, Mamie cried, not only to Nell and Katie, but to Mark, Willie, and Sammy, who had just come in and were now all bright faced. "We're going to move into a big house, like a palace, with twelve rooms and a swimming pool, and a river at the bottom."

The announcement seemed to still them all and to cause them to look at Rupert as if for confirmation or further enlightenment. And it was Nell who said, "Is that a fact?"

"It would seem so, Nell. It's Bill's Christmas box to Fiona, and to you all, I should say."

"Oh, well. Anyway"—Nell shook her head—"she's already given him his Christmas box." Then turning to the children, she added, "Now gang, let's get going. Away to your posts, all of you, and prepare for a happy Christmas. And believe me I never thought we should see it. But thanks to your dear sweet grandmama, she has worked a small miracle. And as my husband says, they do happen."

43

THEY COULDN'T BE TAKEN TO SEE THE HOUSE THE NEXT DAY FOR THE PEOPLE were moving out. So it was the day before Christmas Eve when the whole family piled into the two cars, the second driven by Rupert, who took Mark and Willie, and, of course, it went without saying, Sammy Love. Nell, Katie, and Mamie were seated in the back of Bill's car, with baby, wrapped in two large shawls, a bonnet, and woolly boots, being nursed by Katie.

"You all right, dear?"

"Yes, Bill." Fiona nodded at him.

"Warm enough?"

"Yes, yes; I couldn't help but be in this." She hugged around her the sheepskin coat with which he had surprised her only yesterday. Then she said, "How far is it?"

"Oh, about half an hour's run, a bit more perhaps. You all right back there?"

"Fine." The concerted answer came from the three of them. "But," Nell added, "we will feel better when you get a move on, if this machine works. My old banger would have been away by now."

"Yes, making for the scrap yard."

"Don't you dare insult Maria!" And the laughter this brought about seemed to create the atmosphere for further backchat in the

482

backseat during the journey. In the main, however, Fiona sat quiet, because she felt quiet. The only description she could give to herself with regard to the change in her since that dreadful crying bout was that she was experiencing a kind of silence. Everything she had thought over the last few days seemed to have dropped into this silence and melted away. She didn't know if she liked this feeling or not. But what she did know was that she was thankful unto God that things were right between her and Bill again, and that her mind had accepted the child even while, as yet, her heart was not touched. And yet there were times when she looked at it and it looked back at her that she experienced the very feeling that it was trying to tell her something, and also that there was something bigger than life itself encased in that small body, and struggling to get out. She had told herself that this was mere fancy, a tangent of that feeling she had had before her outburst that she would likely go out of her mind, and end up in the same place as Rupert's fiancée. Nevertheless, it was strange how, since that outburst, the atmosphere in the house had done a complete somersault: everyone now seemed happy, and the child was the focus of it. It seemed as if the child was going to alter all their lives. No, not seemed, it had already done so.

Nell was saying, "And who d'you think's going to clean this twelve-room house of yours, Mr. Bailey?"

"Well, what d'you think I pay you for? And there's not only twelve rooms, I forgot to tell you there's a granny annexe an' all. I thought it would do for Mrs. Vidler."

There were indecipherable noises from the back, while Fiona said, "Yes; yes, it could, dear."

"Over your dead body! Anyway she's not a granny anymore is she? My God, that face. You know, it's funny about faces: those clever bods can't alter expressions in the eyes, and it's the eyes that give away age, more than wrinkled skin."

A short while later Bill got out of the car and, taking the keys from his pocket, unlocked a pair of iron gates, pushed them wide, then took his seat again before driving through a short avenue of trees and onto a broad sweep of pink tarmac, fronting a long two-storeyed house showing three dormer windows in the roof, and a stone-pillared porch covering the front door.

With another key, Bill unlocked the heavy oak door and, pushing this wide, too, he said, "Enter Mrs. Bailey and family." Then looking over his shoulder, he said, "Here are the rest."

When Rupert and the three boys stepped into the hall there was silence among them all for a moment. Then it was Katie who said, in a very small voice, "You said they had moved, Dad. But look, there's the carpets and curtains and . . ."

"They go with the house, Katie; and one or two other things an' all, bits of big furniture here and there, 'cos they're movin' into a smaller place. There was only the two of them, their family were grown up and gone."

Following Bill, they now walked towards one of the doors at the far end of the hall, and as he pushed it open he said, "What d'you think of that?"

No one spoke till Fiona said, "It's a beautiful room."

"And you've seen nothing yet, Mrs. B."

And they certainly hadn't seen anything yet. The dining room brought gasps from them because the dining table and chairs were still there, also a sideboard and a large leather suite.

What was called the study was, to them, more like a small library, with bookshelves covering two walls as well as a huge breakfront bookcase.

It was Rupert who said, "If I remember rightly there was a billiard room somewhere, Bill."

"Aye, it used to be a billiard room, but now it's a kind of games room with exercise machines and God knows what."

"Where? Where?"

Both Willie and Mark made for the door, and when Bill cried at them, "Hold your hand a minute! Keep with the party or else you might get lost. When I've shown you the lay-out, then you may go mad."

The games room brought oohs and aahs from all the children, but it was the kitchen that brought the oohs and aahs from both Fiona and Nell. "It's something you would dream of," said Nell. "Look at the size of this fridge. My, it'll take some filling. And the dishwasher. Oh, Fiona, look." She had walked through another door. "The utility room is nearly as big as our house. Oh, I wish Bert was here; it might give him some ideas to build on at the back of our place; you can hardly get into the kitchen."

Another door led to two smaller rooms, and when Fiona asked Bill what they would have been used for, he, glancing at Rupert and putting on what he imagined to be his voice, said, "The servants, my dear. The servants," whereupon everyone laughed again and repeated, "Oh, yes; the servants, my dear. The servants," while Rupert, not to be outdone and assuming a tone that he imagined was Bill's, said, "Well, boss, I wouldn't mind 'avin' 'em. I can buttle."

"You can what?" Katie was now hanging onto his arm.

"Buttle, miss. Buttle. Be a butler."

"Well, who knows; we could take you on at that." Bill was leading them along a corridor now and so into a separate apartment that consisted of a good-sized sitting room, a bedroom, a kitchen, and a bathroom. And Katie was now crying, "Oh, I could live in this end, and have it all to myself. And look!" She was pointing through a glass door. "It's got a covered patio and a garden."

It was when, a few minutes later, they went into the pool room that they all became speechless for a moment. The water looked deep blue; the bath itself was tiled: the bottom blue, and the sides white. At the near end of the pool was a set of steps in half-moon Roman fashion leading down to the water. At the far end was a diving board. Except for the near end, there was a supporting rail all round at water level. And to the side, there were two dressing rooms.

"'Tain't true, is it?"

They all glanced at Sammy. He was looking up at Bill; and Bill, returning his glance, said, "'Tis true, Sammy. It was a dream, a dream of a lifetime, but it's come true. If you dream hard enough for something it'll come true in the end."

"Are there other people after it, Dad?" Mark's question was quiet yet showing a little apprehension. Bill pursed his lips and said, "Aye; yes, there's other people after it; but there's one obstacle, it's the price. Now come on, come on, you've seen nothing yet."

And how true, Fiona thought as they "toured" the bedrooms: with three of them having a bathroom en suite, as it was called. There were two other bathrooms. These they found along another corridor where the other three bedrooms were. All the bedrooms were carpeted and curtained, and in two of the main ones the beds remained, both with padded headboards. But in the third one there was a four-poster draped in blue satin.

"They must have been millionaires what lived here" was Willie's passing comment.

"How many rooms are there really, Dad?" Katie had a vivid mental picture of relating the wonders of this house to her friend Sue when she went to her party next week, and not only to Sue, but to that swanky piece Maureen Cuthbert and her cronies.

"Well, there's twelve main ones; that's not counting halls and the utility room, nor the attics. Oh, you must see the attics. There's one full of old bits of furniture.... And something could be resurrected from them, I can tell you."

They oohed and aahed through the attics and over the odd bits of broken furniture. And when Bill pointed out there was a small stream running into the mere but told them that they weren't getting him down there today, Rupert offered to go with them. And Nell, being ever tactful, said to Fiona as she held out the child, "Here, take her. I want to go and look at that kitchen, and especially that utility room, so I can describe it to Bert."

"Come and sit down." Bill led the way back into the dining room; and when Fiona was seated with the child in her arms, he stood looking down at her, saying, "Well, what d'you think?"

"It's a wonderful place, Bill, but it's really out of our line, isn't it?"

"What d'you mean, out of our line?"

"Well, what I mean is, the cost. Even if you could get it, it would be a burden on our shoulders, on your shoulders."

"Well, let me tell you, Mrs. B., that it's already a burden on me shoulders because it is ours. It was signed and sealed on Tuesday."

"Bill!"

"Sit yourself down again, woman."

"But ... but how on earth! And it needs more furnishing and ..."

"I know all the buts and ands, I've been through them. And my name's very good at the bank. They would advance me twice as much."

"Twice as much as what, Bill?" There was an anxious note in her voice.

"Well, now, Mrs. B."—he pulled up a chair and sat opposite to her, his knees touching hers—"it's been on the market for over a year. Houses are not selling, not like this, not at this price, not around here. Under the hundred thousand, they are, but when you get up to two hundred thousand plus... *All right! All right!* Sit down, woman. Look, you'll drop her if you're not careful," He put his hand out and laid it on the child. And she said, "Over two hundred thousand?"

"Yes, it was going for two hundred and twenty-five thousand, a year ago. And it was worth it. I looked at it then and laughed. It was just before I got the contract and it seemed as far away then as the contract did. But then I was too busy to think much about it until three months ago when I saw it was still on the market and down to two hundred and ten thousand. And then last month, I understood with a bit of manoeuvring one could get it for two hundred or a bit less, 'cos the old couple wanted to get away and join their daughter down in the west country; and they didn't want to leave their house empty because of the vandals, and believe me, they would have been in in two shakes of a lamb's tail. Anyway, I got them down to a hundred and ninety thousand."

When Fiona closed her eyes, he said, "Look dear, that's nothin' the day. You should see what property's going for in Newcastle."

486

"This is not Newcastle, Bill. But a hundred and ninety thousand. And the interest!"

"Oh, I didn't have to have a mortgage for all that. You know as well as I do, there's quite a bit in the kitty now."

"But it's got to be furnished."

"We can take that in our stride. And we've certainly got lots of bits and pieces back home, haven't we?"

Her face brightened as she said now, "What would that bring?"

"Oh." He put his head back, and then, looking at her again, he said, "I needn't start to reckon up; I've been into all that an' all. You'd get eighty thousand for it the morrow."

"Never, Bill. And look at the town, most people out of work."

"It won't attract the people out of work, dear. But there's all these little factories going up and there's what you call the executive group looking for good houses. Now it's a corner house and it's got a good garden back and front. And apart from the one at the top end it's in the best situation in the avenue. And it's a good repair. Oh yes, you'll get eighty."

"Well, that's something."

"Aye, that's something. But there's something I want to put to you. It's your house. It's your money. *Listen. Listen. Listen.*" He was wagging his finger at her now. "I'm lookin' ahead. This contract is like pennies from heaven but it's not going to last forever, another year or so, or fifteen months, that's if they decide to alter the plans and make that extra row of shops, 'cos as we know there's no more sites like this in these parts. It'll just be smaller jobs, at least here; but I've got a feelin' I can go farther afield now. Yet nothing's ever sure. So you're going into business, Mrs. B., in case I go flat."

"What! What are you talking about?"

"Listen to me, woman. You know Kingsley's garage? Yes, of course you do. Well, you know, it's a scruffy little place, but it wasn't always like that. When Arthur Jones had it, it was a smart affair. He lived above it, and everything was spruce. Then he had to be knocked down by one of his own cars. But since Kingsley took it over ... well, he's as thick as two planks and he's never engaged a decent mechanic, and so they've lost trade and he's selling, or he's tryin' to, and has been for some time. So he's another who won't quibble about bargainin'. So, I suggest, Mrs. B., that you take your eighty thousand and you invest it in the garage business, because, looking ahead, I think we should have our fingers in more than one pie. And people will always be wantin' cars. Many would rather have their own car than their house, or eat. Bloody fools. But there it is, that's life. We could do the place

487

up, put a good man in, a real mechanic, in the flat above. Get some plants and greenery around that front court, and it's a big forecourt. He's got it covered with old run-down bangers now. Well, we won't deal in run-down bangers, not at Bailey's garage ... Mrs. Bailey's garage."

"Oh, Bill!"

"Don't say 'Oh, Bill!' like that. What d'you think really?"

"Well"—she hesitated—"I think it's a good thing to have ..."

"Two strings to your bow."

"Yes; yes, two strings to your bow."

"And perhaps a third, who knows? Anyway, that's settled. Now there's nothin' for you to worry about; all you've got to do is to get this place to your likin', furnished that is, and don't skimp; at the same time don't go mad. Come on." He drew her up from the chair. "Let's go and face the mob and find out if Nell has stripped the utility room yet."

He was making for the door when he turned and said, "We're lucky, you know, to have her ... Nell."

"Oh, I've always felt we're lucky to have Nell, Bill."

"Aye. Well, I'll take some of that back; she's all right in her place. When I think it's just on two years ago, before you went into hospital and thought you were goin' to peg out, that you had it all planned for me to marry her. And she told me plainly that she wouldn't marry me if the rest of the world were dead. And I told her that if she wasn't on earth and was an angel, I still wouldn't look the side she was on, or words to that effect."

They went out laughing, to meet the avalanche coming in the front door.

"It's wonderful, Dad."

"Oh, Mam, there's like a little waterfall at the bottom; it's made up of stones and the water's rippling over it, tumbling and twisting into a little pool."

"Oh, the poet's on his feet."

It was noticeable that Willie didn't turn and snarl at Katie, but said, "Well, clever chops, you said yourself it was bonny."

And it was noticeable, too, that Katie didn't threaten to slap his face, but said, "Yes, it is. It would be lovely in the summer, Mam; you could sit on the rocks and paddle your feet."

"Why would you want to do that when you've got a pool to swim in?"

They looked at Bill in silence for a moment, until Mark said, "You mean that, Dad?"

"Aye, that's what I mean, Mark. I mean that this is your home from now on."

Mark, Willie, Katie, and Mamie, were all clinging round him now, popping and crying out their excitement, while Fiona and Nell stood at one side looking at them; and standing apart were Rupert and Sammy. And Rupert, looking down at Sammy, said in a false whisper, "We'll have to keep our noses clean, Sammy, and try to get an invite to this place."

For answer Sammy said, "Don't matter."

And this caused a bark from Bill that drowned the others' voices: "What d'you mean, it don't matter?" he demanded.

"Well, too far out; not like your other house."

"There's a bus, isn't there? And you can get a bike."

"Don't want a bike. Me da's gonna get a car, a new one."

"Good for him. Then you can come in your da's car, can't you?"

"Might."

"No might about it, Sammy Love. Anyway, you'll be here more than you'll be at home, if I know anything."

"If me da goes along the line I'll have to go to me granny's. Jinny'll not stay."

Bill pushed the children aside, then went and stood over the minute figure, bawling at him now, "Trust you to put a spanner in the works! Everybody laughin' and happy 'cos they've got this grand house an' you puttin' the damper on things. What's up with you? And you." He looked at Rupert, "What's up with you an' all?"

"Well, I'm out in the cold, too, Mr. Bailey. This house is out of my way; I don't see how I'm going to visit so often."

There was a cry from Katie and she was clinging on to Rupert's arm now, shouting, "You can come and live here. You can have the granny flat. I'll cook for you."

"Oh, my God! Then we can expect a funeral."

Of a sudden all their attention was turned towards Nell, who added, "Does anybody realise that the gas, water, and electricity have been cut off in this house? Not that it matters because we haven't any tea, sugar, milk, or crockery. And what I'm needing at this moment is a strong cup of tea. Now do you think, Mr. Bailey, that you can get us home as quickly as you got us here?"

"You know what I'd like to do with you," said Bill, now pushing the tribe out of the door, "I'd like to slap your face for you, both sides."

"Bigger men than you have had that desire, Mr. Bailey, bigger men than you."

So, amid laughter, they piled into the cars and drove away from the house that was to be their new home.

489

44

THE MAGISTRATE WAS ADDRESSING THE MAN IN THE DOCK. "YOU, MR. LOVE," HE was saying slowly, "have acquired the habit over the years of acting first and thinking later. Were we all to hit out when we heard someone speak derisively of us then I for one would have been behind bars years ago."

A titter went round the court at this. Mr. Arthur Fellmore was known for his witty quips. The clerks and solicitors waited for them, and in this case they hadn't as yet been disappointed. It was whether he or the Irishman would come out on top, but, of course, he had the upper hand, and the Irishman was well aware of it. Yet that didn't stop him from saying, "Then you've had a taste of it, yer worship, but bein' more sensible than meself you kept yer hands down an' ..."

"Mister Love!" The magistrate's voice expressed patience. "I do not wish to know your opinion of my mental restraint, but I want you to understand that your actions are not to be tolerated. You were, I am told, in charge of a gang of workers and when the plaintiff was about to carry out an order that you had given him but had the effrontery to express his opinion of you, what did you do?"

"I did what any man in me place would have done, yer worship, I closed his mouth for him."

490

The hammer hitting the desk subdued the laughter.

"I'll thank you, Mr. Love, to listen to what I am saying and not interrupt. Do you understand me?"

"I do yer worship, and I'm sorry. It's me tongue."

It was observed that the magistrate lowered his head and closed his eyes for a moment before going on: "You did not only close the plaintiff's mouth but you broke his nose and put him in hospital for a week."

When someone pushed a paper slowly along the table and under the magistrate's nose, he corrected himself: "Oh, barely two days. Well, that was enough. But since that time I understand the plaintiff has been unable to work and has been suffering from shock."

"Pardon me for sayin' so, yer worship, but he's always shocked by work, even the word shocks him."

"*Silence in court!* I have warned you Mr. Love."

"Aye, yer worship. But God in heaven! It's more than a man can stand to hear him made out as a poor sick individual when we all know he's . . ."

"*Mr. Love!*"

Davey dropped his head, and there followed a heavy silence in the courtroom. When he again looked up it was to meet a warning glance from Bill sitting at the back of the court; in fact, Bill was rubbing his hand through his hair in an agitated fashion.

"I'm afraid, Mr. Love, that you are a man who'll never learn, either to keep his mouth shut or to keep his hands to himself. Now I am going to pass sentence on you, but before doing so I may tell you the bench is taking into consideration that when you used your hands once before, you were the means of bringing to justice two potential murderers who are now serving sentences for their crime. So this fact alone causes us to temper the punishment we might have given to you for your latest episode. Therefore, I will use leniency and commit you to one hundred hours of community work. Also, you will pay a fine of one hundred pounds. And I may add, Mr. Love, that if you are wise you will decide never to appear in this court again, at least when I'm on the bench. Do you understand?"

"I do, yer worship, I do. And honest to God, I promise you you've seen the last of me and me of you. Thank you. Thank you, yer worship."

The court stood; the magistrates departed.

Bill and his solicitor went up to Davey and the solicitor said, "Well, not too bad, eh?"

Davey, who was visibly sweating now, took out a handkerchief and

491

rubbed it round his mouth before saying, "I think it was pretty stiff."

Bill, too, now nodded at the solicitor: "A hundred working hours and a hundred quid. Phew! Yes, I think I agree with Davey."

"You don't know our dear Mr. Fellmore," said the solicitor under his breath. "He must have had a good weekend. I wouldn't have been surprised if he had sent you down for at least three months." He was nodding at Davey. "I can tell you you've got to thank, not only your friend here"—he inclined his head towards Bill—"but one or two friends in the force. They raked out the facts that Potter had been in trouble up in London, nothing very big, all petty; and his worship must have had this made known to him."

"Oh yes, yes, likely." Bill nodded his agreement.

"What'll I have to do in that hundred hours?"

"Oh, all kinds of things. You had better come along with me now to the office. One thing I can tell you, you won't have many weekends free, or even nights, until you've served your sentence." The solicitor laughed now as he added, "You can stop sweating, it's over. But as his worship said, I'd watch those hands of yours in the future."

Following on this remark Davey was put to the test sooner than he could have expected: he was passing by a group of people in the hallway when a voice said, "Community service! He should have been sent along the bloody line, the big-mouthed galoot."

"Now! now! now!" said another voice.

Bill actually felt Davey's body jerk, but he noticed that he looked straight ahead, his eyes very wide, his chin thrust out; the solicitor had noted Davey's reaction and he was quick to remark on it: "You should have ten out of ten for first test passed," he said.

Davey made no remark on this, nor did Bill, for both of them knew how near to another court case Davey had been just a moment previously.

Davey was warmed and touched by the greeting he received when he returned with Bill to the house. Except for Mark, who was at school, all the children were at home.

"They didn't want you as governer at Durham then?" was Nell's greeting when he entered the sitting room.

"No, Nell; no. They don't know what they're missin', do they? Now I ask you."

Fiona said, "Oh, thank goodness it's over. And you won't mind doing community work, will you?"

"Mrs. B., I'd walk on me hands on hot cinders, anything rather than take that van to Durham."

Katie said, "If they had sent you I would have come and visited you. I would. I really would."

"Thank you, Katie, me love; and I'd have been delighted to see you. There wouldn't have been a prettier visitor in that prison."

What Willie said was, "I told him. I told him all along"—he nodded at Sammy—"I told him that they wouldn't dare send you to prison, 'cos you'd knock the he ... " He choked on the word and it brought spluttering laughter from Katie, Mamie, and also Nell, but a look of reprimand from his mother, and so he finished with "Well, what I mean is, he would have seen them off. Wouldn't you, Mr. Love?"

"Well, I would have done me best, lad. I would have done me best. An' what's me son got to say to me? He hasn't opened his mouth." Davey looked around him as if appealing to the others, saying, "Not a word. Not a word."

All eyes were on Sammy waiting for an answer, but for once there was no response, only a thrusting out of the lips and a knobbling of the small chin.

Bill broke the embarrassed silence by handing a glass to Davey, saying, "Get that down you, and then get home and out of those fancy togs and back on the job. And, as Nell says, they'll have the flag out for you."

"Oh aye? I can see 'em, and hear 'em: they'll scoff me lugs off. But what odds."

"If they scoff your lugs off it'll be in a kindly fashion. Should it happen though that one or another should say somethin' that isn't to your likin', Mr. Love, just you remember what his worship said."

"You have no need to press that home, boss, no need whatever. Anyway, thanks for the drink. Thanks for everything." He stood up and looked around him. "And I'll say this: there's one thing I'm sure of in this world, tis I'll never have much money but I feel rich—at this minute I feel a millionaire, 'cos I've got friends like you, large and small, friends like you." On this he turned to make for the door; and when Sammy scampered after him, Willie followed, demanding, "Where you going?"

"I'm goin' home with me da."

"But he's going to work."

"I know that; I've got ears."

"Will you come back after?"

"Aye; aye, I'll come back after. But now *I'm goin' home.*"

"All right, all right, don't bawl. How long will you be?"

"As long as it takes."

Davey had paused to wait for his son and now said to him, "Come on you, an' shut that trap. Tis a pity you take after me, tis that."

The family had followed them into the hall and so Nell, who opened the door, did not immediately close it after Davey and Sammy, for they all stood watching the very tall man and the very small boy walking down the drive together.

When Bill said, "What am I thinkin' about? I could have given them a lift," Fiona put in quietly, "They'll have more time to be together on their own when they're walking."

"There's the phone!" Nell said, and Bill turned quickly away towards the stairs, saying, "If it's for me, tell them I'll be there in the next ten minutes."

After picking up the phone Nell listened for a moment, then, lifting her hand, she flapped her fingers slowly towards Fiona. And Fiona, taking the phone from her, said, "Hello."

"Fiona."

"Yes, Mother?"

"What's this I'm hearing?"

"What are you hearing now, Mother?"

"I've heard you're moving."

"Yes, that's right."

"And, of course, I'm the last to know. I just couldn't believe it. When was all this settled?"

"Just before Christmas, Mother."

"And today is the eighth of January, and you've known all the time."

"Mother!" Fiona's voice lost all its evenness and she was almost yelling now: "You went away on Christmas Eve to stay with friends, didn't you? You didn't tell me what time you were coming back, or if you were coming back. What is more, we weren't on very amicable terms, so you wouldn't expect me to run and tell you what was happening here. Anyway, you made your opinion very plain when we last met. So, yes, we are moving, and soon."

There was a pause before Mrs. Vidler's voice came again, saying now, "And where, may I ask, are you moving to?"

"Well, Mother, for your information, I can tell you that it would be regarded as a small private estate. It is called, Burnstead Mere House."

"*Burnstead Mere?* You can't mean. . . ? You don't mean the Olivers' place? Sir . . . Sir Roger Oliver's house beyond Durham?"

"Yes, that is the house."

"But . . . but it is a large place. It's a . . . "

494

"I know, Mother, it's a large place, with its own swimming pool and large grounds."

"You're flying high, aren't you?"

"Not as high as my husband eventually hopes to fly, Mother."

"Oh, come off it. Don't take that attitude with me. You can't make a silk purse out of a sow's ear, and I've told you that before."

Fiona drew her head back from the phone. She turned and looked to where Nell was standing near the kitchen door and she actually lifted her clenched fist and shook it. Then her mother's voice came again: "And what about me?"

"What about you, Mother?"

"What if I need help and you are miles away? You forget I'm a woman on my own."

"What I don't forget, Mother, is that you are surrounded by your so-called friends. You are rarely in the house; and what is more you are no longer an elderly lady, are you, kicking sixty? You are now, so you would have one understand, a woman in her forties. You could marry again, someone of your own age, whichever one you choose."

"You're being bitchy, aren't you?"

"Yes, Mother, it's my turn, and not before time."

"Well, I can be bitchy, too, dear, and I'll say this: the reason he is putting you in a big house out in the wilds is to hide the monstrosity he's presented you with."

When Fiona dropped the phone onto the stand, placed her hands on the edge of the narrow table, and bent forward, resting her head against the wall, Nell came to her immediately and put her arm around her shoulder. "What is it?" she said. "But need I ask? Oh, she's a devil of a woman that! Come on. Come on. Come and sit down."

Nell now led her into the sitting room, saying hastily, "Don't cry. For goodness sake don't cry; he'll be down in a minute. And if she said . . . oh, I know, it isn't an 'if,' she said something about the child. Well, you know what that'll do to him. Come on. Come on. Pull yourself together. Look I'll get a drink." She quickly poured out a sherry.

"Get that down you," she said, handing it to Fiona. "Oh, here he comes."

Fiona turned and looked towards Bill, but she didn't rise from the couch.

"You all right?"

"Yes, yes."

"Who was that on the phone?"

When she hesitated and looked towards Nell, he said, "Oh, you needn't tell me. What had she to say this time?"

Fiona forced herself to smile. "I told her about the house, and she wanted to know what I was going to do about her, this poor old lady left on her own."

"Oh, tell her we've got a granny flat; tell her not to worry." Then bending over her, he said, "Mrs. Bailey, I'd burn that house down before I'd let her into it. So never let your daughterly compassion get the better of you. You understand?"

"Yes, Mr. Bailey, I understand."

He bent and kissed her; then, looking at Nell, he said, "See that she has a rest; there's plenty time for the packing."

"Yes, master. Will do, master."

"And the same to you." He went out laughing.

Taking her seat beside Fiona, Nell said, "What did she say to knock you out like that?"

"Well, Nell, she said the only thing he was taking the house for was to hide the monstrosity he had given me."

"Oh, my God! She didn't!"

"Yes, she did. And you know something? That's what a lot of people will think. Oh yes, they will. Oh yes, they will. It's the way of the world, and you can't escape it."

45

"COME ON, ANGELA."

"Come on. Come on, Angie, crawl."

"Come on, pet. Come on."

Bill, Katie, and Willie were kneeling at the end of an imitation white fur rug that flanked the large open stone fireplace in which a log fire was blazing. Mark, Sammy, and Mamie knelt to the side of it and all their attention was on the child who lay on its stomach with its elbows half hidden in the pile as it rocked from side to side.

"She's trying. She'll do it! Come on, my angel, come on." Bill held out his hands towards her, and the child, its head up, smiled widely at him, making a gurgling sound. And at this Sammy said, "She won't do it till she's ready."

Fiona, who was sitting on the couch with Nell and Bert, nodded towards Sammy: "You're right, Sammy," she said. "She won't do it till she's ready. I'm told I didn't walk until I was nearly two."

"She'll walk before she's two. Come on, pet. Come on."

Fiona looked down on Bill where he was sitting back on his haunches clapping his hands. How that man loved that child. She loved her, too, but not with his intensity. She doubted that had the child been other than she was he would have showered the love on her that he did. He never came into the house but he made straight for

497

her; and whenever he could he held her, bouncing her in his arms, or holding her high above his head, always taking a delight, it would seem, in her gurgling at him. She was a happy child, she rarely cried. However, she understood from the doctor—a new one since they had come to live here—that, as for walking and talking, she would likely be a late developer. He was a very nice man, this Dr. Pringle. He was one of a small group of three doctors and he had told her that there were eight such children in the practice. And, he had added, they were all happy and lovable. He was very reassuring, and there were times, she had to admit to herself, she needed reassurance. That was one thing she couldn't get from Bill, because he didn't need it; well, if he did, he hid it, and hid it well.

But how different everything had been since they had come into this beautiful house. Sometimes she didn't know whether it was the house or the child; but no, she had to give credit to the child because the children had behaved themselves from the day she had brought Angela home, that awful day when she had been laden down with guilt and shame. And if she was true to herself she must admit that there remained a little of both in her; and she longed to erase it all from her, especially the shame, for why should she be ashamed of this child who had been the means of making her family into a complete unit again? She had been not only irritated but worried by the feeling that had been showing itself between Katie and Willie. Not only did they lash out with their tongues but with their fists. Then their spoiling Mamie had made her quite cheeky at times. Mark was the only one who had remained himself. Yet he went for both Katie and Willie, and, of course, they retaliated likewise. But now all that was as if it had never been: she was often amazed to see how Katie and Willie would give way to each other in nursing the child.

"Look!" cried Willie now, "she's moved her back leg. She's bringing it up."

"She hasn't got a back leg, you idiot!" Katie pushed him. "But yes, she is! She is, Dad. Look, she is."

"She is that," said Bill in awestruck tones as if he was experiencing a minor miracle. "See that, Mrs. B.?"

"What I see," said Fiona, "is that she is being roasted by that fire. Give her here!" She pushed Mark on the shoulder, and he, bending forward, lifted up the child; then, swinging round on his knees, he put her on Fiona's lap.

"A burglar could walk into this place and clear half the house and nobody would notice."

The children sprang up and all eyes were turned towards the door

498

at the end of the long room. And it was Katie who ran forward, saying, "You're back then. You're back."

As she linked her arm in Rupert's he said, "Well, if I'm not, my ghost couldn't keep away."

"Hello there." Bill walked forward to greet Rupert, saying to Katie, "Stop being a nuisance, you. Let the fella get in."

"Katie!" Fiona, too, called to her daughter now, quietly but firmly; then she added, "Take Rupert's coat."

"When did you get back from Scotland? Sit yourself down. Do you want a drink?"

"I got back last night. And yes, oh yes, I could do with a drink."

"Tea or coffee?" It was Katie by his side again; and he smiled at her and said, "May I have something a little stronger, miss?"

Katie looked towards Bill. He nodded, then turned back to Rupert and said, "Would you like it hot? You look frozen. A lot of snow up there?"

Again Rupert answered two questions at once: "That would be very acceptable; hot, and brown sugar." He smacked his lips. "And yes, there was quite a covering of snow. Three-foot drifts in parts. You'll get it next."

"How is Lady Kingdom?"

Rupert turned to Fiona to answer: "Rather lost. They had been married over fifty years, you know; and they'd known each other ten years before that. But her family are very supportive: they all want her to go and live with them, but, as she said, she would then have one leg in Somerset, the other in Jersey, and an arm in Harrogate."

"What's going to happen to the Manor?" It was Nell asking the question, and he said, "Oh, naturally that's got to be sold, Nell. She'd never go back there. Anyway, the upkeep is phenomenal, and it wants so much doing to it. They'll likely pull it down and sell the land."

"Will they now?" Bill's head was nodding, and Rupert replied, "Yes, they will now, Bill. And I was thinking that you should look into it."

"I certainly shall, Rupert, I certainly shall, because the boundary of the estate is cheek by jowl with the last row we're on now. Yes, Rupert, I certainly shall look into it. Anyway, come on into the kitchen and I'll make your toddy."

As Rupert rose, so, too, did Katie, only to be checked by Fiona, saying, "Katie, stay where you are."

"Oh, Mam."

"Never mind, 'oh, Mam.'"

"Could you do with a hot 'un, Bert? No, I'm not enticing you to break the pledge, man, but hot ginger ale isn't bad with lemon. I've had it meself. Good for a cold."

"Thanks all the same, Bill, but I don't trust you."

"My God! What d'you think of that?" He turned to Rupert. "He's tellin' me I'd put a dollop of the hard stuff in."

"Well, that wouldn't surprise me either, Bill."

Bill led the way from the room, saying, "I read somewhere that some bloke said if you could count on one hand two real friends you were lucky. He didn't know what he was talking about."

When the door closed on them, Bert rose from the couch, saying to the boys, "What about a game of table tennis? Sammy and me will take you two on." He nodded from Mark to Willie, and Willie cried, "Fine! Fine!" Then, turning to Fiona, he asked her, "What time's the birthday tea, Mam?"

Fiona glanced at Nell, who just shrugged her shoulders as she said, "Half past four say. You've got a good hour."

As the boys went to scamper from the room, Bert said to Katie, "You coming along?"

"No. What would I do? Just stand and watch."

"We could take turns."

"No, thanks, Bert; I'm all right here. I'm going to read."

"Okay. Everyone to their fancy."

Nell was the next to rise from the couch, saying to Fiona, "Well, I'll go and put the final touches and set another place for Rupert, that's if he'll be staying."

"Oh yes, he will, 'cos he's got no place else to go."

Both Fiona and Nell turned to look at Katie, who then said, "Well, he hasn't, has he? I mean now that the Manor is going to be sold."

Nell again shrugged her shoulders and went out. And Fiona said to her daughter who was curled up in the corner of the couch, "Come here, Katie."

Slowly Katie unwound her legs before hitching herself up towards her mother, who was now leaning forward and placing the child on a cushion in the middle of the large armchair to the side of the couch. Having settled the child she turned to her daughter and, taking both her hands, said, "My dear, I must talk to you about Rupert. Please! Please, don't pull your hands away; and don't look like that, dear. You have been such a good daughter to me this past year; we've never had a cross word and I don't want us to have one now. But . . . but it's for your own good I'm going to say, you must stop—" she was going

500

to use the word pestering; instead she softened it with, "paying so much attention to Rupert."

"*Oh, Mam. Mam.*" The words were a cross between a cry and a protest.

"I know, I know how you feel. I felt like that once, just the same as you do now. He happened to be a greengrocer and I couldn't wait for his weekly visit. Don't . . . please don't pull away from me. Rupert is a man; he is thirty years old. He is admittedly very attractive, but you are a twelve-year-old girl."

"I'm nearly thirteen and older men marry young girls. The film star Frank . . ."

"What film stars do and ordinary people do are vastly different things."

"Do you consider you and Dad ordinary, Mam?"

This was a poser, but Fiona had to say, "Yes, yes, I do."

"Well, you are only thirty-two and Dad is forty-nine; so what are you talking about? There are seventeen between you, and . . . and I could be married when I'm sixteen."

"*Katie! Katie!* What are you saying? And what are you thinking? Oh, I know what you're thinking. Well, let me tell you that Rupert will never marry anyone. Never!"

"What . . . what are you saying? He's already married?"

"No, he's not already married. More's the pity."

"Then why can't he marry?"

"There is a reason."

"I . . . I don't believe you, Mam. You are just saying this to put me off. But it won't; I'll wait. I know how I feel. I'll wait."

"*Katie!*" She now pulled her hands from Katie's and clapped one across her mouth, realising that she had shouted.

And she expected Katie to turn now and fly from the room, but the girl just sat, staring at her, her lips trembling, her eyes wet with unshed tears.

"You're being cruel, Mam. I . . . I love Rupert."

"Katie"—Fiona closed her eyes and brought her chin tight into her neck—"all girls your age go through this pash experience. . . ."

"It isn't a pash. Nancy Burke's got a pash on Mr. Richards and Mary Parkin has a pash on Miss Taylor, and so have other girls. But I haven't got a pash on Rupert. It isn't like that. I know it isn't. *I know it isn't.*"

Looking at her daughter, Fiona thought: Very likely it isn't; these things happen. And she is a sensible girl. She's always been sensible, always older than her years. She . . . she must be told.

Fiona turned and put her hand out and straightened the dribble bib on the baby's pretty frilly dress; then she turned back to Katie and said, "Do you think you're old enough to keep a secret?"

Katie did not reply, and so she went on, "If I tell you why Rupert will never marry, will you promise not to divulge it or let him know you know the reason?"

When again she got no answer from her daughter, only that wide bright-eyed moist stare, she said, "Rupert was to be married to his childhood sweetheart. Everything was arranged. The young girl was a distant relative of Sir Charles and Lady Kingdom. One night just before the wedding, they attended a dance. He had gone to get the car to take her home. When he returned she wasn't there. She was found the next morning in the shrubbery. She had been—" She hesitated, then went on, "she had been raped and hit over the head with some instrument. And this resulted in her being in a coma for a long time, and from then she has never spoken. But she has dreadful screaming fits, and is now in Hetherington House, where she will likely remain until she dies. And she's still a young girl, frozen into the time when that dreadful thing happened. That's why Rupert acted as secretary to Sir Charles, in order to stay near her. And that is why, since Sir Charles has died, he will now remain here in order to be near her, for as he told your father, he feels he is married to her, that she is his wife in everything but name."

Her daughter's face was now drained of colour; the eyes were wide; the moisture had gone from them, and in its place was a look that could only be described as hopelessness. But then Katie's next words contradicted her assumption, for she said, "She could die sometime."

"Oh, Katie, how can you say such a thing. Anyway, she could live for years, years, and years. And let me tell you that Rupert lives in hope of her recovering, no matter what the doctor says, because only a short while ago she called his name, and that was the first time she had spoken. So get it out of your head, girl"—her voice was harsh now—"Rupert is not for you; nor does he want you. He thinks of you as a child. He puts up with your fussing, let me tell you, because he's a gentleman and it would be bad manners to thrust you off."

She watched the colour flood back into her daughter's face, saw the lips tremble and the tears spurt from her eyes. And when her arms went out and pulled her into her embrace Katie muttered, "Oh, Mam. Mam," and she murmured, "There, there."

"Oh, Mam, I'm so unhappy, I . . . I want to die."

"I know, dear, I know; but that feeling will pass."

"No, it never will. It never will."

"I promise you it will. It won't be long before you find another boy; in fact, I know someone who already has his eye on you. In the words of a story, I would say he is enamoured of you. Mark laughs because Roland is always talking about you."

"Oh, Roland Featherstone. He's only a boy!"

"He is fast growing out of being a boy: he's turned fourteen, nearly fifteen and very attractive."

"Oh, Mam, be quiet! Be quiet! I . . . I can't help it about Rupert and . . . and that woman."

"Girl, Katie."

"Well, whoever, I . . . I'll go on loving him."

"That's up to you, my dear, if you want to cause yourself pain. But you've got to also tell yourself that he will never love you other than as a nice girl. Now look, dry your eyes, the others will be coming back shortly. Better still, go out the side door, through the conservatory, and up the back way to your room. Wash your face and put some cream on. You made up very well the other night for the school party, though a bit too heavy in parts, especially round the eyes. Really you don't need mascara; your lashes are dark and long and they enhance your eyes. I'd always go lightly with makeup around the eyes if I were you. Go on now. Wait a moment!" She grabbed her arm. "You won't let Rupert know what I've told you."

"No; no, Mam."

"Go on now, dear."

Meanwhile, in the kitchen, Rupert was saying to Bill, "But I know nothing whatever about cars except how to drive them."

"You're not expected to know anything about cars, man. Mechanics can see to that side of the business. But it needs somebody there with a presence like yours, a fella who can talk to customers and give an air of class to the place. Oh aye, I know, I'm rubbin' it on thick, but you must have the same opinion of yourself if you spoke the truth. Anyway, Fuller and his wife are goin' next week. I took him on the references and they were glowing. He must have written them out himself. Aye, there was one thing he could write all right, his expense accounts. My God! If you saw how much it cost me for him to even run into Newcastle. But when he went to Harrogate and took his wife and two kids with him and stayed in a five-star hotel, well that put the finish to Mr. Fuller.

"Anyway, there it is. There's a flat above, and it's a very pleasant flat. The back looks onto fields, the only farm left in this district I should think. What is more, I want somebody who can give orders in a nice way, an' you're used to that, for you've been the mouthpiece of the old boy for years. . . . Oh, I know. An' so did Lady Kingdom. She said as much to me: 'What would we do without Rupert to soothe the savage beasts that a certain gentleman creates.' She was meaning Sir Charles. And I don't know what screw the old fella gave you, but I'll meet it and a little more likely. You'll also get your cut on sales. As for the fellas there: two are good mechanics, but the third one's goin'. He's simply a greaser and I'm not payin' a greaser mechanic's wages, I can tell you that. And as yet there's only one young fella in the showroom. He'll come on, I'm sure. He had to do the business when Fuller went on his jaunts. From what I understand his wife liked jaunts: hardly a day but they didn't take a jaunt. There'll have to be a lot of reorganizing done; I'll leave that to you. You've been in enough garages, I'm sure, to see the ones you'd go back to and the ones you wouldn't. With the right management and the right workmen that place could be a little gold mine. What about it?"

"I'm very grateful, Bill; you know I can't leave the county. But only this morning I rented a flat for three months."

"Aw, don't worry about that; we'll make that good. Here, shake hands on it."

As they shook hands Rupert said, "Thank you, Bill. You've been a good friend to me."

"I wasn't at first; now, was I?"

"No; no, you certainly weren't: you played the jealous husband to a tee."

"Yes, I did; and that would have gone on, mind, if you hadn't told me the situation. And I shouldn't have been a bit surprised if I'd done a Davey Love on you."

"By the way, how is Davey these days?"

"Oh, the same as ever. If that fella was being hanged you'd have to laugh at him. You know, he made more friends when he was doing his community sentence than half a dozen men would make in their lifetimes. You'll see him later; he's comin' to the tea, so we'll get a laugh if nothin' else. He'll likely shock Miss Isherwood; but then, I don't know."

"Have I met her?"

"Oh no; I forgot. She's come on the scene since you've been away. Our scene, I should have said, for she's been on the scene for longer than this house has stood. She lives in the bungalow just down the road. It's the only other habitation around here. Fiona met up with her when she was out with the pram one day and they got on talkin'.

Our land here belonged to her grandfather. The bungalow has been extended from an old stone cottage which was their original home so she tells us. Yes, her grandfather owned all this land. Of course, it was merely fields then, and he sold it to Mr. Oliver, that was before he was knighted. He built this place, and I am glad he did because where would you find a more lovely house, Rupert, eh? And a happier family—because somethin' seems to have happened to everybody since we came here."

Bill paused and looked away for a moment before he added, "But I don't think that's quite true; I think we might have something to thank the child for. She has linked the lot of us in a chain around her, a happy chain. Anyway"—his voice rose again—"Miss Caroline Isherwood is comin' to Angela's first birthday party. She's a librarian by the way."

"Librarian? Oh. Young, middle-aged, or getting on a bit?"

"Young, my dear sir, young. I don't know her age, but I would say it would be twenty-four, twenty-five; not good-looking, no interestin' face, but very smart. You know, a figure like two lats." He pushed Rupert on the shoulder. "Davey's lost his lady-love, the barmaid, you know. I think it was all to do with Sammy. Sammy didn't take to her. I wonder if he'll take to the librarian? That would be funny, wouldn't it?"

"It would be funnier if the librarian took to Davey."

"Aye, you've said something there, it certainly would. But still, you never know, stranger things happen. Have you finished that toddy?"

"Yes, and it's gone down to my toes."

"Well, let's get back and see if we've been missed. Oh"—he nodded at Rupert now—"you'll have been missed all right, Katie's taken you over. But I'm tellin' you, she's a determined young miss that; you'll have to slap her down if she gets a bit too possessive like. You know what I mean. Young lasses like that want slappin' down. So you slap her down. You have my permission."

"Oh, Bill! I could never slap Katie down. Anyway, she's just a child."

He was about to repudiate this and say, "Katie's no child, lad. Katie's no child," but then if Rupert thought that Katie was just a child, well and good.

46

BILL PULLED HIS CAR TO AN ABRUPT STOP ON THE WIDE FORECOURT OF THE garage, jumped out, and almost ran into the showroom, then wended his way through a number of new cars to the office where Rupert, having seen his approach, had risen from his seat behind his desk. And as Bill came in the door he said, "I can see by your face it's good news."

"Aye, lad; I've clinched it."

"The lot?"

"Aye, the lot. But, of course, there's conditions. I knew there would be. All that matters though is we're all set for another spell. By, lad, it's been hard work."

"Can I get you a cup of tea?"

"No; no, I want more than a cup of tea, man. I'm on me way home, but I thought I'd pop in and tell you because I've got you to thank for this."

"I've done nothing."

"You put me onto it and tipped me off as to who to see an' who to deal with. And there's been some sticky individuals."

"You can take the house down?"

"No, I can't. But that might prove better in the end. It's got to stand in three acres; but I can turn it into some high-class flats."

"Yes; yes, that's an idea."

"Of course that's another thing that'll have to be worked out. But as it stands, it's detached houses with not less than a quarter of an acre. They were adamant on that. And that suits me. McGilroy's got good ideas in that head of his. We'll put up some spankers. Aw, lad." He now pushed Rupert with his doubled fist. "It's been a long haul and I hadn't Sir Charles's voice for me at the table this time."

"And he was always for you. He thought a great deal of you. You know, Bill, he used to say, given the chance earlier on, you could have been a captain of industry. But then you could still."

"Huh!" Bill laughed. "Captain of industry. I'm damn lucky to be second mate, even one of the crew. But no, never one of the crew, not me! I must get back and tell Fiona. By the way, we'll hold the tea for you."

"No, don't do that. I won't be able to get there till about seven."

"Let Mickey close up for you and Joe see to the shop below."

"I'd rather you didn't wait; I'll pop along later. And you know, I can't think it's a year since her last birthday."

"Nor me. Her birthday, as you know, was really on Monday; but Nell was under the weather, had been a couple of days, so we put it off."

They walked down the showroom together; as they reached the door it was pushed open and Bill said in some surprise, "Well, fancy meetin' you here. What you after? Goin' to buy a car? Oh, I can sell you a nice one; it's goin' cheap at the price. Seven thousand five hundred. I'll knock a hundred off to you. What d'you say?"

Caroline Isherwood smiled widely at Bill and immediately took up his attitude. "I'm not interested in anything in that range, Mr. Bailey," she said. "You had a Volvo in last week, in the window there." She waved her hand airily. "It was only thirteen thousand. Have you anything in that range still?"

After they had all laughed together, Rupert said, "She's all ready and waiting. Hang on a minute, and I'll come round the back." But he seemed hesitant to move. Looking at the smart young woman, Bill said, "Why don't you pop in more often and see my wife? You'd be very welcome. We hardly catch a glimpse of you and yet you're only down the road."

"I'm a working girl, Mr. Bailey."

"Aye, I understand that. But there's long evenings and weekends, and you've just said you're on your own. I've thought about you once or twice. Anyway, we're havin' a little birthday party for my daughter. How about it the night?"

Did Bill's sharp eye detect a movement of the head towards Rupert, still standing hesitant? And when she said, "I have tickets for a concert in Durham," he said, "Oh, well; I can't stand up against the concert, I can only put on a turn by a pair called Love, father and son. But I'll bet you won't get as many laughs at your concert as you would from these two."

"I don't suppose we'll get any laughs from this concert; it's a Mozart."

"Oh." Bill pulled a long face. "Mozart. That fella." Then, his eyes twinkling, he looked at Rupert and said, "He plays a ukulele, doesn't he?"

"Go on with you!"

He went out, got into the car, started up the engine, then looked through the side window to where, under the bright overhead lights, they were both standing shoulder to shoulder. And as he put his foot on the accelerator he said to himself, "Aye, aye! How long has that been goin' on?" Then he didn't ask why his mind should jump immediately to Katie: she doted on that fella, although she had stopped pawing him about since her mother had that talk with her last year and put her in the picture. Fiona said she'd just had to, and he agreed with her. Katie was thirteen now, nearing fourteen. It was a tricky age with lasses, as it was with lads. And Katie's brain was away beyond her years in all ways. If her marks came below ninety at school she had a crying match. She couldn't bear to be beaten. Well, life would likely knock that out of her, but it would take time. She had those teenage years to go through. With one thing and another Fiona had her hands full. Oh yes, for there was Willie, too. He wouldn't let himself breathe unless Sammy was about. Then Mamie. My, there was a little madam. She got the surprise of her life last week that one, when he scudded her backside for her. That had given her something to have a tantrum about. All because she couldn't have a gold charm bangle. "I'll send to my grandfather," she had said. "He'll let me have some of my money." Ooh, by, she thought a cuddy had kicked her. And when she was told that arrangements could be made right away for her to go to Wales and stay with her grandparents she howled. And then there was Mark. But there was no girl trouble with Mark. In a way he could wish there was because he spent too much time round his mother. Yet he mustn't grumble about that; the boy had been protective of her before he himself had come on the scene. He must remember that. And Mark was a good lad. And what was more these days and while his mind was on them he must remember, too, that they were all of one accord when it came to the child. But who could help loving her; she gave out love with every breath. And now she was walking and saying a word here and there. And only he himself knew what that meant; even Fiona, as perceptive as she was, didn't realise the effect that child had on him and the feeling she wrought in him. He doubted very much now that, if she had been wholly normal, she would have touched his depth in the way that with her handicap she did.

He went into the house, demanding loudly as he usually did when no one was in sight: "Where is everybody?"

By the time he had taken off his coat, hat, and muffler Fiona had appeared at the top of the broad staircase, calling, "We're up here, dear."

She waited until he reached the landing before asking, "Well, how did it go?"

"It's clinched, lass."

"Really?"

"Yes; yes, really." And putting his hands on her shoulders he bent forward and kissed her on the lips; then, looking into her eyes, he said, "Nothin's goin' to hold that fella back now. The estate contract was big, but this one'll set me name up. These houses will be known as William Bailey's houses. You'll want for nothing: anything you set your heart on in the future you'll have."

"I've all I want, Bill, and more. I've told you dozens of times. This house is to be our home until they all grow up and, as I've said, even after they've gone, and—" She now poked him in the chest with her finger while she added, "and when I'm pushing you round in a wheelchair."

As they walked along the landing he said, "I called at the garage to tell Rupert because, you know, he went a long way in coaching me as to the temperament of Sir Charles's trustees. And who d'you think called in for her car?"

"Well, who? I'm no good at guessing."

"Our neighbour, Miss Caroline Isherwood."

"Well, I suppose ... Was her car in?"

"Yes, I understand her car's been in for some repair or other, but I seem to detect a closer association than manager and client between them."

"How do you make that out?"

"Oh, one of my forty senses. And he won't be in to tea the night. He had previously made an excuse that he couldn't be here before seven. I'd even said we could put the meal back. But no, no. And then Miss Isherwood refused my invitation, too. She was goin' to a Mozart concert. Now, I ask you, Mrs. B., who else is very fond of Mozart if not our dear Rupert?"

509

"Well, you can't blame him, can you?" She put a warning finger to her lips before adding quietly, "Anyway, they could be just friendly."

"Aye, they could. I'm not suggesting anything else at present, but I'm hoping that they get to be more than friendly, for his sake anyway."

"Bill!"

"Well, that's what you're wishin', too, isn't it?"

"Yes; yes, I am, but"—she turned and looked along the corridor from where the sound of raised voices and laughter came—"she'll be upset if she gets to know. I've thought that over the past year she would have grown out of him, but although she behaves herself when he's here, I'm afraid she's still got this thing about him. And I'm sure he's sensed it because he's very tactful in that he doesn't give her any opportunity to get too close. He's either letting Mamie hang on to him or holding Angela. By the way"—her voice lightened—"you must come and see. You know that box of plasticine that Mamie used to play with? Well, apparently she was clearing out her cupboard and she put it on the floor, and Angela toddled over to it, sat down beside it, and started to play with it. I think it was the different colours that attracted her at first. That was a few days ago. I saw her squashing it in her hand and I went to take it from her, because I thought she would mess herself up. But her face started to crumple as if she was going to cry, so I left her to it. Well, about an hour ago she went to the cupboard, I wasn't in the room, but Katie said she pulled the plasticine box out, took off the lid, and picked up a piece of red plasticine and started to roll it between her two hands. And Katie said she made a biggish ball; then a smaller ball, and then tried to stick them together. It was then that Katie came shouting for me because what Angela was trying to do was copy the fat boy on the lid whose head was a round ball and his body a bigger ball. And when I got into the room there she was, looking up at me and pointing to the two plasticine balls. Willie and Sammy were there, too, and apparently what Sammy had done was to roll two pieces longways to represent legs. And when he stuck them onto the body she laughed and laughed. Come and see."

As they entered the playroom they were greeted with a chorus of, "Hello, Dad," and a repeat of Fiona's words, "Come and see! Come and see what Angela's done." But when the child put her arms around Bill's neck Fiona cried, "Oh, your suit."

"Who worries about a suit? How's my clever girl?"

The child, her mouth wide, said something that sounded like, "Di . . . da." And Bill repeated, "Yes, Da . . . da."

510

"Di . . . da. Di . . . da."

Bill put the child down on the floor and she immediately went to the plasticine box, and when Sammy lifted up the two balls and the legs dropped off there was much laughter and booing from the others. And he, kneeling before the child, said, "Well, I'm not as clever as she is, am I Angie?"

The child was obviously enjoying this and she threw herself against him, her arms around his neck, and when they both fell sideways there was more laughter.

Fiona stooped down and picked up the child, thinking as she did so, Nobody's going to stop him calling her Angie now; I should have nipped it in the bud in the first place. But what odds! It was strange, though, how she always threw herself upon Sammy. With others she would put her arms around their neck and hug them tight. But always her attitude towards Sammy was this throwing of her whole self at him. Probably it was because she didn't see Sammy as often as she saw the other children. It could be the way he held her; as he had done right from the very first. He hadn't just nursed her, he had rocked her, continuously rocked her until at times she had to say, "Don't your arms ache, Sammy?"

"Why, no!" He would answer. "Should they?"

Sammy now brought Bill's attention to himself when he said, "Well, I'll be off."

"What d'you mean, you'll be off? You're stayin' to tea, aren't you? Your da's comin'."

"No; no, he's not. That's why I'm goin' home. He . . . he had to come home at dinnertime. He had a pain in his bell . . . stomach. He went and lay down. I just came round to bring Angie's present."

"Pain in his stomach? Had he a skinful last night?"

"No, he wasn't out. He hasn't been out nights this week, not since he broke off with her, his . . . his girlfriend."

"He's broken off with her, final, has he?"

"Aye, so he says. But she'll be after him again."

Bill was bending down to Sammy and he said, "He's not been out at nights at all? Is he bad? Does he look bad?"

"No; no, he doesn't look bad, but he sounds bad. He's not cussin' so much."

"Well, hold your hand a minute. Wait downstairs; I'll run you home."

"I've got me bike; there's no need."

"If I remember rightly the idea was for you to stay the night and go back in the daylight; so go downstairs and wait a minute; your bike can go in the boot. I want to have a word with your da."

511

Bill turned to Fiona, saying, "It's goin' to be a family party this. Rupert, now Davey."

Before Fiona could say anything, Katie, with a worried expression on her face jumped up, saying, "Rupert's not coming? Why?"

"He didn't give me any reason except that he's got another engagement."

"But he said he was coming. He always comes. I mean he comes to all our parties."

"Yes, he does; but tonight he's got an engagement."

"What kind of an engagement?"

Bill's voice startled them all as he yelled at her, "I don't know what kind of engagement; I only know that Rupert is a man an' that he's got his own life to live an' he doesn't tell me who he's goin' to meet or what he's goin' to do with his evenings. Whether he plays Ping-Pong, or squash, or takes a lass out, or what have you, he hasn't got to confide in me, nor you, miss, nor anybody else in this house. So get that into your head."

Fiona said nothing but she followed him onto the landing, and they were going down the stairs before she said, "That was a bit thick."

"It had to come. There'll be trouble one of these days if she doesn't wake up. You'll have to have a talk with her."

"Oh, Bill; I've had a talk with her. She's at an awkward age. It's only time that will talk her out of it."

"Well, all I can say is, roll on time. . . . Oh, love"—his voice dropped—"after such a good day it's a disappointin' evenin'. But there must be something wrong with Davey for him to leave the job, and I want to find out what. I won't be long."

As he made his way to the cloakroom at the far end of the hall the phone rang, and Fiona went towards the marble-topped, half-moon table with the bronze supports that Bill had bought with the other oddments in the house. There was a comfortable straight-backed yellow upholstered chair to the side of it, and as she sat down she picked up the phone and was halfway giving the number when the voice said, "Fiona."

How was it, she thought, that even her name on her mother's lips seemed to carry censure.

"Yes, Mother."

"This is the third time I've tried to get through. I tried twice yesterday."

"Well, we've been here all the time, Mother. Oh, perhaps yesterday—it was so sunny we must have been out in the garden. Such a change to have such a day this time of the year."

She was speaking in a pleasant conversational tone when her mother said, "I have news for you."

"Yes? I hope it's good."

"Well, you'll likely think so, by getting rid of me."

"Oh, Mother! Please, please don't start. Tell me your good news."

"I'm going to be married."

Fiona paused before she said, "Oh ... well, I'm happy for you, Mother." Her mind jumped to Davey—his girlfriend had left. "Is he someone local, Mother?"

"No, he's no one local. He's an American and lives there. I'm going next week."

"To America?"

"Yes, to America. I've been before, you know."

"Yes, I know, but ... but to live there."

"Well, that should please you, dear: no more troublesome mother, no more interfering grandmother. But then I don't get much of a chance, do I? I very rarely see my grandchildren."

"That is your fault, Mother. I've asked you numerous times to come here. I said I would pick you up at any time you liked. But no, you couldn't bear to see the house that Bill had given me; and now apparently you never will. I suppose your future husband is one of those gentlemen you met when you were last in America?"

"Yes, he is; and I was stupid enough to spurn his attentions then."

Spurn his attentions. Dear, dear! She hoped whoever the future husband was he would enjoy her phraseology.

"When are you leaving, Mother?"

"Next Tuesday."

"As soon as that?"

"Yes, as soon as that. The house is up for sale and the furniture is to be auctioned in Newcastle. It's all in hand."

"May I ask if your future husband is in a good position?"

"A very good position, very good. He's in what you call the real estate business. He deals with the buying and selling of big ranches, no small stuff."

"I'm so pleased to hear that; you'll be well taken care of."

"Yes, I'll be well taken care of, Fiona."

"Oh, Mother."

"It's too late, Fiona, for soft talk. You have never understood me. You have never tried. However, I suppose I'll see you before I go."

She found it difficult to answer for a moment, and then she said, "Yes; yes, of course, Mother. I'll come over tomorrow."

"I'll be out all day tomorrow and I'll be very busy visiting friends until next Tuesday. If you have time you can come and see me off

513

at Newcastle airport. As it is the last time we are likely to meet unless I decide to come back for a holiday, perhaps you could arrange to drive me to the airport? I've got to be there by eleven o'clock."

Again she found difficulty in speaking; and then she said, "Yes, Mother, I'll do that. I'll be there."

"Thank you, Fiona."

The line went dead. She replaced the phone and looked to where Bill was standing near the front door. "I can always tell by your face when it's her," he said.

"She's leaving. She ... she's going to America to be married."

"Oh, thank God for double mercies! Now, lass, don't you be a hypocrite and say you're sorry, because she's been tangled in your hair ever since you can remember."

"Oh, you don't know what I ... well, I'm glad she's going to America. Yes, I'm glad she's going to be married. Yes, I am. But I'm sorry for her reasons for going. She's like somebody drowning; she's clutching at straws."

"Oh, I shouldn't worry about that side of it, lass; she'll enjoy it. She'll play the English lady to the last curtain. And you know the Americans fall over themselves for nobility. And she can ape the so-called class to a tee, can your mother. Come on, come on; don't let that worry you. Face up to facts. You've never got on, never. So don't get sentimental about her goin' to America. Anyway, the way planes fly now it's like goin' across the river to North Shields."

He kissed her, then opened the front door and, looking down the drive to where Sammy was standing with his bike, said, "The fact that that lad is wantin' to get home tells me there's something wrong with Davey. Anyway, I won't be long, love." He kissed her again, then went out.

Having put Sammy's bike in the boot of the car, he said to the boy, "Get yourself in."

He started the car, then straightaway turned to Sammy and asked, "Are you worried about your da?"

"Some."

"Some a lot or some a little?"

"He's not like himself, an' he's not eatin' like he used to either, just at times."

"Is he still drinkin'?"

"Aye, I suppose so."

"How much?"

"He gets through two or three cans. I think he must be worryin' about his job."

"Worryin' about his job?" Bill glanced quickly at the boy. "What makes you think that?"

"He was dozing the other night and he woke himself yellin', 'I'm as fit as the next. I can do me job.'"

"Well, he's got no need to worry about his job. He's a good worker is your da."

"I know that. He might be thick about some things, but he's a worker."

Again Bill glanced at him, and now his voice was harsh as he said, "Don't call your da thick. He's no more thick than you or me."

Sammy now turned his head slowly and looked at Bill as he said, "If anybody was sayin' that you an' me da were alike up top, you'd want to knock their bloody ... well *you would*, you'd want to knock their *bloody heads off.*"

Bill drew in a breath that expanded his waistcoat. He wanted to check the boy straightaway for the "bloody," but then how could he? His father's vocabulary was made up of bloody, buggers, and sods, nothing further, just those three words. But the lad was stuck in between the private school wallahs and his da. And it was ten to one his da would always win. At least the lad was sensible enough to tone it down when up at the house.

He made to change the subject now by saying, "Willie tells you're good at maths; you came out on top in the exam."

"Anybody can do that if they can understand the computer. It's that that does it."

"Don't be daft. Where would the computer be without your mind or anybody else's? In the long run they only do what they're told."

Out of the blue Sammy said, "Katie's worried. She's ... she's upset about somethin'."

Bill stared ahead at the two red rear lights of the car some way in front. Nothing escaped this little bloke. "What makes you think that?" he asked.

"Well, she doesn't cry for nowt, not Katie."

He swung the wheel round and entered the side street before he said, "Cryin'? Katie? When was this?"

"Oh, a while back." And then he added, "You want to know somethin'?"

"Aye, aye."

"She's not worried about school."

"Then why did you say she was worried?"

"I was bein' what you could call tactful and evasive."

Tactful and evasive, he said. Put in that way he was certainly pickin' up somethin' from his private education, on one side at least.

"Well, would you mind tellin' me what you're bein' tactful and evasive about?"

"You'll bawl me out."

"I don't see why I should as long as you're tellin' the truth and not tryin' to cause mischief."

"I never try to cause mischief. I don't do that."

"Samuel Love. I've warned you about barkin' at me."

"Aye, well. And I've told you once afore an' all when you called me a liar that I didn't tell bloody lies, 'cos I wasn't afraid to speak the truth. I'm not afraid of nobody."

"Big fella, aren't you? Big fella."

"No, 'cos I've been a little fella for a long time, an' been made to face it."

Well, the private school might be puttin' some long words into his mouth but they couldn't do much to alter that character. It had been formed a long time ago and apparently it knew all about itself. By, aye, it did. He wasn't afraid of anybody 'cos he had been little. He said now, "Well, what's this you think that's troublin' Katie?"

"Mr. Meredith."

The wheel moved sharply under Bill's hands although he was on a straight course. "Mr. Meredith? What's he got to do with it?"

"She's got a thing about him. Always has had since I remember. An' now he's got this other lass. Well, she's not a lass, it's Miss Isherwood from along the road in the bungalow."

"How d'you make that out?"

"I've seen them together twice. I saw them comin' out of the pictures one day; another time I saw them goin' into the park."

"Did you now? Did you now?" Well, there was one thing sure, Katie didn't know about this.

"What are you goin' to do about it?"

He had reached the Crescent and pulled the car to a stop. He turned and looked at Sammy and, putting his hand out and laying it on the boy's shoulder, he said, "I can do nothin' about it, laddie. She'll have to get over it. You see, we all go through these phases. You will an' all. Oh yes, you will." He was wondering why he was emphasising it because the boy had made no denial of what might lie before him, no protest as some boys would have done. Just as Katie was older than her years, so was this little fella. And he wasn't so little anymore either, he was sproutin' all right. "Time'll take care of it," he said. "She'll get over it. But she must work things out for herself. You understand? Nobody's goin' to enlighten her about this. D'you get me?"

516

"Aye, I get you. And you needn't tell me not to open me mouth."

"No, Sammy, no, I needn't. But thanks for . . . well, for tellin' me. Not that I haven't guessed somethin' along the same lines meself; and her mother has an' all."

"You have?"

"Oh aye, yes."

"An' you've still done noth . . .?" He shook his head, then added, "Well, as you say, she's got to work it out. But it's rotten."

There was feeling in the last words as if in some way he had experienced what Katie was going through.

"Come on, out you get."

"It's us, Da." The boy called as soon as he opened the front door, and Davey's answering voice came from a room off the small hall: "What's brought you back so early?"

"I had to drive Mr. B. into town; he was frightened of the dark."

Bill laughed as he followed the boy into the sitting room, there to see Davey pulling himself up from a low black leather chair.

"Hello, boss. What brings you here? Oh—" He pulled his neck up out of the thick sweater, saying, " 'Cos I left the job."

"Sit yourself down. What I want to know is, what took you from the job?"

As his father sat down, Sammy said, "You had any tea, Da?"

"No, not yet. Anyway, I'm not hungry."

"Well, you had better 'cos I'm goin' to make it; and if you don't eat it I'll throw it over you."

As the boy walked out Davey laughed and shook his head, saying to Bill, "See what I've got to put up with? That's what a private school does. Dear God! Havin' to pay money for that."

"He's all right. You'll not have to worry about him, but what about you? Now, what's the matter with you?"

"Nowt, boss, really. I just had a pain in me gut, that's all . . . I'd . . . I'd been runnin' all mornin', so I thought . . . well."

"Have you had the doctor?"

"Doctor?" Davey pulled himself farther up against the back of the couch. "Doctor? What do I want with a doctor? I've had the cramp, a bit of diarrhea. Something I've eaten."

"From what I hear you've had this cramp on and off for some time. And you're not eatin'!"

"Huh! That 'un"—Davey thumbed towards the door—"he's got a mouth as big as mine already. What he'll be like when he grows up God an' His Holy Mother only knows. I tell you, boss, I'm all right. I'll be back on the job the morrow."

517

"You won't be back on the job the morrow. You'll get yourself to the doctor's."

"Not me, boss; I've never been to the doctor's in me life. I came into the world without one and I'll go out without one."

"Big fella, aren't you?"

"Aye, from the head downwards."

"What's happened to you and your lady friend?"

"Oh, we didn't see eye to eye. But truth to tell, boss, it was more Sammy an' her didn't see eye to eye. An' you know, I'd had enough of argy-bargy with the other one and I wasn't gonna have it with this 'un. She had no claim on me, nor me on her for that matter. To tell you the truth, I'm glad it's ended. She was after havin' a wedding ring on her finger. Oh, God Almighty, that scared me. She was all right at first, mind: anything goes; that was her attitude. Then she gets broody, lookin' at bairns in prams. It was then I saw the red light. I think I made him"—he again pointed towards the door—"the excuse. Anyway, you can get too much of a good thing you know." He pulled a face. "I must be gettin' old afore me time. And I don't know whether you've experienced it, boss, likely you have, but some women'd eat you alive, straight on without a sprinkle of salt or a dust of pepper and they wouldn't leave a bit of you for the morrow."

"Aw, Davey." Bill started to laugh. "There must be somethin' radically wrong with you if your nightlife's gone astray."

"Aye, I thought that meself, boss, I thought that meself. Aye, I did. God's truth I did."

"Aw, Davey."

"What d'you really think of the young 'un, boss, I mean your real opinion?"

"What do I think of Sammy? I think he's a fine lad. And I'll tell you somethin' else, I envy you, that you've got a son like him. That's not to say I don't love my youngster, I more than love her, but there are times when . . . well . . . you know what I mean, as one to another, a man thinks of a son. He knows he's goin' to die some day, but in a son he'll live again, more so than in a daughter. You know what I mean?"

"Aye, boss." Davey was looking into the fire now. "Aye, I know what you mean about livin' again in your son. But I hope he makes a better job of his life than I have, 'cos what have I done with it? The only peak I've reached is two court appearances and land meself up in jail, not forgettin' me hundred hours community work. Let's hope he does better than that."

What could he say? It was quite true; that's all Davey had done with his life. Yet, on the other hand, he made people happy. Usually he had only to open his mouth and he caused laughter. And so he was forced to say, "That might be so, Davey, but, on the other hand, you've caused a lot of fun in your time. You've made people laugh who didn't know how to. And don't forget, most of all, you fathered Sammy."

The door was pushed open and Sammy entered, carrying a tray. He started straightaway, "It's nice boiled ham and you like cold sausages," he said. "I've cut the bread and butter thin." And turning to Bill, he said, "I've brought you a cup of tea an' all."

"Thanks, Sammy. That'll be welcome, that's if it's strong."

"Aye, it's strong. I stuck a knife in it and it didn't fall over."

"You'll get your ears clipped me lad"—his father was nodding at him—"with your smart aleck answers."

Bill now watched Davey look down on the plate, then look at his son, and say, "Now I'll have that with a glass of beer in a little while, but I'll enjoy the tea. How many sugars did you put in?"

"The usual. I should know by now, shouldn't I?"

"You see what I've got to put up with? That's what a private school does for you. Begod, he's comin' away from there, and soon."

Bill and Sammy exchanged knowing glances, and when Davey had finished his tea and lay back against the head of the couch, conversation became a little strained; and so Bill rose, saying, "Well, now, I'm not expectin' to see you the morrow or the next day. You get to the doctor's in the mornin'."

"We'll see."

"No we'll see; if it's diarrhea he'll give you something for it."

"Well, that's all it is. I know me inside. But thanks, boss, for comin'." His voice dropped. "I'm grateful. I'm always grateful to you and your family, always: for one big reason at least, and you know what that is. Good night to you."

"Good night, Davey."

At the door Bill, bending down to Sammy, said, "Don't you go to school the morrow; see that he gets to the doctor's, d'you hear?"

"Aye; aye, I hear. But it's easier said than done. He'll likely turn up for work."

"If he does then I'll send him back. Anyway do your best." He ruffled the boy's hair, then went out.

At home Fiona met him in the hall. "How did you find him?" she said.

"To tell the truth I don't know. He says he's got diarrhea, but from what the lad says he hasn't been eatin', and for some time, and he

519

doesn't go out at nights. And you should see him, the look of him; I'd like to bet it's somethin' more than diarrhea."

"Has he been to the doctor?"

"No, and it's going to take an explosion to get him there; he's never been to a doctor in his life apparently. He hadn't one to bring him into the world, he says, and he's not goin' to have one to see him out of it. I don't like it." He took her arm and walked her across the hall and into the long drawing room. "It's odd, don't you think, how he and that lad have got under me skin, under all our skins. I suppose it's because they're laughter makers. But like all laughter makers there's another side to them. And I saw that side the night, and it saddened me: it was as if I, too, was picking up the other side of them, the lonely lost side. . . . Oh, as Davey himself would say, let's stop mummerin' and have a drink. Come on with you."

47

IT WAS BOXING DAY; AS BILL PUT IT, WET SQUIB DAY. ALL THE EXCITEMENT OF Christmas day was over. They were eating the little remains of a turkey, a leg of pork, and a ham. Yesterday had been acclaimed a grand day by all concerned: the family, and those now considered to be part of it—Nell and Bert and Rupert and Sammy—and the visitors: Davey, who apparently was much better in health, and Miss Isherwood. But today the family were scattered about the house, following their own pursuits.

Bill and Bert were playing snooker in the games room; Mark was up in what had been turned into his own bedroom-cum-study, one of the attics; in another room under the roof Willie and Sammy were deep into the intricacies of a new computer game that Willie had been given for his Christmas box; Mamie was curled up on the playroom couch admiring her gold charm bangle as she twisted it round her wrist; while in the third attic, which was still used as a lumber room, Katie stood at the window from which, through the bare trees, she had a glimpse of the distant road that led past the grounds and the bungalow on the outskirts of the paddock.

Downstairs in the drawing room, seated each side of the fireplace, were Nell and Fiona; Angela was asleep on the couch where it faced the fireplace.

521

Nell was bending forward, her hands clasped on her knees. "I've got to tell you, Fiona," she was saying, "I've been putting it off and off. I've fallen pregnant."

"Oh, Nell." Fiona got straight up from her seat and caught Nell's hands and said, "Oh, I am glad for you, I am. I am. Why . . . why didn't you tell me? Why couldn't you tell me?"

Nell didn't glance towards the couch where the reason lay. As she had said to Bert, she wasn't afraid of having a child like Angela, but she was afraid of its being so normal that it would upset Fiona, probably becoming a wedge between them. So she couldn't give any explanation except to say, "I . . . I don't know now why I didn't." Yet even as she spoke the words Fiona knew the reason for her reticence. And she said, "Oh, Nell, Nell. I want you to have a child. Even if she was like Angela I would still wish you to have it. But it'll be all right. And Bert, what does he say?"

"Well, remember how Bill took it when you told him? Somehow similar, he just couldn't believe it. Then he got all worked up and frightened that something would happen to me and began to talk about my age and so on and so on. But inside he's delighted."

"Bill'll knock his block off for keeping it to himself, you'll see." Fiona bent down now and, pulling Nell up to her, she put her arms round her and kissed her, saying, "When is it due?"

"July, early I should say."

"Oh, come on; let's go and tell Bill." She picked up the sleeping child from the couch. "I'll put her in her cot."

As they went up the main staircase Katie was running down the back staircase and letting herself out of the side door. She was wearing her old school coat but had a large scarf round her neck and a woollen hat on. She did not make for the drive but crossed the yard by the stable block, went through the arch that led to the vegetable garden, then on down through the shrubbery and the orchard until she came to the paddock. The paddock had once been the grazing ground of Sir Roger Oliver's horses, and so she kept to the perimeter of it as she knew it was muddy in the middle. At the row of cypresses and the low wall that marked the boundary of the estate she bent down and crept between the boles of the trees.

Leaning over the wall she looked at the cottage just a few yards to the right, and at the newer part built on to it and known as the bungalow. On the road outside stood a car, Rupert's car. She had guessed it was when she had seen it from the attic window. And it wasn't the first time she had seen it there, and it had no right to be there; not now, because yesterday he had been nice to her, ever so nice. When they were playing games he had chosen her and not that lanky Miss Isherwood. She hated her; she acted as if she knew everything just because she had lived here all her life. And what was more, she was two-faced: she had made believe she liked Mr. Love; she had chosen him twice. And when the games room floor had been cleared for dancing and everybody tried to do the Gay Gordons, she had hung on to Mr. Love; she had even leaned her head on his shoulder when she laughed so much; and when he had sung a funny Irish song she had clapped like anything. She was two-faced; she was horrible.

It took but a minute to get over the wall and to the back door of the cottage. To the left was a small window.

Standing close by the door she thought she heard voices, then she was sure when she heard someone laugh. She bit hard on her lip. He was in there talking to her, laughing with her. Well, there was nothing to stop her from calling, was there? She could say that she had seen his car and her mother wondered if he was coming to tea. . . . No, she had better not say that; she had better not mention her mother's name. She would just say, quite ordinary like, "I wondered if you were coming to tea." Yes, that's what she would do. She would just walk in. She would go round the front and ring the bell. She had never been in the bungalow, but her presence would stop them from doing whatever they were doing, talking or laughing, or . . .

Before the thought had time to clarify she heard the laughter again, and instinctively her hand went out to the iron latch on the door. What she meant to do was to rattle it to get their attention, but when she lifted the latch the door swung open and disclosed a small room and in the middle of it a narrow bed. And now from the bed there, looking at her, were two startled faces.

She did not turn and run, nor was she aware of taking two steps into the room, but almost at the moment the man cried, "Katie! Go away," her foot kicked something. She looked down. Two wooden things lying to the side of her feet. One was an old-fashioned wooden pestle bowl, about eight inches deep, the other was the pestle itself. Some part of her mind noted it was just like a potato pounder. She wasn't aware that she had stooped and picked them up, but when they were in her hands she knew she was yelling, "You're filthy! Horrible. Dirty. I hate you!"

She noticed the form of arc the bowl flew in after leaving her hand; then there was a scream and the woman was sitting up holding her head. She had no clothes on. And now as she let the other implement fly from her hand she saw him about to throw the bedclothes back and she heard the dull thud as it caught him on the side of his face; and the next minute, there he was, stark naked, and he had her by the shoulders and he was shaking her.

His hand came out: first on one side of her face and then on the other, and the second blow knocked her flying against the small dressing table.

He had hold of her again and was dragging her to her feet and through her swimming senses she glimpsed the woman now sitting on the edge of the bed: she was moaning and her face was covered with blood; his face too was all blood.

She screamed as his hand gripped her hair and swung her around and threw her towards the door. The next thing she knew she was on her hands and knees on a rough gravel path and she was crying aloud.

She struggled to her feet but could not see the way to go because the tears were blinding her and her head was spinning and her ears were still ringing and both sides of her face hurt. She wasn't really aware of tumbling over the wall or getting up or groping her way through the trees. And she didn't return round the perimeter of the paddock but went straight across it, her shoes squelching in the boggy part, and the mud coming over the tops of them.

When she eventually staggered through the kitchen and into the passage that led to the dining room and met the four adults coming out of the games room, only then did she come to a stop; and they stared at her in blank amazement as she gasped, "He hit m . . . me. He's filthy! Dirty! And he hit . . . me."

"Oh, my God! What's . . . what's happened? You're all blood, girl. Who hit you? Who hit you?" Bill had hold of her now.

"He did. Rupert. He's filthy. He had nothing on, nothing, and he got a hold of me. . . . And she had nothing on, nothing!" She was yelling now. "But I hit them. I hit them both. Her face is all blood. . . ."

Bill was now almost dragging her along the passage, and Fiona at her other side was gabbling, "Why did you go there? What made you? What have you done? Tell me! Tell me!"

In the drawing room Bill pushed her onto a chair and, bending over her, said, "Let's get this straight. You went along to the bungalow and you saw Rupert and Miss Isherwood in bed. Is that it? *Is that it?*" He was screaming at her now, and she was still spluttering, "They . . . they had nothing on. Nothing."

Bill stood back from her and raised his hand and cried, "For two pins I'd knock you from here to hell, girl!"

"Bill! Bill! Go and see what's happened. Please!"

It seemed that he didn't hear her, for he stood glaring down on the distraught girl, but then swinging round he hurried from the room, and Katie muttered, "Mam. Mam, my face hurts, and my knees. Look!"

Fiona looked at her daughter's knees. Her stockings were torn; there was blood oozing through the dust coating them, but she made no comment.

Nell said quietly now, "I'd better get a dish of water," but then, turning to Bert, she said, "No; you go and get it. Get a bowl from the kitchen and a flannel from the bathroom"; she had seen Fiona press her hand tightly across her mouth: "Come and sit down," she said.

"Oh, Nell, what if she's . . . "

"We don't know what she's done. Just sit down."

"I know what I did," Katie said, "*I hit her*. I hit them both."

"What did you hit them with?" It was Nell asking the question, and in a cool voice.

"It hit her anyway, the bowl, right in the face."

"You're a wicked girl; you know that?"

"I don't care. He shouldn't have done it. He has a wife in an asylum. He could have had me; he didn't need to ask. *Yes, he could. Yes, he could.*" She was now bending forward, her head and hands wagging. And Nell and Fiona looked at each other, before concentrating again on Katie. Here was a girl not yet fourteen saying that this man, who could have been her father, could have her for the asking. She was saying, "He didn't need to ask."

As Nell was asking herself, What's the world coming to? Fiona was almost whimpering, "Oh, my God! And she's my daughter." She had always thought that drug-taking by any of them would have broken her up. To her mind there was nothing worse, but she had been proved wrong. Why had life to be like this? Why had growing to be so painful? It had always been painful for the young. But now, this brashness, this blatant offering of herself . . . of her daughter's self . . .

Down the road Rupert was saying to Bill much the same thing at this moment. "Bill, I'm telling you, something will have to be done with that girl or you're going to have trouble. I've been patient; I've tried all ways. Come on, dear." He now led the young woman towards the door. She was holding a large pad of cotton wool over her brow, and Bill said, "Let me have a look."

"No, no." She gently pressed him away.

"It's just missed her eye. My God! That child! That girl is mad.

Just imagine if it had been her eye. As for me, her aim wasn't so straight." He dabbed at the still bleeding cut on his chin.

"Where are you going?" Bill asked quietly.

"I'm taking her to hospital; it will have to be stitched."

"I'm sorry, Rupert. I'm sorry you've been put through this. By God, I'll take the skin off her hide when I get back."

"I shouldn't bother. Her face won't be bleeding tomorrow but it will be showing the imprints of my hands, both sides, and her back likely, too, because I knocked her flying. I . . . I could have killed her. Do you know that?"

"How did she get in?"

"The cottage door was open. I'd been out that way to get some logs for the fire. I never thought about locking it, not till later on." His words now coming between his teeth, he added, "We didn't expect a visitor."

He locked the door now, the door of the bungalow; then taking the young woman's arm, he said, "All right, Caroline, come on. Come on, dear," and led her to the car.

Having settled her and put a rug over her knees, he turned to Bill, saying, "She's spoiled a good friendship. You understand?"

"Yes, yes, Rupert, I understand. And I'm sorry. But it needn't make any difference between us. And for goodness sake, don't let it cut you off from the house altogether. Fiona and the others would miss you."

"It will be impossible to call now. You know that, Bill."

"There's always the daytime when they're at school."

"We'll see. We'll see."

Bill watched the car being driven away. Mingling within him were the feeling of loss and the need to vent his rising anger. But he did not hurry back to the house; when he did enter it, he took off his coat very slowly. He had gone out without a cap. His steps still slow, he made his way into the drawing room.

Fiona and Nell turned towards him, but not Katie. Nell had just finished bathing Katie's knees and the palms of her hands; and as Bill approached she picked up the bowl and put it to one side, and Fiona, rising quickly from the couch, said, "Bill. Wait, wait."

"What for?" He looked at her. "Until she decides to come into our room and split my head open because I'm in bed with you?"

"*Bill. Please!*"

He pressed her aside, not roughly but very firmly; then bending over Katie, he hauled her up by the shoulders and he held her there as he stared into her deepening red face, saying now, "I only wish at this minute that I was your real father, and you know what I would do? I would strip you naked and I would take the buckle end of a belt to you. Today you've not only almost blinded a woman, and might have done the same to a man, but you've broken a good friendship. You spoiled something that I valued, and your mother valued, and it'll take a long, long time to live it down. We're supposed to be in a modern age, and yet what I still want to do is to lift me hand and swipe you to the other end of the room, and out of it, miles away. But Rupert's done that, hasn't he? And it's showing. You know something else? You should be ashamed of yourself the way you've thrown yourself at that fella. No man ever respects a woman, nor does a lad respect a girl, who's cheap. And you've made yourself the cheapest of the cheap this day. Now"—he pointed at her—"while I can remain calm, at least in some control of meself, get yourself out of me sight. An' don't expect any kindness from me for a long, long time. Go on!" He swung her round and thrust her forward, and she ran from him sobbing, like a young girl again and not as Fiona had seen her a short while ago almost like, as her mind had told her, a potential young prostitute.

As Fiona dropped into a chair she said, "How did you find them?"

"It's how the hospital finds her. She's got a split above her eyebrow. Rupert says it's two inches long. The thing just missed her eye. And he's got a split chin."

"She said he hit her."

"Yes, he did, gentleman Rupert. And if I'd been him I wouldn't have stopped where *he* stopped, just slapping her face and throwing her out, I'd have blackened her eyes. You understand what she's done, don't you? She's put an end to a good relationship. What's to be done with her?"

Fiona looked at him and shook her head slowly as she said, "Nothing, except what she does to herself, and that will be punishment enough. What's happened will put an end to a phase that we all go through, only hers is finished long before its time. He had become an obsession with her, and she shouldn't have had to experience that at this age. But now it's over and, if I'm not mistaken, and I hope I'm not, it'll put her off the male sex for a long time."

"You don't say."

"Oh, Bill, please don't take it like that. I'm just trying to put myself in her place. Anyway, your promised attitude towards her in the future will be punishment enough, for you came next in line to him. Anyway"—she moved from him now—"I'd better go and warn the others to leave her alone."

When she left the room Bill turned to Nell and said, "What d'you make of it, Nell? Eh? What d'you make of it?" And before she could answer he added, "And there's you bringing another one into the world. You must be mad. People don't know what they're askin' for when they crave for a family. I was once a middle-of-the-road man with not a care in the world: as long as I got plenty to eat and drink an' I was workin' an' had a bit of pleasure on the side, that was life. And look what I landed meself with."

"You wouldn't have it otherwise, would you?"

"Ah, Nell, I sometimes wonder, more so a few minutes ago down the road when I saw one of the nicest fellas in the world, a real gentleman, bespattered with blood and tellin' me that he had been brought to such a pitch that he knocked a young lass about and had thrown her bodily into the road; and that the close, warm association he had with us all in this house had come to an end. It was then I knew, Nell, that I would have had it otherwise. Oh aye, I would have had it otherwise."

48

"WHAT DO YOU MAKE OF IT, DOCTOR? NOW JUST LOOK AT THAT." BILL PICKED UP a piece of plasticine that had been roughly shaped into a face and, pointing, he said, "There's two holes for the eyes but there's no hole for the nose. The nose has been built up, you see. And look at that. Look at the mouth; then look at mine."

Dr. Pringle nodded while smiling and he said, "Yes; yes, you're right. As you say, the nose is built up and it's a pretty big one; it's like yours except it's a bit outsize."

"Which d'you mean, the plasticine one or mine?"

"Oh, we'll say the plasticine one."

"And look, the piece underneath's representing the body: it's pressed in from what are the shoulders. And there's the buttons on the waistcoat."

Bill now pointed to his own waistcoat.

"Yes, it is remarkable. And you say she did this all herself?"

"Aye. She's done others an' all. Now there's nothing wrong with her mind when she can do that, is there?"

"No, you're right. I don't think there's anything wrong with her mind as far as it goes."

"What d'you mean, as far as it goes?"

"Well, let's say that her brain won't turn her into a scientist or a mathematician."

529

"Well, there's not all that many of them knockin' about, is there?"

"No, you're right there, too; comparatively few against the whole population. But we know that there'll be limitations in Angela's case. She's made remarkable progress as it is: she's walking and talking and is a delightful child altogether. But I think you know that her mental capacity won't go beyond six or seven. You already know that, don't you?"

"I've been told that, but I don't believe it, not with her. And look at that."

He again pointed to the plasticine model. "She started last year by rolling two balls together. Now, and she's not yet three, you show me any other bairn of her age that can do that, make a kind of likeness. Have you got one on your books that can do it?"

"No; no, I can't recall any child at the moment. So we can say she has a special gift, and if she develops it, who knows, she could be a sculptor."

"Aye; aye, she could." Bill looked down on the model and muttered, "She was special from the minute I held her"—he turned and glanced at the doctor—"when I got over the first shock, because you tell me anybody in a similar situation who doesn't get a shock."

"No, that's quite natural; and as you say she's special." The doctor did not add what he was thinking, special to you if to no one else.

They both turned as Fiona came into the room and she, looking towards the low table where the plasticine lay in blobs, said, "Is he boring you to death, doctor?"

"No, no; not at all. I'm finding it very interesting." He pointed down to the moulded head, and Fiona looked at it, too, but made no remark. Bill had a thing about the child's ability with the clay. Granted she kept plying it into all shapes, but she herself didn't see any resemblance to Bill in that piece, nor did she think that the child put the nose on: likely one of the others helped, but they wouldn't say because they, too, wanted to imagine that she had some gift. More than once she had asked herself why she didn't go along with it, and the answer she always got from the first was that she wasn't going to build up any fairy tales about her little daughter. If she continued to progress as she was she would be grateful without imagining that she would one day be an artist.

The doctor turned to her now and, smiling, said, "I think Mamie will live." And at this she smiled, too. "She has a chest cold. Just keep her indoors for a few days. By the way, I haven't visited you for some months now, so you must be a very healthy family. I haven't heard how your friend Nell is. Has she had her baby?"

"Oh yes"—Fiona nodded—"and as you would say, a bonny bouncing boy. They're over the moon. Talk about doting parents."

"Well, that's as it should be."

As they went out of the room Fiona said to herself, Yes, that's as it should be. She was happy for Nell. Oh yes, she was. But at the same time she knew she would never forget the first time she looked down on Andrew, as he was named. The tears had welled up in her and almost choked her. But it had passed. Thank God, yes, it had passed.

As they reached the bottom of the stairs Bill was saying "Sorry we've had to drag you out on a Saturday afternoon ... " when he was interrupted by Mark turning from the telephone table, his hand over the mouthpiece of the phone, saying, "It's a call from America, Mam."

She exchanged a quick glance with Bill, then went and took the phone from Mark.

"Hello."

"Will you take a call from a Mrs. Vidler from the United States?"

"Yes. Oh, yes."

As she waited she thought, Mrs. Vidler. Surely by now it should be Mrs. Benson. She'd had only three letters from her mother in all these months, in fact in almost a year.

Then she heard a voice as if it was coming from the other room, saying, "Fiona?"

"Yes; yes, Mother. How are you?"

"Fiona."

"Yes, I can hear you, Mother."

"I'm ... I'm coming home."

She paused. "You are? For a holiday?"

"No; no, I'm coming home for good. Do ... do you think you could meet me? I ... I'm due in Newcastle about six o'clock in the evening your time next Thursday."

"Are you all right, Mother?"

"Yes; yes, I'm all right, dear. I ... I will explain everything when I see you."

Fiona held the mouthpiece and looked at it. The voice was her mother's and yet not her mother's. "I'll ... I'll have to go now, dear. You'll be there?"

"Yes; yes, of course, Mother. I'll ... I'll look forward to seeing you." She didn't know whether or not she meant those words, she only knew that there was something not right. There must be something not right because she was coming home and not on a holiday, and she was still Mrs. Vidler.

"Good-bye, dear."

531

"Good-bye, Mother."

She put the phone down. There was only Mark in the hall now. She looked at him and said quietly, "It's your grandma, she's . . . she's coming back."

He pursed his lips and said, "Phew, more trouble."

"Yes, perhaps, but she sounded different."

"I couldn't imagine Gran being different, ever."

Katie entered the hall now from the direction of the kitchen, and it was Mark who said to her, "Grandma's coming back."

"Why?"

The question was directed at Fiona, and Fiona shook her head and said, "You know as much as I do. She just said she was coming back, and not for a holiday, for good."

At this her daughter just lifted her shoulders slightly, then turned and went up the stairs and Fiona stood for a moment looking after her. The girl had grown apace in the last year, but there was none of the old sprightly Katie about her anymore; very little conversation; in fact, it was almost nil. Her answers: yes, no, perhaps, why? Strangely, the only one with whom she conducted any form of conversation was Sammy; and that indeed was strange because she had always considered him, in her own jargon, common.

Thinking of Sammy reminded her that he hadn't been in for two to three days, and that was unusual. She could understand his not coming over at nights, but she couldn't remember a Saturday for years now when the boy hadn't been here some part of the day. That's why Willie had gone on his bike to see him.

She called now up the stairs to where Katie was disappearing along the landing: "Look in on Mamie, will you dear?" she said.

She expected no response but she knew her daughter would do what was asked. It wasn't that Katie had become docile, but since that dreadful affair last Boxing Day when she thought she was going to have a defiant sex-crazed girl on her hands, practically the opposite had happened. Katie had become quiet, obedient, but withdrawn into herself, different. In fact, the whole house had become different since Rupert no longer popped in. Only Bill saw him.

One thing that incident had done was to make Rupert take a decisive step in his own life. Within a month Miss Isherwood had sold the bungalow and taken up her abode with him as his common law wife, and they now lived above the garage. She hadn't seen the young woman, but Bill said she had a scar running along the top of her left eye that she would probably never get rid of and it was a miracle that she had the eye at all.

It pained Fiona to see Bill's attitude to Katie: he spoke to her but he never touched her or made a fuss of her like he used to. And there were times when she would catch her daughter looking at him with a mixture of bitterness and sadness in her face. When he had first come on to their horizon she had loved him and vied for his attention; and he had given it to her. But now no more. . . .

It was only a matter of minutes later that Willie, almost throwing his bike against the house wall, ran indoors, crying, "Mam! Dad! Dad!"

To his calling Fiona came out of the dining room and Bill from the study along the passage.

"What is it? What is it?"

Willie stood gasping as he looked from one to the other: "It's . . . it's Mr. Davey, he's bad."

"What d'you mean, 'he's bad'?"

"Sammy's worried. His dad's got to go into hospital."

"When did all this happen? He was at work yesterday."

"Yes; yes, he was, but you said yourself last night, Dad, that you thought there was something wrong with him because the flesh was dropping off him and he shouldn't have been there."

"Aye; aye, I did. Well, I'd better go and see what all this is about. There's no rest for the wicked. It's likely the diarrhea again. I've told him for months now he should go and have that seen to. But he gave it some fancy name, diverticular or something."

Fiona nodded. "Yes; yes, he did: diverticulitis. That can cause diarrhea, so he said. And he was taking some medicine for it, wasn't he?"

"Maybe, but he should see the doctor. Get me coat." He stumped along the passage, and Fiona immediately went across the hall and into the cloakroom and brought his coat and soft hat to him; and as he put them on he said, "There's always something. But I've told that idiot to get to a doctor and not to rely on what somebody else told him to get."

"The doctor came this morning. Sammy wouldn't listen any longer to his dad and he went out and phoned, and the doctor came, said he would get a bed for him by Monday."

As Bill made for the door he said, "Well, this is another of those days: Mamie coughin' her heart out, your granny comin' home, and now this."

About twenty minutes later Bill drew the car up in front of the bungalow in Primrose Crescent, and when Sammy opened the door to him Bill's voice was quiet as he said, "How is he, lad?"

"He's bad, Mr. B., real bad. He's been real bad for a long time, but you can't do anything with him, he's so pigheaded."

Bill went slowly into the bedroom. Davey was in bed. His face looked ashen but his smile was as wide as ever and he greeted Bill with, "I'll break that little bugger's neck. I will, so help me. Haulin' you out on a Saturday afternoon."

"You know what you are, Davey Love, you're a bloody fool, as the youngster said, and a pigheaded one into the bargain. What is it all about?"

"Aw, well, boss, just one of those things."

"Come off it, Davey. What is it?"

Davey looked towards the door. "He'll be makin' tea. I'm full up to here with tea." He tapped his forehead. "If he's made it once the day he's made it a dozen times."

"Never mind that. What's wrong? D'you know?"

"Oh aye, boss, I know. Aye, I know." The smile slid from Davey's face. He looked down over the quilt before adding, "I've known for a long time. It's what they're callin' the big C."

Bill said nothing, he just stared down on this big rough Irishman for whom he had developed a very warm liking amounting to affection. And after a long moment he said, "And you've done nowt about it?"

"Aw, aye. Yes, I've done something about it. I've taken things. Been to mass." Now the grin reappeared, "I had a talk with Him"—he glanced upwards—"but He's of two minds where to send me: bad lads, He said, with good intentions are difficult to place."

"Oh, for God's sake, Davey, stop jokin' about it."

"What d'you expect me to do, boss? Eh? I've had to make up me mind I must face it. I've covered it up from the youngster this long while. I've always sworn at him, but God forgive me I've sworn at him more these last few months than I've done since he was born." He again looked towards the door. "That's the only thing I'm worryin' about, boss, him. He'll have to go to his granny's. I mean, for good."

"For God's sake, man, there's cures the day."

"Aw, aye; yes, I know that, boss. God's good to a lot of folk. But I've known from the start me number's been written down and when it's called out I'll have to jump to it, saying, 'Present, sir!' But seriously, boss, I'd like to thank you and the missis, 'cos you've been kindness itself to the lad. You've shown him another side of life. So could I ask you, boss, that when he's with the old girl you would now and again, when you have a minute, give him a helpin' hand?"

"Shut up, will you! You know without sayin' or askin' that the

534

helpin' hand will be there. An' another thing, I'll promise you this, he won't go to his granny's, 'cos he can't stand her. Up till this week or so he's practically lived at our house anyway. I should send you a bill for his meals."

"Aye, you're right there, boss. Funny, I've often thought about that. You know, about him an' Willie, they're more like brothers than Willie an' Mark, aren't they?"

"Yes; yes, that's true."

"An' they couldn't be two more opposite types, could they now? Your lad bein' nicely spoken an' mine with a tongue like a guttersnipe. And I'm to blame for that. Aye, I'm to blame for that. He's had a rough haul, has the youngster. But life's been different for him since he met up with Willie an' your family. An' boss, you meant that, I know you did, that you'll see to him, and that's all I want to know; I'll be ready any minute now 'cos that's settled me mind."

"Stop talkin' bloody rot! Are you goin' to have an operation?"

"Aye, that's what he said. I go in on Monday."

"Well, that could be the beginning of your cure. And look at it that way, sort of mind over the matter. They're doin' a lot of that stuff the day. Look at me for instance. I'm a case of mind over the matter. I thought I was a big shot when I was nowt, but look at me the day, sittin' pretty. So use that napper of yours. Tell yourself you're goin' to get better."

"Just as you say, boss, just as you say."

"I brought you some tea."

They both looked to where Sammy was coming into the room holding a tray on which there were two cups of tea, a bowl of sugar, and a plate of biscuits.

"Thanks, lad. That's just what I could do with." Bill pulled up a chair to the side of the bed, then, looking at Sammy, he said, "Your da tells me he's goin' in on Monday."

"Aye, and not afore time. Pigheaded galoot!"

As Sammy turned away Davey heaved himself up in the bed and, addressing himself to Bill, said, "D'you see what I mean? Goes to a private school an' speaks to his father in that fashion. Pigheaded galoot. Would you allow Willie to speak to you like that, I ask you? Now, would you?"

"Well, he mightn't use the same words but I often get looks that speak louder than words. Aye, I do."

As Bill drank the strong tea he looked at the man in the bed and he found it difficult to know what to say, so he talked of the family: Mamie's cold, sending for the doctor, Angela's clever way with plasticine. And lastly he asked him had he ever seen anybody with such a permanent grin on his face as was on Bert's since he had become a father. "There's no gettin' a word in," he said, "not even edgeways. All he can talk about is the bairn. You'd think it was the first one that had ever been born. I think he was for usin' his fists on me, an' him the good quiet, religious man, just 'cos I laughingly said that the bairn's mouth was a little outsize. It was yawnin' at the time. He didn't like it. You don't dare joke about his son."

"He's a good man is Bert. He pops in now and again."

"He does?" said Bill in surprise. "Why the hell didn't he tell me?"

"Why should he now? You've got enough on your shoulders. And anyway, as Bert said, you're like a kangaroo hoppin' from one place to another; you were difficult to pin down. An' that's understandable, 'cos this is some job you've pulled off this time, boss. By God, it is that."

"Kangaroo hoppin' from one place to another! Just you wait till I see him. Well"—he got to his feet—"I've got to be goin'. But listen. I'll be along the morrow, and the missis an' all. And don't worry about the lad; let your mind rest there." He bent over and looked into the gaunt bony face as he said softly, "You're goin' to get better. Get that into your head. Do a little talkin' to the Holy Mother that you're always callin' on and see what she can do for you."

"Aye, I'll do that. Yes, I'll do that, boss. An' if anybody can fix it she will." Then, his smile sliding, he put out his hand and gripped Bill's, saying, "I can rest easy now."

At the door all Bill could say to the boy was, "We'll be over the morrow, but pack a case for Monday, you're comin' with us."

And all Sammy said, was, "Aye. Ta."

Davey had his operation on Wednesday morning. He was wheeled into the theatre at half past nine and was wheeled out at half past twelve. And it was four o'clock in the afternoon when Bill spoke to the surgeon; he then drove straight home, went to the drinks cabinet, and poured himself out two good fingers of whiskey.

Standing by his side, Fiona said, "Bad?"

"Couldn't be worse. They just sewed him up again. The surgeon said there was nothing they could do; if they had tried he would have died on the table. It was all over his body. God, what he must have been goin' through all these months. The bloody fool."

"What's going to happen to him now?"

"He'll be in hospital for a time, and then, well ... " He walked away from her and, standing in front of the fire, he placed his glass on the marble mantelshelf, then gripped the edge of it with both hands as he said, "He'll need lookin' after. I'm goin' to bring him here for what time he's got left; he can't stay in that bungalow by himself." Turning sharply towards her now, he said, "I'll engage a nurse."

"No, Bill, no; you needn't do that. Whatever's to be done, Nell and I can do it between us, and be only too glad. If things get very bad, all right, we'll have a nurse, but wait and see what has to be done first."

He drew in a long breath, saying, "I said all that without consultin' you in any way. Sorry. That's how I feel. I mean, he's a big Irish galoot, as Sammy's always tellin' him, but he's brought more laughs into this house than any comedian you see on the screen. An' the lad an' all. They somehow became linked up with the family, you know what I mean?"

"Oh yes, Bill, I know what you mean. I feel the same, and I wouldn't be able to rest if I thought he was in that bungalow all day on his own."

He put his arms out and drew her to him, then said, "And your mother's comin' the morrow. Things never happen singly in this house, do they? Are you worried? I mean about her coming?"

"Yes; yes, I am. There was always a dread when I used to lift the phone that I would hear her say my name, Fi . . . o . . . na, drawn out, just like that. Condemnation in each syllable. I kept thinking about it last night."

"Well"—he now gripped her shoulders—"there's one thing I can tell you, I'm goin' to put me foot down straightaway when she enters that door. I don't care if I vex or please her but I'll make it plain that she's not goin' to upset you again in any way. And . . . oh, my God! I've just thought, will we have to put her up?"

"Oh, I shouldn't think so, she'll go to hotel."

"Yes; yes, that would be more like her, 'cos she wouldn't want to come in close proximity to me, would she?" He smiled now, saying, "You've never noticed or remarked recently on my use of the big words. You should hear me at the board meetings; I astonish meself."

"Oh, Bill, Bill; you sound like your old self again."

"Aye." He turned from her now and picked up the glass from the mantelshelf, saying, "We've all got old selves, haven't we? I wish I could have kept mine with regard to one person in this house."

"You still haven't forgiven her?"

"Oh, I suppose I've forgiven her, but somehow things have never been the same, have they? She's not the same to me, naturally, and I'm not the same to her. An' none of you see Rupert except me; and you used to like him poppin' in and out, didn't you? He gave a bit of class to the place." He wrinkled his face at her and she said, "He was just himself, like Sir Charles used to be: they're at ease in any company. They didn't treat me or you any differently from anyone else. Except on last Boxing Day."

"My God in heaven! I'll never forget that day as long as I live. And that's what I see every time I look at Katie, I see him and that lass bleedin' an' know that she did it, and worse, was capable of doin' it. Ah, well, there's more serious things to hand now. Where will you put Davey? In the annexe?"

"No; no, that's too cut off. There's two spare bedrooms up there. We'll put him in the one looking on to the drive. He'll see the comings and goings from there, that's if he's bedridden all the time."

"Aye, that's an idea." Again he turned and put the glass on the mantelshelf, then, pulling her to him once more, he kissed her hard on the mouth before saying, "You're a good lass, you know. Wonderful, wonderful. And at this minute I could believe in Davey's God and thank Him for you."

49

FIONA WATCHED THE PLANE TAXI TO A STOP. SHE WATCHED THE DOORS OPEN AND the passengers come down the steps. Then she saw her mother, having recognised her more by her walk than anything else. But when a few minutes later they came face-to-face Fiona had trouble hiding the shock she felt.

When she had last seen her mother, the face-lift had given her a false youthfulness, but now, although the skin appeared still tight, she was definitely looking at an elderly woman, not someone just turned sixty. She was further surprised when her mother's arms went about her and her voice murmured, "Fiona. Oh, Fiona."

"Are ... are you all right, Mother?"

"Yes; yes, dear; I'm all right, only tired. I've had a long journey, even before I got on the plane. And then there were the changes and—" She sighed before adding, "How are you, dear?"

"Oh, I'm fine, Mother, fine."

"And ... and the children?"

"They're fine, too."

"I must get my luggage."

"Yes; yes, of course."

Fiona had expected much more luggage than her mother claimed, just two cases. She had taken twice as much with her she recalled.

"Would you like a cup of tea in the restaurant before we start out?" she said.

"No; no, thank you, dear. They give you a nice meal on the plane, and eating helps to shorten the journey.... Are you taking me to your ... I mean, what I mean is, have you made any arrangements about accommodation such as a hotel?"

"No, Mother; I didn't know what you intended to do. I thought you might like to come home with me first."

"Yes; yes, I would like that, Fiona. I ... I have a lot to tell you."

As they drove onto the main road from Newcastle Airport Mrs. Vidler, who had been quiet for some time, said, "It's nice to be back. I ... I never thought I would say that, you know. Just to be back in England, it's a strange feeling."

"Yes; yes, I suppose so." Fiona could find nothing else to say. She felt at odds with this new mother, this different mother, this mother who seemed to be utterly devoid of aggression. She didn't know as yet how to handle her.

As they drove up the drive towards the house her mother now remarked, "It's a lovely house."

Then they were in the hall and she stood looking about her for a moment before turning to Fiona and saying, "It's very beautiful. I ... I never imagined it like this. Oh, hello, Mark."

"Hello, Grandma." Mark came up to her and dutifully kissed her on the cheek; and she smiled at him, saying, "I can't believe it. You've grown so tall. And Willie!" She was now being kissed by Willie.

"Hello, Grandma," he said.

"Hello, Willie. You, too, have grown. But then a lot happens in a year."

Fiona, who was helping her off with her coat, noticed that her mother had lost all her slimness. She'd had an almost sylphlike figure, but she had definitely thickened around the hips and waist; in fact, she appeared plump.

"Come into the sitting room.... Mark, tell Nell we're back. She must be up in the nursery." She turned to her mother. "Nell's got a baby son," she said. "He's upstairs in the nursery with Angela."

"Oh, Nell's got a baby? How nice for her."

This indeed was not Mrs. Vidler.

As they were about to enter the sitting room Bill came running down the stairs; and they turned towards him, and he, now coming slowly up to them, said, "Well, hello, Mother-in-law. You've got back then?"

"Yes; yes, I've got back."

Fiona saw that he was nonplussed, which he certainly was; he was wondering where the old bitch was, the arrogant old bitch, the old bitch that hadn't a good word for him, ever.

"Well, come in and sit down. That was what you were goin' to do, wasn't it, both of you?" he said; and he marched before them into the room talking loudly, as much from embarrassment as from anything else. "Nobody attends to this fire if I don't see to it. I'll get those three lazy young beggars on to that saw and get some logs cut up."

They were just seated when Nell came into the room and she, remembering Mrs. Vidler's manner towards her in the past, said politely, "I hope you had a good journey, Mrs. Vidler."

"Yes; yes, thank you. It was rather tiring, but when you think of it, it's very quick. Just a few hours between here and America. Yet such a vast distance really." Her voice seemed to trail away on the last words. And now Nell said, "I bet you could do with a cup of tea, real English tea."

Mrs. Vidler glanced at her daughter, then said, "Yes; yes, I could. Thank you."

When Nell went out of the room there was silence among them for a moment. And then, to Fiona's and Bill's utter surprise they watched the scourge of their lives, and she had certainly been that, drop her head forward and quickly take a handkerchief from the sleeve of her dress and press it over her eyes.

"Oh, Mother. Mother." Fiona was sitting on the couch beside her now, her arm around her shoulder. "What is it?"

"I'm sorry, dear, I'm sorry. It's just that I . . . I never thought I'd . . . get home again. I never thought I'd be able to see you or . . . or any of the children. But"—she looked up at Bill now through her streaming eyes—"I . . . I won't impose. I promise you, I won't impose ever again. I've still got the money for the house and . . . and I'll get a little place. In the meantime, I can go into a small hotel. I won't impose."

"Be quiet, woman. What are you talkin' about, imposin'? I don't know what's happened to you, but being me I'll tell you straight: it's somethin', in a way, that's done you good. As for imposin', by all means get a place of your own, but in the meantime there's a room for you. That's what you want, isn't it, Fiona?"

Fiona stared up at him, her mouth slightly agape. "Oh yes; yes, Bill, definitely yes."

"Aye, well, that's settled. Now, come on, tell us what happened and what's brought you back?"

Mrs. Vidler dried her eyes, took in a deep breath, and, looking from one to the other, began, "Everything seemed marvellous at first. He had a very nice house, something like this"—she looked about her—"beautifully furnished, and there was a swimming pool attached, and for the first week or two he couldn't do enough. He had proposed marriage or ... well, suggested it strongly in his letters. But there was no mention of that when I got there but a lot of talk about my finances and about me putting money into his estate business, which he told me was making small fortunes. When I told him I wasn't a rich woman, he laughed. You see I had been at this Hydro"—she bent her head again—"stupidly to have this done"—she now dabbed her cheek with her forefinger—"and that cost me a deal of money, more than I could really afford. And he went on that and the fact that I had a house in England and that I even had a daughter married to a"—she glanced at Bill—"a prosperous builder. He kept asking when the money was coming through from the sale of the house. But perhaps you know that it was on the market six months before it was sold. Then one night I had been wined and dined by one of his so-called rich friends and from what was said I realised he thought I was a very wealthy woman but a bit cagey about what I was worth. And I suppose that started me thinking. Then when I got back, unexpectedly early, I found the man I thought of as my prospective husband going through my things. He had actually opened a locked leather case I kept my papers in and also my bank book. Well"—she now swung her head in a desperate fashion—"there was a dreadful scene. He said I'd hoodwinked him, not that he had hoodwinked me. And ... and it turned out that this wonderful house of his had been rented just as it stood for three months, and that was almost up. He ... he called me names. Dreadful. He walked out, took his things and went. That was the last I saw of him. There was a maid in the house and he had told her that I would pay her a month's wages in lieu of notice, and I told her I couldn't because I had very little money left until I got some sent from here. She was very kind to me. She ... she told me that she had known all along he was a fake. And it turned out that he had been married and—" she swallowed deeply before she said, "divorced three times."

"Fiona"— she now looked at her daughter and her lips trembled as she said, "can you imagine how I felt? The humiliation, and to know that I'd been a stupid, a really stupid woman, a stupid ... aging woman. I don't know what I would have done if it hadn't been for that girl, the maid. She knew the town and she got me into cheap lodgings." She shook her head. "And they were cheap lodgings."

"But if that only covered three months, what have you been doin' all this time?" Bill demanded.

"Yes; yes, Bill, what have I been doing all this time?"

It wasn't lost on Bill or Fiona that she had addressed him by his Christian name for the first time, which emphasised the change that had come over this woman. And when she repeated, "You might well ask. Work is as difficult to get there as it is here, more so when you're British, and you have to have a work permit, even for a short time, oh that was difficult, so difficult, and they laugh at you the way you speak, even the way you walk. Anyway, I eventually ended up as an underpaid assistant nanny."

"*Oh, Mother. You?*" She stopped here, and Mrs. Vidler added, "Yes, my dear, an assistant nanny to three dreadful children, spoiled, ruined, and even wicked in the things they did, not only to the other nanny and myself but to others in the household. And all the while I thought of my grandchildren. Yes, dear, my grandchildren. And yes, dear, for the first time I thought how they had been brought up. And I longed to be home, back in England. But I was so ashamed of myself, my stupidity . . . and vanity. If anyone in this world has been brought low, dear, it's been me." She nodded at Fiona.

"You've been a damn fool."

"Yes; yes, Bill, I've been a damn fool."

"What I mean is," said Bill, "you should have wired. You could have had some money sent out to you until the house was sold."

"I thought of that, but I couldn't bring myself to."

"Well, what brought you to it in the end then? Tell us that."

"What brought me to it was that the nanny had had enough and I was left with those three dreadful children. And after three weeks, when I threatened to leave, the so-called mistress told me that she wouldn't give me a reference and I wouldn't be engaged by anyone in that town again. It was my business, she said, being a so-called English lady, that was her term, to improve her children's manners and what was more, to control their actions. It was then I went out and phoned you, dear."

"What about the money for the house? Wasn't that sent on to you?"

"No. I told my bank manager not to send it on because I knew in my heart that I couldn't stay there forever. But I needed to pluck up the courage; and that awful woman, the mother of those three little devils, gave it to me. And I went out and phoned you. I would have got on a plane the next day but . . . but today was the nearest vacancy that was on the chartered flights. Oh, you don't know"—she now

543

looked from one to the other—"what it's like to be back. Oh"—she nodded her head now—"the type of people there are in the world, moneyed people and those who are cut to make it no matter what they do or how they do it, or who they hurt in the process. It's all money there. Without money you're nobody. It's true. You might think that wealth is badly divided here, but you've seen nothing until you go to America. Yet there are nice people there, like the maid. I don't know what I would have done without her. Then there was the nanny. We got on very well together, she and I, supporting each other, until she could stand no more. She was an American, too, and she was a generous girl, not like her employers. They were mean, narrow, except with food." She nodded. "They wasted food. And you know it's dreadful to admit, I . . . I who was always going on diets, I ate and ate. It was my only comfort, and this is proof of it." She tapped her hips now.

"Aye, well, you can say it's been an experience. But now that you're back you're welcome to stay until you get on your feet again an' find a suitable place. And I say the only sensible thing you've done is to leave the money for the house here. By the way, what did it go for?"

"Sixty-two thousand."

"*No!*"

"Yes. It brought a good price, but then it was a very nice bungalow, as you know."

"Well, I can see how that bloke wanted to get his hands on that for his real estate or whatever."

"Oh yes, he wanted to get his hands on it all right. That was the only thing he wanted. He kept pressing me to write to the agent. In fact, in the second month, when nothing had happened, he typed out a letter and got me to send it. It was from then I began to feel uneasy."

"Ah, here's Nell with the tea. Hurry up, woman; you've had long enough to go to the plantation an' pick the leaves."

"Hasn't he got a beautiful drawing room manner?" Nell was speaking to Fiona now, and she answered, "Yes, and I've always admired it, Nell. Such an example to others."

"Is he talking yet?"

"What d'you mean, is he talking yet? Who?"

"Who but young Master Andrew."

"Funny cuts, aren't you!"

Bill now turned to Mrs. Vidler. "It shouldn't surprise me," he said, "but her and Bert have bred a genius. He'll be writing symphonies at three or singin' them because he yells all the time. Be prepared,

Mother-in-law: you'll hear nothing but baby talk in this house from now on."

Nell again addressed Fiona, saying, "And who will lead the chorus?"

"Yes, indeed, Nell, who will lead the chorus?"

And so it went on, cross talk and light chipping to put the visitor at ease for what they were all witnessing was pride having been brought low, and if anyone needed bolstering at this moment, it was this once arrogant, bitchy mother, and mother-in-law; this once proud, impossible woman.

50

IT WAS A FORTNIGHT LATER WHEN BILL HELPED DAVEY OUT OF THE CAR AND INTO
the house and sat him in the drawing room in order to give him his
breath and strength to make the stairs. And just as the arrival of the
child had altered their lives and the routine of the house, so did the
arrival of Davey Love when he came into the house to die. They all
knew, as he did, that he was dying; yet, years later, each individual
was to look back to that time and see it as one of the most peaceful
and happiest times that had reigned in that house.

The en suite bedroom overlooking the drive had a rose pink carpet
with velvet curtains to match, these standing against French grey
flock wallpaper that had a delicate browny pink stripe. The bed, a
double one, had been placed with the head near the window and
opposite on a small raised hearth stood the electric log fire that had
graced Fiona's sitting room in the old house.

Altogether it was a beautiful room, and the first sight of it had
brought tears to Davey's eyes. And when, on that first evening, he
had said, "What better place could God design for a man to die in,"
Bill had exclaimed loudly, "For the Lord's sake, Davey, stop talkin'
like that," only for Davey to come back at him and say quietly, "Come
here, boss. Sit down a minute." And when Bill had obeyed him Davey
said, "Let's get this straight, boss, eh? Me time's runnin' out but me

546

heart's overflowin' with gratitude. Will you believe me when I tell you, I'm happy? I've never been happier in me life. And that's honest to God, who I'll meet up with in a short time." And then he had added on a laugh, "It might be Saint Michael the Archangel, of course. Well, he's a tougher proposition, so I'm told. The situation'll be like everything else down here: when you get to the boss you've got a chance of gettin' a fair hearin'. It's them bods on the way up that have got opinions of themselves. They're the ones you can't get past. And don't I know it. So, boss, let's be happy, eh?"

And so it would seem that everyone in the house had taken their cue from the man who was now the centre of it; and none more so than Katie and, of all people, Mrs. Vidler. Both had taken on the post of part-time nurse.

Mrs. Vidler, at odd times during the day, would sit with Davey, and it would appear that Katie couldn't get back quickly enough from school to take up her position near his bed and chat with him.

When he could no longer stagger to the bathroom, it was Sammy, Willie, and Bill who took over the duties of seeing to his personal needs in that way. Bill made it his business to pop home every dinnertime, and the two boys came in from school just after four o'clock. If he needed attention before that, strangely again, it was Susan Vidler who saw to him. And there wasn't a day went by that the room didn't ring with laughter from one or another. One day in particular was when the priest came to visit him.

Father Hankin was a tall, gaunt-looking man in his early thirties. He was known to be a man of wide views welcoming those of other denominations into conference. But on this day, sitting by the side of Davey's bed sipping a cup of tea, he looked from Fiona to Mrs. Vidler, then to Davey before he said, "There's one thing I want to speak about and I suppose I'm going to affront your good friend here." He now nodded towards Fiona. "But it's about Sammy. Yes; yes, I know he attends his duties. He's a good boy in that way, but he's also attending the Protestant school, now isn't he? And a private one at that."

"Well, all I can say for that, Father, is thanks be to God."

"Well, I can't sort of give you God's opinion of it meself, but mine is, that there's still good teaching in Saint Hilda's. The nuns are splendid teachers; three of them with University degrees, three of them, mind!"

"Aye; and one of them, Father, with hands on her like bloody iron hammers. Pardon me, pardon me." As Davey's head drooped, the priest said, "Well, I agree with you: Sister Catherine has hands on

547

her like bloody iron hammers, but she's got a lot of bloody hard nails to hit there."

Davey had one arm tight round his waist trying to stifle his laughter; Fiona's mouth was wide, and although she had her hand over her mouth the sound of her laughter was loud; and although one would have expected Mrs. Vidler to look askance and say, "Dear, dear, dear! What language!" all she did was bite her upper lip to try and stop herself from roaring like the rest. The priest himself had his head back and his guffaws filled the room. Then, leaning towards Davey, he wiped his streaming eyes as he said, "You see, you're not the only one, Davey, who's been to a special college. And I'd like to bet some of my brethren in the Cloth could beat you hollow."

"I've no doubt 'bout that, Father," replied Davey between gasps.

"Anyway, to come back to the serious subject of education," the priest said, "is it your wish that the boy continues where he is? Now think, think before you answer."

"I have no time to think; I've no reason to think, Father, none at all, none at all. As long as it's possible I want him to stay at that school, then I'd hope he'd go on with Willie to Newcastle. There's a place called Dame Allan's there. . . . She must have been a very good woman to have a school named after her. Aye, she must. I've heard that's a good place for education. An' there's the Grammar school, too."

"Well—" The priest once again leaned towards Davey, saying now, "If that's your wish, it's your wish. But mind, I'll tell you, if he doesn't keep up his duties I'll be after him, and I'll bring Sister Catherine with me an' all. Oh." He turned now and looked from Mrs. Vidler to Fiona and, his head bobbing, he said, "I've got to admit it, between you and me, she'd make her way into the Vatican and scare the pants off the pope, that one."

Again the room rang with laughter.

Christmas was a happy affair. Most of the present opening and the festivities with the exception of the meals had taken place in the sick room. And it was only late on the Christmas night, when father and son were together for a short time, that Sammy, standing near the side of the bed, said, "It's been a lovely day, hasn't it, Da?"

"Wonderful day, lad, wonderful day. You know somethin'? I've said it afore since I came into this house, but I'll say it again and especially for you—an' you've got to remember this—I've never been happier in me life. If heaven is any better than this I wonder why I'm goin'. They're wonderful folks you fell among, lad. And you know something else?" He leaned forward, his eyes bright and moist. "It was all through me teachin' you to swear."

"Aw, Da." Sammy pushed his father in the shoulder; then grinning, he said, "But you're right. Aye, you're right. And I wasn't only swearin', was I? No, no. Four-letter 'uns, and they weren't spelt like our name, were they, Da?"

"No, they weren't, lad, they weren't. But it's funny how things happen, isn't it? So I've done some good in the world after all, 'cos if you hadn't heard me you wouldn't have known half of 'em."

"But you didn't use four-letter ones, Da."

"No." Davey considered a moment before admitting, "No, except once or twice on me own outside the house I might have, but not in front of you. And I didn't want you to use them either. Yet around that quarter there were five-year-olds comin' out with 'em. They knew no better so it was understandable you pickin' them up. But"—he paused—"this is a different life, lad, isn't it?"

"Yes, Da, it is a different life. That's why I always like to come here. I knew there was something I wanted but I didn't know what. Now I do. It was to live in a different way from around Bog's End."

"Well, now, you're gettin' a good start, an' 'cos of it, God helpin' you, you'll grow up to be a good man. Another thing." He now punched Sammy gently. "Make people laugh. Play yersel' down, lad, you know what I mean, an' they'll laugh at you. That's the secret, play yersel' down except among your true friends. Aye, an' even those, 'cos if people think you haven't got much up top it makes them feel better, thinkin' they've got more. You know what I mean?"

"Aye, Da, I know what you mean." And the boy looking at this big gaunt man realised for the first time that his da wasn't as thick as he made out to be, that he had never been as thick as he had always made out to be. It had been a sort of a game with him. His da, in a way, had been wise; but then he hadn't known that, not until now. And until now he hadn't realised how much he would miss him, at least not to the extent that he was going to.

He recalled that his da had made a pact with God to go to mass every Sunday for a year if He did something for him. He wondered if he, too, were to make a pact with Him would it come off? If he said to Him, "God, I'll become a priest if you make me da better." But no; he knew it wouldn't work for the simple reason he didn't want to become a priest. Another thing, it didn't do to make bargains with God. Look what had happened to his da.

"Come on, cheer up!" said Davey now, pushing his finger under the boy's chin. Then he added, "I'm gonna ask you to do somethin' for me.

549

I know you're not one for the lasses, but Katie ... she's a very unhappy lass is Katie. It's all because of what happened this time last year. So you could be nice to her, talk to her. I notice she doesn't talk much to the others."

"She talks to you though, Da."

"Aye; yes, now, that is funny, 'cos you know, she was a snooty piece was Katie. Oh aye, you she thought common, but I knew I was the mud in the bottom of the gut in Katie's opinion. That was when we first came on the scene. But she's a different girl now. She's been through trouble, love trouble, and, oh, God in heaven, there's nothin' worse than that. Oh no. So be kind like to her; don't argue with her or snap back at her."

"I don't, Da."

"No, but you're not very talkative I notice, not with her. With Willie or Mark it's twenty to the dozen, but with her ... "

"Well, she doesn't give you the chance, Da."

"Well, it's up to you to make the chance. Just talk to her. She's like her granny, she's been brought low, 'cos if there ever was a change in a woman it's been in Mrs. Vidler. Don't you think?"

"Aye, Da."

"'Tis an awful thing to bring people low, Sammy. When your ma walked out on us, I meself was brought low. Oh aye, I felt I wasn't a man; all me spunk was knocked out of me, 'specially"—he now pulled a face—"when I saw what she picked in preference to meself. By, talk about the runt of the litter; it was a shame to wipe the wall with him." He gave a sort of giggle now. "And I did wipe the wall with that poor fella. But why in the name of God am I sayin' poor fella. He was a dirty bugger, now wasn't he?"

"Aye, Da, he was a dirty bugger."

They laughed uproariously, and Sammy was on the point of saying, "Stop it, Da! You'll die laughing," but managed to check himself as he thought: he could at that. Aye, he could at that. Yet it wouldn't be a bad way for him to die. But, oh, dear Lord, he hoped it wouldn't be for weeks, and weeks, and weeks.

Bill found a bungalow for Mrs. Vidler. It was on a small estate and it was only a five-minute drive from the house. She was very pleased with it, and for thirty-eight thousand it was well within her pocket and could be considered a bargain, for it was in good decorative repair and the previous owners were leaving the carpets and curtains, which again she found tasteful. The only thing now was to furnish it. She could have moved into it within a week, but on this particular night, while sitting in the drawing room having their

coffee after the evening meal, she said to Bill, "How long has he got
... Davey?"

And Bill answered, "I asked the same question of the doctor only
yesterday. An' what he said was, he should have gone by now, and
he likely would have if he had been in hospital. He was kind enough
to say we had kept him alive much longer than he himself expected.
He was given three months at the most when he left the hospital, but
here we are now at the end of March and we can't hope that he'll go
much longer. He said a week, two or three at the most. But before
that happens he'll increase the dose so that he won't feel any
pain.

"I didn't tell you"—he was looking at Fiona now—"but I found the
youngster cryin' last night, and Willie cryin' with him. They were up
in the bedroom. And I reassured Sammy again that this was his home
now and for always. Then I had to get out else they would have had
me at it. We're either laughin' or cryin' in this house, there seems to
be no happy medium."

"Why I asked was," put in Mrs. Vidler now, "if you'd mind if I
stayed on until it's over. I was always fond of him, you know." She
looked slightly shamefaced now as she added, "In the wrong way, I
suppose; but nevertheless it was there."

"You stay as long as you like, Mother-in-law. I can say now I've
been pleased to have you." Then leaning towards her, he said, "Fancy
me sayin' that, eh?" And she, bending towards him, too, answered,
"And fancy me taking it. The next thing you know I'll be swearing
back at you. That'll shake you." As the laughter filled the room the
door opened and Katie came in. She looked sad as she walked up to
Fiona and, standing by her side, looked down at her, saying, "He
hasn't eaten his supper. And he asked if he could have a cup of coffee,
black. He doesn't usually have it black. Can he have it?"

"Yes; yes, of course, dear. And I'll go up and see."

"You'll sit where you are." Bill put his hand out. "Make a cup of
coffee." He looked at the tall young girl and she at him. "You can
make a cup of black coffee, can't you?"

"Yes, I can make a cup of black coffee."

"Very well then. Go on, take it up to him."

Oh dear, that always pained her. Fiona watched her daughter walk
straight-backed out of the room. The way he spoke to her. Never
unbent. She was lonely, and lost, and she herself couldn't get near
her.

Katie made the cup of black coffee and took it upstairs on a tray.
And when she handed it to Davey, he said, "Now why should I fancy
a cup of black coffee? Eh, Katie?"

"I don't know." She shook her head. "You've never drunk black coffee before, not that I know of."

"No, but I just suddenly thought that . . . well, milk was a bit plain. But why black coffee? Still, let me taste it." He sipped at the cup, then said, "Yes, it's nice. Refreshing. Not so cloyin' as milk, if you get what I mean."

"Yes, I get what you mean."

"Sit down aside me and have a bit crack. Is everybody downstairs finished eatin'?"

"Yes. And we're all washed up. It was the boys' turn tonight."

"How you gettin' on at school?"

"So-so."

"Just so-so?"

"Yes; I . . . I don't seem able to concentrate."

"Well, you used to. You came out top last year, they tell me, miles ahead of the rest. Gallopin' like an Irish cuddy over everybody in your class."

She smiled at him now, saying, "How do Irish cuddies gallop, Davey?"

"Aw, well, bein' Irish, they bring their back legs for'ard first, and havin' done that the front ones are bound to move: the back 'uns sort of kick the front 'uns for'ard. You see what I mean?"

"Well, going on that symbolism, those at the back of the class will come forward and beat those at the front."

He thought a moment before he said, "Aye, you're right, you're right there. But as I said, they were Irish cuddies."

"I wish I had been born Irish."

"In the name of God, why? I ask you, why?"

"So that I could laugh easily. You laugh easily. You make people laugh easily. All Irish people do that."

"Oh no, begod! You're wrong there. Not all Irish folk make people laugh. Some of 'em make people angry an' bitter. Oh, don't get it into your head that all Irish folk are funny. Like every other people, there's some an' some, an' some of the same, if you follow what I mean, are stinkers, although I say it meself an' about me own folk. In any case, most of 'em don't just want to make people laugh. Oh no, lass, all Irish people don't laugh. But I'll tell you somethin'. You should laugh more."

"I've nothing to laugh about except when I'm with you. You make me laugh."

"You think your da's still vexed with you, don't you?"

"I don't think, I'm sure. He dislikes me now. He doesn't hate me but he dislikes me."

"Nonsense."

"It isn't, Davey. Anyway, he's not my real father, so it will be quite easy to dislike me. If he had been my real father he would have forgiven me a long time ago for what I did."

"Did you ever go to him an' tell him you were sorry for what you did?"

"No; no, I couldn't because for some time after I wasn't sorry. I was in a sort of state I suppose. Older people would call it a stupid state, a phase. But I still hated that girl, the woman. He's living with her now, you know."

"Aye, I know. And he deserves some happiness. An' she was a nice enough miss."

"Yes; you danced with her and she laughed a lot with you."

"Aye, she did. An' what's the harm in that?"

"There was no harm as long as it was you, but when it was with him it changed everything."

"And how d'you feel about him now?"

She looked away from the bed and towards the log fire and its flickering flames, and she said, "It's funny, odd, I feel nothing. I wonder why I was so stupid. I'll never be that stupid again. Not over anybody."

"Aw, don't say that. You will one day, 'cos you're goin' to grow into a beautiful woman. With that hair an' those eyes, you'll have 'em runnin' after you like that Irish cuddy."

"Well, it won't matter to me, Davey, if they run after me, because I don't think I'll ever like anybody again, not in the way I liked him. And the awful thing is to know it was of no use. And if a feeling like that can die anything can die."

"That's 'cos you're young, dear. You're just fifteen years old. As you say, you were in a phase. Well, you'll still be in a phase for some time yet."

"I'm not just fifteen, Davey, not inside I'm not; I feel old, well, old in a way because I've experienced something that I shouldn't have experienced for a long, long time. No one of fourteen should have a feeling that makes them feel ferocious. I felt ferocious and I knew I wasn't fourteen inside."

Davey sighed now as they stared at each other, and he said, "What d'you intend to be, dear?"

She put her head to one side, then said, "I've thought about that of late, more so since you came to live with us. And I think I'd like to be a nurse."

"That's good. That's good. But it's no easy job. I was amazed at what nurses had to do when I was in hospital. They worked like Trojans."

"I wouldn't mind the work, but being a nurse you'd be sort of able to disperse yourself or dispense yourself."

"What d'you mean, disperse or dispense yourself?"

"Well, I suppose I mean spread yourself around, not put all your feelings or affections on one person."

"Aw, lass, that's a daft idea. If that's all you're goin' in for nursin' for, I'd give it up now. Yes, I would. Honest to God, I'd give it up now. Spreadin' yourself around. Dear me! Dear me! An' when that fella on the white horse comes ridin' by, you'd have nothin' to give to him, 'cos you'd be skin and bone."

"Oh, Davey, you are funny."

"No, I'm not in this case, Katie, I'm not funny." His face looked serious, as did his voice sound, "Don't think of spreadin' yourself around, hinny, in any way. Keep yourself, what you call, intact. Remember that word, intact, until the fella who's worthy of you comes along. He might come as a surprise or on t'other hand he might be somebody you've known for years, an' you'll look at him as if you're seein' him for the first time. It happens with a man an' all you know. It happened to meself, it did that. I spread meself around an' all, in a way, until I'd nothin' to give to me wife. And what does she do? She walked out on me. But you know all that, don't you?"

He laid his head back on the pillow and, moving his eyes around the room as far as he could see, he said, "'Tis a beautiful room this, Katie, a beautiful room. An' your mother's a beautiful woman, an' your dad is a fine man, one of the best that walks the earth. Loud-mouthed, mind." He lifted his head slightly and grinned at her now. "Oh aye, loud-mouthed, but behind his bellowing he's a carin' man. And he cares for you." He turned his head now and looked at her. "He cares for you deeply. And there'll come a time when you'll just need to put your hand out and he'll be there to hold it."

After a moment of silence she said, "Your coffee's nearly cold. You didn't like it?"

"Oh yes, I did, I mean I do. Look, I'll drink it all up."

"You don't have to."

"Don't I now?"

"No, it was just a passing fancy, wasn't it?"

"Aye, perhaps. I don't know what made me ask for black coffee, 'cos I've never understood the blokes that like it, I mean that like drinkin' it after a meal. Yet there I go, askin' for black coffee. It's fancies I'm gettin' in me old age."

"You're tired. Don't talk anymore."

"You're an understandin' girl, Katie, you're an understandin' girl. Yes; yes, I'm tired. By the way, what's the day?"

"It's Friday."

"And we're in March. I never thought, well to tell you the truth, I never thought to see March. It's the kindness that's kept me here."

She now watched his lips press tightly together and his lips screw up pressing his eyes back into the sockets. And his voice was a whisper as he said, "Will you send your da to me, Katie?"

"Oh yes, yes." She jumped up from the chair and ran from the room, and this time she burst into the drawing room, saying, "He's bad! He's asking for you." She was nodding at Bill and Sammy. "I think he's in pain."

Bill and Sammy rushed from the room now followed by Fiona, and Katie was left with her grandmother. And when the older woman moved towards her, Katie threw herself into her arms, and Susan Vidler, said, "Don't cry, Katie. Don't cry for him. He's had much longer than any of us thought."

"I'm so unhappy, Gran. In all ways, I'm so unhappy."

"I know you are, dear, and I know why. We've both been silly people, but mainly for the same reason. Strange that, isn't it? An old woman and a younger girl making fools of themselves. But it's all in the past. There now, there now. It'll all come right because, as Davey himself would say, you've done your penance and I've done mine."

51

THREE WEEKS LATER, WHEN THEY BURIED DAVEY, IT WAS A BRIGHT APRIL DAY, with the daffodils filling the vases on the graves and the green verge along the path full of them. Fifty of Bill's men were present. One person was noticeable by her absence and that was Davey's mother. She was in hospital having a hip operation. Rupert was also present, but Miss Isherwood, now known as Mrs. Meredith, was not with him. Father Hankin who had said mass over the coffin in the Catholic church was now saying the prayers for the dead. Sammy stood by the graveside and on either side of him stood Fiona and Bill, and next to Bill was Willie, and standing beside him was Mark. Slightly behind them were Mrs. Vidler and Katie. Nell was not present. She had voted to stay behind to see to the other children. She confessed to Fiona she abhorred funerals.

When the first clod of earth hit the coffin Fiona felt Sammy shudder, and as she went to put her hand on his shoulder she noticed Bill's arm come around it. Then one after the other the people dispersed until there was only the family left. And then they, too, moved away.

They were nearing the chapel in front of which all the wreaths and flowers were displayed. And as they paused to look at them a man, who was passing, stopped, and Fiona said, "Hello, Rupert. It was nice of you to come."

"Hello, Fiona." He paused, then added, "I'm sorry he's gone. I liked him. But who didn't when they got to know him." He turned his eyes to the side now, and there standing not two feet away from her mother was Katie. He stared at her for a moment and she at him, and then he said, "Hello, Katie." And another moment passed before she answered simply, "Hello."

Bill now turned from viewing a large wreath that his men had sent and, stepping up to them, he said, "Hello there, Rupert. He was well represented, wasn't he?"

"He was indeed, Bill."

Bill gave a swift glance towards Katie, but her face was utterly blank.

"Would ... would you like to come back for a drink, Rupert?" Fiona said.

"Thank you, but ... but I've got to get back to work." He nodded towards Bill, a half smile on his face now, and added, "Or he'll be asking what does he pay me for. But I'd like to pop in sometime if I may."

"You'll be very welcome at any time."

"I'll do that then. I'll have a word now with Sammy. Be seeing you then." He nodded from one to the other, including Katie, then turned to where Sammy and Willie were looking at the wreaths. Bill, his voice low now, yet in a way light, said, "Well, let's get home," and turned to Fiona, saying, "You take the womenfolk and I'll take the men, the same as when we came."

They walked out of the cemetery and got into the cars, and fifteen minutes later they were getting out of the cars and filing into the house.

It was as they stood in the hall, taking their coats off, that Fiona noticed that Katie was standing apart. She hadn't taken off her coat. She was standing stiffly staring at Bill, and Fiona, in the act of taking Bill's coat from him, made a motion with her head that caused him to turn round; and as he did so and looked at Katie standing, her head up, her mouth open, the tears came streaming down her face and, on a gasp, she cried, "I'm sorry, Dad. Oh, I'm sorry. I'm sorry. I am."

Quickly he went and put his arms about her and held her close, saying, "There, there! So am I, lass. So am I. Come on now, it's all over. Come on into the drawing room and sit down."

Slowly she drew herself away from him. "I'll ... I'll, go upstairs for a minute," she said. "I'll be down directly. I'll just ... just tidy up." Then bending abruptly forward, she kissed him and ran from him up the stairs. And he, turning, first looked at Fiona, then at his mother-in-law, and said quietly, "Back to normal. Thank God for it.

Back to normal." Then glancing towards the passage from where Bert had appeared carrying his son, followed by Nell holding Angela by one hand and Mamie by the other, Bill nodded, saying, "Family en masse." Then addressing Bert pointedly, he said, "You beat me to it. Couldn't get home quick enough."

Bert now looked about him, saying, "Where's Sammy?"

It was Willie who answered, "He's just gone upstairs. He'll be down in a minute."

Sammy was coming out of the bathroom when he saw Katie running into her room. He stood on the landing for a moment wiping his eyes; then walking slowly up to her door he knocked, and after what could have been a full minute she opened it. And she showed her surprise at seeing him standing there, but she said, "You want to see me, Sammy?"

"Aye." He went past her and stood in the room and, looking up at her, because she was still taller than he, he said, "You liked me da, didn't you?"

"Yes; yes, I was very fond of him . . . very. We . . . I mean, I could talk to him. We talked a lot."

"Aye, I know you did. And him and me talked a lot an' all, and about you."

"About me?" She dug her fingers into her chest; and he said, "Aye. And you know what?" He gave a wan smile now, "He told me I had to talk to you."

"He told you that! Why?"

"I don't know except that you weren't talkin' to anybody these days, only to him. And he must have thought when he was gone you still wouldn't talk to anybody, and I'd be better than nothing. But then I don't suppose you will need me to talk to you now."

"But I will, Sammy. Yes, I will." Her voice was urgent now, her expression eager. "You know, you're very like your da. You see, I'm even getting to talk like you."

"Eeh, you'd better not do that"—their smiles mingled—"else I'll get me head in me hands and me brains to play with."

Her smile widened now as she said, "That's exactly what your father would have said."

His face became straight, then his lips trembled for a moment before he said, "I mean to make something of meself, 'cos that would have pleased him. But I'll have to live a long time to repay everybody in this house for what they've done for me."

Her smile became a grin now as she said, "Well, you can start by talking to me and pay it off at so much an hour."

"Aye, that's an idea."

They stared at each other in silence now, and when he slowly put his hand out she took it, and when he said, "I feel sort of lost," she said quietly, "I know the feeling, but it'll pass."

"I'm gonna miss me da. And you know something? He was a wise man and I never knew it until a short while ago."

"Well, I've got one over on you there because I found that out soon after he came into the house."

"You did?"

"Yes."

Again they looked at each other in silence, then he said, "We'd better be getting down," and they turned together and went out of the room, and only became conscious that they were still holding hands when they neared the head of the stairs.

As their hands dropped to their sides they laughed sheepishly, and it was Katie who said, "That would have given them something to get their teeth into, wouldn't it?" And when he answered, "By, aye, it would that, enough to get me thrown out," they again laughed before walking side by side like two people who knew they had discovered something in each other.